The Chronicles of ......

The Legacy of the Elves

Author
Christian Dölder

Publisher
Christian Dölder

Publisher: Christian Dölder

Freidlgasse 12

9400 Wolfsberg

Austria

info@wetherid.com

ISBN: 978-3-9505548-0-9

Cover designed by: Christian Dölder & DALL-E

***

This book is dedicated to my children Patrik Neo, Kristina Karolina and Maria Margareta. Never give up and don't let your imagination be taken away from you!

***

Development of the Story

Chapter 1
Story pacing 35%

Engagement 39%

Action development 41%

Character development 43%

Chapter 2
Story pacing 54%

Engagement 59%

Action development 63%

Character development 61%

Chapter 3
Story pacing 72%

Engagement 79%

Action development 74%

Character development 69%

Chapter 4
Story pacing 86%

Engagement 91%

Action development 92%

Character development 76%

The peoples, the peoples shall forever stand,

let a new era arise across the land.

Scan the QR code to explore a full-size world map, view images and videos, and listen to the soundtrack.

Summary

PROLOGUE..I

CHAPTER 1 1

   AN UNKNOWN PETITIONER.................................... 1
   VRENLI'S DREAM 22
   THE FINAL TEST.. 31
   THE DEPARTURE TO ASTINHOD 50
   AARL'S HUT.. 69
   THE RUINS OF TAWINN.................................... 86
   LAKE TANETH 101
   THE ICE MOUNTAINS 114
   THE CAVE OF THE OUTCAST DWARF 128

CHAPTER 2 143

   THE CITY OF ASTINHOD.................................... 143
   MASTER DROBAL'S TOWER................................ 156
   THE SAGE OF THE DESERT................................ 173
   THE THIEVES' GUILD OF ASTINHOD 191
   VRENLI IN CAPTIVITY.................................... 206
   THE ORDER OF THE DRAGON 220
   BALAE'S WEDDING 234
   THE ESCAPE 244
   SHEIKH NEG EL BAHI...................................... 258
   THE RAGING HORDES 282
   THE DARK FOREST 295

CHAPTER 3 314

   THE JOURNEY TO HORUNGUTH ISLAND 314
   THE LAWS OF THE DRUIDS................................ 336
   THE TUNNEL OF THE GRAY DWARVES 345
   A PACT IS AGREED UPON.................................. 359
   AARL'S VILLAGE.. 380

Horunguth Island in distress 397
The enemy at the gates of Ib'Agier 417
Uprising in Astinhod 431
The return of Princess Lythinda 442
The Underwater Grotto of Irkaar 457
The Mist Moor 471

CHAPTER 4 .... **487**

The Glorious Valley 487
Vrenli's insight 497
The way to Ib'Agier 506
Ib'Agier is refortified 518
The legacy of the elves 536
Betrayed and sold 562

EPILOGUE **579**

AFTERWORD **582**

Prologue

In the thirteenth cycle, after the emergence of the landmasses, long before the Ancient Era began, at the time when the flames in the Northlands had turned to ice and the High Lands had formed on the continent of Mendaris, fearsome, mighty dragons ruled Wetherid. They fought fierce battles with the giant, murderous wolves of Fallgar for the right to rule the land tormented by fire and frost. The cycle of life, of rebirth, was broken and neither the dragons of Wetherid nor the wolves of Fallgar could achieve victory after five thousand years of war. A shadow spread over Wetherid and Fallgar, and a thousand years of darkness followed.

One day, however, the elves, the purest and noblest of creatures, brought a light accompanied by glorious sounding horns across the Southern Sea to the darkened continent, to Wetherid. The darkness was illuminated and the scarred wounds of the land healed so new life could emerge.

20th cycle

It was in the twentieth cycle that the heart of Wetherid began to beat again, and its soul was filled with the "Word of the Father". Ehrondim, the king of the Glorious Elves, wrote down the "Word" in a book and when his time had come, he left the book to Wetherid so that a shadow would never again settle over the land and darkness reign. One cycle later, Wetherid had become a cherished garden in which life sprouted and flourished. The creative gifts of the elves had borne fruit. Humans, dwarves and other races began to feast on its abundant, tasty fruits over the following thousand years. However, as in every garden, Wetherid had also become infested with vermin. Lizard creatures, goblins and underwater creatures began to gnaw on some of the roots unnoticed, laying claim to parts of the paradise garden beds and becoming part of Wetherid.

Towards the end of the twentieth cycle, small settlements of humans began to appear in the north, west, south and southwest of Wetherid. Dwarves began to mine for ore in the mighty mountains to the east, and a strange race of smallfolk who were neither humans, dwarves nor elves settled in the northwest. Soon after, the present-day regions of Wetherid began to emerge and were given their names: "Tawinn" in the northwest, "Astinhod" in the north, "Ib'Agier" in the east, "Thir" in the south, the "Desert of DeShadin" in the southwest and the "Glorious Valley", the home of the elves, in the southeast.

21st cycle

In the twenty-first cycle, the Glorious Elves turned their attention to neighboring Fallgar, sending light into the shadowy darkness. But Fallgar was already populated by creatures of darkness. Orcs, ogres, undead, gray dwarves, mist elves and hundreds of humans, who preferred the shadows to the light, were the new masters of the barren and scarred land. The light of the Glorious Elves was unwelcome, seen as a threat and pushed back with all the power of darkness. Attempts to bring the "Word" to Fallgar were prevented by force of arms. The Glorious Elves had to leave Fallgar to its own devices and thus to the shadows, and turned back to Wetherid, where the Age of the Ancients had begun. Great cities were built and kingdoms arose.

It was the beginning of the age of abundance, prosperity and peace for more than a thousand years.

23rd cycle

In the twenty-third cycle, the inhabitants of Fallgar began to look upon Wetherid with envy and greed. Their dark, poisoned hearts harbored a desire to claim the flourishing land for themselves. Initial attempts to invade Wetherid failed, however. The glaring, burning light and the echoing, aching "Word" put a stop to Fallgar's greed.

Centuries passed.

In an hour of demonic darkness, a child scarred beyond recognition was born in the north of Fallgar, in Druhn, and given the name Rorannis. It was shadow mages who prophesied great deeds for the child and saw in his dark soul a leader who, with their help, would succeed in leading Wetherid back into the shadows.

They were not mistaken. The child grew up to become a fearsome and terrifying ruler. At the age of twenty-six, Rorannis was married to Jehndira, the daughter of Manlatur, the chief servant of the Shadow and the most powerful mage in Fallgar. The blood bond between the people of Fallgar and the Shadow was thus sealed and from the marriage alliance between Rorannis and Jehndira sprang the Entorbis lineage.

It was the beginning of all evil for Wetherid.

Rorannis of Entorbis realized at an early age that the power of Wetherid was based on the Book of the Glorious Elves and that it therefore had to be destroyed - or better still - harnessed. Together with the Shadow Mages of Druhn, under the cover of night, in a magical sphere of darkness, Rorannis of Entorbis traveled to Wetherid, to the Glorious Valley, and stole the book from the son of Ehrondim.

But this act did not go unseen. A circle of mages from Horunguth Island, Guardians of the light and the "Word" who had been granted powerful gifts, stood in the way of the shadow mages.

As in the ancient battle between shadow and light, the opponents clashed.

Rorannis of Entorbis nevertheless managed to escape to the interior of Wetherid, where he hid with the book in an abandoned dragon's lair. Ehrondim's son and a group of elven warriors set off in pursuit. They followed the thief's trail to the Middle Mountains, where the young elf separated from his group and confronted the first of the Entorbis in his hiding place.

The battle between the son of Ehrondim and the ruler of Druhn lasted for many days. In the end, both gave their lives. Neither good nor evil prevailed. The book was lost, the "Word" fell silent and the soul of Wetherid was no longer nourished.

Greed, envy and strife then broke out among the peoples of Wetherid, leading to centuries of war among allies and brothers. It would have been easy for the descendants of Roranni to take over Wetherid, which was almost mutilating itself, had the Glorious Elves and the mages of Horunguth Island not created seven powerful artifacts of light to counteract them.

The "Seed of Life" went to Astinhod. The "Crystal of Seeing" was taken to Tawinn. "The Golden Hammer" was given to the dwarves in Ib'Agier. The "Lute of Peace" went to Kirindor. The "Tablet of Law" was set up in Thir. The "Key of Secrets" went to the Desert of DeShadin and the "Living Glass" remained in the Glorious Valley.

For five hundred years, the seven powerful artifacts of light protected the inhabitants of Wetherid from the Fallgar's attacks, but not from themselves. The seven artifacts were stolen and taken far beyond the borders of the country. Wetherid was almost defenseless as a result. It was only through the efforts of the mages of the Horunguth Island that humans, dwarves, elves and Tawinnians joined forces and drove the gray dwarves, orcs and mist elves that had already invaded Wetherid in the Middle Mountains, back to Fallgar.

Whether it was a coincidence or not, if a group of people had not stumbled across the book by chance in one of the old caves in the Middle Mountains, Wetherid would have faced dark times again. However, the future of Wetherid was in the hands of the humans. As only a few were able to read the old characters, the "Word" began to whisper softly through Wetherid. Loud enough, however, to be heard by the mages of the Horunguth Island.

There was hope again.

25th cycle

With the silent consent of the Glorious Elves, the book remained with the humans, and the mages of Horunguth Island kept a watchful eye on Ehrondim's legacy. By the beginning of the twenty-fifth cycle, the Word was once again widespread in Wetherid, a little of the former peace had returned.

However, the Entorbis family continued to try to take possession of the book from generation to generation. Therefore, the mages of the Horunguth Island chose a few from the peoples of Wetherid and appointed them "Guardians" to spread the Word and protect the book. The Queen of the Elves from the Glorious Valley bestowed special gifts on the "Guardians" to aid them in their task and made them part of the soul of Wetherid. As per Ehrondim's legacy, they were taught to write history and record all the events to ensure posterity and to accompany the Word that had come to life. Bliss and peace reigned in Wetherid.

Until the day when Tyrindor of Entorbis managed to do what only the forefather of his race had managed to do more than one thousand five hundred years ago. Tyrindor of Entorbis was able to steal the Book of Wetherid and even take it beyond the borders of Wetherid to Fallgar

Letter 289

The year is 530 in the twenty-sixth cycle. The Book of Wetherid has been in the Entorbis' possession for sixty years now. How long it will be before they see through our ruse is uncertain. But I can already feel Fallgar's shadow. Closer and closer, faster and faster, it is moving in on the border of our land. Peace still reigns, but the peoples are divided, too weak to oppose the threat. We have been robbed of the artifacts of light. Many of the Guardians have left us, the Word threatens to fall silent once more. Should there be another darkness in Wetherid? A sword of destruction wielded by the young, powerful hand of Erwight of Entorbis hovers over our heads, ready to strike. Never before has the enemy been so close to the target. I am on my guard, listening intently to the wind, looking around with a far-sighted eye and keeping my head down. Only a handful! Will that be enough? Is there any hope?

Chapter 1

An unknown petitioner

It was beginning to get dark. He closed the shutters and dimmed the flame of the oil lamp hanging from the ceiling of the small room. He went to the small cupboard next to the bed, took the book that lay on it and sat down with it in a simple little chair, directly under the dusty lamp, where he looked at the cover for some time before he began to read. With each page he carefully read, the images in his memory became clearer. He saw Tawinn, lying in the northwest of Wetherid, enclosed by two adjacent mountain ranges: the high, mighty and barely passable Ice Mountains that stretched from the border with Astinhod in the north to Kirindor in the south, where the high mountain landscape of the Karwarts reached across to the outer border of Wetherid in the west.

In the north-western corner of Tawinn, in a clearing surrounded by old, thick-trunked oaks, tall beeches, thin-branched birches and mighty maples, was the unfortified village of Abketh. Its inhabitants - the Abkether, as they were called by the humans, dwarves and elves - were a hard-working, ambitious and, above all, cheerful and carefree people who felt safe and protected in their valley. In the settlement of no more than one hundred and thirty houses, there was a store, three inns and a house of prayer with a wooden tower topped by a gleaming golden bell. In the village square, there was a deep well made of stone, which served the women of Abketh not only as a source of water but also, as they called it, a center of conversation.

It was a sunny spring day. The sun's rays were reflected from the stained-glass windows, which shimmered red, green and blue, onto the white alderflowers, the yellow strieglia and the splendidly thriving wonneziras that bloomed in the flower troughs in front of

1

the windows of the small houses. Everything in the quaint and peaceful village went on as usual.

Many of the Abkether were already hard at work in the small-scale wheat, barley and sunflower fields to the north and south of the clearing. The inhabitants of the village were also going about their daily chores. Klersten, the pot-bellied miller, his gray hair caked with flour dust, was busy pushing a few sacks of flour from the mill to the village bakery in his old handcart. As his white work apron protruded a little too far past his knees, he had to take many small steps to avoid stumbling. It was only thanks to his strong, broad arms that he managed to keep the stubborn handcart in check and prevent it from rolling down the small slope and straight towards Ermis, the white-haired rope maker. He was sitting, bent far forward, on a small bench on his ivy-covered terrace, conscientiously and calmly weaving the rope that the rich farmer Olmis had ordered from him two days ago. Ermis would have been scared to death if Klersten's handcart had smashed against his wooden terrace fence.

Further ahead, not too far from Ermis' house, in front of the door of Bells Inn, the pretty, blonde-haired Mina was sweeping the courtyard with a bristly broom, attentively watching the young Abkether strutting across the village square and showing off their brightly polished short swords. A few tens of steps behind, Werlis, who enjoyed the reputation of a good-for-nothing, was lying in the hammock in front of his house as usual.

Werlis was an Abkether just growing into a young man who didn't think much of work, but still wore strikingly fine shirts made of DeShadin silk and silver jewelry. If you took a closer look at Werlis, you could see that strong shoulders were hidden beneath his long curly blond hair. He certainly didn't lack the strength to work, but rather the will, which he often admitted publicly.

Only three or four stone throws away from Werlis' house, the gray-haired Gwerlit, who was many winters old, had her hut surrounded by a wildly growing herb garden. Gwerlit, said to be the wisest woman in all Abketh, was talking to an unknown man in her herb garden.

"You are lucky you came this week, because I would have made a tincture of all the flowers soon," she said to the stranger, adjusting her old silver-gray gown.

"I thank you for letting me have some of them and you can also be sure of King Grandhold's thanks. Since the queen passed away ten years ago, his daughter has meant everything to him," he said.

The stranger bowed his thanks.

"It's terrible what happened to the girl, and very strange too. It's been more than thirty years since I last heard of a similar illness. I think you know what I'm talking about," said Gwerlit seriously.

He nodded.

"My thoughts and suspicions are not far removed from yours. But I am not yet sure whether it is connected to them. I really don't want to rush to judgment. If it is, then we all know what that could mean. Let's hope for the best, Gwerlit," he replied thoughtfully.

"Some of the signs you've told me about indicate that they might have a hand in this," Gwerlit remarked.

She sighed.

"Tyrindor of Entorbis may be an old man whose strength has waned, but his son, Erwight, is now in the prime of life. If he has come full circle, then it is quite conceivable that he will soon turn his attention to Wetherid, if he has not already done so. But as mentioned before, it's still too early to make that assumption public. I hope Master Drobal's plan will be successful, so that clarity can be brought to this whole strange and ominous affair," said the stranger, asking Gwerlit to keep their conversation to herself.

"Don't worry about it. You can be sure of my silence," she assured him and led him to the spot in the herb garden where four moonflowers grew.

She explained to him, in detail, the conditions under which it was possible to grow the rare and extremely demanding plant and what had to be taken into account when harvesting its flowers.

The forty-year-old Vrenli, grandson of the scholar Erendir Hogmaunt, who was on his way to the village square and was just maturing into a man, took a few steps towards the wooden fence that surrounded Gwerlit's herb garden. He looked curiously at the sturdy, middle-aged man, three heads taller than him, who was wrapped in a thick, dark green cloak with a hood.

The stranger was wearing worn dark leather trousers and brown knee-high lace-up boots that looked as if he had already taken tens of thousands of steps in. A few thick strands of his long, wavy dark hair, which reached over his shoulders, almost covered his large, dark green eyes. On his back he carried a fire axe, probably from Ib'Agier, which hung on a leather strap next to his dark wood longbow and bark-woven quiver.

"Probably someone from Astinhod," thought Vrenli, noticing the attentive gaze of the tall man that fell on him.

The stranger then gave him a hand signal to come closer, but Vrenli wasn't sure at first whether the wave was meant for him, so he turned around looking for someone else. When the stranger waved to him again, he opened the garden gate and followed the narrow path that had been trodden into the loose, damp earth and past several green bushes, low-growing shrubs and a variety of different herbs to Gwerlit's house.

Vrenli was no more than three steps away from the two when the stranger's dark green eyes lit up for a moment as he stepped toward him.

"A Guardian here in Abketh? As far as I know, Erendir was the only one. But he left us many years ago," thought the stranger, who was very surprised at the encounter.

He could clearly feel the connection between the Abkether and the Book of Wetherid. The two looked at each other wordlessly for a few moments.

"Very strange, why doesn't he reveal himself? Has he not been given the gifts of a Guardian?" the stranger pondered, trying to explore the innermost thoughts of his counterpart.

He concentrated on his senses, attuned them to his feelings and found what he was looking for deep in a hidden corner.

"I greet you," Vrenli, who froze in shock, heard a voice within him.

Petrified, he stood in front of Gwerlit and the stranger, who placed his hand on his shoulder. Vrenli flinched. His thoughts took on a life of their own, spiraled inexorably for a few moments and were shattered by the fear of impending disaster. Frightened, he looked at the tall man leaning down towards him.

"Don't be afraid, friend. My name is Gorathdin, Gorathdin of the Forest. I am on my way on behalf of King Grandhold to ask Gwerlit for the blossoms of a moonflower," sounded the voice in his head.

"Scared? Yes, I'm scared. I thought I heard a voice," Vrenli confessed in a trembling voice.

"What kind of voice? I didn't hear anything," Gwerlit replied, raising her eyebrows in surprise.

She put her hand to her left ear and listened attentively to the wind.

"The voice sounded inside me," explained Vrenli, pointing to himself.

Gwerlit shook her head.

"You must have been mistaken, my boy. You were probably just frightened by Gorathdin's strange appearance. It's been a long time since someone from outside came to us. Your imagination must have played tricks on you," she reassured him with her gentle voice and stroked his cheek.

Gwerlit felt that there was a connection between him and Gorathdin, and since she knew about Vrenli's grandfather, Erendir, she concluded that the meeting with Gorathdin awakened something dormant in Vrenli. She had known for a long time that it would happen one day. She didn't have a clear idea, but she wished that Vrenli had a little more time before he found out what his destiny was.

Vrenli looked puzzled at Gorathdin.

"She's right. He does look strange. But I'm sure I heard the voice," he mused, lost in thought.

Doubts arose in his mind.

"I'm not going to get sick, am I?" he murmured quietly, touching his forehead.

"Are you not feeling well?" asked Gwerlit worriedly.

"I'm not sure. Maybe I should go home and lie down for a while," Vrenli replied hesitantly.

Gwerlit broke a small twig from a bush and handed it to Vrenli.

"What should I do with it?" asked Vrenli, looking skeptically at the yellowish leaves of the branch.

"I wouldn't be surprised if you got sick. It's a sunny day, but it's still spring and you're out without a cloak. Put three or four leaves in hot water and drink it in small sips, then try to get some sleep and when you feel better, come over again. Who knows when you'll next have the chance to talk to someone from outside," Gwerlit said with a smile and then turned to Gorathdin.

Vrenli said goodbye to them and, thinking about the voice, went back home.

"It may seem strange what I am about to ask you to do," Gorathdin began and paused for a moment.

"I want Vrenli to travel with me to Astinhod and I need your help, Gwerlit. Unfortunately, I can't tell you why," he added.

Gwerlit closed her eyes for a moment and went into herself.

"No explanation is necessary, Gorathdin of the Forest. I think I know what's going on. I will help you, even if I wish Vrenli had had more time," she finally replied.

Gorathdin could not hide his surprise.

"I didn't know you knew about this. So, it's important that we don't tell him about his task. I want him to find out as much as possible for himself. In Astinhod, Master Drobal will tell Vrenli about everything because it seems that he doesn't know about his purpose, has suppressed it or forgotten it," he told Gwerlit, who nodded and followed by Gorathdin, walked back to the house, where he sat down on the steps in front of the entrance and gazed thoughtfully at the cloudless sky.

Gorathdin watched a buzzard circling over the fields outside the village, looking for prey.

"When the circle closes, a shadow will spread across the land and then Wetherid will face dark times," he mused, imitating the bird's call to greet it.

Gwerlit was startled and the jug of water she was about to hand to Gorathdin almost fell out of her hand.

"Forgive me! I didn't mean to frighten you. I was thinking and just greeting a friend," Gorathdin apologized to Gwerlit and pointed to the circling buzzard with his hand.

Gwerlit smiled and handed Gorathdin the jug. He drank and then placed it next to him on the stairs. Gwerlit went into the house and returned a little later with a small, hemp-colored sack.

She sat down on the small bench next to the front steps. She opened the sack and took out a few wonderfully fragrant leaves.

"You have to carefully break off the small green stems and then remove the thin, yellow threads that run through the middle of the leaf," she explained to Gorathdin and handed him a handful of the leaves.

Smiling gently, Gorathdin took them and began to clean the leaves as Gwerlit had explained.

It was after midday when Vrenli got up from the small wooden bench on his terrace. He was already feeling better, although he was still not sure about the voice he had heard. He decided to go back to Gwerlit.

Once there, he knocked on the door, which opened just a moment later.

"Come in, Vrenli. We're having dinner. Are you hungry?" asked Gwerlit, leading the way into the living room.

"If there's enough. I'm a little hungry," Vrenli replied and greeted Gorathdin, who, being too tall and heavy for the small chairs, chose to sit on a chest. Vrenli then sat down at the table.

Gwerlit brought an empty plate and small wooden spoon and sat down opposite them.

"Grab it!" she urged Vrenli.

Vrenli nodded, took a piece of bread and scooped some of the vegetable stew onto his plate with the wooden ladle.

While they ate, Gorathdin began to talk about the city of Astinhod and as he was the only visitor from outside for more than twenty-five years, Gwerlit and Vrenli listened to him attentively. Vrenli was particularly eager to learn and wanted to know everything down to the smallest detail. When Gorathdin had finished his story about the most important events of recent years, he looked at Gwerlit. She nodded slightly and put her hands together.

"You have to listen to me carefully now, Vrenli," Gwerlit began.

She paused for a moment.

"I ask you to accompany Gorathdin to Astinhod," she told him.

Surprise reflected in Vrenli's wide-open eyes.

"I need you to deliver an important message from me to Master Drobal, and I think Gorathdin could use some help on his way back," she said to him.

Vrenli's mouth fell open, and he raised his eyebrows.

"Gwerlit is right. It is important that the blossoms of the moonflower are brought to Astinhod as soon as possible, and I ask you to accompany me there in two days' time, on the full moon, when its buds begin to bloom," Gorathdin added.

"I don't understand...?" Vrenli stuttered and frowned.

"Why me of all people? I'm not the right person for such a responsible task. I haven't even passed the final test yet and then you're demanding that I travel to Astinhod?" Vrenli pressed.

He sighed.

"You misunderstand something, my boy. I'm not demanding that you travel to Astinhod, I'm asking you to. Just like Gorathdin," Gwerlit said gently.

Vrenli thought about it.

"What's with the flowers?" he asked, turning his gaze to Gorathdin.

"I'll tell you about it on our way to Astinhod," he promised.

Vrenli looked disappointedly at Gorathdin because of the short, unexplained answer. He really didn't feel like the right person to fulfill their request. He had doubts and there was also fear. It was not fear of Gorathdin or of the journey to Astinhod. No. It was fear of something he could not describe. Fear that reached far back into his childhood.

"Does the book have anything to do with it?" asked Vrenli, surprised and amazed that he was asking himself this question.

In all the years following the death of his father, and the death of his grandfather shortly afterwards, he had never thought about the book until today and had forgotten everything that had been read to him from it. A shiver ran down his spine. Images from his childhood struck him like flashes of lightning in quick succession. He tried to stop the flood of images that made little sense and only showed fractions of moments from his past. He took a deep breath and composed himself.

Gwerlit stood up and took something from the small chest of drawers next to the table. She took a step towards Vrenli and handed him a small leather pouch. Vrenli opened it and pulled out a finely crafted silver chain with a walnut-sized crystal attached to it.

"The Oracle of Tawinn," Vrenli realized in amazement.

"I want you to take it. It has been in my family for generations, and it has not only served me, but all Abketh, well. It is time for it to be passed on, just as it was handed down to me by my ancestors," said Gwerlit.

"I can't accept that, Gwerlit", Vrenli refused.

"It's a gift from the ancients, take it," said Gwerlit and closed Vrenli's hand around the small leather pouch.

Vrenli lifted the necklace in front of him and looked at the crystal.

"How does it work?" he asked curiously.

"An oracle does not work. An oracle sees! It sees after you ask it what you want to see. Most of the time," Gwerlit's face became serious.

Vrenli's gaze was still fixed on the small crystal that lay cold in his hand.

"I think it will be best if Werlis accompanies you," Gwerlit surprisingly suggested.

Vrenli looked up, startled.

"You've been good friends since you were children. He will certainly accompany you if you ask him to," said Gwerlit.

She glanced at Gorathdin, who nodded in agreement.

"What's Werlis got to do with it?" Vrenli wanted to know.

"Werlis, well, he's your friend, and friends are there to help each other, right?" Gwerlit continued.

Vrenli put the bag away and nodded.

"But I'm not sure if he would actually come with me. I'm not even sure whether I can comply with your request," he admitted hesitantly.

"Can't you two ask someone else to do it?" asked Vrenli.

Gwerlit and Gorathdin were silent for a moment and looked at each other questioningly.

"I want to be honest with you, Vrenli. It's not just about you accompanying me on my journey back and delivering a message from Gwerlit to Master Drobal, it's also about you. But that's all I can tell you about that. Master Drobal will have answers for you," Gorathdin finally revealed.

"About me?" Vrenli asked himself, puzzled, and looked thoughtfully into Gorathdin's eyes, to which he was strangely drawn.

The dark green glow did not cause him any discomfort, on the contrary, he felt warmed inside. Vrenli couldn't explain to himself why that look seemed so familiar. But leaving Abketh and traveling to Astinhod with Gorathdin was not an encouraging thought.

"I really don't know if I'm ready to leave Abketh. I ask for your patience. Before I make a final decision, I'd like to sleep on it," Vrenli announced and stood up from the table.

"Of course, my boy, do that. We really don't want to rush you. I can understand that you have a lot of questions now, but you can only answer most of them yourself," said Gwerlit gently.

"I'll be on my way back in two days, and I'd be delighted if you decided to come with me," Gorathdin said and held out his hand.

Unanswered questions buzzed in Vrenli's head, but he first had to think about what he had experienced and heard before he would demand further answers from them. He said goodbye to them and went to Klersten, the miller, to buy the bag of flour he had left his house for that morning.

"This Gorathdin is very strange. He looks so unusual and yet I feel as if I know him. Maybe grandfather told me something about him? But can it really be that I've forgotten? I should remember his eyes," he thought as he marched towards the village well.

Vrenli stopped for a moment and looked over the low edge down into the darkness. He picked up a small stone from the ground and threw it down into the depths. It took two or three moments before he heard a thud.

"I feel more or less the same as the stone. As if Gwerlit and Gorathdin were throwing me into cold water. I really don't want to refuse their request, but such a long journey certainly harbors many dangers. If I remember grandfather's directions correctly, the road to Astinhod leads through dense forests, wide valleys, over high mountains and deep lakes, and wind, rain, snow and ice will accompany us on our way. I don't think I'm the right person for this," he mused.

Vrenli continued in the direction of Bell´s Inn, where Mina was leaning against the windowsill and stroking her long, wavy blonde hair. When she saw Vrenli, she waved to him with a friendly smile.

"Hello Vrenli. It's a beautiful day today. Isn't it?" she called from afar.

"Greetings Mina. After the winter we've had, it really was time for some warm rays of sunshine. I can hardly wait for summer to finally arrive," replied Vrenli.

Vrenli gave her a smile and was just about to move on when Mina asked where Werlis was.

"Where will he be at this time of night? He's probably still asleep," replied Vrenli with a grin.

"If you see him, give him my regards!" she called after him and smiled sheepishly.

"Does Werlis know that she likes him? He thinks that the girls in the village don't like him. But that's not true. He's brave, strong, a bit rash with his decisions, but he has a good heart. The general opinion of him in the village isn't the best, but that's only because he's wealthy and therefore prefers to sleep rather than work hard," Vrenli thought to himself as he walked towards the mill.

"Come to think of it, Gwerlit is right. If Werlis would accompany me, then I would dare. Although, what Gorathdin said to me sounded very strange. I mean, what does it mean, it doesn't just have to do with his journey and Gwerlit's message for Master Drobal?" he asked himself, knocking on the heavy door of the mill.

Nobody opened the door.

It was late afternoon and Klersten was already in the Guesthouse zur Glocke, washing down the dust of his work with a mug of mead.

"Such bad luck. He's not here," Vrenli said loudly and walked back in the direction of Werlis' house.

"Werlis, wake up! I have something important to tell you," shouted Vrenli from afar.

Werlis shot up from his hammock.

"Are the wolves in the village? Where's my sword?" Werlis exclaimed excitedly.

He looked around in panic.

"There are no wolves in the village, you can calm down. But I must tell you something," Vrenli said to him.

Vrenli put his hand on Werlis' shoulder to reassure him.

"If it's not the wolves, then I wonder what's so important that you're waking me up from my well-earned sleep?" Werlis asked grumpily and lay back in the hammock.

"Oh Werlis, you haven't really earned any sleep for a long time. You haven't done any regular work since your father died and left you all those possessions," Vrenli teased him.

"You are only plagued by envy. Besides, I let every inhabitant of Abketh share in my inheritance. Even crazy old Ingwis," Werlis defended himself.

"I know, I know. That shouldn't be a reproach. Let's not bicker. There are more important things for us to do," Vrenli placated.

"What do you mean by that? Is it already time for the final test? I thought it was tomorrow," asked Werlis.

Werlis, just like Vrenli and all other young Abkether who reached the age of forty, had to learn how to use the short sword, sling and bow and arrow over several months with the Abketh masters of arms and then pass three tests. When the opponents were drawn by lot, it was decided that Vrenli and Werlis would have to fight with the short sword. Only one of them would emerge victorious. The final test, as the Abkether called it, was a village event and was always associated with a festival that lasted several days.

"No, that's tomorrow. So, you have one more day to improve your technique," said Vrenli with a grin.

"My technique doesn't need to be improved. You know I'm the stronger one between us. So, admit defeat straight away and you'll save yourself the embarrassment of fighting me," Werlis countered.

"You're an incorrigible braggart, Werlis. Mere strength is not always enough. In battle, it's not just strength that counts, but also experience, mental superiority, speed and, above all, the element of surprise," replied Vrenli, drawing his short sword and cutting the line of the hammock with a single blow.

Werlis fell to the ground with a loud cry.

"Ow! Are you crazy, that was unfair, I wasn't prepared for that," protested Werlis grimacing.

He rubbed his aching backside.

Vrenli grinned.

"Was that proof enough?" he asked with a laugh and put his sword back in its sheath.

"Yes, yes. I understand what you mean," replied Werlis grumpily.

"Come on, let's go to my place. I must tell you what happened at Gwerlit's earlier," Vrenli urged him.

Werlis nodded and followed Vrenli to his house.

"Now let's talk, what's new?" urged Werlis, who still had his hand on his backside.

"Wait until we get to my house. Patience, my friend," replied Vrenli.

He grinned, although he didn't really feel like it.

Their path led them past the village fountain, where a few women who had lined up to fetch water were chatting like quacking ducks. Among them was Vrenli's corpulent Aunt Lurie, who lived just two houses away. As soon as she saw Vrenli, she took a step towards him.

"You should be helping your mother in the fields rather than wandering around the village with that good-for-nothing. You've certainly got nothing but nonsense on your mind again. Like last week, when you stole your cousin Gerieth's washing from the line and then hid it in farmer Zerwig's hayloft. By the way, I changed my mind and didn't tell your mother about it," she said to the two of them and began one of her long, drawn-out lectures.

Vrenli and Werlis, to whom her words were nothing but chatter, let her go without a word, wished her a pleasant day and then walked on, amidst the laughter of the young girls standing by the fountain.

A little later, they came across old Ingwis, who stepped out of his old, half-ruined hut. Stooped by age, he walked very slowly, using a small, thin stick. He held a bucket in his left hand as he walked towards them.

"In the twentieth cycle, a child was born. It will find the stolen goods," the old man called to the two and went to the women at the village well, where he stood in line to fill his bucket with water.

"What does that mean?" asked Werlis after they had moved on.

"It's one of his fantasies. Ever since he was with the mages on Horunguth Island more than sixty years ago, for reasons no one knows, he has only spoken of a youngling and a father of the world. At least that's what my grandfather told me. He's a poor old man and you shouldn't pay any attention to his babble," replied Vrenli, who opened the door to his house and entered, followed by Werlis.

Before they sat down, Vrenli closed the shutters and lit a candle, which he placed in the middle of the heavy, round oak table.

"Can you finally explain to me what all this strange behavior is about?" asked Werlis and sat down.

He let his eyes glide through the untidy room filled with hundreds of strange things. The combination of disorder, dust, the strange smell and the dim light of the candle, which cast a faint shadow over all the pots, jars, glass tubes, the many books and the strange objects piled up on the floor, made him feel uneasy. Werlis looked at the menacing-looking wooden figure of a Gooter standing on the mantelpiece, its two glittering emerald green eyes shining in the candlelight surrounded the wooden figure with a mysterious aura.

"Every time I look at this hideous thing it sends shivers down my spine," complained Werlis.

"And I tell you every time that there haven't been any Gooters for a long time," said Vrenli, grinning.

"I know, but today I feel as if his gaze is piercing me," Werlis moaned.

He turned his gaze away from the wooden figure.

"Listen, Werlis. My grandfather told me that long before the peoples we know settled in Wetherid, the wolves and dragons battled for millennia over the claim to rule the land. The dragons, who used destructive fire and ice magic as weapons against the huge, murderous wolves, who outnumbered them, inexorably destroyed all life. Powerful beings sent down to Wetherid from another world put an end to the cruel battles and banished the combatants to live out their existence in one body from then on. This creature, which was a mixture of dragon and wolf, was called Gooter," Vrenli told his attentive friend.

Werlis let his eyes continue to glide around the room.

"I don't know how many times I've asked you, but how can you live in this house, I couldn't get a wink of sleep in here," said Werlis, pointing to the various objects in the room.

"My grandfather left me this house. It's messy, that's true, and some things may seem strange, but that's nothing to be afraid of. I've tried to explain that to you so many times, Werlis. Grandfather always had guests from all parts of Wetherid. Each of his guests brought him gifts and over the years the house filled up with them. That cloak hanging on the wall next to the door, for example, was given to him by a guest from the Dark Forest. Or that chalice on the shelf next to the stove," said Vrenli, pointing to the small, silver, richly decorated chalice. "Grandfather was given it by a sheikh from the Desert of DeShadin," he added.

Vrenli looked at the multitude of objects in the room.

"There are so many more here, but unfortunately I don't know what purpose they all serve," said Vrenli and sighed.

"As a child, my grandfather forbade me to play with the presents he received. He said that they weren't toys, but dangerous weapons or magical objects and they didn't belong in children's hands," he said, turning his gaze to the small candle on the table in front of him.

He watched the faintly burning orange-blue flame in silence.

Vrenli remembered.

He was still a small child when the son of Tyrindor, Erwight of Entorbis, the dreaded, fear-spreading Lord Druhns from Fallgar, tried to put an end to what his forefathers had started hundreds of years ago. For reasons that were initially inexplicable, more than a hundred knights from allied Astinhod arrived in Tawinn. They had suffered heavy losses on their arduous and dangerous journey over the Pass of the Ice Mountains and were very weak. They stayed at Lake Taneth for two days until they were joined by a group of ogres, several dozen orcs and some black-clad knights of Entorbis.

A group of merchants from Abketh on their way to Astinhod, who happened to witness this strange gathering, were more than perplexed when they saw the knights from allied Astinhod crossing the lake together with their enemies from Fallgar.

The merchants immediately returned to Abketh with the news and informed the village council of their strange observation. The three old men conferred and concluded that it was very likely that Astinhod had joined forces with the ruler from the east. This conclusion hit the inhabitants of Abketh with full force.

Panic broke out.

A long-forgotten fear was reawakened. Some left the village, packing up their possessions, which were rather modest, and sought shelter in the northern forests. Others buried their gold coins, jewelry and other possessions and hid with their families in the cellars of their houses. Many, however, prepared themselves for an imminent battle against the tall humans and orcs and the giant ogres, although they knew that they would not be able to stand up to the superior forces for long without help. Thanks to a lucky coincidence - some claimed that things had not gone according to plan - a violent, destructive storm that stirred up the waters of Lake Taneth drowned most of the enemy as they were crossing on their rafts.

However, the less than two hundred survivors did not let this stop them and invaded Abketh just a few days later. Vrenli knew from stories, as he had not witnessed the attack himself but was hiding with his mother and grandfather, that his father, Hallweg, had played a considerable part in driving the enemy away before he had fallen in battle.

It turned out some time later that the Knights of Astinhod had acted against their will. They were under the magical influence of the shadow mages allied with Tyrindor of Entorbis and were told to search for something believed to be in Abketh.

"I'd love to know what grandfather's journey of several months, which he set off on just a few days after the raid from Abketh, was all about," thought Vrenli.

He thought he remembered that no one had read the book to him since. When his grandfather returned from his journey, which had taken him all over Wetherid, seriously ill, he no longer had the strength to do so. Vrenli remembered the balmy summer evening when he sat with him on the little bench on the front terrace and asked him to recount some of the adventures he had experienced on his journey.

"I haven't experienced any adventures. Adventures are situations that you are not prepared for. I was just part of a story that had already been written. One day, you too will be immersed in this story. You will find out that there are actually no new situations or tasks to fulfill in life. Everything is part of the story, and you will know this story. Deep down, you will know what you have to do, whatever comes your way," Vrenli heard his grandfather's voice ringing in his memory.

That evening was now more than twenty-five years ago. The words were long forgotten, but today's meeting with Gorathdin reminded him of the book of his grandfather and of some of the things he had said and told him.

Werlis was puzzled by Vrenli's prolonged silence and began to get bored. He began to rock his chair back and forth.

"I absolutely have to find it!" Vrenli suddenly exclaimed, causing Werlis to almost fall over in shock.

"What do you need to find?" asked Werlis, who was only just able to hold on to the tabletop.

His question brought Vrenli back to the here and now.

"My grandfather's book," explained Vrenli.

"Is that why you're keeping quiet? Because of a book?" asked Werlis, shaking his head.

"Yes. It must be here, somewhere in the house," Vrenli replied half-absentmindedly and was about to get up from the table when Werlis held him back.

"Don't you think it's time for you to explain to me why we're sitting here in broad daylight with the shutters closed by the light of a candle?" asked Werlis.

Vrenli sat down again.

"Forgive me. I was just thinking about something. I'd completely forgotten why we were here," Vrenli smiled sheepishly, but his smile was short-lived. He became nervous, got up from the table briefly, went to the window and made sure that the shutters were well closed.

"You have to keep what I'm about to tell you to yourself. Promise me that, Werlis, even if it sounds strange," Vrenli's expression became serious.

"All right, I promise, but now tell me," demanded Werlis. His impatience grew to its limit.

"I don't want people in the village to think I'm crazy, but I heard a voice within me," said Vrenli quietly.

Werlis looked at him questioningly.

"You hear voices? That can't mean anything good," Werlis remarked mockingly.

Vrenli shook his head.

"Not voices. I heard a voice. Before I woke you up, I was on my way to Klersten to buy a bag of flour. When I passed Gwerlit in the herb garden, I saw a stranger standing next to her," he told Werlis and sat down at the table again.

"He waved to me and when I walked over to him and looked into his dark green eyes, which lit up briefly, I heard a voice within me," he continued.

Werlis gasped once.

"At first I thought I was having a daydream or that I was ill, but when he grabbed my shoulder and looked deep into my eyes again, I had a feeling of familiarity. As if I knew that look. I remembered long-forgotten moments from my childhood. I find it difficult to describe. I saw the book in front of me that my grandfather used to read to me in the evenings. I don't even know why I thought about it at that moment, but it has stayed with me ever since.

"I have to find it, Werlis! I think there's a connection between the voice I heard and grandfather's book," Vrenli concluded, looking around the room for a moment.

"Then I should wish you good luck with your search. With all the clutter and the hundreds of things, it won't be easy to find," Werlis replied and grinned.

For him, it was just a book and he didn't understand Vrenli's excitement about it.

"Gorathdin, as the stranger calls himself, asked me for help," Vrenli continued.

"Help with what?" asked Werlis.

"To bring the blossoms of the moonflower to Astinhod. He told me that this was important and that he was traveling on the orders of King Grandhold," Vrenli replied, looking thoughtfully at Werlis.

"You're not actually going on such a long and dangerous journey with this Gorathdin. You don't even know him, Vrenli. I beg you to reconsider," appealed Werlis, looking deep into Vrenli's eyes.

"That's not all. Gwerlit also asked me to accompany Gorathdin. She wants me to deliver an urgent message for her to a mage called Master Drobal," Vrenli added.

He groaned.

"A mage?" Werlis asked in astonishment.

"Yes, one of the mages on Horunguth Island," confirmed Vrenli.

Both were silent for a moment.

"If I decided to comply with her request, would you accompany me to Astinhod, Werlis?" Vrenli asked hesitantly.

"You don't really think I'd risk my life for someone from outside who I've never seen before. Besides, how much help can we both be to him and why doesn't Gwerlit just give him the message for the mage?" Werlis replied, shaking his head.

"Two half-men from the small people of the Abketh, following a stranger to Astinhod. You can't be serious, Vrenli," Werlis added, puzzled.

"I don't feel comfortable with the whole thing myself. If I decide to accompany Gorathdin, I'll have to leave in two days' time. I don't know if I can muster the courage. Gorathdin told me that this journey also has to do with me. I don't know what that means myself. He kept a mysterious silence about it. But something unknown inside me is urging me to go away with him," Vrenli said sadly.

Werlis couldn't help feeling annoyed. He didn't understand why Gwerlit and someone from outside wanted to impose such a burden on his best friend.

"Oh, don't listen to me, Werlis. I can understand why you wouldn't come with me. Don't worry about it. Let's talk about it again tomorrow. After the final test. I'm going to look for the book now, and I still have to tell mother about all this. Oh, that will be something. Just to think what all the relatives and especially my

Aunt Lurie will say when I leave for Astinhod. The Loffers have always been a dramatic family. I hope it won't affect mother that much," Vrenli mused, resting his head in the hand of his left, bent arm.

"You're right. You should sleep on it again. I'll go to Gwerlit and ask her what she's thinking sending you to Astinhod with this Gorathdin. Maybe I'll meet this troublemaker then," Werlis said firmly.

Vrenli tried to dissuade Werlis from this plan, but he was unsuccessful. Werlis said goodbye and let the door slam behind him.

"Oh, Werlis!" moaned Vrenli, who was exhausted from the eventful day.

"Sometimes he really is stubborn," he thought, looking around the room.

"It must be here somewhere. Maybe it's in one of my grandfather's chests. There was a smaller, elaborate one with silver fittings where he kept all the parchment scrolls that he made such a secret of. It could well be that the book is in there," Vrenli said aloud to himself.

Vrenli then began to rummage in a corner among a pile of books, boxes and items of clothing. He quickly realized that it would not be so easy to find this small chest among all the household goods. He lay down for a moment on the narrow wooden bench next to the stove to think about what Gwerlit and Gorathdin had told him. Only a few thoughts later, he was overcome by tiredness and fell fast asleep.

Vrenli's dream

In his dream, Vrenli found himself as a small child in a summer meadow covered with colorful flowers and tall grasses. He was lying in his father's arms under a huge maple tree that was several hundred years old and provided shade. Deer and rabbits jumped past them happily, without any shyness. Birds flew over their heads and sang beautiful songs over the valleys and mountains of Tawinn. It was midday, the sun was at its highest point and its warm, golden rays fell on the old, mighty tree, which began to speak.

"You must take good care of your son, Hallweg. Teach him mental superiority and speed in battle, for only then will he be able to hold his own against opponents two or more heads taller. Teach him, as your father taught you, how to use magical objects and initiate him into the secret of the book," said the tree in a deep, creaky, wooden voice.

"I will teach him everything as it is written," Hallweg replied.

"The course of events can change, but what is written does not. Remember, you don't always have to read a book from beginning to end. That's just a bad habit of the peoples of Wetherid. You can read a book from the middle to the end, or to the beginning, or on a random page of your choice, as you please. Don't always rely on a certain order in life. Everything can change at any time, that's the confusing thing for you because you're not used to it. You live your life according to a preconceived plan. At least that's what you think, but you'll see. You will see. Make the most of the time," said the creaking voice.

The leaves of the maple tree rustled in the rising wind. The next moment Vrenli was in his parents' house, sitting at the table with his father and mother and enjoying supper. Then the village bells suddenly began to ring, urgently and alarmingly. Shouts rang in from the village square outside.

"Fire, fire!" voices shouted in confusion.

The clanging of blades hitting each other and a whole orchestra of arrows whistling through the air could be heard.

"They've entered the village!" Hallweg shouted, jumping up from his chair and running to his weapons. He took them, put his hands firmly around the hilt of his short sword and opened the door.

"Go into the cellar and follow the tunnel to grandfather's house!" he shouted to them and then stormed out into the flaming village, shouting battle cries and readying his short sword.

He was just about to run towards the burning hut opposite to help his friends put out the fire that had broken out on the shingle-covered roof, when a shadow two heads taller than him, screaming loudly, pounced and threw him to the ground. The sharp blade of a sword gleamed in the light of the flames as it hurtled towards his head. At the last moment, he rolled to the side to avoid the fierce blow. Just as the large shadow was about to strike another blow, Hallweg plunged his short sword into its loins. Blood flowed slowly over his blade. The attacker groaned and slumped to the ground.

Hallweg jumped to his feet, his gaze darting hastily through the chaos. About two hundred heavily armed knights and a handful of ogres had invaded the village and set it on fire. They killed anyone who stood in their way. Men, women, children and old people. They searched every house and every hut. Hallweg stopped for a moment, wondering whether he should help his friends put out the fire or throw himself at the attackers, when he heard a loud voice behind him.

"Hallweg, get over here quickly!" the voice called from the mill.

When he turned around, he saw Molekk, the miller's burly son, gesticulating angrily with both hands.

"Five of them have just gone in here. Quick, let's barricade the door," Molekk suggested.

Hallweg nodded and followed him with quick steps to the adjacent barn, from where they pushed an old, heavy cart towards the door of the mill.

"That's it. They can't get out of there. There's only one window and it's at the top," said Molekk, wiping his forehead, taking a deep breath and pointing to the roof of the mill with a sweaty hand.

Cries of despair wafted over from one of the burning houses and made the men shudder. Three of the attackers, who were trying to get an old man to talk, had placed his trembling right hand on a wooden stake and one of them was holding the sharp blade of his sword over it threateningly. But before the old man could answer their question, Hallweg shot two arrows at them in succession. They pierced the lightly armored breastplates engraved with the Astinhod crest and dug deep into their guts through the flesh of their backs. The two victims cried out in pain, screamed and writhed, spat blood and finally fell to the ground dead.

The still-living man flinched, drew his sword and was about to bring it down on the old man's head when the projectile from Molekk's slingshot struck him fatally in the head with full force. The old man looked at his rescuers, shouted his thanks to them and hastily took cover behind the bushy thorn hedge next to his house.

"Back to the mill, Molekk. I have an idea!" Hallweg shouted to drown out the loud sounds of fighting and screaming.

Molekk followed him and when they arrived at the mill, Hallweg explained his plan.

"Get your bow and bring as many arrows as you can find. Come back to me afterwards. We'll let the mill's spinning blades pull us up to the roof. From there we will have a good view of the whole village," Hallweg explained to Molekk.

He nodded and immediately set off for the adjoining house, from which he returned a short time later with his short bow and two full quivers. Both were now standing in front of the old mill. Hallweg grabbed a passing wing with both hands, let himself be pulled all the way up and jumped onto the shingle-covered roof.

He was just about to shout to Molekk to hurry up when a hideous thing several heads taller and spreading an acrid stench moved out of the darkness towards the miller's son.

A club, almost the size of an Abkether, was swung towards Molekk's head by the powerful hand of an ogre that Hallweg could recognize in the light of the flames.

"Duck!" shouted Hallweg from the roof of the mill.

Molekk reacted with presence of mind and was able to dodge the ugly figure's clubbing blow at the last moment. The ogre immediately lunged for another blow, but two of Hallweg's arrows, which he had fired at the thick-skinned, grunting ogre from the roof of the mill, pierced the many-veined, thin skin on its neck. Squealing and grunting loudly, the heavy mountain of flesh took two steps to the right, began to stagger and finally toppled over. The ground shook.

"You see, you have a good view from up here. Now hurry up!" Hallweg called down.

Molekk stood shocked in front of the passing wings of the mill wheel and looked up at the roof.

"Thank you!" Molekk called back. He reached for a wing and was slowly pulled upwards by it.

Once on the roof, they could now, back-to-back, in their position overlooking everything and under the cover of night, shoot their arrows at the attackers, who were easily recognizable by the light of the flames and the burning houses and huts. When they had killed more than a dozen and the rest of the attackers had been driven off by the three hundred armed Abkether defending the village, Hallweg felt a cold, stabbing pain in his back. His senses began to fade, his eyes bugged out, his lungs inflated, blood began to gush from his mouth and finally he slumped down. One of the people trapped in the mill had managed to climb out of the window and onto the roof. He crept up behind them and plunged his sword into Hallweg's back.

Drenched in sweat, Vrenli woke up briefly, tossed and turned a few times and then fell asleep again.

He now saw himself standing with his mother and grandfather at his father's grave. The eldest member of the village council was giving a speech to the assembled villagers.

"He sacrificed his life for the good of us all. Through his courage and his arrows, many of the attackers were killed. May the Father receive him with joy," the old man chanted, stretching his open hands to the sky.

Vrenli's mother burst into tears and was taken into Hallweg's father's arms for comfort.

"He lives on in Vrenli," he said to her and then moved away from the mourners.

A little later, he returned with a scroll of parchment in his right hand and a leather traveling bag hanging around his shoulder.

After a few indefinable images and sounds, Vrenli slipped further into another dream. He was sitting in the middle of a circle of women dressed in silk, shiny white tunics. They were singing a song that was unfamiliar to him.

Once the Father created the peoples of the world,
ended the reign of wolves and dragons unfurled. He then wrote the book of books,
entrusted it to his youth, by his looks.

The peoples, the peoples shall forever stand,
let a new era arise across the land.

The young man began to read the tome,
unaware of how time had flown. He walked by night the path ahead,
recalling the father's words he'd been fed.

The peoples, the peoples shall forever stand,
let a new era arise across the land.

He met a shadow man on the way,
who cast a mighty spell that day.
The book was then taken away from him,
whereupon the young man's search began, grim.

The peoples, the peoples shall forever stand,
let a new era arise across the land.

The youth sought the book in the valley deep,
as a thunderous battle cry did sweep.
Bodies of the dead scattered around, evil had come to the
Glorious Ground.

The peoples, the peoples shall forever stand,
let a new era arise across the land.

Warm rays of sunlight shone through the small gaps in the closed shutters, tickling Vrenli's nose. He woke up and when he heard a rooster's morning wake-up call, he was surprised that he had slept from yesterday afternoon until this morning. He got up from the wooden bench. The melody of the song he had heard in his dream was still in his ears. He opened the window to let the morning in. He took a deep breath and watched as a dog chased after a cat, which eventually fled up a tree. Klersten, the miller, was already on his way to Bendris, the baker, with his handcart full of flour, who used it to bake the Abkether's delicious flatbread. Vrenli went to the wash basin next to his closet and washed the exhausting dreams from his eyes. When he heard the creaking sound of the front door opening, he turned around and saw Werlis standing in the middle of the room with a basket filled with fresh bread and eggs.

"Well rested, Vrenli?" asked Werlis.

"Occasionally you could knock before you enter my house," Vrenli replied somewhat grumpily.

"You must have had a rough night?" asked Werlis, putting the basket on the table.

"After a night like that, you're glad when you wake up again. I'm telling you, I had dreams, terrible. But how come you're already awake? You're usually always the last to wake up," said Vrenli and managed to wring a grin out of his face.

"I thought you'd be happy if we had breakfast together before we face the final test. Besides, I have something to tell you," replied Werlis.

He sat down at the table.

"Then get started without me. I'll just put a kettle of water on quickly," said Vrenli and went to the stove.

He lit a fire while Werlis was already starting to peck at both ends of the eggs he had brought with him.

He then placed them on a plate and broke the bread into bite-sized pieces.

"What I wanted to tell you, Vrenli. Are you listening to me?" asked Werlis.

"Yes, I'm listening to you," Vrenli replied and placed a kettle on the stove.

"Well, I went to Gwerlit that evening. Just as I was about to knock on her door, I heard the stranger from Astinhod, what was his name?" asked Werlis.

"Gorathdin of the Forest," Vrenli helped him out.

"Well, I heard this Gorathdin telling Gwerlit about a beautiful princess," Werlis continued.

"That probably made you curious and you kept eavesdropping. Am I right?" asked Vrenli smiling.

"Believe me, the way that Gorathdin was raving about the princess, even you would have been listening at the door," Werlis defended himself.

"That may well be, but go on," Vrenli urged him as he sucked the contents of an egg with relish.

"I heard this Gorathdin tell Gwerlit that the princess was seriously ill and that the court healers at Astinhod Castle were at a loss. He mentioned a mage who was trying to brew a healing potion," said Werlis, raising both eyebrows.

"And the magician needs the blossoms of the moonflower for this," Vrenli stated and sat down at the table with the kettle full of hot water into which he had put some herbs.

"I'm not finished yet," Werlis continued. "Gorathdin fears that this mysterious illness may be linked to Erwight of Entorbis. Erwight of Entorbis, did you hear that, Vrenli!" Werlis shared aloud.

He was teeming with excitement.

Vrenli nodded and filled his mug with the hot brew.

"He also mentioned a book. I couldn't hear anything more about it because they went into another room. But when they came back, I heard Gorathdin talking about the magic of the elves of the Glorious Valley. Erwight of Entorbis is in search of something that, as I understood it, belongs to the elves. Imagine that Vrenli. Maybe there will be war, who knows," Werlis continued, his eyes wide.

"Who knows," repeated Vrenli, sipping carefully from his hot mug.

"Before I finally decided to knock, I heard Gorathdin say that you will probably go down in history. Did you hear that, Vrenli, you will go down in history," said Werlis excitedly.

Vrenli took notice.

For him, the word history had a different meaning and he immediately thought of last night's dreams.

"Did he say that?" Vrenli asked.

"Yes, he said that you would go down in history. And you know what, if you decide to go with Gorathdin, I will accompany you to Astinhod. I, too, want people to know who Werlis Johnmar was. Do you understand that Vrenli?" asked Werlis.

"Of course I understand that, Werlis," Vrenli replied happily.

"But what did they say to you when you knocked on the door? I'd still like to know," asked Vrenli, taking another egg and slowly sucking it out.

"Well, first Gwerlit told me off for listening at the door, because I didn't even knock, but she opened the door and let her cat out. And then she said to me that if I had a shred of friendship for you, I should go with you," said Werlis, a little ashamed.

"Did Gorathdin of the Forest say something to you?" Vrenli asked curiously.

"Nothing. He just looked at me with his big, dark green eyes. Even though it was so long ago that I almost don't remember what humans look like, I don't think Gorathdin is one of them. Humans don't have green eyes," Werlis replied, widening his eyes to mimic Gorathdin's gaze.

"You're probably right. I've never heard of people with green eyes and his skin shines so strangely. But let's not talk about him any longer. I'm glad that you would accompany me to Astinhod and now that I know that, I think I'll go," Vrenli announced, a broad smile on his face.

"We'll see Astinhod!" Werlis beamed.

The final test

"It's time to get ready for the final test. I'll leave you now and treat myself to a nap in my hammock before I put on my weapons. Meet me at the fountain for lunch," Werlis announced and hurriedly left the house.

Vrenli's thoughts revolved around what Werlis had told him. Erwight of Entorbis was searching for something that belonged to the Elves of the Glorious Valley and he couldn't shake the feeling that it might be his grandfather's book. He finished his cup and glanced at the window, where golden sunrays fell on a dusty pile of books.

"Where would he have kept it?" he asked himself, trying to remember his childhood, but the images of his memory mingled with those of the dreams he had experienced last night.

He couldn't tell the difference between what he had experienced in the past and the images in his dreams. He didn't know whether he had actually experienced what he had seen in the dream or whether it was just a figment of his imagination. But he could remember the book well. He could see it right in front of him. It was a very old book and must have had more than a thousand pages. It was much bigger and heavier than all the other books in Abketh and the purple-colored, leather cover was decorated with ornamental silver fittings. Vrenli could clearly see the strange characters written on the cover.

He knew that his grandfather had read him many stories from it. But no matter how hard he tried to remember at least one of them, he simply couldn't. There was a fog of forgetfulness around the stories that he couldn't see through. But he could still remember his grandfather coming into his room many evenings with the book under his arm, placing it on the small chest of drawers next to the bed, dimming the light, picking up the book and sitting down in the simple little wooden chair by the bed. Before he began to read from it, he had the habit of gazing into the flame of the oil lamp hanging above him for a while, as if he were thinking about something.

Vrenli brushed off his thoughts about the book and returned to his upcoming test. He opened the door to the small chamber next to the stove and took out his father's old combat suit, who was only twenty years older than Vrenli when he died. Vrenli wondered whether he might still be alive if he had taken the time to prepare himself before running out into the burning village. With this thought in mind, he first put on the cotton shirt, as it would soak up the sweat in the exertion of a fight. It took him some effort to squeeze into the tight chain mail shirt made of fine silver threads, which was lighter than it looked and would prevent injury from a sword thrust or a projectile. He slipped into the thick leather trousers and tied the cords that ran along the sides of the barrel. He picked up the brown leather helmet lying on the top shelf and put it on. After closing the door to the chamber again, he adjusted the two thin iron plates that were incorporated into the helmet.

They served to protect the wearer against blows to the forehead and back of the head.

As he walked to the trapdoor that led down to the cellar where his grandfather's weapons collection was kept, he thought that he would certainly have had more fun with all the combat training if he had been allowed to arm himself like this.

"Werlis could hit hard," he muttered to himself, touching a blue, sore spot on his chest.

He opened the trapdoor and was greeted by a cold, musty smell. No one had opened this trapdoor since Vrenli's grandfather returned from his several-month journey through Wetherid seriously ill and died just a few weeks later.

"Far too dark," he muttered and went back to the table in the middle of the room. He took the half-burnt candle, which he lit by the fire in the stove, and climbed down the ladder.

The cellar was dimly lit. Vrenli realized with regret that the many years in the damp darkness had left traces on the numerous objects. He opened the lid of a large, rather rotten box, which only contained the remains of clothes.

Vrenli glanced around the semi-dark, roughly walled room. On a shelf next to the small chamber where the weapons were kept were old, dusty jars with dubious contents. He glanced at the shelf next to it, which was full of dusty, elaborately crafted, thick books, and walked towards it, holding the candle in front of him above his head.

"Maybe I'll get lucky," he thought to himself and carefully took one book after another from the shelf.

But he couldn't find anything special, and above all no book with writing that could still be read. Vrenli knocked the dust off his clothes and walked towards the armory, lifted the heavy bolt and opened the door. This is where Vrenli's grandfather kept the swords, daggers, knives, lances, slingshots, shields, bows and quivers that he had received from his guests over the years. Just to the right of the wall was a holder with a torch, which Vrenli lit with the small flame of the candle.

The small, dusty chamber full of cobwebs brightened. He had only been in here once before. He was still a child when his grandfather was presented with a diamond adorned longsword by a nobly dressed man. When his grandfather was out for a walk with a guest and forgot to lock the door, Vrenli snuck into the chamber. Not much had changed since then, only one or two items had been added to the collection. Vrenli picked up the golden lance leaning against the wall in front of him and looked at the inscription engraved on it.

"May the light of Lorijan always shine for you," he read aloud, wondering what it meant, before putting it back in its place.

He took a step towards the cupboard where the short, curved and long swords, sabres, and daggers were kept, and searched for his father's short sword, which was one of the simplest. What set it apart from the others, however, was its blade was forged in Ib'Agier. No one in all of Wetherid knew better than the dwarves how to smelt the ore from deep within the mountains in fiery furnaces to forge the hardest blades with the resulting metal.

When Vrenli found the short sword, he took it and put it on his belt. He reached for the glass bow and the elaborately woven quiver hanging on the wall in front of him. Vrenli did not know that this was a gift from the Elves of the Glorious Valley. They had made the bow especially for his grandfather, as theirs were at least twice as big as his. Vrenli pulled one of the arrows out of the quiver and examined it. It was made with such care from the finest and hardest wood that it flew further, faster and more accurately than conventional arrows. Vrenli put it back and hung the bow and quiver around his shoulder. Then he extinguished the torch, closed the door and locked it. Now all he had to do was pick up his slingshot from the bench on the terrace, where he and Werlis sat almost every day and practiced their aim by shooting at all sorts of things, and he would be ready for the final test.

He climbed back up the ladder. Just as he was about to close the trapdoor, it occurred to him that the blade of the thirty-year-old short sword would certainly need sharpening.

"There were some grindstones on top of the cabinet with the swords," he recalled.

He climbed back down the ladder, opened the door to the chamber, lit the torch on the wall again and was just about to reach for the grindstones when the cupboard collapsed with a loud crash, followed by the clang of swords falling to the floor.

"All this rotten wood down here is life-threatening. When I get back from my trip, I really must replace them before someone else gets hurt," he said aloud to himself and picked up one of the fine, angular grindstones from the floor.

Just as he was about to stand up again, he noticed a loose stone in the rough masonry wall behind the collapsed cupboard. Amazement and curiosity gripped him, and he began to scrape away the earth around the stone with his short sword. After some effort, he removed it from the wall and laid it on the floor next to the swords. He had uncovered a small cavity and tried to shine the torch he had taken from the wall bracket into the small, dark hole. When he realized that there was something at the very back, he slowly reached out his right hand and hesitantly grabbed it.

"A leather pouch!" he exclaimed in surprise as he pulled the soft object from its hiding place in the wall.

He opened the small, dusty brown bag, which contained a small piece of parchment on top.

"I received these three acorns many years ago from the last living tree creature in the Border Forest. Whoever comes into contact with them without first speaking the following verse will immediately be transformed into a tree," he read aloud and looked at the verse that followed.

"The tree of trees stand by me, it is I who once saved your life, your seed will not hurt me!"

"I was lucky then. It would have been unthinkable if I had touched one of the acorns first," he thought, reading the verse aloud again for good measure before burning the parchment in the flames of the torch.

"These acorns will accompany me on my journey," he said aloud.

He fastened the leather pouch to his belt, closed the chamber and climbed back upstairs. He locked the trapdoor and then went to his washing bowl, dipped a cloth in the water and used it to wipe the blade of his short sword again and again while he carefully sharpened it on the grindstone.

"I've done it! It's as sharp as if it were new," he said with satisfaction and then slid his short sword into the shaft, went outside the door onto the terrace and picked up his slingshot from the small wooden bench, locked the door and made his way to the fountain where Werlis was already waiting impatiently for him.

"What took you so long? We must hurry, the village council and the weapons masters will surely be waiting for us," said Werlis excitedly, not even waiting for an explanation, but walking quickly to the meadows to the north of the village.

When the two of them reported to the three old men for the examination, they were asked why they were late.

"We're sorry we're a little late, but we completely lost track of time helping Gwerlit in the herb garden," Werlis lied.

This was not the first time that Gwerlit, who had a very high reputation in the village, had been used as an excuse for being late and fortunately no one had ever asked her before and so it was this time too. Vrenli and Werlis were sent to the first test, where they had to prove their skill with bow and arrow.

When the two arrived at the northern clearing, Vrenli took a close look at the meadow, because everything was different from the previous months' exercises. To the right of the path that ran right through the middle of the clearing, round targets made of white cotton had been set up on the grass and flower-covered hill. Vrenli estimated the distance at about two hundred and fifty paces, and he knew that not everyone could hit at that distance. About a hundred paces from the left side of the path, a few tree stumps about two paces high rose up on a plain, with pumpkin-sized red helmets on top of them. He assumed that these were the targets he had to hit with his slingshot.

Further down, almost at the end of the path, where the grass was already worn down, there was a circular area marked off with thick ropes where, he assumed, the duel with the short sword would take place. This year there were sixteen Abkether taking the final test. Only eight would pass. Vrenli let his eyes glide past the three stations again when Werlis finally asked him to follow him to the hill.

When they arrived, they were greeted by Armsmaster Narlis, a lean, sinewy man of around seventy. Like all Abketh's weapons masters, Narlis wore laced brown leather trousers and a brown cotton shirt, with a sleeveless leather jacket over it. The golden chain that held his gray cloak together was adorned with an ornate pendant engraved with the mark of the Abketh weapons masters. Next to him, on the meadow floor, lay a short bow made of dark wood, strung with the thin but tear-resistant sinew of a boar. His longbow, which was wrapped in fine silver threads, was leaning upright with its pointed underside against the small wooden platform next to the ground marker. He had hung the quiver, woven from light brown vines and containing a dozen hardwood arrows, next to the small pedestal, on which lay a parchment with the names of the candidates.

Grundlin, Erwog and Jorl, who were not only the same age but also good friends, welcomed Vrenli and Werlis after they had already successfully passed their own test with Narlis.

"Good luck, friends," Erwog wished them and followed Grundlin and Jorl across the meadow and down the path. Armsmaster Narlis made three ticks in red ink on his list and turned to Vrenli and Werlis.

"It's two hundred and fifty paces from the marker here to the targets on the hill," he said, and then explained that they had three attempts to hit the target. He pointed out that they were not allowed to step over the marker and reminded them to take into account the wind and the slope.

"We shot at closer targets on the same level during our exercises. It's impossible to hit the center of a target that's two hundred and fifty paces away on a hill," Werlis objected, discouraged.

"All you have to do is hit the target anywhere," replied the weapons master.

"Then that's good. I thought I wouldn't pass this exam," Werlis remarked.

Narlis gave him a sign that it was his turn next.

"Good luck, Werlis," Vrenli wished him.

"Since I only have to hit the target and not the center, I won't need any luck," Werlis said confidently and smiled.

He stood behind the marker, watched the wind, took his bow, put one of his self-made arrows with hawk feathers attached to the string and shot it at the target, which he missed, albeit narrowly.

"That was close," remarked Vrenli.

"You have two more attempts," Narlis pointed out.

"I'm sure to score this time," Werlis thought to himself.

He plucked the string of his bow, which sounded like the strumming of a lyre.

"You shoot from the bottom up. Don't forget that," Vrenli reminded him.

"I know. I know. I should shoot my arrow steeper," Werlis replied.

He then placed another arrow in the string of his bow and set the firing angle a little steeper. Aiming at the target in front of him on the hill, he tightened the string so much that Vrenli thought it would snap at any moment.

With a whirring whistle, the arrow flew up the hill towards the target, where it got stuck at the far-left edge.

"Done!" exclaimed Werlis.

Vrenli patted him appreciatively on the shoulder.

"You have passed this test, Werlis. You can now move on to the next one," Narlis confirmed and made a tick next to Werlis' name on his list.

Werlis asked to be allowed to wait for Vrenli, who was next. Vrenli followed Narlis' hand gesture, stepped behind the marker, took an ebony-colored arrow, its shimmering silver tip gleaming in the sunlight, from the quiver and placed it in the thin, almost invisible string of his glass bow, which strangely warmed up where he held it.

"Strange, it feels like it's adapting to my grip," thought Vrenli, before tightening it without much effort.

He paid attention to the wind, corrected the launch angle and then released the arrow. Almost silently and faster than the eyes of Werlis and Narlis could follow, the arrow made its way to the center of the target.

"I don't believe that. Was that luck, or were you practising in secret?" Werlis was surprised and stood open-mouthed in front of Vrenli for a few moments.

"A master shot, Vrenli. You hit the center of the target. That hasn't happened for a long time," praised Narlis.

His gaze remained fixed on the glass arch.

"What a strange bow. I've never seen one like it before. May I have a look at it?" he asked.

Vrenli handed Narlis the bow.

"I don't know who made this bow myself. I found it in my grandfather's armory," explained Vrenli.

"How light it is, and it feels so good in the hand, as if it was made for me. Truly, a beautiful bow. You too have passed and can move on to the next test, Vrenli," said Narlis, handing the bow back to him.

Vrenli and Werlis said goodbye, delighted that they had passed the test.

On their way to Armsmaster Jaris, they speculated about who might have made this bow. Vrenli remembered something.

"Grandfather told me that the weapons of the Elves from the Glorious Valley have magical powers. Maybe he got it from them," Vrenli mused.

"As far as I know, the elves live in a dense, impenetrable forest. I don't think they use bows made of glass and even if they did, elves are at least two heads taller than us and a lot stronger. Your bow is as small as one of ours," said Werlis.

"You're probably right. We'll probably never know where the bow came from," agreed Vrenli thoughtfully.

They arrived at the meadow south of the path.

The short, stocky, more than one hundred winter old weapons master Jaris was congratulating Kulis, Werlis' neighbor, on passing his test. With a slightly shaky hand, he made a tick next to his name with a frayed quill and then turned to the two of them.

"Greetings, Vrenli and Werlis. Do you have your slingshot with you?" asked Jaris, raising his.

The two nodded in agreement and began to giggle.

Proving how to use the slingshot should not be a problem for them. Even as children, they had played all kinds of pranks with it. Once they had the idea of shooting at the village bell in the middle of the night, whereupon one hundred and fifty angry, armed Abkether ran out of their houses to the village square and didn't find it funny at all when they realized that the village was not in danger, but that two children had played a trick on them. Vrenli and Werlis were grounded for a few days and their slingshot was confiscated by the village council for several days. Another time, they were just about to shoot apples down from a neighbor's tree behind a wooden fence. After they had successfully brought down about ten, they noticed too late that the neighbor was also in the tree picking apples and had been hit by one of the projectiles. As a result, they were grounded for six days and didn't get their slingshot back like last time.

"So, you two. You have to bring down one of those helmets standing on the tree stumps in front of you. You have three attempts. If you succeed, you've passed the test," explained Jaris, who, like Vrenli and Werlis, remembered their youthful pranks.

They stood together behind the marker and, thinking of their earlier pranks, pulled the smooth, brown leather straps from under their capes, placed the round, peach seed-sized stones in the small leather pockets and began rhythmically swinging the leather straps above their heads. With ease and laughter, they shot one helmet after another off the tree stumps before Jaris even noticed.

"Actually, one of you should just shoot down one of the helmets. It's always the same with you two. You've got nothing but mischief on your minds. Now I have to collect all the helmets because of you and put them back on the tree stumps!" Jaris complained angrily.

"We've passed this test!" shouted Vrenli and Werlis, starting to dance and laughing from the heart.

"Yes, yes. You've passed the test and now make sure you get to your final test," replied Jaris.

He made a shooing gesture and set about collecting the helmets scattered in all directions.

When they had followed the path almost to the edge of the forest, Werlis looked Vrenli firmly in the eyes.

"Now we'll see which of us is the better one," said Werlis.

Vrenli did not answer, for he knew that Werlis could not win against him and his blade from Ib'Agier.

Vrenli approached Armsmaster Turlis, who was overseeing the duel, and greeted him.

"How have you been so far?" Turlis, who was by far the tallest in the village and one of the strongest, wanted to know.

"We passed the test with the bow and the slingshot," Werlis reported proudly, which made Vrenli laugh when the word slingshot was mentioned.

"I'm glad to hear that," Turlis replied, a little surprised at Vrenli's laughter.

The weapons master Turlis was a serious and deliberate man of around seventy. He always had a watchful gaze and his hands, when not otherwise occupied, were always on the hilts of his two short swords, which were ready in the sheaths hanging on the right and left of his belt. Turlis was one of the few who knew how to wield two swords at the same time. He began by explaining the rules of dueling with the short sword to the two of them.

"Don't forget, only one of you will emerge victorious and the loser will have to repeat the final test next year," Turlis reminded them, looking at the two of them seriously.

Vrenli was in a quandary. On one hand, he wanted to pass his test, but on the other, he had to consider that if Werlis lost, he would not accompany him to Astinhod. After some back and forth, he decided that he would let his friend win.

"Let's get started," said Werlis, who had already climbed into the ring and was swinging his short sword through the air as if he were artfully trimming a hedge.

The fight between them did not last long. Werlis knocked the sword out of Vrenli's hand after just a few attacks and Turlis then declared him the winner.

"I won! I won! I told you I was the better of the two of us," Werlis beamed from ear to ear.

Vrenli tried to look disappointed.

"We'll see you again next year," Turlis said to Vrenli, who looked down at the floor in disgust.

"Such bad luck. I was only inattentive for a moment. That's what I get for it now. See you next year, Turlis," Vrenli looked into the ring once more and then set off back with Werlis.

"Don't hang your head. With a little more practice, you're sure to win next time," said Werlis encouragingly, who was delighted with his victory.

At the edge of the clearing, the three old men had already divided the winners and losers into two groups. Once there, Vrenli joined the group of losers and Werlis approached the group of winners with a broad smile. Vrenli realized how important this victory was for his friend and was glad to have made it possible for him to win. It was some time before the three weapons masters came up the path and joined the three old men.

They now called the losers up one by one and informed them that it would be advisable to hold further exercises before they returned for the final test next year. When Vrenli was called up, he only listened with one ear, as his thoughts were on his forthcoming journey to Astinhod and his grandfather's book, which he was determined to find beforehand.

"Vrenli, you should listen to us more carefully," rebuked Armsmaster Jaris, who noticed his inattention, in a stern tone.

"Forgive me. I was thinking," Vrenli said looking at him sheepishly.

"In your thoughts? Well, maybe you'd better concentrate on what we say to you, otherwise you could easily be one of the losers again next year," one of the old men warned him.

Vrenli said goodbye to them and walked towards the group of winners.

"Honoring the winners will take some time. In the meantime, I will go to Gwerlit and Gorathdin and tell them my decision. You'll come with me, won't you?" Vrenli asked Werlis, who was just telling the others in his group about his fight and looked at him expectantly.

"Yes, I haven't changed my mind. I'll come to you as soon as this is over. And don't be angry with me for winning," Werlis agreed.

"I'm not angry with you, Werlis. Not in the slightest. I'm happy for you! I'll see you later," replied Vrenli.

He then made his way to Gwerlit's house. He took the small side path that led from the mill to the Bells Inn. Mina was sitting under the window on the small wooden bench next to the front door.

"Hello Vrenli! Which of you two won the duel?" she asked curiously.

"Werlis knocked the sword out of my hand after just a few attacks," confessed Vrenli, trying once again to look disappointed.

"I'm so sorry for you. You'll have to compete again next year! Please pass on my congratulations to Werlis," replied Mina, smiling sheepishly.

"I'll do that, Mina. I must get going now. See you around," said Vrenli approvingly.

He walked to the village square, where some girls were giggling and chatting. When he saw his Aunt Lurie and Nemlis, the glassblower's wife, standing behind the girls by the fountain, he stopped.

"I really don't want Aunt Lurie to tell me off for having to repeat the final test," he thought, and immediately made a dash for it, walking across Polmis' garden and around the village square.

He followed the wide hedge to its end and walked across the manicured lawn of his Uncle Rados, his mother's brother and Aunt Lurie's husband. He climbed over the small wooden fence and crossed the springtime meadow between his uncle's house and the northern part of Gwerlit's herb garden, which he walked around.

"Vrenli, my boy! How did you fare in the final test?" Gwerlit asked him as she watered the flowers growing along the wall of the house.

She approached and sat down next to Gorathdin on the front steps.

"Hello Gwerlit! Good afternoon, Gorathdin. Werlis has won our duel," he replied.

Gorathdin greeted him.

"Did he? That surprises me. I was firmly convinced that you would win, my boy. One can be so wrong. But you're not going to worry about it, are you? If I remember correctly, your father had to repeat the final test three times and, as we all know, he was later appointed Master of Arms himself," Gwerlit said and put the bucket down.

"To tell you the truth, I let Werlis win. Victory meant much more to him than it did to me. Besides, I talked to him after the conversation with you and Gorathdin about the trip to Astinhod and he will come with me. That's why I didn't want him to lose. I was afraid he would change his mind," Vrenli revealed to them.

Gorathdin listened.

"So you will accompany me, Vrenli?" asked Gorathdin.

He got up from the front steps.

Vrenli looked up into Gorathdin's dark green eyes.

"If I can help you with that and the message is that important to the mage, then I think I'll come with you. Although, there's something I haven't understood so far. You said that this journey also has to do with me and you can't tell me more about it. Well, if the journey is also about me, then I find it very strange why you won't tell me more about it. I am a simple Abkether from the remote valley of Tawinn and have never seen you before in my life and yet I feel like I know you and I am sure I heard a voice when we first met. Even if that sounds a bit crazy," Vrenli shared his thoughts.

Gorathdin looked at Gwerlit, but she only raised her eyebrows and remained silent.

"I can understand your curiosity and that this all seems very strange to you, and I wish I could tell you more about it, but that's not my job. It is Master Drobal's. I don't want you to be worried about it though. Let me put it this way; Erendir had an important task in Wetherid and you are his grandson. You will learn more about it in Astinhod, friend. Be patient," Gorathdin said and sat back down on the front steps.

"Grandfather had an important job in Wetherid? He hadn't told me about that. But that would explain his long journey," thought Vrenli.

"You young people need to be more patient. You can't always know everything right away. Some things you find out at a young age, others only when you get older and some never," Gwerlit philosophized and went inside, returning a little later with a sealed scroll of parchment.

"Here is the message for Master Drobal, my boy. Just give it to him personally. You'll recognize him by the diamond-shaped mark on his forehead. Take care of yourself and Werlis. Good luck, my boy! I'll leave you and Gorathdin alone now. I have to take care of the moonflowers. It's a full moon today," Gwerlit said goodbye with a warm hug, stroked Vrenli's dark, half-length hair and went into the herb garden.

"We have to be in Astinhod within fifteen days, Gwerlit told me, otherwise the flowers will lose their healing powers. So, we don't have much time. We will set off early in the morning. Prepare yourself well for the journey," Gorathdin warned sternly.

Vrenli looked at Gorathdin wordlessly. His thoughts revolved around what Werlis had told him after he had overheard Gwerlit and Gorathdin.

"Should I approach him about the sick princess and what he said about me going down in history? He didn't mention anything to me about Erwight of Entorbis. Maybe Werlis just misheard them," Vrenli thought to himself and decided to wait with his questions. He wanted to look for the book first, which he hoped would answer some of his questions.

"Gwerlit was right about what she said. I'll have plenty of time to talk to Gorathdin about all this," he continued, sitting down next to Gorathdin on the front steps.

The two talked for some time. Gorathdin told him a lot about the city of Astinhod until Vrenli finally said goodbye to him. Gorathdin's story about the city of men made him think. Much of what he heard he thought he had heard before.

He walked home with quick steps. The desire to find the book grew in him and as soon as he entered his house, he began to search for it. He didn't waste a single thought on the fact that he had to repeat the final test and would be leaving for Astinhod in the morning. The only thing that interested him now was finding the book. He felt that there was something special, something important connected to it. But he couldn't place this connection.

As he rummaged through the wooden boxes to the right of the bookshelf, he thought about why he wanted to find the book. Did he want to find it because it belonged to his grandfather? Because it connected him to his childhood, or did it have to do with his father and the dream he had last night?

"What secret did the talking maple tree mean? Was it even grandfather's book? If it wasn't his book, who did it belong to?" he asked himself as the urge that drove him on incessantly grew within him.

He took every single book from the bookshelf next to the fireplace, read their titles and leafed through some of them. But the book he was looking for was not among them. He began to open all the cupboards and chests of drawers and searched through them meticulously. In the hope of finding a secret hiding place, he then decided to remove some slats from the wooden paneling on the walls. But apart from a lot of dust, some spiders and beetles, he couldn't find anything. He continued his search in the kitchen that led into the living room. Here, too, he opened all the cupboards and chests of drawers and looked in all the larger pots. He pushed aside the large glass containers on the sturdy wooden shelf, which contained a wide variety of liquids, rocks and plants. He wanted to make sure that the book was not behind them. He searched under the chests of drawers and behind the shelves, but the book was nowhere to be found, so he opened the door to the small chamber next to the stove and searched through it to no avail.

"I've already looked in the cellar and it's not in the living room, the kitchen or the chamber either. That only leaves the bedroom and the attic," he said aloud to himself, pausing for a moment and wiping the beads of sweat from his forehead.

He went to the table and sat down. Exhausted, he looked around him.

"Is the book possibly not in the house? Did grandfather take the secret of the book with him to his grave? Maybe it's a book about magic. Maybe it holds great power. But why can't I remember anything? Did my grandfather and father teach me magic? Were they powerful magicians? Was Abketh attacked because of the book? Or maybe because of grandfather and that's why he and father had stopped reading it to me, so as not to put the village and me in danger! But where is the book now? I was sure it was here in the house, within my grasp. As if I could feel it," he thought to himself.

Vrenli was shivering from the cold, even though it was already late spring.

He trotted back into the living room and lit a fire in the stove, where he warmed himself up before going into the bedroom, where he continued to search in the wardrobe and in the small chest of drawers next to the bed. As he couldn't find anything, he searched under the bed and behind the wooden paneling on the walls. But without success.

"That leaves the attic," he said aloud and went back into the living room where he used a small pole leaning against the wall next to the bookshelf to open the hatch to the attic and pull down the folding ladder.

Just as he was about to climb up the first rung, there was a knock at the door and Werlis entered, beaming.

"Come on, let's go outside, the village festival has already started," Werlis urged him.

"Maybe later," said Vrenli, half interested.

"Can you help me look for my grandfather's book in the attic first?" he asked him.

Werlis nodded in agreement and followed him up the ladder.

"What's so important about this book?" wondered Werlis.

"It's the book my grandfather used to read to me as a child," replied Vrenli, sweat dripping from his brow.

Werlis stopped in the middle of the ladder.

"It's just a book, Vrenli! You're shaking. Let's look for it tomorrow, or when we return from Astinhod. Don't bother any more, it's already late. Let's celebrate now," said Werlis, worried about Vrenli's distress.

"Are you going to help me or not?" Vrenli's face hardened. He climbed up the last rung.

"If it's so important to you, then of course I'll help you. Although I would have preferred to drink a mug or two of mead with you and the others. Everyone is gathered outside celebrating, Vrenli," Werlis replied and climbed higher up the ladder.

When they realized that the attic was pitch black, Werlis climbed down again, went into the living room and returned with a lit candle. The air under the roof was very dry, almost stuffy. There were cobwebs hanging from the roof posts and walls and when Vrenli took a step down from the ladder onto the wooden floor, he kicked up so much dust that it filled their lungs, and they began to cough. Vrenli wiped away the large, thick nets hanging in front of him with his hand and peered into the half-dark, empty attic.

"That's strange. It's empty. Strange, that doesn't fit in with grandfather at all. There's something wrong here. Come on Werlis, there must be a secret room or something similar in here somewhere," said Vrenli, visibly puzzled and tense.

He urged Werlis on, whereupon the two of them spent half the night searching for loose floorboards, wall paneling and false floors. During their efforts, they talked about the final test and about Gorathdin and Gwerlit.

"I agreed to travel to Astinhod with Gorathdin and told them you are coming with me. You're coming, aren't you?" asked Vrenli, pausing for a moment.

"Of course I'm coming with you. You can stop asking me that," replied Werlis somewhat grumpily.

Time was running out and he began to worry whether they would be able to see any of the village festival at all. Shortly after midnight, dusty and exhausted, they descended the ladder after their fruitless search.

"The book isn't here," Vrenli realized disappointedly and sat down on the bench next to the stove, where a fire was still burning, and looked at Werlis with tired eyes.

"Let's go outside and join the others. It would be a shame if we didn't get a taste of the feast. Think of all the goodies and the mead," Werlis suggested and waited in the already half-open doorway.

Singing and loud laughter drifted in from outside and Werlis was startled for a moment when fireworks were set off, lighting up the sky in red, green and blue.

"I'm really too tired for this, the search for the book has exhausted me too much," Vrenli confessed and put his legs up.

"Too bad. I'll see you tomorrow after breakfast," Werlis said goodbye and closed the door behind him. He still couldn't understand Vrenli's excitement about the book.

Vrenli sat next to the warm fire for some time, gazing into the semi-dark living room. His thoughts were still on the book. He was angry, upset and deeply saddened.

"It's very strange that I couldn't find the book," he thought to himself and wondered where else the book could be since it wasn't in the house.

"I'll ask mother and Gwerlit about it tomorrow, maybe one of them knows where it is," Vrenli decided in his thoughts.

It was only when he went into the bedroom, lay down in his bed and pulled the covers over him that he pushed his thoughts about the book aside and thought about his forthcoming journey to Astinhod.

The departure to Astinhod

The next morning, shortly after Vrenli woke up, he began to pack everything he needed for the long journey into his leather traveling bag; his washing kit, two flints, a drinking bowl, his small knife, a piece of thread, needle and twine, warm socks, thick woolen clothing, a rolled-up sheepskin and an ointment that he had found on one of the shelves during his search for the book yesterday. He tied up the travel bag, made sure that the small pouch with the acorns was still hanging on his belt and went to the small chamber next to the stove where his father's leather armor and chain mail were kept and opened the door. He hesitantly reached for the leather helmet, lifted it up and put it back a moment later.

"I'm going on a journey, not going to war," he said aloud to himself and locked the door.

He walked up to the clothes rack next to the front door and looked at the bow from the Glorious Valley hanging there.

"Actually, this beautiful piece is far too good to take with me on my journey. My slingshot and father's short sword should suffice as weapons," he thought.

He looked at his travel bag and went through its contents again. Before he left his house, he closed all the shutters, checked that the fire in the stove had gone out and, most important of all, went into the bedroom and made his bed.

"When I get back, I'll just fall into my bed and sleep for at least two days," he said to himself as he stretched the fresh sheet over the straw-filled mattress.

He conscientiously folded up the warm, fluffy blanket and placed it on the bottom end of the bed. He shook out the down-filled pillow and placed it at the top end.

"Now just a quick visit to mother and I'll be ready," he muttered to himself as he stepped out of the bedroom and looked around the living room once more.

The wooden slats that he had torn from the wall next to the bookshelf caught his eye.

"Not a pretty sight, really. I'll fix that when I get back," he decided.

n

Vrenli made his way to his mother's house. Fortunately, the conversation with her did not last as long as he had feared it would. He asked her about his grandfather's book, but to his disappointment she didn't know any more about it than he did. When Vrenli told her that he would be traveling with Gorathdin of the Forest to Astinhod, she burst into tears. He was prepared for this; he knew that she would not approve of this journey. He understood that after losing her parents, her husband and his parents, she now only had him and she did not want to lose her only child.

"It breaks my heart, boy," were her words.

But to his surprise, her attempts to dissuade him from his plan were limited.

"You're old enough to decide for yourself now, Vrenli," she said to him.

They drank tea together and Vrenli tried to find out more about his childhood from her. His mother told him one or two stories, but she didn't say anything really significant.

After they had said their tearful goodbyes, Vrenli went to Werlis to run a few errands with him. On the way to the merchant, where they wanted to buy durable supplies such as beans and dried meat, they met Molekk, the son of Klersten, who immediately approached when he saw them.

"Good morning, you two. I've heard that you're leaving for Astinhod today to bring the king a message from Abketh, just like your grandfather once did, Vrenli," Molekk said to the two of them in a good mood.

Vrenli and Werlis looked at him questioningly.

"How do you know we're traveling to Astinhod? And what message are you talking about? I don't understand," Vrenli wondered.

"People hear a lot of things. Why else would you take the long and dangerous journey if it wasn't about something very important. And until now, everything that was important in Wetherid was always connected to Astinhod. But what am I talking about? You should go to Gwerlit, she's been waiting for you all morning. And before I forget, I have something else for you here."

He rummaged in a small bag he had under his cloak.

"Here, take these loaves of bread. I baked them from the fruit flour of the Everfull Tree. They are no bigger than a walnut, but if you put them in water, they will grow into a real loaf that you can eat for several days. Here, take these three pieces and all the best on your journey," he said to them.

Molekk pressed the three tiny pieces of bread into Werlis' hand, who looked puzzled. Werlis thanked him and looked skeptically at the three little things in his palm before stowing them away safely. They said goodbye to him and went to Mr. Rosenstrauch's store, which was only a few houses away.

Vrenli opened the door and a soft chime sounded.

"Good morning, Vrenli. Good morning, Werlis," the small, white-haired man greeted them, adjusting his glasses.

"I have already prepared a package for your journey. Dried meat, beans, a delicious dry cheese, some nuts and dried mushrooms," said the grocer to Vrenli and Werlis with a friendly expression on his face.

The two were astonished.

He pushed the parcel over the counter and when Vrenli went to pay, he turned away from them in a huff.

"I'm not going to ask anything of you. On the contrary, I'll give you another thirty gold coins to take with you. I hope they will be useful to you. You can always use some small change on a long journey," he said with a smile and pressed a small leather pouch into Vrenli's hand.

The amazement of the two grew.

"But I can't accept that, Mr. Rosenstrauch," Vrenli fended him off.

Werlis also shook his head in disapproval.

"Of course you can, Vrenli," Mr. Rosenstrauch encouraged him and smiled again.

Vrenli put the bag away.

"And now make sure you get to Gwerlit. I'm sure she's already waiting for you," he urged them.

Werlis took the parcel with the provisions.

"Thank you very much, Mr. Rosenstrauch," the two thanked him.

They left the store.

"Strange, apparently everyone here knows about our plans," Vrenli wondered.

Werlis shrugged his shoulders.

"That was the first time one of the Rosenstrauchs had ever given anyone anything," Werlis remarked in amazement.

Vrenli raised his eyebrows.

"I find that strange too".

They were just crossing the village square when Armsmaster Jaris asked them to wait.

"Wait a moment. I have a map for you with the way to Astinhod marked on it!" he called out to them. After crossing the village square, he handed Vrenli a fragile scroll of parchment.

"How come everyone knows about our trip?" Vrenli asked him after he had passed the map to Werlis.

"Gwerlit and Gorathdin were at the village feast until midnight, and they mentioned that you are both going to Astinhod with the visitor," old Jaris told them.

"Ah, that explains a lot, of course," replied Vrenli and looked at Werlis, who nodded in agreement. They thanked the weapons master and said goodbye.

"Let's go to Gwerlit and Gorathdin," suggested Vrenli and led the way.

Werlis followed him.

On the way there, they met some villagers who shouted congratulations to them, as if they were setting out to rescue the village from an impending disaster. When they arrived at Gwerlit's house, Gorathdin was already waiting impatiently for them, walking up and down the wooden fence of the herb garden.

"You probably understand 'early in the morning' a little differently than I do! We should have been on the road at sunrise! Wait here, I'll just get my travel bag, then we can set off," urged Gorathdin, about to take a step towards the front steps.

"Wait, we're not ready yet. We still want to talk to Gwerlit and then we have to stow our provisions and put on our weapons," explained Vrenli.

Gorathdin turned around again.

"Gwerlit is not in the house. She was waiting for you, but after a while she went into the forest to collect herbs," Gorathdin said.

"But I wanted to ask her something important," Vrenli interjected disappointedly.

"I'm sorry, but we really don't have time to wait for her. The moonflower blossoms have to be processed in the next fourteen days! Time is of the essence. I'll wait for you here. Hurry up!" Gorathdin said sternly.

The two walked quickly back to their houses, from which they returned after some time with their traveling bags around their shoulders and armed with their short swords and slingshots.

"Let's set off," urged Gorathdin. "I want to reach Aarl's hut before nightfall. If we find him there, we can spend the night with him," he added.

"Do you mean Aarl, the Thirian from the south who lives near the Border Forest?" asked Vrenli.

"Yes, that's the one I mean. Do you know him?" replied Gorathdin.

"I've only heard of him," Vrenli admitted.

"We've avoided the path to the Border Forest until now," Werlis added, somewhat ashamed.

"Have you ever traveled beyond Tawinn and seen the wide green valleys, high angular mountains, broad rushing rivers, crystal-clear lakes and magnificent cities of Wetherid?" Gorathdin asked, pointing with his right hand to the horizon to their left.

"Never until now," the two replied, following Gorathdin along the path that led east from their village of Abketh into the neighboring mixed forest.

They turned around one last time and looked back with mixed feelings.

Leaving their family, friends and the small, quiet, peaceful Abketh behind was not easy for them. On the other hand, they were looking forward to seeing Astinhod soon and with this anticipation in them, they followed Gorathdin to the small path that lay to the right of the road and led across a meadow to the edge of the forest to the east.

Vrenli noticed that he had never been on this path more than two or three times before and that he had never followed it more than a few hundred steps deep into the forest. On second thought, he had to wonder about that. When he and Werlis went hunting or picking mushrooms and berries, they did so in the forest that bordered Abketh to the northwest.

They avoided the eastern forest, which was also called the Border Forest. It had once been traveled through by Abkether on their way to Astinhod, but that was many, many years ago. Vrenli only realized now, as he thought about it, that no one from the village had actually traveled to Astinhod in decades. The path, overgrown with tall grasses and low scrub, remained unused by the inhabitants of Abketh.

"Have you ever thought about why none of us have used this path in recent years, Werlis?" asked Vrenli, who almost tripped over a root sticking out of the ground.

"Watch where you're going and no, I haven't really thought about that yet. Why should I?" replied Werlis, following at a greater distance behind Gorathdin, who stopped to wait for them.

"I mean, isn't it strange? None of us have traveled to Astinhod in the last twenty or twenty-five years," Vrenli remarked.

Werlis asked Gorathdin to walk a little slower.

"Why is that strange? I don't understand what you mean. I don't see the need for any of us to travel to Astinhod," Werlis replied skeptically.

Both began to pant as they tried to keep up with Gorathdin.

"Haven't you noticed that we no longer trade with the other peoples of Wetherid? But what really makes me wonder is that we don't even know what's going on in the rest of Wetherid. We have an alliance with the King of Astinhod, but none of us have been there for so long. Doesn't that surprise you?" asked Vrenli, now starting to walk even faster.

"No, I'm not surprised. Why should I be!" replied Werlis as he climbed over a large stone.

"I'm just saying that it might not hurt to know what's going on in Wetherid, and I imagine the King of Astinhod might be interested to know what's going on in Abketh and Tawinn," Vrenli said in response, dodging the stone.

"You think too much. I don't think people are interested in our village. What's more, it's the only settlement in Tawinn," explained Werlis.

He stopped for a moment and pulled up his ochre-yellow linen trousers. Vrenli was waiting for him.

"And besides, if something were to happen in Wetherid that affected all peoples, the king would certainly send messengers to Abketh," he added and continued walking.

Gorathdin had to wait for them again.

"What do you mean, Gorathdin? You live in Astinhod. Do they talk about Abketh there? And can you please walk a little slower?" Vrenli asked him, puffing along beside him.

"Forgive me, friends. I paid too little attention to your greatness. As far as I can tell, Abketh has almost been forgotten. The path over the Ice Mountains to Tawinn is difficult and, as Werlis has already correctly pointed out, your village is the only settlement there," Gorathdin replied and followed the winding and now somewhat sloping path light-footedly.

"I've had the feeling for a long time that it's very convenient for the village council that Abketh is being forgotten. It seems to me that they want to hide from the rest of the world," Vrenli speculated, looking up at the sky through the treetops.

The sun was high above them, it was midday and the few warm rays that fell through the sea of leaves onto the damp forest floor were soaked up by the tufts of grass and low-growing plants that were now only sporadically growing on the path. The deeper they hiked into the forest, the more the narrow path turned into a dark hollow.

"Watch where you're going!" said Gorathdin, who stepped over some stones and roots.

The loamy, almost reddish-brown earth was swollen with moisture and as the path became slightly sloped, Vrenli and Werlis had their eyes on the ground. They struggled to climb over the roots and stones and had to be extremely careful not to slip and fall. For Gorathdin, the muddy, stony, deeply furrowed hollow path with its many tangled roots sticking out of the ground was not a problem. Werlis watched him as he climbed over all the obstacles without looking at the ground, as if by instinct.

"It seems to me that you spend a lot of time in the woods," Werlis said to Gorathdin, whose eyes glanced through the surrounding trees to the right and left of the path.

"I spent my whole youth in the forest," Gorathdin replied with a smile.

He stopped briefly to help them over a fallen tree trunk that lay across the path. They marched on without stopping.

It was late afternoon and they had already made more than half their way through the Border Forest when the hollow path became flat, covered with moss and leaves again. They followed it for some time until they reached a point where a path leading from the north crossed theirs.

"Wait!" Gorathdin said suddenly.

He gave them a hand signal to stop. His dark green eyes began to light up as he looked up the northern path.

"Is something wrong?" asked Werlis.

"Be quiet. I hear footsteps," Gorathdin remarked and jumped behind the thick trunk of an oak tree that stood next to the crossroads.

"Over here! Quickly! Hide and keep quiet," he warned them, grabbing a branch of the leafy oak at head height and pulling himself up into the tree nimbly and effortlessly.

"Gorathdin? Where are you?" whispered Vrenli, who had crouched down on the ground behind the trunk of the oak tree with Werlis.

"He climbed into the tree," replied Werlis, pointing upwards into the oak.

"I can't see him," said Vrenli quietly, who had spread his brown, furry cloak from the Dark Forest over himself and Werlis and from where the two looked onto the path at a point where he lifted it slightly.

"The leaves on the ground are all damp," whispered Werlis.

"Shh!" warned Vrenli, who was still amazed that he couldn't see Gorathdin up in the tree.

"There are five figures coming down the path," Werlis drew Vrenli's attention.

"Shh, they're people," Vrenli replied quietly.

He put his index finger to his mouth and lifted his cloak a little more.

The five men, dressed in brown leather pants and thick linen shirts, came closer to the crossroads. Vrenli was worried because he didn't know whether Gorathdin was in the oak tree or whether he had escaped.

"What could humans possibly want here? No strangers have been seen near Abketh for years. Is their stay in the Border Forest possibly connected to the appearance of Gorathdin of the Forest?" wondered Vrenli, crouching under the cloak.

"His dark green eyes, his physique and the way he moves. Maybe he really isn't human? If so, then he's not from Astinhod either," thought Vrenli, and the more he thought about it, the more he became convinced that Gorathdin was not human.

"A person with dark green eyes? No, I've never heard of that," he pondered.

The five men stopped abruptly at the crossroads, and it sounded as if they were arguing about which way to go. One of them, a fat, bearded, dark-haired man, divided the others into two groups and pointed with his hand along the eastern path and then to the one leading west.

"Look around for tracks!" he called after the others and, to the horror of Vrenli and Werlis, sat down right next to the trunk of the oak tree they were hiding behind.

Vrenli noticed that Werlis wanted to say something to him and held his hand over his mouth at the last moment.

"Shh!", Vrenli whispered to Werlis and let the end of the cloak slide back onto the forest floor.

Without moving, breathing quietly, they waited for the fat man to move away from the oak. The air under the cloak quickly became stuffy, however, and so Vrenli lifted the end of his cloak again slightly. He looked at the path and tried hard to remember the appearance of the five men, comparing their appearance with that of Gorathdin.

"He could be human in terms of his size and build, but his shimmering skin, dark green eyes and pointed ears speak against it. No. Humans don't have eyes like that and especially not pointed ears. Pointed ears only belong to..." he thought and paused for a moment.

"Elves. Yes, elves. Elves have pointy ears. Now I remember one of the stories my grandfather used to read to me," he remarked to himself.

Vrenli was so pleased that he almost stood up, but luckily Werlis held him back.

"What's got into you? Stay down," whispered Werlis, hoping that the fat man hadn't heard him.

Vrenli let the end of the cloak slide back onto the forest floor.

"Elves have pointy ears and that's why they were often teased by humans. The alliance of the elves. I can almost remember the whole story now," Vrenli thought happily, but his joy disappeared as quickly as it had come.

"But elves don't live in Astinhod. Astinhod is a city of humans," Vrenli corrected his own thoughts about Gorathdin.

He could now remember exactly what his grandfather had read to him from the book about the elves and humans. He knew that there was an alliance between the two peoples and that they lived peacefully side by side in Wetherid. Nevertheless, there were some things that an elf should not do, including joining forces with humans. It was also advisable to keep a certain distance.

"An elf who lives among humans? And what about the voice I heard?" Vrenli asked himself.

Werlis became impatient and unintentionally bumped his left knee into Vrenli's stomach.

"Shh!" he hissed at him.

The air under the cloak became stuffy again and Vrenli slowly and quietly lifted the end again.

"What's that voice I heard all about?" Vrenli continued to ponder. He tried to remember the voice and its sound.

"I'm sure it was Gorathdin's voice," he thought and was startled when a longhorn beetle slowly climbed over his hand.

"Magic! It must be magic. The magic of the elves, yes, it must be!" he thought, pleased that he had come to this conclusion.

A soft cry interrupted his thoughts. Werlis was startled, jumped up from under his cloak and looked around, searching. Apart from the trees, he could see nothing and no one, but when he stepped out from behind the thick oak trunk onto the path, he looked in horror at the fat, bearded man lying dead on the ground in front of him. Strangled! He was just about to call for Vrenli when a hand grabbed him by the back of the neck and pulled him up into the tree.

"Shh!" Gorathdin whispered to Werlis, covering his mouth with one hand and pointing with the other at the two men returning to the oak from the western path.

"Hold on to this branch and stay calm," Gorathdin whispered. Werlis nodded.

Vrenli, who was worried about Werlis, had just stepped out from behind the trunk of the oak tree when one of the two men caught sight of him.

"There's someone up ahead!" one of them shouted and ran towards Vrenli, who was standing motionless and looking at them in fear.

"Kurdek is dead. The little one killed him!" shouted the man dressed in dark suede, drawing a dagger the size of Vrenli's short sword.

Vrenli was about to take a step back when the man running towards him fell to the ground with an arrow piercing his chest.

"An ambush!" shouted the still-living man, hoping that his two friends, who had followed the path to the east, could hear him.

He reached with both hands for two palm-sized throwing knives, which were in small leather sheaths on his chest strap and investigated the oak. Before he could spot anyone in the tree, an arrow hit him and he slumped dead on the forest floor next to the two other men. Vrenli froze. He thought several times about reaching for his short sword, but a great fear paralyzed his muscles and constricted his throat. A hand unexpectedly grabbed him by the back of the neck and pulled him up through the leaves and branches into the oak tree.

"Hide behind the trunk," Gorathdin whispered, pointing to the thick branch behind him.

But Vrenli didn't react, he just looked at him with wide eyes.

"Quick, take care of Vrenli," he whispered to Werlis, who climbed out from a branch behind the trunk of the oak tree.

"Vrenli, reach for my hand," Werlis whispered softly and held out his hand.

"Vrenli! Come on, grab my hand," he whispered emphatically.

Vrenli hesitantly grabbed Werlis' hand and pulled himself onto the thick branch that led behind the trunk of the oak tree.

"Gorathdin is an elf. He lied to us, Werlis. Did you see how he killed the three humans in cold blood and insidiously by ambush? He didn't have the slightest inhibition. He might be a murderer and wanted," Vrenli revealed.

Werlis looked at him in astonishment.

"An elf? A murderer?" Werlis repeated with wide eyes.

Vrenli nodded.

"We have to do something before he kills the other two as well," said Vrenli emphatically.

Werlis thought about it for a few moments before nodding in agreement.

The two men — who had just returned from the path leading to Abketh and saw the others lying motionless on the forest floor — then began to run as fast as they could towards the oak tree. They drew their throwing knives and searched around. Gorathdin was just about to put an arrow in the string of his bow when he was pushed out of the tree by Vrenli and Werlis.

"What are you doing?" Gorathdin shouted as he fell.

He did a somersault and landed upright on the forest floor. The two men immediately pounced on him, threw him to the ground and held him there with all their strength.

"Now we've finally found you, elf," said one of them, laughing maliciously.

Gorathdin was taken aback.

He had never expected that his two companions would throw him at the feet of his pursuers. He had managed to kill three of the thieves from Astinhod from his safe position and it would have been easy for him to get rid of the remaining two who were now pinning him to the ground through the folly of Vrenli and Werlis.

"You will pay for killing our three friends, elf!" the thinner of the two shouted at him and put the blade of his dagger to his throat.

Vrenli and Werlis looked down at Gorathdin, who was in a hopeless situation.

"Vrenli, your folly will have serious consequences for the whole of Wetherid. It's no secret that the thieves of Astinhod have formed an alliance with Erwight of Entorbis," Vrenli heard a voice within him.

"Erwight of Entorbis?" exclaimed Vrenli, attracting the attention of the two thieves.

"Whoever else is up there, if you don't want us to cut your friend Gorathdin's throat here and now, you'd better get down from that tree!" one of the thieves shouted into the oak.

Vrenli looked in horror at the blade on Gorathdin's neck. He realized that he had done something very stupid.

"What do we do now? We can't let them cut his throat, even if he is a murderer," whispered Werlis.

"I'm afraid he's not a murderer, Werlis," Vrenli whispered back quietly, ashamed.

Werlis was confused and looked at Vrenli in astonishment. The thief under the oak once again threatened to kill Gorathdin.

"Have you got your slingshot with you?" Vrenli asked quietly.

Werlis pulled it out from under his cloak and lifted it up.

"I don't think they know there are two of us. I'll go down. Wait for a favorable moment," Vrenli instructed Werlis.

He nodded in agreement, but he wasn't entirely comfortable with the idea. The tree was too densely overgrown for him to hit a target at ground level without difficulty. They looked each other firmly in the eyes once more before Vrenli slowly climbed to the lowest branch of the oak, from which he hesitantly jumped down to the ground. He fell, as expected, right at the feet of the two thieves from Astinhod.

"Who have we got here? A child?" one of them wondered, grabbing Vrenli by the cloak and pulling him up.

Vrenli looked into Gorathdin's glowing, dark green eyes, in which he could not recognize any hatred towards himself.

"I am not a child, but an Abkether and I am traveling to Astinhod with Gorathdin to buy goods. I am a merchant and have gold with me. Let us go and I'll give it to you," he lied to the full-bearded, tanned thief.

Gorathdin did not understand what Vrenli was trying to achieve with his lie.

"Does he really think he can buy our lives," he thought to himself.

The thief began to laugh.

"Gold, you say? And pay us for letting the stinking elf live?" he asked maliciously.

He was still holding Vrenli by the cape at eye level.

"I don't think you quite understand, Abkether. We're thieves, we take what we want!" he shouted at Vrenli, dropped him to the ground and kicked him.

The force of the blow almost knocked Vrenli unconscious, but his will to make amends for the stupidity he had committed saved him. He gasped and writhed on the ground.

"Take the gold, but let us live," he begged the thief tearfully, nimbly taking the small leather pouch from his belt and lifting it up.

The strong, tanned hand of the man, who was two heads taller, hastily reached for the bag.

"What are you up to? There are no gold coins in this bag!" he shouted at him after shaking and feeling the bag.

"No, not this bag. Sorry, I gave you the wrong one in my excitement. Please, give it back to me!" begged Vrenli.

He tried to look desperate.

"You wish!" the thief replied and opened the small leather pouch.

He reached in with two of his fingers. When he touched one of the three acorns in the bag, his gaze became fixed. A paralysis that started in his fingers spread throughout his body.

"What is wrong with you, Frantal?" the other thief, who was holding Gorathdin, called out in surprise, but he got no answer.

Frantal slowly turned into a tree in front of everyone. His hands became branches and his abdomen turned into a tree trunk. It only took a few moments and a multitude of thin branches sprouted from his upper body and head, from which more and more green shoots grew. The other thief let go of the dagger he was holding to Gorathdin's throat in horror.

Werlis, who had watched the transformation in amazement, grabbed hold of himself and hurled a stone at the thief. There was a short shriek as Werlis' projectile hit him on the shoulder. With his face contorted in pain, the thief tried to draw a throwing knife from its sheath. But Gorathdin reacted immediately and pulled his feet out from under him. He threw himself at the thief with his hunting knife, which he pulled from the brim of his boot, and held it to his throat.

"Don't move, or I could easily plunge my knife into your neck," Gorathdin threatened.

His eyes began to light up.

The thief then opened his mouth wide and began to tremble.

"I'm not moving. Relax, we can talk about everything," he whimpered.

Vrenli stood up.

"I'm sorry Gorathdin, I didn't mean to..." Vrenli began.

Gorathdin interrupted him.

"We'll talk about that later. First, I want to find out what thieves from Astinhod are doing in Tawinn, especially near the village of Abketh," he said calmly, still pressing his hunting knife to the thief's throat.

Werlis threw Gorathdin's fire axe down to the forest floor before climbing down from the tree.

"What was in the leather bag?" asked Gorathdin.

"I found the bag in my grandfather's cellar. A gift from a tree creature from the Border Forest," replied Vrenli.

"I thought there hadn't been any tree creatures in the Border Forest for a long time," Werlis objected in astonishment.

"You thought wrong," replied Vrenli.

The two approached the lifeless bodies of the humans and examined them more closely while Gorathdin tried to get information.

"Why are you hanging around in Tawinn? Speak!" Gorathdin demanded sharply of the thief.

He pressed the blade of his hunting knife more firmly against his throat and looked at him determinedly with his glowing eyes.

"We were ordered to prevent the moonflower blossoms from arriving in Astinhod," the thief stammered and swallowed.

"Then Gorathdin was telling the truth after all," whispered Werlis in Vrenli's ear.

Vrenli nodded in shame.

Gorathdin could hear Werlis' words and turned in his direction. These few moments were enough for the thief to twist the ring he wore on his right hand and stab himself with the poisoned thorn that emerged. The poison induced a brief vomiting attack, followed by trembling of all limbs, which quickly led to the thief's death.

Surprised and horrified, Vrenli and Werlis looked at the thief's lifeless body, who had killed himself out of fear of his employer. Even Gorathdin, who had faced death from time to time in his life, was surprised by this act.

"Let's move their bodies away from the path. Or better yet, bury them nearby," Gorathdin suggested.

He then dragged two of the thieves a few steps from the crossroads into the forest, where he dug a pit big enough for five people with his fire axe. In the meantime, Vrenli and Werlis examined the bodies of the thieves for further clues. The only thing they noticed, however, was that they all wore a simple, wide silver ring with the Entorbis coat of arms. Vrenli took one of them and handed it to Gorathdin, who silently put it away. Together they threw the five lifeless bodies into the pit and covered it up again. When they returned to the oak tree, it was already dawn.

"This incident has cost us a lot of time and as it is not possible for you to cross the forest in the dark, we have to set up camp here for the night," Gorathdin said to the two and set about collecting dry branches and twigs.

"What does he mean we can't walk through the forest in the dark? Is he saying that he could?" asked Werlis, opening his travel bag and taking out a piece of dried meat, one of the small loaves of bread they had received from Molekk, a handful of nuts and a bottle of water.

"I think his dark green eyes give him the ability to see in the dark, but I'm not sure. I've made plenty of guesses for one day. Why don't you ask him when he comes back?" replied Vrenli and he sat down on the forest floor next to Werlis.

He was just sprinkling the small loaf of bread with some water when Gorathdin emerged from between the surrounding trees with a good amount of firewood. While he lit a fire, Vrenli and Werlis spread their cloaks on the damp forest floor and laid their sheepskins on top.

"I hope you won't hold it against me that I'm going to rest after I've eaten some of the dried meat. I need to think about what has happened. I ask you to wait until tomorrow with any questions you are sure to have," Gorathdin asked them. The two nodded in agreement while they ate the nuts that Werlis had taken from the travel bag.

When Gorathdin had eaten a little of the dried meat and the Everfull Bread, which tasted unexpectedly good and was very filling, he crouched down with his back against the trunk of the oak tree and closed his eyes.

"This way of thinking is very familiar to me," said Werlis with a grin.

Vrenli yawned.

As it had been an eventful and exhausting day for them too, they lay down on their cloaks a little later and fell asleep next to the blazing fire, listening to the sounds of the night.

Aarl's hut

Their first night spent in the open air passed quietly. Vrenli only woke up briefly once, when Gorathdin put dried branches in the fire at a late hour so that it would continue to burn until dawn. A ray of sunlight, which had found its way through the sea of leaves of the oak, woke Vrenli from his deep sleep. He opened his eyes and saw that Gorathdin and Werlis were already awake.

"Good morning, you two," Vrenli wished them in a sleepy voice.

He stood up and sat down next to them.

"Tea?" asked Werlis, who was heating some water in a small metal container on the almost extinguished fire.

Vrenli nodded in agreement.

"If we keep at it, we'll arrive at Aarl's hut around noon. When he's home, we can get some strength and rest," said Gorathdin as he took one of his arrows from the quiver and began to carve small notches in the wood with his hunting knife.

"It's strange that a human lives in Tawinn. Not far from our village, at that. I've heard he's been living here for over twenty years," said Werlis, taking the metal container from the fire.

"And in all those years he never came to Abketh? Strange," remarked Vrenli.

"He just prefers to live alone," Gorathdin explained and looked up at the sky to check the position of the sun.

"We should set off soon," he let them know.

They sat by the now extinguished fire for some time and drank the hot brew of wild herbs that Werlis had gathered near the oak early in the morning while Vrenli was still asleep and Gorathdin was exploring their surroundings. Vrenli got up, picked up his cloak and removed the damp leaves clinging to it.

"I am astonished to see that you are wearing a cloak from the Dark Forest. May I ask you where you got it?" asked Gorathdin, smiling gently.

"It belonged to my grandfather. By the way, I'm very sorry about yesterday, Gorathdin. I don't know what got into me," Vrenli apologized.

"Fear is one of our greatest enemies and I alone am to blame for this incident. I should have told you more about my mission and myself. It was my mistake not to inform you that the five men were thieves from Astinhod," Gorathdin apologized.

He stood up and kicked out the embers in the fireplace.

"So, the thieves of Astinhod have entered an alliance with Erwight of Entorbis. They wore rings with the Entorbis coat of arms," Vrenli muttered to himself and looked sheepishly at Gorathdin, who knew about his embarrassment and kept silent.

He hoped that Vrenli had not connected yesterday's exchange of ideas with Wetherid's book. So far, he wasn't sure whether Vrenli could be trusted in every respect.

"Something else I wanted to ask you Gorathdin. That voice I heard when we first met and again yesterday, what can you tell me about it?" Vrenli asked him as Werlis went behind the thick trunk of the oak tree to relieve himself.

"As you've probably already noticed, I don't belong to the human race. I am a ranger from the Dark Forest. I am an elf and the voice you heard, well, we elves have certain abilities," Gorathdin lied.

His gut told him that it was still too early to tell Vrenli the truth. He had thought a lot about him last night, but he couldn't find an answer to the question of why they hadn't known about him much earlier.

"So, elves have the ability to exchange thoughts?" Vrenli asked.

"Not all elves," Gorathdin replied, taking his fire axe, which was leaning against the trunk of the oak, and hanging the wide leather strap around his neck.

He reached for his bow, which was hanging at head height from a branch next to his quiver and slung it over his left shoulder. He then freed the leather strap of his quiver, which had become entangled in the thin branches of a bough and slung it over his right shoulder.

"We really should set off now," Gorathdin warned, looking back once more to the place where they had buried the dead thieves before following the path further west, followed by Vrenli and Werlis.

"How is it that you set off for Abketh alone? I mean, the princess of Astinhod is seriously ill and the King is sending a single man on such a long journey, don't get me wrong, you're an elf to boot," asked Vrenli.

"You're very curious," Gorathdin said with a grin.

"I think it's time to tell us the whole story, Gorathdin," demanded Werlis.

The path was now getting narrower, and they finally had to march one after the other. Gorathdin pondered for some time whether he should answer. He observed the surroundings with his sharp elven eyes and became aware of a hare, which was startled by their appearance and sought shelter under the berry bushes and wild thorns a few steps away from them.

Gorathdin's eyes continued to wander through the trees, over the bushes and shrubs until they stopped briefly at two wild boars searching for roots and tubers under the forest floor with their young and then continued past birch, maple, spruce and fir trees. On a small hill deep inside the forest, he discovered a cave on the side facing him, in front of the entrance to which he could make out two forest goblins sitting in front of a pile of animal bones.

"We should hurry, friends! We're not moving fast enough," he urged them. But he didn't tell them what he had seen to their right, more than a thousand paces away, among the trees, bushes and shrubs.

"Gorathdin?" asked Werlis, still waiting for an answer as he began to walk faster to match Gorathdin's haste.

"Forgive me, Werlis. I was thinking," Gorathdin apologized.

Vrenli also took a few quick steps to catch up.

They were on the last stretch of their journey through the Border Forest. Gorathdin looked down at his two companions and decided to tell the story of Princess Lythinda's sudden, strange illness.

"Princess Lythinda and I are, how shall I put it, very close friends and not long ago we decided to go on a two-day ride to Regen, which lies south of Astinhod. Her father, King Grandhold, was not happy about this, but Lythinda convinced him that it would only be to the Crown's advantage if she spent some time among the people in Regen and that she would not be recognized by anyone in the simple outfit she wanted to travel in. King Grandhold finally agreed, but the look he gave me made me realize that I would bear the responsibility.

"The next day we set off from Astinhod's stables. After we had covered half the distance, we stopped at the Three Vines inn to spend the night and taste the excellent wine produced in the Regen area.

"Of course, we were not the only guests on this day, as the harvest festival was being celebrated in Regen. It has always been the custom for guests from all parts of Astinhod to be invited to this event. And so, it was this year too. The inn was full to bursting. Peasants, citizens, nobles, merchants, craftsmen, women and some children from Relvis, Kring, Umlis, Merniton, Wanderbuk and the city of Astinhod sat, stood, danced and sang in the large dining room. To my surprise, there were also inhabitants of the independent county of Kirondor among them. Even songwriters from Hildon, Tumik and wanderers from Wuxtir had come.

"To my astonishment, if the innkeeper had not immediately recognized Lythinda, who entered the inn in simple clothing and

72

only in my presence, and wanted to give us a table, we would probably have ridden on. Lythinda made it clear to the innkeeper that she did not want to be recognized and so we were given a table a little away from the small stage, where guests who had drunk one or two too many cups of wine sang songs which, if they were well known, were sung along by half of those present. Sometimes poems were also recited, but these were usually ended after the first two verses by boos or scraps of food being thrown at the performer. In addition to the performances by his guests, the landlord also hired fire-eaters, jugglers and minstrels, who performed three times a day.

"Princess Lythinda enjoyed being among the simple guests and the wine suited her taste. She drank two cups and was laughing at the minstrels, who were making fun of the noblemen and her father, when a man dressed in dark clothes appeared at the table behind us and bowed to her.

'My lady,' said the stranger, who had pulled his hood low over his face.

"Everything went very quickly.

"I noticed too late how he reached for her hand and said something in a language I didn't understand, bowed again and disappeared into the crowd. Lythinda looked at me in astonishment, but when almost all the guests in the inn began to laugh at a parody of Count Laars, the chief judge of Astinhod, the stranger was quickly forgotten.

"After the show was over and a songwriter from Hildon started a song that we all sang along to, I noticed how Lythinda suddenly stopped singing and her gaze became fixed. When I grabbed her hand and asked her if she wasn't feeling well, I noticed a shadow spreading from her left arm to her shoulder. She didn't answer any of my questions and when I put my hand to her forehead, I realized that she had a fever.

"At first, I thought there might be something wrong with the grilled lamb we had eaten and called for the innkeeper, but he assured me that this was impossible, as more than twenty people had eaten the lamb and no one had complained. I asked him to help me take Lythinda upstairs to one of the guest rooms," Gorathdin explained in detail.

The three travelers were not far from the clearing that lay at the end of the Border Forest to the west.

"We will soon arrive at Aarl's hut. I hope we'll find him. It's already getting dark," Gorathdin remarked as they followed the path through the forest that led to a meadow covered with tall grasses and flowers.

"Go on," Vrenli urged him.

Gorathdin nodded.

"After we had taken her to one of the rooms, I gently placed her in one of the two beds. To cut a long story short, it was obvious that Lythinda was ill. Together with two knights from Astinhod, who were also guests at the Three Vines, I brought her back to the city. As you can imagine, King Grandhold was not happy about his daughter's condition.

After several healers had examined the princess and given her various potions to reduce her fever, with none of them having any effect, the King sent for Master Drobal, the magician from Horunguth Island. He fervently hoped that he would find out what mysterious illness his daughter was suffering from. I have a very friendly relationship with King Grandhold and I could understand the anger he harbored against me. I told him about the stranger in the Three Vines and tried to convince him that it was most likely a planned attack on his daughter. And if that were the case, then even if he had not allowed Lythinda to ride to Regen, they would certainly have found another opportunity to poison her, as I assumed.

He didn't want to believe my suspicions at first, but when Master Drobal entered the bedchamber and I told him what had happened, he supported my suspicions. He told the King that there were rumors that Erwight of Entorbis was looking for allies in Wetherid. But as these were only rumors, King Grandhold was divided. The anger he harbored against me because he held me responsible for what had happened to his daughter subsided after a few days when Master Drobal found a book containing a recipe for making a healing potion that he believed would help Lythinda.

One of the main ingredients was the blossom of the moonflower, which he knew grew in an unknown place in the deep forests of Tawinn, but where exactly he did not know. However, he remembered the village of Abketh and that they would know where to find a moonflower. As I felt it was my duty, I agreed to travel to Tawinn to get Master Drobal a flower. King Grandhold offered to let me be accompanied by some of his warriors, but I told him that I would make much faster progress on my own. I didn't tell him that I wanted to make as little fuss as possible on my journey and therefore decided to set off alone," Gorathdin finished his story.

Suddenly Gorathdin stopped unexpectedly in the evening twilight on the narrow, well-trodden path that led across a meadow to Aarl's hut.

"Watch out! Aarl seems to have dug a pit here to keep out uninvited guests," Gorathdin warned, pointing to a spot on the ground in front of him where Vrenli and Werlis couldn't see anything unusual, even when they looked hard.

"Can't you see the leaves and dried grass lying on the ground here?" Gorathdin wondered, leaning forward.

"Yes, and?" asked Werlis.

Gorathdin smiled.

"Do you see any trees around here?" he asked the two of them.

Vrenli and Werlis shook their heads.

They avoided the pit and followed the path to a small hut surrounded by a high wooden wall. A loud and dangerous barking sound startled Vrenli and Werlis.

"Aarl! I have returned from Abketh with friends!" shouted Gorathdin over the wooden rampart.

"Quiet, wolf! It's only Gorathdin," a loud, powerful voice rang out.

A small gate in the wooden rampart creaked open and a tall, strong, tanned southerner from Thir, with half-long, stringy black hair and eyes radiating a strong self-confidence, stood before them with a large, dangerous-looking wolfhound, which he held by the scruff of his neck.

"Were you successful?" he asked Gorathdin after greeting him.

"I got a handful of flowers from Gwerlit," he replied and introduced his two companions.

"Come in, friends. My name is Aarl and this is Wolf, my friend and companion," said Aarl to Vrenli and Werlis.

The two looked fearfully at the dangerous-looking animal that reached up to their shoulders.

"He looks more like a wolf than a dog," thought Werlis and, like Vrenli, didn't dare to move.

"You don't need to be afraid; he won't hurt you," Aarl let his two little guests know and ordered Wolf to go to his place next to the hut.

The two of them slowly entered the garden with unease. Vrenli immediately noticed the flowers, bushes and shrubs growing along the wooden wall to his right, which was unusual for Tawinn. He glanced around the entire garden. In addition to the colorful blooming keel roses, the magnificent amen lilies, overgrown pommel plants and the intertwined salt roses and hedge ivy, there was a small, well-tended vegetable garden in which larger-than-average pumpkins, carrots, beans, red shining potato and many-bearing galmates sprouted. Between the vegetable garden and the weathered hut grew a wide variety of berry bushes, which Vrenli approached and tasted the blue and red fruits. Wolf, who was lying near the bushes in front of the small terrace, then began to growl. Vrenli didn't know what to do, so he simply stood still and didn't move. Wolf stood up and slowly approached him.

"Aarl! I need your help," called Vrenli, whereupon the sturdy Thirian from the south whistled back to his gray-shaded wolfhound.

"He'll get used to you quickly. Won't you, my boy," he said to Vrenli with a smile and gave Wolf a friendly pat on the back.

"Come on, let's go inside," Aarl urged his guests, leading them up the three low steps that led to the terrace and opening the front door.

In the simply furnished hut, they sat down on a rickety table in front of a small cooking area. Aarl searched for four mugs, which he placed on the center of the tabletop along with a bottle of wine.

"We have discovered one of your pitfalls," said Gorathdin.

"The one on the eastern path, I suppose. The forest goblins still see me as a specialty after all the years I've lived here, so I must protect Wolf and I from their attempts to take us as feast roasts. Those damn creatures still haven't stopped giving me a hard time after all the failed attacks," Aarl told them as he poured them wine.

"Forest goblins?" asked Vrenli and Werlis in amazement.

"Yes, forest goblins. Those hairy little devils with their razor-sharp claws and teeth. How I hate them. A small horde, I think there are about fifty of them, lives north of here near the ruins," Aarl explained angrily.

"But I thought all the goblins had been driven out of Wetherid long ago. In any case, their last attack on our village was more than two hundred years ago. My grandfather told me that before his time, an army of humans, elves, Abkether and dwarves had driven the snow, forest and cave goblins out of Wetherid," Vrenli objected.

"By all appearances, they must have overlooked some of them," Aarl remarked.

"They try to get in here two or three times a year, but my traps and wolf stopped them every time," he added proudly, pouring them another glass of wine.

"You must certainly be hungry," Aarl remarked, got up, went to the cooking area and brought a piece of meat weighing several kilograms from a small chamber, wrapped in large, spicy-smelling green leaves.

"I told you, when you came back, I would prepare us a wild boar roast that you won't forget for the rest of your life," Aarl said to Gorathdin.

He removed some of the leaves and showed him the deep red, juicy piece of wild boar meat.

"I didn't know that Gorathdin and you were friends. Have you known each other for a while?" asked Vrenli.

Aarl looked at him wordlessly for a moment.

"I don't know if you can call seven days long," he replied with a smile and looked at Gorathdin, who was talking to Werlis about wild herbs.

"Only seven days?" Vrenli asked.

"Yes. Gorathdin was on his journey from Astinhod to Abketh when we met in the forest southeast of the ruins. He appeared just at the right moment. It was a favorable twist of fate. I was hunting and had my attention on a boar and was about to shoot an arrow at it when I was ambushed by three forest goblins. Wolf couldn't help me against the attackers as he was having a hard fight with the boar he had tracked down. Gorathdin saved my life, so to speak, as one of those little devils had knocked me unconscious with his club," Aarl recounted, now completely freeing the piece of boar meat from the leaves and beginning to rub it with salt.

"If they hadn't surprised you from behind, you would certainly have dealt with the three of them on your own," Gorathdin objected.

"That may be. But not only did you save me, you also killed the boar," Aarl replied happily.

Aarl lifted the piece of boar meat in front of him with both hands.

"You should get some rest. You still have a long journey ahead of you. I'll prepare the roast in the meantime," Aarl urged his guests.

He poured them some more wine and went out into the garden, where he picked some herbs and put them in the piece of boar meat he had cut in half. He took it to a spot just a few steps away from Wolf's favorite place and laid it on a large flat stone, next to which was a hole in the ground covered with fir and spruce branches. He pulled the large, heavy branches aside, then fetched some thin logs from the pile of wood next to the hut and used them to light a fire in the hole he had dug a day earlier. Little by little, he added larger pieces to the flames and when he thought it was enough, he went into the garden and fetched potatoes, carrots and a pumpkin, which he cleaned by the fire and wrapped in the large, thick leaves of a tan tree.

"The vegetable packet is ready, my boy," he said to Wolf, who had joined him.

While he waited for the wood in the pit to burn down to embers, he wrapped the boar meat in new, fresh leaves.

Gorathdin, Vrenli and Werlis, who had been watching his preparations from the terrace, had dozed off on the long wooden bench where they were sitting. Meanwhile, Aarl placed the wild boar meat wrapped in leaves together with the vegetables in the hot embers. Carefully, he gradually poured the fine pebbly sand that he had laboriously collected for this purpose from the southern stone hills into the hole in the ground.

"We're ready, my boy. Now we just have to wait," he said to Wolf and went out into the dark meadow in front of the wooden rampart to check his traps.

Gorathdin had given him some suggestions on his first visit as to how he could better protect his home from the unwanted visits of the forest goblins, and Aarl had had enough time over the past six days to put some of these suggestions into practice.

It took him a whole day to bring the thorny plants from the nearby forest, which he then hid to the north in front of the wooden rampart, among the tall grasses.

He spent another two days hammering pointed wooden stakes into the ground on the inside of the wall, at a distance of about half a step. Gorathdin had explained to him that if the forest goblins

79

succeeded in overcoming the high wall, at least some of them would die or at least be seriously injured by the tips of the stakes.

Because the forest goblins had once tried to burn down the rampart, Aarl had taken precautions and placed more than ten water buckets, which he filled up once a week at the river Taneth, in various places within the rampart. Aarl checked the water level in all the buckets and, as he still had enough time before the boar roast was ready, he set off for the nearby river with four empty buckets, accompanied by Wolf. It was already night when he arrived at the swampy riverbank, which was covered in mist. He climbed onto the footbridge he had built especially for fetching water and filled the buckets. But as he was about to make his way back, a multitude of small torchlights appeared at the nearby edge of the forest. Wolf began to growl.

"That's all I need. Forest goblins. The whole horde," Aarl said angrily to Wolf.

"Looks like they've decided on a big final blow after all these years. That's at least fifty, my boy," he said aloud.

Wolf bared his sharp teeth and began to pace back and forth restlessly.

Aarl dropped the buckets and since there was at most a distance of seven hundred or eight hundred paces between him and the sinewy, emaciated creatures, he began to run as fast as he could in the direction of his hut.

Wolf followed him.

"Forest goblins, forest goblins. The whole horde!" he shouted from afar.

Gorathdin, Vrenli and Werlis woke up at his warning shouts, hurried into the hut, took their weapons and ran to the rampart, where they climbed onto half-height wooden ladders to the right and left of the gate, which Aarl had leaned against so that he could shoot his arrows at approaching enemies.

"Their last attempt to get in here was no more than three months ago. Strange that they are trying again so soon," said Aarl, out of breath, as he entered the garden through the gate, which he immediately barricaded.

"That's at least fifty," Gorathdin stated, as he could already see the rapidly approaching forest goblins armed with clubs and blowpipes with his sharp elven eyes.

Aarl ran into the hut, where he put on his leather belt with the throwing knives and took his bow and quiver from the wall bracket. He hurried towards the free wooden ladder next to Vrenli and Werlis' and climbed up. He looked out over the wide grassy landscape in the darkness, where a few torchlights were shining brighter as they approached the rampart. There was no wind, and he could already hear the slightly stooped, emaciated creatures, their wizened, earth-colored bodies wrapped in skins, creeping through the tall grass. Wolf sensed the forest goblins coming closer and closer to them and began to bark loudly. The intense, musty smell they gave off caught Wolf's fine nose. He stood behind the gate, snarling, jumping up and down and scratching at it from time to time. Gorathdin's dark green eyes began to light up as the creatures came within range of his bow.

"I didn't think I was so important to them that the whole tribe would come. Strange, they will be expecting greater losses and all this just for a little human flesh," said Aarl to Vrenli, who was standing just a few steps away from him and felt fear at the sight of the strange, menacing-looking creatures.

Gorathdin quickly placed two arrows in the string of his bow and fired them at the approaching attackers. When two forest goblins hit in the middle of the head fell to the ground, Aarl also shot an arrow. Vrenli and Werlis plucked up courage and hurled projectiles from their slingshots down from the rampart at the torchlit pack. Three of the forest goblins were hit on various parts of their bodies, badly wounded and incapacitated.

The leader of the horde, who was clad in wolf skin and wore small deer antlers on his head, stopped abruptly. His shrill, snarling cry, which made Werlis' blood run cold, was the signal to his horde to stop.

"Seems they didn't expect me to have company," Aarl exclaimed delightedly, hoping they would back off.

But to his disappointment, the forest goblins formed into three groups and approached the rampart from different directions.

"Get ready for them. They're throwing their torches!" shouted Gorathdin warningly, pointing with his hand to the few half-full buckets of water.

"Vrenli, Werlis, take care of the water!" shouted Aarl, who fired three arrows at the little devils, as he called them, one after the other. Two of the arrows hit their target.

The three groups of forest goblins had now come close enough to use their blowpipes and some of them were already putting them to their bluish, cracked, dripping lips. Aarl immediately ducked behind the wooden wall.

"Watch out, the arrows are poisoned," he warned the others.

Gorathdin, who did not seek shelter behind the rampart like Aarl, but shot his arrows at the approaching torchbearers, was hit by several small, thin poison arrows. Three of the torchbearers who were not stopped by Gorathdin's arrows threw their burning straw torches at the wooden rampart, which slowly began to burn.

"Gorathdin!" shouted Vrenli, who had seen several of the poisoned arrows hit Gorathdin's body and wanted to run towards him.

"Take care of the fire. Don't worry about me!" Gorathdin called out to his friends.

He then placed two arrows in the string of his bow, several times in succession, and decimated the group of forest goblins heading north-east towards the rampart by almost half. Many of the enraged, snarling creatures coming from the north fell into Aarl's traps and died in pain. Vrenli and Werlis, who struggled to extinguish the fires along the rampart, were shocked to the core as the desperate screams of those who fell into the pits equipped with pointed stakes echoed through the air. The following rows climbed with their bare feet onto the thorny plants hidden in the grass and hissed in pain.

Neither Aarl, Vrenli, Werlis nor Gorathdin noticed how Wolf, who was running up and down the rampart, kept baring his teeth, growling and barking. Suddenly, he leapt with several bounds onto one of the ladders and from there over the rampart onto the meadow, where he lunged at the forest goblins approaching from the north-west with his mouth wide open.

"Wolf! No! Come back!" Aarl shouted as loud as he could down the rampart.

He was able to stop two of the creatures from attacking his friend and companion by hurling his throwing knives at them. Wolf lunged at four of the creatures carrying a moss-covered ladder tied together with branches and vines and tore off several of their limbs with his powerful teeth.

"Good boy. Come back now!" Aarl called out to him.

Just as Wolf was about to answer his master's call, he was struck by several poisoned arrows.

Wolf howled, tucked his tail, turned to and fro and tried to stagger back to the gate, but two forest goblins, not much bigger than Vrenli and Werlis, knocked him to the ground with their clubs.

Aarl's eyes widened in pain.

"Help me!" he shouted, firing several arrows at the forest goblins and then trying to climb over the rampart.

Gorathdin noticed this in time, however, and with several light and airy leaps, he jumped from his ladder onto the one next to it and finally onto Aarl's, preventing him from jumping in front of the rampart at the last moment.

"It's too late," said Gorathdin, holding him by the shoulder.

"Wolf!" cried Aarl, devastated by the loss of his friend.

The forest goblin horde, reduced by more than half, decided to retreat.

"It's over!" cried Gorathdin with relief and climbed down the ladder, followed by Aarl.

He sat down on the ground next to the berry bushes and began to pull out the small, thin, needle-like arrows that had hit him. Aarl opened the gate and hurried to Wolf, who lay dead, just a few paces from the rampart, next to the forest goblins he had mauled. He knelt down and gently stroked his gray fur.

"I'll miss you, my boy," he whispered on the verge of tears, picking Wolf up and carrying him into the garden, where he buried him in his favorite spot.

Vrenli and Werlis stood on the ladders for some time, looking after the departing forest goblins with relief, and joined Gorathdin a little later.

"How come the poison didn't harm you?" asked Vrenli, curious and amazed.

"We elves are immune to plant poisons. An extremely useful gift that has been bestowed upon my people," Gorathdin replied with a smile, whereupon the two helped him remove the poisoned arrows with the utmost care.

It took them some time, and, in the end, they had pulled more than fifteen arrows out of him. Gorathdin took them, looked around the garden and the rampart with his sharp elven eyes and collected the projectiles he had found there so that no one could be injured by them later. He looked out through the open gate into the darkness of the meadow.

"Let's burn the bodies of the forest goblins. Their stench could attract wild animals," he suggested, and Vrenli and Werlis agreed after a moment's hesitation.

They went out in front of the rampart and, a few hundred paces from Aarl's hut, began to lay the bodies of the forest goblins on top of each other.

After clearing the meadow of the hideous creatures, Gorathdin set fire to the disgusting pile. A dark, thick cloud of smoke rose into the sky until dawn, spreading a foul-smelling stench over the entire lowland.

When the three of them returned to the garden after their work was done, it was already morning and Aarl was still sitting on the spot where he had buried Wolf.

"It's always very painful to lose a close friend," Aarl said to them and went ahead into the hut.

"He gave his life to save ours," Vrenli said trying to cheer up Aarl, who was washing off the traces of the fight in the washbasin standing on a dresser next to the hob and nodding silently.

"This is the second time I've lost a close friend," Aarl let them know and placed a bottle of wine and four cups on the table.

"I'm still amazed that the whole tribe came. I already told Vrenli that I didn't know I was so important to them. Surely they were expecting great losses," Aarl continued and sat down at the table with his comrades-in-arms.

Gorathdin thought about what Aarl had said for a moment and came to the conclusion that the forest goblins' attack might not have had anything to do with Aarl, but with him. However, he kept his fears to himself, brushed off the ominous thoughts and tried to enjoy the wine with his friends.

They talked a lot and when Vrenli and Werlis talked about Abketh and kept mentioning the words home, peace, friends and family, Aarl's face became thoughtful. He felt a pang of homesickness.

"I would like to travel with you to Astinhod," he revealed in surprise and looked at them, waiting for an answer.

"I want to leave Tawinn and since I don't really know where to go on my own, you would be doing me a great favor," Aarl let the others know.

Gorathdin looked at Vrenli and Werlis for a few moments. When he felt that they agreed, he agreed to Aarl's request.

"Of course you can travel with us to Astinhod, Aarl. We would be delighted," replied Gorathdin. Vrenli and Werlis were pleased that there were now four of them. They smiled and nodded in agreement.

"You'll no doubt be hungry after all this excitement and work. I'll get the roast boar out of the pit. It will already be cold, but its taste will still delight you, friends, and afterwards we should get some rest, the night was long and tiring. I can feel my muscles aching," Aarl finally said, getting up from the table and walking out into the garden to the fire pit.

He picked up the shovel lying next to it and scooped the fine, pebbly sand out of the hole in the ground until he came across the two parcels. The leaf packet with the vegetables was completely charred, but the roast seemed to have survived well, apart from the slightly burnt underside. He went back inside, removed the charred bits of leaves and scraped away the burnt crust with a sharp knife. He put it on a wooden board and placed it in the middle of the table.

"Here you are, friends. Enjoy your meal," said Aarl and sat down with Gorathdin, Vrenli and Werlis.

The three of them had to admit that they had never eaten such a tasty roasted wild boar before and after they had almost finished it and emptied a second bottle of wine, they spread out their skins on the floor next to the stove, lay down on them and fell asleep.

The Ruins of Tawinn

When Vrenli and Werlis woke up refreshed early the next morning, Gorathdin was already helping Aarl make arrangements to leave his hut in the small clearing near the Border Forest in Tawinn.

"Good morning, friends. There's still some of the roast left and the tea should still be warm," called Aarl to Vrenli and Werlis, who had just stepped out onto the small terrace in front of the hut.

"We'll leave as soon as you've regained your strength," Gorathdin called out to them, to which they nodded and went back into the hut. They sat down at the table and while they talked about yesterday's battle with the forest goblins, they ate the last of the roast boar and drank tea.

"I'm ready, friends!" Aarl announced as he entered the hut, taking his leather belt with the throwing knives from the wall and put it on.

Vrenli and Werlis tied up their travel bags, drank again from their cups and followed Aarl and Gorathdin into the garden.

"I'll be right back," Aarl promised and went to Wolf's grave to say goodbye to him.

As they stepped out through the door onto the meadow in front of the rampart, Aarl stopped for a moment and looked back. He suddenly felt strange. He now had to say goodbye to his home, where he had spent more than twenty-five years of his life.

"I had a good time here," he said, following Gorathdin, Vrenli and Werlis as they walked north across the spring-like meadow.

Their destination was the river Taneth, the largest flowing body of water in Tawinn, with a riverbed more than twenty paces wide and a considerable depth of water. To cross it, they had to walk for half the day across the wide meadow plains and hilly grasslands until they finally reached the bridge to the northwest.

"Our next destination is the Ruins of Tawinn, where we will camp for the night and cross Lake Taneth the next day. We'll have to keep at it. The attack by the forest goblins has cost us a day," said Gorathdin, who was keeping a close eye on the surroundings, for if the attack by the dangerous creatures had anything to do with him, they might come across some of them again.

But when they had left the Border Forest, which lay to the south-east far behind them, and he saw the valley in which the Ruins of Tawinn lay, Gorathdin was reassured.

The narrow bridge made of rope and wood was only a few hundred paces away from them when images of women and children screaming in pain flashed through Vrenli's mind. Behind huge, lambent walls of fire, he recognized the outline of a city. Vrenli stopped in horror and rubbed his eyes.

"Was that a dream?" he asked himself as he stared at the ruins that lay before him on the horizon.

"Vrenli, hurry up!" Werlis, who had gone on with Gorathdin and Aarl, called to him.

Vrenli walked slowly towards his companions. His face was white as a sheet and his eyes reflected horror.

"What's wrong with you?" asked Werlis anxiously.

"I saw terrible pictures in front of me. It was like a nightmare," Vrenli replied, panting with excitement.

"What are you talking about? What pictures?" Werlis asked him, putting his travel bag down for a moment.

"Horrible pictures of dying women and children. And I saw a city on fire," said Vrenli, upset.

"It's probably just the effort of the march, you're tired. Do you want us to take a break?" Werlis offered.

Vrenli shook his head.

"Must have been a daydream," remarked Aarl and walked on slowly.

Gorathdin suspected that Vrenli was having a vision, but he did not speak to him about it, and instead urged him to move on. Vrenli was still thinking about the images he had seen as he followed his companions the few hundred steps to the bridge.

"We should cross one by one. I'm not sure it would hold all our weight," Gorathdin suggested as he stopped just before the narrow, collapsible bridge, whose tree trunks were rotten and whose ropes were brittle.

He was then the first to cross, followed by Aarl, Vrenli and Werlis. Once on the other side of the river, they followed the path that led through the flat valley to the northeast. They could already see the peaks of the Ice Mountains towering into the clouds, two to three days' journey away, on the horizon to the north-east.

"Is it very cold up there?" asked Werlis.

"The Ice Mountains are covered in snow all year round. On the pass, which is the only one in Tawinn that leads to Astinhod, many have frozen to death. Mainly because they wanted to recover briefly from the strenuous climb and therefore stayed out in the cold," Gorathdin replied, pointing admonishingly in the direction of the peaks.

"Frozen to death?" asked Werlis.

Gorathdin nodded.

Werlis looked uneasily at the snow- and ice-covered peaks and pulled his brown cloak tighter.

They hiked north for a while shortly after midday and then all afternoon across the wide plain to the east. In the late afternoon, they reached the first evidence of the once splendid and lively city of Tawinn. The remains of the walls, overgrown with ivy, thorny plants and tall grasses, were once home to noblemen, merchants and farmers who tilled the fields around the city. The path they followed became wide and overgrown with green, bushy grasses, but in some places they could still see the cobblestones with which it was once laid.

There was little evidence of the life that had once prevailed here more than five hundred years ago. Nature had spread over the ruins of the town, reclaiming its property piece by piece. Large, thick oak trees grew on the former village square and a small, dry spruce forest lay where the stables used to be. Vrenli looked at the crumbling town wall, which was only more than ten steps high in some places. Berry bushes, thorny plants and lianas grew on the remains of the former castle, which had crumbled to its foundations and was now home to wild boars, foxes, hares and pheasants.

The travelers crossed the crumbling city until they arrived at the western end, at a round, two-story building that had survived the centuries more-or-less intact. There was no longer a roof, windows or doors, but the foundation walls, apart from a few places, had not yet crumbled.

"This seems to me to be a suitable and safe place to camp for the night," Gorathdin decided and entered through the low but wide archway.

"Let's go upstairs. Except for a few steps, the staircase still seems to be intact," Gorathdin suggested and climbed the steps, light-footed.

His comrades followed him.

The stone floor on the upper floor had collapsed by more than half and there was a hole at least eight paces wide in the western outer wall, next to the staircase, which gave them a view of the ruins of the former city of Tawinn. The atmosphere was gloomy; it was cold and the remaining light of dusk was getting fainter.

"We will spend the night here," Gorathdin said to his friends and laid his fire axe, bow and quiver on the ground.

"Soon it will be so dark that you won't be able to see your hand in front of your eyes and it will get noticeably colder. I'm going to go back outside and collect firewood," Gorathdin announced and made his way back down with Werlis, who offered to help him.

Vrenli and Aarl followed them into the basement a little later, unaware that their night's lodging was a former temple. They looked around curiously. Apart from the stone walls and a weathered floor painting in one of the rooms, they couldn't see anything of interest, so they went back upstairs.

"What will you do in Astinhod?" Vrenli asked Aarl, who was standing next to him in front of the hole in the outer wall and looking out over the crumbling city.

"I don't know yet exactly. I think I will stay in Astinhod for a while and then probably return to my village in the south. I have the feeling that I can only be truly happy there," Aarl replied slowly and thoughtfully.

Just as Vrenli was about to ask him why he had left his village so many years ago, Gorathdin and Werlis returned. Gorathdin had collected a considerable amount of firewood, but Werlis was carrying two pheasants in his hands instead of branches and twigs.

"I came across them and thought it wouldn't hurt to stock up a little more," said Werlis with a grin.

Aarl helped Gorathdin light a fire, while Vrenli and Werlis plucked the pheasants and then put them on two branches, slowly turning them over the fire. They talked about the ruins and conjectured what the former city might have looked like.

By the time the pheasants had finished roasting, it was already pitch black. Vrenli could not deny that there was something eerie about this place. After they had eaten the pheasants, Gorathdin and Werlis began to talk about the Ice Mountains, while Aarl lay down on the bearskin spread out on the ground in front of him and listened to Gorathdin's stories.

But it wasn't long before he fell asleep, snoring in the memory of his Ice Mountains crossing more than twenty-five years ago.

Vrenli stood up from the fireplace, walked to the hole in the outer wall and looked at the ruins, dimly lit by the moonlight. He became thoughtful and his ruminations brought back a memory. He now understood the pictures he had seen earlier near the bridge. The place they were in was the home of his ancestors.

"The Tawinnian people. Now I remember," he rejoiced silently.

He also remembered a page from the book on which there was a picture of a crystal.

"The star of Tawinn. The Star People, that's what they were called before by the humans, elves and dwarves," he recalled, but with his memory came questions.

"Was it so long ago that everyone in Abketh had forgotten the city of Tawinn? How many generations had passed on the history of our people to their children? Am I perhaps part of the first generation to forget the Tawinnian culture or was the forgetting a long time ago?" he asked himself, although he knew that he would not find an answer to these questions on his own.

"Maybe Gwerlit could have told me something about the Old Ones," he thought, and the more he thought about it, the more tired he became.

He was about to avert his eyes from the ruins when he unconsciously reached for the second leather pouch on his belt and noticed that it was getting warmer. He opened it and pulled out the crystal, which shone with a warm, bright blue light.

"The Oracle of Tawinn," he thought.

"Maybe that's the answer to my questions," he murmured quietly.

"Are you alright?" whispered Werlis, who was lying next to Gorathdin and Aarl, who had already fallen asleep.

"I'm just thinking about something, Werlis. Go to sleep," Vrenli whispered to him, whereupon Werlis rolled over and fell asleep a few moments later.

Vrenli stared at the crystal, which he was still holding in front of him. The bright blue light now shone directly into his eyes, and he was startled when he saw an image inside the crystal. His curiosity, far greater than his fear, did not allow him to take his eyes off the image. He saw a wide valley bordered by dense forests to the west and north. To the south he saw large fields of wheat and corn and to the northeast was a lake.

"That's Tawinn," he remarked, whereupon the image began to blur.

But it didn't take a moment for a new picture to emerge. A picture that was full of life. A huge city, surrounded by white walls about twenty steps high, stood in the center of a wide valley. A cobblestone road led from a bridge to the city gate in the southwest. Several guards, dressed in leather armor and armed with short swords and lances, stood at the ivy-and rose-covered round city gate, chatting with some farmers who were pulling handcarts into the city with part of their harvest. The road leading into the town was decorated with magnificent, colorful flowerbeds to the left and right. Every few steps there were oil lanterns which, when it got dark, illuminated the town. The inhabitants were dressed in gray or white tunics. Only the craftsmen or farmers, as it seemed, wore brown cotton work clothes. The language they spoke was foreign to Vrenli.

His gaze fell on a building that caught his attention. It was made of white marble blocks and had three pointed towers that rose to the left, right and center of the front. Several round columns decorated with stucco supported an elongated, dome-shaped roof that covered the steep staircase, which had more than a hundred steps and led to the entrance of the building. Four blonde-haired women in white tunics walked slowly up the stairs and entered the building.

Several guards stood in the long corridor, where fine tapestries and paintings hung on the walls to the left and right in massive, large frames. The four women followed the corridor, which led them into a high, sumptuously furnished hall decorated with wall, ceiling and floor paintings. In the middle of the hall stood a throne carved from white marble, on which sat a rotund, long-bearded old man clad in a robe made of fine fabrics and wearing a shimmering crystal crown.

"We had a king?" Vrenli wondered as he watched the four women approach the throne and bow deeply to what he assumed was the King of Tawinn.

The image began to blur, but, as before, it didn't take a moment for a new image to emerge. A fire was burning on top of the Ice Mountains and Vrenli could hear warning chimes ringing from the temple. Women in white tunics knelt around a huge, precious-looking crystal that shimmered in a bright blue light and stood on a marble pedestal in the middle of the lower hall of the temple. They stared in horror at the image inside the crystal, which showed knights in black armor, several dozen hideous orcs in war paint, and a handful of giant ogres marching across the Ice Mountains. Four of the women kneeling in front of the crystal stood up and left the temple. The image in Vrenli's crystal blurred and the bright blue light went out.

Excited, he went to Werlis and woke him up.

"What is it?" Werlis mumbled with his eyes closed.

"I told you about the crystal that Gwerlit gave me," whispered Vrenli.

Werlis opened his eyes.

"What crystal?" he grumbled, slightly annoyed at his nocturnal awakening.

"The Oracle of Tawinn," Vrenli whispered emphatically.

"Yes, I remember. What about it, have you lost it?" Werlis sat up.

"No. On the contrary, it's here with me and you won't believe what just happened," Vrenli replied.

Vrenli told Werlis, who carefully threw some branches into the fire, what he had seen inside the crystal.

"I'm starting to worry about you. Have you been dreaming again?" Werlis questioned because he couldn't believe what he was hearing.

"No. I wasn't dreaming. I really could see Tawinn more than five hundred years ago and imagine we had a king," Vrenli said excitedly, forgetting to whisper.

Gorathdin and Aarl woke up.

"Forgive me, friends. I didn't mean to wake you up," said Vrenli apologetically.

The two of them looked at him sleepily.

"Why aren't you sleeping?" asked Gorathdin, sitting upright.

"Something incredible has happened," Vrenli replies enthusiastically.

"Forest goblins?" Aarl guessed, still lying drowsily on his bearskin.

"No. I have seen something. Here in this crystal," said Vrenli and took the Oracle of Tawinn out of the leather pouch.

"You saw something in a crystal? I think you're in desperate need of sleep, my little friend," Aarl advised, turning over to continue sleeping.

"Can I have a look at it?" asked Gorathdin.

Vrenli hesitated for a moment before handing him the crystal.

Gorathdin felt the cold crystal, placed it against his forehead for a few moments and closed his eyes. When he opened them again, they lit up briefly.

"Magic," whispered Gorathdin.

"I saw pictures inside the crystal. They showed me the city of Tawinn five hundred years ago. Our ancestors were the Tawinnians. I am quite sure of it. They looked just like us. They were the same height, the same build, only their language was different and they had a king. We had a king! Can you imagine that?" Vrenli shared excitedly.

"Are you sure you weren't dreaming?" Werlis remained skeptical.

"Werlis, I wasn't dreaming. Absolutely not!" Vrenli became restless.

"So, you think we're descended from the Tawinnians? Don't you think we would have been taught that if we were?" Werlis yawned and his eyes almost fell shut.

Gorathdin placed a thick branch in the waning fire.

"We are descended from the Tawinnians, from who else? What do you know of the ancients? Did you think our village has always existed? Werlis, think about it. I beg you. We are Tawinnians!" shouted Vrenli energetically.

"Hm. I don't know anything about the Old Ones, I have to agree with you. But then again, I've never asked myself who they were. But I think it's a bold claim that we're descended from the Tawinnians," said Werlis, shaking his head.

"But it would be conceivable. I don't think it's that far-fetched," said Gorathdin.

Vrenli was determined to convince Werlis that their ancestors were the Tawinnians and took the oracle out of Gorathdin's hands again.

"You don't believe me?" Vrenli played with the fine silver chain.

"Be honest, the story with the pictures about the city of Tawinn sounds a bit crazy. You're probably just tired. Let's talk about it again tomorrow," replied Werlis, who didn't want to hurt Vrenli's feelings.

"Then see for yourself," said Vrenli, holding the crystal in front of Werlis' eyes. Nothing happened.

"Ask the oracle who our ancestors were," demanded Vrenli, still holding the crystal in front of Werlis.

"All right, but only if you promise me that you'll sleep afterwards," Werlis replied.

Vrenli nodded.

"Who were our ancestors, Oracle of Tawinn?" asked Werlis.

Vrenli's eyes began to shine.

"He'll see in a moment," he thought.

But nothing happened.

"I can't see a picture," confessed Werlis, who hoped he could lie down now.

"Wait a moment," Vrenli told him, watching the crystal closely.

"It doesn't even shine in the bright blue light," thought Vrenli disappointedly.

"Let's go to sleep now, Vrenli," Werlis yawned again.

"It doesn't really matter who our ancestors were," he added and lay down.

"You have to believe me. I really did see pictures in the crystal," Vrenli hesitantly put it back into the small leather pouch.

"I believe you, Vrenli, and I can understand your excitement about what you have seen, but you should get some sleep now. We have a long way to Lake Taneth tomorrow," Gorathdin reassured him in a gentle voice.

"You're right. Forgive me for waking you up. It's just that we young Abkether don't really know anything about our ancestors," Vrenli explained and lay down next to Werlis on his cloak from the Dark Forest.

Gorathdin looked gently into Vrenli's eyes.

"I can understand what's going on inside you, Vrenli. I also thought a lot about the history of the rangers in my youth because we had also forgotten our ancestors and it took me a lot of time and effort to establish a connection with the elves from the Glorious Valley. But we really should go to sleep now," Gorathdin said emphatically and lay down again.

Vrenli turned away from the fire and clutched the small leather pouch.

The desire to look into the crystal again did not allow him to fall asleep, so he waited a little longer to make sure his friends were fast asleep before he took the crystal out again and waited for the light blue light. But after a while, when nothing had happened, he wanted to put it back in the leather pouch.

"How I wish I had known what happened to the Tawinnians after the city of Tawinn was destroyed," Vrenli whispered softly.

The crystal lit up bright blue.

Full of anticipation, he placed it next to him on the cloak. It only took a few moments for a picture to appear inside, showing a small group of no more than fifty Tawinnians. The majority of them were women and children, but only a few men who were capable of fighting. They appeared to be fleeing from the enemy, who had completely destroyed the city of Tawinn. They headed east, passing straight through a dense forest to remain unseen by possible pursuers, and then reached a clearing where there was a river to the south, from which they continued west. The group settled down in the shelter of the surrounding woods. Before the image blurred, Vrenli saw a woman pulling a small piece of the crystal from the Temple of Tawinn out from under her tunic, and this small fragment looked very similar to his own.

"Now I have certainty. We Abkether are descendants of the Tawinnians," he thought and immediately wondered who the enemy was that had destroyed the city of Tawinn and killed most of its inhabitants.

Vrenli looked at the crystal.

"Who were the enemies and why didn't anyone come to the aid of the Tawinnians?" he asked the Oracle of Tawinn, whereupon another image appeared inside the crystal that caught his eye.

Vrenli saw many hundreds of heavily armed humans in black armor moving from Fallgar in the east to Wetherid, marching into what appeared to be a city inside a mountain. He watched as many as hundreds of dwarves fled into deep, dark tunnels leading steeply down into the mountain. Ogres and orcs from Raga Gur followed the humans through the city in the mountain, killing many of the dwarves who opposed them. When the attackers had fought their way through, they continued across the mountains towards Astinhod. Vrenli could hear the booming bugles of Astinhod announcing the approaching enemy. A battle lasting several days outside the walls of the city of Astinhod, which the enemy was unable to take, was followed by a siege lasting several weeks.

Vrenli watched as several hundred black knights, dozens of orcs and several ogres formed to the west of the tent camp outside Astinhod and then marched across the Ice Mountains to Tawinn. The remaining army of about five hundred men outside the walls of Astinhod was pushed back to the city in the mountain by the defenders, who were aided by strange-looking creatures, and from there, with the help of the dwarves, pursued back across the eastern border of Wetherid to Druhn.

However, there was no help for Tawinn. The humans, orcs and ogres, who lost more than a hundred men in the snow and ice on their way through the Ice Mountains, set up camp near the city of Tawinn after crossing Lake Taneth on rafts. In the forest between the city and Lake Taneth, they began to cut down vast quantities of trees and used them to build simple, but destructive war machines. After just a few days, they had three catapults and a ballista ready to march on the city, which was less than a day's journey from Lake Taneth.

Vrenli heard a soft, feminine voice accompanying the images he saw. The Tawinnians were not prepared for such an attack. They felt safe in their valley, whose only access was the pass over the Ice Mountains. There was no need for them to learn the art of bearing arms. They were peaceful people and the few lightly armed guards, whose only task was to defend the town from wild animals and the forest goblins that lived in the adjacent forests, were overrun by the humans from Druhn, who were two to three heads taller, the stocky orcs from Raga Gur and the giant ogres from Wahmuther. The voice Vrenli heard fell silent.

The attackers caused a bloodbath in the city of Tawinn, killing women, old people and even children. They searched every house, hall and room. Vrenli could not see who or what they were looking for. The picture showed a mighty, hell-hot wall of flames, several tens of paces wide, burning in front of Tawinn's castle and bathing the city in a dark orange, bluish light. Lamentations, whimpers and cries of fear and despair emanated from the castle, where the king was tied to his throne and executed by two dark-cloaked figures with lifeless eyes before the eyes of some Tawinnians who had sought shelter in the throne room. The images Vrenli saw began to blur and the bright blue light of the crystal went out.

Vrenli cried. He could feel all the pain and anguish of the Tawinnians he had seen in the crystal.

"They didn't hurt anyone. They lived peacefully in their valley. Who was responsible for this terrible atrocity?" sobbed Vrenli, to which a voice behind him replied.

"The Entorbis dynasty, which has dedicated itself to the shadow, to evil, since its inception. They use the power they derive from this for their own selfish ends, and one of these ends is to subjugate, exploit and enslave Wetherid. They exchange love, peace, compassion, helpfulness, tolerance, honesty, honor and respect for hatred, belligerence, self-aggrandizement, greed, intolerance, falsehood, dishonor, malice and contempt for life. To strengthen their power, they commit crimes like this one. Their realm of Druhn lies in the north of Fallgar, which is a land of evil. Cunning mist elves from Marnog Jar, deceitful gray dwarves from Ingar, demonic undeads from Zantranos, angry, ugly ogres from Wahmuther and insidious orcs from Raga Gur dwell there and they all follow the same power, the power of Entorbis and its shadow mages. It casts a spell over the inhabitants of Fallgar. It blinds them, makes them strong and unscrupulous. They are all only looking out for their own advantage," the voice revealed.

Vrenli jumped up, startled, and reached for his short sword.

Gorathdin and Aarl, who woke up as a result, immediately took up their weapons and stood beside him protectively. Werlis first thought that Vrenli had seen something in his crystal again and turned around with half-opened eyes. He almost froze to stone when he saw the glowing outline of a female figure hovering about two steps above the ground.

"Do not be afraid. You don't need weapons," said the female being in a gentle voice.

But none of the four were prepared to lay down their weapons, instead holding them up protectively.

"My name is Lorothe. I was a Tawinnian priestess, and I have come to deliver a message from the ancients to Vrenli," she said.

She floated towards Vrenli.

"To me? What message?" Vrenli stammered and took a step back.

"When you return to your village from your journey, it will be your task from then on to teach the Abkether, as you call yourselves today, the history of the Tawinnians. You must never forget what happened and, above all, who was responsible for it. From now on, you shall be called Vrenli DaFanorlan, which means the preserver in Abketh's language. Bear this name with respect and pride. Preserve the history of the ancients," said the priestess.

A warm, pleasant light shone from her hand onto Vrenli's forehead, on which the image of a star appeared.

"Farewell Vrenli DaFanorlan," she said as her disembodied form slowly dissolved.

Vrenli, Werlis, Gorathdin and Aarl could not quite believe what they had seen and heard and stared wordlessly for some time at the place where the priestess's spirit had disappeared.

Sleep was out of the question that night, so they sat around the fire and gazed into the flickering flames, amazed but also pensive at the appearance of the Tawinnian priestess who had come to them from a long-forgotten time.

Vrenli wasn't sure how he felt. Should he be afraid or feel honored to have been given this task by the ancients?

"Why me? Why not Werlis or someone else? Gwerlit, perhaps. Yes, Gwerlit would be the right person," he thought.

He very much doubted that he was the right person for the job. He was still young, had no children and no wife. He enjoyed a good reputation in Abketh through his grandfather, that was true; he probably had enough influence to fulfill this task. But there was also the village council, which he assumed wanted to hide Abketh from the rest of Wetherid.

"Am I really the right person for this? Am I strong enough to stand up to the village council?" he pondered as Werlis interrupted his thoughts.

"I'm sorry that I didn't believe you. I have thought about it and I now think it is right and important that the history of our ancestors is taught in our village and I am proud that you should take on this task, Vrenli DaFanorlan," said Werlis, standing up and hugging him.

"Thank you, Werlis. I'm glad to have you as a friend," replied Vrenli, wiping a tear from his eye.

"I also consider it a very honorable task, Vrenli DaFanorlan," said Gorathdin, who was glad that Werlis had broken the silence.

"Very honorable," murmured Aarl, who was the only one of them lying on the ground and almost falling asleep again.

"I don't think the title the ancients gave me is a title to be used. Please just call me Vrenli, like before," he asked his friends, smiling sheepishly and telling them into the early hours of the morning what he had seen when he consulted the Oracle of Tawinn for the second time.

Lake Taneth

At the first light of dawn, Vrenli and Gorathdin, who had not slept, woke Werlis and Aarl.

"Wake up, friends. I know you have had little sleep, but we must set out. Lake Taneth is still a day's journey away and I want us to cross it before nightfall," Gorathdin said to the two of them, shaking them gently.

"We have to leave already? But I've only just fallen asleep," yawned Werlis in a sleepy, hoarse voice and looked at Gorathdin with his half-open, swollen eyes.

"It has to be," Gorathdin replied and took his fire axe, bow and quiver.

"Can I at least brew us some tea?" asked Werlis. Gorathdin shook his head in refusal and pointed to the extinguished fire with his hand.

Werlis sighed and stood up.

Aarl rolled up his bearskin, walked to the hole in the wall and took another look at the Ruins of Tawinn.

"I almost feel as if I had only dreamed the encounter with the ghost," he said to his friends, who could see that he had also had little sleep.

"The spirit of the Tawinnian priestess. I thought I was dreaming too," Werlis agreed, rubbing his eyes.

"I wish I had been dreaming," Vrenli stood thoughtfully next to Aarl and looked out of the hole into the cloudy morning sky.

"Your ancestors have chosen you, Vrenli. You should feel honored. I can't understand why you're worrying about it," said Gorathdin, who had a vague idea of what must be going on in Vrenli's mind.

"If only it were that easy," thought Vrenli, wordlessly slung his travel bag over his shoulder and walked down the stairs.

He stayed in the room with the almost unrecognizable, heavily weathered floor painting until Gorathdin, Werlis and Aarl came down the stairs.

The four traveling companions followed the wide path that led from the ruined city of Tawinn to the nearby forest to the northeast. They entered a path branching off to the right across a dewy meadow and followed it to the mixed forest ahead, which they traversed for half the day. They headed north, then east for a while and when the path began to ascend, slightly to the southeast.

Aarl told Werlis at length about the port city of Irkaar in Thir, on the coast of the Southern Sea. As their distance from Vrenli and Gorathdin increased, Vrenli took the opportunity to ask Gorathdin a few questions.

"It's strange! Although I don't actually know you, I'm following you to Astinhod. I have a feeling of familiarity with you, but I would still like to know why you said that the journey also had to do with me, and what task did you say my grandfather had in Wetherid?" Vrenli wanted to know.

Vrenli turned around briefly and made sure that Werlis and Aarl were far enough away.

"I thank you for the trust you have placed in me, Vrenli, but I can't tell you much more at the moment than that it's about a meaningful matter."

Vrenli was disappointed by Gorathdin's answer.

"It's about a book. A very old book," Gorathdin whispered and immediately put a finger to his lips to let Vrenli know that he shouldn't answer.

"Then my feelings and suspicions were right. I knew it," thought Vrenli.

It wasn't easy for him to not ask all the questions that were now running through his head.

"Master Drobal will certainly be pleased to meet you in Astinhod!" said Gorathdin, indicating to Vrenli that he would find the answers to his questions in Astinhod.

"I can hardly wait to meet him," said Vrenli, who understood what Gorathdin was trying to tell him.

Werlis and Aarl, who were still in conversation, noticed that their distance to Vrenli and Gorathdin had increased and began to walk faster until they were finally walking alongside them again. The path zigzagged out of the mixed forest onto a meadow, which they crossed and entered the adjacent dry, initially sparse coniferous forest, which they walked through until late after midday. Werlis expressed his wish to rest.

"I'm hungry, friends. How about you, surely you won't say no to some dried meat," said Werlis with a grin, although he was exhausted.

"Dried meat and bread. Why do I have the feeling that I will soon wish I could remove these two delicacies from my diet," said Vrenli.

Werlis grinned again.

The coniferous forest became denser and Gorathdin asked Werlis to wait until they came to a clearing not far away. As the path they had followed so far was no longer recognizable and certainly not passable due to the dense, overlapping fir and spruce branches, they left it and walked north for some time and then east again until they came to a small clearing overgrown with tall, thin forest grasses, in the middle of which a rock protruded from the ground that could serve as a resting place.

The four travelers put down their luggage and leaned their weapons against the sun-warmed rock on which they then sat down. Werlis took out a piece of well-smoked dried meat, the already slightly smelly cheese and one of the small loaves of Everfull Bread from his travel bag. He pulled his knife from its sheath, used it to cut small, bite-sized slices of the dried meat and placed them on a flat stone lying on the rock. He undid the knot on the thin rope that tied his metal container to the outside of the bag, filled it with his water bag, placed the loaf of Everfull Bread inside and waited a few moments for it to soak up the water. He placed the now handsome loaf of bread next to the dried meat on the stone to dry briefly.

"I'll have a look around in the meantime," Gorathdin announced and disappeared behind the neighboring trees.

Aarl, looking at the few pieces of dried meat lying on the stone in front of him, realized that Werlis' estimate of the quantity was that of an Abkether. He therefore opened his travel bag, took out a smoked wild boar ham and cut several thin slices from it, which he placed next to Werlis' pieces of dried meat.

"I think that will be enough," said Aarl.

Werlis looked astonished.

"You humans certainly can eat a good amount of meat," commented Werlis, pressing his index finger on the loaf of bread to test it.

Vrenli sat in the meadow near them and thought about his grandfather's book.

"Where could he have hidden it?" he asked himself and a few thoughts later came to the question of why Gorathdin knew about the book.

"I hope Master Drobal can tell me more about the whole affair," he thought, unexpectedly remembering a conversation he had overheard his grandfather having with an old man in a gray cloak who had come from outside.

The book in which the Word that has come to life is written.

He had already wondered about this saying as a child and this time, too, it seemed strange and incomprehensible to him. It sounded just as strange as the voice of the stranger who had been talking to his grandfather for two days.

Vrenli's thoughts were interrupted by Werlis, who informed him that Aarl's smoked wild boar ham tasted delicious. "You really must try it," said Werlis, holding up a slice of the pink meat and handing it to Vrenli.

"Fantastic!" praised Vrenli with his mouth full, breaking off a piece of the loaf and topping it with two slices of Aarl's smoked wild boar ham.

"I use a very specific smoking technique," remarked Aarl proudly.

"And what would that be?" asked Werlis with interest.

"That's a secret," replied Aarl with a grin.

Gorathdin, who had returned to his three traveling companions, looked at the dried meat on the stone in front of him.

"You didn't have to wait for me, friends," he said, not understanding why he was being grinned at.

"What is it?" he asked them.

"Nothing. We were suddenly no longer hungry," replied Aarl, who was infected by Vrenli and Werlis' burst of laughter.

Gorathdin finally had to laugh himself, although he didn't know why.

"Put the dried meat back in your travel bag, Werlis," Aarl said, pulling his ham out of the bag and cutting off a few slices for Gorathdin.

"Is there something wrong with Werlis' dried meat?" asked Gorathdin, reaching for the last piece of bread and tasting Aarl's ham.

"Everything is fine with it. We just thought that Aarl's ham tasted a lot better," explained Vrenli.

Gorathdin didn't even try to find out what was so amusing about it.

"Delicious," he remarked.

"A secret recipe," said Aarl and almost started laughing again.

"So, so," replied Gorathdin.

After fortifying themselves, they set off again towards Lake Taneth in the north. By late afternoon, they had left the coniferous forest behind them and entered a wide, initially flat, then rising grassy landscape.

"Beyond this plain, at the foot of the Ice Mountains, lies Lake Taneth," Gorathdin informed them, gazing at the snow-covered peaks shining dazzlingly white in the distance.

"Let's hope the nice weather lasts another two or three days," said Gorathdin, looking up at the bright blue sky.

He knew from his first journey over the Ice Mountains that it would certainly take him a lot longer if a storm came up, especially as he was now accompanied by two Abkether and a human. But he had no more than eight days to bring the moonflower blossoms to Astinhod. If he were traveling alone, he could make twice as much progress, but getting Vrenli to Master Drobal was just as important as the blossoms. There were only a few of them left and he was convinced that Vrenli was an asset to them. He had not yet recognized the power that rested within him, but Gorathdin was confident that Master Drobal would awaken it in him.

The sun's rays shining on the surface of Lake Taneth made the mirrored peaks of the Ice Mountains sparkle like crystals. The wide lake, which stretched from the northernmost corner to the center of the snow- and ice-covered mountain range that bounded Tawinn from Astinhod, could only be crossed by raft. The water was too cold to swim to the other side of the lake, which was more than three hundred paces away. Vrenli looked at the still water and remembered the images the Oracle of Tawinn had shown him. He again saw the knights, orcs and ogres crossing the lake on rafts to destroy the city of Tawinn.

"We'll need a raft," said Aarl, who had come to Tawinn across this lake more than twenty-five years ago.

During this time, he only traveled back to his village in southern Thir once. Back then, when he felt the death of both his parents, he took the long journey and faced the anger, fear and failure that had once caused him to leave his village.

"I thought we were going to cross the lake on Gorathdin's raft," Werlis said, looking around for it.

"I swam across the lake, little friend," Gorathdin revealed.

Vrenli, Werlis and Aarl looked at him in amazement.

"Swam?" Aarl asked.

"Well, the water is cold, but not too cold to unnecessarily stop a ranger on his journey," Gorathdin replied with a smile.

"But Werlis is right. We need a raft. We need to build one and we should hurry. I want us to reach the other side of the lake before dusk," said Gorathdin, looking at the few trees growing along the lakeshore.

"Aarl and I will take care of the tree trunks and you two can start weaving ropes from willow bark," Gorathdin said to Vrenli and Werlis, who nodded, drew their short swords and walked towards the large willow to their right.

They cut off several thick branches and carefully peeled off the brown-green bark. Gorathdin took his fire axe from his back, walked up to a birch and began to strike the trunk of the tree hard. He knew that what he was doing was not what he had been taught as a child, but he had no other choice. He needed the wood to get across the lake with his companions.

"Sorry," he whispered as the first of the four trees he had to cut down fell.

Together with Aarl and with the help of Vrenli's short sword, he split the tree trunks in two. They laid the eight halves next to each other, just a few steps from the lakeshore, with the flat, level side facing upwards. Vrenli and Werlis began to tie the tree trunks together with the braided bark ropes. In the meantime, Gorathdin searched the lakeshore for two branches suitable to use as oars. However, it took longer than he intended and when he finally found what he was looking for and returned to his friends with two strong, straight branches, Vrenli, Werlis and Aarl had already tied the eight trunks together.

"Looks floatable," said Aarl, who was standing next to the raft close to the water.

"Now we just have to build two oars and we can cross," said Gorathdin, who threw the two branches on the ground next to the raft and checked the position of the sun.

They didn't have much time left and he suspected that they wouldn't make it to the other side of the lake before dusk.

Together with Aarl, he split off several small, flat pieces from the remaining logs and tied them to the two branches.

"Let's get it into the water," said Gorathdin after the work was done.

Together they pulled the raft the few steps from the lakeshore into the water. Vrenli and Werlis now realized for the first time how cold the water in Lake Taneth really was. Werlis climbed onto the raft, followed by Vrenli and Aarl. Gorathdin pushed it away from the shallow lake shore before he jumped on, took one of the oars and, together with Aarl, began to row towards the middle of the lake.

Vrenli and Werlis, who were soaked up to their knees, froze in the cold wind blowing across the lake. But it was also this wind that dried their clothes when they reached the middle of the lake after a while. Gorathdin and Aarl decided it was time to take a short rest.

"How deep do you think it is here?" asked Werlis, gazing into the clear, deep water.

"It's hard to say, but since you can't see the bottom of the lake, I estimate at least fifteen or twenty paces," replied Aarl, who had experience in estimating water depths.

He grew up in a small fishing village on the Southern Sea and even as a child he would go out fishing with his father. As Aarl gazed into the depths of the lake, he remembered what had happened more than twenty-five years ago.

He began to sweat, his hands cramped and he started to tremble. If Gorathdin had not urged him to continue rowing, he would have lost himself in his memories and would once again have to face the horrors of his past, as he had done so many times before. Aarl was about to reach for his oar when he almost fell into the cold water in shock when he saw an old man standing next to him on the raft, who had a long, white, matted beard that reached the bottom of the raft and was a head shorter than Vrenli.

"Such a crossing can be dangerous. Especially if you harbor dark thoughts. But I hope that doesn't apply to you," said the old man with a chuckle and, to the surprise of Aarl, Werlis and Gorathdin, pushed Vrenli off the raft into the cold water.

Vrenli stiffened with fright. He slowly sank into the depths of the lake. Aarl was about to reach for the small bearded man when he jumped from the raft onto the surface of the water and, to Gorathdin and Werlis' astonishment, stopped a few steps away from them without sinking. Gorathdin wanted to jump after Vrenli, but a gust of wind threw him back to the bottom of the raft.

"No. No. The Abkether has to make this journey alone," said the old man, chuckling.

"Vrenli, why don't you swim," Werlis called after him full of concern.

But Vrenli did not move and sank deeper and deeper to the bottom of the lake. Gorathdin's dark green eyes began to light up. The old man, who was still standing on the surface of the water next to the raft, felt the anger and hatred that the elf harbored against him.

"You don't have to worry about him, elf," the little old man said to Gorathdin and chuckled again.

With a swinging, circling hand movement above his head, he disappeared before their eyes. Before any of them could jump after Vrenli, a storm arose and the swell increased alarmingly. Gorathdin turned on instinct and saw a huge wave racing towards the raft at high speed.

"Quick, lie down on the ground and hold on!" Gorathdin shouted and threw himself down.

The wave caught the raft and carried it to the opposite shore of the lake. Startled and angry at their unwanted arrival, Werlis, Gorathdin and Aarl stepped off the raft into the cold water, whose swell had subsided with the decreasing wind, and pulled the raft ashore. Werlis stood freezing a few steps from the shore, staring at the middle of the lake, and was startled when a huge carp head emerged from the water behind Gorathdin.

"You don't have to worry about your friend," said the carp and dived down again.

" I am worried, and not a little. Who or what was that anyway?" Werlis asked Gorathdin and Aarl.

"A water gnome," replied Gorathdin, who sat down beside Aarl on the meadow by the lakeside, soaked through.

"I'll light a fire, otherwise we'll freeze to death," Aarl decided and got up to collect some dry branches and twigs from the nearby trees.

"But what about Vrenli?" Werlis called after him.

"We can only hope for the best for him, because we can't help him now," replied Aarl.

As Vrenli slowly sank into the depths of the lake, he was amazed that he could still breathe. All his efforts to swim failed due to the rigidity in which he found himself, which he assumed was caused by the cold water. The deeper he sank, the darker it became around him and eventually he lost his bearings. He no longer knew which way was up or down. However, despite the fact that he was probably sinking towards death, he felt no fear. When he saw a light in front of him, towards which he was sinking, he asked himself whether he was ready to die and answered the question with an unequivocal "no".

"I mustn't lose consciousness now," he admonished himself and was amazed that he still didn't feel any compulsion to gasp for air, which he wouldn't have had anyway.

He sank into the increasingly bright, dazzling, golden light. Vrenli closed his eyes for a few moments. He lost all sense of space and time. But when he opened them again, he found himself floating high above Lake Taneth.

"Have I died and been reborn as a bird?" he asked himself, startled when he saw several hundred heavily armed knights in black armor striding down a path that led from the Ice Mountains to the lake.

He quickly looked around for his friends, who were supposed to be floating on a raft below him. Vrenli wanted to warn them of the approaching enemies. But no matter how hard he tried, he could not see Werlis, Gorathdin and Aarl. He therefore tried to warn them by shouting loudly, but his shouts were stifled before they even left his lips. Vrenli floated slowly towards the western shore of the lake, where three old weeping willows stood. When he caught sight of the Tawinnian priestess who had appeared to him last night, he was surprised. She was sitting on the grass under the drooping, many-leaved branches of the weeping willows with a young man who was a head shorter than her.

111

Slowly, he hovered above their heads. He heard the young man singing a song to the priestess, accompanied by a pair of birds that swooped over their heads.

Bird meadow, flower valley - wonderfully fragrant everywhere
Water rushing in the sun valley - fish and otters everywhere
Love happiness and cheerfulness - have enveloped me
Oh, how delighted I am - as your heart comes close to mine
If you want me, then I want you - Lorothe, I love you
Bird meadow, flower valley - wonderfully fragrant everywhere
Water rushing in the sun valley - fish and otters everywhere

In the bright rays of the sun, the priestess's long, curly blonde hair shimmered golden and the snow-white, silky fabric of her tunic fluttered gently in the wind. Her delicate features were accentuated by her graceful pallor. She gazed, enamored, with her crystal blue eyes at the little man kneeling before her. Vrenli wanted to glide closer to them and warn them of the approaching enemies, but it was too late. An arrow pierced the priestess's heart. She collapsed into the arms of the young man who was still kneeling before her and her white, silken tunic turned red. The weeping young man shouted something Vrenli could not understand and, before the arrow fired at him could hit him, jumped into the lake, from which he did not emerge. Vrenli began to fall. He fell deeper and deeper until he finally plunged into the water below and slowly sank to the bottom of the lake. He noticed glittering points of light moving quickly towards him and suddenly looked into the sad eyes of a huge carp, which opened its mouth wide and snapped at him.

Out of fear, Vrenli closed his eyes and when he opened them again, he had not been eaten by the giant carp, as he had assumed, but was next to the young man, who was now standing on a boat made of snow-white nacre floating in the middle of the lake. He was wrapped in a robe of seaweed and gazed at the enemy returning to Lake Taneth from the direction of the city of Tawinn.

His eyes were filled with pain as he saw the murderers of his beloved rowing towards him on rafts. He began to cry and with each of his tears that fell into the water, the water level of the lake rose considerably.

Slowly, the young man raised both his hands far above his head, whereupon huge walls of water opened to the left and right of the enemy's numerous rafts. Screaming, they fell into the water and sank to the muddy lakebed. He lowered his arms again and with them the walls of water crashed down with a thunderous noise on the murderers of his beloved and buried them beneath them.

"Lorothe, you flower of Tawinn. Your death and the death of your people shall not go unrecognized!" the young man called out into the expanse of the lake and then turned to Vrenli.

"The Entorbis family must be punished for the deaths of your people and those of Lorothe. Do not forget the words of the raftsman of Lake Taneth," the young man emphasized.

Vrenli wanted to answer him, but instead of words he spat out water that he had swallowed when he emerged from the lake near the eastern shore, where Gorathdin, Werlis and Aarl pulled him out.

"You're alive!" cried Werlis delightedly as Vrenli, still dazed from his involuntary journey into the past, opened his eyes.

Gorathdin picked him up and laid him next to the warming fire on Aarl's bearskin.

"That cowardly water gnome just pushed you into the cold water from behind. If I get my hands on him!" grumbled Werlis angrily, pointing towards the lake with a clenched fist and then covering the freezing Vrenli with his cloak.

After they had recovered from the excitement and warmed themselves by the fire, Vrenli described his experiences to them.

"An incredible story," marveled Werlis with raised eyebrows.

Aarl and Gorathdin were silent and thoughtful.

"Unbelievable, but true," said Vrenli.

He lay down on his back and gazed at the starry night sky over Lake Taneth for some time until he finally fell asleep.

The Ice Mountains

When Vrenli woke up, he couldn't remember the dream he had that night. His head was pounding and his limbs ached due to the involuntary bath the day before. He slowly rose from Aarl's bearskin and looked at Werlis, who was no better off. Vrenli's voice was hoarse and his nose was dripping.

"We don't feel particularly well," they let their friends know.

Gorathdin and Aarl scrutinized the pair. They did indeed make a sickly impression. Gorathdin then decided to postpone the ascent into the Ice Mountains for a while.

"Time is running out, friends, but there's little point in us setting off straight away," he said, looking at Vrenli and Werlis, who felt a little guilty as they were responsible for the delay.

"I'm sorry, friends. I really don't feel strong enough to climb the mountains," Vrenli admitted, looking up at the Ice Mountains and sneezing.

"I think we need a strong, hot herbal tea," Werlis suggested, looking sympathetically at Vrenli.

"There's still some firewood left. I'll light a fire," said Aarl and put his travel bag, which he had hanging on his right shoulder, back on the dewy grass.

"If I remember correctly, not far from here, here and there, single-root flowers were growing in the crevices. A decoction with their flowers will restore Vrenli and Werlis' strength in no time," Gorathdin thought, running quickly and light-footed a few hundred steps up the steep path.

"You'd have to be an elf," sighed Werlis.

Gorathdin's speed, strength and stamina impressed him.

"Dark green eyes and pointy ears. No thanks. I'd rather be a bit slower and weaker and take the occasional break," said Aarl with a grin.

Vrenli and Werlis had to laugh and immediately coughed hard.

Aarl lit a small fire on which Werlis heated water. After a short stay on the lakeshore, Vrenli sat down on his cloak from the Dark Forest, which he had laid on the dewy meadow floor as a base and thought about the raftsman from Lake Taneth. Shortly afterwards, Gorathdin returned with a handful of Singleton Blossoms and handed them to Werlis, who prepared a brew from them.

"Just let it boil for a moment," Gorathdin told Werlis and asked Vrenli how he was feeling.

"All my limbs hurt," moaned Vrenli.

He really wasn't in good shape.

"The tea will help you. You'll see, you'll have your strength back by midday," Gorathdin promised and sat down next to him.

After Vrenli and Werlis had drunk the brew from the Singleton Blossoms, they fell into a cozy, warm, deep sleep, from which they only awoke when the sun was high above their heads.

"I haven't slept so wonderfully for a long time," thought Werlis, who woke up before Vrenli and felt much better.

He went to the lakeshore and splashed cold water on his face to wash the sleep from his eyes. Vrenli woke up shortly afterwards and stretched like a cat. He had his eyes fixed on the northern shore of the lake, from where Aarl and Gorathdin were on their way back to the camp site carrying a branch they had strung four fish on.

"We're having fish today. I hope you like fish?" asked Aarl.

Vrenli and Werlis nodded in agreement and smiled.

"We should set off after the meal, friends," urged Gorathdin, as he was worried that they had already lost another half day. He didn't have much time left to bring the moonflower blossoms to Astinhod. Unconsciously, he clutched his chest, where the small leather pouch he kept the flowers in hung.

Gorathdin's thoughts were with the most enchanting creature he had ever met in his long life as an elf. The longing to hold Lythinda in his arms again with a smile had been with him since his departure from Astinhod. But this longing was also accompanied by reproaches about what had happened in the Three Vines and weighed on him as a burden.

"I was foolish. I should have taken better care of her. I let myself get carried away by the happy drinking mood in the pub," he thought and was then plagued by worries.

He gazed into the flames of the small fire on which Aarl was roasting the fish he had caught and remained introverted. Gorathdin was worried about Lythinda first and foremost and hoped that the healing potion Master Drobal would prepare for her would free her from the strange illness that hung over her like a shadow.

However, he was also worried about the kingdom of Astinhod, as Lythinda was the only heir to the throne. He didn't want to imagine what would happen if someone else took over the regency in Astinhod after King Grandhold. No one noticed Gorathdin's worries, which weighed on him like a heavy burden. He fought a battle between hope and hopelessness. He had heard a lot about the loving and hopeful God of mankind. Even though he had often wondered about human double standards and had met many so-called believers who had stolen, cheated and murdered despite their good intentions and values, he decided to pray to their God in hours of inner despair.

"I'm going to take a little walk along the lakeshore until the fish finish roasting," Gorathdin said to Vrenli, Werlis and Aarl, who were sitting around the fire and turning the branches with the fish on them back and forth over the flames.

Gorathdin stood up and walked slowly along the lakeshore to the north. He decided to pray quietly:

"Father,
Creator of all life - my life.

Thank you for all my talents
and abilities that were bestowed upon me.
Give me strength in my struggle
for the good and give me hope
and confidence, in all the difficult
hours of my existence.

Give them light,
who are on their way into the darkness.
Enlighten them with knowledge,
who do not recognize what you have created.

Let the nations endure forever.
Lead them to unity in their struggle
against evil and stand by them.
Amen"

In a miraculous way, Gorathdin's fears and anxieties were replaced by renewed hope and confidence. It was a new and unusual experience for him; a ranger who feared neither the shadow nor the malevolent creatures of Fallgar, a ranger who lived among humans. He had already fought hundreds of orcs, ogres, goblins, underwater creatures from Moorgh, lizard creatures, undead, forest wraiths and shapeshifters, but he had never felt fear or dread before, and he was not used to having to hope for anything. He was a ranger from the Dark Forest, in harmony with nature, he thought, until he felt the desire to live among humans. From that moment on, something changed in him and when he met Lythinda, he experienced the longings of a human. He loved her, but he didn't love her like a ranger, he loved her like a human.

As this human love was now in danger, he sought refuge in the faith of men. Not that he forgot his origins or even wanted to deny them. No. It was more as if he had found something that had always been missing and this miraculously complemented him. Gorathdin went back to his traveling companions and sat down by the fire.

"You've come at just the right moment. The fish are ready," announced Aarl with a smile, pulling the fried fish from the branches.

The smell of the fried fish spreading along the lake shore attracted two otters that emerged from the water just a few steps away from them and pointed their noses into the wind.

"Look, two otters," Werlis drew his friends' attention and pointed to the two small, furry animals.

During the time that the four traveling companions ate their fried fish, the two otters did not move from the spot. It was only when Werlis threw them the leftovers that they greedily snapped at them and dived off with the fish heads hanging out of their mouths.

"We should set off," said Gorathdin and extinguished the fire with the remaining brew from the Singleton Blossoms.

They moved swiftly away from the shore of Lake Taneth and took the path that led steeply into the Ice Mountains. Vrenli and Werlis soon noticed that their travel bags were getting heavier, and they occasionally had to lean on the rock face to their right, so Aarl and Gorathdin offered to take the bags off their shoulders, as they only represented a small additional burden for them.

They followed the path up to the middle of the mountain and looked down one last time at Lake Taneth and the Ruins of Tawinn. The increasingly narrow path, strewn with rubble, made their progress slow. Vrenli and Werlis slipped several times on the loose gravel and therefore continued between Gorathdin and Aarl. The path led them higher and higher up the mountain. Only a few low trees and bushes grew on the slope to their left. As they would soon reach the tree line, Gorathdin took the precaution of collecting dry leaves and branches so they would not be left without firewood on the way ahead.

Far above them, they could already see the snow-covered plateau stretching out in front of the highest peaks of the Ice Mountains.

"The pass to Astinhod leads over these peaks," Gorathdin drew his traveling companions' attention and pointed with his hand to the peaks covered in snow and ice.

It was getting noticeably colder. Vrenli, Werlis and Aarl therefore pulled their cloaks, which had kept them warm during their ascent, tighter. The path they had been following for more than half a day over the summit of the westernmost mountain in the mighty range finally led them to the snow-covered plateau. Gorathdin watched the overcast sky anxiously. The ominous, black clouds forming over the snow- and ice-covered summit of the mountain far ahead of them did not bode well.

"A storm is coming. We should look for suitable shelter," Gorathdin warned his fellow travelers and looked around searching.

Aarl drew their attention to a crevice that had formed between two strange, adjoining rocks and would provide a natural roof over their heads.

"Here on these rocks in front of us is a crevice where we can take shelter," he said to them, pointing to the two broad and high rocks that rose out of the snow to their right, just a hundred paces away. They walked towards them.

"Not exactly comfortable, but still better than being out in the open in a storm," Werlis remarked as they made their way into the crevice.

The sudden icy wind was a harbinger of the approaching storm. Vrenli, Werlis, Gorathdin and Aarl therefore dug their furs out of their travel bags and wrapped themselves in them.

"We should light a fire. When the storm breaks, it will be much colder," Gorathdin suggested and placed a few stones in a circle.

"The idea of it getting even colder further up scares me," confessed Vrenli, who was freezing even though he was wrapped in a lynx skin on top of his cloak from the Dark Forest.

Gorathdin placed a handful of dry leaves in the stone-lined hearth and Aarl tried to light them with the sparks of two flints he struck together.

"The leaves are too damp. It smokes more than it burns," remarked Aarl as he struck sparks on the leaves a few more times.

The sky above them lit up. Lightning struck not far from the crevice and with it began an icy downpour, which only a little later turned into a heavy snowstorm, blowing snow into the crevice again and again and making it impossible for Aarl to light the already damp leaves. Aarl moved closer to Gorathdin and Werlis, who were already sitting very close to Vrenli, who was leaning with his back against the rock face.

"Get ready for a damp and, above all, cold night," Gorathdin predicted and wrapped himself in his fur.

"Impossible!" exclaimed Aarl angrily, throwing the flints on the ground next to him.

He reached for his travel bag and began to rummage in it. After a few moments, he pulled out a small bottle, from which he poured a good amount of the contents onto the dry branches he placed in the fireplace.

"What's that?" Werlis asked with interest and was startled when Aarl struck a few sparks and the branches ignited in a flash of flame.

"This is the finest herbal spirit. Very strong and highly flammable," replied Aarl, warming his hands over the bluish flames.

"Can you also drink the herbal spirit?" Gorathdin asked him and smiled.

"That's what it's actually for," replied Aarl and handed him the bottle.

"Home-brewed," Aarl added as Gorathdin took a big swig from the bottle.

Gorathdin handed the bottle to Vrenli, who fortunately only took a small sip, but it flowed down his throat like fire.

"Strong," he rattled and handed the bottle to Werlis, who sipped from it.

"Very strong, but it warms you up immensely," Werlis remarked with a grimace and handed the bottle to Aarl, who then took a big swig.

Inwardly warmed by Aarl's herbal spirit, they sat around the flames of the small fire, which waxed and waned in the wind. Gorathdin told his companions how he had spent the first and coldest night of his journey alone on the peaks of the Ice Mountains. His words were repeatedly drowned out by thunder. When he had reached the end of his story, Vrenli, Werlis and Aarl fell asleep. Gorathdin placed another branch in the small fire and looked out of the crevice onto the plateau.

The snowstorm had subsided. The distant rumble of lightning let him know that the storm had moved on. He thought about Lythinda for some time, holding the small leather pouch containing the blossoms of the moonflower. His thoughts revolved around the stranger in the Three Vines.

"Was it possibly just a harbinger of another strike the Entorbis were planning against Wetherid?" he wondered. Gorathdin knew that all attempts by the Entorbis to take Wetherid in recent centuries had failed. But the losses of the peoples of Wetherid were becoming greater.

"We have irretrievably lost much of what once helped us in our defense against the Shadow Lords. Do we still have the strength to successfully fend off another blow?" he mused, thinking of the book that was no longer in Wetherid.

The nearby howl of a snow wolf demanded his attention. Gorathdin interrupted his thoughts to sneak out of the crevice onto the dark, cold and snow-covered plain. When the snow wolf howled once more, Gorathdin camouflaged himself. He didn't know if the hunter was just a scout or if there might be a whole pack nearby. Camouflaged from the wolf's eyes and scent, he followed the its scent, which led him to a small hill not more than three hundred paces east of their lair.

His sharp, dark green elven eyes watched the surroundings carefully. When the snow wolf howled three times in quick succession, Gorathdin knew that the animal was not alone. The hunter told his pack about the prey waiting for them in a crevice. Gorathdin wanted to reach for his bow, but he realized that he had left it next to his fire axe in their shelter. He had to make do with his hunting knife, which he carefully pulled from the brim of his boot. He put the knife between his teeth and slowly crawled back to his friends on the snow-covered ground, waking them up and telling them of the approaching danger. Vrenli and Werlis immediately reached for their short swords, which they had leaned against the rock face next to them. Aarl threw off the bearskin he was wrapped in, took a burning branch from the fire and followed Gorathdin, who retrieved his weapons, outside. They stared out into the darkness and waited for the pack of wolves. With his sensitive elven ears, Gorathdin could already hear the panting of eight snow wolves running down the hill towards them. His dark green eyes began to glow as he finally caught sight of them, and he sensed the hunger that was driving them. Gorathdin knew that they would not listen to him if he tried to speak to them. Snow wolves were not like the wolves of the Dark Forest. They followed no laws. They were murderers. They not only killed to feed, they killed for pleasure.

Gorathdin prepared himself for the upcoming battle. Even though he would kill the snow wolves who were hostile to him, he asked for forgiveness in advance, just as his father had taught him as a child. The distance between him and the pack was no more than a hundred paces as he took an arrow from his quiver and placed it in the string of his bow.

"Stay where you are!" he shouted to Vrenli and Werlis, who were just about to scurry out of the crevice with their short swords at the ready.

The two followed his invitation and peered out from behind the rock face. Aarl checked that his throwing knives were loose in their sheaths and waited for the snow wolves to come within throwing range. Gorathdin drew his bow and shot the arrow, which whistled through the air and struck the right shoulder blade of one of the snow wolves, who fell to the ground howling. The pack's leader bared its teeth and urged its hunters on. Aarl dropped the burning branch and threw two of his throwing knives at the two snow wolves running to the right, close behind the pack leader. One of them fell to the ground from the impact of the throwing knife, which hit it in the head, and the other, who was less fortunate, was killed by the second knife hit on the front of its chest. Less than twenty paces separated the five snow wolves from their prey.

Gorathdin knew that he only had a few moments before he would have to fight to the death with the pack's leader. He therefore placed two of his arrows in the string of his bow, which he drew with all his might and shot at two of the snow wolves, who were only a few steps away from him and Aarl. The force of the striking arrows sent the two snow wolves howling backwards, where the white, snow-covered ground turned red. Gorathdin threw the bow into the snow and grabbed his fire axe with small blue-orange flames dancing on its blade. He tightly gripped the handle of his axe with both hands. The eyes of the pack leader and his own collided. Gorathdin watched as the muscles of his opponent's hind legs tensed and with one step the snow wolf leapt at him, snarling. Gorathdin was prepared for this and took a step to the side then turned and cut off its head with a powerful blow.

The three remaining snow wolves howled, snarled and bared their large, dangerously pointed teeth when they saw their leader's head in the snow, but before they could leap towards Gorathdin, two snow wolves fell to the ground, hit by Aarl's throwing knives. The third, however, leapt at Gorathdin and threw him to the ground. Gorathdin held his fire axe above him protectively, fending off the powerful bites. Before Aarl could turn around to help Gorathdin, Vrenli and Werlis, overcoming their people's primal fear of wolves, rushed at the snow wolf, screaming with their short swords at the ready and killing it with several stabs.

"Thank you, my little friends," Gorathdin gasped, pushing the dead snow wolf away from him and standing up.

"We have to get their bodies away from here. The stench could attract other wild animals," Gorathdin said to Vrenli, Werlis and Aarl, grabbing the two hind legs of the wolf lying next to him and pulling it into the darkness to a chasm several hundred paces deep, less than two hundred paces from the crevice.

Aarl fetched a burning branch from the fire in their shelter. Together with Vrenli and Werlis, he pulled one of the snow wolves to the spot where Gorathdin had just thrown his down the precipice and threw the other after it.

Little did they know that the rockfall caused by the falling bodies of the snow wolves had startled a group of snow goblins sitting fifty paces below on a ledge in front of their cave. Vrenli, Werlis, Gorathdin and Aarl spent some time dragging the remaining carcasses from the crevice to the precipice.

By the time they had finished their work and returned to their shelter, where Aarl had thrown some branches on the fire, two of the snow goblins had climbed up a small ascent that led in switchbacks around the eastern side of the mountain onto the snow-covered plain to find out who or what was responsible for the night's rockfall.

The four travelers, who had wrapped themselves in their furs again and were sitting close to each other, were talking about the fight with the snow wolves. They did not notice that the two snow goblins were very close to them, as the hideous creatures had noticed the smoke from the fire, which they could smell from afar, and had followed. With their small, hairy feet, which allowed the snow goblins to creep almost silently over the snow, they climbed up the rock and looked around in search of the fire that was causing the smoke. Gorathdin was startled by a few small stones that bounced down onto the snow-covered ground as the two creatures climbed up.

"Be quiet," he whispered to Vrenli, Werlis and Aarl, who looked at him questioningly.

Gorathdin put his index finger to his lips to emphasize his statement.

His dark green eyes sparkled, and it seemed as if his pointed ears were moving like those of a deer listening intently to the wind. He reached for his fire axe carefully and slowly so as not to make any noise. Vrenli, Werlis and Aarl realized that Gorathdin must have heard something and kept quiet. The two snow goblins who had been lingering on the top of the rock had just noticed that the smoke they had been following was rising from below, on the south side of the rock. Slowly they climbed down the thirty or so steps and spied the light of the flames shining dimly from the crevice. One of them leaned over the crevice from above, holding onto a ledge with one hand, and saw two Abkether, a human and an elf, sitting around the fire causing the smoke.

Before the sinewy, emaciated snow goblin could pull himself back up to tell those waiting on the rock what he had seen in the crevice, Gorathdin's fire axe severed his neck. In a fraction of an instant, Gorathdin leapt out of the crevice and caught sight of the second snow goblin crouching above him on the rock. Gorathdin was about to jump onto the rock when the snow goblin leapt down to the other side of the cliff and disappeared into the darkness. Gorathdin wondered for a moment whether he should try to pursue the fleeing snow goblin, but was prevented from doing so by Vrenli, Werlis and Aarl, who emerged from the crevice and caught sight of the snow goblin's severed head.

"What kind of hideous creature is that?" Vrenli exclaimed in horror, his eyes fixed on the creature's hairy head lying in the snow in front of him.

"A snow goblin," explained Gorathdin, for whom it was now too late to pursue the fugitive.

"Was he alone?" Aarl wanted to know and looked at the headless body lying on the rock above them.

"I'm afraid not. We have to get out of here," Gorathdin replied and crawled back into the crevice, where he took his bow, quiver and the bundle of dry branches that were still left.

"But it's the middle of the night," protested Werlis, looking at Gorathdin in astonishment.

"I don't feel like waiting here until the whole horde arrives. I will lead the way and you must follow me closely," said Gorathdin.

Aarl crawled into the crevice, rolled up his bearskin and extinguished the fire as soon as Vrenli and Werlis were ready to leave.

"Stay close together," Gorathdin warned, looking around the area with his elven eyes.

He listened for sounds and sniffed the wind. When Gorathdin was sure that none of the ugly creatures were near them, he strode east, followed by Vrenli, Werlis and Aarl, across the snow-covered plateau in the darkness. Gorathdin looked around several times to make sure they were not being followed and noticed that it was not easy for Vrenli, Werlis and Aarl to keep up with him. The light of the crescent moon over the tops of the Ice Mountains was just strong enough for them to not lose sight of Gorathdin in the darkness. Werlis and Vrenli fell a few times on the frozen, snow-covered ground.

It was bitterly cold and the several hours they walked wordlessly took almost all the strength they could muster. They had left the plateau behind them and were facing a steep rock face several hundred steps high, and it would not be long before the morning began to turn gray. Gorathdin had doubts as to whether they would be able to conquer the snow and ice-covered walls, weary and exhausted as they were. The ascent would take them half a day and he knew how difficult it would be to find a foothold on this steep wall.

"We need to rest, the climb is exhausting and dangerous," said Gorathdin in a serious voice.

Vrenli, Werlis and Aarl were delighted at the prospect of getting some more sleep. Gorathdin laid his weapons and the smaller bundle of dry branches in a hollow in the snow, which seemed a suitable place to sleep.

"We'll have to do without a fire. It could give us away," Gorathdin warned and looked around.

Convinced that they were not being followed, he crouched down in the hollow.

"It's very cold. I'm freezing," Werlis stuttered, shivering.

Vrenli was no different and \not happy that they were supposed to spend the night here in the hollow without a warm fire.

"I know one way we could keep warm," said Aarl.

Everyone was excited to see what proposal he would make.

Aarl explained to them that he could spread his large bearskin over the cold floor of the hollow. They would stretch Gorathdin's fur over the hollow as a cover and secure it with stones.

"We should at least try," he encouraged Gorathdin and picked up some large stones, which he placed around the hollow.

Aarl asked Vrenli and Werlis to leave the hollow for a moment so he could spread his bearskin on the snow-covered ground.

"You can lie down on it now," Aarl said to the two of them and stretched Gorathdin's fur over them.

Gorathdin weighted down the fur from the outside with the stones he had collected earlier, then lifted the last corner of the fur that had not been weighted down and crawled into the hollow. He reached out to the edge with his hand and placed the stone lying there on the hide.

"Well, what do you say?" asked Aarl, who lay down next to Vrenli and Werlis.

"Very cramped, but I think it will serve its purpose," Gorathdin replied and lay down next to the three of them.

Warmed up inside, they fell asleep shortly afterwards, exhausted but not freezing.

The cave of the outcast dwarf

Aarl was the first to wake up, and as he carefully lifted Gorathdin's fur and stepped out of the snowy hollow, he realized that it was already daylight.

"We did sleep for a while. It was cramped, but it was much warmer than if we had slept outside," he thought as he looked around sleepily.

The snow-covered plateau appeared to him like a white sea, from which the sun's rays were reflected so strongly that he had to close his tired eyes several times. Only after a few moments was he able to see his surroundings clearly. Snow dunes, ice and stone were all he could see. Aarl turned towards the mountain, at the foot of which they had spent the night, looked at the steep rock face covered in snow and ice and wished at that moment that he was back in the south of Thir in his sunny, warm village. Gorathdin awoke and woke Vrenli and Werlis.

"After we've fortified ourselves, we have to set off," he said to the two of them, climbing out of the snowy hollow and realizing that they had slept until well after sunrise.

"I didn't think it would be so restful to sleep in a snowy hollow," said Werlis.

He stretched and reached for his travel bag, pulling out the red and white striped, well-salted dried meat, a bit of cheese, which smelled strong, and the last loaf of Everfull Bread.

"Today we have the most dangerous part of our journey ahead of us," Gorathdin announced, looking at the rock face in front of him.

"How are we supposed to get up there? There's no paved ascent," Werlis remarked as he divided up the dried meat, cheese and loaves.

"There is a fortified ascent about half a day's journey from here, but it would take a whole day. We don't have that time," Gorathdin replied and took the piece of cheese that Werlis handed him.

"We have to climb this wall," Gorathdin added.

Vrenli, Werlis and Aarl looked anxiously at the high rock face covered in snow and ice.

"Once we've conquered this wall, it's only half a day's journey to the pass," Gorathdin explained.

He pulled a rope twisted from hemp out of his dark brown travel bag and checked its tensile strength.

"I'm not sure if it's long enough," said Gorathdin, and he began to measure it with the span of his arms.

"We also have ropes. You said we should take some with us," Werlis reminded him and took the rope out of his travel bag. Vrenli opened his and also pulled out a rope about thirty paces long.

"That's about sixty steps together," Vrenli calculated and handed Gorathdin the two ropes, which were much thinner than Gorathdin's.

"I doubt they can withstand all of our weight," Gorathdin remarked after examining the two ropes.

"They are strong enough to carry the weight of fifty sacks of flour," affirmed Werlis, who had bought the ropes from Ermis, the rope maker, who mainly made them for the craftsmen and farmers in the village.

"But they really are very thin," Aarl also remarked.

"That's deceptive. Thin and light ropes are very popular in our village. But that doesn't mean they are not resilient. Ermis is a master rope maker, none of his ropes have ever broken," said Werlis, trying to appear convincing.

"We have no choice but to rely on Ermis' ropes," said Vrenli and stood in front of Gorathdin so that he could tie the rope around his waist.

"Vrenli is right. We have to trust that they are strong enough," Gorathdin confirmed, knotting the three ropes together and tying them around Vrenli first.

When they were all connected with the rope, Gorathdin climbed up the wall, slowly, with his hands looking for support, followed by Vrenli, Werlis and Aarl. Every ten to twenty steps he had to pull Vrenli and Werlis upwards as they were too small to reach the ledges and notches in the wall.

"It will take us all day to get up there," Gorathdin said anxiously.

"I'm sorry that we're holding you up, but we could never climb up here alone," said Vrenli sadly.

"Of course, it's not your fault that you are so small. Forgive me, friends, I didn't mean to hurt you," apologized Gorathdin, who was just pulling the two of them up onto the small ledge on which he was standing, smiling gently at them.

"We'll make it in time," said Aarl, who had to make some effort to pull himself up.

The four travelers lingered for a few moments on a small ledge about a third of the way up the wall that Gorathdin looked up with concern. The part that was to come was certainly the most difficult. Ice and snow covered the wall completely and there were only a few ledges, but they were too far apart. After they had rested, Gorathdin climbed the few steps where he still had a foothold.

As the gaps between the rocky outcrops and notches grew wider and were finally no longer within reach, he reached for his fire axe, slammed the pointed side of the double blade hard into the ice and pulled himself steadily higher up the wall.

Every time he found a suitable spot, he had to pull Vrenli, Werlis and now Aarl up to him. Not only did they have to struggle with the ice and snow that made the ascent difficult, but there was also an icy wind blowing, which froze their facial hair and caused small, icy lumps to form under their dripping noses. Pulling the hoods of their cloaks low over their faces, they roped themselves up as best they could so as not to overtax Gorathdin's strength.

It was already early afternoon when they had finally climbed half of the rock face. Gorathdin sensed that it would be tight to reach the summit before dusk. He therefore tried to shorten the many breaks they had taken so far. It was getting bitterly cold that even Gorathdin was freezing, but he was not half as cold as his three fellow travelers. The fiery elven blood flowing in Gorathdin warmed him from the inside out. Vrenli and Werlis, who were no longer able to stick their already blue and terribly painful fingers into the icy snow, now used their short swords, stabbing their blades into the icy snow to find the grip they needed.

Occasionally, Gorathdin kept an eye out for black clouds that could cause the weather to change suddenly. But they were lucky because the sun was shining that day. When Werlis asked for a break, Aarl pulled the bottle of herbal spirit from his traveling bag.

"Take a small sip and pass it on, my friend," Aarl said to Werlis and took another big sip himself before handing it to Werlis.

After everyone had taken a sip from the bottle, they were warmed by Aarl's brew for a short while. Their strength was restored, and they made slightly faster progress.

They still had the last third of their ascent ahead of them. It was late afternoon. They didn't have much time left and with the last reserves of strength they had, they climbed and roped their way further up. None of them wanted to spend the night on the rock face. They knew that it could very well mean their death. At the point where they were, the slope of the rock face was not quite as steep and Vrenli followed Gorathdin closely. A moment of inattention caused by tiredness and the cold made Vrenli lose his balance. Staggering, he managed to hold on to the bundle of branches Gorathdin was carrying on his back at the last moment. But the hold was short-lived. Vrenli fell backwards, dragging the bundle with him. The rope around Gorathdin tightened and, out of reflex, he dug the tip of his fire axe deep into the ice and clutched it with both hands.

"Hold on to the rope!" shouted Gorathdin, whereupon Vrenli, without thinking, grabbed the rope and pulled himself up.

The bundle of dry branches fell down the rock face, hitting several ledges.

"Our firewood!" shouted Werlis, looking after the falling branches and twigs.

"I'm sorry," apologized Vrenli, who had a few tears running down his cheeks, which immediately froze.

"Let's keep going," said Gorathdin. He didn't want to lose any more time in addition to the lost firewood.

"It couldn't have been much worse, barring injury or an oncoming storm," he thought as he pulled himself up the last forty steps on his fire axe.

Once they reached the summit, the joy of their arrival was short-lived, as the loss of the firewood dampened their spirits. Everyone had the same thought: a warming fire would have been a just reward. Vrenli felt guilty. He couldn't look his friends in the eye, so he looked up at the sky, where he saw the rising moon.

"We should go on while it's still light," Gorathdin suggested, whereupon Werlis put back the dried meat he had taken out of his travel bag, and was about to slice, with a sigh.

The four travelers looked down at the high, hilly landscape that lay five or six hundred paces below them, at the foot of the wall they now had to descend.

"The pass to Astinhod begins behind these hills and leads over the mountain in front of us," Gorathdin explained as he checked the rope.

The descent from the snow-covered summit, where an icy wind was blowing, proved to be much easier than the ascent. Gorathdin roped his three friends down the length of the rope and jumped light-footedly and unerringly after them.

"You have the skills of a mountain goat — agile and sure-footed. You missed your true calling!" joked Aarl, causing Werlis, who was abseiling down an icy ledge on the rope Gorathdin and Aarl were holding, to laugh out loud.

"Watch out!" Gorathdin called out to him, laughing at Aarl's joke himself.

Vrenli remained silent.

Werlis managed to gain a foothold on the icy ledge. He turned briefly to the side, facing away from the mountain, and looked out over the white, hilly landscape, at the eastern end of which a broad mountain peak rose high into the sky.

"Ready?" Gorathdin asked.

Werlis pulled the rope taut.

"Ready," he replied, whereupon Vrenli, followed by Aarl, abseiled down.

"I don't think you can jump down here," Aarl called up to Gorathdin when he had reached the bottom.

"It's too icy," he added.

Gorathdin looked down the fifty or so steps and realized that Aarl was right. Jumping onto the ice would be too risky, so he tied the rope to a stone and rappelled down.

"And how do we get it down now?" Werlis wanted to know.

Gorathdin did not reply but placed an arrow in the string of his bow and shot it at the upper end of the rope, which was cut by the sharp arrowhead. Vrenli was amazed at Gorathdin's accuracy and thought to himself that even with his glass bow he would have had difficulty hitting it. Gorathdin pulled hard on the rope a few times until it finally snapped and fell down to them. To prevent it from breaking any further, he tied a strong knot at the end.

They completed the last part of their descent just as dusk was falling. Looking for a suitable place to camp, they walked several hundred more steps to the west, past some small snow-covered hills. The looming gray clouds obscured the moon, and it became darker. Vrenli, who had been silent the whole way down, noticed that Werlis and Aarl were freezing and was plagued further by feelings of guilt. He looked around for trees or bushes, but they had long since crossed the tree line. The hilly landscape was buried deep under a thick layer of snow with not a single plant to be found. The icy wind blowing in their faces made progress increasingly difficult.

"We'll have no choice but to dig a hole in the snow. Let's hope we don't freeze to death," said Gorathdin, and he suddenly stopped.

The wind had blown the smell of burnt wood into his nose.

"Wait!" his dark green eyes began to glow.

He looked a few hundred paces ahead of them and could see a small sea of lights on one of the hills.

"I think I can see the light of torches," said Gorathdin to the surprise of his friends, who were unable to see through the darkness.

"We're not alone up here," Gorathdin remarked.

He grabbed his bow and crept towards the lights, followed by Vrenli, Werlis and Aarl.

"Snow goblins," Gorathdin whispered and pointed to the nearby hill that they walked a few more steps toward.

Now Vrenli, Werlis and Aarl could also see the small, bent creatures wrapped in the skins of mountain goats, ibexes and lynxes, their furry faces clearly visible in the light of the torches. They immediately stopped and lay down on the frozen, snow-covered ground.

"That's at least twenty," Aarl estimated, reaching for his throwing knives.

"I wonder what they're doing up here at such a late hour?" whispered Vrenli, watching the creatures closely.

"I don't know. They may be looking for us," Gorathdin speculated.

His eyes fell on a larger snow goblin, clad in a white snow leopard skin and holding a staff of ice in his left hand, pointing at the mound that the other creatures had gathered around. Gorathdin noticed smoke rising from the top of the mound, and he was sure it was not from the snow goblins' torches.

"There must be something in the hill. Let's crawl closer carefully," whispered Gorathdin.

Vrenli, Werlis and Aarl got ready for battle and followed Gorathdin. There were no more than a hundred paces between them and the hill, where they could see four snow goblins pouring masses of snow into a metal pipe smoke was rising out of.

"How did a metal pipe get into this inhospitable area and why are they pouring snow into it?" asked Werlis in a whisper.

"I have no idea," Gorathdin confessed quietly.

Aarl and Vrenli shrugged their shoulders.

"What are we going to do now? I'm cold and tired," whispered Werlis, wiping away the small lump of ice that had formed under his nose with the sleeve of his cloak.

"It's already pitch black, and I have to admit that I'm a little cold too. We could try to go back, or we could wait some more and hope that the snow goblins disappear from here," Gorathdin replied quietly, pulling his fur out of his pouch and wrapping himself in it.

"They'll discover us if we dig a snow hole near here. And go back? I don't know, my toes are freezing and it's already dark. I think it's better if we wait here," said Aarl in a whisper, pulling his bearskin out of the travel bag and wrapping it around him.

"What if they come our way?" Vrenli asked quietly.

"We'll call our bluff," replied Werlis, putting on his coat as well and sticking his short sword into the snow next to him, when suddenly, with a loud crash, a large amount of snow was whirled through the air from the side of the hill. The four friends were startled.

"What was that?" exclaimed Werlis, and before Vrenli, Gorathdin or Aarl could answer, three of the snow goblins were hurled through the air by something unknown.

A dwarf clad in chain armor with red hair and beard leapt out of the hill, circling his axe around him with one hand and protectively holding a shield in front of him with the other, and struck at the snow goblins.

"A dwarf? Here in the Ice Mountains?" wondered Gorathdin, who had traveled a lot in his long life as an elf and had met the most incredible creatures in the most incredible places, but even he had not expected to see a dwarf in this desolate region.

"It's a dwarf, and what a dwarf. Look, he's already beaten five of these ugly creatures to death," said Werlis, who was amazed by the axe-wielding dwarf.

"We should help him," Aarl decided and took two of his throwing knives from their sheaths.

"Yes. Let's help him," Gorathdin agreed, putting an arrow in the string of his bow and shotting it at one of the snow goblins, who fell to the ground screaming.

The snow goblin clad in the white snow leopard skin pointed his staff in the direction of Gorathdin after noticing that one of his party had been hit by an arrow. Four snow goblins immediately ran towards Vrenli, Gorathdin, Werlis and Aarl, but they were killed halfway by two more arrows and two throwing knives.

The dwarf had noticed that he was receiving support from strangers and then cut his way to the leader of the snow goblins. With a powerful blow from his axe, the dwarf cut off the snow goblin's arm that held the ice staff. Vrenli and Werlis plucked up courage and ran at the other snow goblins with their short swords at the ready, bringing two of them down by plunging their short swords into their emaciated bodies. Gorathdin reached for his fire axe and was about to run towards the creatures gathered around Vrenli and Werlis when the red-haired dwarf leapt from a rock towards the snow goblins with his axe held high above his head, ready to strike, and cut off their limbs with quick but fierce blows.

"Thank you!" shouted Werlis, ducking at the last moment before a bludgeon came hurtling towards his head.

Vrenli rammed his short sword into the attacker's back from behind. The snow goblin fell to the ground and with it Vrenli, who had not let go of his short sword, but used his entire weight to ram the blade deeper through the goatskin the creature was wrapped in. The dwarf, looking around for other opponents, saw Gorathdin leaping towards Vrenli, who was still lying on the dead snow goblin's back, performing several somersaults in the air.

At the last moment, Gorathdin prevented the worst by leaping over Vrenli onto the hill and severing the lower body of an ambush attacker with two powerful, cutting blows from his axe.

The dwarf, who had been watching Gorathdin's agility and speed with admiration, was thrown to the ground by the leader, who now held his staff in his right hand. The snow goblin threw off his white snow leopard fur and his mouth formed into a malicious grin, revealing his many pointed and rotten teeth.

He raised his staff, the tip of which glowed red, threateningly above the dwarf, but a moment later he slumped to the ground, gasping and spitting blood. He had received two of Aarl's throwing knives in the back. His staff fell onto a stone and shattered into a thousand pieces. The dwarf looked wordlessly at Aarl for several moments as he stepped out from behind the dead snow goblin.

"Thank you," he finally said to Aarl, who smiled kindly at him.

"We've come at just the right time," said Werlis, wiping the blood of a snow goblin from the blade of his short sword and holding his nose because of the foul stench.

"By all the halls of Ib'Agier! You have indeed come at the right moment. Tell me, what brings a ranger, two Abkether and a Thirian from the south to the cold Ice Mountains?" the dwarf asked out of breath and looked at Vrenli, Werlis, Gorathdin and Aarl in amazement.

"Our journey takes us from Tawinn to Astinhod. And what are you doing here, in this lonely, icy place, so far away from Ib'Agier?" Gorathdin inquired, bowing politely to the dwarf, who had placed his shield on the ground in front of him and was leaning on it.

"That, Mr. Elf, is a long story. And as a thanks for your help against the snow goblins, who are a real nuisance for a dwarf living here in the Ice Mountains, isolated and far away from his home, I will gladly tell it to you over a mug of warm beer and a freshly roasted goat," the dwarf replied and led them into his cave located inside the hill.

Gorathdin and Aarl had to bend down to pass through the entrance, but inside the cave, where the walls and floor were lined with furs, they were able to stand upright.

"Forgive me for not being able to offer you a seat at my table, but I only have one chair. I have never received guests in the thirty years I have lived here. Why don't you sit on the skins on the floor," the dwarf sheepishly admitted.

Vrenli, Werlis, Gorathdin and Aarl were surprised at how cozy and warm a cave could be and looked around curiously. To their astonishment, it was neither damp nor musty, the usual stench prevailing in such places. A small table with a low chair was in the middle of the cave, which was about fourteen paces wide, ten paces long and twelve paces high. A small oil lamp hanging from the center of the ceiling above the table provided a dim light.

To the right of the entrance, where a stone-built stove stood, a metal pipe led through the ceiling to the outside. Off to the side, at the back of the cave, stood a low bed made of wood, on which lay a warm-looking, thick fur. A small cupboard on the left wall next to the entrance was where the dwarf kept his chain armor, which he removed after entering the cave.

Conscientiously, almost reverently, he placed the gloves, chain mail, chain pants and helmet in the cupboard and locked it. He leaned his axe, the handle of which was engraved with dwarven characters, against the cupboard and hung his shield, which reflected the bland lamplight on the other side of the cave, on a large metal peg protruding from the stone wall. The dwarf wore a thick brown cotton shirt under his chain armor and leather pants, which he pulled off and then down over his navel, from where they slid back down at regular intervals.

"It probably came from a time when the dwarf was a bit more corpulent," thought Vrenli, who was observing this ritual.

"My name is Borlix. Borlix from Ib'Agier, or should I say Borlix from the Ice Mountains?" the dwarf introduced himself to his guests, who noticed the sad expression on his face, which he tried to hide behind a grin.

After Vrenli, Werlis, Gorathdin and Aarl had introduced themselves to Borlix, he poured them warm beer from a wooden barrel that stood on the floor to the right of the stone oven.

"Very tasty," praised Werlis, who wondered how Borlix managed to get a barrel of beer in this remote area.

"Every two years, I travel over the Ice Mountains Pass to Astinhod, where I stock up on supplies," Borlix explained when he noticed that Werlis' gaze remained fixed on the small barrel of beer.

While Borlix opened the sturdy wooden door and stepped outside the cave, where he began to dig in the snow at a spot just a few steps away from the entrance, the four friends talked about the battle with the snow goblins and the progress of their journey They were pleased that they had come across the dwarf, whose cozy cave they could warm themselves, fortify themselves, and spend the night in. In the meantime, Borlix had dug out a small mountain goat that he had buried in the snow for safekeeping. He took it back into the cave and laid it on the flat stone slab by the stove. "I'll let it thaw a little before I cut it up and prepare you an Ib'Agier-style roast goat," Borlix announced, beaming.

It was just before midnight when he took the roasted goat out of the stone oven and placed it on the floor in front of Vrenli, Werlis, Gorathdin and Aarl. He sat down with them and cut it into several smaller pieces with a long, sharp knife.

"You wanted to tell us why you live here alone and so far away from Ib'Agier," Vrenli reminded Borlix as he gnawed the tasty, tender goat meat from a bone.

Borlix nodded, poured his guests and himself some more of the warm beer and began his story, which began thirty years ago in Ib'Agier.

"It was shortly after my hundred and twentieth birthday, which I celebrated in The Golden Cup alehouse. A group of five dwarves patrolling the border to the east told King Agnulix about an approaching army from Fallgar, which caused panic in the city. The army commanders immediately began manning the defensive wall in the east. All combat-capable dwarves were ordered to arm themselves as quickly as possible and gather in the inner courtyard behind the eastern rampart. The attack came as a surprise.

With the help of their destructive war machines and magic, they broke through one of the side gates and invaded the halls of Ib'Agier. King Agnulix feared for his people and his city, but as befits a true dwarf king, he gave the order to defend the halls to the last man.

I was an ordinary officer at the time and led a hundred-strong group of axemen. I was stationed with my men at the lake, which was in the center of the hall of living units. But when I saw the hundreds of knights clad in black armor, screaming orcs and grunting ogres coming towards us, I thought it more prudent to order my men to lead the old men, women and children who had gathered around the lake to defend the halls of Ib'Agier deep down into the mines, as I believed they would be safe from the attackers there.

You have to imagine the stupidity of the dwarves. They would sacrifice their elders, wives and children just to protect, how shall I put it, the stone in which they live," Borlix said and the four could see that, for a moment, he was ashamed to be a dwarf.

The pride of the dwarves was known throughout Wetherid, but Gorathdin was not surprised by Borlix. He understood what he meant and respected him for it and from then on looked at him with different eyes.

Borlix continued.

"I disobeyed King Agnulix's order, but saved the lives of many hundreds of dwarves, because, as it turned out later, the enemy was not interested in destroying the halls of Ib'Agier. They marched to the western gates, from where they moved on to Astinhod. They were merely defending themselves against the dwarves who attacked them in the halls.

"We suffered great losses, but the halls of Ib'Agier remained undamaged by the enemy. King Agnulix was a just and wise man, except for what seems to me to be the innate ignorance of the dwarves to protect their buildings with their lives. Despite disobeying his orders, I was decorated for my services. The news of the death of my father, who was a respected paladin, took me by surprise at the award ceremony, which took place before all traces of the battle had been removed. The chief priest of the Holy Hall and King Agnulix offered me the chance to follow in my father's footsteps. I knew about the power of the paladins. I knew about the light of Lorijan, but I also knew the price a paladin had to pay to receive that light.

Faith and religion have never been among my aspirations in my dwarf life. Renouncing alcohol, women and feasts, hours of prayer and meditation and submission to the priests and the goddess Lorijan were not my destiny, so I turned down their offer. King Agnulix decided, as our laws stipulate, that I had to leave Ib'Agier for a period of fifteen years and was only allowed to take the bare necessities with me.

So, I decided to go into exile and the first few years I was away from Ib'Agier were not particularly, how shall I put it, successful. It is difficult for a dwarf trying to live among humans or elves to be accepted because of our size and, shall I say, our pride and the quick temper that comes with it, which often makes us misunderstood.

I had my axe in my hands more often than food, so I decided to head for the Ice Mountains. They may only be half as high as the insurmountable mountains of Ib'Agier, but they are still mountains," Borlix told his four guests, who listened to him attentively as they drank the and feasted.

"But the fifteen years are already over. Why didn't you go back to Ib'Agier?" Vrenli asked in a tired voice.

He could barely keep his eyes open because of the three mugs of warm beer he had drunk.

Borlix was silent for a while and looked around his cave.

"Perhaps I should interpret your unexpected appearance as a sign. A sign that it is time to return to Ib'Agier," Borlix mused thoughtfully.

His eyes took on a certain gleam.

"You can travel with us to Astinhod and from there on to Ib'Agier," Gorathdin offered.

He was delighted that Borlix wanted to end his exile.

"Perhaps I should accept your offer. I'll sleep on it and decide tomorrow," Borlix yawned.

"It's certainly past midnight. We should get some sleep too," remarked Aarl, who had already lay down and covered himself with his bearskin.

"Aarl is right. I can barely keep my eyes open," Vrenli admitted, yawning.

Werlis nodded in agreement.

Borlix removed the remains of the roasted goat and lay down in his bed under the snow leopard skin. Vrenli, Werlis, Gorathdin and Aarl, who were about to fall asleep, were kept awake for some time by the sawing, whistling and humming noises made by Borlix, who was fast asleep, and although their tiredness was painful, they had to laugh about it. When silence finally fell in the cave, they slipped into the realm of dreams with relief.

Chapter 2

The City of Astinhod

When Gorathdin woke up the next morning, followed by Aarl, Werlis and Vrenli, Borlix was already standing in front of the entrance to the cave with his travel bag packed and dressed in his chain armor. He had his axe slung over his shoulder, his shield lying in the snow in front of him and was looking towards the pass that led to Astinhod.

"You're coming with us?" Vrenli asked him in a sleepy voice.

"Since I couldn't really sleep all night, I had enough time to think about my return to Ib'Agier, and yes, I will go with you," Borlix replied, surprised at his guests' sudden laughter.

"Why are you laughing?" Borlix questioningly looked at them.

"It didn't sound like you weren't really asleep," Werlis replied, imitating some of the sounds Borlix had made in his sleep.

Everyone, even Borlix, laughed boisterously.

Vrenli, Werlis, Gorathdin and Aarl returned inside with Borlix, ate the remains of the mountain goat and emptied the barrel of beer. Then they tied up their travel bags and prepared to leave. Borlix looked around the cave, his home for thirty years, one last time. He sadly left behind the belongings he had collected during this time. He hurried ahead of his four traveling companions onto the snow-covered plateau to hide the tears that ran down his round, red-cheeked face and into his long, bristly red whiskers. Borlix himself didn't know exactly why he was crying. Actually, he should be happy that he would soon see the halls of Ib'Agier again.

The ascent to the pass was exhausting and, above all, freezing. Fortunately, there were no clouds in the sky and no storms in sight that could have jeopardized their journey. They followed the path over the pass for two days when they finally reached the side of the Ice Mountains facing Astinhod. Although they were still more than a thousand and two hundred paces above the valley, they could already see the vast fields of wheat, barley and sunflowers surrounding the village of Kring. Gorathdin jumped onto a rock and straightened up.

Far ahead on the horizon, he could make out the city of Astinhod with his sharp elven eyes, surrounded by a mighty city wall of white stone. Three towers rose high into the sky from its center. Gorathdin reached for the small leather pouch hanging on his chest.

"A little more than two days' journey and we will have reached our destination," Gorathdin announced as he looked down at the village of Kring, which they would reach before dusk.

Aarl and Borlix turned their gazes southward, towards the city of Astinhod, which for them was a symbol of homecoming. Aarl still had a long journey to Thir ahead of him, but Borlix would need no more than three days from the city of Astinhod to Ib'Agier.

"Let's go on," Gorathdin urged his travel companions, who were now friends.

He jumped down from the rock onto the mountain path, which was no longer covered in snow but overgrown with grasses and mosses, followed by Aarl, Werlis, Vrenli and Borlix. They had now left the snow and ice behind and low stone pines and larches were already rising to their left and right.

After the five travelers followed the path to the foot of the mountain, they crossed a small, wooded area from which they walked southeast across a grassy landscape. It was late afternoon when they entered a wide path that led through the vast fields of grain towards Kring.

Vrenli and Werlis looked out over the fields, one of which was the size of Abketh. The humans, who appeared large to Vrenli and Werlis, tilled the clay-colored earth with sickles, rakes and shovels, carrying large, woven baskets on their backs that the two could fit inside. Some of the field workers waved welcomingly to the five travelers, although they were surprised at the strangers, for they were an unusual group of wanderers. Five people, four different races, and one didn't have to be very perceptive to realize that they had crossed the Ice Mountains. Vrenli, Werlis, Gorathdin, Aarl and Borlix were aware of the field workers' curious glances, but they paid them no mind, only waved back in a friendly manner.

They were no more than five hundred paces from Kring when they caught sight of the roofs of some simple houses.

"We will share a room at the Golden Chaff. It's the only inn in Kring that offers accommodation to wanderers. Tomorrow our route will take us to Umlis, a small town just a day's walk from here," Gorathdin explained to his friends as they reached the muddy road, on which the wheels of the farmers' heavily laden carts had left deep ruts. It led the five travelers past stables and farmsteads to a small, seemingly insignificant, deserted village square.

On a building that Vrenli first thought was a barn, a lantern hung above a closed wooden door, under which the name of the inn was carved on a weathered wooden panel.

"Don't expect too much. Mostly farmers, field workers, hunters and a few saddlers live in Kring," Gorathdin informed his friends before knocking on the door.

It took a moment for a small hatch to open at the level of Gorathdin's head.

"Who is this, and what do you want?" inquired the gruff voice of a bearded, slightly drunk old man.

"We are travelers on our way to Astinhod and need a warm meal and quarters," Gorathdin replied.

"What in God's name..." croaked the old man and threw the hatch shut again. Vrenli and Werlis looked questioningly at Gorathdin.

"We must have scared him," remarked Aarl.

"Open up," Borlix grumbled and knocked hard on the door three times.

The hatch opened again and, as Borlix was too small to be seen, the frightened eyes of a woman looked at Aarl standing behind him.

"Forgive me, sir. My uncle is a drunkard. He said he had seen the Incarnate One at the door," a timid voice rang out.

A moment later, the door creaked open and a corpulent, slightly stooped, middle-aged woman stood in the doorway. Puzzled, she looked first at Borlix, who was standing in front of her, and then at Aarl, who smiled at her in a friendly manner.

"Have no fear, good woman. We are just weary wanderers looking for a place to stay. My name is Aarl from Thir and these are my friends Borlix, the dwarf, and Vrenli and Werlis, from Abketh. The strange-looking one is Gorathdin, a ranger from the Dark Forest," Aarl introduced himself and his companions and took a step to the side.

"Adlena is my name. Come in," she said hesitantly.

"You'll have to forgive me, but we don't often have guests from outside," Adlena apologized when she noticed that the five travellers posed no danger.

With friendly smiles, Vrenli, Werlis, Gorathdin, Aarl and Borlix entered the small inn, where there was no one except for the bearded old man sitting at one of the eight gray tables in front of a jug of wine. They sat down at the table near the open fireplace and warmed up. Aarl ordered a jug of wine for himself and his friends.

"If you're hungry, I can offer you hot barley stew and freshly baked bread," Adlena suggested, placing a white clay jug and five wooden mugs in the middle of the table.

While they waited for their hot meal, they talked about their battle with the snow goblins and their journey. Adlena brought them another jug of wine before placing a large bowl of steaming barley stew, cutlery and five plates on the table.

After Vrenli, Werlis, Gorathdin, Aarl and Borlix had fortified themselves, Vrenli, who insisted on this privilege, paid five gold pieces for the meal and overnight stay. They then followed a creaking staircase to the upper floor. Adlena opened the door to the guest room on the right and wished them a good night's sleep.

In the small room, lit by a candle, two extra-wide mattresses filled with straw lay on the floor, on which the friends spread out their cloaks, lay down and covered themselves with their furs. Vrenli, Werlis and Gorathdin slept next to the small window on the east side of the room. Aarl and Borlix shared a mattress on the west side.

Early in the morning, when the rooster's wake-up call sounded, everyone woke up except Werlis, who had to be woken up by Vrenli. They stowed their furs, put on their cloaks and went down to the inn, where Adlena had already prepared breakfast. After they had fortified themselves for their journey ahead, they said their thankful goodbyes. As an apology for the misunderstanding the night before, they did not have to pay for breakfast.

They followed the loamy road southwards. Their day's march took them across a wide meadow lowland and through a dense mixed forest followed by a hilly, dry coniferous forest, which they walked through in the late afternoon.

As dusk began to fall, they finally arrived in Umlis, where they spent the night in The Plough inn. As time was pressing, the next morning Gorathdin borrowed a pony and two horses from Mayor Edmarg Humkis of Umlis, to whom he showed a letter of escort from King Grandhold.

"Long live King Grandhold!" the mayor called after them and closed his hand around the ten gold coins that Gorathdin had given him as thanks for his loyalty.

Vrenli, Werlis, Gorathdin, Aarl and Borlix rode on southwards until midday, then eastwards and, after they had left the wide cornfields around Astinhod behind them, Gorathdin stopped his horse and pointed with his hand to the city of Astinhod.

"We made it in time," he said happily and smiled.

The city of Astinhod, home to thousands, stretched majestically before them.

"Never in my life would I have imagined such a huge city," Vrenli marveled, looking at the high, thick city wall, with well-fortified defense towers rising into the sky every fifty paces or so.

They kept up a moderate trot with their mounts towards the city gate, which was not far. Once there, Vrenli and Werlis were amazed at the hustle and bustle in front of the mighty, wide-open gates. Many farmers, merchants and travelers were waiting to enter the city, but the five gate guards only allowed them in after inquiring about their origin and purpose of their intended stay. Gorathdin, who led his fellow travelers, marched past the queue of people, heading straight for a guard.

"Stop! You have to get in line," the guard armed with a lance and sword reprimanded him.

However, he apologized to him only a moment later and bowed.

"Forgive me, my lord. I did not recognize you."

The guard ordered some of the farmers and travelers to clear the way.

"My lord?" Vrenli looked at Gorathdin in surprise.

"A long story and not that important," he evaded and walked through the large archway.

Two guards standing to the left and right behind the gate stopped Vrenli, Werlis, Aarl and Borlix.

"Stop right there!" one of the two guards told them and stood in their way.

"These are my fellow travelers," Gorathdin stated emphatically, whereupon the guard let them pass and looked after the motley group in astonishment.

The five followed a stone-paved street leading to the market square for some time. Vrenli and Werlis looked at the gray facades of the simple houses to their left and right, but the closer they got to the market square, the more magnificent the buildings became. The now white facades were decorated with stucco and there were even small statues on some of the window ledges. Some of the entrances were adorned with marble or dark stone columns.

Arriving at the marketplace, Gorathdin stopped to give his friends time to take in the commotion.

In the center of the crowded square, a white marble basin shot thick jets of water high into the air. All around it were countless stalls lined up by traders who had come from all parts of Wetherid to sell their goods in Astinhod.

Astinhod was a prosperous city and its inhabitants were hardworking and industrious, which brought with it a certain prosperity. People from the DeShadin and Thir deserts, elves, dwarves, a few barbarians and two monks in purple robes touted their goods to eager market visitors: pottery and fine fabrics, carpets, furs, meat, vegetables, fruit, flowers, artfully crafted jewelry, herbs, spices, tea, healing potions, leather goods, weapons and armor. As in any marketplace, the merchants haggled over their prices, which were usually too high. It was not uncommon for the haggling to turn into heated discussions, which occasionally led to an argument. However, the city guards, who ensured peace and quiet in the city with their military clothing made of fine fabrics and their gleaming lances, were usually quick to arrive and settle the loud discussions.

Vrenli and Werlis stopped in front of a market stall where three Scheddifer were selling spices and tea and were amazed at their dark skin color. This astonishment was mutual, however, as the three traders had never seen Abkethers before. Werlis noticed a young man sitting next to the spice and tea merchants' stall on the steps of the water basin, pursuing a pretty girl who was accompanied by a very wealthy-looking man.

"Let's keep going," Gorathdin urged Vrenli and Werlis.

"Just a moment," Werlis asked and approached the painter.

"Forgive me, Sir. Could you paint a picture of my friends and me?" he asked the artist as he followed the artist's quick and precise brushstrokes.

"One gold piece per picture. But since there are five of you, I'll need more parchment, so let's say two gold pieces," he replied, looking up briefly from the picture he was painting.

"Agreed," Werlis agreed.

However, the young man put him off until the next day. Just as Werlis was about to offer him double the amount if he would agree to paint them immediately, Gorathdin urged him to move on.

"There really is time until tomorrow. Come on now!" he said firmly.

Walking side by side, the five crossed the market square to the north. Vrenli and Werlis had just noticed three jugglers showing off their skills on a small wooden stage not far from them when Gorathdin stopped.

"Wait a moment. I have something to do here," Gorathdin pointed with his hand to a tall, strong man with blond hair in two plaits that hung over his shoulders.

The man played a lyre while a large brown bear, standing upright and tied to a thick chain, danced to it. Gorathdin disliked this kind of animal exploitation, so he approached the burly man and asked him to release the bear.

The man, who had something barbarian about him, stared at Gorathdin, who was a head shorter, wordlessly for a few moments and finally laughed out loud.

"Who do you think you are? That's my bear. I caught it myself and I do what I want with it. Mind your own business!" he snapped at Gorathdin in disregard and tugged at his bear's chain, which then opened its mouth wide.

"See to it that you get on, or my bear might suddenly get hungry," the bear keeper irritably hissed and glared at Gorathdin. But when he recognized his elven ancestry, he immediately took a step back. He placed his strong, rough hand on the handle of his axe leaning against a tree trunk next to him where he had placed his lyre.

"I wouldn't dare do that if I were you," Borlix grumbled, whereupon the burly man, who now realized that Gorathdin was not alone, abandoned his plan.

"What do you care how I earn my living, Elf?" he asked in a disparaging tone.

Gorathdin remained calm.

"I'll make you a proposition. I will give you fifty gold pieces if you leave the city and set the bear free," Gorathdin pulled a pouch of gold coins from under his cloak.

"Fifty gold pieces? I can live on that for a year. But what do I do after that? No, Elf, that's not enough. I demand one hundred gold pieces".

The bear keeper's eyes began to sparkle at the thought of the sum.

"Here have a hundred. Take it and make sure you leave the city today," Gorathdin replied and tossed him a pouch of gold coins.

The bear keeper smiled at Gorathdin and looked at Vrenli, Werlis, Aarl and Borlix. He grinned, took his lyre from the tree stump, pulled on his bear's chain and walked a few steps further to an inn, where he tied up the animal before entering the building.

"He's not going to start spending the gold coins with his hands full now, is he?" Vrenli wondered.

"I don't care what he does with the gold coins. But if I still find him here tomorrow with his bear, I'll have him thrown out of the city," Gorathdin replied calmly and walked on.

Not far from the market square, they passed a district that showed Astinhod in a completely different light. It smelled of feces and the inhabitants of this quarter were wrapped in rags or dressed in simple cotton. Dirty children played with a small leather ball on the muddy ground.

The few houses had dirty facades and some of the windows had broken panes of glass or missing shutters. There were even four simple wooden huts far back. Aarl noticed that the majority of the inhabitants were Thirians, and he wondered about the many patrolling city guards.

"Where are we?" he asked Gorathdin curiously.

"There is also poverty in Astinhod. This district is the so-called Shunned Quarter. Women and men who do not or cannot pursue a regular job are housed here for the benefit of others. Between us, with thousands of people living in Astinhod and more than two thousand in the surrounding areas, there are of course criminals and many of them have found shelter here. The idea that the king had when he made this district available to the poor was not to separate them from the other inhabitants, but rather to combat the poverty that was also spreading in Astinhod. Every day, basic foodstuffs are distributed to the needy for a small fee. But I have to admit that many people shamelessly exploit this. Many could work but prefer to rely on the royal family.

What's more, more than ten years ago, thieves and other outlaws joined forces and founded a guild. The Thieves' Guild, as they call themselves, has an estimated one hundred and fifty members who are known to hold underground meetings in Astinhod. This guild is the real problem in the Shunned Quarter and the city of Astinhod," Gorathdin informed his friends, adding that the nobles of the city had been trying for years to convince the King that the inhabitants of this quarter should be relocated from the city to one of the surrounding villages. "However, the powerful landed gentry opposed this proposal and so they had been arguing for years. During this time, the Thieves' Guild had become increasingly influential and now bribed or threatened officers of the city guard to be able to carry out their work undisturbed." Gorathdin continued.

"Why doesn't the King have all the thieves arrested and build a new village for the poor outside the city? He could give them land that they could then cultivate?" Vrenli wondered aloud.

He didn't see the problem as being too big.

"The theory sounds simple, I agree. But the thieves have influence in high places and nobody knows the people who protect them from the law. They are a plague and have to be dealt with.

152

And as for the poor being moved out, I think it's the Thieves' Guild that has found a perfect hideout in a district that is shunned by the rest of the population," Gorathdin explained.

"Politics and crime have always gone hand in hand," Borlix grumbled, to which Aarl nodded in agreement.

They followed the street from the market square, past the Shunned Quarter, to the craftsmen's quarter. Master carpenters, blacksmiths, weavers, shoemakers, goldsmiths, glassblowers and other craftsmen plied their trades here. Borlix stopped in front of a blacksmith's shop and observed the strong, sweaty man wearing a black leather apron, covered in coal dust. He was taking a red-hot piece of metal from the fire of a stone furnace. The blacksmith placed it on an anvil in front of him and struck it with a large hammer several times in succession with short, powerful blows. After only a few moments, Borlix began to criticize him for his imprecise blows.

"Come on, Borlix!" Gorathdin called to him, who had already moved on with Vrenli, Werlis and Aarl.

"Forging is an art," Borlix said after he rejoined them.

"And not every artist is equally good," added Aarl with a grin.

"Indeed," Borlix agreed and turned back towards the blacksmith.

The road that meandered through the craftsmen's quarter turned west and led them into the merchants' quarter, where they noticed that almost every fourth house was an inn. When they saw a sign hanging in front of the entrance to one, they couldn't help but wonder at the name on it.

"Goblin Cave. Who gives an inn such a name?" Borlix wondered aloud and had to laugh.

"I'd like to have a look at this cave," said Werlis. He walked towards the door but was held back by Vrenli's cloak.

"We really don't have time for this now, and besides, it could be dangerous. You don't know what kind of creatures are in an inn called Goblin Cave," warned Vrenli, still holding Werlis by the cloak.

Undaunted, they continued and soon reached a building where halves of lamb, pork and game on large metal hooks hung from its roof beams that reached almost four steps into the street. A short, fat, bearded man with big, strong shoulders was cutting off a large piece of meat with a very sharp-looking knife, wrapping it in parchment and handing it to a woman with two children.

"Can you imagine how much meat the thousands of people who live here eat?" Werlis asked Vrenli, who just shrugged his shoulders as he followed Gorathdin, Borlix and Aarl.

They strolled past a row of stores selling all kinds of things. Once they had left the merchants' quarter behind them, they headed east. They entered a district where tall buildings were lined side-by-side to the left and right of the street.

"Two-story houses. As if they didn't have enough space in the large stone buildings where the humans live. They have to build another - how shall I put it - house on top of their house," Borlix grumbled.

"Seven or eight dwarf families could live in such a building. People always have to exaggerate," he added.

"Sorry, but speaking of exaggeration, I've visited Ib'Agier many times," Gorathdin joked and gave Borlix a mischievous smile.

Werlis, Vrenli and Aarl didn't understand what he meant, but Borlix grinned sheepishly. Wordlessly, they walked past the ornately decorated facades of the two-story houses.

Gorathdin, who was driven by the longing to see Lythinda again and wanting to tell the King about his success in finding the flowers, did not notice the carriage speeding towards them from behind. He was so absorbed in his thoughts that his fine elven ears did not warn him of the approaching danger. The magnificent carriage, drawn by four white horses and adorned with gold, sped towards him and his friends. At the last moment, Aarl pulled Gorathdin aside by his cloak.

"Get out of the way! Count Laars has an important audience with the King!" shouted the coachman, who spurred the horses on with his whip cracking above their heads.

Aarl, who had dodged to the left side of the road with Gorathdin, looked at the shocked faces of Vrenli and Werlis, who had jumped to the right side of the road together with Borlix.

"What on earth! Didn't the coachman see us? We're not that small," Werlis stammered, while Borlix shouted a few dwarven curses after the coachman.

"Humans," he grumbled after venting his anger.

"Very unusual. An inattentive elf," Aarl noted, still holding Gorathdin by the cloak and pressing him against the wall of the house.

"You're right. I was in my thoughts. I let my feelings guide me too much. Feelings which, it seems, are stronger than my instincts," Gorathdin admitted.

"If Lythinda really is as enchanting as you told me, then I'm not surprised," grinned Aarl.

"Which Lythinda?" asked Borlix, who was not yet aware of the reason for Gorathdin's journey.

Gorathdin looked at him wordlessly for a few moments. Borlix noticed his brief silence and walked across the street towards him.

"You don't have to tell me the reason for your journey. It's none of my business. You don't have to feel bad about it. I didn't mean to pry," Borlix placated.

"Can I trust a dwarf?" Gorathdin pondered, as he received looks of approval from Vrenli, Werlis and Aarl that dispelled his doubts.

On their way through the residential district of Astinhod, he told Borlix what had happened to Princess Lythinda in the Three Vines inn. He also told him that he had traveled to Tawinn in the village of Abketh to find the blossoms of the moonflower. Borlix listened attentively and when the name Erwight of Entorbis was mentioned, he grimaced angrily.

"Entorbis. Murderers they were and murderers they are. Feeding on the power of evil in Fallgar. Allies of the shadow. Murderers," Borlix growled and spat on the ground.

None of them noticed the thief who had been following them for some time and had overheard their conversation.

"We should talk further in the castle. Something inside me warns me not to speak so openly here on the streets of Astinhod," Gorathdin suddenly said. He turned around quickly, but he couldn't see anyone.

Having heard enough, the thief disappeared into one of the houses on the road.

They had reached the end of the residential district. The stone-paved street turned off to the right behind the last house. They approached a gate guarded by four soldiers from the lifeguard. Behind the gate was an avenue of birch and beech trees, through which led a path paved with white marble stones.

Master Drobal's Tower

The guards wore heavy, shiny silver armor with the Astinhod coat of arms engraved on their breastplates. When the five travelers arrived at the gate, the guards crossed their long, pointed lances and gripped the gem-studded hilts of their broad-bladed swords menacingly.

"Open the gate!" Gorathdin ordered.

"Tell me your rank, name and desire," demanded the oldest guard.

"I am the Count of Regen and my name is Gorathdin of the Forest. King Grandhold is expecting me," said Gorathdin, who reached into his travel pouch, pulled out the King's letter of escort and handed it to the guard. The guard looked at the royal seal at the end of the letter and stepped aside.

"You may pass, Count of Regen."

The soldiers of the royal guard cleared the way.

The gate was opened and Gorathdin, followed by his friends, walked through. They followed an avenue for some time, which led to a large garden. Aarl was fascinated by the artfully trimmed green hedges, some of which were in bloom, and the rare archbell flowers, clover violet beds and the occasional habermilk cactus, which normally only grew in Desert of DeShadin. Vrenli and Werlis also looked around enthusiastically, overwhelmed by the mighty maple trees and the old, thick-trunked oaks that stood sporadically on the low, well-tended lawn. Just a few steps away, to the left of an oak tree, was a small pavilion. Vrenli and Werlis stopped for a moment and stood for fun under one of the mighty trees that was about forty paces high with a trunk at least seven paces in diameter.

"Your whole nation could gather on this oak tree," joked Gorathdin.

"How easy their lives are," he thought to himself as he watched his two friends begin to chase each other around the thick trunk of the oak tree from the path.

Werlis, who was being followed by Vrenli, turned off behind the tree trunk and ran as fast as his little legs could carry him to the nearby pavilion, where he hid under one of the benches made of fine wood. As Vrenli stopped behind the thick oak trunk to wait for Werlis to come around, he didn't notice that Werlis had long since disappeared.

"Where is he? Surely, he won't have the same idea and be waiting for me on the other side?" thought Vrenli, slowly creeping around the oak trunk.

"He ran over there!" Borlix shouted with a laugh and pointed to the pavilion.

"Not only are they almost as small as children, they also have a childlike disposition. I envy them for that," thought Gorathdin, who almost got carried away by the game had it not been for Lythinda, who was waiting for his help.

"I hope Vrenli will maintain his cheerfulness even after he has learned that life has given him a far more difficult task than simply being an Abkether, or, as the Tawinnian priestess has instructed him, preserving the history of the ancients."

Gorathdin called out to the two to finish their game and, followed by Aarl and Borlix, who didn't have much interest in the plant splendor, continued to a tower rising high in the sky, where they stopped to wait for Vrenli and Werlis.

"This is Master Drobal's Tower," Gorathdin remarked.

"Should I go up and give him Gwerlit's message?" Vrenli asked, looking up to the top.

"There is still time. We must first go to King Grandhold and tell him about the success of our journey. He will certainly be very worried by now," Gorathdin replied and followed the path that led to a wide staircase with many steps. Astinhod's banners waved in the wind to the left and right of the adjacent, half-height staircase walls.

The two men from the bodyguard standing guard outside the staircase were talking to a man sitting on a magnificent carriage that looked all too familiar to the five friends.

"Hey, you there! Be more careful next time. You nearly ran us over earlier," grumbled Borlix.

The coachman gave him an irritated look.

"Look out, dwarf. This carriage belongs to Count Laars," one of the two guards admonished him.

"And if it belongs to the King himself, this man almost killed us before," Borlix angrily replied, which is why Gorathdin gently put his hand on his shoulder to calm him down.

"A little more consideration would be appropriate, coachman," Gorathdin said firmly and ordered the guards to report him and his four companions to the King.

The coachman looked disparagingly at Gorathdin, who, like his friends, was not exactly in a condition befitting court. The dust and dirt of the long journey were visible on their clothes and in some places their cloaks showed small tears. What's more, there was only one human among them, and he was a Thirian to boot.

"Did I hear that right, were those guys talking to me?" the coachman said condescendingly.

"This is Gorathdin, Count of Regen," the guard whispered to him.

"Pah, landed gentry," the coachman replied quietly and made a dismissive gesture with his hand.

Gorathdin, who had heard the conversation between the two, did not react. Far too often in his life he had been insulted by people, treated with contempt, ridiculed and initially driven away. He only understood the reason for this many years later. People were afraid of him. It was the fear of the unknown that drove them to these actions and insults. He used to react to this with anger, but now he only felt pity for those who disregarded him.

The guard who had announced Gorathdin and his friends came down the stairs with quick steps, accompanied by King Grandhold himself. The other guard and the coachman halted their conversation and bowed. Borlix knelt and kept his eyes on the ground. Aarl, who was still a little hesitant, finally followed him.

Werlis stared for a moment at the King of Astinhod, who was a slender but strong-looking man of around sixty. His full brown beard was neatly trimmed and his brown, thick, straight hair, which he wore loose, reached almost to his shoulders. It was barely noticeable that his hair had turned gray in some places, which was covered by the simple golden crown.

"What do we do now? Should we kneel down too?" whispered Werlis questioningly to Vrenli, who was equally perplexed and looked to Gorathdin for help. But he just smiled.

"Gorathdin, my friend!" King Grandhold greeted him warmly and looked at him expectantly.

"My King," replied Gorathdin, barely nodding, to which King Grandhold smiled, reassured.

"You brought friends with you?" the King turned to the companions.

"This is Vrenli and Werlis from the village of Abketh. Vrenli was instructed to seek out Master Drobal," Gorathdin explained briefly and then introduced Aarl and Borlix, whom the King asked to stand up.

"We should continue our conversation in my chambers," he invited Gorathdin and walked up the stairs that led to a large gate with two wings they passed through. They followed a long corridor lined with fine carpets and where hunting trophies and pictures of the King's ancestors hung on the walls. Every few steps there were magnificent, heavy suits of knight's armor, silent showpieces that amazed Vrenli and Werlis. They didn't understand how people could fight in such metal containers, as Werlis called them.

Several castle guards, dressed in splendid uniforms made of fine fabrics, walked up and down the corridor. The two guards standing in front of the door to the throne room opened it hastily when they saw the King with his five followers. King Grandhold entered the magnificent, gleaming golden throne room with quick steps. He strode past the throne of Astinhod, opened the small door that led to his private chambers and entered. From his study, where he wrote most of his royal decrees, received private guests or held secret meetings, he strode purposefully into the adjoining bedchamber.

Inside was what Vrenli, Werlis and Borlix thought was a huge four-poster bed, with a smaller one next to it. Surrounded by a lady-in-waiting, a healer and a priest, the King's daughter lay there, motionless and in the grip of an unknown fever. Gorathdin approached the bed and gently wiped away the small beads of sweat that had formed on Lythinda's forehead with the palm of his hand. Lythinda fixedly gazed at the mural on the ceiling above her.

"Fortunately, her condition has not worsened," the healer said to Gorathdin, who looked at Lythinda with concern and sadness.

Vrenli, Werlis, Aarl and Borlix were enchanted by the princess's grace and beauty. The young girl, who was no more than twenty-five years old, had long, curly blonde hair, which was carefully combed by the lady-in-waiting who sat at her bedside. Her deep blue eyes reflected a sea of emotions and her pale face with its small, delicate nose and thin red lips looked as if it had been painted.

"You should send for Master Drobal," Gorathdin suggested to King Grandhold.

"Master Drobal left Astinhod three days ago. Without much ado, and you can imagine that I was not happy about it. He had a very serious, almost angry look on his face. He didn't want to tell me anything more than that my daughter's illness was probably just the beginning of a greater suffering that could befall us. He told the court healer Palanmar to make the healing potion in his place. The recipe is in the book on his desk in the tower," King Grandhold said.

Gorathdin was irritated by the unexpected, mysterious departure of Master Drobal.

"Master Drobal explained to me how to prepare the potion. I just need to get the book from his tower. Before I forget, the blossoms of the moonflower must not be older than fifteen days," said Palanmar.

"Today is the twelfth day," replied Gorathdin.

"Has Master Drobal given any indication as to when he will return?" asked Vrenli, who was already getting impatient.

"Magicians! Who knows why and where they are going and when they will return? He didn't give the slightest hint. He didn't answer any of my questions. Not even the question of a worried father as to whether the healing potion would help my daughter. He just shrugged his shoulders wordlessly and went back to his tower," King Grandhold complained angrily.

"Something must have happened. Something that has eclipsed Lythinda's illness and requires his full attention," Gorathdin stated anxiously.

"Where did you say the book with the recipe was?" he then asked Palanmar.

"On the worktable in his tower," the healer replied.

"I'll get it," Gorathdin decided, hoping that he might find some clues in the tower as to the reason for Master Drobal's sudden departure.

"I will accompany you," Vrenli said to Gorathdin, who looked at him for a moment without replying.

"I was supposed to meet Master Drobal in Astinhod and no one has explained why. I would at least like to see his tower if I can't meet him myself," Vrenli announced resolutely.

Gorathdin understood and nodded in agreement.

"The blossoms must be processed at midnight," warned Palanmar.

"You will certainly want to rest from your journey. I'll have you taken to your room," King Grandhold offered Werlis, Aarl and Borlix, who, however, expressed the wish to accompany Gorathdin and Vrenli to Master Drobal's tower.

King Grandhold looked at Gorathdin with a smile.

"After the long journey we've been on and the incidents that were not always without danger, it's hard to separate us," Gorathdin replied with a smile.

"Then follow me," he urged his friends, whereupon they left the King's private chambers.

By the time they reached the castle garden, it was already dark, so Gorathdin walked ahead of his friends to the tower.

"Why do you think Master Drobal left Astinhod?" asked Vrenli.

"I only have a vague suspicion and I'd rather keep it to myself," he evaded.

They could already make out the shadow of the tower in the moonlight on the marble-paved path.

Gorathdin walked to the heavy wooden door that blocked the entrance of the tower, which rose more than seventy paces into the sky and had only a single window, just below the battlements of the spire.

"The door is open," Gorathdin noted and looked up, where he noticed a faint light in Master Drobal's study.

"Either Master Drobal is back, or someone else is up there," Gorathdin said, pointing with his right hand to the window at the top of the tower.

"Maybe he just forgot to turn off the light," Werlis pondered.

"I doubt that," Gorathdin replied and reached for his fire axe.

162

"Wait here for me."

Gorathdin was about to enter the tower when he noticed Vrenli following him with his short sword drawn.

"Wait here, Vrenli," said Gorathdin, waving him back with his hand.

"You shouldn't go up alone. If your suspicion that someone other than Master Drobal is in the tower turns out to be true, it could be dangerous and you know that I know how to use my short sword," Vrenli said firmly, looking at Gorathdin with determination.

"All right, then. Aarl, Borlix and Werlis, you guard the entrance. Don't let anyone in or out," Gorathdin instructed his friends, who picked up their weapons and nodded.

Gorathdin and Vrenli followed the winding staircase to the top third of the tower when they heard the sound of breaking glass.

"Shh! I don't think that's Master Drobal," Gorathdin whispered.

They crept quietly up the remaining steps and stopped in front of the heavy wooden door that closed off the mage's study. When Gorathdin tried to carefully and quietly open the door a crack to peek inside, he was surprised to see that it was locked from the inside.

"Maybe it's Master Drobal after all?" Vrenli whispered.

Gorathdin put his pointed elven ear to the door and raised his hand, holding up three fingers.

"I can't hear exactly what they're saying, but I think they're talking to each other in a Thirian dialect," Gorathdin whispered.

"Thirians?" whispered Vrenli in astonishment.

"Thieves," Gorathdin said quietly.

"We should seize the moment of surprise. I'll break down the door and then we'll try to overpower them," he whispered in Vrenli's ear.

"Wait! Shouldn't we let Werlis, Aarl and Borlix know?" asked Vrenli as quietly as he could.

"There are only three of them," Gorathdin replied, swinging out his fire axe and slamming it so hard against the door that it burst into the room with a loud crash that alerted Werlis, Aarl and Borlix.

"Watch out!" shouted one of the thieves, startled by the breaking open of the door.

Gorathdin leapt towards the three and struck one of them down quickly and skillfully with the handle of his fire axe, which he held in the middle of the shaft. The second of the three thieves attacked Gorathdin from the side with a dagger, but Gorathdin grabbed his arm in a flash and twisted it, causing the thief to fall to his knees, whimpering. Instead of helping his two guild brothers, the third jumped over Vrenli, who was trying, unsuccessfully, to stop him by raising his short sword, and ran as fast as he could down the winding staircase of the tower.

"Wait! Werlis, Aarl and Borlix will take care of him," Gorathdin called to Vrenli, who was about to pursue the fleeing thief.

"Let go of me!" shouted the thief, who was still being held by Gorathdin's arm.

Gorathdin's grip tightened.

"You'll break my arm!" shouted the tanned Thirian, who was dressed in brown leather trousers and a similarly colored shirt.

Vrenli noticed that the thief, like Aarl, was wearing a leather belt across his chest with several shafts containing throwing knives.

"What are you doing here?" Gorathdin asked in a sharp tone.

The thief spat contemptuously on the plain, gray stone floor. Gorathdin then twisted his arm so hard that a crack sounded.

"Damned elf! You broke my arm!" the thief screamed, whimpering in pain. Gorathdin grabbed the thief's other arm and pulled him up.

"If you don't want a second broken arm, then answer me!" Gorathdin thundered.

His eyes lit up dark green. The thief, bent over in pain and with tears in his eyes, was being held by Gorathdin and startled when he looked into the elf's eyes.

"We need to steal a book," gasped the pinned man, wracked in pain.

"What book?" Gorathdin asked.

"A book containing the recipe for a healing potion that could help the princess," replied the tormented thief, suddenly turning white as a sheet.

"Vrenli!" Gorathdin exclaimed, pointing with his hand at the other thief, who had just regained consciousness and tried to get up, whereupon Vrenli knocked him to the ground with the hilt of his short sword.

"Who told you to do this?" Gorathdin asked the thief and tightened his grip.

"I don't know," whimpered the thief.

Gorathdin twisted his arm again. The thief contorted his face and begged him to stop.

"Answer me!" Gorathdin shouted at him.

"We belong to Massek's guild. He told us to do it," the thief confessed and tore himself free from Gorathdin's grip.

He looked around briefly, jumped up and ran down the stairs over Vrenli, but didn't get far. The blunt handle of Borlix's double-bladed axe hit him before he could jump over him.

"Vrenli, Gorathdin?" Borlix called up the stairs.

"We're fine!" Vrenli replied.

"What happened up here?" he asked the two of them when he arrived in Master Drobal's study and saw the unconscious thief lying on the floor next to his friends.

"The thieves wanted to steal the book with the recipe for the healing potion," explained Vrenli.

"One of them fell over Werlis down at the entrance, who was worried about the sounds of fighting coming down from above and was about to enter the tower," Borlix reported.

"Is Werlis all right?" Vrenli asked anxiously.

"Yes. Everything's fine. He just has an abrasion on his knee," Borlix reassured him, leaning on the handle of his axe.

"What about the two thieves?" Gorathdin wanted to know.

"Aarl will take care of one of them and the one I met on the stairs won't be waking up any time soon," Borlix said with a laugh, tapping the handle of his axe.

Gorathdin's eyes wandered through Master Drobal's study, which strangely reminded Vrenli of his grandfather's house.

"This must be it," Gorathdin muttered and walked towards the large, round table next to the window, where a pile of old, written parchments, quill and ink, small and larger glass tubes, metal stands, various stones and some test tubes with dubious contents sat on. He leaned over the table and picked up the book lying on the floor. Gorathdin opened it and began to leaf through it. The hundreds of pages were filled with all kinds of recipes for making healing potions.

Borlix grabbed the still unconscious thief lying next to Vrenli and pulled him down the stairs to where the other incapacitated Thirian was.

"Werlis, come up and help me!" Borlix called down the winding tower stairs.

"I'm coming!" he replied and hurried up the stairs. Together they dragged the two thieves down the stairs and laid them on the ground in front of Aarl, who in the meantime tied up the thief that stumbled over Werlis with his belt. While Borlix told Aarl and Werlis what happened upstairs, Vrenli looked with fascination and curiosity at the low, golden, oval bowl, about two and a half steps wide, which stood in the middle of Master Drobal's study. He approached the bowl, paused for a moment and looked at the small, shimmering light blue crystal inside.

Gorathdin, who was looking around for clues about Master Drobal's unexpected departure, did not notice Vrenli climb into the bowl and reach for the small, shimmering light blue crystal. A mist that had slowly formed at the bottom of the bowl began to envelop Vrenli. All at once, it became pitch black around him.

Vrenli tried to move and get out of the bowl, but a sea of lights appeared out of nowhere and blinded him so much that he had to close his eyes. He lost all sense of space and time followed by a state similar to unconsciousness. Gorathdin happened to turn in the direction of the bowl and could not believe his eyes as he saw Vrenli slowly dissolving into the mist.

"Vrenli! What the...?" cried Gorathdin, jumping towards the bowl before he had finished his sentence and reaching into the mist. He grabbed Vrenli by the belt and tried to pull him out of the bowl, but in the same moment, he completely dissolved into the mist. Gorathdin withdrew his hand from the mist and, instead of his friend, he held the small leather pouch containing the Oracle of Tawinn in his hand.

"Vrenli?" Gorathdin shouted so loud that Werlis, Aarl and Borlix could hear the bellow from outside the tower.

Gorathdin gazed into the clearing fog in horror.

"Magic," he thought as he walked towards the window to inform Werlis, Aarl and Borlix about Vrenli's disappearance.

Werlis ran as fast as he could up the winding staircase to Master Drobal's study.

"He just disappeared before my eyes," Gorathdin explained, pointing to the golden, oval bowl.

"Vrenli! Vrenli," cried Werlis and ran towards the bowl, crying.

"That can't be right. How can he just disappear like that?" Werlis sobbed, staring at the bowl in horror.

"Magic," Gorathdin replied.

"But where is Vrenli now?" Werlis' senses began to fade.

Gorathdin was silent for a few moments.

"I don't know," he finally replied, sitting down on the chair at Master Drobal's desk and looking at the bowl in silence for a while.

"He's not dead, is he?" asked Werlis hesitantly.

Gorathdin, still holding the small leather pouch in his hand, did not answer.

"Tell me he's not dead!" Werlis screamed hysterically, slumping down on the floor next to the bowl, crying.

"I don't know," replied Gorathdin, his words almost stuck in his throat.

Werlis straightened up, wiped the tears from his face and stepped into the golden bowl.

Nothing happened.

"What are you doing?" Gorathdin shouted and yanked him back by the cloak.

Werlis fell to the ground.

"I want to follow Vrenli," he replied with a pale face.

"Have you lost your senses? It could mean your death. We don't know what this bowl is all about," Gorathdin warned him.

He held out his hand to Werlis, pulled him up and hugged him.

"But Vrenli is my best friend!" Werlis burst out, his voice drowned in tears.

Gorathdin thought and looked around the room.

"I don't think Master Drobal keeps objects here that mean death if you touch them," he spoke reassuringly to Werlis.

"But where is Vrenli now?" Werlis sobbed.

"I wish I could tell you that. Let's look for clues here in the room," Gorathdin suggested, walking towards the bookshelf, taking out one book after another and reading their titles. Many of them were written in a language he didn't speak and the ones he did understand gave no clues about Vrenli's disappearance.

"What strange objects there are here," Werlis remarked after climbing onto the chair and looking at Master Drobal's desk.

"Please don't touch anything. Who knows what might happen to you," Gorathdin warned him and grabbed his hand before Werlis could touch a test tube containing a brown, viscous-looking substance.

"I can't find anything that could help us. It will be better if we go back to the castle, maybe they can tell us something about the bowl there," Gorathdin decided and went down the tower stairs, followed by Werlis.

"At last! We were getting worried. Now tell us, what happened to Vrenli?" asked Aarl, who was guarding the three bound thieves with Borlix.

Gorathdin told them what had happened up in the tower. Both were left open-mouthed and when one of the three thieves laughed derisively, Borlix acknowledged him with a strong elbow strike. Werlis began to cry again, and Aarl put his hand on his shoulder to comfort him.

"They can certainly help us in the castle. Someone will know what this bowl is all about," said Aarl, whereupon Werlis gathered himself and regained hope.

"Mages. They're all dangerous, just like their objects," Borlix grumbled and motioned one of the thieves to stand up.

"You three will end up in prison!" he shouted and kicked the thief, who did not comply with his request, in the shins.

"You little red-haired devil!" he screamed and began to hop on one leg in pain.

"Let's go," said Gorathdin, and he strode ahead of his friends, who were holding the bound thieves, through the dark castle garden. When they arrived at the staircase in front of the castle, Gorathdin ordered the men of the royal guard standing guard there to take the three thieves into custody and, followed by Werlis, Aarl and Borlix, made his way to King Grandhold's private chambers.

"A golden, oval bowl that stands in the middle of Master Drobal's study?" King Grandhold repeated after Gorathdin had told him about the events in the tower.

"Yes, a golden bowl. It's about two and a half steps in diameter, you can't miss it," replied Werlis.

"I'm sorry about that. I don't know what this bowl is," the King apologized.

"Do you know anything about the bowl in Master Drobal's Tower, Palanmar?" King Grandhold said and turned to him.

The court healer, who was leafing through the book Gorathdin had handed him, looked up.

"I don't know anything about that," he replied briefly.

Werlis gasped for air and began to tremble all over. As tears ran down his cheeks, he began to laugh at the absurdity of his best friend disappearing into a bowl. Gorathdin knelt on the ground in front of him and looked deep into his eyes.

"We will find Vrenli again. Don't give up hope," he said gently and took Werlis in his arms.

"We'll find him," assured Aarl, running his hand through Werlis' short, blond hair.

"Master Drobal will know what has happened to your friend," said King Grandhold, looking first at Werlis and then at his daughter.

"But no one knows when he will return to Astinhod. Who knows what might have already happened to Vrenli," Werlis objected, wiping his nose on his cloak sleeve.

"I have to go to my laboratory to prepare the potion," Palanmar interrupted those present.

He bowed to the King and left the bedchamber with hurried steps.

"I hope the potion will help my daughter. Look at her! How beautiful she is. She is still so young, too young to be punished so severely by life," King Grandhold worried as he paced impatiently up and down the room.

"There's not much we can do for Vrenli today, but tomorrow is another day, Werlis," Borlix comforted him, who, like all dwarves, found it difficult to show his feelings.

"Vrenli will not be forgotten. I will do everything in my power to find out what happened to him. I ask you to understand that I must now turn my attention to Princess Lythinda," Gorathdin said to Werlis.

"We will find Vrenli again. You can count on me," affirmed Aarl, and he put his hand on Werlis' shoulder.

"And on me," Borlix grumbled.

Werlis thanked them. He knew that he could rely on them and that gave him new hope.

Some time passed. Everyone waited anxiously for Palanmar's return. Werlis, Aarl and Borlix had sat down on a narrow bench covered in red velvet on the west side of the room. King Grandhold was still pacing impatiently up and down the room.

"I can't shake the feeling that all the recent incidents, and by that I mean what happened to Lythinda, the group of thieves who followed me to Tawinn, Master Drobal's surprise departure from Astinhod, the three thieves and perhaps Vrenli's disappearance are all part of a plan to harm Astinhod, if not the whole of Wetherid," Gorathdin speculated, interrupting the silence that had fallen in the room.

"Do you think the Thieves' Guild has anything to do with my daughter's condition?" King Grandhold asked.

"The stranger in Three Vines was not a thief and I think it's unlikely that the guild is behind all this. They are thieves, simple men, but someone could take advantage of them and use them as henchmen," Gorathdin replied.

"Do you think someone from the nobility is behind this?" asked the King, who was aware of his enemies in Astinhod.

"Blackmail?" Aarl interjected.

"It's possible," replied Gorathdin.

"But no one has confessed to the crime or made any demands at all," King Grandhold pointed out.

"Also, the Thieves' Guild has split into two groups, at least that's what Count Laars told me today. The town guards apprehended four thieves who tried to flee Astinhod over the city wall last night. They were arrested and interrogated. We have information from them that there have been disagreements within the guild and that some are now following Hattul and the others Massek," King Grandhold announced.

"Did they say why the split happened?" Gorathdin asked.

"As far as I know, the guards couldn't get them to talk," replied King Grandhold.

"Maybe I could help with that," offered Aarl.

"Yes. He could try to get information from them. Aarl is a Thirian and no one in Astinhod knows him. He could be locked up with the thieves under the pretext that he stole something," Gorathdin suggested.

"That would be worth a try," the King said happily. They discussed the necessary steps to have Aarl locked up with the thieves the next day. Gorathdin and King Grandhold knew that the Thieves' Guild had allies in high places, so they had to make sure that what they were about to do seemed genuine. They needed some time to come up with a credible story. As it was already past midnight, Werlis and Borlix felt a growing tiredness and the longer they waited for Palanmar, the sleepier they became.

The lady-in-waiting, who had been sitting silently in a rocking chair next to Princess Lythinda's bed the whole time and, as befitted a woman in her position, was not following the conversation of those present, offered Werlis and Borlix the opportunity to ring for a castle servant to take them to a guest room. The two assured her, however, that they appeared more tired than they were. They didn't want to miss the moment when the princess would be given the healing potion.

More time passed. Werlis and Borlix struggled to keep their eyes from closing and fell asleep in the King of Astinhod's bedchamber. Suddenly, the door opened and Palanmar entered the room with a crystal jar containing a bluish liquid.

"I have followed the instructions in the recipe exactly," he said to King Grandhold, who looked at the crystal vessel with relief and hope.

Palanmar took a delicate silver cup that stood on a small chest of drawers next to the princess's bed and poured a little bit of the bluish liquid into it. He handed the crystal vessel to the lady-in-waiting and was about to put the cup to Lythinda's lips when Gorathdin stopped him.

"Wait a minute. I want to taste it first," Gorathdin announced firmly and held out his hand for the cup.

Palanmar was surprised and questioningly looked at King Grandhold.

"Give Gorathdin the cup," King Grandhold instructed him.

Palanmar handed the cup to Gorathdin, who first smelled it and then sipped it. Werlis, Aarl and Borlix watched intently to see what would happen to their friend. Some time passed and dead silence reigned in the King's bedchamber.

"You can give it to her," Gorathdin finally said, after he could detect nothing unusual about the potion.

Palanmar carefully put the rim of the cup to Lythinda's lips and poured a few drops of the potion into her mouth.

"The recipe didn't say anything about how long it takes for the potion to take effect," he remarked and sat down on the chair that the lady-in-waiting had placed next to the princess's bed.

"Now we have to wait and hope," said King Grandhold, who, despite the late hour, did not feel tired.

Werlis, Aarl and Borlix sat down on the soft, precious carpet on the floor and gazed sleepily at the princess. The time they waited passed very slowly and Werlis, followed by Borlix, was overcome by sleep. Aarl and Gorathdin went over the details of Aarl's planned arrest together once more. King Grandhold sat down on the edge of the bed and held the princess's hand until the early hours of the morning, hoping that his daughter would regain consciousness as the sun rose.

The sage of the desert

When Vrenli stepped out of the golden, oval bowl, which stood in a strange-looking, strange-smelling tent shortly before midnight, he lost consciousness for a moment and when he woke up again, he was lying in front of a tent made of goat and camel skins. A fire was burning next to him, its flames rising into the cold night sky of a desert. Opposite him sat a dark-skinned, sinewy old man whose long, white beard reached down to the chilled, sandy desert floor. The sage of the desert, as he was called by the Scheddifer people, was clad in the fur of a desert wolf and around his neck hung a chain on which the teeth and claws of various desert animals were strung. Vrenli jumped in fright.

"Fear not, Vrenli from Abketh! My name is Nagulaj," revealed the old man, who was sitting opposite him with his legs crossed.

"How do you know my name and where am I?" Vrenli looked around in confusion, but apart from the tent and the fire burning in front of it, all he could see was a sea of sand in the darkness.

Nagulaj did not answer Vrenli's question, but began to talk about an old book, which he said contained all knowledge and in which the magic of the elves from the Glorious Valley rested. The longer Vrenli listened to the stories, the more he concluded that the Book of Wetherid, as Nagulaj called it in his story, could be his grandfather's book. Vrenli asked him questions several times, but Nagulaj did not answer. Nagulaj was so engrossed in his story that he spoke with his eyes closed, and only when he had reached the end, did he open them and look into the flickering flames of the fire in front of him, pausing for a few moments.

"When the sparrowhawks circle in the sky above us, you will set off for Horunguth Island to meet Master Drobal. That's what it says in the Book of Books," he finally announced, looking at Vrenli with his large, dark brown eyes.

"A lot of what you told me about the book seems so familiar to me, as if I already know about it," Vrenli revealed.

"But I would really like to know how I got here, why you know my name and why you told me so much about the book," Vrenli continued.

Nagulaj did not answer.

He slipped his chain over his head and opened it. Slowly, the small, weathered animal bones and teeth slid onto the sandy desert floor, where Nagulaj gazed in silence.

"I have to go back to Astinhod. I'm sure my friends are worried about me," said Vrenli.

Nagulaj got up without saying anything and went into his tent, from where he returned to the fire a little later with a long-stemmed pipe made of dark wood. Vrenli looked at the pipe shaped like a bull's head with red eyes made of two fiery rubies.

"The concern for a friend should never be as great as the concern for your own destiny, which life has given you and which each of us follows, even the simplest man," Nagulaj explained to him, taking a brown ball of dried mataii tree resin from a small pouch and putting a piece of it into the round opening of the pipe.

"Can't I travel back to Astinhod with the bowl?" Vrenli wanted to know.

"That's not possible! As far as I know, the portal bowls can only be used by the mages of Horunguth Island," Nagulaj replied as he pressed the mataii resin more firmly into the bowl of the pipe with his thumb.

"I don't understand. The bowl brought me here, why shouldn't it take me back to Master Drobal's Tower in Astinhod?" Vrenli wondered, got up and went into the tent, where he stood in the bowl and waited anxiously to be taken back to Astinhod.

Nothing happened.

Vrenli sadly went back outside the tent and sat down by the fire.

"I don't understand all this. You say that only the mages of Horunguth Island can travel with the bowl, but then why is it in your tent?" Vrenli groaned and questioningly looked at Nagulaj.

"You'll have to ask Master Drobal that, not me. I don't use the bowl; it was in this place long before I pitched my tent here. A very long time ago," Nagulaj replied.

He pulled a thin, burning branch out of the fire and lit the bull-headed pipe with it.

"That's strange. The most unusual things have been happening since I met Gorathdin in Abketh," mused Vrenli.

"How am I ever supposed to get to Horunguth Island alone or find my way back to Astinhod? Can't you come with me, Nagulaj? Please!" begged Vrenli with a pleading look.

"My destiny is different, Vrenli. The journey you have embarked on together with your friends must not be interfered with. Things must take their course, just as it is written in the Book of Books. I am not allowed to change history. My purpose is to bring you a little closer to yours," Nagulaj replied, taking a puff on his pipe.

Vrenli did not understand what the dark-skinned old man was trying to tell him. His thoughts revolved around Werlis, Gorathdin, Aarl and Borlix, whom he thought he had gotten into trouble for the second time through his carelessness.

"I hope that the blossoms of the moonflower will help the princess so that the long journey was not in vain," he thought, looking questioningly into Nagulaj's large, dark eyes.

Nagulaj offered him the smoking pipe.

"What should I do with it?" Vrenli shyly asked.

"I don't smoke," he added dismissively.

But Nagulaj only made a hand gesture, indicating that Vrenli should pull on the mouthpiece of the pipe.

"Your journey to me was not without reason, Vrenli from Abketh," Nagulaj explained and pressed the pipe into his hand.

Hesitantly, Vrenli put the mouthpiece to his lips and looked at the bull-headed bowl of the pipe as he drew on it. With every puff he took, the two red rubies began to glow brighter and finally in a fiery red light.

After a few strokes, Vrenli felt a pleasant warmth relaxing his muscles. All his worries and fears seemed to have left him. As he listened to the song that Nagulaj began to sing, he noticed a feeling of lightness spreading through him.

"I feel so light. As light as if I could fly," said Vrenli, slowly stretching out his arms and beginning to make wing-flapping movements.

To his surprise, he suddenly found himself floating above the ground in a sitting position.

"Fly home. Fly to the Glorious Valley!" Nagulaj called to him, whereupon Vrenli flew higher and higher, towards the sky, and finally flew over the vast Desert of DeShadin, gazing at the stars before him, to Thir, where he could see the lights of the port city of Irkaar below him.

Vrenli flew over the city towards the east, where, after a while, he saw a vast meadow landscape below him.

Before him lay the mighty mountain ranges that surrounded the Glorious Valley. He headed higher towards the mountain peaks and when he had almost reached them, he was caught by a gust of wind that whirled him through the air. He was afraid of crashing and panic and despair broke out in him. He tried with all his might to fight the wind.

Vrenli felt that he had strayed from his predetermined path. He was no longer flying towards the Glorious Valley, but over the northern mountains to the east, beyond the border of Wetherid.

"Help, Nagulaj!" shouted Vrenli. He had lost control of his flying body.

"Don't fight it. Let yourself drift. Don't be afraid," Nagulaj's gentle voice rang out.

Vrenli tried to overcome his fear. He let the gust of wind carry him further and further south-east. When he realized that his fear was unfounded, he relaxed and looked down at the barren landscape. Leafless, thin-branched trees, thorny bushes and faded grass grew sporadically on the deserted plain. The gust of wind carried Vrenli to the ruins of the city of Zatranos, which lay on the southern border of the valley of Tongar Gor, and suddenly it became frighteningly dark around him, so dark that even the moonlight was unable to penetrate the darkness. Vrenli was shrouded in an impenetrable shadow, from which he emerged a few moments later. He was now hovering above the ruined city and looking up at a hill where he recognized the outline of a castle. He was carried closer. A figure clad in dark clothes and a cloak, sitting on the skeleton of a horse whose eyes glowed fiery, rode out of the castle onto the crumbling bridge above a blood-red river.

A cold shiver ran down Vrenli's spine. As he turned his gaze to the river, he recognized the dead bodies of countless humans, elves, dwarves, Tawinnians, ogres, goblins and other creatures and animals floating in the river. It was their blood that colored the river.

Vrenli turned his attention back to the dark rider who had led his horse to the precipice in front of the crumbling bridge. The figure raised his right hand and pointed north, whereupon the horse's skeleton reared up and neighed. When the figure became aware of Ornux, it paused and a mocking smile played around its lips.

Vrenli was frightened when he saw Ornux, but he listened attentively from a lofty height.

"Ornux, a shadow who dares to enter the realm of the dead. What brings you to me?"

"Azrakel, I come on behalf of Erwight of Entorbis to make an offer. An offer that should interest even a soulbinder like you," Ornux replied, standing imperturbably before the rider.

Azrakel laughed coldly.

"And what offer could that be, shadow mage? What could Erwight offer me that I don't already have?"

With a movement that darkened the air around him, Ornux invoked the power of the shadows.

"The dead of the coming battle for Wetherid, Azrakel. All souls that fall will be yours, added to your ranks of the undead, as your thralls."

Azrakel's interest was piqued.

"All souls, you say? A tempting offer, but why should I trust Erwight of Entorbis? His ambitions are well known to me," he replied coldly.

"Because I stand here to reinforce that promise. Because I am ready to knock you off your high horse should it be necessary,"

Ornux replied, letting the raw, powerful shadow magic pulsate around him.

In a sudden burst of power, Ornux hurled a wave of dark energy at Azrakel. The soulbinder, surprised by the mage's determination, was unable to dodge it. The energy hit him and his horse with such force that both were thrown to the ground.

Azrakel pulled himself to his feet, his gaze now serious as he looked at Ornux.

"You dare to attack me? You have courage, shadow mage. Perhaps ... maybe this alliance is beneficial," he said confidently.

"Courage is necessary to shape the new order, Azrakel. The dead that Wetherid will leave behind will be at your service. Together we can ensure that this battle will be the last," Ornux replied, calming the darkness around him once more.

"Very well, Ornux. I will accept your offer. But remember, the price of betrayal would be your downfall," he said threateningly, his gaze now firmly fixed on Ornux.

"I don't expect anything else," Ornux replied.

Thus, in the darkness of Zatranos, a new alliance was forged, an alliance between shadow and death. Under the leadership of Erwight of Entorbis, this union would lead Fallgar into a new era; an era built on the souls of the fallen.

At the same moment, an army of undead crawled out of the ground in the city below. Azrakel mounted his horse again, spurred it on and jumped with it down the chasm hundreds of steps deep, where he landed in front of the skeletons and half-rotten bodies of the Knights of Zatranos. Under his leadership, the army of the undead marched out of the city towards the north.

The gust of wind suddenly whirled Vrenli through the air so powerfully that he almost threw up. He began to thrash in panic. But shortly afterwards the gust of wind calmed again and carried him further north, where he flew over a fog-covered moor, the musty stench penetrating deep into his nose. At first the thick mist enveloped him so he could not see anything, but as the gust of wind let him glide closer to the ground, he saw the shadows of tall

179

figures whose eyes glowed red in the darkness. The fog lifted and he saw many mud and wooden huts covered in leaves and twigs, standing on the few patches of solid ground. He was carried to Marnog Jar, the city of the mist elves, at the eastern end of Mist Moor. Dozens of spider and lizard riders armed with bows and arrows had gathered in the center of the city in front of the large, mighty wooden sculpture of a spider. Among them stood Ornux, the emissary of Erwight of Entorbis, and Prince Sylvain. It was a moment that, beyond the fate of a hidden city, threatened to affect the fragile balance of the entire world, where alliances were fleeting and enmities deep-rooted.

Vrenli listened, hidden in the mist, as Ornux spoke to Prince Sylvain:

"Prince Sylvain, the world is at the beginning of a change. Erwight of Entorbis has sent me to show you a possibility. A possibility that could change the fate of the mist elves forever," Ornux began, as the silence in the mist carried his words like an echo.

"He offers an alliance, the fruits of which would encompass the Glorious Valley should victory over Wetherid be ours."

"But what will become of Marnog Jar? Of Mist Moor, which offers us not only home, but also protection and identity? How can we give up everything and place ourselves under someone else's banner, just for a piece of land that stands between us and old enemies?" replied Prince Sylvain Fog Crow, his expression marked by pensiveness.

"It's not about being subservient. Erwight sees you, the mist elves, as allies on a path to something greater. The Glorious Valley is just the beginning," Ornux replied with a smile that radiated more patience than joy.

Prince Sylvain paused for a moment.

"If we join this alliance, it will only be on the condition that our people, our freedoms and our heritage remain protected. Marnog Jar and Mist Moor are our foundation; the Glorious Valley must be a place where the mist elves can not only exist, but thrive," he spoke.

"These conditions are respected and Erwight of Entorbis is ready to fulfill them. Together we enter a future in which Marnog Jar will be at the center of a new order," Ornux agreed earnestly.

And so, under the watchful eye of the mist, a new chapter was opened, not without uncertainty, but with a spark of hope for a future in which the mist elves would play a central role in shaping their destiny, strengthened by new alliances and the promise of a better world.

The shrill, distorted sound of horns rang out over Mist Moor, whereupon the spider and lizard riders, followed by a troop of mist elves several hundred strong, rode north.

The gust of wind shot Vrenli accelerating like an arrow into the sky and carried him further inland towards the east. A sea of tents stood on the dark rock-strewn plain of Raga Gur. From the highest peak of a small mountain range in the north, a mighty flame flickered high into the sky.

Vrenli could clearly see the crater filled with glowing lava. He could feel the searing heat of the fire, which never went out and whose light colored the plain fiery red. Hot, molten rock poured out from inside the mountain and flowed slowly down the steep mountain faces. Hundreds of heavily armed orcs had gathered at a burnt forest quarter, no more than a thousand paces from the fire-breathing volcano. Ornux, shadow mage and emissary of Erwight of Entorbis, had set out to renew the alliance with the orcs under the leadership of shaman Gorzod Greywing. But the atmosphere was tense and the air vibrated with mistrust.

"Gorzod Greywing, I bring word from Erwight of Entorbis. He wishes to renew the alliance with your people," Ornux began as he looked at the mighty shaman, whose war paint shimmered in the pale light of the volcanic fire.

"Ornux, the shadow roams our ranks. Why should we place our fate in your lord's hands again?" Gorzod replied, his voice low and penetrating as he gripped the staff tighter in his hand.

"Because the power of Entorbis gives you strength, because our alliance with Raga Gur and beyond can lead to unprecedented power," Ornux replied, but he sensed that words alone would not convince the proud shaman.

The orcs murmured among themselves, their eyes glinting suspiciously. Ornux realized that he would have to find another way to win their approval. In this moment of uncertainty, an idea came to him.

"Gorzod, show us a test of your strength and wisdom. A duel of magic between us. If you win, I will return without having achieved anything. But if I win, you will renew the alliance."

"A duel of magic, then. Very well, Ornux. May the dark power decide," Gorzod laughed in agreement.

The duel began under the eager gaze of the orcs. Ornux and Gorzod faced each other, each of them summoning the dark forces they controlled. But Ornux had no intention of fighting a real duel. With a clever deception, he drew Gorzod's attention to a point behind the shaman while murmuring soft words. An illusion was created, a vision of Erwight of Entorbis himself, granting Gorzod his power and blessing.

"Gorzod Greywing, look! Erwight of Entorbis himself shows you the way. Your strength is undisputed, but together we are invincible!" shouted Ornux as the figure in the illusion knelt down and asked Gorzod to renew the alliance.

Surprised and impressed by the vision, Gorzod lowered his staff.

"If Erwight of Entorbis himself gives us his blessing, who am I to deny this alliance? The alliance be renewed, Ornux. But be warned, the orcs of Raga Gur will not enter the fray lightly."

With these words, the alliance was renewed under new terms. Ornux, relieved at his success, knew that this ruse was a dangerous wager, but one that was necessary to avert a greater catastrophe. The orcs of Raga Gur would once again stand alongside Erwight of Entorbis, but the future remained uncertain, scarred by the shadows that lay over them all.

Three of the pig-faced, sabre-toothed orcs then spurred on their large, furry, horned mounts and swung their lances, red banners waving at their tips, above their heads. Squealing, snarling cries echoed far and wide, whereupon the horde, several hundred strong, moved northwards.

The gust of wind now carried Vrenli northwards along the wide, fiery river over a small mountain range and then further west towards a large, wooded area.

Above a tent camp, in a wide clearing where flames flickered from a fireplace, he paused. Strong, fat, half-naked creatures, at least five steps tall, armed with clubs from which long metal spikes protruded, performed clumsy dance movements to the dull, thunderous drumbeats that sounded across the plain. When the drumbeats stopped, a loud grunt followed, making Vrenli's blood run cold. A five-step-tall ogre stepped out of one of the tents and greeted Ornux, who had come to have a crucial conversation with Gromak Ironskin, the mighty leader of the ogres. The air vibrated with the raw energy that the ogres released in their rituals and dances, a harbinger of the power Ornux sought to tame.

Vrenli had to listen very carefully through the noise of the drum to understand what was being said:

"Gromak Ironskin, in the name of Shadow Lord Erwight of Entorbis, I demand to speak!" Ornux's voice firmly and piercingly rang out, even against the wild grunts of the ogres and the crackling of the hearth.

Gromak, his mighty stature silhouetted against the blazing flames, slowly turned around.

"Ornux the shadow rarely walks without purpose. What does Erwight of Entorbis want from the ogre warriors?" he inquired in a loud and deep voice. His eyes sparkled with suspicion.

"Renewal, Gromak. Renewal of the alliance that will lead Fallgar into a new era. Erwight of Entorbis offers more than promises, he offers the power to take control of your destinies in your own hands," Ornux replied as he raised his hands and softly whispered the words of an ancient, forgotten language.

The shadows around him began to dance, forming images of the future, visions of ogre armies marching invincibly through the lands, led by the dark power that Erwight promised.

"See, Gromak Ironskin, what you and your people can achieve. Unimagined power, strength that will shake the foundations of Wetherid."

Gromak observed the shadow images closely.

"And what does Erwight want in return? Our freedom? Our will?" he challenged, visibly thoughtful.

Ornux made the shadows disappear again and took a step closer.

"No, Gromak. Erwight of Entorbis demands unity, a common endeavor. The freedom of the ogres will be preserved, strengthened by the alliances we forge," Ornux announced.

"Words, Ornux, are like the wind; fleeting and often cold. How can we, the ogres of Wahmuter, be sure that this future will come true?" Gromak spoke, his tone now less challenging and more inquisitive.

"Faith, Gromak Ironskin. Faith and the will to take fate into your own hands. Erwight of Entorbis has powerful enemies, but also powerful allies. Under his leadership, not only will Wetherid fall, but a new world order will emerge. A world in which the ogres take their rightful place," Ornux assured him, underpinning his words with the magic of the shadow that vibrated softly in the air.

A moment of silence enveloped the plains.

"I will take your words to the council, Ornux. If Erwight keeps his word, the ogres will stand by his side. But he should be warned: The loyalty of the ogres is like our wrath; powerful and unrelenting," Gromak finally agreed.

With those words, the conversation ended, and Ornux knew he had taken a significant step towards realizing Erwight of Entorbis' dark visions. The ogres of Wahmuter, once wild and untamed forces, could tip the scales in the coming storm. That night, under the starry skies of Fallgar, the foundations were laid for an alliance that would shake the world.

It was not very long before Gromak, who had been conferring with the council in a tent, came forward again, swung his great club in the air and led the Wahmuther clan northwards.

Once again, the gust of wind caught Vrenli and carried him northeast. He flew over the hilly landscape of Kirbun towards a high mountain range. Hundreds of small caves had been carved into the dark gray, steep, smooth rock faces, from which small shadows roped themselves down to the ground on ropes a hundred paces long. Huge trenches, fifty paces across, lay at the foot of the mountain.

The gust of wind brought Vrenli closer to one of the trenches, which led many hundreds of steps down to Ingar. Slowly the wind died down, allowing Vrenli to glide down into the deep branching tunnels of the gray dwarves.

In the gloomy shadows, deep beneath the mighty peaks of Kirbun, where the passing wind whispered old stories through the barren tunnels, Ornux and Brumir Ironfist, the indomitable leader of the gray dwarves, stood face to face. This was an encounter that would decide the fate of the races.

"Brumir Ironfist, it is with the deepest respect that I come to you, on behalf of Erwight of Entorbis," Ornux began, his words interweaving with the cool tunnel air.

"A shadow that wanders to the gates of Ingar rarely brings glad tidings. What does the emissary of Erwight of Entorbis seek from the gray dwarves if not that which he cannot possess?" replied Brumir, his eyes reflecting the depths of subterranean lakes, in a firm voice.

"Erwight seeks an alliance, Brumir. An alliance that will not only turn the tide of battle but shape the future. Even if the mines of Ib'Agier never belonged to the gray dwarves, we offer something more valuable: a promise to create a new order together once

Wetherid is united under our influence," Ornux replied, emphasizing the gravity of his proposal.

Brumir laughed so loud that an echo reverberated in the cold stone walls.

"Promises are like snow in spring, Ornux. Why should we join an alliance whose fruits we have never tasted?" replied the gray dwarf.

"Because we, Brumir, are at the dawn of an era in which old boundaries will be redrawn. Your skill and knowledge could form the core of this new world. Not as servants, but as shapers and guardians. Ib'Agier may never have been yours, but the future could belong to all of Fallgar. And therein lies your power," Ornux explained, with a quiet fire in his words.

"And what if we decide to follow this path and the battle is lost? What then, shadow mage?" Brumir questioned, his brow furrowed.

"Then, Brumir Ironfist, we will have fought and risen together again. This is not a pact of submission, but of cooperation. Erwight of Entorbis sees you as allies of equal strength," Ornux replied with conviction.

A moment of silence enveloped them, in which the wind seemed to be the only answer. Then Brumir nodded slowly.

"Ornux, your words carry the ring of truth, even if they are surrounded by shadows. I will accept your proposal. But be aware, the trust of the gray dwarves is hard-won. We will be vigilant," Brumir finally agreed.

"So be it, Brumir. Together we will carve a new path through the darkness, a path that leads to a tomorrow where iron and shadow shine in the light of a new world," Ornux spoke, a sense of hope in his voice as he said goodbye to Brumir.

Thus ended their conversation, a dialog between powers that laid the foundations for a possible future. A future in which the gray dwarves might never call the mines of Ib'Agier their own, but in which they could play a role in shaping a new world order. An alliance forged on the thin line between mistrust and hope now carried the possibility of breaking through the shadows and leading into a new age.

Vrenli was carried up again by a gust of wind.

A multitude of diminutive creatures, their silver-gray chain armor reflecting the bland moonlight, climbed out of the gray dwarven city on wooden ladders that reached over the edge of the moat. They followed a path north, which led them to a cleared wooded area where several powerful, destructive war machines were being built. Vrenli flew at great speed over the catapults, ballistae and assault towers, heading north, where after some time he reached the land of Druhn.

He floated further and further over the large, wooded areas, grasslands, meadow lowlands, streams and rivers to the northeast. It was getting much colder and the landscape was covered in snow.

Vrenli could see from afar a frozen lake covered in mist, in the middle of which lay a rocky island where a fortress built of blackstone and dark iron stood, with a flock of black crows circling in the night sky above its five mighty towers. The icy cold enclosed him and he began to shiver. An uneasy feeling grew inside him, a sign of impending danger.

The gust of wind made Vrenli glide slowly towards the dark fortress to within a hundred paces, when suddenly a black shadow appeared above him. Vrenli looked up and saw a large, black crow flying towards him. It grabbed Vrenli with its sharp claws that dug into the flesh on his back through his clothes. Vrenli screamed out. In a dive, the large bird raced with him towards the icy surface of the lake. Vrenli felt the bird's grip loosen. Crying out for help, he plunged onto the icy lake, which broke at the force of the impact. He plunged into the icy water and froze. Slowly, he sank down into the deep, icy darkness. Close to fainting, he closed his eyes. He tried to call Nagulaj's name, but his mouth immediately filled with the foul-tasting lake water.

A warm hand grabbed his shoulder. Coughing and gasping for air, Vrenli opened his eyes and, drenched in sweat, looked at Nagulaj, who was sitting next to him by the fireplace in front of his tent.

"You had a vision. Don't be afraid," Nagulaj said in a gentle voice. Vrenli, pale as a sheet, couldn't get a word past his lips.

Nagulaj handed Vrenli a cup of tea made from desert herbs, which he drank hastily.

"Here, eat," Nagulaj offered and handed him a piece of pulp from the cactus.

Vrenli greedily sucked in the fruity sweetness and recoiled when Nagulaj handed him the pipe again, its contents still glowing.

"There's more for you to see. Don't be afraid," Nagulaj said gently and pressed the pipe into Vrenli's hand.

"I flew over places, towns and settlements far to the east. I saw terrible, terrifying beings and creatures. They were all preparing to move north, where there was a massive, dark fortress that lay in the middle of a lake covered in mist. These places were dark and evil, and I could feel the hatred that their inhabitants carried within them. What does all this mean?" Vrenli asked Nagulaj, who only pointed to the pipe with his bony index finger.

Hesitant and afraid of the unknown, he took a single drag on the mouthpiece. He inhaled the sweet smoke deep into his lungs. He had to cough and gasped for air. He had pulled too hard on the pipe. The smoke from the burning mataii resin billowed out of his mouth and enveloped him. He could no longer recognize Nagulaj because of the thick, acrid clouds of smoke floating in front of him. He closed his eyes for a moment.

When he opened them again and dispelled the last clouds of smoke with a wiping motion of his hand, he saw himself sitting on a branch among the sweet-smelling fruit of a strange tree.

He looked down on a calm and peaceful pond overgrown with ivy and roses, where several silent, white stone sculptures stood. The water in the marble basin shimmered in the violet light of a sparkling crystal lying at the bottom of the pool. A strange-looking youth with long, blond hair and shimmering golden skin sat on one of the steps leading to the edge of the pool. Birds were circling above him, singing a cheerful song. Vrenli's gaze fell on the glass bow and the quiver of silver arrows lying on the step next to the young man. He watched as the young man picked up a book from one of the steps, opened it and began to read it.

"That's my grandfather's book," thought Vrenli excitedly. He recognized it by the purple leather cover with silver ornaments. Vrenli was just about to climb down the tree when the young man closed the book, picked up his bow and quiver from the step and walked away from the pond. Vrenli jumped hastily from the tree, but landed unhappily face first on the forest floor, which was covered in damp leaves. When he straightened up again and looked around, the young man was already more than a hundred paces away.

"Stop, wait for me!" Vrenli called after him, but the young man didn't seem to hear his call.

Vrenli ran after him, but as it was already dusk, he soon lost sight of him. Vrenli followed the narrow path that led him deeper and deeper into the forest. Suddenly he heard screaming in the darkness ahead of him, whereupon he ran towards it as fast as he could. He almost fell in shock when he saw the young man shrouded in a dark shadow. When a tall figure emerged from behind the shadow cocoon, Vrenli froze. He looked into the pupil-less eyes of a face distorted beyond recognition and covered in scars.

"Get away from me, servant of darkness!" the young man shouted and was about to put an arrow in the string of his bow when the figure bent down to take the book that had fallen from the young man's hand.

"No! Not the book. Give it back to me!" the young man pleaded and wanted to jump towards the figure, but the shadow surrounding the young man prevented him from doing so.

With a ghastly grin and the book in his hand, the figure dissolved into nothingness within a moment, while the shadow ball slowly lost density and finally disappeared.

Vrenli looked at the young man, who was kneeling beside the spot where the book had been lying on the floor, weeping.

"Forgive me, father. I've lost the book," he whispered in a low voice. Then he got up and followed the path north. Vrenli brushed off the fright that had gripped him and followed the young man through the night.

"I will find the book again, father. I swear it," the young man repeated aloud as he made his way through the forest.

Vrenli was startled when he heard bugles and a thunderous noise. Cries of despair, weeping and the sounds of fighting reached his ears. Vrenli stopped for a moment, but the young man took his glass bow from his shoulder, put an arrow in the string and began to run in the direction of the screams.

"Wait for me!" Vrenli called and tried to follow him.

But his short legs did not carry him fast enough to catch up with the young man, who could neither see nor hear him.

The deeper Vrenli followed him into the forest, the darker it became and when he could almost no longer see anything, he stumbled over something lying on the ground in front of him. He recoiled in horror: in front of him lay the lifeless body of an elf, its once shimmering golden skin covered in a gray shadow. His mouth was wide open and his dead eyes reflected the horror of the last moment of his life.

It wasn't the young man, as he had first feared, but someone else. Vrenli became afraid. So scared that his lungs constricted and he had to gasp for air. He began to run. Faster and faster, he ran along the path where several dead elves lay. When he could no longer bear the sight of the faces of the dead, distorted by pain and horror, he ran on with his eyes closed and when he again fell over one of the dead, he remained lying on the ground and began to cry. He cried out of the pity he felt for these noble and pure beings.

An initially unintelligible sound coming from a distance grew louder and it sounded more and more like someone was repeatedly calling his name. Vrenli suddenly felt the touch of a warm hand gently stroking his head. He opened his teary eyes and looked at Nagulaj standing in front of him by the fire.

"You should get some rest now, Vrenli. I've prepared a place for you to sleep in the tent," Nagulaj said gently and held out his hand to Vrenli to help him up.

"I saw dead elves and my grandfather's book," said Vrenli.

He spoke slowly, as he was still dazed from the effects of the mataii resin.

"You had another vision, Vrenli. And I would be delighted if you would tell me about it tomorrow, before you set off on your journey to Horunguth Island. But you should sleep now," Nagulaj comforted him gently.

"It was all so real and there was a shadow and a terrifying figure that had stolen my grandfather's book," Vrenli described before lying down on the soft carpet, where Nagulaj covered him with a fur.

"Good night, Vrenli from Abketh," said Nagulaj and he went back to the fireplace where he picked up his pipe from the sandy desert floor and stuffed it again with some mataii resin.

He gazed silently into the starry night sky above Desert of DeShadin.

The Thieves' Guild of Astinhod

It was already midday and Princess Lythinda's condition had not changed. She was still gazing fixedly at the ceiling painting above her bed. Contrary to everyone's expectations, the fever had not gone down and the shadow on her arm was slowly spreading to her shoulder. Palanmar had given her another cup of the healing potion that morning, but it had had no effect.

"All our hopes have been dashed. My daughter has been exposed to this seemingly incurable disease and all my efforts to help her have failed. I will declare this day the black day of Astinhod," spoke King Grandhold, clouded with grief.

"I think it's time we asked the Order of the Dragon for help. Their knowledge of healing is very extensive," Gorathdin suggested.

The king looked at him silently for a few moments.

"You know that the royal house of Astinhod keeps a certain distance from them. I am not sure this is a good decision. My father did allow the Templars to resume their activities in an hour of great need after the Order was crushed a hundred and fifty years ago, but some of the nobles were against that decision. If I ask the Order for help now, it could lead to unrest. The whole debate could possibly start all over again," King Grandhold objected.

He looked thoughtfully at Gorathdin, Werlis, Aarl and Borlix.

"Bah, politics," Borlix grumbled, whereupon the king raised his right eyebrow and gave him a stern look.

"Borlix is right. We mustn't think about politics now. The welfare of Princess Lythinda is at stake and we should leave no stone unturned. I've already thought about asking my father for help. I'm pretty sure his healing skills aren't the most suitable in this case, but as I mentioned before, I don't want to leave any stone unturned," Gorathdin said.

"You're probably right, Gorathdin. We must try everything we can to help her somehow. But the decision to ask the monks of the Order of the Dragon for help is not an easy one for me. I need to think about it alone, friends," said King Grandhold, walking towards the door that led to his study.

"You should fortify yourselves. I'll let you know my decision after you've feasted," he added before the door closed quietly.

He made his way to the palace gardens, where he sat down silently in the pavilion to weigh the pros and cons.

"What's there to think about? After all, his daughter's life is at stake," Borlix grumbled as he stood up from the small stool that the lady-in-waiting had kindly brought him from the library that morning.

"The monks' healing skills are known throughout Wetherid. Many people from the villages and towns of Thir have often made use of them and in most cases the healing potions and ointments have worked," explained Aarl, who clearly agreed with Borlix.

"I've never heard of the Templars of the Dragon. But the name alone makes me uncomfortable," Werlis said and tried to smile.

"Well, King Grandhold is first and foremost King of Astinhod. His kingdom comes first. He put everyone's welfare before his own when he ascended his father's throne. Of course, he is also a loving father, but his hope that someone can help his daughter is fading. He now has a difficult decision to make. Personally, I think his worries are unfounded. But it is not my kingdom and not my decision," Gorathdin explained to his friends and, at Werlis' request, told them who the Templars of the Dragon were.

Just as he was finishing his story, he unconsciously reached for Vrenli's small leather pouch, which was still hanging from his belt.

"That's it!" he suddenly shouted, whereupon Werlis, Aarl and Borlix looked at him questioningly.

"The Oracle of Tawinn! When I reached into the fog that surrounded Vrenli, I grabbed his belt and when it disappeared, I had his leather pouch in my hand," Gorathdin said, waving Vrenli's leather pouch in front of her eyes.

"The Oracle of Tawinn! All is not lost after all. We must ask it about Vrenli!" cried Werlis enthusiastically.

His eyes shone. Before Borlix could say anything, Werlis explained to him what the crystal was.

"I don't know how it works, but let's hope for the best," said Werlis.

"Let's go next door to King Grandhold's study," Gorathdin suggested and, followed by his three friends, left the bedchamber.

In the study, they sat down on a massive table made of dark wood and waited anxiously for Werlis to take the crystal from the leather pouch that Gorathdin had given him earlier.

"Looks like a normal fragment of rock crystal," Borlix expertly stated as Werlis placed the oracle on the table in front of him.

"Oracle of Tawinn. Show me Vrenli. What happened to him?" Werlis spoke in a trembling voice and gazed eagerly at the small crystal, which, to the astonishment of Gorathdin, Aarl and Borlix, began to shine with a bright blue light.

Only a short time later, a small picture emerged inside, showing Vrenli struggling over a dune in the moonlight at night. He was struggling to find his footing in the fine-grained sand and appeared to be suffering from severe thirst. As he tried to descend the other side of the dune, he fell and rolled across the fine sand to the bottom, where he stood up in front of a dried, thick bush. He knocked the dust and sand off his clothes, broke off some branches from the bush and lit a fire with them.

"He's alive!" exclaimed Werlis with Gorathdin, Aarl and Borlix.

"There's a pack of wolves coming towards him from behind the dunes. Look," Werlis remarked. The image inside the crystal began to blur and the bright blue glow went out.

"What about the giant wolves? Oracle of Tawinn, show me what else has happened," Werlis begged the crystal, but nothing happened. He tried again and again, but the glow remained absent.

"Let it go, Werlis. We now know that he is alive," Gorathdin reassured him in a gentle voice.

"But what about the wolves? They'll tear him to pieces," Werlis sobbed and burst into tears.

"Vrenli is tough. He'll cope with the beasts," Borlix announced.

"He wore his short sword on his belt. I could see it clearly. He's not unarmed," Aarl remarked.

"Vrenli is alive! If he wasn't, the Oracle of Tawinn would have shown us. We saw him, albeit not in a completely harmless situation. But he's alive," said Gorathdin.

"He must live," Werlis implored and let the silver chain with the crystal slide back into the leather pouch, which he then tied to his belt.

"All I could see was a sea of sand. What strange place is Vrenli in?" asked Werlis.

"From the looks of it, he's in Desert of DeShadin," Gorathdin replied.

Aarl nodded in agreement.

"But it must be thousands of steps from Astinhod. All the way to the southwest of Wetherid! He'll never make it back alone," Werlis sighed in despair.

Gorathdin, Aarl and Borlix remained silent for some time.

"Listen to me, Werlis. I hope that King Grandhold will decide to ask the Order of the Dragon for help. I promise you that as soon as I have brought Lythinda to them, I will set off with you to Desert of DeShadin in search of Vrenli. But you'll have to be patient a bit longer," said Gorathdin, getting up from the table, walking towards Werlis and placing his hand on his shoulder.

"I'm heading south, I'm happy to take the detour into the desert to help Vrenli," promised Aarl.

Werlis looked eagerly at Borlix, hoping that he too would accompany them. Borlix looked left, right and at the ceiling and finally cleared his throat.

"Well. Hm. Um. Ib'Agier. Yes. Hm. A few weeks more or less doesn't matter now! I'm coming with you, friends," he relented.

"Thank you, friends. I knew I could rely on you. I will never forget that," said Werlis with tears in his eyes.

"Let's go to the dining hall and drink to that," Gorathdin suggested and explained the way there, as he wanted to check on Lythinda first.

"I'll be right behind you," he let them know and went back to the King's bedchamber.

Werlis, Borlix and Aarl had already gathered in the dining room and were just being invited to the table by two servants when Gorathdin arrived.

"How is she?" Aarl inquired.

"There is no improvement in sight. I hope King Grandhold will make the right decision. A decision from his heart," replied Gorathdin and took a seat at the sumptuous table.

Werlis looked at the silver trays. But even the roast suckling pig, partridges, larded saddle of venison, dumplings stuffed with ham, boiled vegetables, soup, eggs, bread and juicy fruit could not restore his lost appetite due to his worries about Vrenli. One of the castle servants approached the table and poured red or white wine, as they wished, into four golden cups that stood next to elaborately decorated golden plates.

The double doors of the dining room opened and a guard informed those present that King Grandhold would be arriving at any moment. One of the castle servants was arranging the cutlery, plates and cups at the end of the table when King Grandhold entered the dining hall with a serious expression on his face. Gorathdin, Werlis, Aarl and Borlix started to rise, but King Grandhold gestured for them to remain seated. Before he sat down, he asked the servants to leave the hall. He took his seat and poured himself a little glass of red wine.

"I've made a decision," he revealed in a saddened voice.

Werlis, Gorathdin, Aarl and Borlix put down their cups and waited anxiously for King Grandhold to announce his decision.

"I, King Grandhold, Lord of Astinhod, will not allow the monks of the Order of the Dragon to be summoned to the castle to help the Princess of Astinhod," he spoke majestically and seriously.

Werlis, Borlix and Aarl's mouths fell open in astonishment.

"That can't be true," whispered Werlis to Gorathdin, who put his index finger to his mouth and stood up from his chair.

"Politics," Borlix grumbled.

Aarl poured himself another cup of wine, which he drank in one go and then put down on the table with a forceful gesture.

"My King! I will take Lythinda to the monks, and I speak here not only for myself, but also on behalf of my friends," Gorathdin said to King Grandhold and bowed slightly.

"Gorathdin of the Forest, Count of Regen, you are contradicting your King," King Grandhold replied with a calmness that Werlis, Aarl, and Borlix were not prepared for.

"But you are not contradicting your friend and a loving father," he added with a smile after a short pause. He got up from his chair, approached Gorathdin and gave him a friendly hug.

"We must keep the journey to the Templars of the Dragon as secret as possible. I have already sent for Army Commander Arkondir. I want him to accompany you with some trustworthy men," King Grandhold explained to Gorathdin.

"Army Commander Arkondir is my and Lythinda's friend. I agree with you completely. We can rely on him," Gorathdin confirmed.

King Grandhold sat back down in his chair. Werlis, Borlix and Aarl were delighted and toasted to their forthcoming mission.

"What about the captured thieves? We talked about me getting information," Aarl inquired.

At the same moment, the wings of the door opened and Army Commander Arkondir stepped into the dining hall.

"You sent for me?" asked the fully armored man of strong build, bowing low before the King.

"Sit down with us. Let's talk openly about what Gorathdin, his friends and I have planned," King Grandhold invited him and assigned him a place at the table.

Gorathdin greeted his friend with a firm and hearty handshake and told him of their secret plan to bring Lythinda to the Templars of the Dragon. He also let him in on his fear that Erwight of Entorbis might have something to do with all the incidents, which he briefly explained to him.

"I thought something similar. The problems with the thieves in Astinhod are increasing day by day. Master Drobal is untraceable, Lythinda lies in an unknown fever. You have left for Tawinn and two Abkether, a southerner and a dwarf are sitting at the King's table," stated Army Commander Arkondir and poured himself a cup of wine.

"I hope I can count on you, my friend," Gorathdin affirmed and raised his cup, ready to clink glasses.

"You know that you can always count on me, Gorathdin! And you too, of course, my King," replied the army commander, whereupon everyone clinked their glasses together.

"The plan has to be made and I need the right, trustworthy men for it. I'm afraid we won't be able to set off before tomorrow evening," Arkondir added.

"You're right. For one thing, we need to get more information about the Thieves' Guild, as I fear they have entered an alliance with Erwight of Entorbis that could be dangerous to us all, and for another, it's better to travel at night anyway to attract as little attention as possible," Gorathdin considered and looked at King Grandhold, waiting for his approval.

"So be it then. I am relying on you, friends," said King Grandhold.

Gorathdin introduced Werlis, Aarl and Borlix to Arkondir and told him about their plan to lock Aarl up with the two thieves who had been arrested last night.

"The best thing to do is arrest him with some of your men we can trust and present him to Count Laars. Think up a credible story for his offense," Gorathdin asked the army commander, who nodded.

"As time is pressing, we should start immediately. I will look after my daughter in the meantime. Good luck, friends," King Grandhold said goodbye.

Army Commander Arkondir had the guards outside the dining hall send for two of his men.

A short time later, a common soldier and an officer arrived in the dining room and were briefed by their commander on Aarl's planned arrest. Aarl took one last sip of wine from his cup and said goodbye to his friends.

"Take care of yourself, Aarl!" Werlis called after him as he was led away by Arkondir's men.

"I will see Count Laars at once and ask him to sentence Aarl immediately due to the seriousness of his offense," Arkondir said and hurriedly left the dining hall.

"Let's hope it all goes well," Borlix grumbled and yawned.

"I think we all need a little sleep after this night, friends," Gorathdin stated and, followed by Werlis and Borlix, went to the room prepared for them close to the King's bedchamber.

"I'll go and check on Lythinda. You don't have to wait for me," said Gorathdin and he closed the door.

Werlis and Borlix lay down on two of the beds and soon fell fast asleep.

Aarl's trial took place before the afternoon and, due to the seriousness of his offense, he was sentenced to five years in prison. The two court guards who took him out of the hall and led him into the underground vaults that lay between the marketplace and the merchants' quarter were not exactly gentle with Aarl. They kicked him several times and the shackles they had put on him were tightly tied around his wrists.

The dungeons of Astinhod were truly not a pleasant place. It was dark, damp and home to countless rats. The thick, black-gray stone walls were covered in fungus, and behind the heavy iron doors, Aarl could hear the prisoners' lamentations.

The officer in charge of the dungeon, who was a friend of Army Commander Arkondir, took Aarl from the two court guards and locked him up with the two thieves captured last night.

"So far, everything has gone as intended," Aarl thought as the heavy iron door closed behind him and locked from the outside. Aarl looked into the dark eyes of his fellow prisoners, who, like him, were from the south of Thir. Throughout the night, he tried to gain their trust by telling them one lie after another. His stories ranged from thieves from Irkaar who allied with Erwight of Entorbis to treasure-hunting tales he had concocted to inflame their greed.

"I'll be out of here by morning. I have friends who will bribe the guards," he told his fellow prisoners confidently and, with a promise to take them with him, he was able to elicit some important information from them, which was of course top secret. As dawn broke, the heavy iron door opened and Arkondir's friend entered, accompanied by four armed men.

"Someone tried to bribe the guards last night because of you. You'll end up in the darkest hole down here for this!" the officer shouted at Aarl and took him away.

The two thieves looked wistfully after their newfound friend, annoyed that their attempt to free themselves had failed.

"Hang on!" one of the Thirians called after him as the iron door was locked again.

Werlis, Gorathdin and Borlix, together with Army Commander Arkondir, had taken all the necessary precautions to get Lythinda out of the city unseen. When Aarl entered King Grandhold's bedchamber, happy that he had been able to coax some secrets out of the two thieves, he looked in amazement at Gorathdin, who was sitting on the edge of the bed next to the princess, wrapped in rags and holding her hand. Aarl's astonished expression changed to a grin when he saw Werlis and Borlix standing next to Army Commander Arkondir in minstrel clothes.

"Here, these are for you," Borlix said to Aarl and handed him a colorful costume that included a jester's cap.

Before Aarl could express his astonishment, Gorathdin explained his plan to him.

"We will hide Lythinda in the cart we will be traveling in. I am a beggar who has joined you, a group of traveling minstrels. You are on your way to Relvis, where you will perform your next play," Gorathdin explained, to which Aarl gave a short laugh.

"Is that the best you could come up with?" said Aarl with a grin as he pulled on the colorful costume.

"You'll have to get out of the city on your own. We'll meet at the abandoned tower. Take good care of yourselves and Lythinda,"

Army Commander Arkondir confirmed and looked expectantly at Aarl, who then reported on his night in the underground dungeon.

"The Thieves' Guild has split. One group is led by Massek, who has formed an alliance with Erwight of Entorbis, and the other, independent, is led by a certain Hattul. Hattul's guild is being pressured by Massek's guild to join the alliance. There have been many clashes between the two groups in recent days. I haven't been able to find out what Massek's guild, or rather Erwight of Entorbis, is up to," Aarl reported.

"You have done Astinhod, if not all of Wetherid, a great service, Aarl of Thir," praised King Grandhold, who stood next to Arkondir, and he shook his hand in thanks.

"As a citizen of Thir, I see it as my duty to uphold the good name of my people. I am ashamed that some of my countrymen break the law, steal, cheat and even murder. You don't have to thank me. I thank you for making it possible for me to help you," Aarl replied and bowed.

"I will immediately arrange for the city and castle guards to be doubled. As soon as Lythinda arrives at the Templars of the Dragon, I will return to Astinhod and personally take care of the two Thieves' Guild," promised Army Commander Arkondir to King Grandhold, who nodded in agreement.

"You should set off with your men, Arkondir. We'll meet at the abandoned tower around dawn, as we agreed," Gorathdin announced and asked him if the cart was ready.

"The cart is in front of the entrance to the castle garden. The guards know about it," Arkondir replied and wished his friend as well as Werlis, Aarl and Borlix good luck.

"I'll wait for you," he said and left the bedchamber in a hurry.

"Get your things. Meet me at the pavilion in the palace garden. I will take Lythinda there together with Palanmar and the lady-in-waiting," Gorathdin instructed his friends. Werlis, Aarl and Borlix said goodbye to King Grandhold and went to their room guised as minstrels to prepare to leave.

As the bells tolled midnight and the city lights went out, a small wooden cart pulled by a dwarf accompanied by two minstrels and a beggar rolled along the cobbled street from the castle garden gate towards the western city gate. Werlis, Gorathdin, Aarl and Borlix avoided speaking all the way to the craftsmen's quarter. A patrol of the city guard stopped the four briefly as they turned into the merchants' quarter, but when they realized they were a group of minstrels, they let the travelers move on. The creaking sound of the cart's wheels on the cobblestones worried Gorathdin as they approached the Shunned Quarter. His unease was not unfounded. Five shadows stepped out from behind a house wall and stood in their way.

"Which way?" came a deep, rough voice, whereupon Gorathdin took the precaution of pulling the hood of his cloak lower over his face so that his dark green eyes would not betray him.

"We are minstrels on our way to Relvis, where we have a performance tomorrow," replied Aarl.

"Minstrels, you say?" one of the men asked.

He walked closer to Aarl and looked at him suspiciously. Gorathdin sensed the danger and slowly reached under the furs in the cart with his right hand. He felt for the handle of his fire axe.

"We must move on, friends. Farewell," Borlix said and was just about to lift the two handles of the cart again when one of the five men walked closer to him.

"Anyone wandering through the dark alleyways of Astinhod this late must have something to hide. Go on, search the cart," ordered the tall man clad in brown leather.

"Who is the girl in the cart?" asked the man standing next to the cart in a Thirian dialect.

"She's my sister and very ill," Aarl lied, and when the tanned man began to look under the furs, Werlis plucked up his courage and bumped into him.

"How dare you? You're not the city guard. Let's move on now!" he demanded, trying to push him aside.

"The little one is apparently unaware of his size. I'll teach him a lesson," said the pushed man and he threw Werlis to the ground, whereupon Borlix struck the man in the stomach with a powerful punch.

Aarl grabbed one of them by the neck and pushed him to the ground, whereupon two others pounced on him. Gorathdin quickly drew his fire axe from under the furs in the cart but was struck down from behind at the same moment. Four more men attacked them from behind. Aarl and Borlix were able to incapacitate five of the nine who rushed at them, but when one of them grabbed Werlis and pressed a dagger to his throat, they gave up.

"Go on, take them to the abandoned smithy. You two go ahead and make sure that none of the city guards notice," ordered the man with the deep, gruff voice.

When Gorathdin regained consciousness, he was lying with his hands tied behind his back next to Princess Lythinda in the cart, which was rolling through several narrow and dark alleyways. He tried desperately to free his hands but was unable to do so and when one of the thieves noticed his attempts to free himself, he threatened him with a dagger. If one of the men had not mentioned the name Hattul, Aarl would not have had the idea that would get himself and his friends out of this situation.

"Wait a moment. I have something to tell you," Aarl began and stopped.

"Go on, keep moving, there's time before we get to Hattul," the man with the deep, rough voice replied and nudged Aarl to move on.

When they arrived at the abandoned smithy, two of them stayed behind with the cart and Princess Lythinda, while the others led Werlis, Gorathdin, Aarl and Borlix into the almost ruined smithy.

Hattul, the leader of Astinhod's independent thieves, sat at a table with four men and played dice. When the thieves had filled him in on their nightly find, Aarl spoke up and announced that they were working on behalf of Massek, or more precisely Erwight of Entorbis. To the horror of Werlis, Gorathdin and Borlix, he told him that the girl in the carriage was the Princess of Astinhod. But when he continued his story and informed Hattul that they had kidnapped Lythinda and that a reward of twenty-five thousand gold coins, which he was prepared to share with them, was waiting for them, his friends understood what he was getting at.

"Twenty-five thousand gold coins... that's a considerable amount. But who can guarantee that you will share it with us if we let you move on?" asked Hattul suspiciously.

"The only guarantee I can give you is my word as a thief," replied Aarl, who knew that honor was highly valued among thieves.

Hattul thought for some time about Aarl's suggestion to share the reward with him. Werlis, Gorathdin and Borlix waited anxiously for an answer.

"What makes you so sure that we won't keep the princess and demand a ransom from the king or Massek?" Hattul probed, fixing Aarl with his gaze.

"If King Grandhold finds out that thieves from Astinhod have kidnapped his daughter, what do you think will happen to you?" Aarl countered confidently.

"And if you demand a ransom from Massek, your guild war will only get bloodier, believe me. So, if I were you, I'd prefer half the reward," Aarl said and sat down next to him at the table.

One of the thieves in the room was about to pull him up from the chair again, but Hattul ordered the man to let him go.

"Four of my men will accompany you to the drop-off point. I hope for your sake that everything you have said is true. You have given your honor as a thief and you know what that means if your story is not true," Hattul said to Aarl, making a quick, cutting motion at his throat with his thumb.

"You have my word as a thief. Let's set off so that we don't arrive too late at the Abandoned Tower, otherwise someone will get suspicious," Aarl affirmed.

He got up from the table and walked towards his friends with a wink.

"All right, then. Jarek, Kunt, Medis and Fengin will accompany you," Hattul announced and stood up.

"They'll be waiting for you at the old oak tree outside the eastern city gate," he added and accompanied them out in front of the smithy, where he looked inside the cart at Lythinda.

"What's wrong with her? Is she ill?" Hattul asked Aarl.

"She's just drugged. My friend, the elf here, is good with poisons," Aarl pointed at Gorathdin and grinned.

"We don't have much time before dawn breaks," Werlis whispered quietly to Gorathdin, who nodded as they walked towards the eastern city gate.

Gorathdin revealed himself to the gate guards, who had been briefed on their mission by Army Commander Arkondir. He then told them about the four thieves who were waiting for them by the old oak tree, just a few hundred paces from the gate. Together with three of the gate guards, they surprised Hattul's thieves, who were taken into custody by the gate guards. Gorathdin, Werlis, Aarl and Borlix hurried to the tower to get there before sunrise.

When they arrived at the crossroads, from which a narrow path led up a low hill to the tower, two of Astinhod's guards were already waiting for them. From a distance, they could see the fire in front of the gate-less entrance of the tower, in front of which Army Commander Arkondir was pacing back and forth, impatiently waiting for them.

They apologized for their delay and were about to inform Arkondir of the reasons for it when a throwing knife struck one of the knights' neck, causing him to collapse dead.

Completely taken by surprise, Arkondir ordered his men to draw their weapons, and Gorathdin, Aarl, Borlix and Werlis also prepared for battle. None of them had expected in the slightest that they would suddenly be attacked by more than twenty thieves from Massek's guild in this remote location.

A fierce, bloody battle broke out between the king's knights, the four friends and the thieves. The losses on both sides were heavy. Werlis was badly wounded by a throwing knife, and if it hadn't been for Gorathdin's modest healing skills, he would have died from the bleeding wound on his shoulder.

"Massek's guild must have more influential allies in Astinhod than I assumed. Only a few knew of our plan," Gorathdin said to Arkondir after he had laid the injured Werlis on the cart next to Lythinda.

"The thieves must be driven out of Astinhod once and for all," Arkondir demanded angrily as he gazed with a heavy heart at the bodies of his fallen men.

Vrenli in captivity

When Vrenli suddenly woke up in the night, he sensed that he was not alone. In the darkness around him, he heard the soft crackling of footsteps and a growl. When he saw that he was surrounded by wolves, he called desperately for Nagulaj. But instead of an answer, only the echo of his own voice reverberated through the cool night air. Nagulaj had disappeared without a trace or explanation. Slowly, the wolves tightened their circle around Vrenli. They thought they had an easy prey in front of them, but when Vrenli, armed with a short sword and a burning branch in his hand, jumped towards one of them and gave it a fatal blow, the rest moved away with their tails between their legs. Only the leader of the pack remained standing in front of Vrenli, baring his huge, sharp teeth as if to let him know that he was ready to fight if Vrenli attacked him. However, Vrenli was so upset that he paid no attention to the wolf's gesture but ran towards him and scorched his brown back fur with the burning branch.

Howling, the big-headed wolf lunged at Vrenli and bit him on the left forearm. Vrenli screamed and dropped the burning branch to the ground. Tormented by pain, he stared for a moment at the bleeding wound. This filled Vrenli with such rage that he forgot the fiery, cutting pain. He rammed the steel blade from Ib'Agier deep into the chest of the wolf that had bitten into his cloak.

A bloodcurdling scream echoed through the silence of the desert.

But before the wolf sank to the ground, dying, it struck Vrenli in the neck with its sharp claws and the last of its strength. Vrenli took a few steps back in pain. Three of the previously fleeing wolves turned back, growling, and circled their dead pack leader. Vrenli covered the bleeding wound on his neck with his injured left arm, which hurt like hell. With the shock of his injury, he remained standing for some time, watching the wolves, holding his short sword in his right hand, ready to fight. He knew that he would not survive another attack. But after several howls, with which the wolves testified to the death of their leader, they hurried out into the darkness.

The cold, night desert wind whipped sand into Vrenli's face and he began to freeze. He staggered to the fireplace, where he shivered and put some dried branches in the fire. With the last of his strength, he tore a piece of cloth from the bottom of his cloak and used it to bandage the wound on his forearm. He pressed the remaining hand-sized flaps of cloth to the bleeding scratches on his neck. He stared painfully into the waning flames of the small fire for some time before he finally lost consciousness.

"Come here, someone is lying over there!" an excited, deep voice sounded the next morning, followed by hoof beats in the sand.

Vrenli looked out from under his half-opened eyelids and directly into two dark brown eyes that belonged to a veiled face. He wanted to reach for his short sword, but a sharp pain prevented him from doing so.

"He's hurt!" the cloaked man shouted to a group of riders dressed in black, mounted on large white horses.

As two of the veiled riders led their steeds towards Vrenli, his eyes fell on their shimmering golden, curved, broad swords that were hung from their horses' saddles and almost his size. Vrenli tried to say something, but he was unable to utter a single sound. The fine dust of the desert sand had settled on his vocal cords. His throat was parched and burning like fire. He needed water, lots of water. Vrenli opened his mouth and stuck out his tongue, hoping that the tall strangers would understand his gesture.

The dark-eyed man kneeling in front of him called out to two of his companions in a language Vrenli could not understand but which sounded familiar. They seemed to be discussing whether they should take him with them or simply leave him to his fate in the scorching sun, injured and without water. Vrenli thought he understood that one of them was in favor of taking him with them, but the others didn't seem to like it very much because a heated discussion broke out.

The veiled men on the horses were apparently not at all interested in taking him with them. One after the other, they spat contemptuously from their horses into the desert sand next to Vrenli. Vrenli was frightened by the loud argument between the five tall desert men.

"I just want water," he thought and tried to clear his dusty throat by coughing.

It was almost midday and so hot that Vrenli was on the verge of losing consciousness again. With his last bit of strength, he pointed to the water bottle hanging from the saddle of the horse standing nearby.

"No water for you, little one," said the veiled man in the local language of Wetherid.

Vrenli briefly thought about trying to reach for the bottle, but lost consciousness again before he could make a move.

Two of the desert men dismounted from their horses and walked to the unconscious Abkether.

"If you absolutely want to take him with you, Alnugh, so be it, but if we are late for Balae's wedding as a result, you alone will take the blame. You know that Sheikh Nam Al Kabun doesn't like to wait," one of the two warned him.

"So, hurry up, search him for valuables and wet his lips or he'll die," Alnugh ordered the two men.

When one of them found the sack of gold coins that Vrenli had received from Rosenstrauch, the merchant in Abketh, and quickly tried to pocket it, Alnugh grabbed him firmly by the back of the neck.

"You won't want to embezzle anything, will you? Get out of here! Put the Abkether in the cart with the other slaves. Hurry up. We have to be in Kajir by tonight and I'll offer this little one to Sheikh Nam Al Kabun as a special attraction. My business sense has never let me down. You'll see, I have a nose for it. Which is more than I can say for you. You would have left him to the desert. You'll see, he'll certainly bring a hundred pieces of gold and two horses. Just let me do it," Alnugh said confidently to his four slave catchers and grinned.

With a loud crack of Alnugh's whip, the slave caravan continued its way to the city of Kajir for the wedding of Balae, the Black Pearl of the Desert, daughter of Nam Al Kabun, the Snake Sheikh, with a new slave named Vrenli.

It was scorching hot; the sun was at its zenith. Two of Vrenli's fellow prisoners in the barred cart begged the riders for water. One of the slave catchers then threw a half-filled bag of water through the bars of the cage.

"Divide it well, that's all there is," the veiled rider called out to them. A dark-skinned, muscular, bald man with an elaborately tattooed face reached for the water bag and slowly began to drink.

"That's enough! Pass the bag!" the slave catcher ordered from his horse.

The tattooed dark-skinned man put down the water bag and leaned over Vrenli, who was sitting against the rusty bars at the back of the cage, sweating, with his arm bandaged and his neck crusted with blood and opened his mouth.

"Here drink, little man. My name is Wahmubu," he introduced himself to Vrenli, who drank greedily from the water bag and

209

blinked his eyes to express his thanks to Wahmubu. Vrenli felt the water mixing with the fine dust of the desert sand in his throat. He began to rattle and cough and spat some of the water he had drunk, which had turned reddish-brown from the dust, onto the wooden floor of the barred cart.

"Thank you," croaked Vrenli.

"You need to drink slower, little man," Wahmubu warned and put the water bag to Vrenli's mouth again. Vrenli now took several small sips to clear his dusty throat. He thanked Wahmubu again, who passed the water bag to one of the other two prisoners.

"My name is Vrenli. Vrenli from Abketh," he spoke slowly and quietly. He was still unsure of his voice.

"Why are we locked in a cage?" Vrenli looked through the bars at the black-clad riders.

"This is a slave wagon," Wahmubu replied.

"A slave wagon? But I'm not a slave. I'm a free Abkether," stammered Vrenli, perplexed.

"You mean you were a free Abkether. Now you are a slave of Alnugh. He will sell you and you will serve a lizard creature for the rest of your life," explained Wahmubu.

"A what?" Vrenli looked at his counterpart with wide eyes.

"Later," whispered Wahmubu, noticing the observant look on the slave catcher's face as he rode alongside the cart.

As the heat became unbearable, Vrenli sat down on the other side of the cage, where the two other prisoners lamented their situation with the soft humming of a song, hoping to escape the scorching rays of the sun for a little while.

The four large wooden wheels of the cart rolled slowly through the fine desert sand. The weight of the cage and the people trapped inside often caused the wheels to sink halfway into the sand, whereupon the cart stopped. Alnugh's men had to get off their horses each time and help the two felty, brown-haired zarukks harnessed to the cart get the stuck wheels moving again. Two of the slave catchers grabbed the two long curved horns of the draught animals and drove them, while the other three pushed the cart.

Vrenli had no idea that they still had a long journey ahead of them through Desert of DeShadin's endless expanse. He looked through the rusty bars of the cage and could see a few snakes slithering through the hot desert sand. Scattered remains of dead animal bones and dried desert bushes were silent witnesses to the scarcity of water in the desert.

When the slave catchers complained to Alnugh about their slow progress, Wahmubu took the opportunity to tell Vrenli about his homeland.

"Two peoples live in Desert of DeShadin. The Scheddifer, in their capital Iseran, ruled by the great reformer Sheikh Neg El Bahi, who united the free nomadic tribes of the northern and eastern desert, and the Snake People, led by Sheikh Nam Al Kabun, in their capital Kajir in the south. We Scheddifer have always been at enmity with the snake people.

This dark brood, who worship the snake god Kajir, is half reptile and half human. They are creatures of darkness. Hundreds of our people were enslaved by them and later sacrificed to their god Kajir. But now, by uniting all the nomadic tribes, we will succeed in thwarting Sheikh Nam Al Kabun's sinister, selfish plan to make his people the ruling people of Desert of DeShadin. This is not the first time that a leader of the snake people has attempted to usurp absolute rule. But all attempts to take Iseran have always been fended off. Our belief in life, freedom and justice has always led us to victory.

This time, however, we don't just have to fight the scimitars and the poisonous thorns that grow from the elbows of these creatures and can kill a person with just one stab.

Sheikh Nam Al Kabun has learned from the failures of his predecessors and now uses all available means to promote the cult of the snake god Kajir. He has realized that fanatical belief can be a dangerous weapon. Cultists of the lizard creatures roamed Desert of DeShadin and converted many of the free nomads to their faith in recent years. Appointed by Sheikh Nam Al Kabun, Kajir's

211

converts do not shy away from atrocities. Using force of arms, torture and the threat of death, they forced many of my people to worship their god. They erected shrines populated by hundreds of poisonous snakes near nomadic settlements, in which huge statues of the image of Kajir stand. These stone buildings are called places of conversion, where dozens of nomads are thrown into the specially constructed snake pools. The hypnotic venom of the green-yellow snakes causes fear and guilt in those bitten and Kajir's converts tell them that only prayer and absolute obedience to their god will alleviate their fear and guilt.

Sheikh Nam Al Kabun has thus gathered an army of fanatical, obedient warriors around him, and if he feels they are numerous and strong enough, he will surely try to take the city of Iseran, which is the center of life in the northern and eastern Desert of DeShadin. The clear lake north of the city feeds the surrounding spice and tea fields, which are the only two trade goods of the inhabitants, who have not lived like nomads for many, many generations. They have forgotten how to survive in the dry, hot, water-scarce desert. If Sheikh Nam Al Kabun succeeds in capturing Iseran, he would destroy the prosperity they have achieved over hundreds of years in one swoop. Poverty, water shortages and the associated outbreak of disease could mean the end of half my people," Wahmubu, whose father led a nomadic Scheddifer tribe in the north, told in detail. Vrenli listened attentively despite his pain and the unbearable heat.

"What you told me sounds terrifying. I've never heard of a snake people before and for the life of me I can't imagine what such creatures look like," confessed Vrenli.

He felt compassion for Wahmubu and the Scheddifer people.

"Thank you for your compassion, little friend. A lizard creature, as we call these beings, is at least a head taller than a human. Its muscle structure is much more pronounced and its shimmering green cornea, which covers its entire body in scales, is difficult to injure. The most dangerous thing about it is the two poisonous thorns that grow from its elbows, followed by its speed and strength, which far surpasses that of a human. It can also get by with far less water than we can. Up to three weeks, which is also the reason why we never tried to destroy the city of Kajir. To lay siege to a desert city, you need water, little friend. Water for weeks, if not months," Wahmubu described as they drove south through the endless sea of sand.

Vrenli writhed in pain and thirst. The little water from earlier was nowhere near enough.

When Wahmubu noticed that Vrenli was about to lose consciousness, he began to sing a song, which the two other prisoners hummed along to. The song told the story of the nomads and their constant struggle for survival in the desert, of water shortages, failed harvests, bad and good sheikhs and their fight against the snake people. In the song, Wahmubu also sang about the current ruler of the Scheddifer, Sheikh Neg El Bahi. When his name was heard, one of the riders struck the bars with his scimitar.

"If I hear that cursed name again, I will kill one of you!" the slave catcher shouted into the cage.

He raised his whip and struck the bars a few times. One blow hit Wahmubu in the face. Blood oozed from a small cut on his right cheek, whereupon he stood up and began to tug at the bars with all his might.

"Open this damn cage door and fight like a man!" shouted Wahmubu, but the slave catcher had already ridden forward to Alnugh.

"I hate these guys. They are renegade, cowardly and despicable bandits. These traitors sell nomads to the snake people," Wahmubu declared and bent down to Vrenli, who was about to get rid of his cotton shirt and helped him. Wahmubu was still angry. He went to the front end of the cage and rattled the bars.

"Do you know what my tribe would do with one of your kind? Do you know?" Wahmubu shouted to the rider.

"You would be buried in the hot desert sand. Only your ugly head would stick out and the sun would be your executioner!" continued Wahmubu.

Wahmubu hit a sore spot in the slave catcher. He had no way of knowing that his brother actually suffered such a fate. The burly, black-robed, veiled rider led his horse back to the cage and with a skillful slash of his scimitar, he struck Wahmubu's left arm through the bars. Blood gushed from the wound, but Wahmubu did not cry out. He just smiled. One of the fellow dark-skinned prisoners quickly tore a piece of cloth from his white overgarment, which covered a thin white linen shirt and trousers, and used it to bandage Wahmubu's injured arm.

"You son of a zarukk!" Alnugh shouted at the slave catcher who inflicted the wound on Wahmubu's arm.

Alnugh pulled out his whip and struck him several times.

"What do you think an injured slave is worth? You freak of a vulture!" he thundered, bringing his whip down on the rider once more.

The slave catcher cried out in pain.

"By Kajir! It's just a shabby slave," he defended himself and spat into the cage.

"What do you mean, shabby slave?" Alnugh wanted to know.

But all he got in response was an annoyed look.

"You fool. This is the son of a nomadic sheikh who will not send his warriors to Iseran if he cares about his son's life. Sheikh Nam Al Kabun will shower me, I mean us, with gold," Alnugh laughed and looked at Wahmubu, who was standing at the bars.

"My father will not allow himself to be blackmailed by Sheikh Nam Al Kabun!" Wahmubu shouted to them.

"That remains to be seen," Alnugh replied, grinning maliciously.

"Iseran will fall and the alliance between the snake people and Erwight of Entorbis will make Sheikh Nam Al Kabun even more powerful. Soon his power will extend beyond the borders of Desert of DeShadin. And for us, that means many new slaves and much more gold. Am I right, Alnugh?" one of Alnugh's five riders spoke up.

"Shut up, you son of a zarukk. No one shall know about the alliance!" Alnugh shouted and cracked his whip at him.

"But they can't tell anyone," defended the slave catcher, who, before he joined Alnugh, had been a good-for-nothing worker in the spice fields around Iseran.

When Vrenli heard the name Erwight of Entorbis, his ears pricked up. He mustered all his strength and crawled closer to the front bars to hear more of the conversation. However, they only discussed the gold they were hoping to get from Sheikh Nam Al Kabun. \ Erwight of Entorbis was no longer mentioned.

"What does Erwight of Entorbis have to do with the snake people?" wondered Vrenli, who hadn't followed the rest of the conversation apart from his name.

His thoughts were with Werlis, Gorathdin, Aarl and Borlix and he didn't feel particularly good about the grief he had surely caused his friends. He hoped that at least the healing potion was working and wished that he had never climbed into the golden bowl in Master Drobal's study to reach for the small light blue crystal.

Unexpectedly, the cart stopped and the slave catchers got off their horses. A heated discussion broke out between them. Vrenli couldn't see or hear everything, as they had moved a little away from the cage. He heard Alnugh's whip snap in the air several times and they shouted at each other in a Desert of DeShadin dialect.

Wahmubu moved closer to Vrenli.

"We have to try to get out of here. I have a plan," he whispered in Vrenli's ear.

"What are you up to?" Vrenli whispered back, his injured arm aching.

Wahmubu whispered his plan.

"Will you have the strength?" he asked Vrenli.

"I think I'll make it, but I'm sure I won't get any further than under the cart," Vrenli replied.

"That's enough! Wait there until it's all over," Wahmubu assured and put his arm on Vrenli's shoulder.

215

"If we make it to my tribe, you will be helped! Our shaman is the best healer in the whole desert," Wahmubu announced proudly.

He handed Vrenli the almost empty water bag.

"Here, take another sip and then stand by," said Wahmubu, signaling to the two other fellow prisoners sitting at the back of the cage and standing full height in front of them to cover their actions from the slave catchers loudly arguing.

"We can't make it, you have to help us, Wahmubu," one of them whispered.

Wahmubu did not react for a moment. He listened to the words of the slave catchers because he was sure that his father's name had been mentioned.

"Wahmubu! You have to help us," he whispered again. Wahmubu crouched down to the two of them and helped them with all his strength to bend the bars apart.

"Done," whispered Wahmubu and he signaled to Vrenli. The gap was just big enough for Vrenli, teeth clenched and close to fainting, to squeeze through and crawl behind the cart onto the hot desert sand. Wahmubu threw his cloak after him. Vrenli grabbed it, rolled under the shady cart and covered himself with it.

At the top of the cage, Wahmubu pressed his palms together as if he were holding an apple and blew into the small opening he left between his two thumbs. A strange, muffled but loud whistling sound was heard, which Wahmubu repeated several times.

Vrenli couldn't see what was going on above him in the cage. He wondered if it was a sign and was about to crawl out from under his cloak to the front of the zarukks when the whistling sound was answered. The whistling became much more powerful and the ground began to vibrate slightly. Frightened, Vrenli huddled under his cloak. The hot sand on which he was lying made the air under the cloak so hot that he neared unconsciousness.

Vrenli almost completely sweated out the little fluid he had left in his body.

The vibration became stronger and the whistling louder. Vrenli could no longer help himself; he had to lift one end of the cloak to be able to breathe. However, the vibration was so strong that he could not only feel it, but also hear it. The desert floor began to shake.

"Wambinis! Wambinis!" Vrenli heard the slave catchers shouting.

From his position, he could only see their feet running towards the cart, but he knew that they were no longer alone.

"Wahmubu's whistles brought help. Probably nomads who live nearby," he thought aloud.

Wanting to see who was coming to their aid, he crawled out from under the cloak and stuck his head out from under the front end of the cart next to the stinking, hairy legs of the zarukks. He hoped to see riders on camels or horses. Nomads who would chase the slave catchers away and free him, Wahmubu and the two other captives.

What he saw, however, were not nomads riding camels or horses. No, Vrenli saw a yellow-brown worm, twenty paces long and with a head the diameter of two ogre shields, sticking out of the desert sand in front of the cart. The green, pumpkin-sized, round eyes sparkled a poisonous green in the sunlight. The desert worm opened its mouth wide, revealing hundreds of sharp teeth, causing Vrenli to flinch and throw on his cloak.

Trembling, he lifted one end slightly and looked out at the monster, whose sinuous, elongated body had more segmented sections than he could count. The body of the worm-like creature was covered with several thumb-thick, overlapping protective plates. Vrenli did not move and hoped that the monster would not notice him. Up in the cage, Wahmubu gazed at the wambini with delight, knowing that few had survived an encounter with one of the monsters, which were older than most other creatures in the desert. It would have taken an experienced, intrepid group, especially one equipped for wambini hunting, to kill such a monster. Spears with long points, forged from a metal originating from Ib'Agier, were needed to slay one. Only a few tribes of the

217

desert hunted wambinis and sold their thick, durable skin, which was used to make tools, armor and weapons, far beyond the borders of DeShadin. Wahmubu's tribe was one of the few who traded this extremely rare and valuable material. The merchants of his tribe traveled as far as Irkaar and sometimes even Astinhod to buy the goods they needed with the proceeds of their sales. Wahmubu had learned the lure of the wambinis from their shaman as a child and he was lucky that one of these worms had been in their vicinity and answered the call.

Vrenli listened to the sounds of battle as the slavers attacked the worm, trembling with fear. He heard swords hitting its thick coat and arrows bouncing off the armored hull. A scream echoed through the hot desert. Vrenli hoped that the desert worm had caught one of the slave catchers. He plucked up all the courage he could muster and crawled out from under the cart. Fearfully, he looked between the legs of the zarukks, who were roaring with excitement, and watched as Alnugh went to the right side of the cart and took a spear from a device. With a shrill yell, he lunged at the enormous worm, which stretched several paces into the air and whose impressive length and stature dwarfed everything around it. Clutching the spear tightly with both hands, he drove the tip into one of the monster's protective plates. The worm hissed loudly, and in just a few moments it had retreated beneath the hot desert sand.

"By Kajir, how I hate these worms!" Alnugh cursed and plunged the spearhead, covered in a green secretion, into the hot desert sand.

He then instructed his men to place the battered man, covered in blood and with his abdomen pierced by the wambini's sharp teeth, on the cart.

The attempt to dress his wounds failed. The bleeding was too heavy and he was already spitting up a dark red liquid. He didn't have long to live.

"Leave me here," gasped the dying man.

Alnugh looked his men firmly in the eye. They all had the same opinion. Alnugh went to the cart and kissed the trembling, whimpering man on the forehead. As he embraced him, he plunged his dagger into the man's stomach and twisted it back and forth several times. A gurgling cry full of blood later, Alnugh had relieved him of his pain.

"Bury him!" Alnugh ordered his men as he wiped his dagger on the clothes of the deceased.

Alnugh then went to the back half of the cage and drove his right arm between the bars. He grabbed Wahmubu by the scruff of the neck and pressed his face against the metal bars with all his strength. Blood began to drip from Wahmubu's nose.

"Not a bad attempt to sic this beast on us! Did you think we couldn't handle it?" Alnugh yelled at Wahmubu.

Alnugh did not mention that he too had learned how to kill wambinis as a young warrior. He didn't mention it because deep in his heart he was still ashamed after all these years.

He was ashamed that he had been cast out of his tribe for killing a young tribal brother. Alnugh could still see the images of him plunging his dagger into Namin's back as if it were only yesterday. He heard the scream of his coveted Lamina as Namin sank to the ground, dead. The angry looks of the tribal elders who condemned him for this cowardly act still pierced him to this day. His love for Lamina and jealousy of Namin turned him into a cowardly murderer who disregarded the tribal laws and circumvented the fair fight for a woman with a despicable act.

Alnugh killed many, and enslaved entire tribes, but never once did he feel remorse for them. However, he still regretted the cowardly murder of his competitor. It wasn't about Lamina and it wasn't about Namin, it was about him. His pride suffered as a result. Alnugh, the bounty hunter, the master slave catcher, became a cowardly murderer out of love. It didn't suit him or the reputation he had built for himself. Alnugh, whose fighting style with the scimitar was unique, who never shied away from a duel, whose courage and fearlessness were known throughout Desert of DeShadin, was a cowardly murderer.

His ruthlessness towards the freedom of others knew no bounds. He enslaved nomads to gain an advantage for himself. On his own account or at the behest of various clients, he roamed the desert in search of strong workers, women and children. Alnugh's name passed through the desert as quickly and devastatingly as a sandstorm. Only a few years after he was cast out of his tribe, he was already feared throughout the land.

When he was younger, he gathered a retinue of thirty mounted men around him. Thieves, murderers and outlaws came from all parts of Wetherid to join him. They raided and plundered many settlements, even those that were well fortified. Under the regency of Sheikh Neg El Bahi, however, the desert gang was crushed. Alnugh and four of his men then entered the service of Nam Al Kabun, the snake sheikh.

Under his patronage, he was able to move freely through the territory that the snake people controlled and claimed for themselves. As the young Sheikh Nam Al Kabun pressed ahead with his plan to become the absolute ruler of Desert of DeShadin, the need for strong slaves to dig for ore in the eastern mountains grew. Ore that was needed to forge the weapons he needed for his army, the army of Kajir. Every three months, Alnugh was therefore personally sent by the sheikh through the realm of the snake people and the surrounding areas of the free nomads to enslave new, strong, young men.

The Order of the Dragon

Gorathdin led his friends and the king's knights, who were on their way to the Order of the Dragon, along a road through a small clearing bordered by a forest east of Astinhod to Ib'Agier, which was an eight-day journey. None of the travelers walking alongside the cart, where the sick Princess Lythinda and the astonished Werlis lay, were therefore surprised when, at dawn, they encountered a group of dwarves who, as it turned out, were merchants accompanied by several well-armed guards.

They greeted each other politely and Army Commander Arkondir asked the dwarves about possible incidents on their way. The highest-ranked guard escorting the merchants and their goods swung his axe through the air.

"There were no incidents on the way here. No one would be foolish enough to attack an armed dwarf caravan," he grumbled, to which the other dwarves agreed, deeply laughing.

"Certainly, Mister Dwarf, few could match you, but be on guard nonetheless! I think you know better than we do that something is going on in the east, in the realm of Erwight of Entorbis," replied Army Commander Arkondir.

When he mentioned the Dark Lord's name, the dwarves clutched the handles of their axes tighter.

"We have to move on," decided the dwarf, whereupon the two groups said goodbye to each other.

"These dwarves are too proud to admit their fear of Erwight of Entorbis," Army Commander Arkondir said to Gorathdin when the caravan was out of sight.

"Your pride is justified," Gorathdin objected.

"Don't forget that they have always guarded the border to the eastern realm. They fought countless battles at the gates of Ib'Agier and fortunately for Wetherid, they were able to stop many who tried to reach us, even if it was sometimes only with the help of the elves and humans. They had successfully prevented ogres, grey dwarves, mist elves and undead from invading here. For my part, I let the dwarves have their pride. They have earned it and I would not interpret the dwarves' gesture as fear. It is more a gesture that shows they are ready to face the enemy," Gorathdin said.

Army Commander Arkondir smiled.

"Gorathdin the Ranger, friend of all peoples," he said, saluting Gorathdin and then putting his arm around his shoulder in a friendly manner.

"You know that we rangers have respect for all living creatures and we only kill when we have to," Gorathdin reminded him.

221

Arkondir nodded.

"I wish we had more rangers in Wetherid. Like it had been before the Raging Hordes settled in our land," Arkondir said.

Gorathdin turned sadly to the neighboring forest. He looked through the trees, saw the animals that lived there and heard the calls of the hawks circling high above the treetops.

"I can't change it. No matter how much I wish I could. Mergoldin, the supreme druid of the Dark Forest, had forbidden us rangers to continue our fight against the Raging Hordes," Gorathdin said, thinking of the words of Mergoldin's druid.

"The battle for the forests is over. They have fought for their place!" sounded in his memory.

Gorathdin sighed with a heavy heart.

"We have to turn right here," Borlix grumbled and looked at the narrow path, which was truly not in good condition and led from the road into the adjacent northern forest.

Thorny plants and roots grew out of the forest floor and it was just wide enough for the cart to fit on. Werlis, who was conscious and suffering from his injuries, had to grit his teeth every time the two wheels of the cart being pulled by two men from Arkondir, rolled over a root or a stone. The days when this path was used were long gone.

The Templars, who dedicated their lives to prayer, meditation and healing, were largely self-sufficient. Only once or twice a year did the monks responsible for the supplies visit the city of Astinhod to buy the goods they needed and offer their healing potions in the marketplace. Since the founding of the Order, which dated back to the age when the era of the dragons had just come to an end, healing potions had been brewed, tinctures made and ointments mixed using ancient, secret knowledge.

The monks who worshipped a dragon, whose power and knowledge they had dedicated themselves to, were shunned and feared for many centuries. It was said that the only surviving dragon of Wetherid was located deep beneath the catacombs of their temple. It was said that this creature demanded human sacrifices in return for providing the Templars with his knowledge of healing, fire and frost magic. Many generations before King Grandhold's reign, the order was crushed by the then reigning King of Astinhod and the area around the temple was declared a forbidden zone. Only King Grandhold's great-grandfather allowed the Order to resume its activities in Wetherid after an application to reorganize had been submitted and reviewed by the royal house.

It was the time when the enemy in the east had almost completely destroyed Ib'Agier. There was a shortage of healers and healing potions, and on the condition that the catacombs deep beneath the temple were thoroughly searched, the Templars began their work again. After the enemies had been driven out of Fallgar and the healing potions of the Templars had given recovery and new strength to the many thousands of wounded warriors of the dwarves, elves, humans and smallfolk, the Order of the Dragon was once again respected and valued. Since that time, many from all parts of Wetherid had traveled to the Templars, asking them for help against diseases.

Aarl knew from stories in his village on the Southern Sea that the Templars brewed a potion that freed them from the plague that the underwater creatures from Moorgh brought in when they came into contact with the inhabitants of the village. The villagers had to catch one of the creatures and bring it to the Templars in the north so that it could be studied and a cure made.

Aarl knew from his own experience that this had not been easy. The creatures that lived in the underwater city in the Southern Sea between Desert of DeShadin and Horunguth Island were shy. If you did see one of them, which only a few fishermen did, you had to be lucky to escape with your life. The underwater creatures, or Moorgher as some called them, had a large fin instead of legs. They had the ability to secrete a corrosive secretion onto their victims, causing severe skin burns. Truly, no one wanted to fight these creatures whose element was water, even if they could survive on land for some time.

Aarl still vividly remembered his own encounter with a Moorgher. Even though it had been countless years since, the ugly scar on his right leg remained. He had pulled his fishing net out of the water, in which a creature resembling a fish had become entangled and splashed Aarl with a strange liquid.

"We'll be there soon," announced Borlix, who knew the way to the Templars of the Dragon best.

Once, when he still lived in Ib'Agier, he used this path many times to buy healing potions for the dwarves.

Borlix remembered. The Templars themselves did not come to the dwarven city after the great battle at Ib'Agier was fought, and that was because King Agnulix accused the Templars of hiding a dragon in Wetherid.

"My men down in the mines heard the dragon," Agnulix confronted the then leader of the Templar Order, who had gathered with the leaders of the peoples of Wetherid in the magnificent but dark stone halls of Ib'Agier.

Agnulix, the king of the dwarves, asked the then King of Astinhod to search the catacombs beneath the temple again, but this time in the presence of the dwarves. However, the King of Astinhod at the time refused and asked the dwarf king if he wanted to accuse the Astinhodians of not having done their job well enough.

"Bah, I'm not accusing you of anything," replied King Agnulix.

"But I'm sure there's a dragon somewhere under the temple. We dwarves would find it. The stony, dark underworld is our element, no one knows how to find their way underground like we do," he explained to the King of Astinhod, who, however, was firmly convinced that there were no dragons in Wetherid and thus ended the conversation.

King Agnulix turned his attention to Ib'Agier's fortification plans and other political issues and never said another word about the alleged dragon.

Borlix looked up at the sky. It was already afternoon and Army Commander Arkondir instructed four of his men to ride ahead and report to Brother Transmudin at the temple.

"I hope the Templars can help Lythinda," Gorathdin murmured as he looked at the four horsemen riding along the path.

Aarl, who was still walking alongside Werlis' cart, urged the group to hurry, as Werlis' condition had deteriorated.

The cart picked up speed and rocked on the stony, rooted path. The travelers stepped out of the forest into a clearing where there was a large temple, which they approached quickly. Brother Transmudin and four of his brothers were already waiting at the large, curved entrance gate. Werlis slowly raised his head and was startled when he saw the Templars dressed in purple robes. The image of a fire-breathing dragon at chest height on the robes had a menacing effect on him.

But when Brother Transmudin pulled back his hood to reveal the face of a bearded and gently smiling old man, Werlis calmed again.

He let his gaze wander around him. A high stone wall, completely overgrown with ivy, lay protectively around the temple and the large garden, in which a wide variety of magnificent plants and trees grew, giving it a paradisiacal appearance. The actual temple, located in the middle of the complex, was built from white and black marble stone. Thick, sturdy pillars supported the semi-circular metal dome that covered the temple, which was open in all directions. The sunlight that reflected off the dome blinded Werlis and he could not tell whether it was gold, silver or another metal. Not far from the temple stood two elongated buildings with straight roofs, which served as sleeping, dining, prayer and study rooms for the fifty or so Templars.

At the behest of Brother Transmudin, two of Arkondir's men pulled the cart through the garden to the temple. Arkondir took a look at the sick Princess Lythinda and the injured Werlis.

After Gorathdin had informed Brother Transmudin of Lythinda's condition, Arkondir called his men to him.

"Secure the entrance gate. Don't let anyone in or out without informing me first. Thondir and Fendalis, you patrol along the wall!" Arkondir instructed his men.

Everyone nodded in agreement, saluted and went to their posts.

Gorathdin, Borlix and Aarl told Brother Transmudin about the current situation in Astinhod, the events on the way to the temple and Werlis' injuries from the throwing knife.

"We will do our utmost to help the princess and the Abkether," Brother Transmudin promised and called one of his brothers to him, who was spraying the crystal roses from the Ice Mountains in the temple garden with a freezing tincture; a necessary measure that made it possible for these flowers to thrive in the temple garden. He asked him to let the kitchen know that they had guests.

Werlis, lying badly injured in the cart in front of the steps at the temple, looked at a huge dragon statue carved out of black stone, in front of which stood a white marble altar. Four monks walked down the steps, carefully lifted Princess Lythinda and Werlis out of the cart and laid them gently side by side on the altar. Gorathdin, Aarl, Borlix, Army Commander Arkondir and Brother Transmudin arrived at the temple just as the four monks stood praying around the altar. They were preparing for the ritual of the dragon to receive the necessary knowledge about the illness and injury so that they could create a suitable cure. Another ten monks in purple robes slowly walked up the steps of the temple and lit the torches around the dragon statue. One of them sprinkled a mixture of herbs into the four braziers, which were aligned with the cardinal points around the statue.

Brother Transmudin asked Gorathdin and his friends to leave the temple and eat in the dining hall in the meantime. The four of them took one last look at Princess Lythinda and Werlis. They then followed a monk into a building across the temple. After walking through several narrow, dark corridors, the monk opened a heavy wooden door and entered the simply furnished, gray dining hall dimly lit by three oil lamps.

Gorathdin, Aarl, Borlix and Army Commander Arkondir sat down at the long, heavy oak table, that could seat at least fifty people. The monk poured wine from a simple clay jug into four of the wooden mugs on the table and then went into the adjoining kitchen.

"I hope they can find out what illness Lythinda is suffering from," Gorathdin spoke to the assembled group.

"I'm sure they can heal Werlis' wounds. I've seen worse beaten men who've been brought back to health by the monks," said Borlix and took a big sip from his mug.

"Let's hope for the best for Princess Lythinda and Werlis," said Aarl, inviting his friends to toast.

The monk returned from the kitchen with a large pot of soup, which he placed on the table in front of the friends. He wished them a blessed meal and departed. While the four of them feasted on the watery soup, Brother Transmudin examined Princess Lythinda and Werlis in detail in the temple. With the help of his two most experienced brothers, he carefully began to undress the princess and applied gentle pressure to various parts of her body to localize her ailments. The monks praying around the dragon statue began to sing a song in a long-forgotten language.

Omnigo darus etner ebig Omnigo darus,
Hanem karuus menhig narus lasmoor.
Ibig inerisus Omnigo darus maslaanus.

Omnigo darus etner ebig Omnigo darus,
karaam optis menhag darus kolarus magnarus.
Ibig inerisus menhig narus lasmoor.

Omnigo darus etner ebig Omnigo darus,
aneruus kamhani maslaanus inberi.
Ibig inerisus Omnigo darus maslaanus.

The smoke from the braziers grew thicker and spread around the statue. A sweet scent tempted Werlis to fall asleep. He felt a hot breath on his body and the sweet smell turned into a corrosive stench that filled his lungs. Werlis' breath caught. He began to rattle. The hot breath became more and more unbearable and when he heard a loud hissing sound, he opened his eyelids and looked into two large, poisonous green glowing eyes.

The smoke around Werlis cleared and he saw the huge, shimmering silver-white head of the dragon Omnigo, who was as old as Wetherid itself. He belonged to the race of silver dragons, masters of fire and frost. Werlis' eyes, which were rolling back, flew open and he lost consciousness for a while. When Gorathdin, Aarl, Borlix and Army Commander Arkondir were ordered by Brother Transmudin to make their way to the altar, Werlis awoke from his swoon.

He opened his eyes and looked at his naked upper body. The monks had removed his bandages and he noticed his wound had stopped bleeding. A dried crust had formed over it and there was a stench of burnt skin in the air. Werlis was still in pain, but it had lost much of its intensity.

"Thank goodness. I feared for his life!" said Aarl with relief when he and the others arrived at the altar and found Werlis, still wondering about his recovery, sitting upright.

Gorathdin supported him as he descended from the altar.

"What about Princess Lythinda?" Gorathdin asked immediately when Werlis was back on the ground.

Brother Transmudin then regretfully explained to those present that it was not possible for them to help the princess.

"I assume it's magic and not a disease," the old monk assumed.

"Magic?" asked Borlix, who was just tall enough to peer out over the altar.

"I'm afraid it's a spell and it's not in our power to break it. We are healers, not magicians. You must take Princess Lythinda to Horunguth Island. She can most likely be helped there, but I fear for her condition. The fever has not risen, but we have not been able to bring it down either and I am worried that she will not survive the long journey in one piece," warned Brother Transmudin.

A disheveled, white-haired monk, who had taken part in the ritual and was apparently also the eldest of the ten kneeling around the dragon statue, pointed Brother Transmudin to the library, which was located under the temple in the catacombs. He was sure that a book could be found there that would shed light on the spell cast on Princess Lythinda.

"It's at least worth a try," said Brother Transmudin, nodding in agreement and instructing his friar to fetch the book in question from the library. The old, white-haired monk questioningly looked at Brother Transmudin as he stood in front of the eastern brazier.

"Go ahead. They are friends and besides, I assume they know about our library in the catacombs," Brother Transmudin replied to his look and smiled at Arkondir, who nodded.

The old monk turned the brazier to the right with all his modest strength. A mechanism was triggered and the huge dragon statue jerked with the sound of stone grinding against stone. An opening appeared in the floor and, upon closer inspection, a descent appeared.

A roughly hewn stone staircase led down into the darkness. Borlix's eyes began to sparkle. Everyone noticed his excitement. He clutched his right hand tightly around the handle of his axe.

"Is everything all right with you, Mr. Dwarf?" asked Brother Transmudin.

"Everything all right? How can everything be all right? I'm the first dwarf to stand in front of the entrance to the dragon's catacombs and you ask me if everything is alright," grumbled Borlix, still clutching the handle of his axe.

Brother Transmudin understood what Borlix meant, nodded to the old monk who was about to descend and invited Borlix to follow him into the catacombs. Borlix thanked Brother Transmudin, gave his friends one last look and followed the white-haired monk, who lit a torch with the brazier, down the steps.

The damp, slightly musty smell that caught Borlix's nose reminded him of his youth. More than one hundred and fifty years ago, he worked for two years in the mines of Ib'Agier, just like every other young dwarf of that age.

Of course, this vault could not be compared to the mines, not by a long shot, but the smell was almost the same. The old monk lit the oil-filled lamps attached to the walls with his torch and the vault was sparsely illuminated. Borlix used the light to examine the construction of the vault.

Since he had counted the steps as they descended, he estimated that they were a hundred paces below the temple. The vault was about eighteen paces high and an estimated seventy paces wide. The walls were made of small, square, smooth-cut stones. Borlix followed the old monk to the side opposite the descent, where there were three heavy metal gates. He immediately recognized that they were from Ib'Agier and immediately struck them with his axe.

"Good dwarf work, very sturdy," he said to the old monk, who was unlocking the right of the three gates.

Borlix followed him into a passageway that was just wide enough for the two of them to walk side by side. The smooth walls of the corridor were painted with pictures, but due to the lack of light, Borlix could not make out what the murals depicted. It was too dark, even for a dwarf. It was only when the old monk kept walking quickly along the corridor that Borlix could occasionally make out the images of dragons in the light of the glowing torch. He saw a red dragon at the entrance of the corridor and a black one roughly halfway through. The dwarves knew about the red and black dragons, many of their legends and songs were about them and the treasures they guarded in their caves.

The two had now reached the end of the corridor and a thick door, this time made of fine wood, blocked their way. The old monk knocked on it with his fist.

"Good work, just the right material to keep the climate in the room constant," he said jokingly.

"But I'm not sure if this door could withstand my axe," Borlix added, gripping the handle of his axe.

The old monk looked up anxiously and wondered for a moment whether Borlix might want to seriously try, so he quickly pulled out a key and hastily inserted it into the lock. Three turns later, he opened the door and stepped inside. Borlix followed him. The air was very dry and the room was already lit up. Borlix immediately noticed the special construction. The room was not roughly walled, but the ceiling, floor and walls were covered with a strangely shimmering metal, its uniqueness catching Borlix's attention.

"I've never seen metal like this before and how is it even possible to cover the walls with it?" Borlix marveled.

However, the old monk just shrugged his shoulders and explained to him that this room had been built long before his time and that he did not know how it was possible. He walked purposefully towards one of the many bookshelves made of fine wood that reached up to the ceiling on all four walls. Filled with hundreds of books from all eras and regions, written in various languages, this library was probably one of the most extensive in the whole of Wetherid. The old monk slowly climbed a ladder and carefully took a book with a thick leather cover from the shelf.

"This is it. Light and Shadow," he revealed and climbed back down the ladder, showing Borlix the book.

They then left the library. On the way back, Borlix asked the old monk about the images of the dragons on the catacomb walls, whereupon he explained to him briefly and succinctly that this was the legend of the Last Battle of the Dragons and walked quickly back to the ascent. Werlis, Gorathdin, Aarl, Army Commander Arkondir and Brother Transmudin were still standing around the altar where Princess Lythinda lay.

"I hope you were able to satisfy your curiosity, Mr. Dwarf?" asked Brother Transmudin with a smile.

"You have a nice little cave here," Borlix replied jokingly. The old monk placed the book on the altar and turned to a page.

"Here it is. Read it for yourself," the old monk urged them, forgetting that the book was written in an ancient language of Fallgar.

Brother Transmudin was well aware of this, which is why he translated what was written and tried to explain it at the same time.

"It says here that shadow mages of the seventh level can seize a person with the help of a shifter and banish their soul from our world. It is also written that, depending on how hard the person fights against this spell, it can lead to fever, skin discoloration and even complete paralysis of the body. However, the physical reactions can be cured with the help of a potion whose main ingredient is a ground horn of the horned bear," Brother Transmudin translated to those present.

"Here is the exact recipe," explained the old monk, pointing to the incomprehensible characters at the bottom of the page.

"I think I have everything in stock except for the ground horn. But I've never heard of a horned bear, let alone seen its horn ground up," he confessed to Brother Transmudin, who was also stumped.

Gorathdin's eyes gazed at the dragon statue in the center of the temple.

"The only horned bear I've ever heard of lived in the Dark Forest. Mergoldin, the Highest Druid, had told a group of young rangers and me one evening as we sat around a fire how he lost his left eye. To cut a long story short, he was fighting a hornbear and he sounded very serious when he said that it was a dangerous opponent," Gorathdin shared his memory.

"We have to take a chance," decided Aarl.

"The three of us will manage," Borlix agreed optimistically.

However, Gorathdin told them that it was not possible for them to come with him.

"You are not rangers; you are not allowed to enter the Dark Forest. Besides, it's too dangerous. I will go alone. You must guard Princess Lythinda and keep an eye on Werlis. He hasn't regained his strength yet," said Gorathdin.

Werlis looked into Gorathdin's dark green eyes, saddened that he could not help him.

Aarl and Borlix offered a few more arguments to travel to the Dark Forest, but deep down they knew that Gorathdin had already made up his mind.

In the meantime, Brother Transmudin instructed his brethren to take Princess Lythinda to his room. Army Commander Arkondir, who had inspected his men while Borlix had been in the catacombs, said goodbye to Gorathdin and went to his officer in the dining hall to discuss a guard plan that would last several days.

"I will leave immediately," Gorathdin announced.

"I wish you good luck, Gorathdin of the Forest. May Omnigo watch over you," Brother Transmudin blessed Gorathdin and squeezed his hands.

Accompanied by Borlix and Werlis, who was supported by Aarl, Gorathdin went to the room assigned to them and prepared himself for his task. There was a knock on the door and Brother Transmudin entered the room. He wished Gorathdin well once again and handed him a flask.

"The liquid freezes wounds in seconds and stops the bleeding. Be careful not to accidentally freeze your joints or bones and remember that you will have a day at the latest to treat the wound," explained Brother Transmudin.

Gorathdin took the bottle and thanked him. He stroked Werlis' hair, who had already fallen asleep on his bed, placed his hands on Aarl and Borlix's shoulders and said goodbye.

"Take good care of Lythinda and Werlis. I hope to be back in a few days," he said and closed the door behind him.

"I wish we could go with him," Borlix sighed and dropped onto his bed in disappointment.

Aarl left the room with Brother Transmudin and followed him into the dining room to question him over a cup of wine about the Moorghers and the plague that had broken out in his village long ago.

Balae's wedding

"The little one has escaped!" shouted one of the slave catchers, running to his horse about to mount when Alnugh stopped him.

"Wait, you son of a zarukk!" Alnugh shouted at him.

"Do you see any tracks leading away from the cart?" Alnugh pointed to the desert floor with his hand.

"Look under the cart!" Alnugh instructed him, whereupon the slave catcher took out his whip and struck it several times under the cart.

"Ow! Damn!" Vrenli gasped.

The slave catcher knelt in the hot, dry sand and bent under the cart.

"Come out, you dwarf, or do I have to get you?" the slave catcher roared, glaring angrily at Vrenli, who crawled out from under the cart.

Alnugh grabbed Vrenli by the back of the neck, lifted him up and asked the other slave catchers what kind of strange dwarf he was.

"A dwarf without an axe, shield or beard. Must be a dwarf child," Alnugh remarked, mocking the slave catcher who was still kneeling in front of the cart.

"Children are paid decently," remarked the man kneeling in the sand.

"It's not a dwarf and it's not a child. The sun must have scorched your mind. It's an Abkether from the north," Alnugh corrected and slapped the kneeling man on the back of the head.

"Lock him up again. Straighten the bars and put the slaves in chains!" Alnugh ordered his men, who immediately followed his instructions.

"Pull!" shouted Alnugh, and the cart set off with a violent lurch.

He urged the zarukks and his men to make faster progress, as they had lost valuable time. Sheikh Nam Al Kabun did not appreciate tardiness, especially when it came to his daughter's wedding and the wedding gift might not arrive on time. Vrenli writhed in pain. The effort of crawling under the cart and out again had caused the wound on his arm to open again. When Wahmubu noticed that Vrenli's bandage was turning red, he called for Alnugh and drew his attention to Vrenli's condition. Alnugh threw a bag of water and a black cloth that he had pulled out of his saddlebag into the cage.

"Looks like the little one won't make it much longer. Try your best to keep him alive," Alnugh shouted to Wahmubu, who picked up the cloth and moistened it with water.

He worriedly looked at Vrenli, who was not in good condition, and pressed the damp cloth to his sweating forehead. Wahmubu feared that the wound on Vrenli's arm had become infected. Vrenli urgently needed something for the pain, fresh bandages and, above all, shade. With his eyelids half open, Vrenli whimpered in pain and gazed into the bright, blazing hot sun. There was not a breath of air to be felt and the sun's powerful rays burned his skin. Wahmubu picked up Vrenli's cloak and fastened it to the top bars of the cage, leaving the back right corner slightly shaded.

Vrenli looked at Wahmubu standing in front of him and providing extra shade with relief. Wahmubu was enormous, a whole head taller than Alnugh. He had a very muscular body and his large, dark brown eyes radiated warmth. Despite the predicament he was in, he stood unbroken in the cage and gazed out at the sea of reddish-brown sand without complaint. Vrenli did not know that Wahmubu was a desert prince and the son of Sheikh Ali Nam Menhi, the leader of the northern tribes.

"In the future, a prince will serve my daughter," Sheikh Nam Al Kabun had announced with a laugh when he instructed Alnugh to kidnap Wahmubu as a wedding gift for Balae.

The cart now rolled slowly up a high dune. Wahmubu reached for the bars to hold on to. The rising, light wind caressed Vrenli's face and cooled him down a bit, but it also blew the fine desert sand into the cage. Vrenli coughed and tried with great effort to turn away from the wind. Wahmubu, observing this, opened the silk scarf he was wearing around his neck and fastened it to Vrenli so his nose and mouth were protected from the dusty, blowing sand.

"Close your eyes," Wahmubu instructed him and closed his own, kneeling on the floor of the cage and lowering his head. He remained in this position until they had crossed the dune and the wind had stopped.

When they reached the other side, Vrenli could already make out a small oasis at the foot of the dune from a distance. Five or six palm trees and a few bushes surrounded the shallow waterhole. When they arrived, Alnugh called for a rest. The cart came to a jerky halt. The slave catchers led their horses and the two zarukks to the waterhole. Wahmubu bent down to Vrenli and carefully opened the bandage on his arm. When he saw the slightly crusted and badly inflamed wound, he called for Alnugh.

"I have to wash out his wound and put a new bandage on him or he will die," Wahmubu said firmly to Alnugh, who thought for a moment and then agreed.

"Hurry up with that. And if you get any ideas, well, my men will not leave your side. They will kill anyone who tries to escape," Alnugh replied with a serious look, sitting down in the shade under a palm tree and thinking about the gold he would receive from Sheikh Nam Al Kabun for the wedding gift and the four slaves.

He stuffed his pipe and enjoyed it in many small, puffing breaths.

One of Alnugh's men opened the cage and freed the prisoners from their chains. With the help of one of the two fellow prisoners, Wahmubu carefully lifted Vrenli out of the cart and gently carried him to the waterhole. From the conversation between Wahmubu and the two fellow prisoners, Vrenli gathered that they were two of Wahmubu's servants.

"Give him a drink and wash his bandages well," Wahmubu instructed the two of them and walked purposefully to one of the bushes growing around the waterhole.

He plucked a handful of the green leaves and some of the star-shaped, yellow flowers then went back to the waterhole. Wahmubu carefully washed Vrenli's wounds with the cool, clear water.

"You have to be strong now," said Wahmubu.

Vrenli blinked and nodded. Wahmubu put the desert bush flowers in his mouth and began to chew on them until they became a paste. He carefully smeared this pulp on Vrenli's wound and the crusty scratch on his neck. Vrenli cried out, his eyes bulging as he lost consciousness. After Wahmubu had moistened the leaves with water and placed them on the wounds, his two servants bandaged Vrenli's injuries on his arm and neck.

Alnugh's men, who had been watching everything closely, accompanied the four back to the cart and chained them together again. Alnugh, who had finished smoking his pipe, gave the signal to set off.

Once they had left the oasis behind them, it was not long before they reached the land of the snake people. They were now no more than three days' journey from the southern border of Desert of DeShadin. Alnugh and his men were visibly relieved, for they would arrive in the town of Kajir, named after the god worshipped by the snake people, towards evening. Wahmubu sat by the side of the unconscious Vrenli from midday until late afternoon, applying wet compresses until the water bag was empty. He and his servants refrained from drinking the whole way.

Dusk fell and the air cooled abruptly. The illuminated town of Kajir could be seen from afar. The cart was rolling along a low dune when Vrenli awoke from his unconsciousness. After less than eight hundred steps, they came to a wide road. By now it had become so cold that Vrenli began to shiver. Wahmubu removed the cloak from the bars and put it on Vrenli.

"I don't know how to thank you," murmured Vrenli, to which Wahmubu only smiled gently.

The cart rolled closer to the town; it was only less than four hundred steps to the city gate. Vrenli could now get a first impression of Kajir. The entire city was surrounded by a huge wall, with round, pointed towers lit by torches rising at regular intervals. High above the center of the city, he could see the huge golden dome of Sheikh Nam Al Kabun's palace. Music played and loud voices called out Balae's name. They stopped in front of the city gate and as one of the five gatekeepers approached the cart, Vrenli froze at the sight. The hairless, scaly skin that shimmered turquoise in the light of the torches, the green, piercing reptilian eyes and the hissing sound the creature made sent a shiver down Vrenli's spine.

Alnugh exchanged a few words with the lizard creature in a language Vrenli didn't understand, whereupon the sturdy gate grille was pulled up and the cart slowly rolled underneath.

There atmosphere was festive in the torch-lit town. All its inhabitants and guests invited to Balae's wedding sang, danced and drank. Jugglers, fire-eaters and sword swallowers performed their skills in several places.

The cart rolled leisurely along the wide road leading to the palace as some of the lizard creatures that had become aware of the cart made hissing noises and provocatively brushed the bars of the cage with their poisonous thorns. As a result, Alnugh had difficulty making the necessary space for himself, his men and the cart.

"How I hate this brood," Vrenli heard Alnugh say aloud to himself and wondered why he was carrying out orders for them anyway.

It took them some time to get through the celebrating crowd. When the cart finally rolled up in front of the palace, Alnugh and his men were asked by one of the palace guards to get off their horses. Alnugh and the lizard creature, which hissed frequently, had a tense conversation. Alnugh then approached the cart and pointed through the bars at Wahmubu. The lizard creature, armed with a large scimitar and a round shield, hissed loudly, formed its pointed mouth into a smile and snaked out the thin, forked tip of its tongue.

"Finally, this beast has understood me," Alnugh muttered to himself and instructed his men to take the captured slaves out of the cage.

Two of the slave catchers climbed into the cage, removed the prisoners' chains and lifted the injured Vrenli out. Wahmubu and his two servants refused to leave the cage at first, but when one of Alnugh's men struck them with his whip, they complied. The hissing, large lizard creature approached Wahmubu and placed a metal ring attached to a chain around his neck.

Alnugh grabbed the chain and pulled Wahmubu like a dog up the stairs leading into the palace. Two of his men followed them with Wahmubu's servants and Vrenli. The lizard creature accompanying them instructed the slave catcher carrying Vrenli to take him to a small outbuilding to the right of the palace.

"Your henchmen must be waiting here," hissed the lizard creature in a broken language of Wetherid.

Two more armed creatures stepped out of the high archway leading into the main building of the palace and approached Wahmubu's servants. Hissing and wagging their tongues, they circled the two frightened desert men and finally urged them to move on with the tips of their scimitars, which they thrust lightly into their backs, and led them into the slave quarters.

Alnugh, leading Wahmubu by the chain, entered the snake sheikh's palace and followed the long corridor leading to the banquet hall, where loud laughter and music could be heard.

As Wahmubu stepped through the large, round archway that led into the banquet hall, filled with hundreds of guests and an exuberant atmosphere, two lizard creatures clad in magnificent robes approached and looked at him with a hiss and congratulated Alnugh, who smiled smugly in response. He yanked on Wahmubu's chain, striding towards the guests invited from all parts of Wetherid and Fallgar and trying to look dangerous to live up to his reputation. Massek, the leader of the Thieves' Guild in Astinhod, staggered drunkenly towards Alnugh and greeted him warmly. Sheikh Nam Al Kabun was standing with a big, fat, ugly ogre at the banquet table set up in the center of the hall, chatting with him about the tender and tasty crocodile meat, when he was informed of Alnugh's arrival by one of his guards. Sheikh Nam Al Kabun looked towards the entrance of the hall and with a wave of his hand, he indicated to Alnugh that he should come to the table. Alnugh yanked the chain.

"Come this way, your new master wants to see you," Alnugh instructed Wahmubu and made his way through the dancing and drinking guests.

The ogre standing at the table blew a foul-smelling breath in Wahmubu's face.

Sheikh Nam Al Kabun proudly patted Alnugh on the shoulder with his scaly, claw-tipped hand and paid tribute to him for the successful mission.

"At your service, Sheikh Nam Al Kabun," Alnugh replied and immediately began to haggle with the sheikh over his payment.

As Alnugh had lost one of his men, he demanded an additional fifty gold pieces and, as the sheikh was in a good mood, he threw Alnugh a bag of gold coins, whereupon Alnugh handed him the chain on which Wahmubu was tied. Sheikh Nam Al Kabun proudly led the desert prince to the center of the banquet hall and asked the guests to be quiet.

"Balae, Black Pearl of the Desert," he began to speak solemnly.

"Today is a special day for you and for all of us. And a special day requires a special gift".

The sheikh yanked the chain and ordered Wahmubu to kneel before his daughter who was sitting next to her newlywed husband on a sumptuously decorated golden chair and accepting gifts from wedding guests. But Wahmubu had no intention of kneeling before any of the snake people.

He stood proudly and looked at the bride and groom with contempt. Sheikh Nam Al Kabun pulled harder on the chain. The ring on Wahmubu's neck pressed on his larynx. He rattled. But instead of kneeling down, Wahmubu spat on the ground in front of the bride and groom. Balae's husband, the commander of Kajir's army, stood up and walked towards Wahmubu. He looked at him sharply with his green reptilian eyes and made a threatening gesture with his hand. Wahmubu was not impressed.

Balae's husband's right elbow slowly approached Wahmubu's face and it didn't take a moment for the poisonous thorn to emerge.

"Kneel before your mistress, kneel before Kajir!" he hissed angrily. However, Wahmubu turned his gaze away from Balae and spat on the ground again, whereupon the strong, clawed fist of Balae's husband smashed into Wahmubu's stomach. He slumped to the ground, groaning.

"That's better," hissed the proud, burly army commander. Sheikh Nam Al Kabun clapped enthusiastically and began his speech all over again. Several praises to his daughter later, the snake sheikh paused briefly and raised his silver goblet.

"A desert prince will be your servant from now on!" he exclaimed, wishing the bride and groom all the best and ending his speech. The guests clapped with enthusiasm. The ogre grunted and threw a few gnawed crocodile bones at Wahmubu's legs.

Two guards stood Wahmubu up and led him to the two golden chairs where Balae and her husband were sitting. Wahmubu let his eyes wander around the hall. A group of gray dwarves approached the bride and groom and presented them with two boxes of dark iron ingots as a wedding gift.

To the right, behind the table, Wahmubu spotted two Moorgher refreshing themselves in a pool of water among the many celebrating lizard creatures. Four emissaries of the Undead City were conversing with humans clad in black robes, bearing the Entorbis crest. On the north side of the banquet hall, in a dark corner, a group of mist elves sat on soft, precious carpets, smoking a huge, glass water pipe together and gazing with their fiery eyes at three burly orcs who were getting drunk at the table, roaring with two warriors of the Raging Hordes.

In the meantime, the group of gray dwarves had made their way to the slave dancers and greedily watched the rhythmic movements of the half-naked desert women. Wahmubu heard one of the drunken barbarians complaining to a slave servant about the food. The burly man tried desperately to explain to the frightened Scheddifer his desire for a suckling pig, lamb or a grilled bear. In

241

his state of intoxication, the barbarian mixed the language of the northland with that of Wetherid. The desert man could not understand the barbarian and handed him a plate of boiled crocodile eggs, whereupon the barbarian lost his patience and knocked the desert man to the ground with a heavy blow from his right hand. The wedding guests laughed out loud and Sheikh Nam Al Kabun, who had seen this out of the corner of his eye, clapped enthusiastically. The servant crawled on all fours to the sheikh's feet.

"You'd better look after my guests!" he hissed and gave him a kick.

Wahmubu tried to free himself from the firm grip of the two guards to help the Scheddifer writhing on the ground and looking at him with pleading eyes. One of them immediately yanked on Wahmubu's chain. The prostrate desert man slowly rose to his feet and, bent over, disappeared into the crowd of revelers.

The guests suddenly screamed and hissed loudly. A huge barbarian gray wolf had torn itself away from its master and jumped onto the table. Scorpion soup, beetle salad with caterpillars, crocodile meat and stewed zarukk eyes were not to the wolf's taste. He growled into the crowd, looking for a victim he could kill and eat. Sheikh Nam Al Kabun grabbed an enslaved Scheddifer, who was serving the guests at the south end of the table, by the neck and dragged him to the north end, where he threw him to the ground in front of the wolf.

"No one should go hungry at my daughter's wedding party!" the sheikh shouted and plunged his poison thorn into the slave's neck.

The wolf leapt from the table onto the desert man twitching on the ground and began to maul him.

Tears welled up in Wahmubu's eyes when he saw a son of the desert lying dead on the ground, mauled by a wolf at a wedding celebration of the snake people. Balae, noticing Wahmubu's tears, slowly rose from her chair stroking the snake coiled around her neck. She walked towards Wahmubu.

"Your pity will be taken from you tomorrow, slave. When the sun is at its zenith, we will perform Kajir's ritual on you," hissed Balae, writhing around Wahmubu and stroking his shoulder and stomach muscles with her taloned fingers. Wahmubu knew of Kajir's ritual and grabbed Balae by the arm.

"You can enchant me, poison me or torture me, but you will never possess my soul!" Wahmubu shouted proudly.

Balae's groom stood up from his chair and knocked Wahmubu to the ground with the end of his scimitar. He then ordered two armed guards to take Wahmubu to the slave quarters.

The room, secured with a heavy metal door and bars on the windows, had around thirty beds lined up next to each other to the left and right of the narrow passageway. When Wahmubu regained consciousness, he saw one of his servants pressing a moistened cloth to his neck.

"The situation is pretty hopeless, Prince," whispered the servant.

"Where is Vrenli?" asked Wahmubu, letting his eyes wander around the room. His two servants then told him that Vrenli had been picked up by two lizard creatures and a man wrapped in a black cloak with lifeless-looking eyes and a black, diamond-shaped mark on his forehead.

"What do you think they intend to do with him, Prince?" asked the older of the two servants. Wahmubu remained silent.

"The description fits one of Erwight's shadow mages," Wahmubu thought.

He knew that this did not bode well.

"We must flee from here. We need a plan as soon as possible," said Wahmubu before briefly telling his servants what had happened in the banquet hall and that conversion to Kajir awaited them all.

"Check the door and the window for weak points," he instructed them, as he sat down on one of the beds and began to meditate.

Wahmubu forgot everything around him and in his mind's eye he saw Mahroo, his tribe's shaman, who had taught him the secrets of the desert and of life since his childhood. Wahmubu began a conversation with the spirit of Mahroo.

The escape

When one of the two lizard creatures accompanying Ornux grabbed Vrenli roughly under the arm and pulled him up, his encrusted wound broke open under the bandage and Vrenli lost consciousness due to the burning pain.

"You'd better watch out, you dolt!" complained Ornux, who was attending the wedding ceremony as an emissary of the shadow mages.

He slowly raised his hand in front of him and pointed at the lizard creature that carelessly pulled Vrenli up.

"Quaj!" shouted Ornux, whereupon a gray ray of shadow beamed from his bony, wrinkled fingertips at the lizard creature, knocking it to the ground.

"Another carelessness like that and the next one will be fatal! If the Abkether dies, we will never know why he was found in Desert of DeShadin, not far from this shaman-juggler," Ornux snorted angrily and instructed the two guards to carry Vrenli carefully into a chamber adjoining the banquet hall.

Sheikh Nam Al Kabun was already waiting for them in the presence of two Knights of Entorbis.

"I hope we get some information from the Abkether. I had to pay extra for him," Sheikh Nam Al Kabun said to Ornux as he, followed by the two guards carrying Vrenli, entered the semi-dark room.

"If his information is of importance to our lord, you will get ten times your stake back," replied one of Erwight's men.

Sheikh Nam Al Kabun hissed and with a flick of his wrist threw everything on the low table in the middle of the room to the floor.

The two lizard creatures laid the unconscious Vrenli on the sheikh's work table. Ornux took a step towards the table, raised his hand and let it slide slowly just above Vrenli's body from his head to his feet.

"He is close to dying," Ornux stated seriously and looked expectantly at Randulin, Erwight's chief emissary.

A silent nod of the head was the agreement that Vrenli should be healed.

Ornux was the only shadow mage who knew the art of healing and who also possessed the ability to transform into a crow, as he had defeated a druid in battle a long time ago and robbed him of his soul.

The mage placed his left hand on the black, diamond-shaped mark on his forehead and stretched out his open right hand over Vrenli's small body. A warm, forest-green light shone from his hand onto the open, inflamed wound, which soon began to close slowly. All that remained was an ugly black scar. Vrenli's eyelids twitched and he slowly opened his eyes, but when he saw the terrifying presence, he immediately wanted to close them again. Sheikh Nam Al Kabun's breath burned in Vrenli's throat as the sheikh bent over him, hissing. He had to cough.

"He's conscious again," hissed the snake sheikh.

"Come on, set him up!" Ornux instructed the two guards.

"Who are you and what do you want from me?" stammered Vrenli, overcome with fear.

He looked at the ugly, black scar on his forearm and was amazed that he no longer felt any pain.

"Who we are is not important," hissed the sheikh.

"Tell us your name and the place you came from. And what interests us most, what were you doing near this shaman?" demanded Randulin in an authoritative and frightening tone, walking closer to Vrenli.

Vrenli remained silent. But when Ornux ran his hand lightly over the black scar, a searing pain shot through Vrenli and he writhed. He began to speak.

"My name is Vrenli, Vrenli Hogmaunt, and I'm from Abketh!" he shouted, tormented by the searing pain.

"I don't know how I got here and I've never heard of a shaman," he lied to Randulin.

Silence filled the room. Those present took a few steps away from Vrenli.

"I'm sure he's lying," the sheikh whispered with a hiss and suggested having the Abkether converted to Kajir alongside the three Scheddifers, since he wouldn't be able lie under the influence of the snake venom.

"We'll question him again afterwards," Randulin agreed to Sheikh Nam Al Kabun's suggestion.

"We should go back to your daughter's wedding celebration so as not to arouse suspicion. As you know, the alliance with the gray dwarves, the mist elves and the Raging Hordes has not yet been decided. Erwight of Entorbis is very keen to do so, but there are still heated negotiations with the Raging Hordes about the division of land. They intend to take the Dark Forest, drive out Mergoldin and cut down the Druids' Tree of Life. In addition, the gray dwarves have not yet been granted the right to mine Ib'Agier's mines. The mist elves want to claim the Glorious Valley as their new home, but as we all know, powerful magical weapons can be made from the wood of the trees in the valley. All in all, we are still a long way from an outcome that satisfies all sides.

The alliance with the ogres, orcs, undead, Moorgher, the thieves from Astinhod and your people is sealed, but as for the others, I still advise caution. Our lord cannot do without the mines of Ib'Agier and the wood of the Glorious Valley. Supporting the barbarians in their fight with the rangers and druids would be too risky at the moment," Randulin explained to the sheikh, who nodded in agreement.

"Take the Abkether to the other slaves," the snake sheikh ordered the two palace guards and set off with Ornux and the four emissaries of Erwight of Entorbis to the banquet hall to rejoin the festivities.

Two guards opened the door to the slave quarters, where Wahmubu was still meditating on the bed next to his two servants. Vrenli was pushed onto one of the beds near the door. The guards hissed, locked the door and went back to their posts.

Vrenli got up from the bed, approached Wahmubu and wanted to tell him about the incident in Sheikh Nam Al Kabun's chamber, but one of the two servants told him not to disturb Wahmubu now.

Vrenli therefore lay down on the simple bed next to Wahmubu and thought about the events that had happened since he had been teleported from Master Drobal's Tower to the desert.

He wished he had never set out from his peaceful village of Abketh. He knew now that there was danger for all of Wetherid, that the Shadow Lord of Druhn had allies and was looking for more comrades-in-arms. He also thought of his grandfather.

"What would he do in my situation? Flee and return to Abketh and try to forget all the horrors?" Vrenli gazed fixedly at the clay-brown, brittle ceiling above him.

"Werlis! What will become of Werlis? I dragged him into all this. He thought he would go down in history if he helped Gorathdin bring the blossoms to Astinhod, but it seems we're facing a war against the peoples of Fallgar," Vrenli thought as despair welled up inside him.

He looked at Wahmubu, who was still in a deep state of meditation.

Wahmubu saw the shaman of his tribe in front of him, pouring water from a small clay bowl onto the sandy ground in front of his tent. Mahroo then began to draw something in the wet sand with a small, thin branch.

When he had finished his painting, Wahmubu recognized a city with four towers and in front of each tower was a desert worm.

Wahmubu understood what Mahroo was trying to tell him and woke up from his meditation.

"Thank the wise men and the Father, you're alive. What have they done to you, Vrenli? How is your wound?" asked Wahmubu, looking in amazement at the black scar on Vrenli's forearm.

"The fact that my wound was healed is pleasing, but the fact that my healer was a shadow mage from Fallgar is less pleasing," Vrenli sighed gloomily.

He and Wahmubu told each other everything that had happened since their separation, and they agreed that they had to flee as quickly as possible.

"We have to report to Iseran and Sheikh Nam El Bahi about what happened in Kajir," decided Wahmubu, who was visibly worried about Vrenli's stories.

"King Grandhold of Astinhod must also be informed," Vrenli remarked.

Wahmubu agreed, because it was also in his interest, as neither his tribe nor Sheikh Neg El Bahi could do anything alone against such powerful opponents.

"But first we have to get out of here. The door looks very sturdy, the window is barred and we don't have weapons. So, what should we do?" Vrenli pondered aloud, looking around the quarters.

Wahmubu's servants stood at the window and rattled the bars anchored in the clay wall.

"We can't get through the window, Prince," said the older of the two.

"Prince?" asked Vrenli in astonishment.

"Prince Wahmubu El Abahi Da Gerweli, son of the Sheikh of the Northern Nomads," the desert man replied formally.

"That really doesn't matter now," Wahmubu waved it off and walked towards the window.

He rattled the bars and tapped the clay wall all around.

"That could work," he finally said and explained his plan to Vrenli and the two servants.

"Vrenli, you need to pretend that the scar on your forearm hurts terribly. I'll call for the guards and ask them for water, lots of water, to make you wet compresses. We need several liters of water to loosen the clay wall around the bars of the window," Wahmubu explained and told them what Mahroo had drawn for him in the desert sand.

"After our escape, each of us must go to one of the four towers to the north, west, south and east of the city wall. As I'm the only one who knows the wambini's lure, you must set fire to the surrounding roofs with the torches we saw on the towers earlier to create enough of a distraction. As it is hopeless to flee to the desert at night without water and sufficient supplies, I suggest that we arrange a meeting point where we can gather after we have completed our tasks. There we can look around for a way to leave the city prepared and unseen. I assume that if our escape is noticed, everyone will think that we have left Kajir and fled into the desert. Since the city is overcrowded with strangers, we won't cause a stir," Wahmubu explained in detail.

"Maybe we'll be lucky and our escape will go unnoticed until the morning hours," Vrenli said optimistically, to which Wahmubu smiled.

Vrenli lay down on the ground and Wahmubu's servants bent over him. He signaled to them that he was ready, called for help and rolled on the floor in pain. Wahmubu knocked vigorously on the door several times and called for help.

After a few moments, they heard the bolt unlocking from the outside. Two guards entered with their scimitars raised. When they saw Vrenli writhing on the ground in pain, Wahmubu explained to the guards that the Abkether's scar on his forearm was hurting and that he had a very high temperature.

"I need a bucket of water to make him wet compresses, otherwise he will die. Sheikh Nam Al Kabun would not be pleased," Wahmubu said to the two lizard creatures as he leaned down to Vrenli and pressed his hand to his forehead.

The guards took another look at Vrenli, who was playing his part excellently after all of his real pain. They said something to each other in the hissing language of the snake people, whereupon one of them left the slave quarters. The one lingering at the door closed it, drew his scimitar and looked intently at the three Scheddifer and the whimpering Abkether lying on the ground. Wahmubu reached for a bed sheet and began to tear off long, narrow pieces. The door opened again and the lizard creature that had left the slave quarters to fetch water entered. It placed a full bucket of water on the floor in front of Vrenli and hissed. Wahmubu thanked him and bowed to the two guards.

Before they left the quarters, they took another look at Vrenli with their poisonous green reptile eyes and tongued him with the tip of their forked tongues. A few moments later, Wahmubu began to soak the long strips of cloth with water and instructed his two servants to pull the water-soaked strips of cloth evenly back and forth along the lower end of a bar.

The rubbing motion of the wet cloth removed the clay wall around the bars layer by layer. After a short time, they had exposed a few thumb widths. Wahmubu now also took a wet piece of cloth and helped the two of them. Two hours later, they were able to lift the bars out of the wall with little effort.

It was midnight and the wedding celebrations were now reaching their climax. Several fireworks were set off at the same time and the music that resounded throughout the city grew louder.

"We have to keep our eyes open for an escape route out of the city. Many of the foreigners will leave Kajir tomorrow," Wahmubu remarked, cautiously sticking his head out of the window.

"I suggest we meet up near the fire-breathers we saw on the way to the palace. If one of us is discovered, he should try to flee the city to throw the lizard creatures off the scent," suggested Wahmubu.

His two servants and Vrenli nodded at the same time. Wahmubu assigned each of them a tower. Vrenli, whom he was most concerned about, was to set fire to the roofs around the eastern tower, as this was closest to the agreed meeting point. He assigned his two servants to the northern and southern towers. He himself would try to lure the wambinis to the western tower, which was close to the city gate.

"When the moon is over the palace dome, you must start the fires at the same time and I will call the wambinis. Don't forget, we'll meet at the fire-breathers," whispered Wahmubu, climbing quietly out of the window and making his way to the western tower.

The whole of Kajir was in an exuberant festive mood. People danced, sang and drank on every corner. The music from all parts of the city was so loud that no couldn't hear their own words. Countless fireworks exploded incessantly in the night sky above the city, illuminating it in bright colors. There was no shortage of scuffles between guests of the different lands and races, but Kajir's guards settled them peacefully, as they had been ordered to do by Sheikh Nam Al Kabun for the special day.

Vrenli took his bearings from the stars and headed east. After following some narrow and dark alleys, he arrived at a smithy. He looked at the huge, heavy, dark anvil standing next to a reddish-brown, bulbous clay furnace. Vrenli wondered for a few moments whether he should try to enter the forge to look around for weapons, when a dancing group of lizard creatures approached him.

Startled, he leaned his face against the wall of the smithy and pretended to vomit. He wanted the group to believe that he was a drunken reveler. The lizard creatures took no notice of him, however, but leapt past him, dancing and hissing. Vrenli turned around and looked after them with relief.

"As long as our escape goes unnoticed, and that could take until the early hours of the morning, I don't have to worry about being caught, it seems," he thought. This gave Vrenli the courage to take one of the wrought irons next to the anvil, break open the window at the back and enter the forge.

Inside it was pitch black. The moonlight that fell through the small window was just enough for Vrenli to make out the outlines of pieces of furniture. He crept carefully from the window through the dark room towards a doorway. He bumped into something hard and was startled. Fireworks lit up the city and for a few moments the room was dimly lit. He had bumped into a wooden shelf, the sharp edge of which protruded into the passageway. He could then see the blacksmith's tools on the wall to the right of the shelf. There were some hammers and wrought iron among them, but they were far too big and heavy for Vrenli to use as a weapon.

When the light from the fireworks went out, it became dark again and Vrenli had trouble not bumping into anything with every step. He therefore decided to stay in his position and wait for another firework display. He fervently hoped that he still had enough time, as he hadn't thought to check the position of the moon before entering the forge. But it wasn't long before the sky over the town of Kajir was illuminated with a light that faded from green to blue. Vrenli could now see enough to get into the next room without bumping into the furnishings. And here he found what he was looking for. The room, illuminated by the blue light of a long-lit firework, was filled with the blacksmith's work. Armor, shields, weapons and more. Vrenli was on the lookout for daggers or short swords, as the scimitars of the lizard creatures were far too large and heavy for him. He found what he was looking for on a shelf next to the armor.

As he couldn't carry anymore more, he only took three of the daggers from the rack and waited for the next firework to escape the smithy quickly. After climbing back out through the window, he placed the three daggers on the floor and tried as best he could to conceal the traces of his break-in at the window. He then put on one of the three dagger shafts and wrapped the other two in his Dark Forest cloak, which he carried inconspicuously under his right arm.

Vrenli glanced at the moon, which would soon be over the palace dome, and hurriedly made his way to the eastern tower. He walked straight past the agreed meeting point and gazed for a moment in amazement at the colored flames that one of the fire-breathers was spitting. Fascinated, Vrenli briefly wondered how it was possible that the scrawny, emaciated lizard creature didn't burn its mouth in the process. He could already see the tall, round tower, lit by torchlight, towering above the city wall, where several houses stood covered in dried palm branches.

"Very good, it'll burn like tinder," he muttered. After following several alleys, he spotted the door that led to the staircase to the tower.

In the meantime, Wahmubu was stopped on his way to the western tower by a group of barbarians and asked for a drink. At first, he thought it was the group that had been in the palace, but when they handed him a cup filled with wine, he was reassured. He drained the cup in one gulp and thanked the burly, rugged men who were pleased that he had emptied the cup so quickly. He then turned into a narrow alley and walked the few steps to the tower. He stopped briefly and looked around for guards. When he saw none, he opened the wooden door in the city wall and carefully crept up the steps to the top of the tower.

His two servants had already reached their assigned towers, which fortunately for them were not being guarded and were waiting impatiently for the moon to pass over the palace dome.

Wahmubu was less fortunate because when he reached the top he saw, just in time, two-armed lizard creatures standing with their backs to him. He squinted up into the night sky from under the tower roof. He didn't have much time left, as the moon would be over the palace dome at any moment. So, he lay down on the ground and crept quietly closer to the two lizard creatures, who couldn't hear over the loud music and the wedding guests singing and shouting. Quickly and purposefully, Wahmubu reached for the shaft hanging from the left guard's belt, pulled out the dagger, jumped up and, before the two realized what was happening, Wahmubu plunged the tip of the dagger into the guard's neck. Hissing and gurgling blood, he slumped to the ground and looked at Wahmubu with wide eyes.

253

The other hissed, snaked the tip of its forked tongue out of its mouth and raised its right elbow, from which its poisonous thorn grow, to stab Wahmubu. The latter was able to dodge just in time. The lizard was about to pull the shimmering golden scimitar from the shaft hanging from its belt on the right with its left hand when Wahmubu seized the opportunity, covered the lizard creature's mouth with his left hand and plunged his dagger into his opponent's ribs with his right. Wahmubu let go of the stuck dagger stuck, grabbed the lizard's head from behind with his right hand and snapped its neck with a powerful, quick forward-backward movement.

The moon was now over the palace dome and Wahmubu had to hurry. He threw the two lifeless bodies from the tower over the city wall.

"The wambinis will take care of you," he whispered after the falling bodies.

He looked out into the dark desert and, hoping that some of the desert worms were near, imitated their call several times. Wahmubu turned his gaze to the city when he noticed that some of the roofs had already caught fire and was reassured that everything was going as discussed. He looked out into the dark desert again and let out a few more decoy calls.

As expected, the tower began to vibrate. Wahmubu smiled. Several wambinis had answered his call. Slowly, he descended the stairs from the top of the tower and made his way to the fire-breathers, where he hoped to meet Vrenli and his two servants.

Manahe, one of Wahmubu's two servants, was about to leave his tower when a lizard creature, who had noticed the fire on the roofs near the northern tower, came up the winding staircase and surprised him. Startled, Manahe looked into the lizard's reptilian eyes, swinging its scimitar and striking a deadly blow. Wahmubu's servant slumped to the ground, bloodied and dead. Hissing and fizzing, the lizard creature then alerted the tower guards, who were sharing a drink on the other side of the street. The fire, which was slowly spreading across the rooftops, was now noticed by several of Kajir's warriors. The celebrating people and guests were startled by the shrill sounding of the alarm bell from the palace dome. In the commotion that broke out in the city, Wahmubu, his servant and Vrenli, who had gathered by the fire-eaters, looked around for Manahe, confused and waiting.

"He's not coming," said Vrenli nervously, handing them the daggers he had taken from the smithy.

"Let's wait a little longer. I hope they haven't picked him up," Wahmubu replied, looking at the water bags, scraps of food and clothes left behind by the excited crowd and starting to collect them. Vrenli helped him.

The music fell silent and all over the city, the former revelers, flustered like a hive of bees, ran through the streets with buckets of water. Of course, there were also some who were unperturbed by all the commotion and continued to drink, dance and sing. The presence of the city guards increased and soon one hundred armed warriors of Kajir had gathered in the city center and split up according to the three cardinal points where the fire was raging. However, when a thunderous roaring sound was heard at the main gate, most of the guards rushed there. At the sight of five huge desert worms' bodies sticking halfway out of the desert sand, they immediately lowered the heavy gate bars, closed the wings and barricaded them with thick wooden posts.

Vrenli, Wahmubu and his servant hid in a dark alley and changed their clothes with the ones they had picked up earlier to look as inconspicuous as possible. Wahmubu's servant carried the two bags of water and a small brown leather bag filled with food that they had stolen from a group of gray dwarves who were helping put out a fire. Newly clothed, they crept through several small, dark alleys and finally came to a wide path that led them to Kajir's stables. Three carts offered them an escape route. After Wahmubu removed the wooden cover from one of the locked carts and saw the brown iron ingots stacked to the brim, he knew that luck was on their side. They immediately began to rearrange the ingots so that they could fit in the middle of the cart. Wahmubu pulled the wooden cover closed from inside. It was getting dark.

After a good while, the excitement in the city had died down. The roof fire in the affected districts was quickly extinguished. As the damage was not extensive, most people went back to celebrating Balae's wedding with meat, wine and music. The crowd did not know that the fire had been started deliberately. The majority were convinced that one of the fireworks had started the fire. Even the wambinis, who were driven away by Kajir's warriors, only caused minor damage to the main gate. There were a few cracks in the city wall and a handful of lizard creatures were killed, but the attack by the desert worms was dismissed as a coincidence.

However, Sheikh Nam Al Kabun was informed of the incident at the northern tower by one of his men.

"A slave set the fire," he informed Sheikh Nam Al Kabun who was a cautious and thoughtful regent.

He did not believe a single perpetrator could set fires in three different parts of the city.

"Fire and the wambinis at the main gate? No, that wasn't the work of a single person," he thought. But before he could express his doubt, Alnugh interrupted him.

"I heard that wambinis attacked the city gate?" he asked the sheikh.

"You heard right, and there was also a fire in three different parts of the city," confirmed Sheikh Nam Al Kabun.

"Three fires and the attack of the wambinis, makes four. The four slaves. Wahmubu, his two servants and the Abkether!" shouted Alnugh.

"That would be possible," agreed the sheikh and instructed two of his guards to go to the slave quarters immediately.

It wasn't long before the two returned with the news that the slaves had escaped.

"Send riders in all directions immediately. They must be found!" their ruler hissed at them, letting his poisonous thorns grow from his elbows and lashing out with his forked tongue.

When the large-scale search party returned at dawn without the fugitives, Sheikh Nam Al Kabun was so enraged that he rammed his two thorns into the warrior who had informed him of the failed mission and decapitated him with his scimitar. Balae, who was standing next to him, tried to calm her father down.

"How do we look to our guests? Now that we've entered an alliance with Erwight of Entorbis," he hissed angrily at his daughter.

Balae's husband offered to take up the pursuit of the slaves. However, Sheikh Nam Al Kabun rejected this out of consideration for his daughter.

"In three days, we will attack Wahmubu's tribe. I want you to take care of it, my son," Sheikh Nam Al Kabun told him and was about to leave the banquet hall in a huff when Ornux and Randulin approached him.

"Stop, Sheikh Nam Al Kabun. This is not the time to waste your strength over such a ridiculous incident. Remember the alliance and what you promised," Randulin warned with a serious expression on his face.

Sheikh Nam Al Kabun hissed, but quickly came to his senses and took back the order he had given his son-in-law.

"But what about the Abkether?" he hissed at Randulin.

"We'll take care of him, we know his origin and his name," Ornux reassured him.

"Vrenli from Abketh!" hissed the sheikh, before ordering the palace guards to end the wedding ceremony.

Vrenli, Wahmubu and his servant held their breath as they realized that someone was approaching the cart they were hiding in.

"We're leaving!" a powerful voice rang out.

"The wedding celebration seems to be over. Let's hope we're not discovered," Wahmubu whispered, as he carefully and quietly adjusted some of the iron ingots they had piled over their heads.

The carts began to move and the barbarians pulling them talked about the festival, the fire and the attack by the wambinis on the way to the main gate. They were very pleased with the brown iron that Sheikh Nam Al Kabun had given them as a gift. They could make good use of it, as an alloy of dark and brown iron was particularly in demand for making weapons. Weapons that they would soon need when they joined the alliance with Erwight of Entorbis.

At the main gate, heavily armed guards checked everyone who wanted to leave the city of Kajir. When the barbarians arrived with their three carts, they were checked by two of the gate guards. They looked at the iron ingots in the cart and, seeing nothing suspicious, let the group move on. The cart moved northeast at a moderate pace.

Sheikh Neg El Bahi

The three carts, which had been rolling through the dry, hot desert since the morning, came to a halt at the small oasis where Wahmubu had treated Vrenli's wounds two days earlier. The barbarians took a break to water their horses and rest under the shady palm trees. The hot, dry desert was truly no place for the barbarians of the Raging Hordes, who originate from the cold north country.

Vrenli, Wahmubu and his servant held their breath as one of them approached their cart. Wahmubu knew they wouldn't last much longer inside, as the brown iron ingots piled up around them had already heated up so much that the air in the small cavity where they were huddled became stuffy. Once again, they needed an escape plan.

"I'm not sure, but I think there are eight or nine," whispered Wahmubu.

"A fight is futile," Vrenli remarked in a whisper.

Wahmubu's servant nodded.

They had escaped from Kajir, but their current situation seemed hopeless. The carts set off again, leaving the small oasis behind them. For Vrenli, Wahmubu and his servant, the heat and, above all, the stuffy air inside was almost unbearable. The water bags they were carrying were already empty. Vrenli became restless. He was thirsty and had to get rid of his clothes or he would die in the heat.

"Vrenli, please hold on," whispered Wahmubu, holding his left arm tightly.

"I can't stand it any longer. I have to get out of here!" gasped Vrenli.

If there had been enough light inside the cart, Wahmubu and his servant would have been able to see Vrenli's bright red face drenched with rivers of sweat pouring from his forehead. It was already past midday and they were still a little more than two days' journey from the border of Desert of DeShadin to the east.

Suddenly the barbarians began to shout something incomprehensible to the four in the cart. The clattering of hooves from several horses coming towards them rang out. It wasn't long before Vrenli, Wahmubu and his servants flinched at the hiss of arrows smashing into the cart's wood. War cries and the clashing of swords resounded inside the cart, followed by a brief silence, interrupted by loud, jumbled voices.

"These are Sheikh Neg El Bahi's riders. I recognize the dialect they speak," exclaimed Wahmubu delightedly and immediately began to remove the brown iron ingots from above their heads.

The wooden cover opened with a crash and Wahmubu, sticking his head out, was almost hit by an arrow fired at him by an archer on a black horse. He immediately put his hands above his head to show the shouting Iseran riders that he was unarmed.

"I am Wahmubu, son of the tribal leader of the northern nomads!" he shouted as loud as he could.

The leader of the riders, hearing this, rode slowly toward the cart and raised his hand above his eyebrows to shield his gaze from the bright sunlight.

"Wahmubu? How on earth did you get into this cart?" asked the masked rider in astonishment, dismounting from his white horse.

Wahmubu looked at the bloodied, lifeless bodies of the barbarians and, followed by his servant and Vrenli, who immediately attracted the attention of the desert men, climbed out of the cart and told Iseran's riders about his abduction and what had happened in Kajir.

"Sheikh Neg El Bahi increased the patrols around the larger nomadic tribes, the mines and the border of the desert when he was told of the many foreigners crossing his kingdom. You are lucky that we passed by here and confronted the barbarians. Their response was to attack us. They must have feared for their goods," said the leader of the riders, glancing at the shiny brown iron ingots.

"My name is Jefmadan and I lead these riders. It will be best if you come with us to Iseran and tell Sheikh Neg El Bahi personally about what has happened." Wahmubu agreed but asked to make a detour to the northern desert first to inform his father of his well-being. The leader of the riders of Iseran agreed.

"And who does the child belong to?" Jefmadan asked as he lifted his black tekatkat slightly and swung himself back into the saddle.

"I am not a child. My name is Vrenli and I come from Abketh, far to the north of Wetherid," Vrenli replied with a certain pride.

Wahmubu informed the riders about the Abkether's small size, whereupon their leader apologized to Vrenli with a respectful bow. Two riders led their horses towards Vrenli and Wahmubu's servants and pulled them up onto the saddle behind them.

"Wahmubu, you're riding with me," Jefmadan said and held out his hand to pull him onto the horse's back.

As they rode north, the two talked about the snake people. Wahmubu told Jefmadan everything he had seen and heard in Kajir. The heat and the ride in the saddle made Vrenli tired. He fell asleep clutching the Scheddifer riding in front of him tightly.

"We should ride west at the next dune," suggested Wahmubu.

Jefmadan nodded and spurred his horse on. Wahmubu looked at the ever-approaching low mountain range that stretched from near the border in the east to the west, south of Iseran. The ancient rock, which had silently stood in the sun since Wetherid's existence, was only a few hundred paces high and in some places overgrown with bushes, shrubs and cacti. The smooth, lateral rock faces were colored a brownish red by the fine-grained sand that the desert winds blew up incessantly.

It was already afternoon when Iseran's riders stopped their horses in front of the narrow path leading steeply into the mountains. The rider in front of Vrenli woke him up.

"We have to walk, little man," he said to Vrenli and helped him dismount.

The riders led their horses by the reins up the winding, loamy path.

Vrenli was still sleepy when he saw a desert troll peering out from behind a rock. He didn't know whether he was still dreaming or already awake and rubbed the sleep and dust from his eyes. The ugly creature was the size of an ogre, but because it lived in the desert where food was scarce, it had a lean appearance with its rib bones protruding through the bare, wrinkled skin of its upper body. The troll's matted, black hair hung down to the ground and his body, naked except for a fur wrapped around his waist, was stained by the desert sand like the rock of the mountains in which he lived. He clutched a club with his scrawny, bony fingers, on which grew very long, razor-sharp fingernails. Nobody noticed him except Vrenli.

"Wh - wha - what's that?" stuttered Vrenli, pointing to the rock with his hand.

The riders of Iseran immediately drew their scimitars from their scabbards and wanted to run towards the desert troll, but Jefmadan ordered them to wait.

"The desert troll is alone, he poses no danger," Jefmadan reassured his men, who put their scimitars back in their scabbards.

"Desert trolls are stupid, but not so stupid that one alone would attack a group of ten men," Wahmubu added.

The riders led their horses further along the path. Vrenli could feel the pursuing, hungry eyes of the desert troll on the back of his neck and therefore sought to be close to Wahmubu, quickly walking beside him. The ascent into the mountains took longer than Jefmadan had expected and by the time they reached the top of the ridge, dusk was already falling. They decided to set up camp for the night near a sheltering group of rocks. Jefmadan instructed two of his men to light a fire and assigned three of them to keep the first watch of the night.

"It could well be that the desert troll will return, and possibly not alone. Be on your guard and ready for battle," warned Jefmadan and set off with two of his riders to scout the surrounding area.

The two warriors of Iseran, who were searching for firewood in the surrounding bushes and shrubs, returned to the group of rocks with two bundles of dried branches and twigs and lit a fire, around which Vrenli and Wahmubu sat down. The other desert men, together with Wahmubu's servant, prepared a supper that they all ate together shortly after Jefmadan had returned with his people.

Vrenli stared into the orange-blue flickering flames and listened to the crackling of the burning branches. He saw Werlis, Gorathdin, Aarl and Borlix in front of him.

"Ah, friends, when will I see you again," he thought, sighed and lay down on his cloak from the Dark Forest. Wahmubu, who was sitting close to him, covered Vrenli with the fur of a zarukk so large that it could have covered him three times over. Warmed by the fire and the fur, Vrenli slowly slipped into the realm of dreams, still thinking of his friends.

The night was starry and bitterly cold. Wahmubu, the only one, apart from the three guards, who had not slept so far, was listening to the desert wolves howling at the moon when his fine ears suddenly heard heavy breathing and the snapping of branches nearby.

"Wake up!" shouted Wahmubu and pulled a burning branch from the fire, raising it in front of him. The warriors of Iseran immediately jumped up, looked around and drew their scimitars.

Just a moment later, three desert trolls leapt out from behind a rock and pounced on one of the men standing guard away from the fire. With their enormous strength, they tore at his limbs. Death cries rang out, mingling with the howling of wolves in the dark desert night. The two other guards charged at the desert trolls from the opposite side with their scimitars at the ready. However, the trolls immediately knocked the weapons out of the attackers' hands with their huge clubs.

Vrenli woke up startled.

He caught sight of the desert trolls, had the presence of mind to take a burning branch from the fire and hurled it into the matted, long, black hair of the creature standing with its back turned to him and fighting with three of the desert men. The matted hair began to burn brightly, causing the troll to throw itself to the ground, rolling back and forth and letting out squeals. Jefmadan leapt over the fire and dealt the burning creature a death blow. The blade of his short sword turned the slimy dark brown of the troll's blood.

Vrenli looked around for Wahmubu, who was cutting off the right arm of one of the desert trolls with a powerful blow using the scimitar he had taken from the dead warrior of Iseran. The troll then threw himself at Wahmubu, eyes wide open, with a bloodcurdling scream. Both fell to the ground and started a fight to the death.

The third desert troll, who was swinging his mighty club to ward off the blows of Iseran's warriors, dropped his club in surprise and ran off into the darkness with huge, quick strides.

Jefmadan's men immediately rushed to Wahmubu's aid, hacking at the one-armed desert troll's back with their scimitars' sharp blades.

It took the strength of four warriors to lift the lifeless body of the troll from Wahmubu, who was already gasping for air. Wahmubu slowly stood up bent over and stayed in this position for a few breaths.

"Thank the Father, you're alive. I thought the monster crushed you," Vrenli said with relief and put his arm amicably on Wahmubu's back.

"Almost," he groaned, breathing heavily, then straightened up and looked around.

When he heard a pleading whimper, he turned around and approached the badly injured Iseran warrior lying on the ground to help him. Jefmadan tried to get an overview of the casualties and wounded. He counted three wounded and one dead.

"One of your men is badly injured!" Wahmubu called out to him.

Jefmadan hurried to him, bent over the wounded man and looked at the bruises, red and blue from blows with a club, and the many bleeding cuts that a desert troll had inflicted with its sharp nails.

"I hope that he will be able to hold out until we reach my village. He can be helped there," said Wahmubu, who looked after the seriously injured man as best he could.

Jefmadan patted Wahmubu on the shoulder with thanks and instructed two of his men to bring the two injured men next to the fire and bury the dead man. Wahmubu's servants and one of Jefmadan's warriors removed the traces of the fight and threw the bodies of the two desert trolls over the steep rock face to their right. In the little time they had left to sleep, Wahmubu and his servant tended to the wounded. Jefmadan and two of his men guarded the camp for the night, while Vrenli tried to sleep despite the tension.

As dawn broke, the group prepared to descend from the low mountains. They followed the steeply descending, narrow path until midday, when they finally reached the plains covered with fine sand in front of the mountains. They were now able to ride their horses again and reached the border to the northern part of Desert of DeShadin, where Wahmubu's tribe lived, before late afternoon. They rode until dusk and finally came across a small nomad camp where they spent the night and tended to the injured.

In the cool of the next morning and with rested horses, they made rapid progress. They reached Wahmubu's tribe before noon. A sentry standing on a simple, wooden lookout tower in the sand about a hundred paces from the nomad camp, which consisted of well over a hundred tents, announced the approaching riders with a shrill, fast-sounding bell call. More than thirty heavily armed riders immediately gathered at the lookout tower. They were just about to ride off to encircle the approaching riders when one of them recognized Wahmubu.

"The prince is alive!" he shouted, repeating his call until the sheikh of the northern tribes, accompanied by his main wife, Wahmubu's mother and a handful of his personal bodyguards, arrived at the lookout tower. Wahmubu jumped off his horse and ran towards his father, hugged him and then kissed his weeping mother several times.

"I'm fine," Wahmubu assured his parents.

"But we have a seriously injured man from Sheikh Neg El Bahi's horsemen with us. His wounds must be treated immediately," he explained to his father, who then ordered two men from his bodyguard to take the injured man to Mahroo.

Overjoyed that his only son had returned home unharmed, Wahmubu's father called for a party and invited everyone who had come with Wahmubu.

"Father, we have to get to Iseran as quickly as possible. I must tell Sheikh Neg El Bahi what I saw and heard in Kajir," Wahmubu objected.

Jefmadan nodded in agreement.

"Kajir? The snake people are responsible for your disappearance?" Wahmubu's father asked in astonishment.

"Please, come into my tent, let's at least have a cup of tea while you tell me what happened," the sheikh invited Jefmadan, who dismounted from his horse and bowed to the leader of the northern nomadic tribes. Vrenli, who was helped off his horse by one of Iseran's riders, attracted the attention of the assembled nomads. It was the first time they had seen an Abkether. Until now, they had only heard of them from stories and were puzzled by his small size and pale white skin.

"Follow me," said Wahmubu's father, walking quickly back to the nomad camp and entering his tent, the largest of them all, followed by Wahmubu, Jefmadan and Vrenli.

The tent, which looked rather plain from the outside and was sewn from goat, zarukks and camel skins, resembled a palace on the inside. Thick, intricately woven wool carpets lay on the floor and lighter and finer carpets hung on the tent walls. Most of the furnishings were made of fine wood and decorated with gold or silver fittings. The spacious tent consisted of several subdivisions. The middle section of the tent could hold a good hundred people. To the left and right were seating areas covered with fine carpets that could accommodate up to ten people. Ornate golden water pipes stood in the middle of each seating area. Young girls wearing belly-baring costumes and covering their faces with golden veils brought the guests fruit in golden bowls and hot tea in small, ornately decorated silver cups.

Wahmubu sat down and gave his father a very detailed account of everything that had happened since his abduction. He took special care to tell him even the smallest detail about what he had heard and seen in Sheikh Nam Al Kabun's palace.

"I saw gray dwarves, mist elves, undead, barbarians, orcs and ogres, thieves from Astinhod and a group of Erwight of Entorbis. My friend Vrenli also told me about a shadow mage called Ornux," Wahmubu told his father, who listened to him anxiously.

"You're right, you must tell Sheikh Neg El Bahi about this, don't waste any time. Ten men from my bodyguard will accompany you," the sheikh said to Wahmubu, standing up and hugging him.

Jefmadan thanked the sheikh and bowed.

"Be careful, my boy!" said the old, white-bearded man, who wore a diamond-studded turban, fatherly to Wahmubu and then turned his gaze to Vrenli

"Tell me, young man, what brings you to Desert of DeShadin?" the sheikh wanted to know.

"It's a very long story and I'm afraid we don't have time for me to tell you," Vrenli replied politely and bowed.

"I must travel to Astinhod and tell King Grandhold about the events in Kajir. But I have no horse, no water, no food and I don't know the way," sighed Vrenli, looking first at Wahmubu and then into his father's kind eyes.

Before he could offer Vrenli help, Wahmubu put his hand on Vrenli's shoulder.

"I ask you to accompany us to Iseran and tell Sheikh Neg El Bahi about the shadow mage Ornux, then I will take you to Astinhod myself, little friend," Wahmubu suggested.

Vrenli was silent for a few moments.

"Nagulaj told me to travel to Horunguth Island. Werlis, Gorathdin, Aarl and Borlix are certainly already very worried and King Grandhold must be informed about the events in Kajir. Now Wahmubu is asking me to travel with him and Jefmadan to Iseran. How am I supposed to decide?" Vrenli asked himself and looked wordlessly at Wahmubu, his father and Jefmadan.

He took a sip of hot tea and unconsciously let his hand slide to his belt.

"The Oracle of Tawinn. Yes! I'll ask it what I should decide," he thought, but realized just then that the small leather pouch was no longer on his belt. Disappointed, he looked up. Wahmubu was still waiting for an answer.

"If I can help your people with that, then I will come with you to Iseran. But after that, I really must go back to Astinhod and I hope you really will accompany me there, Wahmubu," Vrenli finally said as his heart told him to help the Scheddifer. Wahmubu smiled.

"Thank you, little friend, and I am true to my word, I will accompany you to Astinhod, Vrenli," Wahmubu promised and bowed to his Abketh friend.

"Let's get going," Jefmadan suggested, bowed to the sheikh and left the tent, followed by Wahmubu and Vrenli.

They walked past several smaller tents in the direction of the paddocks.

"Just a moment," Wahmubu asked as they arrived at the waiting riders of Iseran.

Jefmadan looked at him questioningly.

"I just want to quickly check on the injured man," explained Wahmubu and went to Mahroo's tent a little way off.

When he entered the tent, he saw the man lying in the middle on one of the soft carpets on the floor, covered in cuts. He had opened his eyes but was too weak to speak. He smiled, strained, at Wahmubu and blinked. Mahroo, who was sitting next to the injured man arranging some animal bones on the ground, looked up and lifted a small doll that looked like a desert troll in front of him. Wahmubu noticed that the doll was missing an arm. The shaman simply smiled at Wahmubu without saying a word. Wahmubu returned the old man's smile, bowed and left the tent.

Ten of his father's bodyguard, in their black tekatkats decorated with golden embroidery and covered faces, were already sitting heavily armed on their horses when Wahmubu arrived. Wahmubu quickly helped Vrenli into the saddle, swung himself onto his horse and nodded to Jefmadan, who gave the signal to set off.

"If we push our horses to the limit, we can be at Sheikh Neg El Bahi in Iseran in two days. We will spend the night with nomadic tribes along the way!" Jefmadan shouted to his riders and those of Wahmubu's tribe and spurred his horse on.

They made rapid progress on the first day. They rode southwest, skirting the mountains that bordered the northern and southern Desert of DeShadin. They only stopped twice at smaller nomadic tribes to water their horses and fortify themselves. The tribal leader of the nomads who lived on the border to the southern part of the desert was an uncle of Wahmubu and treated them particularly well. After they had completed the first day of their journey, they decided to accept Wahmubu's uncle's offer to spend the night in one of their best tents. When the riders wanted to set off further west the next morning, Wahmubu's uncle asked them to wait. He insisted that three of his best warriors should ride with them, which Jefmadan did not refuse. They set off and, after riding through the dry, hot sea of sand until midday, they rested at an oasis.

None of them expected to encounter a group of lizard creatures who had been commissioned by Sheikh Nam Al Kabun to convert free nomads to the Kajir. A fierce battle broke out immediately. However, before any of Jefmadan's or Wahmubu's riders could be killed or even injured, half of the lizard creatures lay dead on the ground. The few others were captured and tied up.

After Vrenli, Wahmubu, Jefmadan and their riders had recovered from the fight, watered their horses and washed away the fight's traces in the small waterhole, they continued their journey to Iseran without further incident. They reached their destination before dusk fell.

The city of Iseran, which was almost the size of Astinhod, was the largest of all the settlements in Desert of DeShadin and was regarded by the Scheddifer people as their capital. Iseran was home to more than ten thousand people and the thick, mud-walled city walls rose like a bulwark from the desert floor.

The pointed tower of the palace, which was located on the north side of the city, rose so high into the sky that it could still be seen from the crest of the mountains to the east. At the place of worship of the devout desert people, located in the center of the city, was a garden that Vrenli estimated was the size of his village of Abketh. Iseran's marketplace was bustling with activity, with several hundred people selling or buying goods. Iseran was the trading center of Desert of DeShadin and traders from all regions of Wetherid often made weeks-long journeys across the ocean of sand to make a good deal. They could get double and sometimes even triple the price for their goods. Metal traders from Ib'Agier, timber merchants from Kirindor, cattle and grain traders from Astinhod and fishmongers from Thir loudly advertised their wares. Wahmubu, Vrenli and Jefmadan, who had arrived at the palace, were received by a vizier, who then informed Sheikh Neg El Bahi of their arrival.

Their waiting time was sweetened with a sumptuous meal, music and dancers in belly-baring costumes. Vrenli felt intoxicated by the strange-sounding hypnotic music and the desert women moving rhythmically to it. The mataii wine he drank several cups of also played its part.

A heavy, elaborately decorated golden gate opened on the north side of the hall. A group of young women, throwing colorful flowers on the floor, walked through the archway, followed by four burly men carrying a golden palanquin.

They placed the palanquin on the ground in front of Vrenli, Wahmubu and Jefmadan. The red silk curtain of the palanquin was pushed aside, and, to Wahmubu's delight, Princess Manamii stepped out gracefully. Vrenli noticed how Wahmubu's eyes began to sparkle.

The princess walked slowly towards the three visitors. Jefmadan immediately bowed to her.

"I am glad that you are alive, Wahmubu. I received word that you were missing," said Princess Manamii, hiding her true feelings of a caring, loving woman.

Wahmubu bowed his head.

"I am also happy to see you again! What you have heard is true. Two of my servants, my little friend and I were abducted by slave catchers. But as you can see, we were fortunately able to free ourselves," Wahmubu told the princess, who then invited the three of them to talk to her about what had happened.

She sat down next to Wahmubu, Jefmadan and Vrenli on a stool covered in purple velvet on a carpet woven with gold thread.

Wahmubu then gave a detailed account of what had happened, focusing particularly on the alliance and the plans of the snake people.

"That really isn't good news. My father will arrive any minute," said Princess Manamii, looking at Vrenli with wide eyes.

She stood up nervously, whispered something in Wahmubu's ear and hurriedly left the hall. It was only a few moments before Sheikh Neg El Bahi entered the hall, without any special announcement, with two of his viziers and Princess Manamii. Vrenli, Wahmubu and Jefmadan stood up and bowed to him.

The very old, almost elderly, but still upright, rotund man with a long white beard and kind eyes, sat down with his two viziers and Princess Manamii at the round, heavy marble table not far from Wahmubu, Vrenli and Jefmadan.

"Please, join us," the sheikh asked the three of them.

His gaze fell on Vrenli.

"An Abkether, here in Desert of DeShadin? What brought you here and what is your relationship to Wahmubu?" the sheikh asked.

"My name is Vrenli, Vrenli Hogmaunt, and as you have correctly noticed, I come from Abketh. What led me, or should I say brought me, to Desert of DeShadin is a long story. My relationship with Wahmubu was that of a fellow prisoner and developed into a friendship during our escape from Kajir," Vrenli replied and looked at Wahmubu, who nodded and smiled in agreement.

"Hogmaunt?" repeated Sheikh Neg El Bahi with raised eyebrows.

Vrenli nodded, whereupon the sheikh remained silent for a few moments.

"Mr. Vrenli, I would like to speak to you in private after Wahmubu has told me his request," said Sheikh Neg El Bahi to Vrenli, who was just as astonished by his request as Wahmubu, Jefmadan and the two viziers.

Only Princess Manamii was not surprised.

Wahmubu began to tell the sheikh about his abduction, the meeting with Vrenli, Balae's wedding celebration and the hostile guests from Wetherid, Ornux and the emissary of Erwight of Entorbis. Sheikh Neg El Bahi listened attentively to Wahmubu and every time he mentioned the gray dwarves, mist elves, ogres, orcs, barbarians or undead, the sheikh looked into his daughter's eyes and then turned his gaze to Vrenli.

Wahmubu went on to talk about his escape from Kajir and the lizard creatures that had captured them at the oasis on their way here.

"We have already tripled the patrols, but in view of what you have just told us, I think it would be advisable for us to send armed riders to the respective nomadic tribes in the western, northern and eastern desert," suggested one of the viziers attentively listening to Wahmubu.

Sheikh Neg El Bahi agreed to his proposal and ordered him to begin preparations immediately.

"I will go to the barracks immediately and inform the officers. We will need about four hundred riders for this," the vizier announced, bowed and left the hall with quick steps.

The twenty or so tribes that lived under the regency of Sheikh Neg El Bahi in the Scheddifer-populated regions of Desert of DeShadin had to be protected from the converts of the snake people.

This was also intended as a sign that Sheikh Neg El Bahi was aware of Erwight of Entorbis and Sheikh Nam Al Kabun's plans.

"Twenty well-armed riders per tribe is not an army, but we will set an example," explained Sheikh Nam Al Kabun.

The people around the table nodded in agreement.

The remaining vizier suggested informing the traders coming from the various regions of Wetherid of what was happening and giving those who wanted to leave the Iseran and Desert of DeShadin escorts to the border.

"This is how we strengthen our alliances with the various peoples of Wetherid," the vizier explained.

Sheikh Neg El Bahi also agreed to this proposal but urged caution so that panic would not break out in the city.

After Wahmubu had finished his story, he said goodbye to those present and, together with Princess Manamii, went for a walk in the palace garden.

Sheikh Neg El Bahi instructed Jefmadan to ride back on patrol and turned to Vrenli.

"Would you please follow me to my private chambers?" asked the sheikh, getting up from the table.

Vrenli nodded and followed him.

Sheikh Neg El Bahi walked wordlessly through the hall towards his chambers and informed the guards at the door that he did not want to be disturbed. He then entered the room, followed by Vrenli.

"Sit down, my friend," the sheikh said kindly to Vrenli and took a seat himself on his chair behind a white marble table. He plucked some grapes from the vine lying in a golden bowl and savored them.

"So Hogmaunt is your name," said Sheikh Neg El Bahi and looked thoughtfully at Vrenli.

"Yes, Vrenli Hogmaunt. But why are you surprised by my name?" asked Vrenli.

Sheikh Neg El Bahi stood up from his chair, walked to one of the huge windows and looked down on the city.

"I knew a Hogmaunt from Abketh, is he perhaps a relative of yours?" asked the sheikh.

Vrenli told him that the only two male Hogmaunts, apart from himself, were his father and grandfather and that both had passed away. Sheikh Neg El Bahi was saddened by this news and became thoughtful.

"Many, many years ago - it was the time when Tyrindor of Entorbis tried to take Wetherid - my father sent me to Astinhod to renew the alliance with the then king. A mage from Horunguth Island, Master Drobal, who served as an advisor to the king, told me about a book of the highest importance that was in Abketh. He asked me to travel with him to Tawinn. That's where I met Erendir Hogmaunt," the sheikh said, waiting eagerly for Vrenli's reaction. However, he did not mention that his grandfather was a Keeper of the Book.

"That was my grandfather," Vrenli confirmed proudly.

Sheikh Neg El Bahi was delighted to see Erendir's grandson sitting in front of him, approached Vrenli and hugged him warmly.

"My boy, grandson of Erendir. I'm glad you're here," said the sheikh, on the verge of tears.

"Please tell me what happened to your grandfather. You said he died?" asked the sheikh.

Vrenli told him about his grandfather's illness and his unexpected death when he had returned from a months-long journey to Abketh. With a slight tremor, the sheikh placed his hands on Vrenli's shoulders and looked at him deeply and sympathetically.

"Tell me, did your grandfather tell you anything about a book?" he wanted to know from Vrenli.

Vrenli nodded.

"He read it to me, just like my father," Vrenli replied sadly, as he couldn't remember anything about the book apart from a few stories that had come back to him over the past few days and weeks.

Vrenli continued to tell the sheikh about his encounter with Gorathdin and the voice he had heard inside him.

"I've also had a few dreams," Vrenli continued, taking a deep breath.

"It's all very confusing for me," he added, recounting how he was taken to Desert of DeShadin, his encounter with Nagulaj and then bursting into tears.

"I really hoped that Master Drobal would answer all my questions. How am I ever supposed to get to Horunguth Island on my own?" sighed Vrenli sadly.

He was desperate and all the fears, doubts and horrors of his journey seemed to take possession of his soul at the same time. He began to tremble.

Sheikh Neg El Bahi stood up, walked towards him and gently hugged him.

"My boy, don't cry. Didn't your grandfather tell you that the magic of the elves from the Glorious Valley lies in the book? The book in which the Word that has come to life is written. Didn't he tell you?" Sheikh Neg El Bahi thought for a moment, wondering whether he should share his thoughts with Vrenli, but when he saw him lying so desperately in his arms, he pushed it aside.

"I can't remember almost anything connected with the book. It's as if a dark shadow lies over my memory. It was all so long ago. And I've lost sight of the book since my grandfather died. Please tell me everything you know about it," Vrenli asked.

Sheikh Neg El Bahi sat down on a narrow bench at the back of the room, asked Vrenli to sit next to him and briefly considered how he should explain the meaning of Wetherid's book to him.

"Listen to me, my boy," he said gently and began with the historical background of the book, which he knew from legends, lore and his own experience.

"Long before there were humans, Abkether, dwarves, elves and the multitude of other living beings and creatures in Wetherid, mighty dragons and huge, fearsome wolves lived here. At first, they lived peacefully side by side, but one day they began to disobey the rule of life. They became disobedient to the Father. Their constant struggle for power, their greed and senseless murder only ended when the Father sent powerful beings who then proclaimed his word to put an end to the fighting and misdeeds of the dragons and wolves," the sheikh said when he was interrupted by Vrenli.

"I know this part of the story. I know about the Gooters. Although I didn't know that the book was connected to it. Grandfather didn't tell me," Vrenli explained.

Sheikh Neg El Bahi nodded and continued with his story.

"The King of the Elves then wrote down the Word of the Father so that it would be preserved for all eternity. At least that is the general opinion. There are different views on this. But that is not important now. The Book of Wetherid not only contains the history of the creation of our country, but is also filled with stories, advice and laws of coexistence. It served not only sages, scholars, learners, religious leaders, priests, healers and seers, kings and leaders, and the common man, but also the peace of the whole of Wetherid. An indescribable power flows from the words of this book. Some claim that this power is greater than the magical formulas of the elves of the Glorious Valley described in the book. You must know, Vrenli, that there has not always been peace in Wetherid over the past thousand years, and I am not just referring to the Entorbis' attempts to take Wetherid. No! There were times when the dwarves from Ib'Agier were at enmity with the humans and the humans in turn with the elves. Many of the races were at war with each other. Thirians with the Astinhoders. Scheddifer with both. Only the long-forgotten Star People stayed out of the disputes. During this time, a group of humans, later known as the Keepers, joined forces. They traveled through Wetherid and proclaimed the Word to those who longed for peace. This task did not always evade danger, as some of the warriors were so taken with the power of the book that they wanted to use it for their own ends. It was the Guardians' task to prevent this," Sheikh Neg El Bahi told in detail, interrupting his explanations for a moment.

He went to his table and poured himself and Vrenli a cup of water.

"Who were these Guardians and how were they chosen?" Vrenli asked curiously.

"You'll have to ask Master Drobal about that, my boy," replied Sheikh Neg El Bahi.

Vrenli thought of Gorathdin, who had also put him off to Master Drobal when he had asked him the important questions that were close to his heart.

Vrenli sighed.

"How did Grandfather get the book from Wetherid and where is it now? It couldn't be found at home," asked Vrenli.

Sheikh Neg El Bahi cleared his throat.

"The book is in Fallgar, my boy, it was stolen by Entorbis in the last battle of Wetherid against Tyrindor," the Sheik replied and sighed.

"But that would mean that all our lives are in danger, or even worse, that we are already close to the end," Vrenli shouted desperately.

"It's not quite so bad," Sheikh Neg El Bahi reassured him and told him that when he was with Master Drobal at Vrenli's grandfather's house in Abketh, he had been given some pages from the Book of Wetherid for safekeeping in Iseran. He stood up and walked towards the tapestry hanging in front of them.

He pulled it to the side and there was a door behind it.

"Follow me," he urged Vrenli.

Sheikh Neg El Bahi opened the door and stepped into the small, semi-dark room. In the middle stood a half-height pedestal on which, under a glass dome, was a scroll of parchment.

"Are these pages from the Book of Wetherid?" Vrenli asked.

He felt a slight excitement.

"Yes, my boy, these are the pages that your grandfather and Master Drobal gave me," confirmed Sheikh Neg El Bahi.

He then explained to Vrenli that after all the incidents that had taken place in Desert of DeShadin, he had concluded that the pages in Iseran were no longer safe. However, he did not tell him that he recognized a Keeper of the Book in Vrenli; Master Drobal would have to reveal this to him.

"I fear that Erwight of Entorbis knows that some pages from the Book of Wetherids are in Desert of DeShadin and it is only a matter of time before he tries to take Iseran with the help of his allies. You must take the pages to Master Drobal in Astinhod," Sheikh Neg El Bahi explained his fears.

"But Master Drobal has disappeared, he's not in Astinhod. In any case, I don't think I could make it to Astinhod on my own, especially with the missing pages of the Book of Wetherid," Vrenli admitted, looking sheepishly at the fine carpet.

"Master Drobal has not disappeared, my boy, he is on Horunguth Island, working with the other mages to find out what plan is behind the events that have taken place in Wetherid so far. Take the pages to Astinhod. They are safer there than here anyway and wait for Master Drobal's return," advised the sheikh.

"But then why doesn't anyone in Astinhod know about Master Drobal's whereabouts?" Vrenli wanted to know.

"I assume that this is a precautionary measure by Master Drobal. As you yourself know, Erwight of Entorbis is trying to find allies throughout Wetherid and you can be sure that he has found them in many places," replied Sheikh Neg El Bahi.

"But why do you know about Master Drobal's whereabouts?" Vrenli asked.

Sheikh Neg El Bahi pointed to the golden, oval bowl on the wall in front of them.

"He was here with me about two weeks ago and we exchanged news," revealed the sheikh.

Vrenli approached the bowl and immediately thought of Werlis, Gorathdin, Aarl and Borlix.

While Sheikh Neg El Bahi slowly raised the glass dome, he sang a song that Vrenli knew well.

Once the Father created the peoples of the world,
the reign of wolves and dragons unfurled.
He then wrote the Book of Books,
entrusted it to his youth, by his looks.

The peoples, the peoples shall forever stand,

let a new era arise across the land.

The young man began to read the tome,
unaware of how time had flown.
He walked by night the path ahead,
recalling the father's words he'd been fed

.

The peoples, the peoples shall forever stand,
let a new era arise across the land.

He met a shadow man on the way,
who cast a mighty spell that day.
The book was then taken away from him,
whereupon the young man's search began, grim.

The peoples, the peoples shall forever stand,
let a new era arise across the land.

The youth sought the book in the valley deep,
as a thunderous battle cry did sweep.
Bodies of the dead scattered around,
evil had come to the Glorious Ground.

The peoples, the peoples shall forever stand,
let a new era arise across the land.

He then lifted the glass dome from its pedestal and placed it
carefully on the floor. Slowly, almost reverently, he reached for the

rolled-up pages of the book, put them in a leather bag and handed them to Vrenli.

"Here, my boy! Take them, grandson of Erendir Hogmaunt. Take care of them and hurry on your way to Astinhod. I wish I could accompany you, but I fear that I am too old to undertake such a long journey," said the sheikh in a depressed voice and sighed.

"But my daughter Manamii will accompany you. She will renew the alliance with Astinhod in my name and in the name of the city of Iseran and the Scheddifer people. We must reunite," the sheikh continued.

Vrenli was not entirely comfortable with the whole thing. He had a great responsibility and the thought of the long journey and the many dangers that might await him were already weakening him, even though he knew that Wahmubu and Princess Manamii would be accompanying him.

"If only Werlis, Gorathdin, Aarl and Borlix were with me," he thought as he looked at the sheikh, who was waiting for an answer from him.

"I don't really know what to say. Everything you've told me sounds incredible, although much of it sounds very familiar to me. However, given the events of the last few weeks and what I have heard in Kajir, I think your fears are to be taken seriously. I will do everything I can to help avert the impending danger. Even if I don't really understand everything that's going on. I will try to find Master Drobal so that I can finally get answers to my questions and I will also travel to Astinhod with Wahmubu and your daughter to bring the book pages to safety. But I'm not entirely comfortable with all of this," Vrenli said.

"I believe in you, Vrenli. You'll manage it all! I'm convinced of that," replied the sheikh and patted Vrenli on the shoulder.

They both went back to the sheikh's chamber.

Once there, he rang for a palace servant and instructed him to take Vrenli to a guarded guest room.

He said goodbye to Vrenli with a hug.

"Take good care of yourself and the contents of the leather bag. Tomorrow morning, I will make all the necessary arrangements so that you and Manamii can set off for Astinhod," the sheikh informed him.

Vrenli bowed to Sheikh Neg El Bahi and followed the palace servant into his room, where he took the pages of the Book of Wetherid out of the bag and studied them carefully.

However, he was unable to understand the strange characters that he had seen several times as a small child when his father or grandfather read the book to him. He stayed in bed for a while, looking at the pages spread out in front of him, then suddenly jumped up and called for a palace servant to bring him a needle and thread.

Vrenli locked the door then took his cloak and began to slowly unravel the lining at the bottom. He went to the washing bowl on a chest of drawers next to the door, took the silk cloth lying next to it and wrapped it several times around the pages, which he then carefully pushed into the inside of the cloak. He painstakingly sewed the bottom of his cloak back up along the unraveled seam.

He then took one of the candles from the seven-burner stand and sealed the seam with the hot wax. Then he lay down in bed and fell fast asleep.

The next morning, when one of the palace servants led Vrenli to the lavishly laid table, Wahmubu and Manamii were already sitting there.

"I will not let you go alone; besides, I have given Vrenli my word to accompany him," Wahmubu emphatically emphasized to Manamii. Vrenli knew immediately that the sheikh had already spoken to his daughter about the upcoming journey to Astinhod. He took a seat in silence and ate some fruit.

The door to the dining room opened. Sheikh Neg El Bahi entered. Wahmubu stood up, bowed and immediately told him that he wanted to accompany Manamii and Vrenli. The sheikh looked at his daughter. He knew that she was a good fighter. She was a

Scheddifer assassin, but she was a woman and his daughter, so Wahmubu's wish to accompany her came at just the right time.

"So be it," said Sheikh Neg El Bahi succinctly and called for one of his viziers.

He ordered his ten most capable riders to escort the group to the desert border.

"From the border to Astinhod, you are on your own. It would be too conspicuous if several Iseran riders were seen going to Astinhod," warned the sheikh.

He sat down at the table with them and began to explain to his daughter, Wahmubu and Vrenli the quickest way to Astinhod.

"Keep north near the border of the desert; to the south you may encounter underwater creatures from Moorgh. After the border, continue northwest. If you see Zeel, which is west of Irkaar, then you have strayed too far west. Do not try to travel on the known paths and trails and beware of the Raging Hordes north of Thir. Their village is no more than a two-day journey northwest of its border. Once you reach Wanderbuk, it's not far to the city of Astinhod. Four or five days to the north. Stay away from the Dark Forest to the west. The druids are easily angered if the peace of the forest is disturbed," the sheikh explained and then led them to the stables north of the palace.

Vrenli, Wahmubu and Manamii were provided with gold, weapons, food and the fastest horses the nomads had. Jefmadan, who had brought Vrenli and Wahmubu to Iseran, was given the task of accompanying the three with his men to the border of Desert of DeShadin.

The Raging Hordes

The closer Vrenli, Wahmubu, Manamii and the ten riders led by Jefmadan approached the border, the more the vegetation increased. In place of the low-growing thorny plants, bushes and cacti, half-tall pines, berry bushes and, in some places, yellowish-brown tufts of grass grew. As Vrenli looked high above himself into the sky, he saw a screeching falcon on the lookout for mice and lizards. The strong rays of the sun burned Vrenli's skin, but here, where the desert climate mixed with that of the sea, there was a steady breeze that cooled him slightly.

From the border mountains in the north, a shallow stream flowed past them towards the south, where it finally flowed into the Southern Sea, thousands of steps away.

They had been riding through the scorching, dry desert for three days now and Vrenli had only really slept through the night once, and that was last night when they stayed with Wahmubu's tribe. Wahmubu's father was very proud that his son was accompanying Manamii and Vrenli and he urged his son to finally ask for Manamii's hand in marriage when they returned. Wahmubu promised to it much to the delight of the desert princess.

Vrenli was happy for the two of them and as they had been riding side by side for some time now, Vrenli's eyes often fell on the desert princess. Her dark, shimmering skin glistened in the sun. Like all Scheddifer people, Manamii was tall and had a very muscular, sinewy build for a woman. Her striking, angular facial features were not hidden by her pinned up long, thick, black hair. She had large, deep brown eyes, long black eyelashes and narrow, raised black eyebrows. Her lips were full and dark red, which was typical of all desert women.

Initially, Vrenli was unaware of Manamii's true profession. It wasn't until he observed her deft handling of a dagger, throwing knives, and a crossbow that he began to suspect her skills were not just for show. Her masterful techniques and extensive knowledge of poisons hinted at a life spent training in the art of silent killing from her early childhood. Manamii had also perfected the arts of stealth and surprise attacks, wearing light leather armor that enhanced her speed and agility in battle. Despite her royal status as a princess, she was every bit a warrior.

As Vrenli glanced at Wahmubu, who sat upright in the magnificent saddle of his noble white horse, he reflected on the contrasts between them. Wahmubu, a desert prince and proud warrior with healing knowledge, could be as gentle as a lamb or as fierce and aggressive as a desert wolf. Observing them together, Vrenli mused, "They were actually made for each other." His thoughts, however, were abruptly interrupted by Jefmadan's call to halt. He pointed with his hand to the still sandy ground.

"Underwater creatures from Moorgh have come this way," Jefmadan said to his riders, looking around.

"These are definitely their tracks," Wahmubu confirmed, looking at the wavy drag marks in the sand. Manamii stood on the back of her horse to get a better view of the terrain.

"I don't see anything suspicious. It's probably been a while since they came this way," Manamii told Wahmubu and Jefmadan.

"Let's ride north and then further east along the mountains," Jefmadan suggested, pulling on his horse's reins and leading it towards the northern border mountains, which they soon reached. Vrenli was pleased that the air was much cooler at the foot of the mountains.

The group was riding less than fifty paces from the smooth, shady, steep rock faces when they suddenly heard the thunderous sound of falling boulders.

Jefmadan looked up.

"Desert trolls!" he shouted and ordered everyone to follow him. He spurred his horse on and galloped towards the cactus forest in front of them. The desert trolls jumping down from the rock faces initially tried to run after the riders, but as the Scheddifer's horses were far too fast for them, they soon gave up the chase.

"That was more than close! We'll soon reach the border and we shouldn't stop until then!" Jefmadan shouted to the others as they rode about four hundred to five hundred paces into the forest of colorful, flowering cacti.

They all spurred their horses on and rode as fast as they could behind Jefmadan towards the valley just a few thousand paces ahead.

It was shortly after midday when the fourteen riders rode out of the valley into a sparsely vegetated grassy landscape. Jefmadan gave the signal to halt and led his horse towards Wahmubu, Manamii and Vrenli.

"We have made it! The border to Thir lies ahead of us," announced Jefmadan, pointing to the horizon in the south, where the Southern Sea lay far ahead of them. Vrenli was fascinated by the huge masses of water. He sucked in the salty, fresh air and stretched. Manamii gave Vrenli a smile when she noticed his delighted look.

"Those tiny little dots on the water are fishing boats," Wahmubu explained, placing his hand protectively over his eyebrows to avoid being blinded by the glare of the sun.

Vrenli looked intently to the south and when he saw the black dots, he thought of Aarl, who had told him about the southern fishermen.

"Let's take a break here and look after the horses," Jefmadan suggested and instructed five of his warriors to explore the surrounding area.

Manamii and Wahmubu tied their horses to an umbrella acacia and then prepared a simple meal for everyone.

Vrenli talked with Jefmadan. They exchanged stories about the customs of the Scheddifer and Abkether while the other five Iseran warriors tended the horses.

When the other riders returned from their exploration, they all ate together and then rested under the shade of the trees.

They rode on and after a while came to a paved path that led to Irkaar.

"From here, you must ride on alone. Keep to the north," said Jefmadan, who held out his hand to Wahmubu and Vrenli.

He bowed to Manamii.

"I wish you good luck on your long journey. Take care," Jefmadan said goodbye and rode back west with his men.

Vrenli, Wahmubu and Manamii rode towards an initially low-growing, sparse forest after they had left the foothills of the mountains to the north behind them.

"Let's ride through this forest, off the beaten track," suggested Wahmubu, leading his horse through the low pines and bushes into the forest.

After less than five hundred steps, they were disappointed to discover that it was impossible to cross the wilderness, which was overgrown with thorny bushes, dense shrubs and vines, with their horses.

"We can't get any further here with our horses," remarked Wahmubu, jumping off the saddle and helping Vrenli and Manamii dismount.

He whispered something into the two mounts' ears and sent them back to Iseran.

The three then tried to make their way north on foot through the unfamiliar surroundings for Wahmubu and Manamii. With the sharp, broad blade of his scimitar, Wahmubu began to cut a path through the thorny bushes, slowly but steadily paving the way for them.

After some time, beeches and oaks mingled with the low-growing pines. Instead of the thorny bushes and shrubs, which no longer thrived due to the lack of sunlight, the forest floor became overgrown with grasses, mosses and mushrooms. They were now making much faster progress. They penetrated deeper and deeper into the forest. Many paces high, dense fir trees took the place of the low-growing pines. The forest terrain became increasingly hilly and the many deep ravines they had to avoid made it difficult to keep going.

Vrenli, for whom the forest was a familiar environment, was the first to notice that they had strayed too far to the east.

"We have to go more to the northwest," he said to Wahmubu, who went ahead of them and then changed course.

They reached a deep ravine that Vrenli almost fell in had he not grabbed onto the branch of a fallen tree at the last moment.

"That was close, little friend," Wahmubu remarked and tried to look up through the dense treetops to check the sun's position in the sky.

"It's already approaching evening, we should look for a suitable place to camp before it starts getting dark," he told Vrenli and Manamii.

He looked around, searching for a way around the ravine in front of them.

"Let's try over there," Vrenli recommended after spotting a small clearing to the west.

Wahmubu and Manamii agreed and walked carefully along the edge of the ravine.

When they reached the clearing, they entered a dry coniferous forest, which they walked through until dusk.

Vrenli looked up at the sky and checked the position of the North Star.

"I think we've lost our way! The sheikh said that we should see the North Star ahead of us when we get out of the border area," Vrenli told the two with regret.

"We have to keep further north," Wahmubu explained. Manamii remained silent.

"Let me think for a moment," Vrenli asked.

He was just about to sit down on a fallen tree trunk when he heard a loud knock followed by the crunching of slowly breaking wood.

"Is there a settlement in this area?" asked Wahmubu.

Vrenli shrugged and admitted that he had never actually left the borders of Tawinn before and had no idea where they were. Manamii reminded them of her father's words, who had warned them about the village of the Raging Hordes in the west.

"Is it possible that we've gone too far east after all?" Manamii asked the two of them.

"Could well be. But that would mean we've been going in the wrong direction since the afternoon," replied Vrenli.

"If you ask me, we should head back west and then further north," he added.

"It's already dawning. There's no point in going any further. We should set up camp here for the night," decided Wahmubu and set down his large leather bag filled with dried zarukk meat, dried fruit, a bag of water and some herbs from Desert of DeShadin.

Vrenli and Manamii nodded in agreement.

Wahmubu started to pick up dry branches from the forest floor when Vrenli told him not to.

"We don't know who or what caused the noises earlier and I think it would be wiser not to have a fire tonight," suggested Vrenli.

Wahmubu nodded and threw the branches back on the ground. Manamii sat down on the damp, leaf-covered forest floor. Wahmubu and Vrenli crouched down in front of the trunk of an oak tree. While Vrenli told Wahmubu and Manamii about Abketh and his friends, they relished the sweet, dried fruit.

It was getting dark. The sounds of the day turned into the sounds of the night. The loud call of an owl, whose den was nearby, rang out. The rustling of dried leaves startled Vrenli briefly. When he noticed a hedgehog crawling out from behind a bush in its nocturnal search for worms and caterpillars, he was reassured.

Wahmubu took three dried strips of zarukk meat from the travel bag and handed two of them to his fellow travelers.

"I miss my friends very much," sighed Vrenli, staring sadly into the darkness.

"You'll see them again soon. When we arrive in Astinhod, you can tell them about your adventures in Desert of DeShadin over a cup of wine or two," Wahmubu comforted him and smiled.

A short howl from a wolf not far away made Vrenli flinch. He had not yet forgotten his painful encounter with the desert wolves.

"Maybe we should light a small fire," suggested Wahmubu, but Vrenli denied it.

Manamii reached into one of the many small leather pouches she had hanging from her belt, took a pinch of a powder in her fingertips and sprinkled it on her small silver shield, lying beside her on the forest floor. The metal began to glow faintly. They now had just enough light to look at each other.

"What's that?" Vrenli wanted to know.

"Moon powder. It intensifies the moonlight," Manamii explained and lay down in Wahmubu's arms.

Both fell asleep shortly afterwards. Vrenli lay down on his cloak from the Dark Forest and listened to the sounds of the night for a while until he too was finally overcome by sleep.

The next morning, Manamii was woken by a dangerous growl. Four wolfhounds had surrounded them. She nudged Wahmubu lightly with her elbow and he slowly opened his eyes. However, Manamii's movement was noticed by the dogs, who paced nervously back and forth. One of them bared its teeth and howled. Vrenli awoke frozen in fear. Before Wahmubu and Manamii could reach for their weapons, barbarians armed with huge axes appeared and glared at the three lying on the ground.

"We are harmless traders," Wahmubu lied and slowly stood up. A dog was about to pounce on Wahmubu when one of the barbarians held it back by the hair on its neck.

"Search them and tie them up. Then take them to the village," the largest and fattest of the barbarians ordered the other four. Wahmubu, who was counting the barbarians and wolfhounds, thought that a fight was hopeless when he noticed Manamii reach for her belt and pull a throwing knife from its sheath. Wahmubu reached for her hand and shook his head.

"There are too many," he whispered to her.

Manamii let go of the handle of her throwing knife.

"Luckily for you, you surprised me in my sleep," Manamii said and submitted to the barbarian, who took the throwing knife from her and then tied her up with rope.

"Take their things!" the leader ordered his men and pushed Wahmubu in front of him.

The three were led through the forest by the five burly barbarians dressed in furs and accompanied by their wolfhounds.

They reached a wide clearing where several fallen trees lay rotting. In the middle of the clearing was the village of the Raging Hordes. At the four corners of the village, aligned with the cardinal points, tower-like wooden scaffolds rose close to a ten-step high wooden rampart that surrounded the village. In front of the rampart, pointed wooden stakes protruded menacingly from the ground.

Vrenli looked fearfully at the four heavily armed, tall and muscular barbarians standing guard in front of the village gateway. Their grim, bearded faces did not bode well. From a distance he could hear the loud, bellowing voices of the villagers and he got an idea of why the barbarians were called the Raging Hordes by the peoples of Wetherid.

He remembered Gorathdin's tale of rough and violent Northmen as they crossed the Border Forest together. Gorathdin had told him that a hundred and thirty years ago, when an ice age broke over the north country, the clan of barbarians had moved over the northern pass to Wetherid. The pack tried to forcefully claim land near Relvis. However, they were driven off by an army led by the then King of Astinhod.

The barbarians who survived fled south, where they fought another battle with the elves of the Dark Forest. With the help of the mighty druids, they pushed the barbarians back from their realm. The attackers, who suffered heavy losses, then moved further south, where they devastated the village of Wanderbuk and settled southwest of it in a huge, dense forest area.

Their population grew rapidly and as they lived mainly on game - agriculture and livestock farming were alien to them - they had to extend their hunting grounds further and further. They penetrated deeper into the open and untouched forest area.

Over the years, the peoples of Wetherid had come to accept the barbarians' existence and even entered trade relations with them. As they were excellent and well-organized hunters, they had game meat, hides, horns and tallow at their disposal. The druids of the Dark Forest, however, looked with disfavor on the clan of the Northmen. They disliked the cruel hunting methods and their large-scale hunts left traces of destruction in Wetherid's forests. When it became increasingly common for the barbarians to enter the Dark Forest to hunt rare animals for pure profit, Mergoldin, the Highest Druid, declared war on the clan leader.

Not long afterwards, a bloody battle broke out in the surrounding forests of Wanderbuk. The barbarians, helpless against the might of the druids and their allied wild animals, as well as the deadly arrows of the elves, suffered heavy losses. Had Mergoldin not shown leniency at the time, the barbarians would have been wiped out.

"Even if they do not obey our laws and are hostile toward us, we must respect their right to live," Mergoldin spoke to the assembled druids and elves at the time.

However, Mergoldin also warned the barbarians never to set foot in the Dark Forest again, as this would mean their end. More than forty years had passed since then, and like their ancestors in the Northland, the barbarian clan split up when it reached a certain size. About half of them moved a four-day journey to the east, where they settled in a wooded area north of the Vast Plain to build a new village and open a new hunting ground.

Loud roaring laughter from the guards at the village entrance brought Vrenli back from his memories.

Together with Wahmubu and Manamii, he entered the west village of the Raging Hordes as a prisoner. The clan leader was Erik, Warwik's older brother. The two dark-skinned men from Desert of DeShadin caused astonishment among the barbarians arriving at the village square. Only a few of them had ever seen a Scheddifer before. A horde of children playing in the earthy village square ran towards Wahmubu and Manamii. They placed their dirty hands on their dark skin. Two of the older children struck Wahmubu's legs with their wooden swords, and the others threw small stones at Vrenli and Manamii. The eyes of the women and men dressed in leather and wrapped in furs pierced the three prisoners. Some of the villagers, who stood in a circle around them, began to stamp their feet vigorously on the ground.

"Bring the dark-skinned beauty to my hut!" a deep voice shouted.

A bear pelt hanging in front of the entrance to the large main house on the village square was pushed aside and a tall, muscular barbarian appeared. He had blond hair hanging in his face and was wrapped in a thick bearskin. He looked at her grimly.

The crowd in the village square fell silent as Erik, the son of Trom, stepped out of the main house and walked towards the three prisoners. He glared angrily at Wahmubu.

"What are you, inhabitants of Desert of DeShadin, doing here in our forest?" Erik wanted to know.

None of the three answered.

Erik turned his eyes to Manamii's tanned body and stared at her lustfully. Wahmubu noticed this and wanted to go after Erik, but Vrenli stood in front of him. '

"We are merchants traveling to Astinhod to buy goods," Vrenli replied.

"Nobody asked you, Abkether," Erik replied scornfully. "Let the desert man answer!" Erik ordered and looked at Wahmubu again.

"We are traders, as our friend already mentioned," Wahmubu confirmed and pulled Manamii closer to him by her arm.

"You look more like lovers to me. What's the Abkether doing with you, is he a trader too?" Erik continued, looking down at Vrenli.

"Is it forbidden for an Abkether to trade?" Vrenli countered, whereupon Erik's strong arm grabbed him by the scruff of the neck and lifted him into the air.

Vrenli began to kick his legs and, as he was close enough to Erik's upper body, he pushed his right knee into his stomach. Erik gasped for air and let Vrenli fall to the floor.

"Lock up the desert man and the Abkether and take the dark beauty to the main house!" Erik ordered the two barbarians standing next to the prisoners. Wahmubu tore the rope that bound his hands behind his back and struck the two barbarians down.

"Don't touch her!" he shouted at Erik.

However, he only laughed and knocked Wahmubu to the ground with the powerful blow of his right hand. Several barbarians immediately pounced on him and held him so tightly to the ground that he lost consciousness.

Erik cast another lustful glance at Manamii and went back into the main house. The barbarians, who took the unconscious Wahmubu and Vrenli into a hut locked with a thick wooden door, stole Wahmubu's golden jewelry and then searched Vrenli, where they found a leather bag and a pouch full of gold coins. The two barbarians then left the hut and locked it with a thick beam. Wahmubu regained consciousness a few moments later. He took a quick look around the small, dark hut and when he realized that Manamii was not with them, he ran against the thick wooden door with all the strength he could muster and tried to break it down. But the door held firm. Wahmubu sank to his knees. It was the first and last time Vrenli saw him cry. He gently put his arm around Wahmubu's shoulders and finally began to cry himself.

Erik sat on a heavy wooden chair in the middle of the main house and stared at Manamii standing before him with her hands tied behind her back and guarded by two of his men. Manamii's dark skin was glistening with sweat as she struggled to free her hands from the shackles.

"Wild as a cat," the barbarian holding her remarked, placing his large hand on one of Manamii's breasts.

293

Manamii acknowledged this by spitting at him and kicking him in the shin. Before he could raise his hand against Manamii, Erik ordered his two men to leave the main house.

"Watch out, Erik, she's got a strong kick," laughed the barbarian and locked the door.

Manamii stood in front of Erik with a contemptuous look.

"I like it when you fight back," said Erik, grinning lecherously.

He stood up from his chair and walked towards Manamii. He grabbed her breasts with his two strong hands. Manamii turned her eyes away from Erik but did not resist. She knew that her only way of getting out of this situation untouched was to make him believe that she liked him.

She therefore began to kiss him hesitantly. She tried to make Erik believe that she was enjoying it and finally Erik cut the ties on her hands. Manamii put her left hand around Erik's neck and kissed him again. With her right hand, she reached into one of the small leather pouches hanging from her belt, took some of the powder between her fingertips and blew it into Erik's eyes.

"I can't see anything, you damned witch, what have you done to me?" he screamed and before he could call for help, Manamii punched him twice in the groin.

Erik sank to the ground like a stone, whereupon Manamii rushed as fast as she could to the opposite window, opened it and climbed out.

With quick but silent steps, she crept from the back of the main house towards the nearby rampart. She climbed up the tree posts, jumped over the sharp wooden stakes to the ground and crawled into the adjacent forest, where she ran as fast as she could. When she was sure she wasn't being followed, she stopped and hid under a fallen tree trunk to catch her breath.

She was in a better position than Wahmubu and Vrenli, but she didn't have weapons or food and, above all, she did not know where she was and in which direction she had run.

However, she knew that she was alone and that Wahmubu and Vrenli couldn't help her. She was not only worried about them, but also about the pages of the book Vrenli was carrying. She decided to stay under the tree trunk until dusk and hoped that with the help of the stars she would find which direction to go to get to Zeel whom she assumed must lie somewhere to the southeast.

She was aware of the danger of crossing the forest alone in the dark, so she looked for a suitable branch to defend herself against wild animals. Time passed very slowly under the tree trunk, but finally night fell and Manamii could see the North Star rising in the sky. She now knew where west was.

The Dark Forest

To make faster progress, Gorathdin left his heavy fire axe from Ib'Agier with Werlis, Aarl, Borlix and Arkondir. Its weight would only hinder him as he walked through the Dark Forest. He was armed only with the traditional weapons of the elven rangers: a short sword, bow and arrow and hunting knife.

It was already midnight, but the darkness in the forest was no obstacle for an elf whose eyes were as sharp as an eagle's and pierced the darkness like an owl. It made no difference to Gorathdin whether he walked through the forest by day or night since he knew every path and footbridge. He knew the deep ravines, steep hills and rushing streams. He had often walked through every coniferous and mixed forest, no matter how dense, and he remembered every clearing, no matter how small.

He was Gorathdin, the half-breed, and the Dark Forest was his home. He was the first child in the history of Wetherid to be born from a love affair between a druid and an elven woman, so he did not always have it easy in his youth.

The druids of the Dark Forest did not regard him as one of their own. The magic of the Tree of Life, which would have given Gorathdin not only the powerful magic of the druids but also the ability to transform himself into an animal of his choice, was denied to him by the council. They did not approve of the love affair between one of their own and an elven woman.

Nevertheless, Gorathdin had half the blood of a druid in him, and so he had the ability to speak with animals. The trees also often came to his aid with their strong, gripping roots and branches. He owed these two gifts to his father, who also taught him the laws of the druids, which Gorathdin always tried to follow. He had never killed a living creature in the forest out of pure lust. He hunted only to feed himself, and he met his need for wood as best he could with what the trees freely provided to the creatures of Wetherid.

His parents, who could not live together because of the strict laws, therefore decided that Gorathdin would grow up with his mother. He learned to use ranger weapons in his early youth and was more skilled with them than most of his peers. The ability of the elves of the Dark Forest to camouflage themselves, to see over long distances and in the dark, to hear all and sense danger, he owed to the elven blood that flowed like fire within him.

Gorathdin grew up to be an excellent hunter. Tracking and killing game was easy for him and the traps he devised and built never ceased to amaze the oldest and most experienced rangers. He lived happily among his people for more than a hundred years, but as he was a half-breed, he always sought contact with humans.

After he had grown into a man, he expressed the wish to live among them for some time. Although his parents were not happy with his decision, they respected it and allowed him to leave the Dark Forest.

The first years he spent among humans were some of the darkest in his life. He encountered rejection, ridicule and violence. But he did not give up. He learned the customs and habits of the humans. He adapted to them and quickly discovered that he found it easier to be accepted in larger settlements or villages. He therefore decided to move to Astinhod, where he had lived for more than seventy years. He was the only inhabitant of the town descended from elves who had gained respect and renown in those years.

He was even appointed Knight of Astinhod and Earl of Regen by King Grandhold for his services to Astinhod and the whole of

Wetherid. Gorathdin had known King Grandhold since he was a small child, and over the years they became friends.

Gorathdin gained the king's complete trust. He was at the king's side when he married the queen, who died ten years earlier, forty years ago. He held her daughter, the lovely and beautiful Princess Lythinda, in his arms as a small child and often rocked her to sleep.

Neither King Grandhold nor Gorathdin himself could have foreseen the feelings that arose between her and Gorathdin as Lythinda matured into a woman. Because of their different races, King Grandhold disapproved of their love. He felt betrayed and taken advantage of by Gorathdin and a deep wedge divided their friendship. Gorathdin tried to explain to King Grandhold that he and Lythinda were more-or-less at the same stage in their lives. He even claimed that they were almost the same age, but his arguments fell on deaf ears. It was only when Master Drobal pointed out to King Grandhold that there were some relationships between humans and elves in Wetherid and that the long life of the elves would pass to his daughter if they received the blessing of the Queen of the Glorious Valley that King Grandhold changed his mind. Had it not been for the incident in the Three Vines inn, Gorathdin and Lythinda would already be a bride and groom.

Gorathdin ran through the forest as fast as the wind. He leapt light-footedly over every obstacle in his path. When the sun began to rise, he was only a two-day journey from the center of the Dark Forest. As he had been running all night, he decided to take a short rest and lay down in the dewy moss under an oak tree.

He looked at the ancient, mighty trees that surrounded him.

"I'm back, my friends," he said quietly, whereupon the branches of the trees moved as if by a breeze, as if to welcome him.

As the sun rose, many animals began their daily search for food. Gorathdin encountered hares, deer, wild boar and greeted a lynx that had retreated from its nightly hunt to a thick branch of a beech tree. Gorathdin was glad to be home again and, assuming his whereabouts would not go unnoticed by other rangers and the druids, he walked on without disguising himself. He knew that there could be a transformed druid behind almost any animal in the Dark Forest.

There were no large settlements of rangers, as they only lived in small groups and usually slept in trees or used a natural shelter. Only a few of them built dwellings from twigs, grasses and leaves. When Gorathdin arrived at a small clearing in the middle of which stood a solitary weeping willow, he stopped and concentrated on all his senses. He was looking in the direction of the trees bordering the clearing when his gaze stopped at a beech tree. A ranger had retreated into the tree with his wife and a small child when they heard someone approaching from a distance.

"Eldor min helvajar!" called Gorathdin and raised his hand in greeting. The ranger and his wife leapt light-footedly from the beech tree onto the grassy ground with a somersault. The child, lingering, hid behind the broad trunk. Like them, Gorathdin had pointed ears and glowing dark green eyes, but his human features immediately told the two rangers who he was.

"You must be Gorathdin, the half-breed," the ranger recognized and bowed to Gorathdin.

"Yes. That's what they call me here in the Dark Forest," Gorathdin replied with a smile and bowed.

"What brings you back after such a long time?" the ranger wanted to know.

Gorathdin initially wondered whether he should tell the truth and finally decided, after some back and forth, to tell the two of them about his search for a hornbear.

They were rangers like him and Gorathdin trusted them. However, he did not tell them the reason he was looking for a hornbear, and the elven couple did not ask.

Gorathdin knew that it was very unlikely that a hornbear was in this area, as their preferred habitat, the grassy hills with their many dens, was to the west. Hornbears also needed a river in their immediate vicinity, as fish were their preferred prey, and there were none to be seen, heard or smelled here.

Nevertheless, Gorathdin asked the two rangers if they had seen any of the hornbears that had lived in Wetherid in the time of the dragons and giant wolves. As expected, they answered his question in the negative.

"It is not advisable for you to go hunting for one alone," warned the elf man.

"I can accompany you if you wish," he offered Gorathdin.

"I am very grateful for your offer, but I do not want to put you and your family in danger," Gorathdin replied and bowed politely.

The ranger also bowed and, with a great leap, he and his wife jumped back into the beech where their little son was waiting for them.

"I wish you good luck and may the Tree of Life protect you!" the ranger called down from the tree and camouflaged himself.

Gorathdin ran on. He penetrated deeper and deeper into the forest. He had been running for a whole day now without a long rest and he decided to stop his haste for a moment. He walked slowly along a narrow path, breathing in the coniferous scent of the pine forest deeply and singing a song.

There, where the forest is densest of all.
There, where the light through the branches can fall.
There stands the tree since time's first dawn.

Its breath sweeps like the wind through the wood,
Its deep roots holding firm as they should.
Its limbs, so mighty and so grand,
Cannot be broken by the strong wind's hand.

There, where the forest is densest of all.
There, where the light through the branches can fall.
There stands the tree since time's first dawn.

The creatures of the wood are its friends.
The druids of the wood, its brethren's amends.
The protector of every ranger's child blend.

There, where the forest is densest of all.
There, where the light through the branches can fall.
There stands the tree since time's first dawn.

Over and over, he repeated the verses of the song that his
mother had sung to him every night before going to bed.

Singing, he wandered past the old, mighty fir trees as a delicate
female voice returned the song.

Gorathdin stopped, turned around and took his mother in his
arms as she stepped out from behind a fir tree. She kissed
Gorathdin on the forehead, just as she had done when he was a
small child.

"Gorathdin, my boy, how glad I am to see you again. I felt that
you would come soon," she said in a soft, sweet voice.

A small, crystal-clear tear flowed down her right cheek.

"Don't cry, mother. You should be happy that I'm here,"
Gorathdin replied, catching his mother's tear with his index finger.

"They are tears of joy, even if they are also tears of sadness, my
boy," she revealed with such a youthful smile that one wouldn't
guess she is two hundred and sixty years old.

"Why sadness?" asked Gorathdin.

"Every visit from you also means a new farewell," she said with
a smile, several tears escaping from her dark green eyes.

Gorathdin had not been home for more than twenty years now
and was therefore glad that he would get some time with his
mother, even if time was pressing. He followed her to the thick-
branched, tall fir tree he had built her a tree house in many, many

years ago, after returning from a journey from the Glorious Valley, where he had first seen elves living in treehouses.

Without much effort, Gorathdin and his mother jumped up the thick branches of the fir tree and entered the dwelling. They sat down on the wooden planks and Gorathdin began to tell his mother about the past twenty years.

He also told her that he had been appointed Knight of Astinhod and Count of Regen. As his mother didn't think much of human titles, but didn't want to offend Gorathdin, she smiled and congratulated him.

When he told her about the sick Princess Lythinda and the feelings he had for the young human, his mother looked up, worried.

"Don't you think you'll get the girl into trouble with that?" she worried, reminding him of his own background and that he hadn't always had it easy because of it.

"Times have changed, mother," Gorathdin assured her. He took his mother's hands, placed them in his and told her that Master Drobal had told him of many marriages between elves and humans.

"I hope that's the case for you," she replied and squeezed his hands.

While his mother told him about the past years in the Dark Forest, Gorathdin lay down on the thick branch that protruded through the open window and fell asleep.

When he woke up some time later, before dawn, his mother had already prepared a deliciously fragrant meal for him. Gorathdin looked out of the window at the sky.

"I wasn't actually planning to sleep that long," he confessed, accepting the lavishly filled bowl she handed him.

While he ate, Gorathdin told his mother that he was looking for a hornbear whose ground-up horn was an important ingredient in a healing potion that he hoped would, at the least, reduce Princess Lythinda's fever.

"You know that hornbears are immune to the magic of the forest," she warned, her face turning serious.

Gorathdin nodded.

"Ask your father, he'll know where you can find one," she suggested.

Gorathdin nodded again.

"That's what I was going to do, mother. I really have to leave now. I hope you understand," he urged.

She nodded and brushed her white-blue hair out of her face.

"Be careful, my boy, hornbears are very dangerous. Even the druids have respect for their strength," she said.

Gorathdin said goodbye to her, kissed her on the cheek and jumped down to the forest floor, landing almost silently.

"Goodbye, mother!" he called up the fir tree.

"Watch out for the forest wraiths!" she called out to him.

Gorathdin did not answer, but only smiled.

He had heard this warning from her too often. Even as a small child, she shouted it after him every time he went into the forest alone. Gorathdin hurried. Like a shadow, he scurried past the surrounding trees, always heading southwest.

The closer he got to the center of the Dark Forest, the darker it became around him even though it was already almost noon on the second day of his journey.

After he reached a section of forest littered with rotten, fallen tree trunks, he noticed the flash of a blade to his right, about four hundred paces away. Loud, creaking noises rang out.

"Forest wraiths," he whispered to himself.

He camouflaged and crept cautiously in the direction of the creak. It was not the first time he had encountered these creatures, which were as old as the forest itself. Their large bodies resembled rotten tree trunks, home to larvae and worms. Their scrawny arms and legs, which looked like withered, bony branches, could grow many steps long in a matter of moments to wrap around their victim. Their strength exceeded that of an elf many times over.

They were fearsome opponents, even for the most experienced rangers.

However, there were two things that forest wraiths feared and every ranger child knew about them.

Fire and woodworms. Fire that could quickly burn their dry, rotten bodies and the small gnawing insects that ate them from the inside.

Gorathdin scurried behind the trunk of a larch tree. Just a few paces in front of him, he saw a ranger fighting with two forest wraiths. The elf skillfully dodged every attempt by the woody, creaky creatures to wrap their branches around him. He twisted and ducked, jumped forwards, backwards and into the air. He was nevertheless caught by one of the thinner, twig-like growths, but he cut them with his hunting knife.

If Gorathdin had had his fire axe from Ib'Agier with him, he would have pounced on the two forest creatures immediately. But since he didn't have it, he had to think about whether and how he could fight them with fire or woodworms, because arrows wouldn't harm them.

He looked around and, not wanting to cause a forest fire, he decided to go for the small, gnawing insects. His eyes quickly searched for dead, rotten tree trunks, three of which he could make out in the immediate vicinity.

Carefully and quietly, he crawled to the nearest ones, cut off the partly dry and rotten bark with his hunting knife and checked them for the small, wood-eating insects.

"Wonderful," he thought to himself.

With his skin color matching the forest floor, he crept closer to the forest wraith, wrapped in his dark green cloak.

His gaze fell on two rotten branches on the ground in front of him. Hoping they were colonized by woodworms, he picked up a branch and hurled it at one of the two forest wraiths standing with their backs to him.

The forest wraith who had been hit turned slowly with a creak and looked with its large, round eyes at Gorathdin, who threw another rotten branch.

After a loud, distorted, crunch that sounded like a deep laugh, the forest wraith began to move its woody body slowly in Gorathdin's direction. Gorathdin rose and hurled the large piece of bark at the forest wraiths with all his might. On impact, the rotten branch shattered and in just a few moments the forest creature was populated with hundreds of the tiny wood-eaters. A long, muffled, creaking cry rang out, whereupon the forest wraiths fled with long, quick strides.

The other forest wraith was still attacking the ranger with its continuously sprouting branches. Gorathdin pulled his hunting knife from the brim of his boot and rushed to the elf's aid. With countless, quick cutting movements of the blade, Gorathdin severed the bulbous head from the woody body of the forest wraith, falling to the ground like a dead tree trunk.

"Thank you for your help, friend," the brown-haired ranger dressed in dark green linen spoke to Gorathdin and bowed.

"You were lucky that my path led me past here. A fight with two forest wraiths alone is almost hopeless," replied Gorathdin and bowed.

"How true, how true. I could not have evaded their attempts to entangle me for much longer. May I know your name, friend?" asked the ranger, whereupon Gorathdin told him his name.

"My name is Temeth. I live not far from here with my family and my brother's family at the small waterfall in the north. I would like to invite you for a meal as thanks for your help. My wife Zathriel is an excellent cook," the ranger suggested.

Gorathdin declined with thanks and told him that he was looking for a hornbear and that time was short.

"Seven days ago, as I was walking past the hill pasture west of the Tree of Life, where the Shadow Brook flows towards Wanderbuk, I saw one from a distance," Temeth reported and Gorathdin thanked him.

The two exchanged a few more words and finally said goodbye. Temeth looked after Gorathdin, who began to walk faster towards the west for some time until he finally disappeared from his field of vision.

As dusk fell, Gorathdin had already left the dense mixed forest behind him and arrived at the end of a young coniferous forest. He was now filled with the strengthening power of the Tree of Life standing nearby. With this power inside, he ran faster and lighter than before. There were only about eight hundred steps between him and the druids' stone circle, which stood in the oldest part of the forest. Thick-trunked, ancient, mighty oaks and beeches, alders and ash trees overgrown with lianas and elms covered in ivy stood like an impenetrable bulwark around the center, which Gorathdin entered reverently.

He walked slowly under the dense crowns of the venerable trees and greeted the thick-trunked witnesses of life, as the laws of the druids demanded.

The damp forest floor, bathed in perpetual darkness by a dense blanket of leaves, was overgrown with man-sized, whimsical mushrooms and shimmering mosses. Gorathdin could already see the small clearing ahead of him, shining in the pale, bright blue light of the Tree of Life. When he arrived, he laid down his weapons in front of the stone circle where the Tree of Life stood, as prescribed by the laws of the druids.

Just as he was about to enter the circle, a deep, grumpy voice sounded behind him.

"It's been a long time since you were last here, son," said the voice.

Gorathdin turned around and looked at a one-eyed bear that had reared up to its full height. Water dripped from its shaggy, soaked brown fur onto the forest floor.

"You took a night bath, father?" Gorathdin asked with a smile.

A whirring, whistling sound was heard, whereupon a warm green light, growing brighter, enveloped the bear.

In a fraction of a moment, the bear disappeared. An old man with a white beard reaching down to his waist and shoulder-length silver-gray hair stepped out of the bright light, closed his dark green tunic decorated with silver embroidery and embraced Gorathdin.

"I've missed you, father," Gorathdin confessed and returned the hug. They both looked at each other for a few moments, smiling wordlessly.

"I wish you could leave the Dark Forest and visit me in Astinhod with mother from time to time," Gorathdin said, causing his father's gaze to turn serious.

"You know that my place is at the side of the Tree of Life, son," his father reminded him and entered the stone circle.

"I know, father," sighed Gorathdin.

"Follow me. We have a lot to talk about," Gorathdin's father urged him.

Gorathdin nodded and followed him into the stone circle filled with bright blue light. They walked slowly towards the Tree of Life and sat down beneath its many-leaved, silvery branches. Gorathdin placed his hand on the thick trunk's smooth, shimmering silver bark.

"I missed you too," he whispered, whereupon one of the branches slowly lowered and gently stroked his hair.

"Leave us for a moment, brothers," Gorathdin's father whispered into the tree, whereupon a druid in the shape of an owl fluttered into the night sky. Another druid, who had taken the form of a lynx, jumped down from the branches to the forest floor and crept out of the stone circle into the darkness.

"Now that we are alone, speak, my son. Something is bothering you," Gorathdin's father gently urged him.

"I would like to ask you and the Tree of Life for permission to kill a hornbear," Gorathdin replied.

"I have known for a long time, my son, that you are searching for a hornbear. You know that nothing that goes on in the Dark

Forest remains hidden from us druids. Our friends, the animals, tell us everything they hear and see," his father replied.

"I already thought so. But please listen to why I have to kill the hornbear," Gorathdin begged and began to tell his father about his journey to Abketh and the spell Princess Lythinda was under.

"As you know, my son, we druids only kill in self-defense. I cannot allow you to kill a creature of the Dark Forest, even if it is a very unpopular one," his father replied firmly.

"But understand, father, it's about the well-being of the woman I love," Gorathdin explained emphatically and tried to convince him with further arguments.

"I cannot allow you to do so, even though I understand your reasons very well. I am bound by the laws of the druids, my son. You must ask the Tree of Life," he replied to Gorathdin, who nodded.

His father stood up and, followed by his son, walked to the center of the stone circle, where he held his staff high above his head and recited a verse in the language of the trees.

A forest green light radiated from the tip of his staff and blended with the current light blue light. A mist rose and enveloped the stone circle.

"Mergoldin, my guardian, you summoned me?" a deep, slow and somewhat creaky-sounding voice sounded from the fog.

"My son, Gorathdin, would like to ask your permission to kill a hornbear," Gorathdin's father spoke into the mist.

"I need its horn to help the Princess of Astinhod," Gorathdin added.

A few moments of silence passed.

"How can killing a creature from the Dark Forest be of any help?" asked the deep, slow voice.

Gorathdin thought about this legitimate question for a moment. He began to tell the voice about his feelings for Princess Lythinda, of Vrenli, Werlis, Aarl and Borlix, and that he feared that the Erwight of Entorbis from Fallgar had set his greedy eyes on

Wetherid, and also mentioning the pages from the Book of Books that remained in Wetherid.

Silence reigned.

Gorathdin and his father waited for an answer from the Tree of Life. After some time, the voice from the mist began to speak again.

"Entorbis! How I despise that name. For generations, this name has brought nothing good with it. What others create, cherish and nurture, this spawn of the shadow destroys with passion. Entorbis!" the voice raged.

"Give me permission to kill the hornbear. I beg you in the name of Lythinda, in the name of Wetherid and in my name," Gorathdin called into the mist and knelt down imploringly.

"So be it!" the voice replied, and the fog lifted.

"Thank you!" cried Gorathdin.

There was no answer.

"I knew that the Tree of Life would agree if you mentioned the name Entorbis," said Mergoldin, taking on the form of a bear again.

"Follow me. Even before you got here, I was able to track one down," growled Mergoldin.

"At the night bath?" Gorathdin inquired and picked up his weapons sitting outside of the stone circle. The bear nodded and walked westward through the night. Only when dawn broke did they change direction and head south towards a dense mixed forest, which they crossed by midday.

"The hill pasture begins up ahead. We have to be careful. As you know, hornbears don't get along well with their relatives," Mergoldin grumbled as he put his paw in the place of his missing eye.

Gorathdin camouflaged himself and followed his father to the nearby hills with countless caves.

Mergoldin turned his nose to the wind.

"The stream is north of here. If we follow it, we will come directly to a hornbear's den," Mergoldin told Gorathdin.

When they arrived at the two-paces deep and twenty-step wide torrent, Mergoldin suddenly stopped and sniffed the wind.

"If my sense of smell doesn't deceive me, and it never has, then I smell orcs. They can't have been in the forest for long, or I would have been told," Mergoldin grumbled.

"How did they get to Wetherid unseen?" asked Gorathdin.

"Either through Mist Moor with the help of the mist elves, where they then took the tunnel of the gray dwarves, or they came to Irkaar by sea," Mergoldin replied.

"We should go and see what they are doing here. They must have assumed that their stay in the Dark Forest would not go unseen. Either they are very stupid or very sure of themselves," Mergoldin pondered.

Gorathdin nodded.

The two moved upstream until they came to a clearing where five heavily armed, stinking and sweating orcs were sitting around a fire. Cautiously, Gorathdin and Mergoldin, still in bear form, crept closer to the enemies from Fallgar. The grunting language of the orcs was difficult for Gorathdin to understand, but he thought that the five warriors from Raga Gur were talking about an animal.

Mergoldin waved his mighty bear head in the direction of the orcs sitting around the fire. Behind them stood a cage with a captive hornbear.

"We're in luck," whispered Gorathdin.

"I don't know if you should call that luck," Mergoldin replied skeptically.

"We'll save a lot of time after we've finished with the orcs," Gorathdin whispered and placed an arrow in the string of his bow.

"Don't be so hasty, my son, there are still five of them," Mergoldin warned.

"Better we drive them apart. That way we can take them on one by one," Mergoldin suggested with a grumble.

Gorathdin nodded in agreement.

"I'll prepare some traps," Gorathdin spoke quietly and crept slowly and stealthily to the opposite side of the clearing, where he disappeared behind the neighboring trees.

He looked out again from behind the trunk of a fir tree at the five orcs, grabbed the strong branch above his head and quietly pulled it down towards him. He stretched the branch back and forth, grabbed a vine growing along the thick trunk of the fir tree and wrapped it around the stretched branch. He then took his bow from his shoulder and shot four arrows with all his strength through the branch, which he then stretched behind the tree trunk and wrapped a piece of the vine around. He then tied the liana to a root sticking out of the ground.

He checked that the arrows were firmly stuck in the branch and placed his right index finger on one of the points that had pierced the branch before taking a few steps towards two berry bushes that he prepared the next trap behind.

Gorathdin peered around. His eyes fell on a hazelnut bush with thick branches. He approached it and chopped off five straight branches as thick as a man's arm with his hunting knife. He sharpened the tops of the branches and buried them behind the two berry bushes so they stuck out of the ground more than halfway at an angle, tip first. Since Gorathdin did not know how much longer the orcs would sit around the fire, he hurried with his last trap.

He wandered through the thicket towards the nearby torrent in search of mist mushrooms. When he got there, Gorathdin had already collected a considerable number of mushrooms. Mist mushrooms owed their name to the fine, yellowish powder dust trapped in their large caps. When the caps broke, a dense yellow mist escaped.

He carefully placed the collected mushrooms in the grass a few steps away from the streambed. Then he went back to the fir tree in the clearing and signaled to his father that he was ready to attack.

Mergoldin transformed back into the shape of a human and waited for another sign from his son. He stepped out from behind the trunk of the fir tree, placed an arrow in the string of his bow and shot it at one of the orcs.

Hissing and whistling, the arrow flew across the clearing towards the orcs and hit the one sitting with his back to Gorathdin on the right shoulder blade. A squealing, snarling cry echoed across the clearing. Four of the orcs leapt to their feet and ran in the direction the arrow had been fired from, broad-bladed daggers drawn and axes raised.

That was the signal for Mergoldin, who raised his staff high above his head. He spoke a verse in the language of the trees and then aimed the tip of his staff at the spot where the rearmost of the orcs running in Gorathdin's direction stood. Green light radiated from the tip of the staff onto the ground in front of the running orc, whereupon strong, intertwined roots grew out of the earth and embraced the Raga Gur warrior.

Mergoldin changed into a bear and pounced on the immobilized orc. Mergoldin struck him with several powerful blows until he slumped to the ground, covered in blood, and then set off in pursuit of the remaining four.

Gorathdin waited in front of the fir trunk until the first orc was close enough. He looked at the furious, axe-wielding orc with his dark green elven eyes, turned around and severed the vine holding the arrow-pierced branch with his hunting knife. The branch sprang forward and the four arrowheads pierced the orc's chest, throwing him backwards with the force of the blow.

Gorathdin turned around and looked at the three orcs following him, cursing furiously. He slowed his pace and ran just fast enough for his pursuers to believe that they would catch him at any moment. Just as one of the orcs threw his axe at Gorathdin, he suddenly leapt into the air. With a somersault he leapt high over the two berry bushes and continued running towards the torrent. The orc, who was the first to run through the thorny bushes, ran straight into the thick, sharpened branches jutting out of the forest floor. The orc toppled forward, grunting in pain, and before he could reach for the branch that had dug into his left thigh, Mergoldin pounced on him.

Gorathdin, now pursued by only two orcs, jumped far over the mist mushrooms right across the stream. He crouched down in the tall grass on the other side, took two arrows from his quiver, placed them side by side in the string of his bow and waited.

The orcs ran over the mist mushrooms, immediately breaking the caps, and causing a huge, yellowish cloud of dust to swirl into the air. The two coughed, spat and ran straight into the stream without stopping, where they were up to their necks in water. Two whirring arrows hit them in the middle of their foreheads. The water in the stream turned blood red.

Mergoldin, who had just arrived at the streambed, waded into the water and washed the orcs' blood from his mouth and paws. Gorathdin jumped into the stream and began splashing around, which Mergoldin, still in his bear form, returned with a fierce swipe of his paws into the water. For a moment, they felt transported back to Gorathdin's childhood when they played together almost every day.

"Let's get the horn," said Mergoldin and, followed by Gorathdin, ran back into the clearing to the dead orcs' campfire, where a stunned hornbear lay in a metal cage just a few steps away.

Gorathdin was about to take a step closer to the cage when he saw a black crow circling above him that immediately flew off to the east when it noticed his gaze.

He was just about to plunge his hunting knife into the stunned hornbear's heart when Mergoldin growled.

"It is not necessary to kill him, my son. All you need is his horn," Mergoldin objected.

Gorathdin nodded and asked for forgiveness.

He carefully placed his hunting knife on the front of the hornbear's head and, with great effort, cut off its horn.

"A bloody affair," Gorathdin stated, the hornbear's blood dripping from his hands to the ground.

"Less bloody than if you had killed him, my son," Mergoldin replied and transformed back into his human form. He slowly stretched his hand across the front of the hornbear's head and a warm, forest-green light radiated from his palm, closing the bleeding wound.

Gorathdin and his father, the highest druid of the Dark Forest and guardian of the Tree of Life, talked for a while at the orcs' campfire until Gorathdin finally made his way back to the Order of the Dragon with the horn in his pocket. Mergoldin opened the cage door, took on the form of a one-eyed bear again and strolled slowly back to the center of the Dark Forest.

Chapter 3

The journey to Horunguth Island

O n his way back to Werlis, Aarl, Borlix and Arkondir, Gorathdin had enough time to think about the group of orcs who had captured the hornbear. The longer he thought about it, the stronger his conviction became that their stay in the Dark Forest must be connected to him and Princess Lythinda in some way.

"The Shadow Lord's henchmen, blindly following his orders to get a share of the spoils when Erwight of Entorbis' shadow has settled over Wetherid. This must be prevented at all costs!" he thought and began to run faster, as if he could already feel the shadow close behind him.

As he turned north to shorten his way back, he thought about why the orcs had taken the hornbear alive. The only reasonable explanation he could come up with was that the orcs had known about his plan and wanted to set a trap for him. That in turn raised more questions.

"Where did they get the information that I was going to the Dark Forest, and how did they know about the horn?" Gorathdin asked himself.

This question occupied him for two days, and on the third day, on the last leg of his return journey, he thought he had finally found an answer.

"There must be a traitor. Someone that King Grandhold trusted!" he thought aloud.

Startled by this thought, he stopped for a moment and looked up at the night sky illuminated by the full moon.

"Don't let it be Werlis, Aarl, Borlix or Arkondir. Father in heaven, I beg you!" Gorathdin whispered to the stars. His trepidation was wiped away by a moment of clarity. "It can't be Werlis, he didn't even know of my or Princess Lythinda's existence before I came to Abketh. Aarl? Aarl lived far away from all events and he had several opportunities to end my life unnoticed. Borlix? No. A dwarf making common cause with Erwight of Entorbis, that can't be. The hatred of the Shadow Lord is rooted too deep in his people for that.

That leaves Arkondir. The Army Commander of Astinhod, who, like me, has often saved my life in battle. My friend for more than thirty-five years. Out of the question!" As he mused, he could see the lights of the monastery ahead of him in the distance.

He began to suspect that one of the monks from the Order of the Dragon might be a traitor.

He gathered all his strength and ran out of the forest towards the clearing.

He decided not to enter through the gate but jumped over the high wall into the monastery garden. Quietly and stealthily, he crept past the flowers, bushes, hedges and shrubs, heading for the lodgings. He cautiously entered the old walls. Like a predatory cat, he crept along the long, dark corridor to the room his friends were sleeping in.

He quietly opened the door and scurried silently to a bed.

"How are you, little friend?" he whispered in Werlis' ear. The latter jumped out of bed, groping for his short sword, and was about to call for help when Gorathdin pressed his hand to his mouth.

"Shh, don't wake the others. Come on, let's go outside," whispered Gorathdin and slipped out of the room again.

Werlis followed him to the monastery garden, confused.

"Why are you sneaking up to my bed like an assassin and why can't we talk inside? It's cold out here!" protested Werlis sleepily.

Gorathdin stopped behind a large, dense bush.

"Keep your voice down, my friend," Gorathdin whispered, placing his index finger on his lips in warning and telling Werlis what had happened in the Dark Forest.

"I can't say for sure, but I think it might have been an ambush!" Gorathdin revealed.

Werlis' eyes grew wide.

"But how did the orcs know about your plan?" Werlis asked quietly.

"That's what gives me food for thought, my friend" Gorathdin replied, looking around.

"Do you think we have a traitor among us?" Werlis asked uncertainly, also looking around.

"Could easily be possible" whispered Gorathdin.

"You don't seriously believe that Aarl or Borlix could be traitors after all the trials we have overcome together, or even an army commander from Astinhod?" Werlis doubted incredulously, looking Gorathdin straight in his dark green eyes. He waited eagerly for an answer.

"To be honest, I don't know what to believe. I don't think so. I've thought about it a lot, but can I really be sure?" Gorathdin pondered.

His voice sounded depressed.

"The way I see it, the traitor can only be one of the monks. I'd put my hand in the fire for Aarl and Borlix, and Army Commander Arkondir is a long-time friend of yours. You don't think he ...?" asked Werlis.

His face became serious.

"No. You're probably right that it's one of the monks, but we can't be too careful," Gorathdin replied quietly.

"I want you to take the horn, Werlis!" Gorathdin decided.

He pulled the horn out of his pocket and handed it to him.

"There's still blood on it!" Werlis remarked and hesitantly reached for it.

"I will leave the monastery and return through the gate again. Watch out for the horn!" Gorathdin whispered and was just about to sneak away when Aarl appeared behind them.

"Gorathdin, you're back!" Aarl rejoiced in a loud voice.

"Shh!" warned Werlis, putting his index finger to his lips.

Aarl immediately pulled a throwing knife from its sheath.

"What has happened? Are you being followed?" asked Aarl, looking around carefully.

"No, I'm not being followed!" whispered Gorathdin.

"But then what are you doing out here in the middle of the night?" Aarl asked, looking at them in amazement.

Gorathdin cast a questioning glance at Werlis, who returned it, looking at his hand.

Gorathdin was just about to tell Aarl about what had happened in the Dark Forest when Borlix came out of the building, yawning, and walked towards the hedge where he had heard faint whispers.

"By all the halls of Ib'Agier, what are you doing here? Oh, Gorathdin, you're back!" he shouted in a loud, grumpy voice.

"Shh!" the three hissed at the same time.

Borlix's eyes glided through the dark garden.

"What's going on here?" he inquired, this time in a hushed, but still too loud, voice.

"Pssssst!" was the simultaneous response from the three.

"So, tell me, what is it? I saw Aarl leave the room and Werlis' bed was empty!" said Borlix, now whispering. Gorathdin looked at Werlis questioningly again.

The latter looked at his hand with a smile. Gorathdin decided to initiate Aarl and Borlix.

"You... you didn't think that one of us...? Really!" Borlix grumbled in a huff.

Aarl could understand Gorathdin's caution.

"One of the monks is most likely a traitor!" whispered Werlis, advising caution.

"I will leave you again, friends, and return through the gate in a moment. Perhaps one of the monks is acting suspiciously," Gorathdin explained to his friends.

Everyone nodded in agreement.

Gorathdin made his way to the wall, jumped over it and headed towards the gate. Werlis, Aarl and Borlix crept quietly back to their room and lay down in their beds as if nothing had happened.

Gorathdin knocked on the mighty gate outside, whereupon a few moments later the small viewing window below his head height opened.

"Mr. Gorathdin, you're back!" the monk behind the window greeted him and opened the gate.

He informed Gorathdin that Brother Transmudin had gathered with some other monks for a nightly prayer at Omnigo's statue and made his way to the temple.

"Were you able to get the horn?" the monk asked.

Gorathdin pretended not to hear the question and followed him in silence. The path to the temple was lined with low torches, but their flames were extinguished by a sudden shower of rain. The monk now began to walk faster.

"Come on, Mr. Gorathdin, you're going to get all wet!" the monk urged him.

Gorathdin paused for a moment and looked up at the cloudy night sky.

When they finally arrived at the temple, soaked through, they found Brother Transmudin kneeling at the statue with several monks saying a prayer.

"Please wait here until they have finished praying. Brother Transmudin will surely come to you immediately," the monk asked and ran through the rain back to the gate.

As Gorathdin's waiting time dragged on, he sat down on one of the covered steps and watched the raindrops falling and bursting on the ground as they were greedily absorbed by the dry earth.

Brother Transmudin, who had finished praying, approached Gorathdin from behind, put his hand on his shoulder and asked him if he could get the horn. At first, Gorathdin did not know how to answer, so he inquired about Princess Lythinda's condition.

"To my regret, her fever has gotten worse," said Brother Transmudin, briefly lowering his gaze.

"Do you have the horn?" repeated Brother Transmudin.

Gorathdin let his gaze wander over the monks kneeling by the statue. He hoped that his return would cause one of them to act conspicuously. But the monks kept their eyes firmly fixed on Omnigo.

"I have the horn!" Gorathdin revealed, looking Brother Transmudin firmly in the eye and hoping that he might make a treacherous gesture.

"Very good, my friend," replied Brother Transmudin and smiled.

"I will send for Brother Theramond immediately so that he can start preparing the potion!" the monk announced happily and instructed one of his brothers in prayer to tell Brother Theramond about Gorathdin's successful mission.

Some time passed, during which Brother Transmudin asked Gorathdin about his journey to the Dark Forest and whether he had possibly met the druid Mergoldin, who was, so to speak, an acquaintance of his.

"The druid guards the Tree of Life and I guard the statue of Omnigo, which makes us both Guardians!" explained Brother Transmudin.

He did not know that Mergoldin was Gorathdin's father.

Gorathdin said that he had fought a long, exhausting battle with the hornbear and that he had not met the druid Mergoldin.

"I'm proud of you!" said Brother Transmudin and patted Gorathdin on the shoulder appreciatively.

Brother Theramond, the old monk who had led Borlix into the catacombs beneath the temple, stepped out of the library towards

Brother Transmudin and Gorathdin. He carried a torch in his left hand and held the old book, wrapped in cloth to protect it from the rain, in his right.

"Do you have the horn?" the old monk asked.

Gorathdin nodded, hoping to detect a telltale sign in Brother Theramond, but the old monk only smiled.

"I'll start preparing the ingredients right away!" announced Brother Theramond, holding out his hand expectantly for the horn. However, Gorathdin asked him to wait a moment because he wanted to tell Werlis, Aarl and Borlix about his success first and show them the horn.

"Bring the horn to my laboratory. Brother Transmudin will show you the way," said the old monk and walked away.

"I will wait for you here and say another prayer," said Brother Transmudin and walked towards the statue. Gorathdin hurried to the lodgings.

"Has anyone been acting suspiciously?" Werlis asked quietly as Gorathdin entered the room and sat up in his bed.

"No, but we have to be on guard. You can give me the horn back now," replied Gorathdin.

Werlis reached under his bed, pulled out the horn and handed it to Gorathdin.

"I'll take it to the old monk in his laboratory so that he can grind it up and mix it with the other ingredients," Gorathdin told his friends.

Aarl and Borlix rose from their beds.

"Better we accompany you!" Borlix suggested and reached for his axe.

Gorathdin agreed.

Together, the four of them made their way to the temple, where Brother Transmudin had just finished his prayer.

"Follow me!" he urged the four of them and led the way to Brother Theramond's laboratory.

The building was located on the opposite side of the temple, just behind the hut where the monks kept their gardening tools.

Brother Transmudin knocked on the heavy door, which Brother Theramond then opened.

"Come in and lock up behind you!" said the old monk, and he went back to the large, angular wooden table covered with glasses and containers of various lengths and widths.

A small oil lamp hanging from the ceiling was the only source of light in the room and cast a shadow over all the books, strange tools and equipment.

"It looks like Vrenli's home in here," Werlis remarked quietly, thinking of his friend with concern.

As no one had heard Werlis' remark, he was left alone with his worries about Vrenli. He sat down on one of the large chairs and watched the old monk as he made his preparations.

Brother Theramond filled some of the jars on the table with dusty powders, dry flowers and different colored liquids.

"I need the horn now!" announced Brother Theramond.

He stretched out his hand, whereupon Gorathdin reached into his pocket and handed him the still bloodstained horn.

The old monk looked at the horn, grabbed it hesitantly, took it to a low cupboard and cleaned it in a bowl of water. He then dried it with a cloth, laid it on the table and examined the one-foot-long, thick, gray-shaded horn in detail.

He thought about the easiest way to pulverize it and tried to scrape at it with a sharp knife, but the blade became blunt rather than just a single particle detaching itself from the horn.

The old monk grabbed a hammer from a box under the table and tried to smash the horn with a few light blows at first, then with increasing force. However, the horn withstood the hammer's blows without any apparent damage.

"Very stubborn!" remarked Brother Theramond and placed the horn in a press that he used to press all kinds of plants. He turned the large wing screw into the thread as hard as he could, and when

Gorathdin realized that the old monk's strength was not enough, he helped him turn it.

But the horn remained intact.

"Give me the horn!" Borlix demanded confidently and held out his hand.

Brother Theramond looked at the dwarf questioningly.

"Give me the horn!" Borlix repeated, whereupon the old monk, with Gorathdin's help, opened the wing screw on the press.

He took out the horn and handed it to Borlix, who placed it on the stone floor in front of him. He raised his axe, the back of which was shaped like a hammer, and brought it down on the horn with a mighty blow. When the hard steel from Ib'Agier hit the horn, propelled by the dwarf's tremendous strength, not only did the horn shatter into many small pieces, but so did the stone floor underneath.

"Hard steel from Ib'Agier!" Borlix shouted with a laugh, swinging his axe at the splintered horn a few more times.

"That's enough!" instructed Brother Theramond, who was worried about his floor.

Gorathdin, Aarl and Werlis laughed, while Brother Transmudin was still amazed by the dwarf's powerful punch and the rigidity of the steel melted in Ib'Agier.

"Unbelievable!" Brother Transmudin finally said.

His gaze remained fixed on Borlix and his axe for a few moments.

He then picked up some of the small pieces of horn, put them in a stone mill and began to grind them.

"A handful of the powder should be enough, at least that's what the recipe says," he informed those present, looking at the pieces of horn still scattered on the floor.

"That's enough for ten more potions," he remarked as he set about collecting them and putting them in an empty test tube, which he then filled with a blue liquid and placed in a large cupboard with the others.

He then went back to the stone mill, picked up the small bowl under the two heavy stone slabs and emptied the contents into one of the jars on the table. He then attached the jars filled with the powders, leaves and liquids to the thin glass tubes that ran like a labyrinth from the right to the left end of the table.

He lit small oil lamps under some of the tubes.

He took one of the glasses in his hand and began to shake it several times. Werlis looked in amazement at the glass objects on the table, some of which began to fizz and bubble. When all the ingredients were prepared according to the recipe, Brother Theramond poured them into a cast-iron pot filled with hot water hanging over the open fireplace.

"The whole thing has to boil for a good while now, then the potion will be ready" the old monk explained them.

"In the meantime, I will go and see Princess Lythinda. Would you please lead me to her?" Gorathdin asked Brother Transmudin, who nodded.

"Yes, of course, come, follow me. She is under the supervision of two of my brothers in the room next to mine!"

He left the laboratory with Gorathdin.

Werlis, Aarl and Borlix stayed behind and guarded the potion.

Gorathdin and Brother Transmudin entered the room where the feverish and starry-eyed Princess Lythinda was. She was lying in a simple bed under the supervision of two monks.

"I want to be alone with her," Gorathdin asked Brother Transmudin.

"Of course!" he replied and walked away with his two brothers.

Gorathdin knelt before Princess Lythinda on the bed, took her hand and kissed it tenderly.

"The potion will lower the fever, my love, and we can then take you to Horunguth Island. I'm sure the magicians will be able to free you from the spell," Gorathdin said to her quietly, leaned over her and kissed her on the mouth.

He remained kneeling in front of her bed until there was a knock at the door and Brother Transmudin and Theramond, Werlis, Aarl and Borlix entered.

"The potion is ready!" announced Brother Theramond delightedly, walking towards the bed and about to pour the potion from the small, bulbous bottle, into the princess's mouth when Gorathdin held him back.

Brother Theramond shuddered and spilled a few drops of the poisonous green liquid.

"What's going on?" the old monk asked Gorathdin in astonishment.

"Please wait. I want to try the potion myself first," Gorathdin replied firmly.

"But ... but you're not ill! Who knows what effect the potion has on a healthy person!" protested the monk.

But Gorathdin insisted.

"It's all right, Theramond. Let him try it," Brother Transmudin placated him, whereupon the old monk handed Gorathdin the bottle. Gorathdin took a big swig, grimaced at the bitter taste and paused for a few moments.

"You can give it to her now," he finally said and handed Brother Theramond the potion, whereupon he brought the opening of the bottle to Princess Lythinda's lips and slowly poured the potion into her mouth.

They waited anxiously for some time, during which Brother Transmudin placed his hand on the princess's forehead at regular intervals to check her temperature. They waited hopefully until the early hours of the morning, when Brother Transmudin finally looked up in delight.

"Her temperature is dropping," he said, taking his hand from her forehead.

"Indeed, she's much cooler already," Gorathdin remarked, very pleased.

Werlis, Aarl and Borlix clapped their hands with joy.

"Now we have to make the right decision. Should we take them back to Astinhod and wait for Master Drobal there, or take them to the distant Horunguth Island?" Gorathdin pondered aloud.

The room was filled with a moment of silence.

"What about Vrenli?" Werlis finally asked, breaking the silence.

"I haven't forgotten Vrenli. I am still true to my word. The thing is, I can't get Princess Lythinda to Horunguth Island on my own. I need your help, friends. If you give it to me, we will find a way to track down Vrenli. The border of Desert of DeShadin is only a three-day journey from Irkaar. It's practically on our way. I don't know how we're going to do it yet, but I'm sure we can combine our plans to find Vrenli and bring Princess Lythinda to the mages. Or we can bring her back to Astinhod, hope that Master Drobal will return soon, and set off in search of Vrenli, as we decided before. I'm in favor of combining the two, but it's up to you, friends!" Gorathdin announced. He sat down next to Princess Lythinda and stroked her face. Another, now longer, silence filled the room.

Again, it was Werlis who broke the silence.

"I agree with your wish to bring the princess to Horunguth Island and I hope that we will also find Vrenli," said Werlis, who was feeling a little queasy out of concern for his friend.

"I can't promise, but I think we can count on the help of my village, at least as far as the princess is concerned. My village is close to Desert of DeShadin's border. One of us could watch over the princess there while the others go in search of Vrenli," suggested Aarl.

"That sounds like a good plan!" Borlix agreed.

"Then it's decided?" asked Gorathdin, to which Werlis, Aarl and Borlix nodded in agreement.

Gorathdin smiled gently.

"I knew I could rely on you!" he said happily, hugging one after the other.

"The road to Horunguth is long and dangerous. I cannot justify letting you go alone, especially in the state Princess Lythinda is in. If you wish, I will accompany you," offered Brother Transmudin.

Gorathdin looked questioningly at his friends. Werlis was the first to nod in agreement, followed by Aarl and Borlix.

"We would be delighted if you would accompany us and put your healing knowledge at our disposal," said Gorathdin to Brother Transmudin, who then instructed the two monks waiting outside the door to dress Princess Lythinda in a robe to conceal her royal origins on the journey.

"I want you to take charge of the monastery. You are the eldest of us, you know what to do, Brother Theramond," said Brother Transmudin.

The old monk nodded and wished everyone a safe journey.

He looked at Princess Lythinda again and moved away with quick steps.

"We should leave as soon as possible!" urged Gorathdin and asked Borlix to bring him his fire axe from their room, as he would be staying here with Princess Lythinda.

"I'll take care of the food for the journey," Brother Transmudin said and made his way to the kitchen.

"We should keep an eye on Brother Transmudin," Aarl said to Werlis and Borlix as they walked down the long corridor to their room.

"Either he's a good-hearted person or he's the traitor and just doesn't want to lose sight of us," added Aarl.

Werlis and Borlix nodded.

"You can't be too careful with anyone, especially if they're not a dwarf, as my grandfather used to say," joked Borlix, looking suspiciously at Aarl and Werlis before bursting into a hearty laugh.

Werlis and Aarl, who thought for a moment that Borlix was serious, then joined in his laughter.

Once in their room, they began to tie up their travel bags, take their weapons and Borlix put Gorathdin's fire axe over his shoulder.

They looked around the room again and made their way back to Gorathdin. Werlis was just about to open the door to the princess's room when he heard Gorathdin singing a song to her. He knocked briefly before opening it. When he entered, followed by Aarl and Borlix, he found Gorathdin sitting by the princess's bed, wiping a tear from his cheek that had found its way to freedom.

"I'm worried about her condition. She no longer has a fever, but who knows what effects the spell will have. The journey to Horunguth is long and dangerous and after everything that has happened to us in the last few days and weeks, I fear for her safety," Gorathdin said worriedly to his friends when he saw them at the door.

"The five of us will make it!" replied Werlis optimistically. Aarl nodded in agreement. Borlix handed Gorathdin the fire axe.

"We will protect Princess Lythinda with our lives," growled Borlix, swinging his own axe briefly through the air.

"Are you ready to leave?" Gorathdin asked as he put on the leather strap of his fire axe.

"You can't be more ready!" Borlix replied, stamping the handle of his axe on the ground.

Brother Transmudin entered the room and informed them that the cart was ready.

Gorathdin carefully lifted Princess Lythinda out of bed and carried her to the gate, where an old two-wheeled cart was waiting for her. Two of the monks were busy stowing away the provisions. With their help, Gorathdin carefully placed the princess on the soft, fur-lined loading area.

"Unfortunately, we cannot provide mounts. As you know, we live very modestly. But at least we have a donkey to pull the cart," explained Brother Transmudin, stroking the black fur of the small, hoofed animal that one of the monks was leading to the cart.

Gorathdin was just about to call for departure when Brother Transmudin interrupted him.

"By Omnigo, I almost forgot the most important thing. I'll be right back!" he shouted and hurried along the cobbled path to the accommodation.

The three looked questioningly at each other.

"Very suspicious," whispered Borlix.

However, not much time passed and Brother Transmudin returned to the cart holding a bag in front of him.

"The medicines, I almost forgot them!" he announced with a smile and hung the bag around his left shoulder.

Almost all the monks had arrived at the gate in the meantime to say goodbye to them.

"May Omnigo protect you!" shouted the old monk Theramond. With these words, the five set off to bring Princess Lythinda to Horunguth and find the missing Vrenli.

It was early morning when they left the monastery behind and followed the narrow path southwest until midday. When they arrived at a well-traveled, wide path that connected Astinhod in the west with Ib'Agier in the east via the tunnel of the gray dwarves, they stopped briefly.

"We can buy horses in Astinhod," suggested Aarl. Gorathdin was deep in thought.

"Gorathdin, are you listening to me?" Aarl asked.

Gorathdin looked at him absent-mindedly.

"Forgive me, I was just thinking about whether it would be wise to return to Astinhod with Princess Lythinda. The Thieves' Guild would find out about our return immediately. Besides, I would like to avoid following the known paths and trails to the south. I'm sure Erwight of Entorbis has other allies and spies. Maybe even animals," Gorathdin replied.

"I understand your concerns, but there's no other way to Thir and without mounts we'll need at least four or five days longer," Borlix objected.

Gorathdin was silent for a while and stopped on the path shortly afterwards.

"There's another route where horses wouldn't be of any use to us anyway. But I'm not sure yet whether we should use it," Gorathdin finally revealed.

Werlis, Aarl, Borlix and Brother Transmudin looked at him questioningly, as they were unaware of any other route to the south than the one leading from the city of Astinhod via Regen to Zeel.

"Which path are you talking about?" Aarl wanted to know.

"I'm talking about the path that leads through the Dark Forest," replied Gorathdin.

"We can't travel through the Dark Forest. No one can. You should know that better than anyone. What about the ranger elves, druids, wild animals, forest dragons and who knows what other creatures dwell there," warned Brother Transmudin.

"The forest is haunted!" Borlix grumbled in agreement.

"The forest is not haunted! But you are right, you are not allowed to enter the Dark Forest and under normal circumstances I would not consider it. But something warns me not to take the familiar path to the south," Gorathdin explained.

A discussion flared up between Gorathdin, Aarl and Borlix about the potential dangers that might lurk on the known paths and trails, as opposed to those that would surely await them in the Dark Forest.

"Friends, we're wasting precious time!" Brother Transmudin, who had stayed out of the discussion, drew their attention.

Werlis nodded in agreement.

"What do you mean by precious time? I'd rather waste precious time than my precious life. The forest is haunted, I say!" grumbled Borlix.

Aarl agreed with him.

"I'll follow Gorathdin, whichever way he wants to go!" said Werlis.

"Let the Dark Forest be my concern!" Gorathdin spoke firmly, and his dark green eyes lit up.

Aarl and Brother Transmudin agreed to take the path through the Dark Forest. Borlix, who held on to the route via the city of Astinhod for some time, finally gave in to the majority in annoyance.

"But I warned you!" grumbled Borlix, following his friends at a short distance.

"Let me worry about that!" he grumbled mockingly as he followed them south across the meadows to the right of the path, where they finally set up camp for the night.

The next day, they continued until the afternoon. Gray clouds were gathering over the high mountains of Ib'Agier in the west when they arrived at the edge of a forest.

"The Dark Forest begins up ahead. Stay close together and near me!" Gorathdin warned.

"I'm not entirely comfortable with this," confessed Aarl, a cold shiver running down his spine.

Werlis took the donkey's reins and walked alongside him.

Mighty trees, many hundreds of years old, stood guard at the edge of the forest. As they walked beneath them, Werlis got an idea of where the forest got its name from. After less than half a mile, it became much darker around them. Only in a few places did the sun's rays penetrate the sea of leaves. They were not far from a narrow path that Gorathdin was about to take with his friends when a pack of wolves stood in their way.

The pack leader, a fierce-looking, snarling brown wolf, jumped at Gorathdin's feet. The donkey on the cart reared up and Werlis, Aarl, Borlix and Brother Transmudin were startled.

Gorathdin remained calm. He was not afraid of the big, brown wolves. Brother Transmudin, on the other hand, leapt towards the cart and held his bag of healing potions protectively in front of him.

Borlix swung his axe and Aarl stood with two throwing knives ready for battle next to Werlis, who drew his short sword with one hand and held the donkey's reins with the other, fearing that it would break free.

"Wait!" cried Gorathdin, raising his hand.

Sniffing, the wolves began to circle the cart, while the pack leader glanced at Werlis and growled. But when Gorathdin's dark green eyes lit up, the pack leader fell silent.

"Let's move on!" Gorathdin spoke firmly, whereupon the pack leader began to bare his teeth again.

The dark green in Gorathdin's eyes glowed.

"Let us through!" he repeated in a loud voice.

To the astonishment of his fellow travelers, the big brown wolf began to whimper, suddenly lay down on his back in front of Gorathdin and stretched his four paws upwards. Gorathdin bent over him, gently stroked his belly fur and whispered something in the wolf's ear, whereupon he jumped up and moved away from the travelers with his pack.

"We can go on!" said Gorathdin to his friends, who looked at him in amazement.

The howling of the wolves, which were still nearby, made Werlis flinch.

"Why are they howling?" Werlis asked, frightened.

"They're registering us," replied Gorathdin.

"To whom?" Werlis wanted to know.

"They report our arrival to all the inhabitants of the Dark Forest," Gorathdin explained, looking up.

A large white owl flew over their heads and let its call echo through the forest.

"I told you, this damn forest is haunted! But nobody listens to me!" grumbled Borlix, gripping the handle of his axe tighter.

"Let's keep going!" Gorathdin urged his friends and headed for the path leading south.

From there, however, their progress was slow. They had to stop several times and lift the wheels of the cart over roots and stones protruding from the ground. With great effort, they managed to complete the first fifth of their journey through the Dark Forest before dusk fell.

They still had a three-day march to the south ahead of them, where they had to cross a high mountain range. From there, they had to travel through Thir to the coast of the Southern Sea, to Irkaar, in order to find a way to reach Horunguth Island from there.

"We still have a long way to go," Gorathdin addressed his friends, who could clearly see the exertion of the second day of their journey. Werlis, for whom the march was the most strenuous, had already fallen asleep in the cart next to Princess Lythinda.

"We should look for a place to camp for the night. It's getting darker. I can hardly see a thing," suggested Aarl.

Brother Transmudin, noticeably exhausted, nodded in agreement.

As they passed an ancient, mighty oak tree, Gorathdin was about to give the signal to rest, when he spotted a group of camouflaged rangers crouching on several thick branches in the tree with bows drawn.

An arrow whizzed past Borlix, who immediately held his axe protectively in front of him, and stuck in the planks of the right-hand side of the cart. Borlix and Aarl threw themselves to the ground behind the cart and looked around, searching.

Brother Transmudin, who had led the donkey for a while, held the reins tightly and ducked behind the draught animal.

"Eldor min helvajar!" shouted Gorathdin into the oak.

"Who are you and who gave you permission to enter the Dark Forest?" asked one of the rangers in the tree, unmasking himself so he could be seen by everyone.

Aarl carefully drew one of his throwing knives, but before it could come to blows, Gorathdin answered the ranger's question.

"I am Gorathdin of the forest, the son of Mergoldin!" After a short silence and subsequent whispering from the elves in the tree, the others also revealed themselves.

"Greetings, Gorathdin, son of Ilirinda. Speak, what are the humans, the half-grown man and the dwarf doing here? Have you forgotten the laws of the Dark Forest after so long?" asked a voice from behind the trunk of the oak.

Gorathdin's dark green eyes began to light up.

"Who are you? Show yourself, come out from behind the trunk!" he called upwards.

A ranger with blond hair plaited into a braid at the back, who must be about the same age as Gorathdin, leapt to Gorathdin's feet with a jumping somersault.

"Regindar!" cried Gorathdin, happily hugging the ranger standing in front of him.

Werlis, awakened by the commotion, was startled and dived back under the furs.

"Gorathdin, my old friend!" Regindar greeted him and returned the embrace.

"What do you mean old, I'm a year younger than you!" Gorathdin countered with a smile.

Aarl, Borlix and Brother Transmudin stood next to Gorathdin. Werlis looked out from under the furs.

"Tell me, what's the deal with your companions? The druids will not be pleased and you can assume that they already know about your appearance," Regindar warned.

"I know I'm doing something forbidden, but I'm afraid I have no other choice," Gorathdin replied, pointing to the cart with his hand.

"Who is the girl?" Regindar asked curiously when he had looked inside.

"This is King Grandhold's daughter, Princess Lythinda," replied Gorathdin.

"What's wrong with her, she has such a lifeless look, is she ill?" asked Regindar, leaning over the edge of the cart.

"That's a long story," Gorathdin replied with a sigh.

"Then tell me about it. You look very tired anyway. We've set up a camp nearby, where you can rest and regain your strength undisturbed," suggested Regindar. Gorathdin and his friends were delighted by the invitation and followed the rangers to the fire.

While they refreshed themselves, Gorathdin introduced his friends and told Regindar everything that had happened since his stay at the Three Vines inn.

"It's a long journey to Horunguth and there are many dangers along the way. My men and I could accompany you as far as the Border Mountains in the south," offered Regindar.

"Thank you very much for your offer, but I cannot accept it. I don't want you to break the laws of the Dark Forest because of me," Gorathdin refused.

"Gorathdin, my friend, how often did we break the laws of the forest and those of the rangers in our childhood and youth?" Regindar reminded him with a smile.

"We were young back then. People were lenient with us," Gorathdin replied with a grin.

Regindar performed a high jump, twisted and turned and landed with both feet on the ground.

"I'm still young!" he shouted and laughed.

"My friend, we will accompany you to the Border Mountains. I would rather risk banishment from the Dark Forest than expose my friend to the dangers that lurk here. I could never forgive myself if anything were to happen to you. Now, get some rest. In the meantime, I'll send two scouts south," Regindar decided decisively and jumped over Borlix's head with a somersault, poking him in the nose with one finger.

"Damn elf!" Borlix grumbled sleepily, to which Regindar laughed.

"A dwarf in the Dark Forest, that hasn't happened for two hundred years," Regindar chuckled and disappeared into a tree.

Borlix mumbled something incomprehensible after him. It then fell silent in the rangers' camp.

One of the elves took off the donkey's harness, led it to a place where lush forest herbs grew and gently stroked its black fur.

Gorathdin sat by the fire for some time next to Werlis, Aarl, Borlix and Brother Transmudin, who had fallen asleep on the soft, moss-covered forest floor. At midnight, he lay awake next to Princess Lythinda in the cart and fell asleep a little later.

It was early morning when Regindar returned to the open camp in the forest and woke Gorathdin.

"My scouts told me about a group of forest wraiths south of here. We'd better go around them to the west!" suggested Regindar.

Gorathdin stretched, jumped out of the cart and sat down by the fire.

"You mean we should go past the center of the Dark Forest?" Gorathdin asked as he placed some branches in the fire.

"I know what you're thinking. But sooner or later, one way or another, we'll have to justify ourselves to the druids," Regindar replied.

"You're probably right. Let's bypass the forest wraiths," Gorathdin reluctantly agreed.

He got up, woke his friends and explained to them the new plan.

"Right past the center of the witches' forest? Does that have to be?" grumbled Borlix, getting up tiredly and stretching his legs.

"If you'd rather fight with a group of forest wraiths, then we can go further south," Gorathdin countered.

Borlix grumbled something into his thick, red beard.

Accompanied by Regindar and his men, the travelers set off west. As they made slow progress with the cart, they were on the road for more than a day.

Brother Transmudin, who was looking carefully at the plants in the forest, was amazed by the variety of different forest herbs. As he passed a shrub of remembrance, he asked Regindar if he could pick some leaves from it.

"Go ahead, Brother Transmudin!" replied Regindar, whereupon the monk happily plucked a handful of the coveted and extremely rare leaves. They stepped out of the mixed forest they had been walking through and stopped briefly in a meadow overgrown with brown and gray forest grasses, behind which a dry coniferous forest opened up.

The laws of the druids

"The center of the Dark Forest is not far away. Keep quiet. Do not disturb the peace of the druids. It's bad enough that you're here at all!" Regindar warned Werlis, Aarl, Borlix and Brother Transmudin, who all nodded silently.

After they had fortified themselves, they crossed the forest meadow and, led by Regindar, entered the coniferous forest. They now headed south towards the Border Mountains, two days away. Again, Brother Transmudin saw something that made his eyes sparkle.

"That's a very rare shade plant!" he exclaimed enthusiastically, pointing with his hand to a tiny little plant growing next to the trunk of a larch tree.

"May I be allowed to pick this little plant?" asked Brother Transmudin politely.

Regindar nodded.

The monk was just about to bend down when he was startled by the call of a white owl sitting in a larch tree in front of them. With a few flaps of its wings, it suddenly flew down and straight towards Borlix. It quickly and unerringly grabbed his helmet with its strong, sharp claws and circled above his head.

"By all the halls of Ib'Agier. You cursed fowl!" Borlix growled and raised his axe threateningly.

The owl opened the grip of its claws and the helmet fell to the ground. Borlix bent down and just as he was about to pick it up, he saw the forest-green tunic of a druid.

"What are you doing in the Dark Forest, especially with a dwarf? Speak!" the druid demanded angrily.

Dwarves were not exactly popular with the druids because of their great need for wood, which they burned in vast quantities in their smelting furnaces. Borlix had already noticed the druid's hostility when was still in owl form.

"You, rangers, answer!" the druid ordered angrily. No one answered.

"Who allowed this monk to steal our plants?" he asked them, casting a dark look at Brother Transmudin.

"I... I didn't know... that it was forbidden!" replied Brother Transmudin, stammering.

"Not only are you forbidden to enrich yourselves with the goods of the forest, you are also forbidden to enter the Dark Forest at all!" the druid shook and stamped the forest floor with his staff.

"But I am a healer. I'm not enriching myself!" Brother Transmudin defended himself quietly, intimidated by the druid's trembling voice.

"Empty chatter. Am I going to get an answer from you, ranger?" the druid said threateningly, taking a step towards the intruders as he pushed Werlis aside with his staff.

"Enough!" Gorathdin shouted firmly and stood protectively in front of Werlis, whereupon the druid looked at him in astonishment.

He was not used to someone speaking to him in this tone and raised his staff in anger.

A green beam of light shot from its tip towards Gorathdin. To the druid's astonishment, however, it was deflected into the night sky just before it could hit Gorathdin. The druid was about to raise his staff again when Gorathdin snatched it from his hand and threw it to the ground.

"I've had enough of your looking down from above! Your way of separating yourself from all the inhabitants of Wetherid! I despise you and your self-proclaimed laws! Just because you are a Guardian of the Tree of Life does not give you the right to treat everyone who enters the forest as an enemy!" said Gorathdin, his eyes shining.

The druid straightened up to his full height.

"Who do you think you are, ranger?" the druid's voice trembled.

"How dare you despise the ancient laws of the forest and break them at the same time!" the druid added angrily, looking grim.

Gorathdin's dark green eyes were now glowing as if they would explode in thousands of flashes of fire at any moment.

"Tell me your name, elf, so that I know against whom I have to direct my power!" the druid demanded.

Gorathdin remained silent.

The druid began to chant, raised his hands, which began to glow with a green light, and just as he was about to strike Gorathdin with all his might, growling sounded behind him.

"Enough!" it bellowed.

One more enough was too much for the druid. He turned around and was about to turn his power against the stranger behind him when he looked in amazement at a one-eyed bear.

Werlis, Aarl, Borlix and Brother Transmudin, who could not believe how Gorathdin was talking to one of the powerful druids, dared not move. Regindar and the other rangers had thrown themselves on the ground in front of the druid for fear of the consequences.

"Mergoldin, you're here? Why are you stopping me from teaching the intruders a lesson? Did you not hear how that ranger spoke to me?" the druid asked Mergoldin in an angry voice.

"Bah, nothing but words. You can't be after the lives of everyone who speaks their mind!" Mergoldin growled angrily and straightened up.

"But they have invaded the Dark Forest, that's against the law!" protested the druid.

"These laws date back to a time when Wetherid was populated by creatures of darkness. The law was meant to protect the Tree of Life from their greed for its power. It is not right to equate good and well-behaved citizens of Wetherid with these creatures of darkness. However, this does not mean that everyone is free to roam the Dark Forest as they please or to enrich themselves with its goods. We must protect the Tree of Life from its enemies. Yes, that is our destiny. But we must be wise enough to distinguish friend from foe," said Mergoldin.

"You talk like that ranger!" the still angry druid replied disparagingly.

"The ranger is my son!" Mergoldin replied seriously.

"The half-breed?" the old druid asked.

Mergoldin remained silent.

"You may be the highest of us druids, Mergoldin, but that does not give you the right to disregard our laws and the laws of the forest. You are bound by the instructions of the Druid Council and the Tree of Life. Even you will not stop me from enforcing our laws!" said the druid, raising his hands threateningly at Gorathdin.

A bright blue beam of light appeared out of nowhere and enveloped the angry druid, who was unable to move. He was held in place as if by an invisible hand. A deep, creaky, slow voice sounded from the darkness.

"You have chosen to be an owl and from now on you shall live your life as one!" the voice announced and then fell silent again.

The druid in the bright blue beam of light turned into a small, gray owl in front of everyone's eyes and flew off into the night sky, calling. Silence reigned, and no one dared to speak.

"You can continue your journey," Mergoldin finally said and asked his son for a word.

"Go ahead!" Gorathdin instructed his friends. Mergoldin changed into human form and embraced Gorathdin.

"Father, I can't believe what you've done. The Druid Council will banish you from the forest!" Gorathdin said worriedly.

"What did I do?" Mergoldin repeated in astonishment.

"The only thing I did was speak the truth. Just like you, my son. The bright blue light did not come from me, it was the light of the Tree of Life. It made the judgement itself," replied Mergoldin.

Gorathdin was visibly relieved.

"What are you going to do now, father?" Gorathdin asked.

"I will convene the Druid Council and propose that our laws be changed," replied Mergoldin.

"But what about the laws of the forest?" Gorathdin wanted to know.

"The laws of the forest are the laws of the forest. I have no influence over them," said Mergoldin, placing his hand on his son's shoulder and wishing him a safe journey.

"Take care of yourself, son!" Gorathdin heard his father shout as he hurried after his friends.

"You never mentioned that you had a druid for a father," Werlis remarked as Gorathdin arrived at the cart.

"Because it's not important," Gorathdin replied and smiled.

For two days they hiked southwards, through dense and dry coniferous, old deciduous and dark mixed forests. They walked around ravines, up and down hills, through forest meadows and across small and large clearings until they finally arrived at the foot of the Border Mountains at dusk.

"There's a tunnel halfway up!" Regindar revealed, pointing with his hand to the rock face in front of them, which was overgrown with dry grasses, bushes and shrubs.

"I know that a clan of gray dwarves from Ingar, who came to Wetherid from Fallgar before the time of Entorbis, dug for ore here," Gorathdin replied.

"Gray dwarves lived here?" Werlis asked in amazement.

"It was a long time ago, a very long time ago. They dug the tunnel long before Ib'Agier was built. Long before the time of humans," Borlix told him and stroked his long, red chin beard a few times, muttering something unintelligible and looking up the rock face.

"I can't say when it was last used, but I hope it hasn't collapsed," Regindar said worriedly.

"Whether built by honest or treacherous dwarves, things built by dwarves don't collapse. Not even in three thousand years," Borlix declared proudly.

"I hope Borlix is right. If we can use the tunnel, we'll save ourselves a seven-day march around the mountains," Gorathdin explained.

"We should set up camp here for the night. It's too late to start the ascent," suggested Regindar.

Gorathdin agreed.

He knew that the ascent to the tunnel would take half a day but as they had to leave the cart and the donkey behind, they should be well rested. They would need all the strength they could muster to carry Princess Lythinda to the top.

Werlis and Aarl set off in search of firewood, while Borlix stood silently, eyes wide open, in front of the mountains and explored them in detail. He was interested in the shades of the rock, the fractures in the cliffs, the slope of the walls, where they were overgrown, where water collected in stone niches.

Brother Transmudin took some provisions from the cart and began to prepare a simple evening meal.

"I'm going to build a stretcher for Princess Lythinda," Regindar announced and began to search the surrounding area for branches and vines, which he used to build a sturdy stretcher with the help of two other rangers.

Gorathdin sat down next to Werlis and Aarl at the campfire and talked to them.

When Brother Transmudin had finished preparing the thick stew and gone to hand Gorathdin a bowl, he declined with thanks, while all the others ate hungrily. Gorathdin stood up and lay down in the cart next to Princess Lythinda. He kissed her tenderly on the forehead and placed another fur over her. It was a cool late spring night. A light wind was blowing and clouds covered the sky. Gorathdin placed Princess Lythinda's hand tenderly in his and fell asleep.

Two of the rangers kept watch some paces away from the campfire while Regindar told those gathered around the fire about his youth with Gorathdin until, one-by-one, they fell asleep.

As dawn broke, the rangers were already ready for their return journey.

"It's time for us to leave," Regindar said to Gorathdin as he arrived at the campfire and woke Aarl, Borlix and Brother Transmudin.

However, Werlis could not be woken up.

Regindar and the rangers said their goodbyes. Gorathdin hugged his old friend and the group of forest elves set off quickly to the north.

"Take good care of the donkey!" Brother Transmudin called after them, waking Werlis up with his call.

With half-open eyes, he got up and staggered sleepily to the cart, where he lifted the skins covering Princess Lythinda to make sure she was still alive.

"I had a terrible dream. I dreamt that Erwight of Entorbis appeared and shrouded Princess Lythinda in a dark mist," he told his friends as he sat down by the campfire and continued with more details. When the fire had burned out and they had finished Brother Transmudin's tea, they prepared to leave.

Gorathdin and Brother Transmudin lifted Princess Lythinda out of the cart and placed her onto the stretcher built by Regindar. Aarl and Borlix volunteered to carry the stretcher.

When all their travel bags were tied up and their weapons put on, they set off and after half a mile entered the steep, scree-covered narrow path that led up into the Border Mountains.

"Watch where you're going!" Aarl, who was leading the way, warned Borlix, who was carrying the stretcher from behind.

"Stop pulling so hard!" grumbled Borlix, to which Aarl laughed.

The two of them carried Princess Lythinda more than halfway up the mountain. When their strength waned, Gorathdin and Brother Transmudin took over.

The narrow path then led along a steep rock face to their left. To the right was a precipice that was now several hundred steps deep. In some places, the path was so narrow that Brother Transmudin, who did not have the skill of an elf, had to be careful not to lose his balance.

After half a mile uphill, there were now almost insurmountable boulders on the path instead of scree. Borlix pushed his way to the top and cleared the way for Gorathdin and Brother Transmudin by pushing the boulders into the abyss to his right.

The path led ever higher into the mountains.

They soon reached the tree line. It was getting much cooler. Aarl therefore put his bearskin, which he pulled out of his travel bag, over Princess Lythinda.

The path now led around the mountain.

"Look, here!" shouted Werlis, pointing to the bracket in front of them on their left.

Thin metal pillars had been driven into the rock face every twenty steps, connected to each other with a thick, rusty rope.

Borlix tore at it to check its stability.

"It still seems to be holding!" he remarked, scraping at one part of the rope with the blade of his axe until he had freed it from the layer of rust.

Shiny silver, twisted metal threads appeared.

"It's a steel cable. Indestructible," grumbled Borlix.

They now made faster progress as they could hold on to the rope and no longer had to pay so much attention to the abyss to their right.

It was already afternoon. The sky was cloudless and they had almost reached their destination. Suddenly falling stones turned out to be the mountain's answer to a herd of ibex jumping over the rocks.

They reached a flat rocky landscape where they rested. Gorathdin looked north towards the huge foothills of the Dark Forest below them.

"Here! Look, you can see the peaks of Ib'Agier!" Borlix shouted and pointed to the east, where Wetherid's oldest and highest mountain range lay.

A long-forgotten feeling took possession of Borlix and after pondering it for some time, cutting it into small bite-sized pieces and chewing on it, he recognized the taste.

It was homesickness.

After everyone had rested and regained their strength, Aarl and Borlix took the stretcher again.

"But it's my turn!" protested Werlis, who also wanted to do his part.

"Thank you, my little friend," said Gorathdin and winked at Borlix, who then carefully placed the two handles of the stretcher on the ground.

Gorathdin did not want to offend Werlis and although he knew that the stretcher would be far too heavy for him, he at least let him try.

Werlis bent down to grab the handles and realized as soon as he tried to lift the stretcher that the load was too heavy for him.

"The climb must have weakened me," he said and groaned.

"Yes, really very exhausting," gasped Brother Transmudin, who wanted to show solidarity.

Borlix took over the stretcher again and, together with Aarl, walked behind Gorathdin across the rocky plains.

They had already climbed more than half of the mountain range. The fresh, constantly blowing wind blew cold on their faces. After crossing the plain, they reached a steep rock face into which several dozen low steps leading upwards had been hewn.

"I've never gone further than this myself," Gorathdin told his friends.

"We can't possibly carry Princess Lythinda up here in the stretcher," Borlix remarked, looking at Gorathdin expectantly.

"I will carry Princess Lythinda up alone," replied Gorathdin.

He carefully lifted her out of the stretcher and was just about to put his foot on the first step when Brother Transmudin asked him to wait.

"It's windy and cold," he said to Gorathdin and quickly put a coat over Princess Lythinda.

Followed by Borlix, Werlis and Brother Transmudin, Gorathdin climbed higher and higher up the steps, holding Princess Lythinda in his arms. Aarl, who had agreed to take the empty stretcher to the top, was the last to follow them.

The tunnel of the gray dwarves

Before they had even reached the end of the steps carved into the steep rock face, they could already see the half-collapsed entrance to a tunnel above them that would lead them to Thir.

A cold, damp, slightly musty smell reached Borlix's nose, which he breathed in deeply.

"Just like at home!" he grumbled.

345

His friends didn't understand what he meant and looked at him curiously.

"The smell coming from inside the mountain reminds me of Ib'Agier," Borlix explained.

"I would describe it more as a stench!" commented Werlis, holding his nose.

Aarl laughed and Borlix rolled his eyes at this remark.

Gorathdin climbed from the last step onto the flat ledge in front of the tunnel entrance and waited for Aarl to put the stretcher down once he had reached the top. He carefully placed Princess Lythinda on the stretcher and covered her with two thick furs.

"I've heard that the tunnel is thousands of steps long. It will certainly take us a whole day to get to the other side," Gorathdin told his friends.

He sat down next to the stretcher for a moment and looked at the boulders lying in front of the tunnel entrance while he warmed Princess Lythinda's cold hands.

"Hopefully the tunnel is in better condition than the entrance," Werlis remarked and sat down next to Gorathdin, waiting.

Borlix, Aarl and Brother Transmudin walked closer to the entrance and took a look into the dark tunnel. Brother Transmudin was the first to realize that they had no torches with them.

"Torches, I hadn't thought of that!" Gorathdin admitted angrily.

"How could we have forgotten the torches!" Borlix, a dwarf used to using semi-dark tunnels and corridors, was annoyed as complete darkness was a problem even for him.

"What if we make some? We could try wrapping scraps of cloth around a branch and lighting them," suggested Aarl.

"I'm afraid they wouldn't burn long enough and the draught in the mountain would extinguish them immediately anyway. But if someone has oil with them that we could soak the scraps of cloth in, it will work," explained Borlix.

But as none of them had any oil with them, they were at a loss.

Aarl, Borlix and Brother Transmudin sat down next to Gorathdin and Werlis. Some time passed before Brother Transmudin finally stood up and looked once more into the darkness of the tunnel.

"Should we turn back?" he asked his companions.

No one answered.

"I have an idea!" Werlis exclaimed loudly after a while, reaching into the bag he was carrying under his cloak and pulling out the Oracle of Tawinn.

"That's our salvation!" Borlix remarked happily.

"Now we just have to make it glow," said Werlis, lifting the crystal in front of him.

"Oracle of Tawinn, please, shine!" he pleaded, full of hope.

Nothing happened.

The crystal remained lightless and cold.

"Maybe we should ask it," suggested Aarl.

"Do you want to keep it glowing with a thousand questions while we cross the tunnel?" grumbled Borlix, tapping his forehead with his index finger.

"Why not?" replied Aarl and asked Werlis for the crystal.

But despite all the questions Aarl asked the Oracle of Tawinn, it did not begin to glow.

He then handed it to Gorathdin, whose attempts were also unsuccessful, whereupon their perplexity grew ever greater.

"We'll never get through this dark tunnel. What do we do now? Should we turn back? Who knows what has happened to Vrenli in the meantime? I'm already worried sick and now we're going to lose another four or five days, possibly more!" complained Werlis as the crystal suddenly lit up briefly.

"Did you see that?" he asked the others, who nodded.

"It lit up when you mentioned Vrenli's name," Gorathdin remarked, his eyes fixed on the crystal.

"The brief flash would not suffice as the only source of light, friends. Or do you want to call out Vrenli's name over and over again for all eternity?" grumbled Borlix, ruining Werlis' joy.

"I'm afraid we'll have to turn back then," Aarl sighed sadly and handed the Oracle of Tawinn back to Werlis, who put the crystal in his pocket.

"I could go through the tunnel alone with Princess Lythinda and then we could meet in Irkaar," suggested Gorathdin.

"I wouldn't advise it. Who knows what has taken up residence in there over the past hundred, or rather thousand, years. When I think of the old, abandoned mines deep under Ib'Agier, I could tell you stories," Borlix objected.

"Even if you manage to get through the tunnel, you'd still have a long way to go to Irkaar, and don't get me wrong, but traveling through Thir as an elf with a starry-eyed young human woman in your arms is suicide," said Aarl warningly.

Gorathdin agreed with his two friends' objections.

"Well, there might be another possibility," Brother Transmudin spoke up.

"And what would that be?" Gorathdin asked eagerly.

Brother Transmudin hesitated for a few moments, but finally he managed to convince himself to tell them about the fire and frost magic that had been taught in the Order of the Dragon since ancient times until the royal ban a hundred years ago.

"You know Brother Theramond. He is the oldest brother of the order and, how shall I put it, he did not abide by King Grandhold's father's ban. He continued to practise fire and frost magic and when I was appointed head of the temple, he initiated me into this magical art. I have broken the king's law. But I assure you that Theramond and I are the only ones who still know this ancient knowledge," reported Brother Transmudin.

"Well, what do you think of me now?" he asked, embarrassed.

"That's excellent!" exclaimed Gorathdin delightedly.

"This is our salvation!" agreed Aarl, who, like Borlix and Werlis, began to laugh with joy.

Brother Transmudin was clearly confused by their reaction.

"But don't you understand? Practicing fire and frost magic is punishable by death!" he emphasized emphatically.

"I don't see any king guards or anyone else from Astinhod here, apart from Gorathdin, but he's not really from there," Borlix grumbled and grinned.

"Nobody will find out about it!" Gorathdin promised and placed his hand on Brother Transmudin's shoulder.

"Nobody!" Aarl and Werlis assured them in unison.

The travelers stood in front of the tunnel's entrance and swore an oath not to tell anyone about Brother Transmudin's forbidden abilities. The head of the Order of the Dragon, who regained his gentle smile after his fellow travelers had sworn the oath, stood at full height at the tunnel entrance, raised his hands imploringly above his head and spoke a verse in an unknown language.

Omnigo darus etner ebig Omnigo darus,

Hanem karuus menhig narus lasmoor.

Ibig inerisus Omnigo darus maslaanus.

Brother Transmudin began to draw circles with his hands. Instantly, his fingertips caught fire and this fire slowly spread through his circular hand movements. A fireball the size of Werlis' head appeared between the monk's hands.

Werlis, Gorathdin, Aarl and Borlix watched this miracle with amazement and respect.

"What do you think, is it big enough? I can make it even bigger!" said Brother Transmudin, who did not take his eyes off the fireball.

"That ... should be enough," Borlix stuttered.

Brother Transmudin strode forward into the tunnel, followed by the others. The fireball hovered in front of them, illuminating the dark rock walls at the entrance.

"As we don't know what awaits us in the mountain, we'd better keep quiet. Stay close together," warned Gorathdin.

They followed the tunnel, which was only a few steps wide, for about a mile into the mountain, when Brother Transmudin suddenly stopped.

"What is it?" Gorathdin asked quietly.

"Look!" replied the monk, sending his fireball slightly ahead with a wave of his hand.

The tunnel ended abruptly. A gigantic stalactite vault stretched out before them, littered with numerous stalagmites protruding from the floor and hanging from the ceiling. Borlix stepped closer to Brother Transmudin.

"Looks like the gray dwarves not only wanted to mine ore here, but also build a small town," Borlix remarked, looking at the smoothly hewn walls of the vault, into which several square chambers about twenty-by-twenty paces wide had been carved.

"I'm sure they were intended as accommodation," Borlix realized and his eyes wandered through the high vaults as far as the light from the fireball would allow.

"Looks to me like they stopped after the first construction phase," Borlix thought aloud and stroked his long, red beard a few times.

"What stopped them from finishing their plan?" Borlix pondered in silence.

"Let's go on slowly!" Gorathdin urged his friends.

Brother Transmudin retrieved his fireball with a wave of his hand and stepped out of the tunnel onto the wide path that he assumed led to the opposite side of the vault. Large shadows of the unfinished, rough-hewn stone pillars that stood to his left and right were cast by the light of the fireball onto the semi-dark path. Slowly, marveling at the unfinished structures, the travelers made their way to the approximate center of the vault when Borlix sniffed a familiar scent.

"Wait, friends!" whispered Borlix.

"What is it?" Gorathdin inquired.

"That smell, can't you smell it?" he asked quietly,

Werlis, Aarl and Brother Transmudin shook their heads. Only Gorathdin, who drew in the air deeply, could perceive anything.

"What's that?" Gorathdin asked Borlix.

"Cave goblins!" Borlix replied, holding up his axe ready to fight.

"Cave goblins?" Werlis repeated incredulously.

"We dwarves also call them the rats of the deep," Borlix replied in a whisper.

"Rats?" Werlis asked.

"We dwarves gave them this name because, like the small rodents, they live in the dark depths and feed on bats, lizards, insects and other creatures that live inside a mountain," Borlix explained.

"Are these cave goblins dangerous for us or not?" Gorathdin pressed impatiently.

"Immensely dangerous. These child-sized, blue-skinned, hairless creatures with their pointed, half-rotten teeth are very aggressive. Their red, glowing eyes bear witness to their pact with evil," explained Borlix.

"Go on!" Werlis urged Borlix and stood very close to Gorathdin, almost disappearing under his cloak.

"They have been a nuisance for as long as we dwarves can remember. They shoot poisoned arrows at their opponents with their short blowpipes. Many of them are also armed with clubs. But the most dangerous are their magical warlocks," Borlix continued.

"So we should be on our guard," said Aarl.

Gorathdin's eyes roamed the city under construction.

"Over here, to the right behind the stone bridge, at the other end, there are two of these creatures," whispered Gorathdin, setting down the stretcher together with Aarl and reaching for his fire axe as small blue flames began to dance on its mirror-smooth blade.

"We'd better keep moving," muttered Brother Transmudin.

"Looks like they haven't noticed us yet," whispered Borlix, whereupon Gorathdin put the leather strap of his fire axe back on.

Brother Transmudin reduced the flames of his fireball many times over so as not to attract the attention of the two cave goblins.

"Come on, let's make sure we get to the other side of the city, or whatever is to be built here," Gorathdin said very quietly, lifting the stretcher with Aarl and following Brother Transmudin, who often had to stop briefly to send his fireball a few paces ahead. The light from the flames was not always enough to illuminate the dark path ahead.

Apart from the sounds of the travelers' footsteps and the occasional bursting of water droplets falling from the stalactites, the mountain was absolutely silent. When they had almost reached the other end of the vault, Gorathdin spotted a group of about fifteen cave goblins standing in front of the tunnel leading out of the vault before anyone else could see.

"Wait!" Gorathdin whispered, raising his hand in warning. "Cave goblins. Up ahead, at the exit," he let his friends know.

Brother Transmudin hid his fireball behind a protruding rock face to their left and gazed intently into the darkness before him. The darkness was broken only by the light of a small fire the group of cave goblins sat around. His gaze fell on a larger one standing apart from the group, staring into the blazing flames. The large cave goblin was wrapped in a cloak patched together from rat skins and was leaning on a wooden staff, at the end of which was the skull of what Brother Transmudin assumed was a large cave rat.

"Watch out for the taller one with the staff. He's a warlock!" Borlix warned.

"Let's get Princess Lythinda away from here," Gorathdin whispered to Aarl, who nodded.

Carefully and quietly, they carried the stretcher into one of the half-finished stone chambers in the vaulted wall to their right and placed it on the floor inside. Gorathdin signaled Werlis to come over to them.

"I want you to look after her," Gorathdin whispered to Werlis, who stood in the darkness next to Princess Lythinda's stretcher with his short sword drawn.

Werlis reached into his pocket and pulled out the Oracle of Tawinn. He put the fine silver chain attached to the crystal around his neck.

"Vrenli!" he whispered softly, whereupon the crystal lit up for a few moments. Werlis looked around the rough-hewn stone cave with a glance.

"Nothing but stone!" he thought and crouched down next to the stretcher.

Gorathdin and Aarl crept quietly back to Brother Transmudin and Borlix.

"Can you make the fireball float over the goblins' heads?" Gorathdin asked Brother Transmudin quietly.

"I think so, but then we're in the dark," he replied.

Gorathdin nodded.

"That is my intention," whispered Gorathdin.

Brother Transmudin and Borlix looked at him questioningly.

"I plan to strike down three or four of them before they can get to us," Gorathdin told the two of them, instructing Aarl to sneak closer to the cave goblins.

"You'll stab them in the back if they run towards us," whispered Gorathdin, to which Aarl nodded.

He crept crouched down to one of the stalagmites reaching from the floor to the vaulted ceiling in front of them, pulled two of his throwing knives from their sheaths and signaled to Gorathdin that he was ready.

"Borlix, take good care of Brother Transmudin, without his fireball we are lost," Gorathdin whispered to Borlix, who gripped the handle of his axe tightly with both hands and nodded.

Gorathdin placed his fire axe on the ground beside him, took his bow from his shoulder and put an arrow in the string. He signaled to Brother Transmudin to send the fireball over the heads of the cave goblins. The monk made a quick movement with his right hand in the direction of the vault exit, whereupon the fireball hurtled towards the group of cave goblins and stopped mid-air just above their heads.

"Maannuuu!" came the warning cry of one of the dark-loving creatures, causing the cave goblins to jump up and recoil in fright from the flames. They held their bony, wrinkled hands in front of their eyes to protect themselves from the glaring light.

Gorathdin took advantage of their confusion and shot an arrow at his intended target. The arrow flew at high speed with a loud whirring sound towards the cave goblin warlock. As soon as he heard the buzzing, he threw himself to the ground to protect himself.

Still lying on the ground, he swung his staff up and pointed it in the direction the arrow had been fired. A bright light flashed above the heads of Gorathdin, Borlix and Brother Transmudin. The cave goblins jumping up and down around the warlock on the ground grabbed their blowpipes and clubs and ran towards their attackers, shrilly shouting.

Gorathdin reacted immediately and fired several arrows in succession at the creatures rushing towards him. He managed to kill three of them before they reached the stalagmites Aarl was hiding behind.

"Moggnarrr, Moggnarrr!" shouted the angry mob, jumping up and down and running towards Gorathdin, Borlix and Brother Transmudin.

The cave goblin warlock, who had righted himself in the meantime, raised his staff high above his hairless, wrinkled head and let a loud whistle through the vault, whereupon Aarl, who had not taken his eyes off him the whole time, jumped out from behind the stalagmites.

He purposefully threw his two throwing knives at the warlock staring into the dark vaulted ceiling above him, waiting for something. With a loud, gurgling cry, the tall cave goblin slumped to the ground.

In the meantime, Gorathdin was able to kill three more of the red-eyed creatures jumping up and down with three well-aimed shots. Just as he was about to put another arrow in the string of his bow, Borlix stood in front of him.

"Brother Transmudin, get the fireball back!" shouted Borlix, looking ahead intently.

Since he was unable to see through the darkness like Gorathdin, he only saw the narrow red eyes of the small, blue-skinned creatures coming towards him. Brother Transmudin reacted immediately and waved the fireball back. Aarl used the passing light to approach the cave goblins running towards his friends from behind. Before they could put their blowpipes to their cracked, grayish lips, they slumped to their knees, gasping. Aarl had skillfully slit their throats.

The few remaining cave goblins had almost reached Brother Transmudin, who now had a close-up view of the ugly creatures dwelling in the dark depths of the mountains. They were only a few steps away from him menacingly swinging their clubs. Seeking shelter, he stood behind Borlix, who was already circling his axe around him.

Gorathdin grabbed his fire axe and leapt towards the cave goblins, striking their bluish, wrinkled bodies with swift, powerful blows. Four of the creatures dodged Gorathdin's blows and leapt towards Borlix, only to be decapitated by his whirling axe blade. Werlis, frightened by the sounds of battle, whispered Vrenli's name over and over again and approached the cave entrance, short sword drawn, to peer out at his friends in the pale light of the crystal.

Brother Transmudin had taken a few steps away from the fighters. He now sent the fireball floating in front of him hurtling towards the still living cave goblins. They immediately caught fire and rolled onto the ground. Horrific, pain-filled screams rang out as the creatures burned to death.

Borlix and Gorathdin quickly put an end to their torment.

"Done!" Borlix grumbled, pulling the blade of his axe from the cave goblin's body and wiping the black, stinking blood from its wrinkled, burnt skin.

Aarl collected his throwing knives again and did the same as Borlix.

"Do you hear that?" asked Gorathdin, listening attentively with his pointed elven ears.

He took a few steps towards the stone cave where Werlis and Princess Lythinda were hiding.

"What is it?" Borlix and Aarl asked.

"That fluttering sound," Gorathdin replied.

"I can't hear anything," Aarl confessed, listening into the darkness in front of him.

Borlix and Brother Transmudin also shook their heads.

"Quick to the stone cave!" shouted Gorathdin and ran towards Werlis, followed by the others. He was waiting for them in the dark entrance, which was only lit up by the fireball.

"Have you finished them off?" Werlis wanted to know.

"Yes!" replied Gorathdin and bent over Princess Lythinda.

"I need a break!" gasped Brother Transmudin and made the fireball disappear with a wave of his hand, whereupon it became pitch black in the narrow cave.

Gorathdin could hear the fluttering sound getting louder and walked closer to the entrance with his dark green glowing eyes. He looked out at the stone buildings.

"Something's going on out there. Wait here for me," he instructed the others, camouflaging himself and slowly creeping out into the darkness.

The fluttering noise fell silent. Gorathdin lingered for a few moments and looked around, but he couldn't see anything suspicious, so he crept back to his friends.

"Come on, let's go further. But be quiet," whispered Gorathdin.

Brother Transmudin created a new fireball, using its light to walk back along the path leading through the vault.

"Rats!" growled Borlix, who was carrying the stretcher with Aarl. He lifted it up higher to step over the lifeless bodies of the cave goblins.

They were only a few hundred paces from the exit of the vault when Brother Transmudin caught sight of the dead warlock's staff lying on the ground in front of him. He picked it up and broke it over his knee. The loud crack of the staff breaking startled the giant bats that had responded to the warlock's call. With shrill cries, they fluttered their huge wings down from the ceiling of the vault onto the intruders, inflicting bloody cuts with their sharp claws.

"Damned, bloodthirsty brood!" Borlix scolded, circling his axe above his head.

"Help!" Werlis screamed and threw himself to the ground, holding his hands protectively over his head.

Aarl threw a throwing knife at the bat that attacked Werlis, only to be attacked himself by two of the monstrous bloodsuckers the next moment.

Brother Transmudin tore the bat, which had bitten into his neck and clawed its way into his robe, from his body and pressed his left hand onto the bleeding wound.

He then directed the fireball at the flock of bats above their heads with his right hand. But the animals' bloodlust eliminated their fear of fire and light. Several of them were burnt to death, but there were too many for Brother Transmudin to chase away with the fireball.

"By all the halls of Ib'Agier. We'll attract the attention of even more cave goblins!" grumbled Borlix, turning in circles with his axe.

Aarl had already thrown all his throwing knives and was trying to fend off the bats' attacks with his dagger. Gorathdin circled his fire axe over Princess Lythinda to protect her from the sharp claws and painful bites of the bloodsuckers. Since he did not defend himself, his face was covered in blood.

"There are too many!" shouted Gorathdin.

Brother Transmudin then made the fireball disappear and it went dark for a short time.

"Brother Transmudin, the fireball, quick!" shouted Borlix desperately.

The monk stretched out his right hand to the bats and spoke a verse, whereupon a moment later an icy wind blew over their heads and froze the wings of the bats. They then fell to the ground like stones.

"What's going on, where's the fireball?" Borlix stammered, looking around blindly.

"Right away!" announced Brother Transmudin and created a new fireball that illuminated the icy bats lying on the ground around them.

"Well done, Brother Transmudin. Quick, let's get out of here!" urged Gorathdin and picked up the stretcher with Aarl's help.

They walked quickly towards the tunnel in front of them.

"The ice will only hold them back until it starts to melt," warned Brother Transmudin, who, followed by Werlis and Borlix, entered the tunnel.

The bite wound on his neck, which he was still clutching with his left hand, burned like fire and he tried to find a small flask in his pouch with his right hand as he walked. When the tunnel rounded to a corner, they stopped for a moment.

Gorathdin asked Borlix to take his place at the stretcher and then wiped the blood from his face with his cloak. Brother Transmudin asked a trembling Werlis to hold the bag with the healing potions for a moment and began to search for something in it. Once he had found the small bottle he was looking for, he

358

dripped a little of the contents onto the bite wound on his neck. The bleeding stopped immediately, whereupon he pulled a cloth from the pouch and asked Gorathdin to bandage his neck.

"Forgive me, friends! I shouldn't have broken the warlock's staff," said Brother Transmudin contritely.

"Forget and forgive!" Borlix placated and followed his friends down the long tunnel to the exit.

"Daylight!" shouted Werlis delightedly as they emerged from the tunnel and he caught sight of the sun setting behind the horizon in the west.

Brother Transmudin made the fireball disappear, put down his pack and turned his attention to his friends' injuries. When all their wounds had been treated, they climbed down the steps carved into the rock on the side of the mountain facing Thir until they reached a ledge.

Aarl looked down at his home.

Far back on the horizon lay the Southern Sea. He would soon be confronted with the horrors of his past again, but he was confident that the wound in his heart, similar to the one on his leg that had already healed, would soon heal for good. The travelers soaked up the last rays of the setting sun and recovered from their march through the darkness.

They followed a winding path downhill for more than a mile. When it became too dark to continue, they set up camp under a large pine tree and spent the night there.

A pact is agreed upon

Manamii's escape led her further and further south-east in the darkness. She hoped that she would soon reach the village of Zeel, northwest of the port city of Irkaar. Manamii fell several times over roots protruding from the ground, fallen trees or stones and scratched herself on thorny plants. She was often startled by the sounds of the night. But her concern for Wahmubu, Vrenli and the pages of the book kept her running through the dark wilderness. Manamii did not realize that she was too far east of Zeel, running towards a lake several thousand paces from her destination.

In the meantime, Erik had regained his feet in the main hut in the village of the Raging Hordes. Dazed, he called out to his men and ordered the two barbarians who burst through the door to take up the pursuit of the desert woman.

"Take the dogs with you!" he ordered, visibly annoyed, as he carefully felt his aching genital area.

"That witch, if I get my hands on her, then...!" he roared, clenching his fist.

He left the main hut and marched angrily towards the wooden hut where Wahmubu and Vrenli were being held captive.

"Bring her back to me!" he shouted at the five barbarians who had gathered in the darkness at the village square with three wolfhounds to find Manamii.

"Look for her!" shouted one of the barbarians to the dogs, who immediately picked up Manamii's scent and ran unerringly out of the village to the northeast.

Erik unlocked the door to the wooden hut, entered, grabbed Wahmubu by his clothes with his strong right hand and pulled him up.

"Who is this witch? Your wife? Fiancée? Answer me!" Erik trembled.

Wahmubu remained silent.

He suspected that Manamii had escaped. Vrenli, who had fallen asleep with his hands tied behind his back, woke up as Erik continued to attack Wahmubu. He rolled skillfully to Erik's feet and sank his teeth into his calf with all his might. The barbarian let out a bloodcurdling scream, turned away from Wahmubu and kicked Vrenli hard in the stomach with his right foot. The force of the kick hurled Vrenli across the hut, where he writhed in pain as tears streamed down his cheeks. Wahmubu saw his chance, rose and tried to throw Erik to the ground with a powerful shoulder kick, but Erik turned to the side to avoid the blow. Wahmubu fell forward, hitting his nose on the ground and coming to rest at Erik's feet.

"As soon as my men have brought this witch back, I'll feed you three to the dogs!" he shouted at them, gave Wahmubu another kick and left the hut in a huff.

Some time after Erik had locked the door, Wahmubu straightened up and wiped his bleeding nose on his overdress. He helped the still sobbing Vrenli, lying on the ground and holding his cloak from the Dark Forest with all his might, stand up.

"We have failed!" Wahmubu confessed dejectedly. "The pages of the book are in the hands of the barbarians and the woman I love is probably wandering through the forest in the dark," he added sadly, sitting down in the middle of the hut and staring at the wooden walls.

"If I were you, I'd be glad that Manamii was able to escape. Who knows what that barbarian would have done to her otherwise. She will surely return with help and as for the book pages..." said Vrenli, placing his hand on his cloak.

"I sewed them into the lining of my cloak before we left Iseran," Vrenli added.

Wahmubu looked up.

"You've done well, Vrenli. Maybe we still have a chance after all. You're right, one should never stop hoping," Wahmubu affirmed and lay down on the floor.

"We should try to get some sleep. Let's hope you're right and Manamii returns with help," he murmured and then closed his eyes.

Vrenli thought about their situation and about his friends in Astinhod for some time.

"The village of the Raging Hordes is well fortified and Erik has more than three hundred men around him; it won't be easy for us to get out of here. Manamii should come back with a small army," thought Vrenli.

Faced with the unlikely rescue, his hope began to fade. He lay down on his back next to Wahmubu, stared into the darkness for some time and fell restlessly asleep.

Manamii, whose knees were already bloody from her frequent falls, decided to take a short rest after all. She was desperate, she didn't know for sure whether she was on the right path, and if she did somehow make it to Zeel, she still faced the uncertainty of whether the village would help her at all. She didn't even know if the people of Zeel were capable of going into battle against the Raging Hordes. Exhausted, she crouched down, hid her face between her knees and tried to catch her breath. The barbarian wolfhounds following Manamii's trail were already close behind her. When a sudden howl cut through the silence, Manamii jumped up and sprinted east with the last of her strength.

As the morning dawned and she still hadn't arrived in Zeel, she began to doubt that she would ever make it there, but as the forest grew thinner, she saw a clearing ahead of her after only a few hundred steps, and she regained hope.

A nearby howl sounded and Manamii began to run towards the clearing in front of her with the last of her strength. But instead of the village she had hoped for, she only saw a small lake. Despair overcame her, tears streamed down her cheeks and her strength dwindled. The sounds of her pursuers rose menacingly close behind her. The saving thought of jumping into the lake to throw the dogs off her scent gave her a final surge of strength. When she arrived exhausted at the lake shore, she jumped headfirst into the cool, refreshing water. She submerged and swam towards the middle of the lake. As she came up for air and looked back, she saw five barbarians running out of the forest towards the clearing, following their dogs.

Manamii still had a head start and hoped that the dogs had lost her scent. She swam towards the northern shore of the lake. Once there, she looked around again and saw the dogs sniffing the ground where she had jumped into the lake, angrily pacing up and down.

Completely exhausted, she dropped into the damp grass on the lake shore and warmed herself in the rays of the morning sun. She knew she didn't have much time. Her pursuers were barbarians, but they weren't stupid enough not to find out soon that she had jumped into the water. Nevertheless, she had to close her eyes for a moment and rest. She had been without sleep for two days now. Only a few moments passed before she fell asleep, eyes closed in the warm sunlight, completely exhausted.

Manamii's pursuers had split into two groups in the meantime. Three of the barbarians and two dogs circled the lake from the north and the other two, with one dog, headed for the opposite shore from the south. When they reached the western shore of the lake, their dog began to growl and bare its teeth. It had scented Manamii and began to run northwards, picking up speed.

Just as the dog was about to pounce on Manamii, who was still lying on the lake shore, an arrow hit it with full force as it jumped. Manamii jumped up at the howl of the hit dog and looked around, startled.

Two of her pursuers ran towards her. Manamii turned in the direction from which the arrow had been fired and looked at a tall elf. He was clad in a dark green cloak, holding a longbow in his right hand and waving to her with his left.

Manamii was about to wave back when the strong arm of a barbarian grabbed her by the back of the neck and pinned her to the ground. Two loud screams later, the barbarian released his grip. Manamii jumped up, turned around and saw that her tormentor and the other barbarian had been hit in their shoulders by two throwing knives.

Manamii immediately ran towards the ranger and realized that he was not alone, but accompanied by a Thirian, a dwarf, an Abkether and, as she assumed, a monk. A stretcher lay in the grass next to him with a young woman resting on it.

Werlis, Gorathdin, Aarl, Borlix and Brother Transmudin, who had been walking south from the Border Mountains since the morning, stood in front of Manamii. They were surprised to meet a desert woman here in the wilderness.

"Help me. They're going to kill me!" she begged them.

The two barbarians were not held back for long by the knives in their shoulders and ran towards Manamii with their axes raised. Two more throwing knives from Aarl stopped the wounded, grim-faced attackers halfway. They fell to the ground, dead.

"Please help me!" Manamii pleaded again.

"What is a desert woman doing so far north, alone and pursued by two barbarians?" asked Gorathdin, and before Manamii could answer, the three other pursuers arrived at the lakeshore with their two wolfhounds.

"Give us the witch!" roared one of the barbarians, raising his axe threateningly as he saw his two dead clan brothers lying on the grass in front of him.

"What has she done?" Gorathdin asked, putting an arrow in the string of his bow and aiming at one of the two snarling dogs.

"None of your business, stinking elf. Give her to us!" retorted another of the battle-ready barbarians.

"The barbarians have captured me, my fiancé and an Abkether who was traveling with us!" she explained hurriedly, grabbing Gorathdin's arm for protection.

"An Abkether?" Borlix asked brightly.

"Yes, an Abkether, just like your friend here!" replied Manamii, pointing to Werlis.

"Do you know his name?" Gorathdin asked.

"His name is Vrenli!" replied Manamii.

The five friends smiled happily at each other.

"Vrenli is alive!" Werlis cheered overjoyed.

As one of the barbarians took a step towards Manamii, Gorathdin fired his arrow at the targeted wolfhound. The second, who was about to leap, succumbed to a throwing knife from Aarl.

Borlix ran towards the three barbarians and struck one of them down with a mighty axe blow, turned around and used the handle of his axe to jab the one standing next to him in the groin. The barbarian fell to his knees and Werlis rammed the blade of his short sword into his back from behind. Gorathdin leapt at the third barbarian and brought him down with two swift successive punches. Borlix was about to slay the man on the ground with his axe when Gorathdin stopped him.

"Stop, let him live!" Gorathdin objected.

Borlix looked at him in astonishment. "Why?" he wanted to know, hovering his axe above the barbarian.

"We need information," Gorathdin explained.

Borlix nodded and slowly lowered his axe, whereupon Aarl tied up the barbarian lying on the ground.

"Thank you!" Manamii said with relief and threw her arms around Gorathdin's neck.

"Where is Vrenli?" asked Werlis impatiently.

"He and my fiancé Wahmubu, prince of the northern nomadic tribes, are being held captive by the Raging Hordes! Their leader is called Erik," she replied.

Gorathdin nodded.

He knew the location of the village of the Raging Hordes and that there were at least three hundred armed men there.

"As far as I know, they hold no grudge against the Scheddifer. How is it then that they captured you?" Gorathdin inquired further.

Manamii sat down on the grass and began to tell her saviors about the events in Desert of DeShadin.

"Erwight of Entorbis!" Borlix grumbled and cursed after Manamii told him about the Shadow Lord's plan. Manamii's eyes fell briefly on Princess Lythinda.

"What about her?" she asked, getting up and walking towards the stretcher.

"She's ill," replied Brother Transmudin, who wasn't sure whether the desert woman could be trusted.

With Gorathdin, however, it was different, he knew from the first moment he had looked deep inside her that she, just like him, served the Book of Wetherid. She was a guardian, a sister. He trusted her and so he told her the reason for their journey and that their destination was Horunguth Island. Gorathdin was well aware that his openness towards the strange desert woman puzzled his travel companions.

"We can trust her," Gorathdin affirmed, looking at his friends.

Werlis, Aarl, Borlix and Brother Transmudin then hesitantly introduced themselves to Manamii.

"We have to free Vrenli," emphasized Werlis anxiously.

"Of course we have to," agreed Aarl, while Borlix nodded.

While Gorathdin pondered a rescue plan, Brother Transmudin tended to the wounds on Manamii's knee.

"We'll find a way to free Vrenli and Manamii's fiancé, but it won't be easy," Gorathdin remarked.

"Bah! Let's just go into the village and get them out of there. Whoever gets in our way... well, you know!" Borlix grumbled, swinging his axe through the air.

"No, my friend, it's not that simple," Gorathdin replied, informing his friends of the approximate number of barbarians and the fortifications around the village.

"We need an army to get in there," declared Manamii.

"I'm afraid we don't have an army, princess," Borlix remarked politely.

"I can see that for myself. But the village of Zeel is around here somewhere, we can ask for help there," she suggested, her gaze lingering on Aarl.

"I don't think we'll find any help there. The inhabitants of the village avoid fighting with the Raging Hordes," explained Aarl, shaking his head.

"I'm afraid we're on our own," Gorathdin concluded.

"But we can't leave Vrenli in the lurch!" protested Werlis, standing up and nervously walking up and down the lakeshore.

"I could ride to Iseran if they sell me a horse in Zeel and ask my father for help," suggested Manamii.

Aarl stood up and began to pick up some dry branches along the lakeshore.

"I'm afraid we don't have the time. Erik, the clan leader of the Raging Hordes of the West, will soon realize that his men are not returning. He won't wait long to kill Wahmubu and Vrenli," Gorathdin clarified as he approached Princess Lythinda's stretcher, took her hand and sank into his thoughts.

Some time passed.

In the meantime, Aarl had lit a fire and Brother Transmudin began to prepare a simple meal. Werlis and Borlix, who were sitting on the ground next to the fire, were discussing various rescue plans. Manamii stood near the lakeshore and looked across to the other side.

"I think that could work!" Gorathdin finally announced and stood up.

"Listen to me, friends!" he begged.

Everyone looked up.

"Aarl, you will pose as one of Astinhod's thieves and lead me to the barbarian village as your prisoner. Tell them I am the son of Mergoldin and a gift from Erwight of Entorbis to reinforce the alliance we seek. We will cause a great commotion among the barbarians!" Gorathdin explained and, before any of his friends could voice their objections, he turned to Manamii and continued.

"Manamii, you are an assassin, do you think you can sneak into the village unseen during the excitement to free Wahmubu and Vrenli?" Gorathdin asked her.

His friends were surprised because Manamii had never mentioned that she was trained in the art of silent killing.

"I can do that!" Manamii assured him confidently.

Gorathdin looked at Borlix.

"I want you to accompany Manamii and keep the way back clear for her," he continued.

Borlix nodded.

"Of course!" he grumbled, clutching the handle of his axe.

"Werlis and Brother Transmudin, you stay here with Princess Lythinda," Gorathdin said in conclusion, to which the monk nodded.

"I'd rather go with you and free Vrenli. He's my best friend. You have to understand that," objected Werlis.

"Of course I understand that. But you must guard Princess Lythinda for me, Werlis. Please! I need Aarl and Borlix on this mission," Gorathdin explained, looking deep into Werlis' eyes.

Werlis understood.

"All right, so be it. But woe betide you if you return without Vrenli!" said Werlis, somewhat angrily.

"I have another question. How do you imagine we'll get out of the village unharmed?" interjected Aarl, playing with one of his throwing knives.

"You disappear as quickly as you can. Say that you are expected back with an answer from Erik and demand a reward to make it look real," Gorathdin replied.

"But what about you?" Aarl asked, whereupon the others also wanted to know how Gorathdin was going to get out of the barbarian village.

"Don't worry about me," replied Gorathdin.

"But we're worried about you!" protested Werlis, whereupon Borlix stood up.

"Don't worry, bah!" he grumbled and kicked a stone towards the water.

"How are you going to escape the village alone if they know you're Mergoldin's son? Disappear into thin air? I didn't know rangers had that ability," Borlix grumbled again and sat back down by the fire.

"They won't kill me. I'm worth more to them if I stay alive," replied Gorathdin.

"But they will keep you prisoner, maybe even torture you," Werlis pointed out.

"I'll improvise," Gorathdin replied calmly and took the bowl handed to him by Brother Transmudin, who had stayed out of the conversation.

"Please trust me again, friends. We must free Vrenli and Wahmubu. It's important," Gorathdin begged. Manamii nodded in agreement.

Gorathdin looked at everyone for a few moments.

"Of course we have to, but you're putting yourself in great danger," said Werlis worriedly.

"If anyone has a better suggestion, name it," Gorathdin replied and waited.

A general shake of their heads.

Manamii stood up, approached Gorathdin and sat down next to him. After whispering something in his ear, she stood up again, sat down by the fire, took the bowl Brother Transmudin had handed her and began to eat.

"I can't shake the feeling that Gorathdin and Manamii are hiding something from us," Borlix muttered to Werlis, Aarl and Brother Transmudin.

"We should get going," Manamii suggested and stood up.

Gorathdin kissed Princess Lythinda on the forehead, said something to her in the language of the forest, which none of those present understood, and laid down his weapons beside the stretcher.

"Take good care of her," he asked Werlis and Brother Transmudin.

"We'll do that. And you take good care of yourselves," replied Brother Transmudin who began to collect the empty bowls around the fire.

Gorathdin leaned down to Werlis and hugged him. "We'll get Vrenli out of there! Be vigilant," he whispered in his ear.

And with these words, Gorathdin, followed by Borlix and Aarl, who handed Manamii four of his throwing knives, walked north around the lake. They had been traveling all day, and when they finally arrived at the large clearing where the village of the Raging Hordes lay, it was already midnight.

"You can tie my hands behind my back now," Gorathdin instructed Aarl, who then pulled out a short rope. "Make it tighter, it has to look real," said Gorathdin, whereupon Aarl tightened the rope.

"Are you really sure you want to do this?" Borlix worried.

"I'm sure of it. Let's go, Aarl!" Gorathdin replied firmly.

Aarl grabbed Gorathdin's arm and walked towards the torch-lit entrance to the village. A barbarian standing guard on one of the lookout towers alerted the villagers of the two approaching strangers. A group of heavily armed Northmen arrived at the entrance shortly afterwards and blocked Gorathdin and Aarl's way into the village.

"Who are you and what do you want here?" a big, fat barbarian asked them in a growling voice.

"My name is G...!" Gorathdin was about to reply, but Aarl hit him lightly on the back of the head with his hand.

"You're quiet!" Aarl hissed at him.

Gorathdin lowered his head.

"I am a thief from Astinhod, traveling at the behest of Erwight of Entorbis. I have a gift for the clan leader of the Raging Hordes," replied Aarl, very convincing in his role.

"Who is the ranger?" the barbarian asked.

"He's a gift, now go and tell Erik!" spoke Aarl in a firm tone.

"Wait here!" the barbarian ordered and went back into the village. Two wolfhounds sniffed around Aarl and Gorathdin, who did not move from their spot.

"Take them to the main house!" a voice called out from behind the entrance.

Two of the barbarians then led Gorathdin and Aarl into the torch-lit village. On the way to the main house, the inhabitants stepping out of their huts gave Gorathdin a dark look. Erik was already standing in front of the main house on the village square, waiting for the two strangers.

"You bring a gift from Erwight of Entorbis?" asked Erik, looking at Gorathdin with contempt.

"Yes, clan leader of the Raging Hordes," replied Aarl.

"Well then, where is it?" Erik inquired as his eyes scanned the surroundings.

"Here!" Aarl replied and pushed Gorathdin to the ground at Erik's feet.

"What are you talking about? A ranger?" grumbled Erik grimly.

"Not just any ranger," replied Aarl, pausing for a moment.

"This is the son of Mergoldin. The half-breed," said Aarl, pointing to Gorathdin lying on the ground, attracting the attention of all the barbarians present.

"The son of Mergoldin? Is Erwight of Entorbis sure about that?" Erik wanted to know.

"Of course, and he wants to give him to you as a gift, as a sign of his trust," replied Aarl.

Erik's eyes began to shine and a smile spread across his face.

"By the gods of the north! I thought I couldn't trust this dark figure!" Erik shouted delightedly, whereupon the barbarians gathering in the village square began to roar and clap their hands enthusiastically.

"The son of Mergoldin. This is truly a gift!" cried Erik, grabbing Gorathdin by the scruff of the neck and pulling him up to him. "You! You will help me expand our hunting grounds!" Erik said to Gorathdin and shook him.

"If your father ever wants to see you alive again, he will do well to comply with all our wishes!" Erik threatened, grinning shabbily.

Gorathdin's dark green eyes lit up.

"My father will never give in to your demands!" he countered, trying to free himself from Erik's grip.

"We'll find out soon enough!" Erik announced triumphantly and punched Gorathdin hard in the face. Two of the barbarians grabbed Gorathdin's arms and held him down.

"Surely you will be kind enough to reimburse me for the expenses of my long journey?" Aarl demanded, holding out his hand waiting.

Erik laughed and threw him a small bag filled with gold coins.

"This calls for a celebration!" Erik shouted to the now fully assembled inhabitants of the village, who roared and stomped their feet on the ground.

Meanwhile, Manamii smeared her already dark body with the damp, dark-black forest soil. If she hadn't smiled at Borlix, revealing her white teeth, he wouldn't have been able to recognize her in the darkness. The loud, bellowing chant of the barbarians let them know that Aarl and Gorathdin had been successful. Manamii checked the contents of the small leather pouches hanging from her belt and made sure that the throwing knives she had received from Aarl were loose and light in their shafts.

"Good luck," Borlix whispered to her, whereupon Manamii crept carefully and quietly across the forest floor towards the rampart that surrounded the village. She squeezed through the pointed wooden poles sticking out of the ground at an angle and skillfully and light-footedly climbed the high rampart. Once at the top, she jumped down the other side silently.

She crept up to several huts and carefully peered through their windows in search of Wahmubu and Vrenli. When she arrived at a smaller, windowless hut to the west of the main house, she quietly unlocked the door, opened it a crack and peered inside.

"Wahmubu, Vrenli," she whispered softly.

"Manamii!" shouted Wahmubu delightedly.

"Shh, be quiet!" Manamii warned him.

She entered the dark hut.

Vrenli woke up and was about to call Manamii's name, but she beat him to it and put a hand over his mouth to placate him. "Where's the bag with the book pages?" she asked Vrenli quietly, holding her breath in fear of the answer.

"The barbarians took my bag. But the book pages, they're here in the lining of my cloak," replied Vrenli, to which Manamii exhaled with relief.

"How did you escape? Are you alone?" asked Wahmubu.

Manamii did not answer.

She cut Vrenli and Wahmubu's shackles with Aarl's throwing knife.

"Follow me, but quietly," she whispered, peering cautiously out of the door. When she didn't see anyone, she crept outside, followed by Wahmubu and Vrenli.

They were walking, crouched, around the corner of the main house, where there was a loud party going on, when they came across a drunken barbarian relieving himself behind the wooden wall. Before he could realize what was happening, Manamii had blown an instantly acting sleeping powder into his face. Wahmubu caught him just before he could fall to the ground.

"Let's take him behind that hut over there," whispered Manamii and helped Wahmubu and Vrenli drag the heavy Northman away from the main house.

They gagged and bound him and then crept towards the rampart. Once there, Manamii climbed over it without much effort, but when Wahmubu tried to follow her, Vrenli held him back.

"I don't think I can do it," he whispered to Wahmubu and looked up the high rampart.

Wahmubu knelt down in front of Vrenli.

"Get on my back!" he urged Vrenli and bent down.

Vrenli climbed up, clutched Wahmubu's neck and let him take him over the rampart, where Borlix was waiting for them on the other side, smiling.

Vrenli jumped off Wahmubu's back and ran towards Borlix, who immediately took him in his arms. Tears of joy at their reunion sprang from their eyes.

"Where are Werlis, Gorathdin and Aarl? Are they all right? How did you know I was captured by the Raging Hordes?" Vrenli asked, speaking quickly.

"There's no time for explanations now. Come on, my boy, let's get out of here!" urged Borlix.

Manamii nodded and, followed by the three of them, stepped into the thicket ahead. On their one-day march back to the lake, Borlix and Vrenli told each other what had happened since they had parted.

When the four of them arrived at the small lake where Werlis and Brother Transmudin were watching over Princess Lythinda, they were overjoyed. Werlis gave Vrenli a big hug and kissed him on both cheeks. They had countless stories to share with each other.

In the barbarians village, Aarl sat with Erik at a large oak table in the main house and toasted to the gift from Erwight of Entorbis. He explained to the clan leader that he would be expected back in Astinhod as soon as possible with an answer regarding the alliance.

"Tell Massek that the Raging Hordes will join the alliance!" Erik bellowed, standing up and raising a mug of mead over the heads of his men.

A few mugs later, Aarl said goodbye to Erik and left the main house, where the barbarians were having a raucous party that lasted until the early hours of the morning. In the middle of the village square, Aarl looked at Gorathdin, who was standing there tied to a wooden post.

"Good luck, my friend," thought Aarl as he walked through the entrance, out into the clearing and from there into the forest. As he searched his way through the darkness, he hoped that his friends had managed to escape.

Before dawn the next day, Aarl arrived at the eastern shore of the lake, where Vrenli, Werlis, Borlix, Brother Transmudin, Wahmubu and Manamii were sitting around a fire. Vrenli and Aarl's joy when seeing each other again was dampened by the uncertainty about Gorathdin's well-being. They would have loved to know what would happen to their friend, who remained a prisoner of the Raging Hordes.

The morning dawned and Gorathdin was still tied to the wooden post. The two barbarians guarding him, the only ones in the village who had not taken part in the feast, were yawning with fatigue.

"I need to talk to Erik," Gorathdin said to the two of them.

"What do you want from him?" one of the guards grumbled sleepily.

"I have important information for him. Bring him here!" demanded Gorathdin, whereupon one of them stood up and shuffled to the main house, yawning.

Some time passed before Erik, looking grumpy and yawning, stumbled out from behind the bearskin covering the door to the main house and staggered towards Gorathdin.

"I'm warning you, if your information isn't important, you're in for a treat!" grumbled Erik.

"How is it that the great Erik, clan leader of the Raging Hordes of the West, does not take what he desires?" Gorathdin shouted so loudly that he woke many of the sleeping villagers.

The doors of some huts opened and sleepy, grumpy-looking barbarians with disheveled hair stepped out.

"What are you trying to say, elf?" asked Erik angrily.

"I'm saying you're a pathetic coward!" Gorathdin's voice rang out again through the silence of the awakening village. Erik began to boil with rage.

"I'm going to... you... you ...!" Erik struggled for words, his face red, and stepped so close to Gorathdin that he could feel his breath, which smelled of mead.

"Go ahead, beat a man tied to a stake. Show your men how cowardly you are!" Gorathdin shouted in Erik's face.

The barbarians standing in the village square, wrapped in furs, became restless. No one had ever spoken to their clan leader like this before.

"Very well, I can see where you're going with this, elf!" hissed Erik.

"It will be my pleasure to shut your cheeky mouth!" he shouted and ordered his men to untie Gorathdin from the wooden stake.

The villagers, now almost completely assembled and excited by the impending duel, began to chant Erik's name.

"Erik! Erik! Erik!" their voices boomed.

Several formed a circle around Gorathdin and their clan leader.

Erik gave them a sign to let go of Gorathdin, whereupon he slowly walked towards Erik, who was standing in the middle of the human circle. He closely observed the clan leader of the Raging Hordes, who was a head taller and a good deal heavier, waiting for him ready for battle. He studied the barbarian in the few steps he still had to take.

As soon as Gorathdin was within reach of Erik's strong hands, they grabbed him and embraced him. Erik lifted Gorathdin up and squeezed his arms together with all his strength. Every vertebra in Gorathdin's back ached. As the pain became more and more unbearable, Gorathdin hit Erik's nose with the front of his head.

Blood flowed.

Erik's tight clutched arms broke free from Gorathdin. Erik cried out in rage and tried to punch his opponent with his right hand. Quick as a weasel, Gorathdin dodged the blow and leapt behind Erik. Before he could turn around, Gorathdin landed three powerful blows to Erik's kidneys.

Erik writhed in pain.

Gorathdin tried to take a step away from Erik when he grabbed him by the hair and pulled him to the ground. Just as Erik was about to lunge at Gorathdin, he rolled to the side and, without using his hands, jumped up from the ground and brought Erik down with a kick to the stomach. Gorathdin jumped on top of Erik and choked him. But Erik, who was much stronger than Gorathdin, broke free of the hold and grabbed him by the right arm, throwing him off.

The crowd went wild.

"Erik, Erik!" the barbarians shouted and stomped their feet.

Erik ran towards Gorathdin, who was lying on the ground, and tried to kick him. But Gorathdin parried skillfully, grabbed Erik's foot and threw him to the ground with a jerky movement. Gorathdin now clutched Erik's neck with his legs. He squeezed so tight that he began to gasp.

Erik tried unsuccessfully to free himself from Gorathdin's grasp. The barbarians around them became restless. They feared that the ranger would kill their clan leader.

Erik cried out in pain, and when Gorathdin saw one of the barbarians enter the human circle, he squeezed his legs even tighter around Erik's neck, causing him to tremble all over and gasp greedily for air, whereupon the barbarian stepped out of the circle again.

Against all expectations, Gorathdin released his grip and stood up.

Erik was still lying on the ground, gasping, when several barbarians rushed at Gorathdin to avenge their clan leader's defeat.

"Leave him!" croaked Erik and raised his hand upwards. The barbarians looked in amazement at their leader, who slowly rose and massaged his neck.

He coughed and rattled a bit, but after a few moments he recovered. Gorathdin had sat down in the middle of the broken circle and waited for Erik to approach him.

"You could have killed me, ranger. Why didn't you do it?" Erik wanted to know.

"We were fighting for honor. There was no reason to kill you," replied Gorathdin.

Erik nodded.

"You have won. You're free to go!" Erik announced as his sharp gaze pierced the crowd, whereupon some of the villagers made way.

"Listen to me, Erik, clan leader of the Raging Hordes of the West. I have no intention of leaving your village until you have sat down with me and spoken to me about the animosity you harbor against the inhabitants of the Dark Forest!" Gorathdin declared firmly.

Erik listened and looked thoughtfully at Gorathdin.

The ranger had defeated him in a fair fight in front of his men and now he was trying to thwart the alliance with Erwight of Entorbis. He was boiling with rage, but somehow, he liked the way the fearless ranger was causing a stir in his village.

Erik had to admit to himself that he had respect for Gorathdin and even felt sympathy for him.

Still, he had to be careful what he said to the ranger now, because he didn't want to lose his reputation in the village.

"Having Gorathdin killed would be an option. Or I could demand another fight from him. But the elf is quick and an excellent fighter," thought Erik. Gorathdin was still looking at him, waiting for an answer. But Erik continued to think and finally decided on a completely different solution, which he thought was not a bad one at all.

"Takes some getting used to, but not bad," he thought and put his hand around Gorathdin's shoulder in a friendly manner.

"You're a good fighter. If I was any younger, I wouldn't have made it so easy for you!" Erik said so loudly that every one of his men could hear.

"Let us celebrate. To Gorathdin, the conqueror of the once unconquerable clan leader of the Northmen!" shouted Erik, hoping his men would be carried away.

"To Gorathdin, the conqueror of Erik. To Erik, our clan leader!" some of the men began to shout and soon the whole village was roaring.

"You are a wise man," Gorathdin whispered and followed Erik into the main house, where they sat side-by-side at the large oak table. Some women placed barrels of mead, wooden platters of dried meat and bread on the wide tabletop.

"I have a confession to make," Gorathdin began, just as Erik was about to drink.

"I am not a gift from Erwight of Entorbis and your two prisoners have been freed in the meantime. You know, the Desert Man and the Abkether," whispered Gorathdin.

Erik, who almost choked at first, looked at Gorathdin in silence for a moment and then laughed out loud.

"Who needs them anyway? Two less mouths to feed!" he finally replied and downed his cup.

"Listen, Erik. I don't have much time; we should talk in private. If possible, before you're completely drunk," Gorathdin demanded, looking at his cup.

"Follow me!" Erik replied, filling his mug with mead and stepping outside to go to the main house.

Outside, Gorathdin revealed to Erik the true purpose of his coming. He did not describe everything, but enough to convince Erik of the advantages of farming and animal husbandry compared to the arduous life of hunting. Gorathdin understood Erik's objections about not being able to give up hunting altogether, as game meat, hides, horn and tallow were their only trade goods.

"No one is asking you to give up hunting altogether. But you must convince your men to stop hunting in the Dark Forest," Gorathdin explained.

Gorathdin placed a hand on Erik's shoulder and looked deep into his eyes.

"Erik, you are a proud warrior and your people adore you. But the Entorbis are playing a false game. Their promise of power and domination is an illusion that only leads to ruin," he said.

He paused to make sure his words were having an effect.

"King Grandhold and his kingdom stand for honor and justice. An alliance with him would not only strengthen your clan, but also secure its rightful place in the world," Gorathdin continued.

"Hunting in the Dark Forest is a dangerous endeavor that costs more than it earns. It is a path of destruction that keeps you and your people from true greatness."

Gorathdin saw Erik thinking.

"Imagine how much we could achieve together if we joined forces instead of losing ourselves in old feuds. King Grandhold respects strength and would welcome you and your clan as equal allies."

"Let us pave a new path for your people, a path of peace and prosperity. It is time to put old enmities behind us and fight for a better future," Gorathdin concluded, hopeful that his words had reached Erik's heart and mind.

Erik, who was no longer the youngest, but experienced enough to decide what was best for his clan, agreed.

"Here, take this ring. It will help you if you ever come into conflict with my brother's clan," said Erik, pulling a ring off his finger and handing it to Gorathdin, who accepted it, thanked him and placed his hand on Erik's strong shoulders.

"I'm counting on you!" Gorathdin said, but instead of going back inside with Erik, he made his way to the small lake in the west, hoping to find his friends safe and waiting for him.

Aarl's village

When Gorathdin arrived at the clearing before midday the next day, he ran towards the lake in front of him, jumped in and swam towards the eastern shore. He enjoyed the refreshingly cool water, which, for a moment, made him forget for about the worries and fears that had accompanied him since his departure from Abketh.

Manamii and Wahmubu sat arm in arm near the water and talked about what they should do now.

"Father said that the book pages would be safest in Astinhod, but perhaps we should accompany Gorathdin, Werlis, Aarl, Borlix and the monk to Horunguth after all. I think the mages of the island will know best what to do with the pages," Manamii said to Wahmubu, who remained silent for some time, staring out at the lake. He turned around and looked at Werlis, Aarl, Borlix, Brother Transmudin and Princess Lythinda.

"I'm worried about the snake people and their alliance with Erwight of Entorbis. With the support of the shadow mages and perhaps the thieves and the Raging Hordes, they could take Iseran. You know what that would mean," Wahmubu shared his concerns.

Manamii nodded and looked at him in silence for a while.

"Do you really think Astinhod will be spared? We should accompany them. I think the book pages are safest in the Tower of Mages. They can defend themselves against the shadow mages from Fallgar. Astinhod's knights can hold their own against the forces of Erwight of Entorbis, the gray dwarves, mist elves, orcs and ogres, but not against the undead of Tongar Gor and the Shadow Mages of Druhn," Manamii explained to Wahmubu, who nodded.

"You're right, Manamii, we should accompany them if they want us to," he agreed.

Manamii suddenly jumped up in alarm.

"Someone's swimming in the lake!" she shouted, whereupon everyone made their way to the shore.

"A barbarian?" asked Borlix, reaching for his axe and staring intently out over the lake.

"I don't think so. Seems too small for a barbarian to me," remarked Aarl, taking a step closer to the water.

Everyone looked excitedly at the middle of the lake and their joy grew as the stranger swam closer to them.

"It's Gorathdin!" exclaimed Vrenli delightedly.

Werlis jumped into the lake and swam towards Gorathdin. Vrenli almost jumped in after him, but he remembered the book pages in the lining of his cloak in time. He stopped and waved to the ranger.

"By all the halls of Ib'Agier, you've managed to escape!" growled Borlix.

He held out his hand to Gorathdin and pulled him out of the water. To Wahmubu's displeasure, Manamii jumped up to Gorathdin, hugged him and kissed him on the cheek. Werlis, who had been pulled out of the water by Aarl and Borlix, approached Vrenli. The two of them had regained their almost forgotten, carefree smiles and were jumping around happily together in front of Gorathdin. In an instant, Gorathdin grabbed Vrenli and lifted him up.

"My friend Vrenli, do you even know how worried we were about you? Is it so common for you Abkether to reach for magical objects, or rather, to climb into them?" Gorathdin teased him in a stern undertone.

Vrenli lowered his eyes.

A moment later, Gorathdin slowly let him slide back to the ground, knocked him over with his cloak and pounced on him. Gorathdin instinctively knew where to tickle Vrenli so that he wouldn't be able to stop laughing.

"Werlis, help me!" Vrenli begged, laughing, whereupon Werlis tore off a tuft of grass, jumped onto Gorathdin and began tickling his pointed ears.

Gorathdin laughed out loud.

Vrenli crawled out from under him and, together with Werlis, tickled Gorathdin so much that he was in tears of laughter.

Their play was interrupted by Aarl.

"We really should set off. It's at least another two days' walk to Irkaar and I want to leave the forest before dusk. The woods ahead are teeming with wild boars," Aarl warned them, who only began to laugh louder.

"Wild boars!" snorted Werlis.

"We fought with forest, snow and cave goblins, were attacked several times by thieves, wandered through the most dangerous of forests, Vrenli saw lizard creatures and was captured by barbarians, and you... you now want to tell us that we have to watch out for wild boars!" laughed Werlis, writhing on the ground.

Aarl began to grin and ended up laughing himself. It wasn't long before Borlix, Brother Transmudin, Manamii and Wahmubu joined in the laughter.

"Aarl is right, we should set off, not because of the boars, but we still have a long way to go," Gorathdin agreed.

What he did not tell his friends, however, was that he sensed a shadow moving from Fallgar to Wetherid and that he was worried about the land and its peoples because of all that had happened. Not only did he want to get to Horunguth Island as quickly as possible for Princess Lythinda's sake, but he also wanted to talk to Master Drobal about everything that had happened. And then there was Vrenli, who, unbeknownst to himself, was a Keeper of the Book of Wetherid. Gorathdin sensed that the pages of the book were in danger. Which confirmed Manamii's father's request of Vrenli to bring the pages of Iseran to Astinhod.

Gorathdin stood up and walked towards Princess Lythinda's stretcher. Her gaze was still fixed, almost lifeless. He took her hand, held it for a while and then sat down by the fire to dry his clothes.

In the meantime, his friends were preparing to continue their journey.

Manamii and Wahmubu approached Gorathdin and offered him their help.

"We can use all the help we can get. It's not just about Princess Lythinda's well-being, but I fear for all of ours!" Gorathdin said, accepting their offer gratefully after giving his friends a questioning look and nodding in agreement.

Thus, the original seven travelers became nine, who marched south for two days.

Before nightfall on the second night, they arrived in Irkaar, where they stopped at a questionable inn frequented mainly by sailors. Gorathdin did not fail to notice the scurvy-stricken, long-bearded men gazing curiously at Princess Lythinda as they poured mead down their throats from large clay jugs. They went straight to their rooms without eating or drinking so as not to cause a further stir. Borlix and Aarl found it difficult not to go down to the guest room to drink a mug or two of mead. They certainly deserved it, they both thought, but the look on Gorathdin's face spoke volumes.

The next morning, they traveled further southwest. Just before dawn, they reached the north side of Aarl's village with its vast wankini fields. Aarl could hardly wait to pick some of them and bite into their juicy, sweet flesh.

"Eat up, friends. Help yourselves. They're delicious!" he urged the others, who accepted his invitation.

While his friends feasted on the sweet fruit, he looked across the fields to the small fishing village.

He was visibly pleased to return to his birthplace after such a long time, even if the thought of his deceased parents saddened him somewhat and he was still a little afraid of facing his past.

After everyone had feasted on the wankinis, they headed south across the fields and entered the small, unfortified village of no more than fifty simple wooden huts.

Werlis immediately noticed hammocks hanging from the terraces of almost all the huts, where many of the villagers were sleeping.

"They know how to live. It's midday and they're sleeping outside their huts," Werlis said with a grin.

"The village of your dreams!" Vrenli replied and laughed.

Aarl then explained to them that his people lived mainly off fishing and growing wankinis.

They went out in their boats before sunrise and cast their nets. In the evening, when it got cooler, they went out into the fields to water them.

"Then it's probably not the village of your dreams after all. People work here, not only during the day," Vrenli teased Werlis, who grinned in response.

Due to its proximity to the port city of Irkaar, where inhabitants from various regions of Wetherid and some from Fallgar were staying, the travelers hardly caused a stir in Aarl's village. The only astonished looks from the villagers were directed at the starry-eyed Princess Lythinda on the stretcher, dressed in a monk's robe. On their way to the hut of Aarl's parents, Aarl greeted some of the villagers and when they arrived, he looked in amazement at the small, well-kept garden and the neat-looking terrace.

He noticed that the planks of the wooden hut were coated with a shiny glaze. The flower troughs in front of the windows were filled with magnificent anthuriums.

"Wait here for me. Something is wrong. Everything looks so neat," Aarl told his friends, who waited in the garden.

Aarl suspected that someone had taken up residence in the hut and carefully lifted the beam that locked the door, opened it and entered. He was surprised to see that the hut was not inhabited but was in a tidy state.

"I don't understand," he muttered to himself and looked around the two rooms in the large hut. When he returned to the terrace, he saw his friends talking to a woman. From a distance, he couldn't make out who it was, so he approached the stranger.

"Aarl, I knew you would come back one day!" the pretty, tanned woman in her fifties welcomed him with a beaming smile.

"Marlina!" shouted Aarl and immediately took her in his arms. The two of them looked at each other lovingly.

Gorathdin assumed that their reunion would be long-lasting and therefore asked Aarl if he and the others could go into the hut.

"Go ahead, friends. Make yourselves at home. I'll be right behind you," replied Aarl, without taking his eyes off Marlina.

Borlix and Brother Transmudin carried Princess Lythinda into the hut, took her to the room next to the kitchenette and laid her on one of the two beds inside. Gorathdin, who had followed them, sat down on the edge of the bed and placed Princess Lythinda's hand in his.

"I'll stay with her for a while," he said to Borlix and Brother Transmudin, who left the room and sat down at the table by the window next to Vrenli and Werlis.

"Gorathdin is staying with her," Borlix let his two smaller friends know. Vrenli and Werlis nodded silently and looked out through the window at the sea, which was no more than fifty paces from them.

Borlix got up again after a while, walked towards a low bench at the back of the room and lay down on it.

"Time for supper," said Brother Transmudin and was just about to open the provisions bag when Aarl and Marlina entered the hut.

"I've brought you fresh fish and some wankinis," Marlina announced, smiling, to everyone's delight.

"Excellent. Thank you very much," replied Brother Transmudin who wanted to take the fish from her, but she insisted on cooking for everyone.

"But you're welcome to give me a hand," she told Brother Transmudin and Manamii, who had offered her help as well. The three of them began to prepare the fish in a tasty wankini sauce. Vrenli, Werlis, Wahmubu and Aarl waited impatiently for the evening meal. Tired from the long walk, they sat at the table.

Aarl fetched wankini wine from a chamber, placed four cups on the table and filled them. "The older the wine, the better it tastes," Aarl remarked.

Wahmubu declined with thanks and explained that he did not drink wine, mead, beer or anything similar. Aarl shrugged his shoulders, took Wahmubu's cup and emptied it. After he had poured himself, Vrenli and Werlis another cup, he looked at the snoring Borlix with a grin.

Aarl took a big sip from his cup and began to tell Vrenli and Werlis about his youth. Vrenli noticed how Aarl and Marlina kept exchanging amorous glances. As he was about to address Aarl, Gorathdin came out of the room and sat down at the table with them.

"Just in time. Dinner's ready!" Marlina announced and, together with Manamii, placed a large cast-iron pan in the middle of the table.

Borlix woke up.

"That smells fantastic," he grumbled and took a seat at the table.

"I hope it not only smells fantastic, but tastes fantastic too," Marlina replied with a smile.

Everyone grabbed the food.

While they enjoyed the meal, Marlina talked about her youth with Aarl.

After everyone had eaten their fill and expressed their subsequent tiredness, Marlina and Aarl left the hut and went outside onto the terrace, where they sat down on a small bench and began to reminisce.

Gorathdin, who had slept in the bed next to Princess Lythinda for some time, woke up around midnight and quietly walked past his sleeping friends out onto the terrace. He found Marlina asleep in Aarl's arms. Aarl, however, sat awake, gazing thoughtfully into the darkness of the sea and listening to the sound of the waves.

"Sit down with us," Aarl invited Gorathdin when he noticed him.

"I don't want to disturb you. I couldn't sleep anymore. It's too hot for me. Even at night," Gorathdin explained.

"You're not interrupting, my friend. Have a seat. Marlina is already asleep and I can't sleep," said Aarl in a depressed voice.

"What's bothering you, Aarl? Aren't you glad to be back?" Gorathdin asked quietly, not wanting to wake Marlina.

"Yes and no," replied Aarl.

Hesitantly, he began to tell Gorathdin why he had left his village and moved to the vicinity of Abketh. More than thirty years ago, when he still lived here with his parents, he had two good friends, Dramis and Marlina, who was young then and just maturing into a woman.

Not a day went by that they didn't spend together doing all the things three teenagers could do.

Over the years, Aarl began to develop feelings for Marlina and one day he decided to confess his love to her. Little did he know that Dramis had confessed his own feelings to Marlina a week earlier. Marlina didn't tell Aarl, but she gave him the same answer she had already given Dramis: that she was still too young for love and that she didn't want to lose the friendships that meant so much to her.

Aarl was disappointed by this answer, but because he didn't want to lose their friendship either, he accepted Marlina's decision without holding a grudge against her.

Weeks passed. It was high summer and the fish that usually swam near the coast were now to be found two nautical miles further out. It was the first time Dramis and Aarl wanted to row out to sea to fish without their fathers. They met early in the morning at Dramis' father's boat and checked the nets before rowing out to sea at dawn. They had been going out with their fathers and casting nets since they were children and were aware that if a dangerous storm arose, they would have trouble getting back to land. But as they saw no clouds in the sky, they were in good spirits and rowed two nautical miles out and cast their nets.

But the two were not just interested in filling their nets, they had more plans. They wanted to catch the big hammerfish, which had been roaming their fishing grounds for weeks. They wanted to prove to everyone in the village that they were real fishermen and, above all, men, so they prepared themselves well for their big project. Dramis had a bag filled with pig's blood with him to lure the hammerfish and Aarl had stolen two sharp harpoons from his father's shed.

They rowed half a nautical mile west from where they had set the nets, threw the thick, wide-meshed net intended for catching larger fish overboard and dragged it behind them. While Dramis dripped a little bit of the pig's blood into the water from time to time, Aarl rowed further and further west.

When the bag was almost empty and the two had already given up hope of catching the hammerfish and were about to row back, Dramis noticed that something had become entangled in the net. He slowly began to haul it in. It was heavy, so he asked Aarl to help him. Just as he was about to lend a hand, something emerged from the water, grabbed Dramis, pulled him overboard and went under with him. At the last moment, Aarl got hold of the rope attached to the net and began to pull on it with all his might, but it tied itself so tightly to his hands that they began to bleed.

The burning, cutting pain increased, but before he had to let go of the rope, he wrapped it around the wooden post at the bow and prevented the end of the rope from going overboard. The boat began to rock violently and Aarl fell over. His right leg hung over the edge of the boat where, to his horror, a hideous, terrifying, frog-like figure emerged and sprayed a burning ooze at him.

Aarl grabbed one of the oars and began to strike the underwater creature several times, and it finally dived away with a hissing sound. There was no sign of Dramis and no matter how often Aarl called out its name, there was no answer.

In almost unbearable pain, Aarl rowed back to the coast at dusk, where he got out of the boat, close to fainting, and called for help.

Aarl could still remember how the villagers looked at him when he told them what had happened out at sea, whereupon Marlina, in tears, told those present about Dramis and Aarl's confessions of love.

"You killed him!" she screamed at Aarl and ran off crying.

No one in the village believed the story about the underwater creature that supposedly dragged Dramis into the depths. Everyone agreed that once Aarl's leg wound had healed, he would have to leave the village. There was no place for a murderer here in the village, they shouted to Aarl as his father carried him into their hut.

His parents were desperate. They believed their son's story, but the others in the village were against them so they had to resign to their son leaving the village.

In the days that Aarl lay in bed in great pain with a fever, fishermen increasingly reported sightings of the underwater creatures near the coast and people began to believe Aarl's story.

But Aarl was certain that he would leave the village as soon as his leg was well again. His disappointment at Marlina's accusation that he had killed their mutual friend was too great. In the two weeks it took for his wound to heal, he did not leave the hut once.

When the day came for Aarl to pack his things, his parents and many of the villagers who had apologized to him tried to dissuade him from going. Kneeling on the terrace and crying, his mother begged him not to go. But Aarl's mind was made up and even Marlina's apologies and pleas did not dissuade him.

"So, now you know everything," Aarl concluded his story, relieved.

"I have failed. I couldn't save my best friend," he added.

He was on the verge of tears.

"You did what you could. It wasn't your fault," Gorathdin comforted him gently and put his hand on his shoulder.

The two of them sat on the terrace for some time, gazing out at the foaming sea. When Marlina opened her eyes, she immediately knew why Aarl had tears in his eyes and began to kiss him gently. Gorathdin said goodbye to them, went back into the hut and lay down again.

When Vrenli woke up the next morning, everyone was already sitting at the table drinking tea.

"I've saved you a few wankinis," Manamii offered Vrenli, who nodded gratefully and sat down at the table, drowsy.

"It's more than twenty nautical miles to Horunguth Island. We need a ship," remarked Aarl, who wanted to further accompany his friends and travel companions.

"A ship? By all the halls of Ib'Agier. Do you think you can get a dwarf on a ship? A rocking thing made of planks. I'm supposed to take to the water on something like that?" Borlix grumbled in horror.

"How did you think you were going to get to the island?" Werlis asked him.

"Well, to be honest, I hadn't thought about that yet," Borlix grumbled quietly into his beard, which made everyone laugh.

"But a ship..." he grumbled again and drank a little of the tea made from desert herbs.

"We have to go back to Irkaar. Only there can we find a ship to take us to the island," suggested Brother Transmudin.

Vrenli, Werlis, Borlix, Wahmubu and Manamii agreed with him, only Aarl and Gorathdin held back.

"I don't think it will be easy to find a captain to take us to the Isle of Mages. It is said among the sailors that the island is cursed and that monsters living in the depths of the sea guard it," explained Aarl.

Gorathdin did not think it advisable to bring Princess Lythinda back to the port city anyway.

"Thieves, pirates and some of the inhabitants of Fallgar are staying there. Just remember the inn. Irkaar is a dangerous city and that's also why I wanted to travel on to Aarl's village with Princess Lythinda as quickly as possible," Gorathdin explained to his friends.

"I don't want to risk being held up just before we reach our destination," he added.

They all understood Gorathdin's concerns, but as they had no better suggestion than Brother Transmudin's, they kept quiet.

"I'll go alone," Aarl broke the silence. After his friends had discussed the pros and cons, all but Borlix agreed.

"But Aarl said that all sailors are afraid of the island," Borlix reminded his friends.

"I'll get us a ship. But I'm afraid it's going to be expensive," announced Aarl, who got up from the table and was about to set off when Brother Transmudin handed him a bag of gold coins.

"You'll certainly need them," he said with a smile and closed the door behind Aarl.

Werlis lay down in the hammock on the terrace for a while and felt completely at home. Meanwhile, Vrenli chatted animatedly with Brother Transmudin, who told fascinating stories about the Order of the Dragon.

Borlix wondered what the other dwarves would say if they found out that he had traveled on a ship. He tried to wash down his unease with a few cups of wankini wine.

A short time later, he was drunk and fell asleep in his chair.

Gorathdin did not leave Princess Lythinda's side all day. Manamii and Wahmubu went for a long walk along the coast and Marlina and some of the villagers began to prepare a feast for Aarl's return.

From time to time she came to the hut with a few women and men to introduce them to Aarl's friends.

In the meantime, Aarl rode on Marlina's white horse along the coast towards the harbor town of Irkaar. Even from a distance, he could see the sails of the single-masted ships anchored in the harbor. Irkaar was the third largest city in Wetherid after Astinhod and Iseran. However, the city had a bad reputation due to its trade relations with Fallgar. Its inhabitants, who were mainly seafarers, traders or fishermen, cared little about this. What mattered to them was the sound of gold coins, and Aarl had a few to hire a brave, fearless captain who would agree to take him and eight other passengers on board and bring them to Horunguth Island.

When Aarl arrived at the stables outside the town, he dismounted his horse and handed the reins to a stable boy.

"Take good care of the horse, boy!" he warned and gave the boy a gold coin, which he bit into to make sure it was genuine.

Aarl followed the narrow footbridge that led down to the harbor. A crowd of children playing further down the jetty came running up and begged him. Aarl knew that if he gave them a coin, he would not be able to get rid of them, so he tried to scare them away. Laughing, begging and screaming, they ran in circles around him and were not impressed by his shooing hand movements.

Just as Aarl was about to move on, he noticed someone reaching for the pouch on his belt. He grabbed the stranger's hand in a flash, faster than the boy could pull it back, and held it tightly.

"You probably thought you could steal from me!" said Aarl in a sharp tone, whereupon some of the smaller ones began to cry.

"Listen to me. I'll give you a gold coin if you tell me who is the most intrepid captain in Irkaar!" Aarl offered the children, took a gold coin from his pouch and lifted it up in front of them.

"Captain Roobar!" announced the boy, whom Aarl was holding by the hand.

"Roobar," repeated Aarl, letting go of the boy and handing him the gold coin.

"Where can I find Captain Roobar?" he asked the boy, who held out his hand waiting for Aarl to understand that this information would cost another gold coin. Aarl took another gold coin from his pouch, which he previously hung around his neck as a precaution.

"If he's on land, you can find him in the Drinking Sailor," the boy replied and reached for the gold coin, but Aarl held it between his fingers.

"And where is the Drinking Sailor?" Aarl asked.

"Right by the harbor. Where the big winch is that lifts crates out of the ships," the boy replied, whereupon Aarl gave him the gold coin and continued to follow the jetty down to the harbor.

Once there, he looked around. The harbor square was crowded with people from all regions of Wetherid and he could even sometimes spot gray dwarves, mist elves and other dark figures from Fallgar in the crowd.

It was a hive of activity. Dock workers passed Aarl, dragging heavy crates or wheelbarrows. He tried to get closer to the ships via the harbor square but was stopped every few steps by merchants. They pulled Aarl by the hand to show him their wares. There was nothing that wasn't on offer.

When Aarl saw the large winch near the water, he freed himself from the pushy merchants and walked purposefully with quick steps to the ships' moorings.

He stopped at the large wooden tower to which the oversized winch was attached and looked around. A dark-skinned desert woman approached him from the crowd and offered him her amorous services. Aarl declined with a smile and asked her where he could find the Drinking Sailor, which must be very close by.

Annoyed by Aarl's refusal, the desert woman pointed to the house behind him.

Aarl thanked her, turned and walked the few steps to the entrance of the inn. He opened the door and stepped inside.

The heavily smoky, dark dining room had space for up to a hundred guests. Opposite it was a stage on which two dark-skinned women danced to the sounds of a drunken old man's lyre. They were cheered and applauded by three barbarians sitting at a table directly in front of the stage.

On the way to the bar, Aarl noticed a mist elf sitting alone at a table in a dark corner, studying a map. Aarl sat down at the counter and asked the fat, full-bearded southerner behind it smoking a pipe if Captain Roobar was here.

"Are you here to ask questions or to have a drink?" the innkeeper gruffly snapped at him.

"Both. Give me a cup of wankini wine!" replied Aarl, placing a gold coin on the counter.

The innkeeper quickly grabbed the money and then nodded his head towards one of the tables where a group of sailors were sitting.

"The tall one with the white hair and the headscarf," said the landlord, taking a puff on his pipe.

Aral approached the table.

"Are you Captain Roobar?" he inquired.

"Who wants to know?" he replied.

"My name is Aarl. I come from the fishing village west of here," Aarl replied.

Captain Roobar looked him up and down.

"I see, and what do you want? My crew is complete, if you're looking for work," replied Captain Roobar and turned away.

"I'm not looking for a job. I need to talk to you in private," Aarl insisted.

"Forget it. Say what you have to say or get lost!" Captain Roobar snapped at Aarl, who threw his bag of gold coins onto the table.

"I want to speak to you in private," repeated Aarl.

Captain Roobar opened the bag and looked inside.

"Let's go outside," he finally decided, stood up and walked to the door.

The two left the Drinking Sailor and went down to the jetty. Captain Roobar walked ahead towards one of the ships moored there.

"Watch out when you cross the plank," Captain Roobar warned Aarl.

Aarl nodded and followed Captain Roobar into his cabin. The captain sat down behind the chart table and poured Aarl a cup of rum.

"What can I do for you, Aarl?" he inquired curiously.

"I'm looking for a ship to take me and eight other people to Horunguth Island," Aarl started and drank from his cup.

Roobar looked up when he heard the name of the island.

"Nobody goes to that island, not even me. It's cursed!" declared Captain Roobar as he poured himself a refill and emptied the rum in one go.

"Me and my friends have to go to the island," said Aarl emphatically.

"There's nothing to do, my friend. I'm not going to Horunguth!" replied Captain Roobar.

He slid the bag of gold coins across the card table back to Aarl.

"Keep it!" Aarl refused and pushed the bag with the gold coins back to Captain Roobar.

"I'll give you another one if you change your mind!" offered Aarl.

Captain Roobar poured himself and Aarl more rum and fell thoughtfully silent.

"There are a good hundred gold coins in the bag, times two, that makes two hundred gold coins. I can pay my crew for the whole month with that," he thought and took another sip.

"I'll make you a deal. You pay me with a second bag of gold coins and I'll take you to within a nautical mile of Horunguth Island. From there, you can row over in the dinghy," he finally said.

Aarl didn't think twice and agreed.

"We're in business!" agreed Aarl, raising his cup and clinking glasses with Captain Roobar.

"I have one more request. Can you pick us up with your ship at the fishing village west of here?" asked Aarl, even before they had finished their drinks.

"That's all right. Be on the coast by midnight tomorrow. A dinghy will pick you up," agreed Captain Roobar and he emptied his cup.

"See you tomorrow at midnight then," Aarl said goodbye.

He went back to the stables where he had the stable boy bring him Marlina's horse and he rode back to his village as quickly as possible.

He happily shared the good news with his friends. Shortly afterwards, Marlina knocked on the door and collected everyone for the welcome party held in Aarl's honor. That evening, Aarl cleared up any misunderstandings between himself and Marlina. The two of them danced and talked until the early hours of the morning. They also spent the entire next day together. Shortly before midnight, Aarl promised Marlina that he would marry her as soon as he returned from Horunguth Island and then followed his eight companions along the path to the coast.

Horunguth Island in distress

Aarl could already see the position light of Captain Roobar's ship, which was less than half a mile from the coast. A dinghy was launched and two sailors rowed it towards the coast.

"Aarl?" called one of the two sailors, and when he answered, a sailor dressed in gray canvas put down his oar, got out of the boat and pulled it closer to land.

"Hurry up, the wind is favorable!" the sailor urged those waiting.

Aarl got in and made sure there was enough room for his friends and especially for the stretcher with Princess Lythinda.

Vrenli and Werlis followed him and sat next to each other at the stern of the boat. Manamii and Wahmubu took a seat at the bow. Gorathdin and Brother Transmudin lifted the stretcher on the side of the boat, while the sailor in the boat helped Aarl lay the stretcher on the bottom of the boat. Gorathdin and Brother Transmudin got in and sat to the left and right of the stretcher.

"Borlix! What's wrong? Come on!" urged Aarl.

Borlix stood rooted to his spot and stared at the small dinghy.

"Come on!" Gorathdin urged him, waving his hand.

"I ... can't," Borlix stuttered, already feeling dizzy at the sight of the light swell.

"Get in, dwarf!" shouted the sailor holding the boat and pulled Borlix by the arm.

"Go on!" Aarl urged him again.

But Borlix only gazed fixedly at the water. His pupils began to dilate more and more. He lifted his leg as if he wanted to take a step, but after a moment he put it back on the solid ground.

"I can't do that. We dwarves are not meant to travel over water. We need solid, stony ground," grumbled Borlix.

The two sailors became restless.

"Come on now, don't be a coward!" Vrenli finally said.

Borlix looked up.

"Me a coward? No one has ever said that to me! Wait, I'll help you!" Borlix grumbled and took three quick steps into the water, which was now up to his stomach. He tried to pull himself up the side of the boat but found it difficult. Gorathdin grabbed him by the cloak and pulled him into the boat.

Borlix straightened up to his full dwarf height and was just about to take a step towards Vrenli to tell him off when the boat began to rock.

"Wha ... Wha ... What's going on here?" Borlix stammered.

He began to stagger and would almost have fallen on Princess Lythinda had Gorathdin not pulled him onto the plank seat in time.

"Sit down. We're casting off!" the sailor instructed, pushing the boat off the shore and then pulling himself into the boat.

"By all the halls of Ib'Agier, I'm in a boat," grumbled Borlix as he clung to the seat with all his might.

It took several strokes of the oars before Borlix turned his gaze away from the bottom of the boat and looked out over the dark masses of water. The gentle swell rocked the dinghy in a steady rhythm. With each stroke of the oars, they drew closer to Captain Roobar's ship floating before them like a giant shadow.

When the dinghy finally docked on the port side of the long ship, a sailor threw a rope ladder down into the dinghy, where one of the two sailors caught it and held on. "Climb up!" said the other sailor, who was holding the dinghy to the side of the ship with a hooked pole.

Aarl was the first to climb up, followed by Vrenli and Werlis.

"Throw a rope down for the girl!" the sailor holding the rope ladder called upwards.

"That's not necessary," Gorathdin objected and, together with Brother Transmudin, lifted Princess Lythinda from the stretcher.

Gorathdin placed her delicate, fur-wrapped body over his shoulder and reached for the rung at head height. The sailor looked at Gorathdin in astonishment.

"You don't want to go up with her alone, do you?" he asked, pointing up the high ship's side.

"That's far too dangerous," he warned Gorathdin.

The sailor swung the rope ladder from right to left and pointed upwards again with his hand. But Gorathdin was not deterred. He would rather take the risk of falling off the rope ladder with Princess Lythinda than leave her fate to an unknown sailor on a reckless captain's ship.

"Keep it taut!" Gorathdin ordered him and reached for the rope ladder again.

He held Princess Lythinda with his right hand and pulled himself up with his left, rung by rung. Brother Transmudin followed them closely, ready to intervene should Gorathdin lose his balance.

Manamii and Wahmubu, who helped the sailor keep the rope ladder taut, climbed up after Gorathdin had reached the top with Princess Lythinda.

Borlix, who was the last of the travelers still in the dinghy, regained his stare when the sailor waved to him and pointed upwards with his hand.

"Friends, perhaps someone could give me a hand!" Borlix called up, whereupon Aarl picked up one of the ropes on the deck and threw it over the railing to Borlix in the dinghy.

"Tie the rope around your stomach. I'll pull you up!" Aarl called down to Borlix.

"You... you... can't be serious?" Borlix stammered, but the sailor who had been holding the rope ladder was already tying the rope around his stomach.

"Ready?" Aarl called out, not waiting for Borlix to answer, and immediately began pulling hard. Borlix was heavier than he thought. It took him some effort not to lose the rope from his hands.

When Vrenli and Werlis realized that Aarl couldn't do it on his own, they helped him.

"Pull now, pull now!" shouted Werlis and, together with Vrenli and Aarl, pulled hard on the rope several times until they heard a dull bang on the side of the ship.

"Not so fast," grumbled Borlix, who was knocked against the side of the ship by the rapid pulling of the rope and held his helmet to his head as a precaution. The three on the ship began to pull on the rope again, only this time not quite as quickly.

Wahmubu, who was standing away from Aarl, Vrenli and Werlis, spotted Borlix's helmet coming up over the railing and hurriedly ran towards it, offered Borlix his hand to help pull him on board. Borlix thanked him and immediately sat down on the wooden floor so as not to lose his balance.

"Ships are not for dwarves," he said to his friends, who had just been greeted by Captain Roobar.

"It will take us a day and a half to reach the island," Captain Roobar informed his passengers and instructed one of his crew to show the passengers to their quarters. A short, rotund Thirian led Gorathdin and Brother Transmudin, who were carrying Princess Lythinda, down a staircase below deck.

"You must make yourselves comfortable in the storeroom," the sailor explained in a croaky voice, pushing aside a wooden crate that was blocking their way into the storeroom.

"The ship is not designed for passenger travel. There is only one shared cabin for the crew and Captain Roobar's," he informed them.

Gorathdin and Brother Transmudin searched for a suitable place for Princess Lythinda in the large, semi-dark room laden with wooden crates and sacks and lit only by a small oil lamp.

Captain Roobar, who in the meantime gave the signal to weigh anchor, invited Aarl into his cabin for a cup of rum. Manamii and Wahmubu sat down in a lonely spot on deck and gazed arm in arm into the vastness of the dark sea.

Vrenli and Werlis went up to the helmsman on the upper deck, sat down next to him on a wooden plank and watched him at work.

"Is it difficult to steer a ship?" asked Werlis after a while.

"Steering a ship is a responsible task that takes years to learn!" replied the full-bearded, stocky Thirian, holding his hands firmly around the steering wheel.

As Werlis continued to pepper him with questions, the helmsman invited him to take the big wheel for a few moments.

Werlis was delighted to accept this invitation.

"Vrenli, look, I'm steering the ship!" shouted Werlis, who was too small to hold the steering wheel at the top and was therefore gripping the two handles on the underside.

He moved the two wooden handles from right to left, causing the ship to move in serpentine lines for a short time.

The old Thirian nimbly reached for the steering wheel again.

He explained to Werlis that the helm had to be handled with care, as the rudder reacted to even the slightest movement and how to do it correctly. Werlis listened attentively to the helmsman and when he had finished his explanation, Werlis asked him another question.

"Why do you keep looking up at the starry sky?" Werlis wanted to know.

The helmsman smiled and explained to the inquisitive passenger that he could find his way on the water with the help of the stars.

"Let the man do his job!" Vrenli finally admonished, stood up and went below deck.

Borlix had not yet moved from the spot where he had sat down when he was pulled on board by Wahmubu. But when he saw Vrenli going below deck, he overcame his fear and took slow, small steps to the stairs leading down to the storeroom.

In the meantime, Aarl and Captain Roobar were chatting in his cabin and drinking their third cup of rum.

"What about the agreed payment?" asked Captain Roobar, his eyes shining.

"You'll get the gold as soon as we arrive safely at the island," replied Aarl, who suddenly realized at that moment that he and his friends hadn't given any thought to their return journey. He therefore asked Captain Roobar when he would be sailing back to Irkaar.

"In about a month. After we drop you off, we'll be heading for the islands of Keem and Leewich," replied Captain Roobar, pouring rum.

"Hm. A month," Aarl muttered, finishing his cup of rum and about to say goodbye to Captain Roobar when he asked about Princess Lythinda.

"She is a nun of Brother Transmudin and seriously ill," Aarl lied.

However, Captain Roobar was not satisfied with this answer. He wanted to know what they wanted with a seriously ill girl on the cursed island. Aarl politely explained to Captain Roobar that this was not his business, wished him a good night's sleep and went below deck to the storeroom. He lay down next to his friends, who had made themselves a bed for the night among the many wooden crates and sacks. But he couldn't fall asleep for a long time because he was thinking about how they would get back to Irkaar from Horunguth Island.

When the next morning dawned, everyone was already on deck except Borlix, who hadn't been able to sleep all night due to the rocking of the ship. He had only fallen asleep when his friends left the storeroom and joined the crew in eating and exchanging trivialities until the afternoon.

As dusk began to fall, Brother Transmudin went back below deck to watch over Princess Lythinda.

"Three more nautical miles!" shouted Captain Roobar from the foredeck.

"I think I can already see the island!" shouted Werlis, who was standing at the railing. His friends came up to him and looked at the outline of the island.

"So, this is the feared and shunned Horunguth Island, the home of the Mages of Light," grumbled Borlix, who had drifted sleepily towards them from the lower deck and had to hold on to Aarl's arm to keep his balance.

"I really hope that Master Drobal is on the island," said Gorathdin, whose elven eyes had already caught sight of the mages' tower.

"Manamii's father, Sheikh Neg El Bahi, told me that Master Drobal and the other mages were conferring in their tower about the incidents related to Erwight of Entorbis. If he hasn't traveled back to Astinhod or somewhere else in the last few days, he should be on the island," Vrenli whispered in Gorathdin's ear.

"Then there is hope," replied Gorathdin and went back below deck to Princess Lythinda and Brother Transmudin.

The ship had sailed to within a nautical mile of the island when Captain Roobar gave the signal to drop anchor.

"As agreed, we're a nautical mile from the island," said Captain Roobar, who was standing next to Aarl at the stairs leading up to the helmsman.

After thanking him, Aarl went below deck and prepared to leave the ship with his friends. When the travelers had said their goodbye to Captain Roobar and his crew, they boarded the dinghy accompanied by two sailors.

"Don't forget the gold!" Captain Roobar called after them.

"As soon as we get to the island. As agreed!" replied Aarl loudly.

Captain Roobar waved after them for some time as the dinghy made its way towards Horunguth Island. To the surprise of his friends, Borlix was remarkably quiet and did not complain, although this could have been due to his slightly greenish complexion.

Row stroke by row stroke, the boat, rocking in the swell, drew ever closer to the island.

"One of you should get out and pull the boat closer to land. You're not getting me out of here!" demanded the darker-skinned of the two sailors when they were only a few steps away from the shore.

Gorathdin then jumped out of the boat and pulled it ashore in the small bay. Then he helped Wahmubu and Brother Transmudin lift Princess Lythinda out.

When all but the two sailors had gotten out of the boat, Aarl tossed them a bag filled with gold coins.

"As agreed!" he called out to the two of them.

The sailor who had caught the bag opened it and inspected its contents. Then they rowed back to Captain Roobar's ship.

Horunguth Island resembled a rocky mountain peak jutting out of the water, devoid of life except for a few seagulls circling overhead. On a stony hill, a huge white tower rose high into the sky. Its top shimmered in a bright blue light.

The travelers climbed over the rubble and the lumps of stone lying around and headed towards the elevation on which the tower stood. As they were on the north side of the rocky island, they had no idea that that the underwater creatures were trying to break through an invisible barrier that lay protectively around the mages' tower with their corrosive secretions.

Gorathdin led his friends and discovered a climb that led to the tower. They now made faster progress. Halfway up, they heard strange hissing and fizzing noises.

"Do you hear that?" asked Vrenli, listening attentively.

Wahmubu nodded and put his hand to his ear.

"It's just the spray hitting the rocks on the island," Aarl reassured them, wanting to move on.

But Gorathdin gave him a hand signal to wait.

"Stay here. I'd better check!" Gorathdin decided, and he camouflaged himself and crept cautiously up the path. He followed the sounds that came from the other side of the rock, slightly above his current position.

He climbed further towards the west side of the island and when he saw what was making the sound, he ducked behind a large rock. He carefully peered over the sharp edge. About a hundred paces from the white tower, three or four dozen male and female creatures were spraying their sticky secretions seemingly into nowhere. More and more of them emerged from the seawater and crawled up the rise towards the others. Gorathdin was puzzled by the actions of the creatures from Moorgh. He continued to watch them and after a while he noticed that the yellowish secretion did not splash to the ground in front of them but stuck to something invisible. Astonished by what he had seen, Gorathdin made his way back to his friends waiting impatiently for him and questioningly looking at him.

"What's going on over there?" Vrenli wanted to know.

"Creatures from Moorgh are trying to get to the white tower," Gorathdin replied, giving all the details he had.

His friends were very disappointed to be faced with another problem so close to their destination.

"How many of these beasts are there?" asked Aarl.

"I estimate a hundred or more. New ones are still coming out of the water," replied Gorathdin.

"A hundred or more?" Borlix repeated in astonishment, dropping his axe and sitting down on the stony ground in despair.

"We can't possibly fight against such superior numbers," Wahmubu remarked.

Manamii nodded.

Werlis sat down next to Borlix with his head bowed, and Aarl followed him. Vrenli looked up to the tower on the side facing them and searched in vain for an entrance or window.

"It doesn't look like we can get into the tower from this side," he said sadly and sat down.

"I could try to stop the Moorgher with my frost magic so that we can run to the tower," suggested Brother Transmudin hesitantly.

"I'm afraid there are too many of them and they can spray their secretions very far. Some are also armed with tridents and spears," replied Gorathdin.

"Maybe we should turn back," said Wahmubu, looking at the others with heavy eyes.

"Speaking of turning back, friends. Um... I think we forgot to think about the way back to Irkaar. We're on an island twenty nautical miles from Irkaar," Aarl remarked.

His friends responded with several moments of silence, eyes wide open and mouths agape.

"By all the halls of Ib'Agier! It can't be that none of us have thought about the way back," grumbled Borlix.

He picked up his axe and let it hurtle towards a large stone, which cracked in half, and scowled at Aarl and Gorathdin.

Despair broke out among the travelers.

"Don't worry about the way back. Master Drobal will take care of it," Gorathdin tried to reassure them.

"Will he?" Borlix asked suspiciously.

"Yes, he will. Now let's think about how to get past Moorgh's creatures and into the tower," Gorathdin confirmed, sat down and began to think.

Vrenli and Werlis looked up at the tower and exchanged questioning glances. Wahmubu got up, sat down on a rock a few steps away and tried to contact his shaman, Mahroo.

Borlix picked up small stones one by one and threw them down into the bay, while Brother Transmudin poured water into Princess Lythinda's mouth.

"You and I could try to sneak past the Moorgher unseen," Manamii suggested to Gorathdin.

"I think that's too risky. If Moorgh's creatures discovered one of us, they would certainly make sure that there weren't any more of us on the island," Gorathdin objected.

Manamii accepted his concerns.

"Let's go further up to the tower. Maybe we'll find a way to make ourselves known to the magicians at the top," suggested Vrenli, and as it was the best suggestion so far, they decided to carry on.

"We can't use the climb from here. It leads over to the other side," Gorathdin explained, whereupon they climbed the last two hundred or so steps over the scree to the tower.

Aarl and Brother Transmudin, who had shouldered Princess Lythinda's stretcher, had difficulty finding their footing, so Gorathdin helped them keep their balance.

Borlix, who led the group, suddenly bumped into an invisible obstacle and toppled over backwards. At the last moment, Vrenli caught him by the cape before he could slide down the slope.

"How could this happen?" asked Vrenli, holding Borlix by the cloak.

"I have no idea. I was walking up here and suddenly there was something there, like I'd hit a wall," Borlix explained, slightly confused.

With Vrenli and Werlis' help, he stood up and pointed in front of him with his hand. Vrenli walked towards the spot and a few steps further.

"There's nothing here," he realized and waited for the others. Borlix now walked on slowly and bumped into something again. He tried to walk on and when he realized that he couldn't, he tried a little further to the left. But he couldn't pass there either.

"That can't be right," Borlix grumbled in amazement.

Werlis, who couldn't believe what he was seeing, tried to walk past Borlix, but he too bumped into an invisible barrier. He then tried to feel the circumference of the invisible barrier with his hand. He felt in the air in front of him and it felt as if he was standing in front of a wall.

Manamii stepped out from behind Aarl and Brother Transmudin and walked past Werlis to Vrenli.

"I didn't notice anything," she said, standing next to Vrenli.

Now Wahmubu also went on and came across an obstacle at the same place where Werlis and Borlix were standing.

"I can't get past here," he said in amazement.

Confusion spread among the travelers, and when Gorathdin walked to Vrenli and Manamii without encountering an obstacle, it only grew.

Werlis, Borlix and Wahmubu groped through the air with outstretched hands. They tried to push the invisible barrier away, but despite their best efforts they were unable to do so. Brother Transmudin and Aarl slowly walked towards Vrenli, Gorathdin and Manamii with the stretcher. Brother Transmudin, who led Aarl, also bumped into the barrier.

"Let me try," said Aarl and asked Wahmubu to hold the stretcher for him. But even Aarl couldn't go any further at that point.

Werlis tried a few more steps to the left and right, but to no avail.

The travelers were now divided into two groups. One stood behind the barrier and the other in front of it.

"Something's not quite right here. The sailors are probably right and the island is cursed," grumbled Borlix.

He raised his axe and struck the barrier with all his might, causing the blade to vibrate from the impact. But the barrier held firm.

Brother Transmudin asked Borlix to take his place at the stretcher, which he did. The monk stepped in front of Werlis, Wahmubu and Aarl, raised his hand and let a few flashes of fire fall in front of him, but they were deflected to no effect in all directions.

The friends instinctively ducked.

"That's magic. Probably some kind of protective spell to keep uninvited guests away," he remarked disappointedly.

"But why can Vrenli, Manamii and Gorathdin get through, and we can't?" said Werlis perplexed.

Gorathdin began to understand.

"I think I know why, friends," he announced.

"And why?" Vrenli wanted to know.

"Master Drobal will explain that to you," replied Gorathdin.

Now Manamii also understood why only the three of them could pass through the barrier.

Vrenli looked at Gorathdin confused.

He had a hunch, but he didn't want to voice it at the moment.

"Keep quiet and wait for us here. We will inform Master Drobal," Gorathdin instructed his friends.

"I'd better stay here," Manamii decided cautiously. Gorathdin agreed and made his way to the other side of the tower with Vrenli.

"We'll meet Moorgh's creatures, but don't be afraid, they can't get past the barrier," Gorathdin told Vrenli as he climbed over some boulders.

As the two emerged from behind the tower, Vrenli caught sight of the underwater creatures spurting secretions. As he had never seen a resident of Moorgh before in his life, he took a few steps closer to them.

When the creatures caught sight of Gorathdin and Vrenli, they began to hiss and some threw spears and tridents at the pair, but the invisible barrier protected Vrenli and Gorathdin from their projectiles.

Vrenli stood directly in front of one of the underwater creatures and looked deep into its slitted, yellow-green eyes. The creature, which resembled an upright frog, opened its mouth wide and flicked out its split tongue. Vrenli could see its countless fine, pointed teeth and took a step back.

"Come on!" Gorathdin urged him and pulled on his cloak.

The two walked briskly towards the tower's doorless entrance and entered. A winding staircase led upwards. Gorathdin hurried up the steps, but as Vrenli was much slower than him, Gorathdin had to stop a few times to wait for him. Vrenli finally needed a few moments to catch his breath.

"Come on, there's no time to lose!" urged Gorathdin and pulled Vrenli up the last few steps.

Once they reached the top, they entered a large room with high ceilings. Vrenli looked around enthusiastically. The round walls were covered with thousands of sparkling crystals. Transparent, glass columns rose from the floor up to the cylindrical roof. Corridors with high bookshelves containing a multitude of neatly arranged books led along the right-hand side of the sparkling tower wall.

In the middle of the room, on a low marble column, stood a head-sized crystal ball from which a broad, bright blue light shone up to the top of the roof. Vrenli heard a steady, low, whirring sound that seemed to emanate from the shining crystal. A few steps away stood a round, solid white marble table at which five old men dressed in white tunics were sitting and, to Vrenli's amazement, talking with their eyes closed.

When Vrenli, dazzled by the beauty of the hall, carelessly bumped into one of the purple velvet-covered benches around the magicians' table, one of the old men opened his eyes, jumped up from his chair and grabbed the staff leaning next to it.

"Intruders!" the mage shouted, raising the tip of the staff above his head.

"Stop!" Master Drobal reassured them, his eyes fixed on Gorathdin and Vrenli.

"They're friends!" he added.

The mage, who had stood up, slowly lowered his staff.

"Forgive our unannounced intrusion. We are not alone, there are friends of ours behind the invisible barrier and the entrance to the tower is teeming with Moorgh's creatures," Gorathdin explained hurriedly.

The magicians at the table looked at him in amazement.

"Where are your friends?" Master Drobal wanted to know.

"They are on the north side, behind the tower, but they can't cross the barrier," replied Vrenli, who would have preferred a more favorable time for the long-awaited meeting with Master Drobal. Vrenli was worried about his friends behind the tower; he feared for their lives.

"Because of Moorgh's creatures, which have been trying to get into the tower for two days, we can't drop the barrier," one of the mages at the table objected.

"We just need to open it for a few moments. We can send lightning down in front of the tower. Gorathdin's and Vrenli's friends must then use the time of confusion to pass through the barrier," suggested Master Drobal to the other mages.

After some unspoken thoughts, they agreed to Master Drobal's proposal.

"Gorathdin, inform your friends of our plan. When you see light blue lightning coming down from the top of the tower on the south side, walk through the barrier with them," instructed Master Drobal, walking towards the shining crystal ball.

Gorathdin nodded and made his way back behind the tower, where he explained to his waiting friends what they had to do when he gave them a sign.

In the meantime, Vrenli stood in the middle of the room and watched as Master Drobal, together with another very old and frail-looking magician, placed his hands on the shining crystal ball.

Small, finely lined flashes then formed inside the sphere, which shot upwards into the roof of the tower and finally beyond it in a bright blue beam of light that grew larger.

Down in front of the tower, Gorathdin did not take his eyes off its top, and when he saw the bright blue lightning bolts striking in front of the tower, he signaled his friends to run to the other side of the barrier.

This time, nothing stopped them.

They skillfully avoided the creatures of Moorgh, who retreated towards the water. They reached the entrance to the tower and followed the stairs to the top, where Vrenli, Master Drobal and four other mages were already waiting for them.

Like Vrenli before them, everyone was amazed and delighted by the sparkling hall.

"Who are all these strangers, Drobal?" asked one of the mages sitting at the table who stood up, followed by the others.

The loud voices of all those present, who were crisscrossing the room, made it impossible for Master Drobal to explain.

"Brothers! Please sit down. I will try to explain everything to you!" Master Drobal called out twice, whereupon the magicians sat back down on their chairs.

"You too, friends! Please sit down!" Gorathdin said in a loud voice to his eight companions.

Vrenli and his friends then took a seat on the benches around the table.

Vrenli, Werlis, Brother Transmudin, Aarl, Manamii and Wahmubu sat down next to each other on one of the benches.

Borlix had one all to himself and Gorathdin remained standing next to Princess Lythinda, who was lying on the stretcher.

Master Drobal waited until all were quiet then rose from his chair and gave each of the travelers a glance.

"Listen to me, brothers!" asked Master Drobal after he had turned to the other mages at the table.

"I would like to introduce you to some friends of mine. Friends indeed. Even if some of them have never met me before," announced Master Drobal with a gentle smile, infecting those sitting around him.

"On my left are Vrenli and his friend Werlis, from Abketh. Vrenli is the grandson of Erendir Hogmaunt, whom you knew," Master Drobal explained to the other mages, who smiled kindly at Vrenli after they were told that he was Erendir Hogmaunt's grandson and greeted him with an approving nod.

"The elf standing before you is called Gorathdin of the Forest. He is the son of our dear friend Mergoldin. Gorathdin enjoys my full trust," continued Master Drobal.

The mages looked deep into Gorathdin's dark green eyes and nodded.

"The young woman lying on the stretcher next to Gorathdin is Princess Lythinda, daughter of King Grandhold. Her condition is extremely critical, but I've already told you about that before," he explained and paused for a moment.

The magicians looked at Princess Lythinda attentively.

Master Drobal turned to Brother Transmudin.

"The monk sitting on the bench next to Vrenli is Brother Transmudin. He heads the Order of the Dragon," said Master Drobal, raising his right eyebrow as his brothers suddenly got up from their chairs.

"What is a traitor of the Order of the Dragon doing here, and their supreme leader at that?" asked the old mage, who previously worked on the crystal ball with Master Drobal, in a sharp voice.

Brother Transmudin did not know exactly what the old man was alluding to and was irritated by the attack on him.

"Why do you call me and my order traitors? Are you alluding to long-forgotten, untrue accusations?" replied Brother Transmudin who stood up.

The mages at the table began to talk loudly to each other. Master Drobal called for silence.

"I beg you, brothers, be careful with your choice of words," Master Drobal warned firmly.

"We'll talk about the Order of the Dragon in due course," he added, whereupon Brother Transmudin took his seat again.

Master Drobal continued with the introductions.

"Next to Brother Transmudin sits the Thirian Aarl, who has accompanied Vrenli, Werlis and Gorathdin since Tawinn. On the bench opposite is the dwarf Borlix, the son of Regorox, a paladin who served under King Agnulix in Ib'Agier," said Master Drobal, looking at the two with a smile.

The other mages at the table nodded to Borlix. They ignored Aarl.

"I would also like to introduce Princess Manamii, daughter of Sheikh Neg El Bahi, from Desert of DeShadin, and her fiancé Prince Wahmubu, son of the leader of the northern nomadic tribes," announced Master Drobal, bowing to the two of them.

The mages at the table nodded to Manamii and Wahmubu. Master Drobal paused for a few moments and began to walk slowly around the white marble table.

"Everyone here, whether they know it or not, has served and continues to serve the Book of Wetherid. Vrenli, Gorathdin and Manamii are Keepers of the Book and with the help of their friends, who joined them for one reason or another, Vrenli was able to bring us the pages of the book from the city of Iseran in the first place," Master Drobal explained, mentioning some of the adventures the travelers had experienced up to this point.

Vrenli looked questioningly at Gorathdin.

"How did Master Drobal know about all this?" Vrenli asked himself silently and, as he had done twice before, a voice rang out inside him.

"Vrenli, Keeper of the Book! The time of answers will come!" the voice rang out and Vrenli was sure that it was not Gorathdin or Manamii's voices.

Werlis looked at his best friend in amazement.

"We've known each other for as long as I can remember, and as if it wasn't enough of a surprise that our ancestors chose Vrenli to be the keeper of our people's history. No! He's also a Keeper of the Book of Wetherid, which is the subject of so many stories," Werlis thought.

Borlix, Aarl, Brother Transmudin and Wahmubu were surprised when Master Drobal mentioned the Book of Wetherid. The four of them had previously thought that the book was just a legend and were all more surprised when they learned that Vrenli, Gorathdin and Manamii were its Keepers.

Aarl was surprised when Master Drobal started talking about other continents because he thought it was just sailor's yarn. Nothing more than stories told by drunks in the taverns of Irkaar.

"What many of you probably don't know is that the Book of Wetherid was stolen from Tyrindor of Entorbis several decades ago," Master Drobal continued.

Excitement broke out among some of the travelers.

"But!" said Master Drobal, whereupon silence returned to the room.

"But before it was stolen, some pages were removed from the book. So, the book was not complete. Some of the pages that dealt with the origins of the Wetherid peoples were hidden in Abketh, Astinhod, Ib'Agier, Iseran, Irkaar and the Glorious Valley," continued Master Drobal.

Some in the hall breathed a sigh of relief.

"However, I fear that Erwight of Entorbis, the son of Tyrindor, has recently found out about this and is already trying to get hold of the missing pages. The spell on Princess Lythinda could be proof of this. I fear that this is his way of trying to force King Grandhold to hand over the pages that are in Astinhod. Fortunately for all of us, however, he did not reckon with Gorathdin, nor with you, who have now brought Princess Lythinda to us. Since Gorathdin, Vrenli and Werlis left Abketh, the Shadow Lord has not only tried to obtain the missing book pages from Astinhod. No. He has also entered alliances with various peoples and creatures from Fallgar and Wetherid. He's trying to build a force like no other. I think his plan is to weaken Wetherid's borders. The snake people from Desert of DeShadin, the underwater creatures of Moorgh, goblins long thought to have been driven out, the thieves from Astinhod, the Raging Hordes, the gray dwarves, mist elves, undead, orcs, ogres and a shapeshifter from Fallgar have already joined this alliance and, above all, the Shadow Mages of Druhn are directing their lord's plans. Erwight of Entorbis has already gathered a huge army of allies around him and his spies are spread across Wetherid on land, sea and in the air. We face a force that the otherwise valiant dwarves alone can do nothing against, and Ib'Agier will be its first target. We must inform the leaders of Wetherid and ask for their help. That is what we, the Council of Mages on Horunguth Island, have decided," Master Drobal told his attentive listeners.

After a long period of silence, commotion broke out again and this time Vrenli, Werlis and Manamii were among the distraught. Only Gorathdin, Master Drobal and the four mages at the table remained calm and waited patiently until the others' excitement had subsided.

"Erik, the clan leader of the Raging Hordes of the West, gave me his word to enter into an alliance with King Grandhold," Gorathdin reported to Master Drobal and the mages, breaking the general silence.

"Very good, that means one less ally for Erwight of Entorbis. What about the Raging Hordes of the East?" asked Master Drobal, looking hopefully at Gorathdin.

"Erik gave me this ring," he replied and lifted it up.

"It is proof of our newfound friendship. This ring will also help me bring his brother over to our side," Gorathdin explained.

Master Drobal shook his head in disapproval.

"You cannot travel to their clan north of the Vast Plains now. You don't have time for that, Gorathdin. You are needed elsewhere," replied Master Drobal, pausing briefly and looking at the other four mages seriously.

The oldest of them nodded silently.

Gorathdin waited just as eagerly as everyone else to see what suggestion would come from Master Drobal's lips.

"We did not count on the actions of the Order of the Dragon and the events in Astinhod. Someone else will have to try to persuade Erik's brother to form an alliance. We need all the help we can get. Not just from the barbarians, but from all the peoples of Wetherid. But we'll get to that later. Gorathdin, you and Princess Lythinda must return to Astinhod as soon as we have freed her from the spell," Master Drobal explained and before Gorathdin could ask why, the eldest at the table stood up, pointed his staff at Brother Transmudin and sent a piercing, dark look after him.

"I demand to finally be told why my order is being accused of being traitors!" Brother Transmudin croaked to the mages at the table in a dry voice.

"Come and see for yourself!" replied the old magician, sweeping his staff across the mirror-smooth tabletop.

A picture appeared.

"Come to us, friends. See what happened a few days ago," Master Drobal encouraged Vrenli, Werlis, Gorathdin, Aarl, Borlix, Wahmubu and Manamii.

The enemy at the gates of Ib'Agier

Astonished by the magic that brought the pictures to life, the eight friends looked at the tabletop with the magicians.

"This is the Hall of Kings in Ib'Agier!" remarked Borlix, who, like Vrenli and Werlis, was standing on one of the mages' chairs to be able to see the tabletop at all.

"Yes, that is Ib'Agier. Take a good look, friends!" confirmed Master Drobal.

King Agnulix sat on his stone throne on the north side of the huge hall carved into the mountain, at the top of a large rock, behind which an image of Ib'Agier's builder, King Ewendarix Hammerbein, was carved into the wall like a giant. King Agnulix gazed sadly down at the ground in front of him, where the charred corpses of hundreds of miners lay spread out before him.

"By all the halls of Ib'Agier! Who or what can do such a terrible thing!" shouted King Agnulix to one of his paladins, who were blessing the dead with the priests of the Holy Hall.

"We don't know yet, Sire. But to find out what was going on down there, we sent a force, fifty-strong, into the mineshafts," replied the paladin.

A hurried messenger entered the Hall of Kings with quick steps and knelt before King Agnulix.

"Sire, our patrol on the border of Fallgar reports approaching enemies. Some of them bear the Entorbis crest on their armor. Among them are gray dwarves, undead, orcs, mist elves and ogres. They are only a day's march from Ib'Agier!" the messenger excitedly and quickly reported.

"Erwight of Entorbis on his way to Ib'Agier?" asked King Agnulix, who couldn't believe what he was being told.

"Forgive me, Sire, I cannot confirm that Erwight of Entorbis himself is among the approaching foes, but his insignia is clearly visible on the knights' armor and shields. The banners of Marnog Jar, Tonga Gor, Raga Gur, the Whamuther and Ingar are among the approaching army. All of Fallgar is on its way to Wetherid!" reported the messenger, puffing and pale as a chalk.

"Well then! Once again, the enemy is moving to the gates of Ib'Agier and we must try to stop them by any means necessary. For Ib'Agier, for Wetherid! Sound Hammerbein's horn. Call for my commanders and let the paladins line up. Bring me my armor and weapons!" King Agnulix shouted through the hall, whereupon several dwarves immediately set off to do their king's bidding.

"I would be surprised if the incident in the mine had nothing to do with the approaching enemies," the king grumbled.

He walked down the steps carved into the rock and put on his heavy, golden armor with the help of two dwarves. He picked up his golden hammer and struck the stone floor with all his might, the vibration of the blow almost knocking the two dwarves standing next to him off balance.

"Let them come, I'm ready!" King Agnulix thundered defiantly and walked past the charred miners towards the round, gray stone table in the middle of the hall. His army commanders were already waiting for him there.

"How many men strong is the approaching army, Korblix?" asked King Agnulix.

"Hard to say, Sire, according to the reports, about a thousand men," replied Army Commander Korblix, standing opposite King Agnulix at the table.

"And how many men do we have ready for battle, Horndomix?" the king asked the white-haired army commander standing to his left, carrying his silver helmet under his right arm.

"More than two thousand men, and if we arm the miners who didn't fall victim to the flames, we'd have five hundred more," replied Army Commander Horndomix.

"Are the enemy carrying fighting machines?" King Agnulix asked Army Commander Korblix.

"I've been told nothing about fighting machines, Sire," he replied.

King Agnulix looked at his army commanders silently and began stroking his long black beard, which reached down to his stomach.

"What is Erwight of Entorbis up to? He should know that we have at least two thousand men ready to fight and he's only coming with an army of one thousand. And how, by all the halls of Ib'Agier, is he going to take the defensive walls and gates of Ib'Agier without catapults, ballistae and assault towers?" King Agnulix spoke to his army commanders, who merely shrugged their shoulders.

"Well, whatever. Let's give them a proper welcome. Army Commander Horndomix, man the defensive walls and towers with archers. In addition, thirty axemen are to be stationed on each defense tower. I want all the smelting furnaces fired up! Smelt ore and bring it to the eastern defensive wall. If the onslaught is too great, pour the hot, molten metal onto the enemy and before I forget, there must be a paladin on every defense tower. Undead from Tongar Gor are among the enemy!" ordered King Agnulix.

"As you command, Sire!" saluted Army Commander Horndomix who left the table with quick steps.

"If the enemy succeeds in taking the defensive walls or breaking through the gates, I want two hundred and fifty archers to barricade themselves in the courtyard behind the main gate. Three hundred lancers are to stand ready at the main gate and see to it, Commander Korblix, that there are at least ten paladins among the archers and lancers to give the undead a proper welcome. A force of a hundred axemen should be enough to protect the paladins!" King Agnulix ordered.

Army Commander Korblix bowed and hurriedly made his way to the inner courtyard behind the eastern defensive wall, where a main gate and two smaller side gates blocked Ib'Agier's halls from enemies.

"How many mounted men do we have, Army Commander Melchodix?" King Agnulix asked the youngest dwarf in the group.

"We have around three hundred warbuck riders, Sire!" replied Army Commander Melchodix.

"Divide them between the two side gates. We could easily have to make a sortie to protect the main gate!" ordered King Agnulix.

Army Commander Melchodix then set off for the west gates, where Ib'Agier's stables were located, to carry out the king's order.

"Commander Hoogorix, you take care of the incident in the mines. I want you to go down with two hundred men. Take all available paladins with you. The Holy Light of Lorijan will illuminate even the darkest tunnels. I would be greatly mistaken if something devilish is not going on down there. It would be a strange coincidence if the incident in the mines wasn't connected to the approaching enemy!" King Agnulix said to Army Commander Hoogorix, who bowed and left the Hall of Kings with quick steps.

The chief priest of Lorijan approached King Agnulix and asked for permission to bless the men going into battle.

"Hurry up Groblix! Give them your blessing. Fill them with the Holy Light of Lorijan. For the good cause. For Ib'Agier. For Wetherid!" shouted King Agnulix.

Groblix made his way to the Hall of Lorijan to pray before sending his brothers to the Hall of Warriors to bless the armed dwarves of Ib'Agier.

Groblix knelt before the golden statue of Lorijan and asked for the Holy Light to illuminate the halls of Ib'Agier with all its inhabitants and to blind the approaching enemies. Groblix also asked for light in the deep mines of Ib'Agier. After saying his prayers, he set off with two priests of Lorijan to the eastern side of the mountain range where the city of Ib'Agier was carved into the stone by the dwarves more than fifteen hundred years ago.

On the border of Fallgar, as well as on the side facing Wetherid, defensive towers many paces high rose from the thick stone ramparts at the foot of the mountains. Forged from the ore that the dwarven miners brought up from the depths beneath the mountain and smelted into steel in the fiery furnaces, they once forged the mighty main and smaller side gates that protected the halls of Ib'Agier to the west and east from enemies.

The six defensive towers in the east were already manned by archers, axemen and paladins when one of the priests climbed the first of the towers to bless the dwarves stationed there with the light of Lorijan. The archers, armed only with chain mail and trousers and visorless steel helmets, looked almost insignificant in comparison to the paladins with their large golden shields and mighty, gleaming golden hammers, clad in golden armor and winged helmets that reached far over their faces.

The priest first blessed the archers and then the heavier-armed axemen, who, as befitted good dwarves, swung their axes through the air and struck their round shields with them once. The paladin knelt before the priest of Lorijan, who said a lengthy prayer. A golden light from the hand the priest raised above the paladin's head shone on his armor and illuminated it. When everyone had been blessed, the priest went back down the stone steps. He walked through the courtyard near the main gate, past his brothers who were blessing the archers, axemen, paladins and spearmen armed with long spears, and towards the nearest defense tower.

Army Commander Horndomix, who was responsible for manning the defensive wall and towers, reported to King Agnulix that his orders had been carried out.

"How much time do we have left?" asked King Agnulix, who walked onto the wide stone terrace outside the Hall of Kings with Army Commander Horndomix and looked at the mighty defensive wall of Ib'Agier to the east.

"Not much more, I'm afraid, maybe until dawn," replied Army Commander Horndomix as he tried to investigate the distance beyond the borders of Fallgar towards Druhn.

"I hope Hoogorix will report to us from the mines before the enemy arrives," grumbled King Agnulix into his long, black beard.

Just as he turned to go back inside, the halls of Ib'Agier shook. Stones came loose from the walls and some of the thick, massive stone pillars threatened to collapse. Desperate cries of women and children echoed through the air as they ran to the safety of their mountain-carved dwellings. But some had already been injured and some killed by falling stones.

"By all the halls of Ib'Agier! I thought they didn't carry war machines!" King Agnulix shouted in horror, trying to keep his balance.

"Sire, I believe the vibration came from underground. From the mines!" Army Commander Horndomix spoke in horror, thrown to the ground by the vibration.

"Send another hundred men down immediately!" King Agnulix ordered.

"But Sire, we need the men on the rampart," replied Army Commander Horndomix, straightening up again after his objection.

"We have enough men to defend ourselves against the enemy from Fallgar. Let's go now. Don't waste any time!" urged King Agnulix. "I need to know what's going on down in the mines," he grumbled.

Army Commander Horndomix made his way to the Hall of Warriors, from where he and another hundred men walked into the Hall of Furnaces and from there descended the many hundreds of steps into the old mines. The loamy, damp floor and the smooth, dark rock walls reflected the light of the torches as they followed the labyrinth of corridors that led deep down under the mountain.

Most of the narrow, low corridors had been built during the reign of King Ewendarix Hammerbein.

Army Commander Horndomix had trouble leading his men along the right path. They lost their way several times and then had to go back up several tunnels. A former miner, who had been serving as an axe fighter for several years, therefore asked Army Commander Horndomix to take the lead.

"Go ahead, Kluumix, you know your way around the old mines a lot better than I do," Army Commander Horndomix agreed and stepped behind Kluumix into a steeply descending tunnel, which they followed for some time.

The breeze coming from the depths not only extinguished some of the torches, but also carried desperate cries of help upwards.

"Faster, men!" Army Commander Horndomix urged the dwarves armed with axes, spears and shields as they hurried down the tunnel. Their hurried steps were accompanied by the loud rustling of their chain armor.

When they reached the end of the tunnel, which led into a vault, the cries grew louder.

"Which of the four tunnels do you think they took?" pondered Army Commander Horndomix, looking at the four dark entrances.

Some dwarves, with their torches still burning, began to search the ground for tracks.

"I think they've taken this one!" one of them finally shouted, pointing his torch at the tunnel entrance on the far right.

"Hm. Actually, there were only ever three tunnels leading out from here," Kluumix wondered.

One in the group pointed out to the others some stones and bricks lying on the ground next to the entrance.

"Looks like the tunnel was bricked up and someone uncovered it," remarked Army Commander Horndomix, who picked up one of the bricks and looked at it in the torchlight of the dwarf standing next to him.

"Men, we follow this tunnel!" he growled resolutely and stepped into the entrance together with Kluumix and a torch-bearing dwarf.

They followed the tunnel, which was noticeably narrower and lower than the ones they had used before. Strangely enough, it got warmer and warmer halfway through.

"The deeper we descend, the colder it should get, not warmer," Kluumix remarked, wiping the sweat from his forehead.

Some of the dwarves were already sweating so profusely that sweat was pouring down their foreheads, over their long beards and dripping onto the loamy ground.

They were only a few hundred steps away from the end of the tunnel when the cries of help became louder. Now they could also hear cries of despair.

The further they went, the hotter it became and some of the dwarves began to lose their senses. When they reached the end of the tunnel, Army Commander Horndomix and Kluumix stopped as if petrified and looked in horror into a huge, smoky vault, in which wide, high flames raged and whose floor was covered with burnt dwarves. A huge silver dragon, reaching almost to the ceiling and constantly spewing its fiery breath onto the walls of the vault, was attacked by the few dwarves still alive. They slashed at the thick, scaly armor of the primal creature with their axes.

Again and again, some of the dwarves were hit by the liquefied rock that flowed like lava from the ceiling and burned to death, screaming in agony.

The silver dragon swept some of the dwarves against the vaulted walls with its mighty tail. Only the six paladins, surrounded by thick swathes of smoke, were able to temporarily blind the dragon with their shields and hammers, from which the light of Lorijan shone, and stop the monster from spitting its fiery breath at them and some of their brethren.

"By the hall of Lorijan! A dragon! Then the men who reported eerie noises in the depths of the mines were right!" shouted Army Commander Horndomix, terrified.

"Escape back into the tunnel! You must tell King Agnulix what's going on here. I don't know how much longer we can hold out here!" shouted one of the paladins.

Army Commander Horndomix gathered himself and immediately hurried back upstairs with Kluumix and ten of the dwarves, where they ran as fast as they could into the Hall of Kings.

"A dragon? In our mines?" exclaimed King Agnulix in shock and dropped back onto his throne.

"Yes, Sire, a giant silver dragon! It's trying to melt the ceiling!" replied Army Commander Horndomix with horror still in his eyes.

"Quick, bring me the map showing all the vaults, tunnels and passages in the mine! Quick!" shouted King Agnulix, whereupon a short, stocky dwarf in miner's clothing immediately rushed into the Hall of Furnaces to fetch the map in question.

"If your mind still works and it's true that there's a dragon down in the mines, that would mean that that rotten scoundrel of a monk who called me a madman in front of King Grandhold's father back then was lying. I knew I could believe my men! Damn it all, why didn't I insist on exploring the catacombs beneath the Temple of the Order of the Dragon? They stretch in a branching system of tunnels all the way to Ib'Agier!" King Agnulix shook angrily, before despair crossed his face as the map of the mine was presented to him. He could see where the vault with the dragon was located.

"The dragon wants to bring down the Hall of Lorijan and deprive us of the Holy Light. We would be at the mercy of the army of the undead. Now I'm beginning to understand," muttered King Agnulix.

He was silent for some time, during which he gazed gloomily at the stone painting of King Ewendarix Hammerbein.

"Should I be the last of us?" King Agnulix asked himself, lowering his gaze.

"Send for Groblix!" he shouted, bending over the map of the mines again.

Not much time passed and the Chief Priest of Lorijan, followed by two of his brothers, entered the Hall of Kings and approached King Agnulix.

"A silver dragon is trying to bring down the Hall of Lorijan!" revealed King Agnulix, looking up from the map. Groblix's eyes widened as he heard King Agnulix's words.

"Lorijan protect us. Then it's true, Omnigo is alive!" Groblix shouted loudly.

His two brothers knelt and began to pray.

"I know of no power that could kill the dragon and stop it from bringing down the Hall of Lorijan. We are doomed!" Groblix despaired.

"Six of the paladins are blinding the dragon with the Holy Light," Army Commander Horndomix reported to Groblix.

"Omnigo shuns the Holy Light, but it cannot kill him and it will only keep him from bringing down the hall for a while. We need help, King Agnulix!" warned Groblix, clutching the golden pendant of Lorijan tightly on his chain.

"Send messengers to Astinhod and tell King Grandhold about the events in Ib'Agier!" King Agnulix ordered Army Commander Horndomix, who then hurried out of the Hall of Kings.

"Who knows how many days we have left and to make matters worse, the enemy from Fallgar is at our gates. When will these Entorbis finally be put to an end," grumbled King Agnulix and, followed by Groblix, strode outside onto the stone terrace. He looked angrily at the gates of Ib'Agier where the Knights Erwight of Entorbis, gray dwarves, mist elves, orcs, ogres and undead were positioning themselves.

"I'll send two priests to the mines. Who knows how long Lorijan's light will be able to strengthen the paladins," Groblix anxiously suggested.

With an approving nod, King Agnulix turned his attention to the defensive towers. There stood his archers, firing a ceaseless hail of arrows at the enemies no more than three hundred paces from the defensive wall. The heavily armored knights bearing the banner of Entorbis did not flinch at the archers' arrows, although some of them were mortally wounded.

Loud war cries rang out.

The enemy's archers now returned Ib'Agier's hail of arrows. But they only hit a few of the dwarves ducking behind the thick stone walls of the rampart and towers.

King Agnulix watched as several troops of orcs carrying long ladders, followed by dozens of undead, approached the northernmost of the defensive towers. Most of the orcs were killed halfway there, and the undead that had been hit by the paladins' blessed arrows went up in smoke.

"Well done!" thought King Agnulix who turned his gaze towards the main gate, where a shapeshifter was transforming into a stone creature in front of the guards on the rampart. It began to beat at the steel gate with its powerful stone arms. The dwarves above the gate poured down hot, molten ore from large, cast-iron troughs. A roaring, muffled cry rang out as the liquefied ore covered the shapeshifter and froze it in place.

The image on the marble table began to blur and finally disappeared.

"What kind of spell was that, and did what we just saw actually happen?" Borlix, who was almost falling off his chair with excitement, wanted to hear from the old magician.

"What I showed you happened two days ago," the old magician replied, leaning his staff against the table.

He sat down again and fixed Brother Transmudin with a dark look.

"This ... can ... not be!" stuttered Brother Transmudin, as white as a sheet.

"You bet it can!" thundered the old magician, banging his fist on the tabletop.

Brother Transmudin searched desperately for an explanation.

"Omnigo lives in the catacombs, deep beneath our temple, I must admit. But please, let me explain to you why the Order of the Dragon has been denying the existence of Omnigo for generations! Please, friends, listen to me first before you pass judgment!" asked Brother Transmudin, and he began to tell those present about long-forgotten days. Of the days when the dragons still ruled Wetherid.

"When the dragons' time was up, he was the only one to survive in the depths of the underground and had found a new home there. A group of humans who had discovered the dragon by chance while exploring for valuable ores, artifacts and other treasures realized that Omnigo held no grudge against them, but that the opposite was true. Omnigo asked them to keep quiet about his existence. In return, he agreed to share his knowledge of healing and initiated one of them into fire and frost magic. In return, he simply asked for food to be brought to him from time to time. The group then swore an oath not to tell anyone of Omnigo's existence. They were also the ones who had laid the foundations of the Order

428

of the Dragon. You have to believe me, friends, Omnigo lived in Wetherid long before us and he had never harmed anyone in centuries. I can't for the life of me imagine why he would try to bring down the Hall of Lorijan. Unless..." Brother Transmudin told the attentive audience and paused for a moment.

"Unless what?" Borlix asked impatiently.

Brother Transmudin was silent for a few moments.

"Unless Brother Theramond is making common cause with Erwight of Entorbis. But I doubt that. He is the eldest of us. I can't believe he would use Omnigo for his own ends," continued Brother Transmudin.

"It is more than irresponsible not to inform the peoples of Wetherid about the existence of a dragon!" the old mage spoke in a sharp, punishing tone.

"We shouldn't waste time assigning blame now. King Agnulix, yes, all of Ib'Agier needs our help," intervened Master Drobal.

His and Brother Transmudin's eyes met.

"I think I can stop Omnigo from going ahead with his plan, but I don't know how much longer the paladins will be able to hold out. Ib'Agier is far away," said Brother Transmudin in a depressed voice, looking down to the ground in shame.

"And don't forget, friends, we're on an island without a ship," remarked Aarl.

Borlix muttered a dwarven curse and shook his head.

"You can be in Ib'Agier in less than a day by air," said Master Drobal to Brother Transmudin, who, like his friends, didn't understand how they were supposed to do that.

"Master Drobal is right. Follow me, friends," Borlix joked and began to make flapping movements with his hands as he jumped around the room like a chicken.

"Tell the dwarf chicken to sit down!" one of the mages at the table demanded of Master Drobal, who then gave Borlix a warning look and told him to sit down again.

"Who can guarantee that we can trust Brother Transmudin?" the old mage expressed his doubts.

"I'm afraid there's no guarantee of that and we have no choice but to trust him anyway. Our strength alone will not be enough to take on a silver dragon," Master Drobal replied rationally.

The other mages finally agreed to let Brother Transmudin fly to Ib'Agier.

"I want to go with him! My brothers and sisters need my help. I hope you understand that!" Borlix said, looking questioningly at Master Drobal and his friends.

"Of course we understand," replied Gorathdin.

"But it's not up to us to decide," added Vrenli, looking at Master Drobal and waiting for his response.

"Borlix can fly with Brother Transmudin," agreed Master Drobal, who was not at all inconvenienced by this, and walked towards one of the windows.

He looked down at Moorgh's underwater creatures, who were still tirelessly trying to break through the barrier.

Master Drobal passed the tip of his staff, from which a bright blue light shone into the sky, through the window and let out a loud whistle. After a few moments, during which Master Drobal remained looking out of the window, his whistle was returned. A haldakie appeared in the sky above the tower and flew towards the window, lingering in front of it, slowly flapping its wings.

"Brother Transmudin, Borlix. Come closer and get on his back. My friend here will fly you to Ib'Agier," Master Drobal instructed the two.

"By all the halls of Ib'Agier! Was it not enough that a dwarf sailed on a ship, must I now fly with this beast?" grumbled Borlix, looking at the huge bird wearing a black leather saddle decorated with silver embroidery on its back. Its feathered body was armored with thick, light-colored suede, while a helmet made of fine dark ore protected its head.

"Get on! There's no time to lose!" urged Brother Transmudin, who had already taken a seat on the haldakie's saddle.

Borlix hesitated.

He didn't really know how to get onto the bird.

Aarl and Gorathdin noticed Borlix's hesitation, stepped up to him and helped their friend ascend. After a final exchange of encouraging gestures, the haldakie rose with powerful wing beats and set course over the sea towards Ib'Agier.

Uprising in Astinhod

Master Drobal returned to his seat from the window.

"Before we take care of Princess Lythinda, you should first find out what has happened in Astinhod since you left," said Master Drobal, sliding his staff across the tabletop. Once again, those present observed as a living picture was created on the tabletop.

"I recognize the city of Astinhod," Gorathdin remarked, leaning further over the table.

The picture showed the town's market square eight days ago. Gorathdin immediately recognized that something was wrong, for the square was deserted and a large wooden platform had been erected in the place of market stalls, with a wooden structure standing in the middle. As the image came into focus, Gorathdin realized that it was a gallows.

"What does that mean?" he wondered, looking up from the tabletop.

"The gallows are for King Grandhold's murderers," Master Drobal replied sternly.

Gorathdin's face froze as this news caught him completely off guard.

"That can't be, your magic must be wrong!" Gorathdin objected vehemently.

His heart began to beat faster and faster. The fiery elven blood boiled in his veins.

"Alas, it is the truth, Gorathdin of the Forest. It is the gallows on which Army Commander Arkondir is to be hanged!" replied one of the mages at the table.

Master Drobal immediately put his hand on Gorathdin's shoulder to reassure him. Gorathdin's dark green eyes glowed.

"The king dead? Army Commander Arkondir his murderer? What has happened?" Gorathdin asked angrily.

His hope that Wetherid could simply shake off the impending danger had died. There was only one way to counter Erwight of Entorbis' greedy desire. Master Drobal was right, Wetherid now urgently needed to unite and renew its alliances. Gorathdin hoped that all his prayers would be answered and that the nations would continue to exist.

"Look, it started shortly after you left!" said the old mage, breaking through Gorathdin's unspoken thoughts. With the tip of his staff, the mage blurred the image of the gallows in Astinhod's market square and created a new one. Everyone leaned far over the table.

The two thieves, Massek and Hattul, sat together at a simple wooden table, somewhere underground in Astinhod.

"I warned you about this. You should have accepted my offer to enter an alliance with Erwight of Entorbis," Massek rebuked Hattul.

"Who could have guessed that that sneaky Thirian Aarl would tell us such a lie," replied Hattul.

"You are too gullible, my friend. Did you really think that Erwight of Entorbis would hire two Abkether, a ranger, a dwarf and a Thirian to kidnap the Princess of Astinhod for him? And for a paltry twenty-five thousand gold pieces at that. Did it not occur to you that I would have personally taken on this most honorable task if Erwight of Entorbis had wanted me to?" Massek asked in a sharp tone.

Hattul did not answer.

"Be that as it may. The king has put a bounty of ten thousand gold pieces on your head after Army Commander Arkondir told him about your bungling. Be sure, after his last words - bring him to me, dead or alive - you're as good as dead, Hattul!" Massek announced, grinning maliciously.

"What are you trying to say? You don't want to hand me over to the king, do you? Me, a thief like you," asked Hattul, aghast.

He began to sweat; his hands were already shaking.

"What are you thinking, my friend? I'm not going to break our codex, even if your guild, how shall I say, doesn't get along with mine. But..." Massek replied, not finishing his thought.

"But what?" Hattul wanted to know, his throat tightening.

"But... if your men don't join me again, as they once did, then someone who might not care so much about the codex might not keep his mouth shut," threatened Massek, giving him a sardonic smile.

Hattul turned white as a sheet and began to gasp for air.

"Doesn't the climate down here suit you? Do you want to go back upstairs and take a carefree stroll through the city?" Massek asked with a sneer and a grin.

"You sneaky scoundrel!" Hattul gasped.

"Thank you for the compliment," Massek countered and unsheathed his dagger.

With a determined thrust, he rammed the blade into the tabletop right next to Hattul's hand.

"Well, the way I see it, my friend, you only have two options: Either you and your men join us or the gallows await you!" Massek clarified, rising from his chair and stepping behind Hattul, who stared motionlessly into the semi-dark room for some time and finally nodded in agreement.

"All right, then. We'll join you. But you must guarantee I can leave Astinhod unharmed," Hattul agreed.

After all, he had no other choice.

"I'll have you taken out of the city unseen, my friend, and I'll also give you five hundred gold pieces on the way. But first you have to do something for me," Massek replied.

"What more do you want? Isn't it enough for you that I'm leaving the city and you can now command my men?" Hattul angrily asked.

"Surely, you'll do me a little friendly service?" Massek said with a malicious grin.

"What do you want?" asked Hattul sharply.

Massek leaned towards Hattul's ear.

"I want you to kill King Grandhold," Massek whispered, pulling his dagger from the tabletop.

Hattul tried to get up, but Massek's dagger rested menacingly against his throat.

"You ... You ... You're not serious, are you?" Hattul stuttered, lifting his head slightly and swallowing over the blade on his larynx.

"You bet I mean it, my friend! The orders of Erwight of Entorbis are to always be taken seriously," Massek emphasized, pressing the blade of his dagger firmer against Hattul's throat.

"How do you imagine that? That I simply walk into the throne room, past the castle guards and slit the king's throat in the presence of his bodyguard?" asked Hattul in a hushed voice.

Massek put his dagger back in its sheath and sat down at the table again. Hattul breathed a sigh of relief.

"Not quite, but something like that. Listen to me," Massek began and explained his plan to Hattul.

"My men captured Army Commander Arkondir while he was on his way back to Astinhod from the Order of the Dragon. All his men were killed and no one knows that we have him in our power, so the king will think he is still with the monks in the temple. He won't miss him for the next two or three days and, as you probably know, in two days the Chief Justice Count Laars will return to Astinhod from his country seat near Merniton. On that day, Army Commander Arkondir will be found in the king's bedchamber with the dagger you used to kill the king. Shortly afterwards, he will be sentenced to death," Massek described.

"Do you really think that anyone in Astinhod would sentence Army Commander Arkondir to death even if he was found with a dagger in the king's bedroom?" Hattul doubted and laughed out loud.

"My friend, I notice that you are not aware of the influence Erwight of Entorbis has in Astinhod," Massek replies.

"All his influence will not help him to portray the king's commander as a murderer," Hattul objected.

"Listen to me, Hattul. Count Laars will not be Count Laars," Massek emphasized emphatically.

"I don't understand, what do you mean Count Laars won't be Count Laars?" asked Hattul, visibly puzzled.

"A shapeshifter will arrive in Astinhod tomorrow," Massek informed him.

"A shapeshifter? I thought there were only a handful of them left, somewhere deep in the east," replied Hattul.

"Erwight of Entorbis is more powerful than his enemies think. He has gathered beings around him that you have never heard of in your life. The shapeshifter is coming tomorrow. That's what Erwight of Entorbis has ordered." Massek said firmly.

"I hope you don't forget that any mage will see through the shapeshifter immediately," Hattul pointed out to Massek.

"Master Drobal isn't in Astinhod and he won't be coming back here any time soon, the Moorgher will see to that," Massek replied confidently.

"The plan might work, but what I still don't understand is, what does Erwight of Entorbis gain from King Grandhold's death? I mean, of course he's taken out the king, but the earls, commanders, officers, even the common man, they'll all try to stop Erwight of Entorbis from taking Wetherid. And what about Princess Lythinda? When she returns, she will ascend to the throne as the daughter of King Grandhold," Hattul mused.

"Don't worry about Princess Lythinda. The shadow spell on her can only be broken by the light of Lorijan in the Holy Hall of

Ib'Agier. And Erwight of Entorbis will take care of the dwarves very quickly," Massek replied and laughed out loud.

"Then I'll see you in two days," said Hattul, wanting to get up from the table and leave the room, but two of Massek's men blocked his way.

"I think it will be better that you are our guest for the next two days," Massek said with a sardonic grin. He then ordered one of his men to go to the abandoned forge to announce to Hattul's men that their leader had made an alliance with Massek and Erwight of Entorbis and that he would be in a meeting with Massek for two days.

"My men won't buy this story!" protested Hattul, who was not happy about his forced stay.

Massek turned to Hattul and tore the golden chain from his neck, from which hung a pendant in the shape of a ship.

"Here, show them this and tell them that Hattul gave it to you as proof that you are telling the truth!" Massek instructed the thief, who then left the room and made his way to the abandoned smithy.

The image at the marble table in the Tower of Mages blurred and Gorathdin was about to say something when a new image appeared.

"Look what happened two days later," Master Drobal revealed to those present.

Count Laars was riding back from his country estate to Astinhod, accompanied by four guards, when a group of Massek's thieves stood in their way. The guards immediately drew their swords, gathered around Count Laars and brought their horses into position.

"Clear the way! You are preventing Count Laars of Astinhod from riding on!" one of the guards demanded of the group of men standing in front of them on the hollow path.

The men did not answer, but only drew their throwing knives.

"Thieves! Ride over them!" shouted one of the guards before he fell dead off of his horse, hit by a throwing knife.

Count Laars was just about to spur his horse on when one of the thieves grabbed the reins and another cut it in a flash. Count Laars fell from his horse onto the damp, earthy forest floor.

"To me, guards!" shouted the count, lying on the ground, but before the three guards could hurry to their master, they were killed by Massek's men.

"Look what you've done. You, you... you scoundrels!" the count shouted at the thieves, standing up and trying to wipe the damp earth off his white shirt. But he was immediately kicked back to the ground by one of the thieves.

"Nobody allowed you to stand up!" the tall, full-bearded Thirian snapped at him.

"How dare you speak to me? Do you even know who I am?" the count said indignantly.

"Of course I know who you are, Count Laars, Chief Justice of Astinhod!" replied a voice in the same tone as the count's, who looked up from the ground at the thieves and couldn't believe what he was seeing.

"How ... How is that possible?" he stuttered as he saw himself, or someone who looked like him, standing next to the thieves.

The shapeshifter changed back into his natural form. A hideous, hairless and toothless creature, stood hunched over in front of him, looking at him with empty eyes.

The count was just about to lose consciousness when the tall, full-bearded thief grabbed him by the hair, yanked his head back and cut his throat with a skillful move.

"For the Shadow Lord!" shouted the thief, wiping the blood from his knife on Count Laars' white shirt.

"Go on, bury them!" the shapeshifter ordered in a low, very slow voice. Four of the thieves stripped off the clothes of the dead guards before burying them. Once the work was done, they slipped into the uniforms of the fallen, mounted their horses and waited for the shapeshifter to take on the appearance of Count Laars. They then rode to Astinhod together.

In the meantime, Hattul had snuck into the royal palace in Astinhod with four of his men. Two men guarding the King's bedroom had been bribed by Massek with gold and lands, which they would receive as soon as Erwight of Entorbis had taken Astinhod. Hattul quietly opened the door to the bedroom and crept over to King Grandhold, who was asleep in his bed. As he unsheathed his dagger and pondered whether he really should kill the king or whether it might be better to flee, to get out of Astinhod once and for all and go to Irkaar where he could sign on a ship and sail the islands of the Southern Sea, he began to tremble.

Hattul was a southerner and had lived in Astinhod for more than twenty years. He still remembered exactly how he came to Astinhod with his father, who traded fabrics. He was overwhelmed by the size of the town, its buildings and gardens. He saw the marketplace with the many people and merchants who came from all parts of Wetherid to offer their wares. When two of the city guards marched proudly past him with their long spears and elaborate uniforms made of fine fabrics, he knew that he would not return to Irkaar, but instead try to become one of the proud guards who protected the city of Astinhod and its inhabitants. Hattul had no idea at the time that he would not be accepted into the city guards because he was a southerner. He knew nothing of the thieves who lived underground or in abandoned houses and whose only job was to steal from the honest inhabitants of Astinhod.

Hattul worked as a helper in the marketplace for two years after he was refused entry into the city guard. He remembers clearly when a thief stole a golden chain from the stall of a merchant from Desert of DeShadin who he worked for. He followed the thief, several years his senior, through the many narrow streets of Astinhod and saw him disappear into an abandoned smithy with the gold chain in his hand. He followed the thief, but when he arrived at the smithy, he could not spot him. It was very dark, so he opened the shutters on one of the windows and then searched the three rooms in the smithy to no avail. Just as he was about to leave, he heard noises coming from under the wooden floor. He looked around for a trapdoor but could not find one. He sat down at the table in the middle of the forge and let his eyes wander around the room.

Being a very observant young man, he noticed that the door to a large, heavy cupboard was not fully locked.

"Could it be that there's a secret passage here?" he mumbled, went to the cupboard and opened the door. He saw a handle on the floor inside the cupboard, which he pulled hard. The base of the cupboard opened with a slight creaking sound. In front of him, a narrow wooden ladder led down into darkness. At the prospect of a reward and with the hope that the merchant might put in a good word for him to the city guard, he decided to climb down the ladder. It was dark, and as he reached the last rung of the ladder, someone pulled his legs from under him. He fell to the dark, hard stone floor and lost consciousness.

When he woke up some time later, he was sitting in a semi-dark room, tied to a chair.

"He's awake," a voice spoke. The shadow of a strong man approached him. A cold, strong hand pressed around his neck.

"Who are you and what are you doing here?" the shadow asked him threateningly.

"I was following a thief who stole a golden chain and if you help me find him, I'll share the reward with you!" explained Hattul.

Several voices laughed out loud.

"Are you looking for me?" mocked the young man, holding an oil lamp in front of his face and grinning maliciously.

"You vile thief! Give back the golden chain you stole and let me go!" Hattul shouted at him.

"Thank you for the compliment, my friend," the thief replied and laughed.

"Listen to me, you honest southerner. Haven't you noticed how you're treated in Astinhod? Haven't you noticed that you can't pursue an honorable profession here and that you can never join the King's army? You are a southerner, like most of us, my friend," said the thief.

Hattul could still remember the many arguments the thief had persuaded him to join the Thieves' Guild of Astinhod, as he stood in front of the bed where King Grandhold slept, supposed to kill him.

"So that's what it's come to, from thief to murderer," thought Hattul.

Determined, he took the dagger and stabbed several times. The white silk bed linen turned blood red.

Two thieves soon brought the bound and gagged Army Commander Arkondir into the king's bedroom. One of them struck him on the back of the head with the blunt side of his dagger, causing him to fall unconscious to the floor.

"Quickly now!" whispered Hattul, taking the gag from his mouth and cutting the shackles. The two thieves laid Army Commander Arkondir on the floor next to King Grandhold's bed. Hattul pressed the bloody dagger into his hand. The three left the room and crept out of the castle through one of the long corridors.

"That happened two days ago. And tomorrow, Army Commander Arkondir will be brought before the shapeshifter who has taken on the appearance of Count Laars. He will sentence him to death. We also know that the thieves are planning an uprising in Astinhod after Army Commander Arkondir is to be hanged. This must be prevented. Princess Lythinda must return to Astinhod as soon as possible and take the throne," Master Drobal said.

"But this Massek said that the shadow spell can only be broken by the light of Lorijan in the Holy Hall of Ib'Agier," Gorathdin objected, very saddened by the King's death.

Vrenli, Werlis, Wahmubu and Manamii could hardly believe everything they had just seen and heard. They looked at each other without a word.

"It is true that only the light of Lorijan can break the shadow spell, but we don't necessarily have to travel to Ib'Agier to do so," the old mage revealed, pointing his staff at the floor next to the crystal ball, where a golden bowl stood that looked exactly like the bowl in Master Drobal's Tower in Astinhod.

"We will bring the light of Lorijan here, friends," announced Master Drobal and went to the bowl.

"Bring Princess Lythinda to me and place her near the bowl. I'll be back in no time," instructed Master Drobal, climbing into the bowl and disappearing in a bright blue flashing light.

He reappeared a few moments later in a golden bowl in front of the statue of Lorijan in Ib'Agier, much to the astonishment of the three priests kneeling in front of it and saying their prayers.

"Hurry, call for Groblix!" Master Drobal shouted, flashing a bright blue lightning bolt from his staff to emphasize the urgency of the matter.

Quickly, some of the monks ran out of the hall.

Only a short time passed when Groblix, in the presence of King Agnulix, approached Master Drobal.

"How glad I am to see you here, Master Drobal!" exclaimed King Agnulix.

"Greetings, King Agnulix!" replied Master Drobal and bowed briefly to the dwarf king.

"A welcomed support," said Agnulix, delighted.

"I'm afraid I must disappoint you, King Agnulix. I have come to help Princess Lythinda of Astinhod. She is under a shadow spell and only the Holy Light of Lorijan can break it," explained Master Drobal, whereupon King Agnulix could not hide his disappointment.

"But you will soon receive help from Brother Transmudin, the leader of the Templars of the Dragon. He will try to dissuade

Omnigo from his plan to destroy the Hall of Lorijan in Ib'Agier. A dwarf named Borlix is traveling with him and will support you with his axe," said Master Drobal to King Agnulix, who could not quite follow the mage.

"The supreme leader of the Templars of the Dragon is coming to Ib'Agier soon? The leader of the traitors?" King Agnulix repeated incredulously.

"I don't think he is the traitor. But we don't have time to discuss that now," Master Drobal replied firmly and bowed to the king.

"Trust me, Agnulix, King of the Dwarves. There's no time to explain everything to you right now. But as I said, you are not alone. We are with you," he assured him and explained to Groblix that he should channel the Holy Light of Lorijan into the golden bowl after he traveled back to Horunguth.

"I will channel the Holy Light of Lorijan into the bowl, Master Drobal," confirmed Groblix, whereupon Master Drobal climbed into the bowl and reappeared in the Tower of Mages a short time later.

The return of Princess Lythinda

Only a few moments after Master Drobal's return to Horunguth Island, a bright, golden ray of light that filled the entire room shot out of the golden bowl next to which Princess Lythinda lay on the floor. A hissing and sibilant cry rang out. A shadowy figure escaped from the princess's body, shot up and dissolved into smoke in the bright light of Lorijan.

"What on earth was that?" shouted Werlis in amazement.

Before anyone could answer, Princess Lythinda opened her eyes.

"Where am I? What happened?" she murmured in a low voice. Her eyes began to shine when she saw Gorathdin standing in front of her.

"Who are all these people, Gorathdin, my love?" she said, frightened.

"They're friends of mine. You don't have to be afraid," he assured her in a gentle voice and supported her as she tried to stand up.

"Why was I laying here on the floor and what strange place is this?" she inquired as her eyes glanced around the room.

"You are on Horunguth Island," explained Master Drobal, to whom Princess Lythinda smiled when she saw him.

Gorathdin took Princess Lythinda in his arms and stroked her long, blonde hair tenderly.

"You must be strong now, my love," he said to her, taking her hands in his and telling her what had happened since their trip to Regen.

She couldn't follow the variety of events that Gorathdin told her so quickly and was therefore slightly confused.

"If everything happened as Gorathdin told me, then I owe you all a great debt of gratitude," Princess Lythinda said in a soft voice and sat down, weakened, on one of the chairs at the marble table.

"My father will reward you all richly, you have done him and Astinhod a great service," she announced majestically.

"Tell her!" Master Drobal urged Gorathdin, whereupon Princess Lythinda looked at him with concerned, clear blue eyes. Gorathdin went to her chair, took her hand and knelt down in front of her.

"Your father, King Grandhold, has been murdered," he revealed in a gentle voice, wiping the tears that were slowly running down her delicate cheeks from her face.

"My father is dead?" she sobbed, to which everyone nodded silently.

When she tried to get up from the chair, she toppled forward. Gorathdin just managed to catch her and pressed her gently against him.

"Your father, King Grandhold, was a good and just ruler. His death has hit us all hard, but you must be strong now. Astinhod needs you. The atrocious crime must be solved and the real culprits punished," Gorathdin said to her.

"The real culprits?" Princess Lythinda repeated in a trembling voice, unable to believe what she had just said.

"Yes, the real culprits," Gorathdin affirmed.

Master Drobal told her about the shapeshifter and the thieves and that Army Commander Arkondir was held responsible for the King's death.

"Arkondir, my father's murderer? Never. He was always loyal to him and to me. Gorathdin, he is your friend. You know he would never be capable of that!" Princess Lythinda contradicted desperately as she placed her hands on Gorathdin's cheeks.

"Arkondir is not the murderer, and we must go to Astinhod to save him from the gallows. You must ascend your father's throne before Erwight of Entorbis' plan to incite an uprising in Astinhod can be realized," Gorathdin told her, to which Princess Lythinda nodded, slowly regaining her composure.

"I will accompany you," said Gorathdin, looking at Master Drobal.

"Of course, you must go with her and one of us must accompany the two to unmask the shapeshifter, brothers," Master Drobal took the floor and looked at the three other mages.

"I'll go with them," the oldest of them offered.

"So be it then. Princess Lythinda and Gorathdin of the Forest, you will fly to Astinhod. Master Wendur is able to use the bowl and will therefore arrive before you. When you have gotten the situation under control, send the Knights of Astinhod to Ib'Agier. King Agnulix can still hold off Erwight of Entorbis' army on his own, but I fear that this attack is just one of many. He needs all our help," said Master Drobal, who went to the window and summoned another haldakie.

He then walked quickly to a high cupboard, opened it and took out a magnificently decorated longsword.

444

"This is for you Gorathdin. Your fire axe from Ib'Agier has certainly served you well so far, but now it is time for you to take up your inheritance as the Guardian of the Dark Forest. Here, take the sword. It belonged to Gronondir, who was a guardian like you," Master Drobal revealed solemnly and handed Gorathdin the sword, its blade glowing a bright forest green as Gorathdin gripped the hilt.

"It's beautiful! And how well it sits in the hand. It is perfectly balanced. Thank you, Master Drobal," Gorathdin replied, putting the sword on and feeling the glassy middle section of the blade. He then hung his fire axe on the cupboard wall, somewhat melancholy.

"The sword was forged a long time ago in the Glorious Valley. Shortly after the Living Glass was brought there. There is nothing in all of Wetherid or Fallgar that could make this blade burst in battle and the green light in the glass never extinguishes," Master Drobal explained and motioned Gorathdin to mount the haldakie.

Princess Lythinda said goodbye to everyone present and thanked Vrenli, Werlis, Aarl, Manamii and Wahmubu for their help. Then she climbed onto the haldakie behind Gorathdin, which flew the two of them to Astinhod, where they were to meet the Mage Wendur in Master Drobal's Tower.

"Now for you, Vrenli," said Master Drobal and turned in his direction.

"As far as I know, you have something for me," he said to Vrenli, who at first didn't know what Master Drobal was talking about and looked at him confused.

"The pages of Iseran's book, Vrenli," he clarified with a smile.

"You still have them, don't you?" he asked, raising his right eyebrow briefly as he became concerned that Vrenli might have lost the pages.

"The pages of the book. Yes, of course. Sorry, I didn't know what you were talking about at first," Vrenli replied and took off his cloak.

To the astonishment of those present, he began to carefully undo the seams on the underside of the cloak with his knife. He then pulled out the rolled-up pages of the book and handed them to Master Drobal.

He immediately checked their authenticity by passing his staff, which shone with a bright blue light, over the sides.

"Listen to me, friends," said Master Drobal, and everyone looked at him.

"We have managed to get Iseran's book pages into our possession. The pages that were in Astinhod are now here with me in the tower. If we can also secure the missing pages from the Underwater Grotto near Irkaar and those from the Glorious Valley, then we will finally have what Erwight of Entorbis desires so much. And as the Circle of Mages of Horunguth Island has decided, we will bring all the missing pages from the book to Ib'Agier," said Master Drobal, looking hopefully at the scroll in his hand.

"Forgive me, Master Drobal, I may only be a simple man, but I doubt it's a good idea to take the pages to Ib'Agier. It seems to me that we would be taking them directly to Erwight of Entorbis, who, as we know, already has an army of a thousand men stationed outside the halls of Ib'Agier," Aarl said, worried.

Vrenli, Werlis, Manamii and Wahmubu agreed with his objection.

"Given the many alliances Erwight of Entorbis has forged - including with the snake people of Desert of DeShadin, the Wahmuther clan from the east, the thieves of Astinhod, the Templars of the Dragon, the mist elves, gray dwarves and undead - the scattered book pages throughout Wetherid are in danger. For this reason, we, the mages, have decided to inform the leaders of Wetherid's peoples of Erwight's plans. It is imperative that all allied parties send their forces to Ib'Agier to support King Agnulix. By joining forces, we can make Ib'Agier a fortress, the safest place in all of Wetherid. As you know, Erwight of Entorbis has allies and spies in all the major cities. With their help, he could take possession of the missing book pages without much resistance. That is why we have chosen Ib'Agier as our base; this is where we will confront Erwight of Entorbis," explained Master Drobal.

After thinking about it, they agreed that Ib'Agier was a good choice.

"Since Ib'Agier needs all the support it can get, I ask you, Manamii and Wahmubu, to travel back to Desert of DeShadin. Unite the nomadic tribes and ask Sheikh Neg El Bahi for support. It may be a long way from Desert of DeShadin to Ib'Agier, but with the Scheddifer's horses, at least an army of five hundred men can arrive in Ib'Agier in two to three weeks," Master Drobal asked Manamii and Wahmubu.

"We will arrive in Ib'Agier with support as soon as possible. You can count on that," Manamii promised and bowed to Master Drobal.

"I will unite the nomads of the north and the south," Wahmubu announced.

Master Drobal called a haldakie, who waited outside the window until the two had said goodbye to those present. The haldakie then flew the two to Iseran in Desert of DeShadin.

"Well, friends, we should devote ourselves to our task. I will accompany you to the Underwater Grotto of Irkaar and the Glorious Valley. We must get the pages and it is important that Vrenli accompanies me to Ib'Agier afterwards. I hope that Aarl and Werlis will accompany us," said Master Drobal to Vrenli, Werlis and Aarl, who agreed without hesitation.

"Are we going to fly too?" Werlis asked excitedly.

"There are two entrances to the grotto, one is on the small peninsula east of Irkaar and the other is a nautical mile from Irkaar, a hundred paces underwater. In my opinion, it is safer to use the underwater entrance. Don't forget that there are already three haldakies flying over Wetherid. You can be sure that this will not go unnoticed by Erwight of Entorbis. What's more, the haldakies can't land on the water. We have to choose a different way of traveling," explained Master Drobal.

"But shouldn't we get rid of Moorgh's creatures in front of our tower first?" one of the two mages sitting at the table interjected.

"I would be very grateful if you could both look after it. I still have to make some preparations for my journey. Make sure that you are in constant contact with the crystal, it is important that you channel its energy to Ib'Agier," Master Drobal spoke and went to one of the bookshelves to look something up in a book that he took out from the top.

The two magicians got up from the table and went to the crystal, where they placed their hands. It didn't take long for a bright blue light to shoot up from the crystal ball to the top of the tower. Each of the two magicians then went to one of the tower's windows.

With the help of their staffs, they sent burning bolts of lightning down on the Moorgher below. One of them began to speak in a language none of the three friends understood. He raised his staff, leaned it back slightly over his head and when he had finished the spell, he swung his staff out and hurled hundreds of spears of bright blue light at the Moorgher, which, together with the other mage's firebolts, killed more than half of them. The survivors fled back into the water as fast as their webbed, mutilated-looking legs would allow.

"I don't think they'll be back any time soon," said the mage who had hurled the spears from his staff. The other mage at the left window rained down a hail of ice in front of the tower.

"To be on the safe side," he added and went back to the crystal ball with the other mage, where they put their hands again.

This time they closed their eyes and slowly spoke verses that neither Vrenli, Werlis nor Aarl understood. Small twitching flashes formed inside the crystal ball.

"Send three bolts of lightning to the main gate of Ib'Agier when you have charged the crystal ball. It is time for King Agnulix to know that he is not alone," instructed Master Drobal, who was ready to leave.

He carried an old leather bag around his shoulder, held his staff in his left hand and an old-looking, thick book with a red leather cover in his right.

"Come on, friends, let's go down to the water. We still have a lot to do and the way to Ib'Agier is long and full of dangers," he said and went ahead of them.

"Farewell, brothers," he said goodbye to the two magicians before descending the tower stairs.

"Take care of yourselves!" the magicians called after them.

Meanwhile in Astinhod, Commander Froland entered the throne room in the presence of Count Laars, two officers and ten knights.

"Who dares to enter the throne room of our deceased King and also has the insolence to sit on his throne?" shouted Count Laars into the hall.

Gorathdin's dark green eyes began to glow and he was about to reply when Mage Wendur tapped him lightly on the shin with his staff.

"Before you is Princess Lythinda of Astinhod and she is claiming her rightful place on the throne!" the mage replied.

"Princess Lythinda of Astinhod? I doubt it. We were told that Princess Lythinda died trying to learn the forbidden fire magic from the Templars of the Dragon," the count replied, whereupon Brother Theramond stepped out from behind him.

"That's exactly what happened! The former leader of the order, Brother Transmudin, who is responsible for this crime, has been missing since the incident," confirmed Brother Theramond, who avoided Gorathdin's gaze and stared at the ground.

When Wendur noticed the intensity with which Gorathdin's dark green eyes began to glow, he tapped him lightly on the shin again.

"As far as I know, Count Laars, anyone who lays claim to the throne must justify themselves to the nobles and advisors. Whether or not this is the true Princess Lythinda is a moot point. What matters is that she has laid claim to the throne of Astinhod!" explained Mage Wendur firmly.

"Forgive me for asking, but you look very much like one of those mages of Horunguth to me, and as I am the Chief Justice of Astinhod, it falls to me to investigate the cowardly murder of King Grandhold. A mage from Horunguth Island named Drobal is suspected of aiding and abetting the king's murder and since he cannot be found in Astinhod, which adds to the suspicion of aiding and abetting, perhaps you can tell me where he is?" asked Count Laars loudly.

"You wouldn't want to informally interrogate an old man in the middle of the night, who has also had a very long journey, would you?" Wendur interjected with a gentle smile.

"You're right, it's late. We'll talk more tomorrow when we examine the girl's claim in all formality, as the law in Astinhod stipulates," the false count replied in conclusion and ordered the officer on his right to take the three of them to a guarded room in the castle.

"Why didn't you unmask the shapeshifter?" Gorathdin asked when they were alone in the room.

"I think it would be wiser to find out who is on Erwight of Entorbis' side first," Wendur explained and lay down in one of the four beds.

"If I'm right, tomorrow, before Princess Lythinda officially claims the throne, the shapeshifter will try to sentence Army Commander Arkondir to death. He will not want to risk Princess Lythinda ascending the throne first and then overturning the death sentence. He knows that she and Army Commander Arkondir are friends. He will do everything in his power to make her out to be a liar. Our task will be to prioritize her hearing over the conviction of Army Commander Arkondir. I don't know how we're going to do that yet, but I'm sure I'll have a plan by tomorrow," Wendur revealed and closed his eyes.

It was just midnight when Gorathdin was woken by a noise at the window. He opened his eyes briefly and clearly saw two dark-clad men carefully opening the sliding window. He waited until the first of them was in the room and, just as he was about to pull the other through the window, he jumped up and pushed them both out again. With a cry, the two of them, still trying to hold on to the thin ivy on the outer wall of the castle, fell to the ground, where they lay motionless.

The two guards outside the room opened the door and entered the room.

"What are these noises about?" one of the two called out, waking up Mage Wendur and Princess Lythinda, who looked around questioningly.

"It's not good for Astinhod's security if you're already being attacked by riffraff in the royal castle," Gorathdin stated, pointing to the window with his right hand.

One of the guards walked up to it, leaned out and saw two dark figures lying on the ground below.

"They were definitely thieves! Since the cowardly murder of our king, they no longer shy away from the castle guards. Several break-ins in the castle have already been reported. Count Laars therefore had the guards doubled and announced that he would take care of the thieves in Astinhod as soon as King Grandhold's murderer was hanged," reported the well-armed guard.

"I doubt that," Gorathdin replied and went back to bed. The guard closed the window and apologized to Princess Lythinda for the incident.

"Am I allowed to say something?" he asked her.

"Go ahead, speak," Princess Lythinda encouraged him.

"I wish you good luck for tomorrow. Astinhod needs you, my Queen," he said and bowed.

"The nobility, led by Count Laars, cannot rule over Astinhod, My Lady," the other spoke up.

"I thank you. I will ascend my father's throne tomorrow and ensure peace and security in Astinhod again," she promised the two guards, who then left the room.

"It's better if I stay awake," Gorathdin whispered to Princess Lythinda and Wendur, who thanked him and fell asleep again.

The rest of the night passed without further incident and early in the morning there was a knock at the door. A castle servant informed the three that Count Laars was waiting for them in the dining room.

"He is very sure of his role," Gorathdin remarked.

"That is a good thing. Since I made him believe that I cannot recognize his true form, he has become careless," Wendur replied and suggested that Gorathdin accompany Count Laars to the court hearing and tell those present about Princess Lythinda's return.

The three of them then made their way to the royal dining room.

"How can this creature allow itself to sit in my father's place and enjoy breakfast," Princess Lythinda whispered to Gorathdin and Wendur as they entered the dining room.

"Count of Regen, please sit with me," the shapeshifter invited Gorathdin, who complied.

"How is it that you support the claims of this girl and run-of-the-mill mage? As a nobleman, you should be on Astinhod's side, not on the side of two liars," he mocked as he gnawed on a pheasant leg.

"Well, I think we'd better let the other nobles and advisors judge that at the hearing," Gorathdin replied.

"As you say, Count of Regen. As you say," returned Count Laars, and he continued eating with relish.

The three watched the shapeshifter as he stuffed himself full of meat and refrained from eating anything themselves.

An officer from the castle guard entered the dining room and announced that all participants were present.

"Well then, I'll see you after I've sentenced the king's murderer," said Count Laars and indicated to two castle guards to keep a watchful eye on the three of them.

"Not so fast, Count Laars. I will accompany you, it is my duty to help you convict King Grandhold's cowardly murderer," said Gorathdin and followed the count into the castle's assembly hall.

As the two entered the hall, Gorathdin saw his friend, Army Commander Arkondir, in a very poor state. He was sitting on a bench in front of the podium where Count Laars was seated next to two other judges. In a semicircle around Army Commander Arkondir sat ten nobles, some advisors, two other army commanders and a few officers who attended the hearing.

"The people of Astinhod against Army Commander Arkondir!" announced the court crier, whereupon everyone in the hall rose to their feet.

Count Laars called the first two witnesses. They were the two knights who were standing guard outside the King's bedroom door and found Army Commander Arkondir with the bloody dagger in his hand. Just as the two were about to step forward, Gorathdin suddenly stepped in front of the podium where the three judges were sitting.

"Honored attendees. I would like to let you know that Princess Lythinda of Astinhod is in the castle. Out of respect for her grief over the death of her father, I ask you to leave the judgment on the cowardly murderer to her," Gorathdin spoke to those gathered.

"Count of Regen, you are disturbing the trial. Sit down in your seat!" Count Laars snapped at him in a sharp tone.

A murmur broke out among those gathered and Army Commander Arkondir looked questioningly at Gorathdin.

"Princess Lythinda of Astinhod lays claim to her father's throne and we must hear her out before we judge her father's murderer," Gorathdin continued firmly. The murmuring of those present grew louder and ended in a loud discussion. Count Laars tried to restore calm in the hall by tapping his small wooden mallet on the tabletop several times.

"Count of Regen. I must ask you to leave the hall. The title of count does not give you the right to disrupt a court hearing!" shouted Count Laars and beckoned three guards to him.

At the same moment, the door to the courtroom opened and Princess Lythinda stepped into the hall with Mage Wendur at her side.

"Princess Lythinda is back!" cried several voices in a jumble and some of those present bowed to her.

"Quiet, please!" demanded Count Laars, who was getting slightly nervous.

"I will not allow an elf, a runaway mage and a girl pretending to be Princess Lythinda of Astinhod disrupt a court hearing!" he roared into the hall.

"Officers, take the three of them out of the hall and put them in custody until the trial is over and the king's murderer is convicted. We will deal with their fate later!" ordered Count Laars.

Two of the officers and an army commander stood up to take the three out of the courtroom as the two judges stood up.

"Wait!" shouted one of them.

"Princess Lythinda is the rightful heir to the throne of King Grandhold. Let her speak!" demanded the other judge.

"Princess Lythinda is dead! The girl is an impostor!" shouted Duke Grendewald, a former advisor to the king, at the top of his voice.

Count Laars agreed with the duke's statement. And another heated discussion broke out in the hall.

Count Laars once again gave the order to take the three out of the hall and put them in custody. One of the army commanders was about to grab Princess Lythinda by the arm when two castle guards stood in front of him.

"Army commander, get away from the princess!" one of them demanded.

The commander was about to draw his sword when Gorathdin grabbed him with his left hand and put his hunting knife, which he pulled out of his boot, to his neck.

"Don't touch her!" he threatened and his dark green eyes began to glow.

The two officers present were about to throw themselves at Mage Wendur when a bolt of lightning from his staff hurled them both far across the hall.

"Guards! Guards! Arrest the three rebels!" shouted Count Laars, whereupon ten armed guards entered the hall at a run.

When they saw Army Commander Arkondir, Gorathdin, the Mage Wendur and Princess Lythinda, they stopped and knelt before Princess Lythinda.

"My Lady, you're back!" one of them exclaimed.

He laid his sword at her feet and ordered his men to do the same.

"This is rebellion!" shouted Count Laars, tapping incessantly on the tabletop in front of him with his little hammer.

Duke Grendewald stood up and ordered the guards to take up their weapons immediately and lead the three out of the hall. He threatened them with the gallows if they did not comply with his order.

"Enough now!" thundered Mage Wendur in a trembling voice. But as the silence in the hall would not return, he took his staff, raised it in the air and let the lower end crash to the floor. The shock caused pictures to fall from the walls and some of the chairs in the hall to topple over.

"I said quiet!" he repeated.

Everyone looked at him in horror. A bright blue light shone from Wendur's eyes onto Count Laars, allowing him to see the creature in its natural form.

"Your game is over!" he said in a deep and serious voice to the shapeshifter, who was struggling to maintain Count Laar's appearance in his excitement.

Those present noticed with horror that the count's skin color changed and for a fraction of a moment the count's face blended with the ugly grimace of the shapeshifter.

"Take them away!" croaked the shapeshifter.

But Mage Wendur raised his staff and fired a bolt of light that hit the shapeshifter with full force. All of its limbs twitched, emitting rattling, hissing noises. Another flash of light hit it and now everyone could see the ugly creature.

Those present in the hall were shocked.

The shapeshifter, who wanted to use the confusion in the hall to escape, was now caught by a purple beam of light coming from Wendur's staff and slowly lifted into the air. The shapeshifter hissed and made the strangest contortions to free himself from the beam of light.

"See the being that blinded you to the truth!" the mage spoke to the hall and let the shapeshifter glide high above the heads of the nobles, advisors, officers, commanders and judges.

"An army of Erwight of Entorbis, one thousand strong, stands before the gates of Ib'Agier. The dwarves are waiting for Astinhod's help. Crown Princess Lythinda and send your knights to Ib'Agier!" he shouted into the crowd and let the shapeshifter slide back to the ground.

Gorathdin strode to the Shadow Lord's ally, drew his longsword and decapitated him with a single blow. Those present froze at the sight of the creature cut in two.

Princess Lythinda stepped up to the judge's podium and ordered the guards to arrest Duke Grendewald, her father's former advisor, the two officers and the traitorous commander.

"Commander Arkondir is innocent; the true murderer of my father is the thief Hattul, who acted on the orders of Erwight of Entorbis. Rise up, Army Commander Arkondir, you are free!" Princess Lythinda announced majestically and gave him a brief smile.

"Thank you, My Lady," replied Army Commander Arkondir and knelt in front of her.

"What are your orders, my Queen?" he asked her.

"Send as many men as Astinhod can spare to Ib'Agier as quickly as possible. I also wish for the thieves in Astinhod to be dealt with severely. The guards in the castle must be tripled and the defensive walls and towers must be manned!" Princess Lythinda ordered him.

"As you command!" he replied and smiled at her.

"And now for you, gentlemen. I want you to follow me into the throne room and crown me Queen of Astinhod!" she commanded those present in the hall.

The coronation of the new Queen of Astinhod did not take long, and when the people were told of Princess Lythinda's return and her regency, a festive mood broke out in Astinhod.

"I will accompany Army Commander Arkondir and his men to Ib'Agier," Gorathdin said to her as they sat side-by-side at the banquet table that evening.

"I know you have to do that, my love," she replied.

"Please give my thanks again to your friends and take care of yourself!" she called after him as he rose from the feast table with Army Commander Arkondir and set off for Ib'Agier with an army of a thousand men that had gathered outside Astinhod's city walls.

The Underwater Grotto of Irkaar

As Vrenli, Werlis, Aarl and Master Drobal followed the path down towards the sea, they walked past the dead bodies of Moorgh's underwater creatures. The ugly sight made them all walk faster. When they arrived at the bottom of the small bay, the waves were crashing hard against the cliffs.

"It looks like a storm is coming," Aarl remarked, looking anxiously at the black clouds that were moving from Irkaar to the island.

Vrenli and Werlis nodded in agreement.

"Are you ready?" Master Drobal, who was unperturbed by the approaching storm, wanted to hear from the three of them.

When they nodded, he gripped his staff in the middle with both hands and let it glide over his head in twisting movements. With a whirring sound that got louder, he whirled the staff faster and faster through the air. He now began to swing the staff in a circular motion over himself and his three friends. The whirring noise was so loud that Werlis had to cover his ears.

Master Drobal began to speak slowly in the ancient language of Wetherid. Vrenli noticed the outline of a huge, transparent, gaseous sphere forming above his head. In an instant, Master Drobal let go of the staff and, in the blink of an eye, the staff swung from the ground to the left and then to the right, over their heads and back again.

The circular movements of the staff became so fast that it could no longer be seen. A transparent sphere had formed around the four.

"Don't touch it!" warned Master Drobal.

Vrenli, Werlis and Aarl felt themselves moving slightly away from the ground and floating towards the water inside the sphere.

"Don't be afraid, friends," Master Drobal reassured the three, who were standing inside the sphere with their eyes and mouths wide open.

They looked down at their feet, which were slightly above the surface of the water.

"How on earth do you do that?" Aarl marveled, but Master Drobal just smiled.

The sphere floated purposefully across the water towards the city of Irkaar.

"Look, friends, a group of dolphins is following us!" exclaimed Aarl, pointing with his finger at their companions swimming alongside the sphere. From time to time, the dolphins took a leap into the air and dived back into the water. Vrenli and Werlis, who had never seen this spectacle before, were thrilled.

The wind that blew around Horunguth Island turned into a powerful storm the further they moved away from it. The swell became stronger and stronger. They were now directly under the dark clouds that Aarl had noticed earlier. It began to rain, but the raindrops bounced off the gaseous shell of the sphere.

"I think it will be better if we continue our journey under the water," Master Drobal decided and made a few downward circling movements with his hand.

The sphere then plunged into the water and slowly sank below the surface, where it quickly became dark due to the cloudy sky.

Master Drobal therefore let a beam of light emerge from his right hand, which was transmitted to the sphere. The shell of the sphere began to glow. Vrenli, Werlis and Aarl could now see the colorful schools of fish swimming around them as they passed by.

"I'd like to know what it looks like at the bottom," Werlis said to Master Drobal with an expectant look. Without hesitation, Master Drobal steered the sphere deeper down. Once it had reached the sea floor, the sphere set course for the city of Irkaar again.

"We are now at least two hundred paces below sea level. Look!" said Master Drobal.

The three watched the underwater world from inside the sphere in fascination. Strange-looking fish with three glowing eyes on antennae swam around the sphere. Next to them, fish with wide open, large mouths covered with numerous razor-sharp teeth slowly glided past. These fish, covered in thick scales and as big as Aarl, moved leisurely along their course. A vast, brightly colored plant world grew over the rocky seascape that opened up before them. The sandy seabed was occasionally gently stirred up by fast-crawling crustaceans and shell-like sea creatures.

"What a wonderful place," said Vrenli to Master Drobal, who nodded and then slowly let the sphere rise again to just below the surface of the water.

"The underwater grotto is to the east of Irkaar. It is very large and reaches under the small peninsula that lies on the border of the Glorious Valley," he explained to the three of them as he propelled the sphere to make faster progress.

"I've never heard of a grotto," confessed Aarl to Master Drobal.

"The grotto has a land entrance, but it has long been forgotten. Long before the city of Irkaar was built, the grotto served as a temple for underwater creatures. There they prayed to their gods of the sea. When the people who came across the sea settled on the coast, there were long disputes between the two peoples. As the humans fished, the underwater creatures claimed the sea for themselves, and they repeatedly attacked the southerners' fishing boats and destroyed their nets. This led to the land people organizing themselves and driving the underwater creatures out of the coastal waters. Their temple was also destroyed in the process. The creatures fled to the west, where they built the underwater city of Moorgh. This city is located between Horunguth Island and the border waters of Desert of DeShadin. The grotto, half of which is under the surface of the water, subsequently served as a refuge for fishermen from approaching enemies for centuries. When the city of Irkaar was built, however, the grotto was forgotten. It was only when Vrenli's grandfather, together with us mages, wanted to hide the pages of the book that had been cut out that Master Wendur remembered the grotto, which he thought would be the ideal place to hide the pages containing the history of the southerners," Master Drobal told his friends.

"Does that mean my grandfather separated the pages that contain the history of the various peoples living in Wetherid?" Vrenli asked.

"That's exactly how it was! Your grandfather was of the not-at-all-wrong opinion that if the pages containing the history of the peoples of Wetherid were removed from the book and hidden, it would be incomplete and thus protected from misuse. The book is now in the second generation of unlawful possession of the Entorbis, but to date they have been unable to find the missing pages. They therefore cannot use the book against Wetherid," Master Drobal told his attentive friends.

The sphere now slowed down and glided past a huge coral reef populated by countless shoals of fish.

"We will soon arrive at the entrance to the grotto, friends. It is at the underwater mountain range in front of us," announced Master Drobal, pointing north with his hand and letting the sphere slide slowly into the depths.

"Look, there!" shouted Aarl, pointing with his hand to the grotto entrance, where two Moorgher were swimming up and down.

"Looks like the grotto isn't as deserted as you thought, Master Drobal," said Vrenli, whereupon Master Drobal let the sphere slide backwards.

"I wasn't expecting that. I can't use my magic against the Moorgher from inside the sphere. Friends, we must change our plan. We must use the land access," Master Drobal decided and let the sphere glide to the east side of the peninsula. It made a wide arc around the underwater mountains, then he slowly let it surface. The sphere floated on the surface of the water towards the steep cliffs that separated the peninsula from the water.

"We have to look for a suitable place to go ashore," Master Drobal decided and let the sphere float along the rocky coast towards the mainland.

"There seems to be a small bay up ahead," Aarl remarked, pointing with his hand in the direction where the peninsula connected to the mainland.

"Very good! We'll go ashore here," decided Master Drobal, whereupon the sphere slowly slid out of the water and came to a halt on the pebble-covered beach.

Master Drobal spoke a sentence in the ancient Wetherid language and made a wiping motion in the air with his hand. The sphere then slowly dissolved, beginning above their heads.

"Let's go to the land entrance of the grotto. We climb up this rock face here, then we can walk along the cliffs to the south side of the peninsula. The entrance to the grotto is at this rock that rises up there," said Master Drobal, pointing with his hand to the southernmost tip of the peninsula, where a high rock rose up less than two hundred paces from the water.

The climb up the rock face caused Master Drobal some difficulties, but with the help of Aarl, he reached the top before Vrenli and Werlis. The four of them walked south along the cliffs. The sound of the waves lashing against the steep cliffs kept them walking in silence. After a short walk, they were only a few paces away from the cliff when they were surprised to see a wall about two paces high surrounding the rock. Vrenli was the first to spot a wooden tower with several ropes hanging to the ground behind the rampart.

"What's that?" he asked Master Drobal.

"I have no idea. I've never seen this before," he replied to Vrenli, looking at the wooden structure in amazement.

"Hide behind the bushes. I'll take a closer look," said Aarl and crept closer towards the rampart.

He could see inside through a gap between two of the wooden posts.

"That's all we needed," he muttered and slowly crawled back to his friends.

"Gray dwarves, dozens of them," Aarl told his friends.

"They are pulling up baskets full of rocks with the ropes. I've also seen some of them descending into the cave, equipped with shovels and pickaxes, not to fight but to work!" continued Aarl.

"They must be looking for the missing pages of the book," Master Drobal realized with a horrified expression on his face.

"Then the Moorgher on Horunguth Island were just a diversion," Vrenli remarked.

"How do they know that some of the missing pages are in the grotto?" wondered Aarl.

"I don't have an answer to that," replied Master Drobal.

"They know the book pages are in the grotto, but it seems they don't know exactly where. That would be the only explanation as to why they are digging," said Aarl.

"What should we do now? The four of us can't fight dozens of gray dwarves alone and don't forget the Moorgher we saw underwater. That would be suicide," Werlis said, worried, and looked at Master Drobal.

"I'm less worried about a few dozen gray dwarves and a few Moorgher and more concerned about how they knew the book pages were in the grotto," Master Drobal said and stomped on the ground with his staff, causing the earth to shake.

Shortly afterwards, the four heard excited cries from the gray dwarves running out of the grotto entrance.

"The grotto is threatening to collapse! Everyone out!" shouted a gray dwarf in a loud voice that echoed over to the four.

Master Drobal waited a few moments before raising his staff in the air, reciting a verse in the ancient language of Wetherid.

A rain of fire then poured down on the gray dwarves in front of the entrance to the grotto. Some of them who had caught fire tried to smother the flames by rolling on the ground. Others jumped straight from the cliffs into the water while the rest tried to escape back into the grotto.

Master Drobal caused the earth to shake again, whereupon the gray dwarves ran into the nearby thicket and threw themselves to the ground in fear.

"Follow me! We have to get to the grotto," said Master Drobal, walking quickly ahead.

While they were still running towards the wall, Master Drobal fired a bolt of lightning from his staff, which punched a hole in the wall. The four of them climbed through the hole and ran to the entrance of the grotto.

Vrenli, Werlis and Aarl were just about to walk down the torch-lit tunnel when Master Drobal gave them a sign to wait.

"I will seal the entrance as a precaution," he announced and, with the help of his staff, created a wall of bright blue light that closed off the land entrance to the grotto.

"Be careful! There could be Moorgher in here. I doubt that the two guards at the underwater entrance were the only ones," Aarl warned, checking that his throwing knives were loosely sheathed.

Vrenli and Werlis drew their short swords, held them in front of them and followed Aarl and Master Drobal into the steeply descending tunnel.

They walked no more than a hundred steps when they arrived at a small rocky outcrop where a staircase, roughly carved into the stone, led down into the grotto.

Vrenli looked down from the ledge and saw a small lake covering half of the floor. The grotto was not particularly large, but Vrenli estimated that at least fifty people could fit inside. Collapsed columns, broken sculptures and statues bore witness to a long-forgotten time. The rock walls were damp, but Vrenli could make out colorful drawings on them in the dim light of the torches the gray dwarves had set up for their excavations.

The four of them descended the narrow staircase.

"Look at these tons of holes in the ground," Aarl pointed out to the others.

"The gray dwarves must have been here for days," Vrenli remarked.

Werlis noticed that the top layer of stone had been removed from one of the walls. There were baskets filled with rubble and debris all over the grotto. A heavy-looking stone table stood on the side of the grotto not covered with water. The gray dwarves had left shovels, pickaxes, chisels and hammers on it in their hasty flight from the quake.

"The altar is still standing. We're in luck," said Master Drobal happily, taking quick steps towards the massive table and sweeping the remains of the gray dwarves off the tabletop with his staff.

He then began to draw circular and square lines on the tabletop with his stick.

A hidden drawer on the side of the thick tabletop facing the water opened with a soft click. Master Drobal was about to reach into the opening when several Moorgher emerged from the water behind them.

Aarl reacted quickly and threw two of his throwing knives at the two Moorgher coming towards Vrenli and Werlis.

"Moorgher!" shouted Werlis, and together with Vrenli, he slashed at one of the creatures with his short sword causing the Moorgher to spray its corrosive secretions at them.

Werlis was hit by the secretion on his right forearm. He cried out, tormented by burning pain, and dropped his short sword on the ground. Another creature reached for him with its clawed hands and tried to pull him into the water, but Vrenli cut off its arm with a powerful blow.

In the meantime, Aarl was able to finish off two more Moorgher with his throwing knives.

"Quick, come to the altar and hide behind it!" shouted Master Drobal, who took a roll of paper from the drawer and immediately fired several bolts of lightning from his staff at the Moorgher.

The Moorgher then retreated into the water, throwing spears. Master Drobal only just managed to avoid one of the spears and sought shelter behind the altar next to his friends.

"There are at least five of them still alive and who knows how many may still be underwater," said Aarl, peering cautiously from behind the altar.

The Moorgher, frightened by Master Drobal's lightning, tried to splash their secretions behind the altar from the water.

"If they get a few paces closer, it doesn't look good for us," Aarl remarked.

"It burns like fire!" shouted Werlis, who was lying on the ground behind the altar, his voice distorted with pain.

"You've been badly hit, Werlis! It doesn't look good," replied Aarl, who could well empathize with Werlis' pain. The skin on his forearm was in danger of disintegrating completely.

"Help me, Master Drobal!" cried Werlis, tormented by pain.

"Hang in there, my boy," said Master Drobal.

He stood up quickly behind the altar and drew a line with his staff along the water, stretching from the right to the left side of the grotto. He spoke a short verse, whereupon a huge wall of fire flared up at the edge of the water.

"That will hold them up for a while," Master Drobal announced, kneeling down next to Werlis and examining his forearm that was still dropping secretion onto the ground.

Werlis' eyes went black and he lost consciousness.

"I'm afraid there's not much more we can do," said Master Drobal in a depressed voice.

"You have to help him. I beg you!" said Vrenli, holding Werlis in his arms.

"Make sure you don't come into contact with the secretion," warned Aarl.

"I'm not a healer, but I'm afraid we'll have to remove his forearm," Master Drobal said seriously.

"No!" cried Vrenli.

"You're crippling him!" he shouted at Master Drobal in despair.

"The secretion has completely destroyed the skin tissue and is now eating into his flesh. Look at his upper arm, the skin is already beginning to disintegrate slightly. He will die from the pain. His arm can no longer be saved," explained Master Drobal, placing his hand gently on Vrenli's head.

"You have to understand. It has to be," he spoke to him gently.

Vrenli burst into tears.

For a few moments he saw himself and Werlis in Abketh again, as they fought each other on the day of the final test when Werlis defeated him with the short sword.

"He's still so young. He was one of the strongest in our village. Is there really no other way?" Vrenli asked Master Drobal with tears streaming down his face.

"I'm afraid not. I'm sorry," replied Master Drobal.

Aarl dared to look at the water.

The wall of fire was still burning and kept the Moorgher from approaching.

"Lay him carefully on the ground and make sure his right arm is far enough away from his body," Master Drobal instructed them.

Vrenli, who couldn't bear to see what Master Drobal was about to do, closed his eyes. Master Drobal touched Werlis' right arm with his staff and turned it to ice. "Cut off the arm right at the elbow," he then instructed Aarl.

Vrenli cried out and dropped to the ground when he heard Master Drobal's words.

Werlis' body twitched briefly as Aarl cut through the frozen arm with his dagger. When Vrenli saw Werlis' forearm lying severed on the ground next to his body, he gasped for breath and lost consciousness.

"I must cauterize the wound or he will bleed to death when his upper arm thaws," Master Drobal said to Aarl, who nodded in agreement.

The top of Master Drobal's staff began to glow.

With a cry from Werlis that echoed through the grotto, he pressed the glowing rod against, gaping stump. Werlis' upper body shot upwards and his eyes popped out. He turned white as a sheet and fell back to the ground, where he lost consciousness again.

"It is done," Master Drobal spoke softly to Vrenli and gently shook his cloak.

Vrenli opened his eyes and crouched down next to Werlis. He gently stroked Werlis' face.

"Forgive me, my friend," he whispered, before bursting into tears again.

"We will have to carry him. I'm afraid he'll be unconscious for a long time, probably a few days," said Master Drobal.

"Have you got the pages of the book?" Vrenli wanted to know, taking Werlis in his arms.

"I took them," said Master Drobal, who could not smile at the fortunate twist of fate - the gray dwarves had not destroyed the altar and in turn hadn't found the pages of the book - because of what had happened to Werlis.

"We should think about how to get out of here," suggested Aarl.

"The gray dwarves will surely have recovered from their fright by now and I doubt we'll have such an easy time getting past them this time, especially with the unconscious Werlis," Master Drobal spoke and looked around.

"Can't we just dive under the Moorgher with the sphere?" Vrenli wanted to know.

"I'm afraid the sphere offers no protection from the Moorgher, my boy," Master Drobal replied.

"The flames are getting smaller and smaller," remarked Aarl.

"I can create a new wall of flame, but that won't really help us either, as the Moorgher will simply dive down and the fire won't harm them," Master Drobal replied with a slight sigh.

"That means our only option is to kill the Moorgher in front of us and hope there aren't any more of them under the water, so we can dive away from here in the sphere through the water," Aarl stated.

Master Drobal nodded in agreement.

"Aarl, stand in front of the altar and when the wall of fire disappears, wait until the Moorgher see you and then come back to us immediately. I will use the spell of a hundred spears," said Master Drobal to Aarl, who then crawled to the front of the altar, held two throwing knives in his hands and waited for Master Drobal to make the wall of flames disappear.

He stood up behind the altar and let his staff glide over the wall of flames, which grew smaller until they finally went out. The Moorgher, who had retreated into the water to protect themselves, slowly swam closer.

When they caught sight of Aarl, they reared up in the water and threw spears at him, spraying their secretions in his direction. Aarl jumped up from the ground, hurled two of his throwing knives, which found their target in one of the Moorgher, and rolled over the large altar to the other side, where he threw himself to the ground.

The Moorghers' spears fell to the ground just behind Master Drobal´s and Werlis heads. Master Drobal now slowly raised his staff above his head.

"Nehrweg anibaris mechjot, loohnamis hundus!" he spoke, firing hundreds of bright blue flashes of light, which turned into massive iron spears in flight, at the approaching underwater creatures.

The Moorgher were pierced by the spears, but one of the creatures closest to the altar managed to spray its secretion before it was killed by a spear. The corrosive liquid hit the stone slab of the altar and the upper half of Master Drobal's staff, which immediately began to disintegrate. Out of reflex, Master Drobal dropped his staff and rolled backwards.

"Watch out!" he shouted to warn his friends.

Aarl rolled to the edge of the altar and looked at the water, where more than eight underwater creatures were floating dead on the surface. Two more lay on the ground just a few paces from the altar.

"They all seem to be dead," Aarl noted, standing up carefully behind the altar.

"That's all we need," grumbled Master Drobal as he saw his staff, which was dissolving in the secretion, lying on the ground.

"We're doomed!" Vrenli despaired, not bothering to get up.

"I may have been robbed of a powerful tool, but that doesn't mean we are lost," replied Master Drobal, who was visibly angry at the loss of his valuable staff.

He informed them that he could not create the sphere that would bring them out of the grotto without the help of his staff.

"I'm going to have a look at the exit underwater," announced Aarl, jumping into the water with his dagger between his teeth.

"The way out seems to be clear!" he shouted as he resurfaced after a short time. He gasped for air and pushed aside one of the dead underwater creatures floating on the surface.

"But it's hopeless. We'll never be able to hold our breath long enough to get out through the exit and emerge on the other side," Aarl said to Master Drobal.

"We also have to think about Werlis. He's unconscious. He would drown after just a few moments," said Vrenli, who was still holding Werlis' unconscious body in his arms.

Master Drobal walked towards the water, stretched out his right arm above the surface and opened his hand. A small, bright blue ray of light shone from his diamond-shaped mark to the surface of the water, which he slapped a few times with his palm.

He then went back to Vrenli and Werlis and sat down on the floor next to them.

"I hope that Werlis will survive the shock he will experience when he regains consciousness and realizes that his right forearm is missing. We must make sure that we find a settlement on our way to the Glorious Valley where Werlis' wound can be treated," said Master Drobal to Vrenli.

"Gorathdin mentioned that there is another Raging Hordes village northeast of Irkaar, halfway to the Glorious Valley. He gave me this ring in case we need their support," explained Vrenli, holding up the ring.

"There are two shadows coming up from under the water. Moorgher!" Aarl suddenly shouted and was about to run to the altar when Master Drobal, to his astonishment, stood up and walked to the water, where two snow-white dolphin heads were slowly emerging from the water.

"Friends!" said Master Drobal, stroking the two marine mammals on the head.

"We need to be taken out of this grotto and to a small beach northeast of here," Master Drobal asked the dolphins, who bobbed their heads up and down as if agreeing to Master Drobal's request.

Vrenli, who stood up behind the altar to see who or what had come up out of the water, looked at Master Drobal in amazement, as did Aarl.

"Not only druids have animals as friends and can communicate with them," revealed Master Drobal, who had regained his smile.

"I'll ride the dolphin on the right with Werlis. You two take the one on the left and don't be afraid," said Master Drobal to Aarl and Vrenli as he got into the water and sat down on one of the animals. Aarl carefully picked up Werlis and placed him between the dolphin's fin and Master Drobal. He then climbed onto the back of the other dolphin, on which Vrenli had already taken a seat.

"Let me sit by the fin," Aarl asked Vrenli, who then sat down behind Aarl and clutched him tightly from behind.

"Friends, swim as fast as you can. We have an injured person with us. We can't let him drown!" shouted Master Drobal, holding on to the dolphin's fin.

The next moment it dived down and, with two passengers on its back, swam like lightning to the exit of the grotto. From there, it swam two hundred steps upwards and resurfaced in just a few moments.

"Well done, friend," Master Drobal praised the dolphin and stroked its head.

It didn't take long for the second dolphin to appear with Aarl and Vrenli on its back. Together they reached the small beach with their swimming friends, where they went ashore and said goodbye to their helpers.

The Mist Moor

As it was already getting dark, Master Drobal decided that they would spend the night on the beach. Aarl collected dry driftwood that had been washed up on the beach and dried by the hot rays of the southern sun during the day. As he wanted to make sure they had enough wood to keep the fire burning all night, he decided to break off some branches from the small bushes growing on the rock face in front of him.

When he returned to his friends with a considerable amount of firewood, he found Vrenli already asleep next to Werlis. He noticed that Vrenli had spread his cloak from the Dark Forest over Werlis and was now shivering a little himself, due to the cool wind blowing in from the sea. To give Vrenli some warmth, he lit the campfire close to him and hoped that the heat from the flames would be enough to warm him.

"I dread the moment Werlis comes to and realizes the absence of his right forearm," Aarl whispered softly to Master Drobal, who was gazing out into the darkness of the night towards the sea.

"He will learn to deal with it. You have to make him realize that he could easily have died and that he was actually lucky. It will take some time, but I am firmly convinced that he will come to terms with it. I'm more worried about Vrenli. It's not good for him to talk himself into feeling guilty because that can hurt a hundred times more and far longer than Werlis' wound, which will heal. Werlis is young, he still has a long life ahead of him, he will find his way," said Master Drobal to Aarl, who was sitting on the ground next to Werlis.

"Are you really convinced that we can stop Erwight of Entorbis at Ib'Agier?" he asked Master Drobal in a serious voice.

"If Brother Transmudin can stop Omnigo from his plan to bring down the Hall of Lorijan, Princess Lythinda ascends her father's throne, Gorathdin comes to Ib'Agier with an army, Manamii and Wahmubu bring their warriors from Desert of DeShadin and we get the help of the elves from the Glorious Valley, then we have a good chance that Erwight of Entorbis' forces can be defeated at the gates of Ib'Agier. Let's hope for the best," he replied to Aarl.

"Werlis' wound must be treated in the village of the Raging Hordes of the East. It's a five-day march from there to the Glorious Valley, and after that it will take us at least another twelve days to reach Ib'Agier. We will be on the road for more than three weeks and we don't know whether our friends have been successful. Is there really no way to take the air route?" Aarl wanted to know from Master Drobal.

"Haldakies are beings from another world, Aarl, and without my staff, which is charged with the energy of the crystal ball from Horunguth Island, I have no way of summoning a haldakie. We have no choice but to walk, at least as far as the Glorious Valley. There I can contact my two brothers in the tower and ask them to

472

send two haldakies to the Glorious Valley," said Master Drobal as Aarl threw some dried branches into the fire and then lay down next to Werlis.

The three friends were woken from their sleep several times during the night by Werlis' cries of pain. Before the morning dawned, Werlis developed a severe fever. He was sweating so much that his clothes were soaked in sweat. The moist compresses that Master Drobal put on him to bring down the fever only helped a little.

"Why don't we take Werlis to Irkaar? That's only one or maybe two days' journey away?" Aarl asked Master Drobal.

"I've already thought about that possibility. But going to Irkaar is too dangerous. Erwight of Entorbis' henchmen are there," replied Master Drobal.

"I could go to Irkaar alone and get a healer," Aarl suggested.

"No. It is and remains too risky. We can't trust anyone in Irkaar," Master Drobal replied emphatically.

"We have to head north," he added.

"Come on Vrenli, let's build a stretcher for Werlis with the driftwood!" called Aarl to Vrenli, who was still sitting by the fire with Werlis.

When the stretcher was finished, the four of them headed north. They marched through the coastal region with its low vegetation until dusk. Master Drobal kept applying wet compresses to Werlis to bring down the fever as best he could.

On the morning of the third day of their journey, which passed without any particular incident, they crossed a sparse forest which, to their disappointment, ended at a high rock face. Aarl and Vrenli tried to go around the rock face in both directions without success.

Werlis was running a very high temperature and the bumpy journey on the stretcher had not necessarily helped his recovery. He was writhing in increasing pain. Master Drobal then decided to take a break.

"I fear that Werlis is no longer able to continue the journey. He really needs to rest. I'm worried whether he'll even make it to the Raging Hordes. And we don't have time to find another way," Master Drobal said worriedly and put the stretcher down together with Aarl.

All three stared silently at the steep rock face and then at Werlis.

"I will go to the village of the Raging Hordes alone," Vrenli finally said.

However, as he looked around, he realized that he didn't know the area he was in at all. He had no idea where exactly the barbarian village was.

"I'll go with you Vrenli," announced Aarl who looked at Master Drobal expectantly.

"Go, friends, I will wait for you here with Werlis," Master Drobal said approvingly. He sat down next to Werlis, placed his hand on his forehead and began to sing a song softly. It seemed that the singing calmed Werlis down a bit.

Vrenli and Aarl climbed up the rock face and, once at the top, headed north-east. The path through the low-growing forest with its shrubs, bushes and thorny plants was arduous and their progress slow.

"We've been traveling for some time now, but there's no sign of a barbarian settlement. I doubt that they live anywhere here in this low-growing forest," Vrenli remarked and followed Aarl, who climbed through a thorn hedge.

"I've never been to the village of the Raging Hordes of the East myself," Aarl confessed.

"I only know from stories that they are said to live north of the plain, before the entrance to the valley that leads to the realm of the Queen of the Elves," he added.

To reassure Vrenli, he began to walk east.

"When we reach that level, it shouldn't be far away," he said.

After a while, they reached a mixed forest, which they were able to cross quicker. As the forest thinned out and they reached its end, they could see the wide plain where the entrance to the Glorious Valley was located.

Wide meadows overgrown with colorful flowers lay before them. The light wind that blew here caused the tall grasses to undulate.

A flowery smell surrounded them.

"Like a green sea!" said Vrenli, whose mood brightened a little at the sight of the plain.

"Are those tents back there on the horizon?" he asked Aarl, pointing east with his hand.

"Tents?" Aarl repeated.

"I think they're tents," confirmed Vrenli, who took a few steps back into the forest and climbed a beech tree to get a better view.

"Tents! They are tents!" cheered Vrenli and climbed back down the tree.

"The Raging Hordes of the East!" he shouted delightedly and began to run towards the tents.

"Wait!" Aarl called after him.

Vrenli stopped and questioningly looked at him.

"What is it?" he wanted to know.

"I hardly think the tents are those of the barbarians. Barbarians don't live in tents," said Aarl.

"Maybe it's an outpost, or maybe they're going to Ib'Agier to help King Agnulix," Vrenli replied.

Aarl brushed aside Vrenli's statement with his hand.

"The village of the Raging Hordes is somewhere north of here," Aarl said, pointing north with his hand.

"Here somewhere in the woods," he added.

"But whose tents are those then? Maybe they belong to the elves?" Vrenli wondered.

"That could well be the case. Maybe they've set up guard posts on the plain because of the attack on Ib'Agier," Aarl pondered.

"Let's go over and ask them for help," suggested Vrenli.

"We'd better be careful," replied Aarl who lay down on the grass and, followed by Vrenli, began to crawl towards the tents.

Every few paces he stuck his head out of the tall grass to estimate their distance from the tents.

"What's that stench?" asked Vrenli, holding his nose due to the disgusting smell the wind was blowing in their direction.

Aarl sniffed.

"Ogres. Damn!" he whispered, signaling Vrenli to stay down and keep quiet.

He carefully lifted his head out of the grass. There were a good fifteen tents in front of them and he could see two ugly ogres, probably acting as sentries, a little less than forty paces ahead of him.

A stranger, who was clearly not an ogre, approached the two guards and began to converse with them. Aarl could not hear what they were saying, but when the figure took a few steps in his direction, stopped and looked out over the plain, Aarl recognized a mist elf, his head bald. He was clad in black leather and wore a gray cloak. He held his bone bow firmly in his right hand and scanned the plain with his red eyes.

The hairless head of the mist elf repeatedly swiveled from south to east and then north. He remained in the same place for some time. Finally, he took an arrow from the braided quiver on his back and pointed the tip north. The two ogres standing next to him, armed with large spiked clubs and shields, grunted as they looked intently to the north.

The mist elf talked to the two guards for a while and then went back to the tents.

"The mist elves have led a troop of ogres through Mist Moor to Wetherid," Aarl said to Vrenli.

"Mist Moor?" Vrenli inquired.

"Mist Moor lies in Fallgar. A vast bog surrounded by a constant dense fog. It borders the foothills of Ib'Agier and the southern mountains that surround the Glorious Valley to the southeast.

Constant darkness reigns there. A place avoided even by the peoples of Fallgar. It would be impossible to lead an army through Mist Moor, but it seems feasible for a small force like the ogres before us," Aarl told Vrenli, who looked at him, worried.

"They're blocking access to the Glorious Valley. But let's think about how we can get past them unseen later. Think of Werlis. We have to find the barbarians' village," said Vrenli and headed north through the undergrowth ahead of them.

"You're right, we should hurry," Aarl agreed and followed Vrenli through the mixed forest that lay ahead of them.

It wasn't very long before they had left the mixed forest behind them and arrived at a small clearing. A dense coniferous forest spread out on the other side, which they entered and continued north. Fallen trees indicated the nearby village of the barbarians.

Two wolfhounds guarding the area around the village quickly tracked down Vrenli and Aarl and began to howl loudly. A group of barbarians felling wood nearby with their heavy axes became aware of the intruders.

Vrenli, who was standing with his back against the trunk of a fir tree, drew his short sword.

"Back off!" he shouted at the two wolfhounds and let his short sword glide through the air. The wolfhounds, however, were not afraid of Vrenli's movements and growled menacingly at him. Aarl slowly picked up a broken branch from the ground and drew their attention to himself.

"Come on, you beasts!" he shouted, holding out the branch as the group of barbarians suddenly emerged from behind the surrounding trees.

"What are you doing here? This is our land, get out!" one of the barbarians snapped at the two.

"We're friends of Erik," said Vrenli, who was still standing with his back against the fir tree.

"An Abkether and a southerner? I doubt it, but it's not up to me to decide. Follow me!" the barbarian growled and called the two wolfhounds back.

Vrenli and Aarl now walked to the wooden gate of the fortified village, accompanied by the barbarians and their wolfhounds, who were still growling at Vrenli.

"Looks just like Erik's village," Aarl noted.

"All of us Northmen's villages look like this," the barbarian grumbled and walked to the village square, where there was also a main house.

"Wait here!" he ordered Vrenli and Aarl.

Two of the woodcutters who had entered the village with them guarded them. It took a while before the door to the main house finally opened and a tall, muscular, somewhat aged barbarian stepped out.

"Erik?" marveled Aarl, who stood open-mouthed as he saw someone who was the spitting image of Erik.

"I am Warwik, leader of the Raging Hordes of the East," the barbarian replied in a strong voice.

"Erik is my brother," he added.

"You look very much like him," Vrenli noted.

"That may be so, and now tell me what you want here," Warwik grumbled.

"My name is Vrenli and I come from Abketh. This here is my friend Aarl from the small fishing village near Irkaar. We need your help. We are not alone, two other friends of mine are southwest of here. One of them has a high fever and is unconscious. We need your help. Please, surely you have a healer in the village," Vrenli asked urgently.

"What do I care about your friends? We have our own problems. My scouts reported a troop of ogres and mist elves coming through Mist Moor from Fallgar. I can't spare any of my men, let alone our healer. Now leave my village!" Warwik instructed them firmly.

Vrenli dug the ring Gorathdin had given him out of his pocket and lifted it up in front of him.

"How did you get hold of my brother's ring?" Warwik wanted to know, immediately recognizing the ring in Vrenli's hand.

"My friend Gorathdin of the Forest received it from Erik as a token of friendship. Gorathdin entrusted it to me. He told me that if I needed help from the Raging Hordes of the East, I should show you this ring," Vrenli replied.

Warwik stared at the ring for a few moments without saying a word. He turned around and walked back to the main house, where he stopped for a moment in the entrance.

"Alright, I'll help you," he agreed and ordered one of the barbarians standing guard outside the main house to send three men and the healer with the two strangers.

"Take three wolfhounds with you. You might run into ogres or mist elves," Warwik ordered the barbarian and was about to go into the main house when Aarl asked him to wait.

"We saw a troop of ogres and mist elves on our way here," Aarl said to Warwik, who turned and walked towards him.

"Where and how many?" Warwik wanted to know.

"I can take you there," Aarl offered.

"And what about the Abkether's injured friend?" Warwik asked.

"Vrenli will find his way back without me," replied Aarl, looking Vrenli firmly in the eyes.

Vrenli understood that he had to seize the chance to drive the ogres and mist elves from the plain.

"Yes, of course I can find my way without Aarl," said Vrenli to Warwik, who called another barbarian to him.

"Four men, three wolfhounds and the healer will accompany the Abkether south," he told him and asked Aarl to come into the main house.

"Take ropes with you!" he shouted to the barbarians standing with Vrenli in the village square and closed the door behind Aarl.

Warwik offered Aarl a seat at the large table in the middle of the main house and poured him and himself a cup of honey wine.

"Where exactly did you see the ogres and mist elves?" asked Warwik, taking a big sip from his mug.

"Their tents are on the plain that sits before the entrance to the Glorious Valley," Aarl replied and took a sip of the honey wine.

"Were you able to see how many of them are there?" Warwik inquired further.

"I could count fifteen tents, but I don't know how many ogres and mist elves are there," replied Aarl.

"Fifteen, you said," Warwik remarked, and while he was thinking, he drank more honey wine.

"Then there are at least fifty ogres and who knows how many mist elves," he concluded after a while.

"I wonder what they're up to," Warwik mused.

Aarl wondered whether he should tell Warwik about the events and their plans but decided to only tell him about the Erwight of Entorbis' army at the gates of Ib'Agier.

"Erwight of Entorbis, you say?" Warwik repeated.

"Yes, an army of the Shadow Lord," replied Aarl, who knew that an alliance between the two was under discussion.

"Your brother Erik did not enter into the alliance," Aarl finally spoke and waited for Warwik's reaction.

"What do you know about it?" Warwik asked in a sharp tone.

"Well, as far as I know, Erik has decided to enter into an alliance with King Grandhold," Aarl announced, concealing the king's death.

"Grandhold? Does he actually know what he wants?" Warwik grumbled and drank his cup empty.

"Listen to me!" Warwik urged Aarl.

"I will ride to my brother to get more men and if what you told me is a lie, then you can start praying, if you southerners do that at all," Warwik warned with a serious face.

He threw a fur coat over his shoulders and left the main house.

"Make sure the southerner stays in the village," he ordered the two guards outside the door of the main house and beckoned several men standing in the village square to join him.

"We're riding to Erik, bring me a horse!" he shouted and left the village a little later with ten heavily armed men.

Aarl sat at the large table in the main house for a while longer and drank another mug of honey wine. A barbarian with two braided pigtails hanging down the left and right of his head opened the door and led Aarl to his quarters, which was a small hut right in the village square.

"Warwik does not want you to leave the village before he returns," the barbarian spoke and gave Aarl a fur blanket for the night.

Although it was still daylight, Aarl lay down on the fur blanket he had previously spread out on the wooden frame that looked like a bed and fell asleep after a while.

For two days, Aarl had remained more-or-less a prisoner in the village. When he awoke one morning, he was filled with great joy at the sight of Master Drobal, who opened the door and approached his bed.

"How long have you been here?" asked Aarl, stretching as he stood up from the wooden frame.

"We arrived last night," replied Master Drobal.

"Last night?" Aarl repeated.

"Yes. Seems you had some sleep to catch up on," Master Drobal replied and smiled.

"Are Vrenli and Werlis all right?" Aarl wanted to know.

"Well, Vrenli is feeling very guilty and the barbarian healer is looking after Werlis. He is still unconscious, but the healer said that he will wake up in a few days. Vrenli has stayed with Werlis in the healer's hut," said Master Drobal.

"A few days until he wakes up? We don't have that much time," remarked Aarl.

"I know. We will travel to the Glorious Valley without him," replied Master Drobal.

"Does Vrenli know about it yet?" asked Aarl.

"No, not yet. I want him to get a good night's sleep before we set off," revealed Master Drobal.

"Are you sure the healer knows what he's doing? I mean, they're barbarians," doubted Aarl.

"I think that's why he knows what to do. He should have experience with severed limbs," said Master Drobal, who managed to keep a smile on his face despite the seriousness of the situation.

"Warwik rode to his brother in the west to get reinforcements and confirm the truth of my story," Aarl said.

"You didn't tell him anything, did you?" Master Drobal probed.

"Of course not. I only told him that Erik wanted to form an alliance with King Grandhold," Aarl replied.

"Then it's all right," Master Drobal said reassuringly.

"Vrenli told me about the ogres and mist elves. It's a mystery to me how they were able to lead the fat and clumsy ogres through Mist Moor," Master Drobal said to Aarl, to which he just shrugged his shoulders.

"If Erik confirms to his brother what I have told him and gives him some men as reinforcements, then we can drive them off the plain. Our path to the Glorious Valley would then be clear," said Aarl, to which Master Drobal nodded in agreement.

"If we're lucky, we can be in the City in the Trees, or rather the Glorious Valley as you call it, in three to four days. There I can make contact with the other mages. I need to know what is going on in Wetherid and especially in Ib'Agier," said Master Drobal with a serious face.

Several successive, dull and loud knocking noises coming from a hollowed-out tree trunk announced Warwik's return.

Master Drobal and Aarl left the hut and went out into the village square. Warwik returned to his village with a good hundred heavily armed horsemen. When he saw Master Drobal and Aarl, he rode slowly towards them and dismounted his horse.

"You have told the truth, Aarl. Even if not the whole truth," Warwik said to Aarl and looked him firmly in the eyes.

"What do you mean?" Aarl wanted to know.

"My brother Erik has made an alliance with the Queen of Astinhod, but you have kept the death of King Grandhold from me," Warwik grumbled, his face brightening only a moment later.

"The clan of the Raging Hordes of the East supports the alliance that Erik has made with the Queen of Astinhod!" he loudly shouted, whereupon the barbarians who had gathered in the village square began to roar.

Master Drobal and Aarl were both delighted and reassured when they heard the word queen.

"They've done it!" Master Drobal said happily.

"Why didn't Erik come with you?" Aarl asked.

"An officer of the queen came to my brother's village a day ago and asked him for support against the enemy at the gates of Ib'Agier. My brother set out with two hundred and fifty men to do his part for the alliance," Warwik replied, taking his war axe from its holder on his horse's saddle and standing in the middle of the village square.

"Get ready, men. We'll set off as quickly as possible to drive the ogres and mist elves from the border of our land, which the Queen of Astinhod officially granted us!" Warwik shouted, swinging his heavy axe through the air.

The village square began to shake as the assembled barbarians stomped their feet on the ground.

"It's time to tell Vrenli that we're leaving for the Glorious Valley without Werlis," said Master Drobal and, followed by Aarl, went to the healer's hut.

"We can't just leave him here!" protested Vrenli when Master Drobal told him his decision.

483

"You must understand. He is not in a position to undertake such a long journey," Master Drobal said, placing his hand on Vrenli's shoulder.

"Remember our mission. He will be well looked after here in the village; the barbarians have made an alliance with the Queen of Astinhod," he added.

"With the queen? Does that mean that Gorathdin and Princess Lythinda were successful?" Vrenli inquired, a spark of hope in his eyes.

"I guess that's what it means," Master Drobal confirmed, smiling gently.

"Come on now. It's time. Warwik has returned with reinforcements from his brother to drive the ogres and mist elves from the plain," Aarl said to Vrenli, who kissed Werlis on the forehead in farewell and said goodbye to the healer.

With a heavy heart, he followed Master Drobal and Aarl to the village square, where Warwik and his men were preparing for the upcoming battle.

"We don't have any horses for you, but if you want you can ride behind my riders, or you can join the foot troop," Warwik offered the three of them.

"We will join the foot troop," replied Master Drobal, and he set off with Vrenli and Aarl to the village gate, where the foot troop had already gathered.

"Avoid interfering in the fighting. We have more important things to do than fight a troop of ogres and mist elves," Master Drobal whispered to his friends as the barbarians set off.

Warwik led his three hundred and fifty men through the forest to the south and from there onto the plain where the enemy had pitched their tents. The two ogres standing guard north of the tent camp blinked in disbelief as they saw the barbarians and two packs of wolfhounds charging out of the forest towards them, bellowing war cries and baring their teeth.

"Barbarians!" echoed through the plain.

The mist elves immediately positioned themselves on the north side of the camp and fired their arrows at the approaching horde of barbarians. Some of Warwik's and Erik's men were hit by the arrows. Warwik signaled his men to halt.

"Send the wolfhounds ahead!" he ordered, whereupon the two packs rushed towards the mist elves.

They were able to kill some of the wolfhounds before they even reached them. But the more than ten survivors pounced on their victims and mauled several of them in a matter of moments.

A handful of mist elves drew their curved daggers and faced the wolves. The barbarians, who were no longer under arrow fire, spurred their horses on. Shouts and the clanging of steel on steel echoed through the plain. The camp was overrun by the Raging Hordes. It took three barbarians each to kill one of the huge hulks of flesh wielding heavy spiked clubs with their long, muscular arms. However, the barbarians outnumbered them and so the battle did not last long. The attackers' losses were low, but the enemy was completely destroyed.

Warwik instructed his men to burn the tents and bodies of the enemy. The thick, black smoke rising into the sky could be seen from afar, bearing witness to Warwik's victory over the invaders from Fallgar. The barbarians collected all the usable weapons that lay scattered in the grass around the battlefield.

Warwik stood in front of the blazing fire as Master Drobal, followed by Vrenli and Aarl, walked towards him.

"You have done Wetherid a great service," praised Master Drobal and bowed briefly to Warwik.

"As advisor to the royal house of Astinhod, I ask you to guard the border to Mist Moor. Do not allow anyone from the Moor to enter Wetherid. Build ramparts. Secure the border to Mist Moor," Master Drobal urged him.

"We will do our best, mage," Warwik replied. He called his men over and told them that from then on, the Raging Hordes of the East would be the guardians of the border to the Mist Moor.

Warwik then issued instructions for the construction of an outpost.

"I want a hundred men to guard the outpost at all times," he ordered his men.

Master Drobal, Vrenli and Aarl thanked Warwik for the horses he had given them, for his help and for letting Werlis stay with them. They told him that their journey would take them to the Glorious Valley and that they would be back in a few days.

Warwik in turn, followed by his warriors, settled down on the grass and began to draw lots for the first hundred men who were to be stationed on the border for two months.

Chapter 4

The Glorious Valley

The next morning, Master Drobal, Vrenli and Aarl rode south across the plain, where two high mountain ranges formed the entrance to the Glorious Valley. The beauty of the plain, overgrown with colorful flowers and tall, diverse grasses, which presented its full splendor of color in the light of the sun, made the three quickly forget the battle with the ogres and mist elves.

The two mountain ranges that lay to the west and east in front of them grew larger the closer they rode towards them. The gentle hills at the foot of the mountains grew into high rock faces.

The entrance to the valley that opened up before them was no wider than a thousand paces. The sparse rays of sunlight that found their way down turned the green-covered path into a barren gravel path of boulders and stones that had fallen from the rock faces over time. They rode along the path through a ravine for some time, when they finally noticed that the ground beneath their horses' hooves was becoming loamy and covered with scattered tufts of grass and moss. They approached the forest that bordered the entrance to the valley.

A sudden gust of wind from the inside of the valley caused the hoods that Vrenli and Aarl had pulled over their heads for protection to blow backwards. Master Drobal looked up the rock faces, now hundreds of steps high, paused for a moment and then turned his gaze towards the forest they had been riding towards for hours.

"Let's camp here for the night. The horses are tired and so am I," suggested Master Drobal as he led his horse to a mighty, solitary oak tree.

487

Aarl got off his horse and then helped Vrenli dismount. They both searched the surrounding area for firewood while Master Drobal unrolled the thick furs they had received from Warwik. They talked for some time around the fire that Aarl lit before they gave in to their deep-seated tiredness and fell asleep.

The next morning, Aarl noticed a suspicious noise coming from the forest.

"Our arrival has been noticed," he pointed out to his two friends and plucked at Master Drobal's tunic.

"That's what I thought. Nothing and no one escapes the elves from the Glorious Valley," replied Master Drobal in a sleepy voice.

"Is there still a long way to go?" Vrenli wanted to know.

"We have to follow the path that leads through this forest to a large clearing. Behind the clearing is a small lake that divides the valley in two. We have to leave our horses there. Once we cross the lake, it is not far to the city of the elves," replied Master Drobal.

"If we hurry, we can be at the lake before dusk," he added, rolling up his coat and untying his horse. Vrenli and Aarl packed their things and got on Aarl's horse together.

They then followed the path that led through a dense mixed forest. After covering about half the distance to the lake, they decided to take a short break.

Aarl opened the bag of rations he received from the barbarians for the march. To Vrenli's disappointment, there was only dried meat and a loaf of bread left in the bag.

"I can't see any more dried meat," Vrenli confessed and left the path, walking a few paces into the forest.

"Where are you going?" Aarl wanted to know, who had sat down on a stone by the side of the path and started to eat.

"I'm collecting berries," replied Vrenli, bending down, picking some of the dark blue wild berries and eating them straight away.

They talked for some time until Master Drobal finally gave the signal to leave.

As they rode along the narrow path, Vrenli often looked up into the treetops. It seemed to him as if they were being followed by a shadow that jumped from treetop to treetop.

"I don't think we're alone," whispered Vrenli to Master Drobal and Aarl.

"A scout of the elves. He has been following us since we entered the gorge from the plain," explained Master Drobal.

As the three of them stepped out of the forest into the clearing, they looked out over the wide lake that stretched across the valley from the mountain range in the north to the mountain range in the south.

Dusk was falling.

The three friends hurried and arrived on the western shore of the lake before nightfall.

Aarl, together with Vrenli, began to search for dry firewood under the trees that stood scattered along the lakeshore, while Master Drobal went to the small wooden footbridge that reached a few paces into the lake. Next to the jetty was a raft attached to a rope that reached to the other side of the lake.

"We'll cross the lake on this raft tomorrow!" Master Drobal called to Aarl and Vrenli, who returned with a considerable amount of firewood.

While Aarl lit a fire, Vrenli joined Master Drobal on the jetty and looked out over the lake.

"What is that strange, violet-colored light glowing up the entire forest at the other end of the lake shore?" Vrenli asked Master Drobal.

"This forest is home to the elves of the Glorious Valley. In its center is their city. The purple light you see comes from the crystals the elves use for light. If you look closely, you can see that it shines high up into the sky. That is the tree of the Queen of the Elves," Master Drobal explained to his little friend.

"Now that you've said it, I can see it," said Vrenli, looking intently towards the middle of the forest in front of him.

When Vrenli and Master Drobal returned to the campfire, Aarl was already asleep on the ground.

"We should get some sleep too," said Master Drobal to Vrenli, and he lay down on the ground next to the fire, where he unrolled his fur. Vrenli stayed awake for a while longer. His thoughts were with Werlis and as the flames of the fire grew smaller, he threw some branches into it and lay down on his fur on the ground next to Aarl and Master Drobal.

When Vrenli opened his eyes in the morning and looked towards the lakeshore, he saw Aarl and Master Drobal already standing on the raft next to the small jetty.

"Hello! Wait for me!" he called to the two of them, stood up and walked over to the raft, which Aarl and Master Drobal were checking for its buoyancy and stability. After Vrenli had taken a seat on the raft, Aarl stood on the side of the raft facing the water and began to rock, shifting his weight from right to left. With a yell, Master Drobal fell off the raft into the water, whereupon Vrenli and Aarl began to laugh out loud.

"You could help me instead of laughing your heads off!" Master Drobal shouted and then laughed heartily himself.

As he tried to pull himself out of the water and onto the raft, the raft began to rock violently again and this time Vrenli and Aarl fell into the water together.

The three of them began to splash each other with water like children. Aarl dived under the raft to push Vrenli under the surface from behind.

"The pages of the book!" Master Drobal said, and immediately swam the few paces to the lakeshore, where he jumped out of the water, threw his soaked bag on the ground and knelt down.

He opened the bag, took out a cylindrical object and carefully unscrewed the lid.

"Everything's all right. They're dry!" Master Drobal called to Vrenli and Aarl, who had pulled themselves onto the raft.

"Let's set off," Aarl said to Master Drobal, who climbed onto the raft soaking wet. Slowly, Aarl and Vrenli pulled on one of the two ropes together and the raft moved towards the middle of the lake. It took them some effort to get to the middle, but suddenly, when they got there, the raft began to move much faster towards the opposite shore of the lake.

"Have you noticed that too?" Vrenli wanted to know.

"Yes, we're speeding up," replied Aarl, and he let go of the rope, but the raft was still moving towards the lakeshore at the same speed.

When Vrenli also let go of the rope and the raft continued to move forward, they looked at each other confused.

"Look, there are elves on the lake shore pulling on the rope," Master Drobal recognized and pointed in front of him, where three elves were pulling on a rope and waving to them.

"Manda Goij!" one of the three elves called out to them as the raft docked at the jetty.

"Manda Goij!" replied Master Drobal.

The three elves bowed to him, which Master Drobal returned.

"What does Manda Goij mean?" Vrenli wanted to know from Master Drobal.

"It's elvish language and means 'Welcome'," he explained, whereupon Vrenli and Aarl greeted the elves with a Manda Goij and bowed to them.

Vrenli looked closely at the three elves and noticed that they were slightly different from the elves in the Dark Forest. Their eyes did not shine like the dark green of Gorathdin's or like the red of the mist elves' Vrenli had seen on the plain before the valley entrance. Their eyes shone with a violet light.

He also noticed that all three elves had snow-white hair styled in a plait that reached down to their backs. Their skin was also much lighter than that of the rangers. When Vrenli took a closer look, he noticed that their skin shimmered slightly golden. Silver rings shone on their fingers and each of them wore a silver necklace, from which hung a pendant with a strange symbol that Vrenli could not interpret.

The hilts of their scimitar daggers were studded with purple crystals and the blades gleamed silver. One of the three elves had a bow the size of an Abkether slung over his shoulder. When Vrenli saw the silver arrows in his quiver, he was amazed.

"Did you see that? They have silver arrows," Vrenli whispered to Aarl.

"That's silverwood from the silver tree, Vrenli," explained the elf, who had not missed Vrenli's remark thanks to his keen hearing.

"How do you know my name?" Vrenli asked him in astonishment. But the elf just looked at him with his violet eyes and smiled silently.

"Let's set off. The queen is waiting for you," he finally said and went ahead of them into the adjacent forest, which was clearly no ordinary forest.

Vrenli saw trees that he had never seen before in his life. Mighty oaks towered high into the sky, their trunks the diameter of an Abkethian house. Bushes and shrubs with silvery leaves and forest flowers that shone in a variety of colors grew on the forest floor. Some of them were as tall as Aarl, with petals that looked like bells. When Vrenli touched one of them, a soft chime sounded.

Lianas with white flowers hung from the trees and when Aarl accidentally brushed against one, hundreds of white butterflies flew into the air. Wild berries the size of a human hand grew on bushes.

Vrenli couldn't resist and picked one of the berries. "I hope these are safe to eat," said Vrenli, whereupon one of the elves nodded, picked a berry himself and ate it with relish.

Vrenli followed his example.

The fruity, sweet juice of the berry was the juiciest Vrenli had ever tasted.

"They're fantastic!" exclaimed Vrenli enthusiastically, picking another berry and putting it in his bag.

"For later," he said, to which the elves smiled at him.

A doe came out from behind the trees with her fawn and walked past them without fear. When Vrenli turned around, he noticed that the two deer were even following them for a few steps, completely unafraid. A pair of birds flew over their heads and when one of the elves began to sing, the birds flew towards him and perched on each of his shoulders, accompanying his song with their singing.

"What a peaceful place," thought Vrenli, but his contentment was interrupted by a pack of wild boars appearing on the path in front of them with their young.

Vrenli was about to draw his short sword when one of the elves placed his hand on the hilt.

"You don't have to worry," the elf spoke reassuringly as he walked up to the boars, picked up one of the newborns and stroked its little head gently.

"What a strange place," muttered Vrenli, who was surprised that the wild boars had not attacked them.

"There is no danger for you in the Glorious Valley," one of the elves explained to the three.

His gentle smile suddenly disappeared as a black crow flew over their heads.

"Kondijr Maasaga," whispered one of the elves, whereupon Master Drobal immediately searched the treetops.

"What was that?" asked Vrenli.

"Just a crow," Master Drobal placated, reaching into the void with his right hand.

"Oh, I forgot. Force of habit," he said, trying to smile.

Vrenli knew that he was hiding something from him, but as they were not alone, he refrained from questioning him about the crow.

The three friends followed the elves through the forest for some time when they suddenly heard a voice above their heads.

"Manda Goij!" the voice called, loud and friendly.

Vrenli and Aarl looked up into the treetops, where several elves were standing on wooden platforms connected by rope bridges.

"A sentry," explained one of the elves, noticing the question on the tip of Vrenli's tongue.

A few hundred paces after the guard post, they passed a pond surrounded by white marble sculptures.

"Drink up if you're thirsty," one of the elves urged the three friends.

Master Drobal, followed by Aarl and Vrenli, went to the pond illuminated by a violet-colored light radiating from a crystal in the water. Master Drobal put his hands together and filled them with water.

"Not everyone is allowed to drink the water of the elves," he remarked and carefully let the water flow into his mouth.

"Loomar jakodji!" said one of the elves.

"Loomar jakodji!" Master Drobal replied with a smile and bowed.

"Drink up, friends! The water of the elves is said to prolong life. Loomar jakodji. Here's to a long life!" said Master Drobal to Vrenli and Aarl, who then drank the water.

Refreshed, they followed the three elves along a path paved with white marble blocks, next to which, about every twenty steps, stood elaborately crafted lanterns one both sides, in which warm purple crystals were attached. Artfully carved sculptures made of white stone stood between the adjacent trees and bushes. The three followed the elves through a large glass archway on which red and white roses bloomed.

"Are there no houses here?" Vrenli asked Master Drobal, who then pointed ahead with his hand.

Vrenli remained standing with his mouth open. He gazed at an architectural marvel. A tree so tall that it seemed to reach into the sky, and whose trunk had a diameter the size of the village of Abketh, stood before him. The immensely thick branches contained storeys and terraces of white stone, glass and wood.

Large archways in the tree trunk, decorated with glass and silver, suggested that there were rooms behind them.

A curved glass staircase lit by lanterns led up from the foot of the tree trunk. It was guarded by elven warriors dressed in silver armor and carrying long, silver lances and large, oval, silver shields.

Vrenli, Aarl and Master Drobal walked slowly up the wide glass staircase, led by the three elves. When they were close enough to one of the guards, Vrenli could see the thin glass bow, similar in design to his own, on the elven warrior's back. Next to the glass bow hung a glass quiver containing silver arrows. When Vrenli took a step towards the elven warrior, Master Drobal immediately pulled him back by his cloak and urged him to continue. The higher they followed the glass staircase, they could see more of the Glorious Valley and when they reached the top, they could even see the gorge far ahead that they had entered the valley through.

Aarl was just leaning over the edge of the glass staircase to reach for one of the fine silver branches hanging down from above when he almost lost his balance.

"Take care!" one of the elves warned and smiled.

They followed the elves up the glass staircase to a plateau of white stone. On the opposite side was a large oval-shaped entrance that led into the interior of the tree. Vrenli was fascinated by the way the white stone archway was carved into the tree as he walked underneath it.

A large hall filled with a warm, purple light opened up before them. The walls were covered with a dark, shiny varnish, the color of which Vrenli could not make out exactly because of the violet light. Elven warriors stood lined up against the dark wall around the hall. All the furniture inside the tree was made of precious woods, only the throne of the Queen of the Elves was made of Living Glass. Glass from which small, thin branches sprouted green leaves. Vrenli was overwhelmed by the interplay between the glass and wood.

When he saw the Queen of the Elves sitting on the throne and smiling gently at him, he burst into tears, touched by the beauty and kindness she radiated. Her slender body was wrapped in a white, silken tunic with silver embroidery. Her snow-white hair reached down to her bare feet on the floor. Her doe eyes, which shone with a violet light, adorned her striking, youthful face.

Vrenli knelt in front of her on the ground covered in fresh leaves.

"Forgive me," he said to her.

No matter how hard he tried to stop his tears, he simply couldn't. Aarl didn't know exactly how to behave, so he knelt next to Vrenli. Master Drobal bowed to the queen and remained standing next to Aarl and Vrenli, looking at her.

"Manda Goij," the queen spoke in a soft, sweet voice that went through Vrenli's bones.

"Manda Goij, Elerionel, Queen of the Elves from the Glorious Valley!" Master Drobal replied to the welcome.

"I can already guess what brings you to me in these dark times. Fallgar is trying to seize Wetherid, as it has done so many times before!" said the queen, looking deep into Master Drobal's eyes.

There were several moments of silence in the Queen's Hall.

"Wetherid and its inhabitants need your help. I have come to ask you for the pages of the book," Master Drobal revealed.

"Why do you think the pages are safer with you than with me in the Glorious Valley?" the queen asked.

"I'm afraid they're not safe here," Master Drobal admitted in a depressed voice.

"Even Erwight of Entorbis' army could not take the Glorious Valley. Tell me, who would have the power to invade my valley and steal the pages of the book?" the queen asked Master Drobal in a serious voice, whereupon he began to tell her about the alliances that Erwight of Entorbis had made with the various peoples of the East and even with some Wetherids.

"The shadow mages have gained power since their last defeat. They managed to seize the souls of their slain opponents," Master Drobal explained seriously and began to tell the queen about all the incidents in Wetherid and the plan of the mages of Horunguth Island.

"I understand," said the queen and stood up from her throne.

"It's late and I need to think about what you've told me. We'll talk more tomorrow," she said in a familiar tone, ending the conversation, and instructing two of the elven women standing next to her at the throne to take the guests to quarters and bid them farewell.

Vrenli's insight

"Don't you find it strange how quickly the queen broke off the conversation?" Vrenli asked Master Drobal and Aarl as they followed the two elven women up a spiral staircase that led from the glass staircase to one of the upper floors where their quarters were located.

Master Drobal did not answer but put a finger over his mouth. Vrenli understood that he did not want to talk about this in the presence of the two elves.

When they arrived at their quarters and the two elves said goodbye to them, Master Drobal waited until the sound of their footsteps had moved away from them. He closed the door behind him, sat down on one of the four beds and answered Vrenli's question.

"As you know, the Book of Wetherid was stolen from the elves a long, long time ago. However, it was found by the humans, who settled in Wetherid much later, in one of the many abandoned dragon caves. The book then remained in their possession for hundreds of years. Although the humans knew that the book must be something special, they were unable to recognize or harness its power, as it was written in the ancient language of Wetherid. It took another three hundred years before a handful of people who had studied the ancient characters for years finally deciphered them and translated them into the current language of Wetherid.

When they realized what the book was about and understood its contents, they decided to entrust it to us mages on Horunguth Island. At the time, we were more than pleased that the book had been found. Our coven had long protected the book from those who craved its power. When the dynasty of Entorbis found out about the book, they tried everything to get hold of it. They formed an alliance with the shadow mages of Fallgar, who are said to have stolen the soul of the black dragons. The rulers of Druhn then joined forces with their new allies against the mages of Horunguth Island. Many of my brothers died trying to protect the book.

The enemy was finally defeated by us, and the five surviving magicians had to find a way to protect the book from misuse. We tried to seal it magically and cast protective spells on it. But all attempts were unsuccessful. The book inexplicably resisted all magic. After much deliberation and weeks of helplessness, one of us suggested that we take the book to an alchemist known throughout Wetherid, your grandfather, Vrenli, and ask him to find a way to protect it at least physically against misuse.

We came to him in Abketh with the craziest and most fantastic ideas, ranging from putting corrosive substances on the cover to trying to shrink the book. Our suggestions were crazy, but the fear that the book could fall into the wrong hands drove us on.

Your grandfather, who had listened to us attentively at the time, just looked at us wordlessly over the edge of his glasses, which he had pushed up to the tip of his nose. He finally shook his head, opened the book and tore out a few pages. Friends, you have to believe me, I wanted to sink into the ground at that moment. All our magic wasn't enough to make the book unusable for the enemy, but an alchemist from a village far in the north of Wetherid, which was barely the size of the castle garden in Astinhod, simply tore a few pages out of the book and looked at me silently," Master Drobal told Vrenli and Aarl, who listened to him attentively.

"In your grandfather's house, Vrenli, a plan was hatched to remove the pages containing the history of the peoples of Wetherid and Fallgar from the book and hide them in five places in Wetherid. Your grandfather, Vrenli, thus became a Keeper of the Book. He asked us to keep the book for a few weeks to study it. We agreed and only found out much later that he had made a copy of it. When we confronted him, however, we understood his arguments. He explained to us that, on the one hand, Wetherid's history had to be preserved for posterity in case the book was stolen and, on the other, that if you were going to remove pages from a book, it was only natural that you should have a complete copy because life doesn't always go according to a preconceived plan. But he emphasized that only the original book retains its magical powers. A transcript, however accurate, could not replicate its power. The original book, with the missing pages, was then returned by us to Horunguth Island, where it was safe for many years until Erwight of Entorbis' father made another attempt to take it. My brothers and I knew that we couldn't do much against the shadow mages' magic without support. We therefore decided that four of us should travel to Astinhod with the book and deliver it to King Grandhold's father. Master Wendur sacrificed himself by defending the tower on Horunguth against the enemy for as long as he could to give us enough time to prepare against the enemy in Astinhod. We were convinced that the king's army would be strong enough with our help. However, we had not expected that the shadow mages would succeed in casting a spell that would allow them to steal the soul of a living being and thereby control its will," Master Drobal continued his story and took a deep breath.

"When I gave the book to the king at the time, I didn't know that he was under the influence of a shadow mage. As a result, Tyrindor of Entorbis managed to take possession of the book. He traveled to Astinhod to have the book presented to him by the king. I can still see it in my mind's eye as he raised the book in the air with both hands and laughed out loud. His laughter was short-lived, however, because when he opened the book, he noticed that some of the pages were missing. When he started shouting in rage at the shadow mages and the king, and the confusion in the throne room was at its height, my brothers and I managed to escape," Master Drobal said.

"I'm sure you know the rest of the story, Vrenli," he added.

"Under the influence of the shadow mages, the armies of the King of Astinhod marched through Wetherid to find the missing pages of the book for Tyrindor of Entorbis," Vrenli replied, nodding.

"What I don't know, however, is how Tyrindor of Entorbis was driven out of Wetherid," Vrenli confessed, looking inquisitively at Master Drobal.

"It was the elves from the Glorious Valley who rushed to aid the other peoples of Wetherid. The elves could not be controlled by the shadow mages. They are different from all other creatures because their souls form a community. An elf from the Glorious Valley does not live for their own goals. They live for the community. They know no greed, envy, pride, lust, gluttony, anger, laziness or murderous desire. Nevertheless, many Knights from Astinhod, as well as elves from the Glorious Valley, died when they clashed at Abketh. The spell of the shadow mages was finally broken when the elves blew their horns and proclaimed the Living Word. The people from Astinhod then came to their senses and realized the extent of their deeds, whereupon their rage against

500

Tyrindor of Entorbis grew immeasurably. Together with the elves from the Glorious Valley and us mages from Horunguth, they then drove Tyrindor's army and the shadow mages out of Wetherid," Master Drobal recounted.

"As I feared that Erwight of Entorbis would also try to take possession of the missing pages when his father Tyrindor died, I made various arrangements with my brothers. At my request, King Grandhold's father appointed me advisor to the royal house. We were in constant contact with the Keepers of the Book, except for you. I don't know how, but your grandfather had managed to, how shall I say, hide you from the other Keepers. No one knew of your existence until Gorathdin of the Forest came to Gwerlit and asked her for the herbs I needed to make the healing potion. Close contact with a Keeper of the Book was necessary to recognize you as such," Master Drobal explained, glancing at Aarl, who only understood half of what Master Drobal was saying and had therefore fallen asleep on his bed.

"I fear that the army Erwight of Entorbis has sent to the gates of Ib'Agier is only the vanguard. We know of the alliances with the undead, mist elves, gray dwarves, ogres, thieves, the lizard creatures from Desert of DeShadin and the underwater creatures from Moorgh. Each of these groups is interested in breaking the alliances between the peoples of Wetherid and Astinhod. They will go to war with Erwight of Entorbis and there will be far more than a thousand of them. I estimate that he will go to Ib'Agier with a force of at least five thousand men, unless he manages to get hold of the missing pages of the book first. Since the pages from Astinhod, Iseran and Irkaar are with us and the pages of the Glorious Valley are with the Queen of the Elves, I fear that we do not have much time left. The greed for wealth, land and power has always driven the Entorbis dynasty," said Master Drobal to Vrenli, who had many questions on his mind.

"The book was stolen from the young man from the Glorious Valley. The elves initially suspected that it had been stolen by Gooters, but it soon turned out that someone else had stolen it. At least that's what I was told. So, who stole the book from the young man?" Vrenli wanted to know from Master Drobal.

"Gooters never existed, and wolves never ruled Wetherid together with the dragons. Gooters are a myth and I can't tell you how this myth crept into Wetherid's history. Dragons, on the other hand, lived in Wetherid and they were indeed the most powerful beings. Omnigo is a living example of this. I didn't understand many parts of the book either, but that's the way it is with books. Who can understand everything as the author or authors of a book meant it at the moment it was written," Master Drobal replied and gently smiled.

"They say that the pages of the book fill themselves. Is that true?" Vrenli wanted to know.

"I'm afraid this is a misunderstanding. The Keepers have always seen it as their duty to write down the incidents and events that took place in Wetherid in the Book. You have to interpret the old language correctly. The book 'fills itself' through the events that take place in Wetherid. It was therefore not necessary to make up a story and write it down in the book, at least that was never the author's intention. Of course there are exceptions, the Gooters for example. Nobody today can say for sure what the author really had in mind when he wrote about the Gooters in the book," explained Master Drobal.

"By the author, do you mean the creator of the world and the stars?" Vrenli asked.

"According to tradition, the Father sent his word into the world. We know that the book was written in the old language, which was elven," replied Master Drobal.

"Why do people talk about the Word coming to life? How can a word live?" Vrenli asked inquisitively.

"Because the Word was written down and also spread orally, it reached many in Wetherid and many a person aligned their life with the Word. That is how it came to life. Of course, it is not just a word. What the Father said contains many words. Thousands, even thousands upon thousands," replied Master Drobal.

"So, you believe in a creator? The Father?" Vrenli continued to ask.

"I am a magician and I have been given many gifts. I can influence the elements. Travel long distances in a matter of moments. I am old, very old, so old that I was there when the Father sent his youth to Wetherid," Master Drobal explained and held out his hand. A bright blue light radiated from the diamond-shaped mark on his forehead.

Vrenli was startled for a moment, but when Master Drobal asked him to reach into the warm blue light, he calmed down again.

"What exactly is the power of the book or the magic that it talks about?" Vrenli inquired further.

"Well, it's a fact that there are some spells in the book that are very powerful. Anyone who has a flair for magic or is a mage themselves will recognize this when they hold the book in their hands. These spells are referred to by some as the magic of the elves and have always been a thorn in the side of anyone hostile to Wetherid. The book also holds another power, and I dare say that this power is more powerful than anything else," replied Master Drobal.

"What power do you mean?" Vrenli asked.

"You'll soon find out for yourself," replied Master Drobal, who noticed that Vrenli was not satisfied with this answer.

"But if everything you've told me is true, why did I see everything completely different in my dreams?" Vrenli continued to ask.

"Well, first of all, dreams are dreams. They certainly contain messages, but you have to interpret them correctly. How often can you realize when you are awake, albeit usually too late, that things are not always what they appear to be and in dreams this happens even more often," replied Master Drobal.

"There's one more thing I'd like to know. Why didn't the elves try to get the book back from the humans?" asked Vrenli.

"That's a fair question, but only the queen knows the answer. You can ask her yourself tomorrow. It's late, we should make sure we get some sleep before we head back to the Raging Hordes and then on to Ib'Agier," said Master Drobal, lying down and closing his eyes. Vrenli gazed out the window for a while, from where he could see the valley in the twilight. He then tucked Aarl in, lay down in the empty bed and fell asleep.

When Vrenli and Aarl woke up the next morning, the bed Master Drobal was sleeping in was already empty.

"Come on, let's go and find Master Drobal," suggested Vrenli, and he left the quarters with Aarl.

On their way to the throne room, they met one of the elves who had led them from the river into the city. He wished them a good morning and told them that Master Drobal was taking a walk with the queen and that they should wait for him in the throne room, where there was something for them to eat.

Vrenli and Aarl made their way inside the tree, where the two elven women who brought them to their quarters last night approached them and led them to one of the glass tables, where the two took their seats. They poured sweet berry juice into the cups on the table in front of them and moved away. Vrenli and Aarl looked around the throne room. It wasn't long before the two elven women returned with silver trays in their hands and placed them on the table in front of them.

"I hope we have met your taste. We have roasted mushrooms, winter moss salad, honey, wild berries and fresh bread," said one of them, smiling kindly.

Aarl, who was fascinated by the throne room and hadn't really been listening to her, began to search for meat on the tray. "Am I seeing this right? They've forgotten meat, eggs and milk," he grumbled quietly.

"Help yourself! It's delicious!" said Vrenli, who was eating the winter moss salad and roasted mushrooms.

Staring at the food in front of him, Aarl finally reached for the honey, broke off a piece of bread and began to eat.

"I think I'll stick to honey and bread, somewhat plain, but at least better than the rest," he remarked quietly.

One of the elven women noticed that Aarl was eating nothing but honey and bread and slowly approached him. "Would you prefer something else to eat?" she asked him politely.

"I wouldn't say no to meat, eggs and milk," replied Aarl, smiling at her.

"You'll have to forgive me, but our people don't eat meat or eggs. And we don't drink milk either. We live on what grows on the forest floor or on the bushes and trees," explained the elf woman, and she apologized to Aarl.

"No meat? No eggs? No milk?" Aarl asked incredulously.

"I'm sorry," she apologized again and moved away from the table.

"For not eating meat, their warriors look quite strong," Aarl remarked, glancing at the guards in the throne room.

"Yes, quite strong, so what they eat can't be bad. Why don't you try it? It's really delicious," Vrenli emphasized and smiled.

Aarl hesitated at first, but then he finally tasted the fried mushrooms.

"Actually, not bad at all," admitted Aarl, who a few moments later had eaten almost everything on his plate and couldn't believe that he was completely full and didn't feel a bit stuffed.

Just as Vrenli had finished the last sip of berry juice and put his cup down on the table, he looked towards the entrance, where he saw Master Drobal and the queen enter.

"Good morning, friends! I see you have already sampled the delicacies of the elves," said Master Drobal and sat down at the table with them.

Vrenli and Aarl rose from their chairs and bowed to the Queen, who was seated on her throne and conversing with an elven warrior wearing heavy, elaborately decorated silver armor.

"We will stab Erwight of Entorbis' forces in the back. He won't expect us to get to Ib'Agier through Mist Moor," the queen said to the elven warrior, who raised an eyebrow when the queen mentioned Mist Moor.

"But, Your Majesty, there are many dangers lurking in Mist Moor and what about the mist elves who live on the border of the Moor? You know that even some have built a small town in the middle of it," the elf objected.

"I appreciate your concerns and you are right that Mist Moor is a dangerous place. We will most likely have to accept that there will be casualties when going through the Moor to Ib'Agier, but my mind is made up," the queen replied emphatically.

"As you command, my Queen!" said the elf and bowed to her.

"The elves from the Glorious Valley will march through Mist Moor to Ib'Agier with two thousand men. I wish you to make all the arrangements so that we can set off in two days' time!" the queen commanded majestically. The elf nodded, bowed again and hurriedly left the throne room.

The way to Ib'Agier

"It looks like you've reached an agreement with the queen," Aarl remarked happily.

"We had a long talk in the morning and I was able to convince her that the pages of the book are safest in Ib'Agier. She promised to support King Agnulix. Her army, as you have just heard, must pass through Mist Moor. So far, however, no large group has managed to cross it without suffering heavy losses. But we don't have time for the elves to take the much longer route north via Astinhod and from there west to Ib'Agier. Besides, stabbing Erwight of Entorbis' forces in the back is a good plan. We have to take that risk. He won't expect that," Master Drobal revealed to the two, who nodded in agreement.

The queen gave them a sign that they should come to her in front of the throne.

"I have a gift for you, Master Drobal!" she announced and, with a wave of her hand, made a small branch grow out of her throne, which grew bigger and thicker. When the branch was large and strong enough, she put her hand around it and murmured something in elven language. The branch detached itself from the throne and fell to the ground. From there it floated slowly into the queen's open hand. After she had stomped the branch hard on the ground, the thin twigs and dark green leaves fell away and she held a shiny, dark staff in her hand. She rose from her throne and walked to one of the large, purple-glowing crystals that stood on the glass pedestals in the throne room. She gently tapped the crystal with the staff, causing a violet-colored light to shine on the wood.

"I noticed that you are traveling without your staff, Master Drobal," said the queen and presented him with her gift.

"Thank you very much for this wonderful gift," replied Master Drobal, bowing to the queen and feeling the wood of the staff.

The queen let her eyes slowly drift to the other two guests.

"I must ask you to forgive me for not being able to pay more attention to you until now, Vrenli and Aarl," she said to the two of them.

"In light of the seriousness of the situation, we fully understand, Your Majesty!" replied Vrenli.

"Master Drobal told me about your adventures on the way to the Glorious Valley. I would like to thank you, on behalf of all the elves, for your contribution to protect Wetherid from Erwight of

Entorbis and his allies," said the queen, bowing her head slightly to Vrenli and Aarl.

"May I ask you a question, Your Majesty?" asked Vrenli, shyly.

"Go on!" she encouraged him.

"Why didn't the elves from the Glorious Valley reclaim the Book of Wetherid from the humans?" he wanted to know.

The queen smiled.

"You are truly your grandfather's grandson. I remember very well how he stood here before me many years ago and peppered me with question after question. Well, as the name suggests, it is the Book of Wetherid, and humans are part of Wetherid. When a few found out what the book was about and started writing down the events of Wetherid, there was no reason for us to reclaim the book. We even appointed them Keepers of the Book. We shared some of the gifts we had been given with them and taught them to better understand the ancient language of Wetherid. We were in contact with the guardians, met and even celebrated together," explained the queen.

"But what about the elven magic in the book? Weren't you afraid that it might be used against you?" Vrenli continued to ask.

"The magic of the elves! Of course, I've often heard this persistent rumor. Our magic is within us, given to us at an early age. It does not reside in a book. The power that the book possesses is the Word of the Father come to life. His Word is like a powerful, bright light that displaces the shadow. Is it magic? If you want to put it that way, yes, perhaps. But it is not the magic of the elves from the Glorious Valley. I must confess that we were not averse to the rumor because hostile minds feared it. On the other hand, as we know, this rumor also aroused the desire of some to appropriate this power for their own ends," the queen replied.

"You said the Keepers have special gifts. But I can't detect any special power in myself," Vrenli doubted.

"Vrenli Hogmaunt! You too have the gifts of the Keepers within you. Some of them are still dormant, but there will be situations and events that will awaken these gifts in you. The Seven Artifacts and the Ice Flames in the Northland will strengthen your abilities. But you will have to wait for that in the near future. I can't tell you any more about it now. But the time will come when we can talk about it in more detail," the queen gently informed Vrenli.

"We shouldn't delay the queen any longer and don't forget that someone else is waiting for us," Master Drobal reminded them, attracting Vrenli and Aarl's attention.

"Aren't we going to travel to Ib'Agier with the elves? Surely it would be much safer for us?" asked Aarl.

"Well, considering the queen's gift, I will try to summon a haldakie. The faster we get to Ib'Agier, the better, and the air route is the fastest," replied Master Drobal.

"But wouldn't it be better if you brought the missing pages directly to Ib'Agier with the help of the golden bowl?" Vrenli interjected, causing Master Drobal to pause.

"You should tell them about it," said the queen, taking her seat on her throne again.

"What's happened?" Vrenli and Aarl asked excitedly.

"My two brothers, who used the crystal in the tower to send lightning bolts to the gates of Ib'Agier, attracted the attention of the shadow mages. I am sorry to tell you that they did not survive," said Master Drobal in an extremely depressed voice.

Aarl and Vrenli could see how deeply affected he was.

"Of the original fifteen mages of Horunguth Island, only Wendur and I are still alive today," he murmured into his long white beard, shaking his head.

"So! Our crystal was stolen, the golden bowl was destroyed and all the books were burned. Without the bowl in the tower on Horunguth Island, we won't be able to use all the other bowls," explained Master Drobal, pointing with his hand to the bowl on the floor near the wall to their right.

"They were useful tools, but they were not so crucial that we should give up hope in their absence," said the queen, who rose from her throne, signaled the three to follow her and strode out of the throne room onto the terrace.

"Behold the army of elves from the Glorious Valley!" she spoke proudly, pointing down to the clearing where hundreds upon hundreds of elven warriors were preparing for their imminent journey to Ib'Agier. The silver armor of the swordsmen sharpening their blades and polishing their shields reflected the light of the sun shining through the treetops. The archers checked the strings of their glass bows and some of them carved their arrows from thin silver tree branches. The silver lances of the lancers, which stood in elaborately crafted weapon holders, were being counted and then handed out to the elven warriors, who had positioned themselves in six rows, one behind the other.

"There. Look to your right!" said the queen.

From the surrounding forest, one by one, about fifty elven warriors rode on bears and larger-than-average white wolves, blowing their silver horns adorned with gold. The bright, booming sound filled the entire valley. The bears and wolves, wearing saddles with silver fittings on their backs and their heads and flanks armored with silver armor, reared up threateningly at the sound of the horns.

Vrenli and Aarl were thrilled by the spectacle.

"I wish you good luck on your journey through Mist Moor," said Master Drobal, raising the staff he had received from the Queen of the Elves in front of him. A purple ray of light shot into the sky and Master Drobal let out a shrill, loud whistle. Vrenli and Aarl gazed eagerly into the sky, waiting for the haldakie. When they saw the large wings above them, they were delighted.

But suddenly the sky above them darkened. There was the deafening caw of hundreds of crows, which swooped down on the haldakie and attacked it with their sharp claws and beaks. It was so loud that Vrenli had to cover his ears. The haldakie tried in vain to defend itself and grabbed some of the attackers with its huge claws, but there were too many of them. The haldakie fell to the ground dead.

"Kondijr Maasaga! The Shadow Mages' henchmen!" Master Drobal called out loudly, whereupon the archers among them immediately shot their silver arrows at the black cloud of crows.

They managed to decimate the band by more than half, but the survivors swooped down on the elven warriors below and attacked them.

"Ornux must be among them! They need a leader!" Master Drobal called over to the queen and tried to locate the Shadow Mage in the tangle of birds.

When he spotted a crow that was bigger than the others, he raised his staff and sent a few purple flashes into the sky. But the large crow skillfully dodged them. The queen recited a few words in the language of the elves and gently placed her hands on one of the branches beside her that reached down from above. In just a few moments, all the branches and twigs of the tree began to sprout, reaching out towards the crows like living claws, wrapping themselves tightly around them and bursting them under their merciless grip. Only the large crow escaped. It cawed loudly three times and flew off to the north.

"Ornux!" Master Drobal called after him as he raised a clenched fist to the sky.

With quick steps, he followed the glass stairs down from the tree and ran to where the haldakie lay dead on the ground with countless small, bleeding wounds inflicted by the crows. A bright blue light shone from Master Drobal's diamond-shaped mark onto the haldakie, who then slowly dissolved in front of him.

Vrenli and Aarl, who had followed Master Drobal, stood next to him and looked up into the sky, searching and full of fear.

"So, our plan to fly to Ib'Agier is probably dead," Aarl remarked.

"Looks like it. It would be pointless to summon another haldakie. The shadow mages are prepared for it," agreed Master Drobal.

"Perhaps we should consider traveling through Mist Moor with the elves after all," suggested Vrenli.

"That way is dangerous and takes many days. We will use another, secret path, one that leads through the mountains. The path through the mountains is not without danger. The path is narrow and unpaved, but a small group can make it. We can arrive in Ib'Agier at least three days before the elves," explained Master Drobal.

"What will happen to Werlis if he is still not ready for such an arduous journey?" asked Vrenli, worried.

"We'll think about that when we get to him. We should say goodbye to the queen now and set off," said Master Drobal, and he walked back to the glass staircase where the queen was standing and waving to them.

"Here are the book pages from the Glorious Valley. Three wolf riders will take you to the barbarians. I hope to see you again in Ib'Agier," said the queen. She bid goodbye to Master Drobal, Vrenli and Aarl, who then went to the wide clearing in front of the tree.

"Randa koul!" the queen called down to them from the tree as the three rode off on the wolves' backs.

The elven warriors spurred their wolves on and never paused. Before nightfall, they had reached the edge of the forest, behind which lay the barbarian village. The three friends said a grateful goodbye to the elven riders and walked the few steps through the forest to the clearing where the barbarian village lay.

A barbarian on the lookout tower announced the arrival of the three to the village. As Vrenli entered the village through the large gate, he saw Werlis sitting next to a fat, shaggy barbarian in the light of the torches. They were sitting on one of the benches dotted around the village square. Vrenli ran up to the two of them and when he got close enough, he realized that the fat barbarian was also missing an arm. He was wearing a leather cap on the stump of his right arm. When the barbarian saw Vrenli approaching, he got up and went to one of the huts that stood to the north of the village square.

"Werlis!" cried Vrenli, delighted, and he hugged him gently.

"How are you?" he asked him.

Instead of answering, Werlis burst into tears.

Vrenli hugged him a little tighter and finally began to cry himself. The two of them stood crying for a few moments in the village square.

"Are you in pain?" Vrenli finally asked.

Werlis nodded.

"It's the worst at night. I can't get a wink of sleep," replied Werlis.

"I'm so terribly sorry for everything," Vrenli sobbed in a trembling voice.

"You don't have to be sorry. It wasn't your fault," replied Werlis, hugging Vrenli tighter with one arm.

"But I'm responsible for you setting off on this journey," Vrenli objected.

"Do you remember when I said at the beginning that I wouldn't risk my life for a stranger from Astinhod?" Werlis asked him.

"Yes, of course," replied Vrenli.

"Well, luckily I still have my life," said Werlis who tried to smile.

"Oh, Werlis, how can I ever make it up to you," sighed Vrenli.

"Take the missing pages to Ib'Agier. Don't worry about me," Werlis replied.

"You have to come with us. You can't stay here with the barbarians. Your home is Abketh," said Vrenli emphatically.

"I would only be a burden for you. Please go without me. Remember the importance of your mission," replied Werlis.

"I'm not leaving without you. I can't leave you here with the barbarians as a cripple!" Vrenli blurted out, only realizing what he had said after he finished speaking.

"I'm sorry, Werlis, I didn't mean to..." Vrenli stammered.

"That's all right. I'm just a cripple," said Werlis, whereupon Vrenli began to cry again.

"Listen, Vrenli. Gerold, the fat barbarian who was sitting on the bench with me earlier, is a living example of how a one-armed man can still do anything in his life. He is one of the most feared fighters in the village and he can chop down a tree in just a few moments. You should have seen it! He offered to train me. He said that an axe or sword wielded properly in the left hand can be just as dangerous as if it were wielded in the right," Werlis told him enthusiastically.

Vrenli was pleased when he noticed the sparkle in his friend's eyes as he continued to talk about Gerold.

"Are you sure you want to stay here until we get back? It could be weeks, if not longer, Werlis," asked Vrenli.

"I'm staying here!" Werlis insisted emphatically.

In the meantime, Master Drobal and Aarl, who gave Vrenli and Werlis time to talk alone, told Warwik, who had joined them from the main house, that the elves from the Glorious Valley were moving through Mist Moor to Ib'Agier and inquired about the situation on the border.

"We have built a wall with two lookout towers. A hundred men are guarding the border. Fifty of them are my men and the other fifty are Erik's men. If the mist elves try to lead anyone through Mist Moor again, they will be in for a treat," Warwik replied proudly.

"Don't underestimate the mist elves, they prefer to attack in the dark when they have the advantage," warned Master Drobal.

"We have two packs of wolfhounds on the border," Warwik replied, glancing at Vrenli and Werlis, who were walking towards them.

"Werlis, little friend," Master Drobal greeted him, picking him up carefully and kissing him on the forehead.

Aarl hugged Werlis as Master Drobal placed him back on the ground.

"How are you?" Aarl asked.

"At night, the wound hurts so much that I can't get a wink of sleep, but during the day the pain is limited," Werlis replied.

"You mustn't give up, my boy. Be strong. Even a one-armed man can enjoy life. You will learn that almost everything you did before with your right hand can also be done with your left," Master Drobal encouraged Werlis and placed his hand on his head.

"I know, I made a friend among the barbarians. He is also missing his right arm and he offered to train me. Speaking of which, I won't be coming with you to Ib'Agier. I already told Vrenli that I would only be a burden to you, and your mission is too important for that. Important for all of Wetherid," Werlis explained.

"Let's discuss this in the main house over a cup of honey wine," Warwik suggested and went ahead of them.

Werlis, who had already asked Warwik's permission to stay longer in the village, reaffirmed his wish to remain here, and since he was right in his argument that he would only delay them, no one contradicted him.

Vrenli told Werlis about the Glorious Valley, the huge tree where the elves live, about the queen, the crows and that they had ridden here on wolves almost as big as horses.

"You're exaggerating, wolves as big as horses!" Werlis doubted and laughed.

For a moment, everyone forgot that Werlis had lost an arm. They talked for some time and drank several mugs of honey wine until they were finally so tired that they had to go to sleep. Werlis, who was still sleeping in the healer's hut due to his pain during the night, wished everyone a good night's sleep.

As usual, Master Drobal was the first one awake the next morning when the others opened their eyes and walked out of their hut onto the village square with a slight headache from the honey wine.

"Five of my men will accompany you to the foothills. It will be best if you go through the forest, so you remain unseen," Warwik said to Master Drobal, who was standing with him in the village square.

"Good morning, friends. We have to leave soon, so make sure you wake up," Master Drobal said to Vrenli and Aarl with a smile.

"Next time I'll stop after two cups of honey wine," remarked Aarl.

Vrenli nodded in agreement.

"I'm going to check on Werlis," Vrenli announced and went to the healer's hut.

To Vrenli's surprise, Werlis was already awake and trying to poke a stick he was holding in his left hand into a small metal ring hanging on a thin chain from one of the posts of the healer's hut.

"Gerold showed me this exercise," said Werlis when he saw Vrenli coming.

"We'll be leaving soon, Werlis," Vrenli told him in a depressed voice.

"Take good care of yourself and don't worry about me. I'll wait for you here, Vrenli. I hope you come back soon," said Werlis and put his left arm around Vrenli's shoulder.

"Promise me you won't start crying now," he added.

The two talked for a while and Werlis showed Vrenli another exercise that Gerold had given him to sensitize his left hand. Aarl and Master Drobal came to say goodbye to him.

"I wish you good luck on your journey to Ib'Agier, friends!" said Werlis, who was on the verge of tears.

"We'll be back as soon as possible," Vrenli assured him and hugged him.

"Don't give up!" Aarl encouraged him and patted his left shoulder.

"Werlis of Abketh, I thank you for what you have done for Wetherid so far," Master Drobal spoke formally and kissed him on the forehead.

"Take care of yourselves!" Werlis called after them as they left the village with the five barbarians.

Half a day's journey later, they arrived at the bottom of the foothills in the north. They said goodbye to their companions and followed the path that led them upwards.

When they were already several hundred paces up in the mountains, they turned around one last time and looked at the forest where the village of the Raging Hordes of the East was located.

The path through the mountains took them far above the tree line. The part of their journey covered in snow and ice was exhausting and cost them a lot of time. The furs that Warwik had given them for their journey kept them warm during cold nights they spent sleeping on the icy ground. After seven days of snow and ice, they finally reached the third peak of the mountain range that separated Wetherid from Fallgar in the east, frozen, hungry and exhausted.

As they looked northeast of the summit, they could already see the high defensive towers of Ib'Agier far ahead of them.

"Two more days and we will have reached our destination," announced Master Drobal, who dug his staff firmly into the snow-covered ground to find his footing.

The three were relieved when they were finally able to leave the narrow, snow- and ice-covered descent behind them the next day and set off on the section of their journey overgrown with low shrubs and grasses.

A storm came up unexpectedly in the afternoon.

"We should find somewhere to shelter. These pitch-black clouds above us don't bode well," warned Aarl, who turned left behind a steep rock face to his right.

"Wait here for me! I'll have a look around. Maybe we'll be lucky and can take shelter from the storm in one of the alcoves," he said to Master Drobal and Vrenli.

Aarl soon found what he was looking for and led his friends under a low rocky outcrop, which sheltered them from the icy wind and heavy rain.

Ib'Agier is refortified

When the rain subsided and the sky began to clear again, the three followed the path once more, which led them onto a wide mountain plain. They hiked for several hours through the rocky, barren landscape, from where they climbed to the last peak of their journey. They spent the night halfway up, and the next morning, they descended into the high landscape dotted with many hilltops. At a wide mountain ridge, they finally reached a high, thick wall that blocked the entire mountain side from west to east.

"We're here, friends!" Master Drobal called out in an exhausted voice.

"At last!" Vrenli groaned and looked around.

"But where are the great gates of Ib'Agier people talk so much about?" Vrenli asked, when all he could see was a small iron gate in the wall.

"They are on the east side of the mountain where you can get to Fallgar from," replied Master Drobal.

"I can't wait to sleep in a bed again," said Aarl, trying to open the gate.

"It's locked," he told his friends, whereupon Master Drobal tapped on it several times with his staff.

A small hatch in the middle of the gate opened a moment later and two eyes stared at the three friends.

"Who are you and what do you want? Ib'Agier is in a state of war. Better turn around and go back to where you came from!" growled a voice from behind the gate.

" King Agnulix is expecting us," replied Master Drobal.

"Tell me your names!" grumbled the dwarf.

"This here is Vrenli and Aarl, and I am the magician Drobal," he introduced himself and his companions.

"Drobal, you say?" the voice behind the gate repeated.

"I am a mage from Horunguth Island. Now open this gate at last, I told you that King Agnulix awaits us!" urged Master Drobal in a serious voice.

"Wait here!" the voice replied.

Some time passed.

Master Drobal knocked on the gate several times with his staff.

"I should just destroy it," he grumbled impatiently.

The grinding sound of the bar opening behind the gate reassured Master Drobal, and he smiled as a burly dwarf with bright red hair and equally red whiskers opened the gate.

"Forgive me for keeping you waiting so long, gentlemen, but Ib'Agier is still in a state of war and my orders are clear," the dwarf apologized and asked the three to enter.

Master Drobal and Aarl had to duck as they entered through the archway. They found themselves in a small courtyard and looked around. Two groups of thirty dwarves sat to the left and right of the gate with their shields and axes lying on the ground beside them.

"My name is Tormenix, and I am the group leader of the southern rampart. Normally there are only five of us here, but after the attack, King Agnulix ordered that the southern rampart be more heavily guarded," the dwarf reported, leading the three of them to a tunnel entrance that led into the interior of the mountain.

"Does that mean the attack is over?" asked Master Drobal in astonishment.

"The enemy gave up after two weeks and retreated, weakened. But King Agnulix will certainly tell you about it," replied Tormenix as he walked quickly along the tunnel.

They reached the end of the tunnel and entered a plateau carved into the rock, high above the city of Ib'Agier.

"Don't go too close to the edge!" warned the dwarf, and he loudly whistled three times.

With a loud crunch and the rubbing sound of ropes, an iron cage slowly moved up the precipice.

Tormenix opened the bars and entered the cage.

"Come inside!" he urged the three.

Master Drobal, Vrenli and Aarl hesitantly complied with his request. The dwarf locked the bars and whistled loudly again, whereupon the cage slowly moved down. Vrenli and Aarl, who were in Ib'Agier for the first time, were amazed at the dwarves' city, which was bigger and more beautiful than they could ever have imagined. A labyrinth of stairs led up to hundreds of caves carved into the stone around the steep, smooth rock faces of the hollowed-out mountain. Diamonds, sapphires and opals protruding from the carved rock sparkled along the torch-lit paths that led from one cave to another. Each of the dwarven dwellings had heavy, intricately crafted iron doors and colorful, ornately painted stained glass windows.

In the huge mountain wall to their left was a high archway decorated with golden ornaments where they entered a spacious hall.

"This is the entrance to the Hall of Kings, behind which is Lorijan's Hall," explained Tormenix when he noticed Vrenli and Aarl's astonished looks.

When they reached the bottom with a jolt, the two dwarves who had been operating the iron crank opened the cage for them and greeted them warmly. Vrenli, Aarl and Master Drobal followed Tormenix along a street paved with darkstone that led them to the center of the city. A small lake, fed by the waters of a stream that flowed south from the Hall of Kings, lay directly opposite. The lake was surrounded by a high white marble wall. At all four points of a compass, steps led up to a plateau that protruded several paces into the lake. Several thick metal pipes, from which several thinner ones led to the countless staircases of the residential units, rose from the middle of the lake up to the ceiling.

"What purpose do these metal pipes serve?" Vrenli, who was looking at them with fascination, asked Tormenix.

"They provide running water in the caves," the dwarf replied proudly and continued along the road, past a large statue that stood in a rock garden just a few paces behind the lake. It depicted a grim dwarf who had placed his axe on the front of his shield.

"Who is that?" Vrenli asked Tormenix.

"This is King Zergonix, the founder of Ib'Agier," he replied and continued towards the smelting furnaces.

Once there, they paused for a moment. Vrenli and Aarl gazed into the fiery cauldrons and watched as dwarves brought ore up from the mines deep below the mountain and melted it down.

"We're almost there," Tormenix informed them and walked the last two hundred steps from the Hall of Kings a little faster.

When they arrived at the huge, golden-gleaming archway, Tormenix stopped in front of the six heavily armed dwarves guarding the entrance to the Hall of Kings and announced the guests to them.

"I have to get back to the south wall," he said to them and hurried off.

Master Drobal, Vrenli and Aarl, accompanied by two guards, walked under the golden archway into the Hall of Kings. There they saw King Agnulix from afar, sitting majestically on his throne. Standing around him were Gorathdin, Borlix, Army Commander Arkondir, Manamii, Wahmubu and several dwarves wearing heavy, shining golden armor.

"Gorathdin! Borlix!" Vrenli began to shout, but before he could call out the names of Manamii, Wahmubu and Army Commander Arkondir and run towards them, Master Drobal held him back by placing his staff in front of him.

"Don't forget, we have a king ahead of us," he whispered to Vrenli and Aarl, who waved to his friends.

"Welcome!" said King Agnulix, who became aware of them by Vrenli's shouts.

Master Drobal, Vrenli and Aarl bowed to King Agnulix, who got up from his throne and walked towards Master Drobal.

"We put the enemy to flight before help even arrived from Astinhod and Iseran," King Agnulix reported happily to Master Drobal, who bowed again and smiled gently.

"I expected nothing less from the dwarves," replied Master Drobal as he and the others present followed King Agnulix to the table of thick stone that stood to the right in front of the throne.

"Sit down with me and tell me about your journey," the king ordered them.

Vrenli and Aarl sat down on the right side of the table together with Gorathdin, Borlix, Army Commander Arkondir, Manamii and Wahmubu. Master Drobal began to tell King Agnulix about their journey, while Gorathdin inquired about Werlis, who had not come to Ib'Agier with them.

Vrenli told his friends everything that had happened since their separation and when he got to the incident in which Werlis lost his arm, tears were streaming down his face. All his friends were shocked and horrified by Werlis' fate.

Aarl then told them about the battle with the ogres and the mist elves on the plain and gave a detailed account of the Glorious Valley.

"You have to imagine, friends, the elves who live there don't eat meat or eggs and they don't drink milk!" he revealed to them.

"I can understand that about the milk. Only cows and goats drink milk. We dwarves drink beer and sometimes water. But no meat? No eggs? That can't be right! Then what do they eat?" asked Borlix in amazement.

"Forest fruits, mushrooms, honey and mosses!" replied Aarl, grinning at Borlix, who was sitting next to him with his mouth open.

"Now tell me, what happened in Ib'Agier?" Vrenli turned to the group, overcoming his sadness.

"When we arrived in Ib'Agier with our army from Astinhod, the battle between the dwarves and Erwight of Entorbis' army had already been fought. The dwarves suffered losses of more than four hundred men, but the enemy suffered many more," Gorathdin reported.

"Is Princess Lythinda well? Why isn't she with you, Gorathdin?" Vrenli asked curiously.

"She wanted to ride with us to Ib'Agier, but I thought it wiser for her to stay in Astinhod. After King Grandhold's death, the balance of power between the nobles is not particularly good. Her diplomatic skills are needed there to keep the peace," Gorathdin replied.

Vrenli nodded in agreement and turned to his two Scheddifer friends.

"We arrived with five hundred riders two days after Gorathdin and Army Commander Arkondir," Manamii said, sitting hand in hand with Wahmubu at the table.

"Is Erik also in Ib'Agier with his barbarians?" Aarl asked his friends.

"Yes, he arrived with the army from Astinhod," Gorathdin replied, whereupon Vrenli told him about Warwik.

"Where is Brother Transmudin and what about the dragon down in the mines?" Aarl wanted to know.

"Brother Transmudin was actually able to stop Omnigo from bringing down Lorijan's Hall. It turned out that Brother Theramond was in cahoots with Erwight of Entorbis. Omnigo began digging, or rather melting, a massive tunnel months earlier. It led from the catacombs beneath the Temple of the Dragon to the mines of Ib'Agier. The dragon's fire is so hot that it melts rock," Gorathdin reported.

"But where is Brother Transmudin now?" Aarl asked.

"He is down in the grotto with Omnigo, who is now smelting ore for the dwarves, which is urgently needed for a new fortification in Ib'Agier. The enemy has caused severe damage to the defensive wall and the main gate and King Agnulix's men need new weapons. I was able to convince King Agnulix that this was certainly not the last attack, so he gave the order to refortify Ib'Agier. With the help of the thousand men from Astinhod, Erik's men, the riders of Manamii and Wahmubu, the work has been underway for two days. Army Commander Arkondir suggested setting up an outpost a few hundred paces from the gates to the east to hold back the war machines that the enemy will surely approach with," Borlix said.

"The foot troops from Iseran should arrive in two days. Another four hundred men," informed Wahmubu.

"We set out with over a thousand men, but a messenger from my father reached us before we reached the border of Desert of DeShadin and told us of an attack on Iseran by the snake people. We had to send reinforcements back to Iseran. I hope that Iseran's defenses held up," Manamii said, looking at Wahmubu with concern.

"It certainly held up," Wahmubu reassured her and placed his hand tenderly over her shoulder.

"The elves from the Glorious Valley are on their way through Mist Moor with a thousand men. I expect them to arrive here in less than three days," Vrenli announced.

"Why are they going through Mist Moor, isn't that madness?" Gorathdin wondered.

"Since we knew nothing of the dwarves' victory, Master Drobal and the Queen of the Elves decided to stab the enemy in the back," replied Vrenli.

"Before I forget! Here! Take the pages of Ib'Agier's book, Master Drobal," said King Agnulix, handing Master Drobal a thin iron tube containing the rolled-up pages of the book.

"So, my friends have already told you about our plan," Master Drobal said with a gentle smile and thanked the king.

"Here are the pages from Astinhod. Princess Lythinda gave them to me. She found them under the ground cover in the pavilion of the castle garden where King Grandhold had proposed to her mother many years ago. The king's estate contained a letter with several personal clues as to where the pages were hidden," Gorathdin said, handing Master Drobal a small, sealed chest made of gold.

Master Drobal then rummaged in his leather bag, which he had placed next to the stone chair along with his staff.

"Here friends! The book pages from Iseran, Thir, the Glorious Valley, Ib'Agier and Astinhod," he announced in a depressed voice.

"You should be happy about that, Master Drobal! Why does your face appear as though you've failed?" King Agnulix wondered, patting Master Drobal on the shoulder appreciatively.

"We have only achieved partial success. The pages from Tawinn are missing! And I'm afraid I have to confess that I have no idea where they might be. Vrenli's grandfather kept them and, as we know from Vrenli, he didn't tell him anything about their whereabouts," replied Master Drobal, looking at Vrenli.

"But if you don't know where the pages are, the enemy won't find them either! So there's no need to be sad. That's how I see it," grumbled Borlix.

"Erwight of Entorbis didn't know where to find the other pages either, and yet he sent his henchmen. He and his allies will not rest until they have taken all the pages of the book," explained Master Drobal.

"He has to take Ib'Agier first and we know how to prevent that," King Agnulix objected.

"I have to disagree with you King Agnulix. I've had a lot of time to think about why Erwight of Entorbis attacked Ib'Agier. I am convinced that he has a diabolical plan. He made several alliances within Wetherid to help him find the book pages. At the same time, this also gives him a force within Wetherid's borders. We also know that he is already trying to infiltrate the ruling houses, or rather, diminish their power through targeted attacks. Remember the capture of Wahmubu and the assassination of King Grandhold. The alliance sought with the Raging Hordes to take the Dark Forest and the druid who was turned into an owl by the Tree of Life. He was a defector for sure. I also think he's already plotting something in Irkaar. We saw a lot of mist elves and gray dwarves coming by sea during our last stay. In Tawinn we met several goblin clans, something is brewing there too. Also, don't forget the mist elves and ogres that you said were stationed off the border of the Glorious Valley. The underwater creatures from

Moorgh on Horunguth Island. And finally, Omnigo under your halls and a feigned attack on the gates of Ib'Agier," Gorathdin explained.

An eerie silence fell among those gathered.

"Gorathdin is right in what he says! I saw through Erwight of Entorbis' plan even before I left Astinhod and traveled to Horunguth Island. My brothers and I therefore decided to take the pages of the book for ourselves and gather the might of Wetherid in Ib'Agier. Erwight of Entorbis should know that the pages are here. He will now send all his allies to Ib'Agier to bring it down. We chose Ib'Agier because the dwarves have the most experience in attacks from Fallgar and it is on the border of the Shadow Lord's realm. And even if Erwight of Entorbis wanted to take the book pages, he would first have to take Ib'Agier to be able to lead his assembled army to Wetherid, because to lead his army to Wetherid by sea, he would need hundreds of ships, and he doesn't have them," concluded Master Drobal, interrupting the silence.

"Excuse me, friends. I will ride to the outpost and see how the work is progressing," announced Army Commander Arkondir, bowing to King Agnulix and hurriedly leaving the table.

"He is very worried. He fears that Erwight of Entorbis' force will attack in a few days. He expects up to five thousand men. He was firmly convinced that the thousand men the Shadow Lord had sent to Ib'Agier were just a diversion. He didn't know what it was, but he said he had a bad feeling, which, of course, we now know was justified," Gorathdin said.

"Master Drobal also spoke of an army of five thousand men," Aarl remarked, to which Master Drobal nodded in agreement.

"Something has been bothering me since we left the Glorious Valley. I'm sure Ornux led the crows that descended on the haldakie, and what I've wondered all the way here was why no one tried to stop us from getting to Ib'Agier. We traveled undisturbed. Do you understand what I mean? Ornux knew where we were. He could easily have followed us or set up an ambush," Master Drobal mused thoughtfully.

Brother Transmudin walked through the golden archway into the Hall of Kings and smiled as he saw his friends gathered around the table.

"But someone is missing here. Where's Werlis?" he asked after greeting Master Drobal, Aarl and Vrenli. Vrenli gave him a brief summary of what had happened since they parted.

"If only I had gone with you, I might have been able to save his arm," he sighed sadly.

"You have done Ib'Agier and all of Wetherid a great service by preventing Omnigo from bringing down the Hall of Lorijan. You have nothing to blame yourselves for," King Agnulix said to Brother Transmudin, who took a seat next to Borlix.

"What will become of the pages of Tawinn now? I have a bad feeling that Abketh might become the target of an attack," Vrenli expressed his concern to Master Drobal.

"Vrenli is right! We have to do something. But what? We could send messengers to Astinhod so Queen Lythinda can send reinforcements to Abketh. But that would take weeks, and I'm afraid we don't have that much time," Master Drobal explained and looked at Gorathdin, who shrugged his shoulders.

"What about the Oracle of Tawinn? Can't you ask it where the book pages are?" Aarl asked Vrenli.

"It would be worth a try," he replied, pulling out his leather pouch and placing it on the table.

He took out the crystal hanging on the silver chain and lifted it up in front of him.

"Oracle of Tawinn! Where are the pages of the book that my grandfather hid?" asked Vrenli in a stern voice.

The crystal began to shine with a bright blue light.

Everyone waited in anticipation.

A picture began to form in the small crystal. Those present stood up from the table and moved closer to Vrenli.

The picture showed Vrenli's grandfather wandering around the Ruins of Tawinn at night a long time ago. He entered a building with a huge hole in the upper floor. He lit a torch and went into a room with weathered floor paintings. He knelt down and began to pry two of the gray bricks out of the floor with his dagger. He then dug a small hole and placed a sealed glass container in it. He buried the hole again, placed the two bricks on top and covered the area with fir branches.

The crystal in Vrenli's hand went out.

"But I know this place! We were there. I walked past it with Aarl!" exclaimed Vrenli.

The crystal almost fell out of his hand.

"So the pages of the book are hidden in the Ruins of Tawinn. We have to get to them before the enemy does," Gorathdin concluded, looking at Master Drobal.

"I will fly to Tawinn and fetch the pages. It's risky because Ornux will surely find out about it quickly, but it has to be done, friends," announced Master Drobal.

"I'll be back in two days at the latest," he added.

He said goodbye to everyone present and, with a wave of his hand, brushed aside all the objections that his friends shouted after him as he made his way towards the plateau.

When he arrived at the plateau above the main gates, he raised his staff in the air and let out a whistle.

It took a while, but soon the silence of the night was broken by loud, powerful wing beats. The haldakie landed gently in front of Master Drobal and let him climb onto his back. Just as the owl flew away with Master Drobal on its back, Gorathdin arrived on the plateau with quick steps and saw a large crow soaring into the night sky from a rocky outcrop.

"Ornux! I knew it!" cried Gorathdin and hurried back to the Hall of Kings, where he told his friends about what he had seen.

Four dwarf women entered the hall with golden trays and served a sumptuous supper to those present at the table.

"Let's hope for the best, friends!" grumbled Borlix, who finished his mug of mead in one go.

The friends sat around the table until long after midnight, discussing the defensive measures for the impending attack from Fallgar.

Borlix then led Vrenli, Aarl and Gorathdin into one of the residential caves located above the golden archway.

"Sleep well, friends. I'll see you tomorrow. King Agnulix intends to visit the outpost and would be delighted if you would join him," Borlix said then left.

However, he did not mention to his friends that he had been appointed a paladin of Ib'Agier and had been enlightened with the light of Lorijan. He wanted to surprise them with it tomorrow.

The next morning, everyone met in front of the main gate in the east, where work was still going on. The ore that Omnigo was smelting deep beneath the mines was brought by miners in wheelbarrows to the main gate, where the dwarves had built a smelting furnace in which the liquid metal was reheated and turned by blacksmiths into sturdy square plates that were used to repair the extensive damage to the gate.

King Agnulix rode ahead of the friends on a grey ibex with mighty, gilded horns, together with one of his army commanders and a paladin in golden armor. "Didn't Borlix want to come with us?" Vrenli asked Aarl, who was riding a horse next to Vrenli's pony.

Before Aarl could reply, the paladin rode up to them on his white warhorse and flipped up the visor of his golden helmet.

"Borlix?!" exclaimed Vrenli in surprise.

"Yes, the king has forgiven me for my mistake and made me a paladin for my services to Ib'Agier and Wetherid. This would not have happened without you, Gorathdin and Werlis. If you had not happened to pass by my cave in the Ice Mountains, I would still be living there today. I am grateful to you for that. Now I have followed in my father's footsteps after all!" Borlix announced, beaming, and rode back to the side of King Agnulix and his commander, who was in charge of the outpost with Arkondir.

Even from a distance, they could already see the hundreds of dwarves ahead of them, digging deep trenches two hundred and fifty to three hundred paces long and ten to twenty paces deep. They stretched from the adjacent forest in the north to the high rock faces in the south. There was a trench every hundred paces in the direction of Ib'Agier's gates.

Thick, high and wide iron plates were pulled onto the narrow level by the dwarves with the help of rolling tree trunks, sunk upright into the ground at various points near the trenches with rope hoists supported by thick wooden posts.

"We will position fifty archers behind each of these massive slabs," explained Army Commander Arkondir, who was standing in front of a tent bearing Astinhod's coat of arms. King Agnulix, followed by Borlix and the army commander of the dwarves, dismounted his horse and looked around the outpost.

"The long, deep trenches that we dig in the earth have different functions. The first trench, which is slightly longer and deeper than the others, is covered with branches, twigs, leaves and grass, as you can see. Its purpose is to prevent the enemy's war machines from getting close to the defensive wall. We hope that we can stop the majority of them with this first trench. The second trench, filled with oil, serves as a deadly trap for those who make it past the first trench. Positioned behind powerful metal screens, the archers are ordered to ignite the oil with flaming arrows as soon as the enemy reaches this point. Immediately afterwards, they are ordered shoot a rain of arrows on the flaming attackers. The third trench, reinforced with robust metal plates, serves as a retreat and strategic trap. Lockable entrances are currently being installed in it, allowing the archers to retreat after firing their arrows and deal a surprise blow from behind to the enemy crossing this trench. The fourth and final trench, just two hundred paces from the gates, is still within range of the archers on the ramparts and towers. This trench is currently being equipped with a deadly mixture of wooden and metal spears, which are embedded vertically in the ground to create an almost insurmountable obstacle," the dwarf commander described the sophisticated defenses to his king and the astonished audience.

"Why are aisles being cut into the neighboring forest?" King Agnulix asked.

"Firstly, we need the wood for our barricades and secondly, the riders of Iseran and Astinhod will hide in the forest together with the barbarians and attack the enemy from the flank when the time is right," explained Army Commander Arkondir.

King Agnulix nodded a few times in agreement.

"You've both done a really good job. I have the highest regard for you," he praised the two generals.

"Thank you, Sire!" they replied at the same time and saluted.

"Bear in mind that there will also be undead among the enemy. You should position some paladins with your archers," Borlix suggested, whereupon King Agnulix put him in command of the paladins needed at the outpost.

"We will be finished with our work in two days," Army Commander Arkondir said before bending over the battle plan again with the dwarf army commander.

King Agnulix rode back to the defensive wall with Borlix and his friends, where he checked the work on the damaged areas. Borlix said goodbye to the king and his friends there and made his way to Lorijan's Hall, where he assigned fifteen of the thirty paladins gathered for a prayer before the statue of Lorijan to support the archers at the outpost.

In the meantime, Vrenli and his friends climbed one of the defense towers to the right of the main gate to get a better view of the plain in front of the gates.

Gorathdin asked the archers, who were talking loudly up in the tower, to leave them alone for a while as they had something important to discuss.

After the dwarves had willingly left their post, Vrenli, Gorathdin, Aarl, Wahmubu, Manamii and Brother Transmudin stood on the high tower and looked to the east, where dark clouds were forming in the sky and moving in their direction.

"When do you think Erwight of Entorbis will lead his force to Ib'Agier?" asked Vrenli.

"It's hard to say. In a few days, maybe weeks," Gorathdin speculated.

"I could consult the Oracle of Tawinn," Vrenli suggested after watching the dark clouds for a while.

"It would be worth a try," Gorathdin agreed, whereupon Vrenli pulled the chain on out of his leather pouch.

He briefly thought of Werlis, who had returned the Oracle of Tawinn to him on the day of their reunion, which clouded his thoughts.

"Oracle of Tawinn! Show me when Erwight of Entorbis' forces will attack Ib'Agier!" said Vrenli, holding the crystal in front of his eyes. After a few moments, it began to light up and Vrenli could make out an image.

A mighty force marched from the east to Ib'Agier. At their head rode Erwight of Entorbis, the shadow mage Ornux, the king of the gray dwarves, the prince of the mist elves, the king of the undead, a fat, ugly ogre and a shaman of the orcs in war paint. Hundreds of black crows flew above them in the light of a full moon. Vrenli could hear their loud caws, which rang through his bones. He saw war machines pulled by ogres and gray dwarves behind an army of many thousands of men. Knights in black armor and cloaks bearing the crest of Entorbis rode out of a forest towards the right flank of the army.

On the left flank, mist elves rode giant spiders and lizards. The image slowly began to blur and finally disappeared.

"They come on the night of a full moon," Vrenli remarked.

"We have a waxing moon so if they attack us on the next full moon, we still have three days," Gorathdin concluded.

"What do you think, friends, should I ask the oracle who will win this battle?" asked Vrenli uncertainly.

"I wouldn't advise it!" replied Gorathdin.

"But it might help us," replied Aarl.

"Or it could harm us, whichever way you look at it. If the oracle shows that we will lose the upcoming battle, how do you think we will face the enemy?" Gorathdin interjected.

"I agree with Gorathdin. We would be scared, panicked and weakened before the battle even began," Wahmubu affirmed.

"But what if we win? We would be motivated and fearless!" replied Vrenli, to which Aarl nodded in agreement.

"Let's put it to the vote," suggested Brother Transmudin, as they were divided.

"Anyone who is in favor of me asking the oracle about the outcome of the battle should raise their hand," said Vrenli who raised his own hand, followed by Aarl and Manamii, who hesitated at first.

"That would be a draw," Vrenli stated and questioningly looked at Gorathdin.

"Then the decision is up to you, Vrenli. But please, think about it carefully. Can you really handle it if the oracle shows our defeat?" asked Gorathdin, looking Vrenli firmly in the eyes. Vrenli took a quick look at each of his friends, glanced at the dark clouds that were approaching and finally pulled the Oracle of Tawinn out of his leather pouch.

"I need certainty," he said to Gorathdin. He lifted the crystal high above his head, took a deep breath and closed his eyes for a moment.

"Oracle of Tawinn! Show me who will emerge victorious in the upcoming battle!" Vrenli implored and opened his eyes.

A black crow swooped down from the sky towards Vrenli and snatched the crystal from his hand. Before any of them could react, it flew over their heads with the crystal in its beak, high into the sky.

"The oracle!" cried Vrenli.

Brother Transmudin reacted quickly, created a fireball and hurled it upwards towards the crow.

But the fireball missed its target.

"Ornux!" shouted Gorathdin in a trembling voice, drawing his longsword and raising the blade threateningly into the air.

"We'll be facing each other soon!" he shouted into the sky.

"After all, we know that they will attack on the night of the full moon," remarked Aarl.

"Let's tell the king," suggested Brother Transmudin and walked angrily down the stairs from the fortified tower.

Vrenli looked to the east, where the crow flew away with the crystal.

"Forgive me Gwerlit," he whispered and followed his friends down the stairs from the fortified tower, from where they went into King Agnulix's hall.

King Agnulix stood at a table, bent over a map with his army commanders, discussing the internal defenses.

"Erwight of Entorbis will attack on the night of a full moon," Gorathdin informed him and told him everything Vrenli had seen in the Oracle of Tawinn.

"The next full moon is three days away," noted Brother Transmudin when Gorathdin had finished his report to the king.

"Inform Army Commander Arkondir and everyone else. Tell them that they don't have much time left!" King Agnulix ordered his army commanders, who immediately informed their officers.

"So, three more days," repeated King Agnulix and then sat down on his throne, deep in thought.

"It's been a long day friends, we should give ourselves a rest," said Brother Transmudin.

Everyone nodded and went to their quarters together.

Over the next two days, Vrenli and his friends helped the dwarves work on the fortification. On the evening of the second day, Master Drobal returned to Ib'Agier on his haldakie. As Gorathdin had feared, the haldakie was attacked by Ornux's crows. Master Drobal was able to fend off the attack, but the injured owl could only fly slowly as a result, which is why Master Drobal needed a full three days to complete his mission. On top of this, goblins were sneaking through the Ruins of Tawinn and almost prevented Master Drobal from taking the book pages.

Now that all the missing pages of the book had been gathered in Ib'Agier, Vrenli, Gorathdin, Aarl, Borlix, Brother Transmudin, Master Drobal, Wahmubu and Manamii decided to join King Agnulix in a celebration that lasted until the early hours of the morning of the full moon.

The legacy of the elves

"Tonight we will have a full moon, and as you all know, Erwight of Entorbis will most likely lead his forces to Ib'Agier!" King Agnulix spoke to all those gathered in the Hall of Kings shortly after midday.

He asked his army commanders whether all the necessary preparations and measures had been completed.

"The outpost is ready and the riders from Astinhod, Iseran and the barbarians will take up their position in the forest before dusk. The archers and the paladins under Borlix's command are already in position!" reported Army Commander Arkondir to King Agnulix and saluted.

"The defense towers are occupied, Sire. Just as you ordered. The damage to the main gate and the defensive wall has been repaired!" reported the dwarf commander in charge.

"The lancers, axemen, archers and six paladins are ready in the courtyard in case the enemy breaks through!" said a dwarf with red braids and a heavy double-bladed axe in his right hand.

"The mounted lunge force is already in position with its fighting trestles and a four-hundred-strong foot troop of the knights from Astinhod is in position to support them. However, we are still waiting for the four hundred men from Desert of DeShadin!" reported Army Commander Rednix, adjusting his breastplate.

"Is there any news about your warriors, Manamii and Wahmubu?" asked King Agnulix.

"They should have arrived in Ib'Agier yesterday. I have sent some riders in their direction and expect to hear from them before dawn," Manamii replied.

"Let's hope they arrive in time," said King Agnulix, stroking his long, thick white beard.

"How many men are at the west gates?" King Agnulix wanted to know.

"Three hundred men, Sire!" a dwarf replied.

"That should be enough in case someone tries to attack Ib'Agier from Wetherid," said the king.

"What about the rampart?" he asked Tormenix.

"One hundred and twenty men are ready, My King," he replied.

"Then to my last question. Are the ballistae ready at the defensive wall to the east?" he asked a small, stocky dwarf standing next to two others carrying compasses and rulers.

"Yes, my king! We built three additional ballistae in the morning and since the dragon has melted a lot of ore, we will use iron balls instead of stones!" replied the short, stocky dwarf.

"The elves from the Dark Forest will secure Ib'Agier with the druids from the west," Gorathdin interrupted, unprompted, but to the delight of the king and those present.

"Well then, let the enemy come!" shouted King Agnulix, raising his golden, gem-studded war hammer into the air.

"For Ib'Agier, for Wetherid!" he shouted, whereupon everyone in the hall repeated his call.

Groblix and several priests stepped out of the Holy Hall and into the Hall of Kings and began to bless those present. Master Drobal signaled his friends to follow him into the Hall of Lorijan. Once there, he stood next to the gray bowl on the floor next to the statue.

"Friends, today is the day that will determine the fate of Wetherid. If we lose this battle, Erwight of Entorbis will try to reach Astinhod. If he succeeds, he will ascend to the throne and take over all of Wetherid in a short time. Wetherid will never be the same again," said Master Drobal to his friends, who looked seriously at each other.

"I wish you all good luck in this battle!" he added, hugging each of them.

"May the power and light of the Father be with you!" he said, whereupon a bright blue light shone from his diamond-shaped mark onto the friends, filling them with hope, warmth and strength.

"My place will be here at Groblix's side," Master Drobal let his friends know.

"I'm going down to Omnigo," announced Brother Transmudin, handing each of them a flask.

"A few drops on a wound will stop the bleeding," he said and went down into the mines.

"I will ride to our riders in the forest," Wahmubu said, kissing and hugging Manamii and walking to his horse standing in front of Ib'Agier's main gates.

538

"I can't leave Borlix out there alone," Aarl decided and made his way to the outpost.

"Now as for us, friends! When you see a bright blue light in the night sky above the peaks of Ib'Agier, come to the Holy Hall as quickly as you can," Master Drobal said to Vrenli, Gorathdin and Manamii, who looked questioningly at him. "If Erwight of Entorbis succeeds in penetrating Ib'Agier and taking the missing pages of the book, his power, and that of the shadow mages, will grow. They could become invincible opponents," warned Master Drobal with a serious expression.

"Where are the missing pages?" Vrenli asked.

"I took them down to the mines with Brother Transmudin. I find it hard to imagine Erwight of Entorbis or any of his allies taking on Omnigo," replied Master Drobal.

"I don't quite understand, what does Omnigo have to do with the missing pages and why are they down in the mines? Do you really think they're safest with the dragon?" Vrenli wanted to know.

"Last night, when you were all asleep, I asked Brother Transmudin to take me to the mines. I saw Omnigo, lord of fire and frost, and I must tell you, it was better that you didn't come with me. When I entered the vault, I found a huge, terrifying beast from long forgotten times. Omnigo was ceaselessly melting rock with his fiery breath to uncover ore for the dwarves. I asked Brother Transmudin to speak to Omnigo and ask him to keep the metal cylinder that King Agnulix had made for the pages safe. The dragon agreed and then punched a hole in the stone floor with his tail where Brother Transmudin placed the cylinder for me. Omnigo then sealed the hole with liquid ore. I didn't dare get too close to the dragon," Master Drobal told the three friends, who had been listening attentively.

"You told me about a power that is supposed to be more powerful than the magic of the elves," Vrenli recalled.

"Will this power help us against the enemy?" asked Vrenli.

"I said that I believe it is more powerful than the magic of the elves. It is still too early to make a final judgment. But this power I spoke of is with us, friends," he replied to Vrenli, who was not entirely satisfied with the answer.

"Take care of yourselves and don't forget to hurry to Lorijan's Hall as quickly as you can if you see the blue light!" Master Drobal warned and hugged each of them again. Then he approached Groblix, who had just entered Lorijan's Hall, and began to talk to him.

"I will go to Army Commander Arkondir, friends, he needs all the help he can get at the outpost," Gorathdin said and set off.

"I am going to the gates in the west and will lead my warriors to the strike force when they arrive in Ib'Agier," Manamii announced and left the Holy Hall.

Vrenli stood alone in front of the statue of Lorijan and thought about where his skills as an Abkether might be most useful. He went back to the Hall of Kings, where Tormenix told King Agnulix about two one-armed men, a barbarian and an Abkether, who were standing at the southern wall asking to be let in.

"They said they wanted to help Ib'Agier defend against the enemy," Tormenix informed the king.

"Werlis! It must be Werlis and Gerold!" shouted Vrenli and asked the king to let them in, as they were friends of his.

King Agnulix agreed, whereupon Vrenli excitedly followed Tormenix to the rampart.

"Let them in!" shouted Vrenli from afar as he ran out of the tunnel towards the rampart.

"Open the gate!" Tormenix ordered the heavily armed dwarves guarding the small gate.

"Werlis!" shouted Vrenli delightedly when he saw him and the barbarian at the gate.

"Vrenli!" replied Werlis, running towards him and hugging him with his left hand.

"But you said you were going to stay with the barbarians," Vrenli wondered with tears in his eyes.

"I changed my mind. Gerold encouraged me to come with him and go to war against the enemy," replied Werlis, his eyes shining.

"Oh, Werlis, I'm so glad you're here," said Vrenli, gently hugging him.

"Thank you so much for bringing Werlis to Ib'Agier," said Vrenli, extending his hand to Gerold in gratitude.

"Having only one arm doesn't mean we can't help defend Ib'Agier!" replied Gerold, grabbing Vrenli's hand.

"Now I know where the best place for us is!" exclaimed Vrenli, to which Werlis, who didn't understand what he meant, looked at him confused.

"We'll use one of the ballistae located on the eastern defensive wall," explained Vrenli and, followed by the two of them, made his way to there.

On their way there, Vrenli filled them in on Ib'Agier's defenses and told them about the book pages and the incidents in the last few days. When they arrived in front of one of the huge metal constructions that looked only remotely like a conventional ballista, Vrenli approached one of the officers and explained that he and his two friends wanted to operate one of them.

He also asked him to explain to them how it works.

"The most important thing is that you get a feel for how far the iron ball is thrown. And you have to be careful not to hit your own people who are at the outpost. You can change the direction of the throw with these three levers and the strength of the throw with these two," the officer explained, pointing to the various levers at Vrenli's head height.

"One of you needs to head to the defensive wall and guide the lever operator with precise instructions on the throw's direction and force," he directed. Upon hearing this, Werlis promptly volunteered for the role. "I'll take care of the iron balls," said

541

Gerold, picking up one of the balls, which weighed a centner, with his left hand and placing it in the throwing device.

"Then I'll take care of the levers," said Vrenli.

"Now try to hit one of the trees in the forest to our right," the officer told them.

Werlis went up to the wall and climbed the battlements to get a better view.

"Can you see the forest, Werlis?" Vrenli called up the wall.

"Yes, to our right, about five hundred paces away!" he called back.

"How far to the right?" Vrenli wanted to know after he had moved the lever a little to the right. Werlis drew his short sword and pointed toward forest.

"Can you see my sword?" he asked Vrenli.

"Yes, I see it!" shouted Vrenli and pushed the lever a little further to the right.

"Stop!" shouted Werlis.

The officer now showed Vrenli another lever, which he was to pull towards him once the direction and distance of the throw had been set.

Vrenli then pulled the lever and the iron ball was hurled over his and Werlis' heads towards the neighboring forest, where it smashed into the ground with a tremendous force just a few steps away from the trees.

"Twenty, maybe thirty steps too few. But the direction is right!" shouted Werlis.

"Try it again!" the officer urged them, going to one of the other ballistae and checking its lever.

Vrenli, Werlis and Gerold spent some more time familiarizing themselves with the ballista.

In the meantime, King Agnulix stood on the plateau in front of the Hall of Kings with two of his army commanders and watched as his men and those of the allies made their final preparations. The sun had now almost completely set behind the mountains of Ib'Agier and King Agnulix could already see the faint rising full moon behind it.

One of the two army commanders pointed to the several hundred riders who rode through the main gate to the nearby forest and disappeared under the treetops.

King Agnulix saw a golden light shining in the distant plain in front of him at the outpost. He then knew that Borlix and the paladins had begun to bless the arrows of the archers behind the high, thick metal plates. Some were covering themselves with branches to hide from the enemy's view.

"I hope that the warriors of the Desert of DeShadin and, above all, the elves from the Glorious Valley will arrive in time," muttered King Agnulix as he saw a sea of light far on the horizon.

"They're coming!" he shouted, whereupon loud gongs rang out, coming from golden metal disks that dwarves were hitting with golden hammers.

Gorathdin and Army Commander Arkondir, standing at the front line, felt the ground beneath their feet begin to vibrate slightly. Torches, carried by the foot soldiers of Erwight of Entorbis' force, shone like a sea of lights, drawing ever closer to the outpost. Behind them, tall, dark outlines of the war machines rose into the sky, emitting loud, creaking noises.

Gorathdin's dark green eyes began to light up. He took his bow from his shoulder and stuck more than twenty arrows into the ground in front of him. The hundred well-armed dwarves gathered around Gorathdin and Army Commander Arkondir, heavily armed, began to tap their shields with their axes. Gorathdin pointed his hand to the sky above the approaching army.

"Hundreds of crows!" he said to Army Commander Arkondir, who was lowering his visor and checking his armor.

Two riders carrying the banner with the Entorbis crest split off from the approaching army and rode slowly towards the outpost.

"Just what we need," Gorathdin said to Army Commander Arkondir, who didn't understand what he meant.

"They will discover our trenches. Let's ride to them quickly," Gorathdin explained.

"Two horses! Quick!" he shouted.

Two dwarves then hurriedly led the horses forward. Gorathdin and Army Commander Arkondir, who took the banner of Astinhod with him, jumped on their horses and rode towards Fallgar's two riders.

"Erwight of Entorbis lays claim to Wetherid. He offers to spare everyone in the city if you hand over your weapons and Ib'Agier. If Ib'Agier resists, no one will be spared!" said one of the two black riders to Gorathdin and Army Commander Arkondir.

Army Commander Arkondir then dismounted his horse and rammed the banner of Astinhod into the ground with all his might.

"You are on Wetherid soil. In the name of the Queen of Astinhod and the peoples of Wetherid, I demand that you and your men withdraw immediately!" Army Commander Arkondir replied firmly to the rider.

The rider drew his sword, knocked down the banner of Astinhod, loudly laughed and rode back in the direction he had come from with the other rider.

"That was close. The first trench is only a few steps behind us," remarked Gorathdin, who rode back to the outpost together with Army Commander Arkondir.

Five horsemen riding at the head of the enemy, several thousand strong, stopped about two hundred paces from the first trench. The light of the full moon dimmed as hundreds of crows flew over the army and the heads of the five horsemen.

The resounding trumpets of the black knights rang out, followed by the thunderous drumbeats of the ogres, which mingled with the bright metallic sound of the gray dwarves' axes striking their shields. A loud, bellowing scream from the orcs followed the muffled war horns of the mist elves, accompanied by the hideous, howling cries of the undead.

One of the five riders in the lead, a fat, ugly ogre, raised his hand and let it swing down resolutely to the west.

The war drums of the ogres began to sound again, whereupon the front line of the army, followed by several war machines, began to move towards the gates of Ib'Agier.

Gorathdin looked tensely at the catapults, ballistae and high siege towers that were slowly rolling towards them behind the foot troops of the orcs, ogres and gray dwarves. When they were only a few steps away from the first trench, the archers of Erwight of Entorbis and the mist elves began to advance, accompanied by the black knights who rode their horses on the flanks.

The foot troops now marched over the first trench. But when the heavy war machines were pulled over it, many broke through the branches, twigs and planks with a loud crash and got stuck.

A horn sounded, calling for a halt.

Some of the foot troops turned back and tried to pull the ballistae, catapults and three defensive towers out of the trench, which they almost succeeded in doing. But before the rear ranks could rush to their aid, Army Commander Arkondir signaled his archers to fire a flaming hail of arrows at the first trench. Hundreds of flaming arrows flew, whistling through the air and fatally striking several enemies. Those who were not hit released the war machines, several of which had caught fire.

A horn sounded three times.

The archers of Erwight of Entorbis and the mist elves then returned a hail of arrows. A hail of poisoned arrows from the mist elves and the archers from Druhn rained down on the dwarves and humans from Astinhod. However, most of the arrows bounced off the thick iron plates the defenders sought shelter behind.

Only a few arrows hit their intended target.

When the attackers' army commanders realized that their warriors' arrows were not having the desired effect, they sent the mist elves riding large spiders and lizards towards the defenders' archers. The spiders and lizards leapt over the first trench with ease. One of the spider riders stopped briefly and instructed his spider to stretch a web over the trench. The other spider riders followed his example, and within moments the first trench was covered by strong webs. Some of the ogres and gray dwarves put the undamaged ballista and the defensive tower back into action and, followed by the rest of the army marching across the trench, moved on towards the gates of Ib'Agier.

Gorathdin and Arkondir gave another signal for a hail of arrows. However, the nimble spider and lizard riders split up in different directions and from there rode in a roundabout towards the second trench, behind which Astinhod's and Ib'Agier's archers were entrenched. When the first of them noticed that the ground below was giving way, they spurred their mounts on. The signal to ignite the oil in the trench sounded too late and many of the attackers were able to jump the second trench unharmed. It was only when the fire arrows of the archers behind the second trench ignited the oil that a huge wall of fire flickered out of the trench and burned many mounted dark elves to death.

The spiders and lizard riders, who had previously managed to jump over the ditch unscathed, pounced on the archers behind the metal plates.

Gorathdin, noticing this, immediately sent the dwarves' axemen forward as support. Army Commander Arkondir signaled for another hail of arrows, which the archers not being attacked by the giant spiders and lizards launched. A sea of arrows rained down on the orcs, ogres, gray dwarves, mist elves and Druhn knights from behind the wall of flames.

Perplexed and seeking shelter from the hail of arrows, they ran around behind the high wall of flames.

In desperation, they sent messengers back to the army leaders, who stood at least six hundred paces behind them, at a safe distance. It took some time for Erwight of Entorbis to confer with the king of the gray dwarves, the prince of the mist elves, the king of the undead, the fat ugly ogre and the shaman of the orcs.

When the messenger returned to the wall of flames with new orders, he ordered the ogres and gray dwarves to move the ballistae and catapults that had not fallen into the first trench into position.

"Fire on the iron plates!" ordered a gray dwarf wearing dark ore armor and standing among a group of ogres.

It didn't take long for the catapults and ballistae to fire ammunition at the iron plates. The iron could not withstand the force of the heavy rocks and wooden stakes and toppled backwards. Some of the defenders' archers, who sought shelter behind the iron plates and were unable to jump to the side in time, were crushed.

A hail of arrows from the attackers followed and decimated the defenders' archers by half.

Army Commander Arkondir then gave the signal to retreat. The survivors, some badly injured, dragged themselves back behind the trench that lay just outside the gates of Ib'Agier. Borlix, who was standing in front of the third trench with a small group of archers, was about to retreat when a spider rider appeared in front of him and struck him violently on the helmet with his scimitar as he rode. Borlix lost his balance and fell backwards to the ground. Through the opening in his visor, he saw the poisonous stinger of a spider that had positioned itself above him and was holding him with two of its eight legs.

With great difficulty, Borlix grabbed his axe lying next to him and parried a few stabs with it. The mist elf sitting on the spider said something to his mount in a language Borlix couldn't understand and dismounted. The spider then began to spin a number of fine, but barely severable, threads around Borlix with its web gland located behind the stinger. In a few moments, his legs were completely wrapped. The mist elf, who was standing next to the spider and Borlix, laughed maliciously.

Borlix tried to hit him with his axe. However, the mist elf dodged the blow, jumped towards Borlix and knocked the axe out of his hand with his scimitar. The spider above Borlix hissed and opened its mouth wide, revealing hundreds of tiny teeth. It slowly moved its venomous stinger towards Borlix, who looked around desperately for his shield but couldn't find it anywhere.

"By all the halls of Ib'Agier. This is the end for me! Lorijan help me!" Borlix cried out desperately and tried to roll to the side, but the mist elf standing next to him prevented him from doing so. The rider flipped back the visor on Borlix's helmet with the blade of his scimitar and grinned at him with glowing red eyes.

Gorathdin, who had noticed Borlix's hopeless situation from a distance, ran as fast as he could towards his friend in distress and shot an arrow at the mist elf while he was running, which hit him in the middle of his forehead and threw him to the ground.

With a somersault in the air, Gorathdin leapt onto the spider's back and plunged his hunting knife into its neck with all his might. The arachnid collapsed and landed on Borlix, who groaned violently from the weight pressing down on his body.

"Gorathdin!" shouted Borlix, taking a deep breath before lifting the spider up a little with his strong arms.

"Pull!" Borlix demanded Gorathdin, who then pulled him out from under the spider with a jerk. Gorathdin struggled to cut the spider threads wrapped around Borlix's legs with his dagger. Borlix waited impatiently and still lying on his back, looked up at the sky above him.

Hundreds of black crows circled, cawing above them. Ornux had sent them to support the attacking spider and lizard riders.

With their razor-sharp claws and beaks, they hacked at the lightly armored archers. The dwarf axemen who arrived at the third trench to support the archers were almost completely wiped out by the lizard and spider riders of the mist elves.

Gorathdin drew his longsword and carefully cut the spider threads on Borlix's legs.

"Thank you!" said Borlix, reaching for his axe, which Gorathdin handed him, and picking up his shield that lay a few steps away from the dead spider.

Together they hurried past a row of fallen mist elves, archers and axemen, straight towards Army Commander Arkondir, who was waiting for them with a few men next to the hatches on the third trench. The two had to hurry to get there before the flock of crows arrived.

As he ran, Borlix glanced over his shoulder at the wall of flames, which were now almost extinguished. In some places, Erwight of Entorbis' knights were already leaping over the ditch on their horses and galloping towards him and Gorathdin at ever increasing speed.

"Give the signal for the riders in the forest!" shouted Borlix to Army Commander Arkondir, who was standing in front of an open hatch.

"But what about the crows?" he called to Borlix, who then stopped, placed his golden shield on the ground in front of him, knelt behind it and began to pray for the light of Lorijan.

"Give the signal!" shouted Borlix, who was delighted to see the arriving troops from the Desert of DeShadin joining the defenders.

Gorathdin, who had already arrived at the hatch, nodded to Army Commander Arkondir, who then blew a horn. At the same time, a bright golden beam of light shot from Borlix's shield and spread into the sky. The crows, blinded by the light, cried out and flew back to their master, cawing.

Wahmubu's and Manamii's riders from the Desert of DeShadin, the knights from Astinhod and the mounted barbarians, led by Erik and Warwik, drove their horses from the northern forest straight towards the attackers, who had jumped over the second trench. Defenders and attackers clashed, and a fierce battle broke out.

Azrakel, the Soulbinder, who was at the back of the battlefield, raised his sword to the sky. In response, an army of undead slowly freed themselves from the earth's grip. Gorathdin watched as they laboriously rose from the ground between the second and third trenches with their decayed bodies and slowly dragged themselves towards the other allies of Erwight of Entorbis. They charged at the defenders' horses, which reared up and threw off many of their riders. The undead then pounced on the unfortunates and mauled them.

Borlix didn't know what to do at first. If he turned Lorijan's light on the undead, the crows would be able to join the fight again, but on the other hand, only Lorijan's light could stop the undead. Borlix felt that he was losing the strength that the light demanded of him.

He looked at Gorathdin, who realized that something was wrong with his friend. He quickly ran across the third trench towards Borlix.

"The paladins in the third trench, they have to come out. Now!" Borlix called out to Gorathdin before he could reach him.

Gorathdin turned around as quickly as he could and ran towards the closed hatches.

"Borlix needs the paladins!" he shouted as loudly as he could and, once there, struck the hatch with his longsword.

A paladin hesitantly climbed out and looked out onto the battlefield. Gorathdin pointed with his hand at the undead charging over the horses and riders of their allies. "Paladins to the top. Undead!" shouted the dwarf, who, like Borlix, wore golden armor.

Several hatches opened. The paladins climbed out of the trench and charged towards the attackers. The light of Lorijan shone from their blessed axes, hammers and golden spears. Every undead that was hit by a beam of light dissolved into dust, screaming.

A muffled horn sounded over the plain.

A paladin with a long black beard swung his hammer over his shield as he chased after some fleeing undead. Suddenly he spotted

Ornux's flock of crows flying menacingly down from the forest towards the paladins.

"The crows of the shadow mages!" he called warningly to the other paladins, who then abandoned their pursuit of the undead.

Together, they rammed their shields into the earthy ground and began to say a prayer. Shortly afterwards, golden light shone in the dark night sky above them. Once again, with the help of Lorijan's light, the crows were driven away. The paladins then marched back to the third trench.

Gorathdin and Army Commander Arkondir used the moment to get an overview of the battlefield.

Most of the archers and axemen lay dead on the ground before them, near the extinguished wall of flame at the second trench. Many of Wahmubu's and Manamii's riders lay half mangled beside their horses. Some of Warwik and Erik's riders lay there as well. Astinhod's knights and the surviving barbarian riders, who were currently fighting with some of the ogre and orc troops, realized their numerical inferiority and turned their horses towards the third trench, blowing their horns in retreat.

Gorathdin ordered the remaining archers to fire several hails of arrows in the direction of the retreating horsemen to cover their backs.

"We don't exactly have few casualties," he then said to Army Commander Arkondir.

"Unfortunately, yes. I had hoped we could keep them down. But all these sacrifices were not in vain. The enemy has only a few war machines left, the mist elf riders have been defeated and the undead that did not crumble to dust have fled into the nearby forest. They fear the light of Lorijan too much to take part in the battle again. Our riders were also able to roust the ogre and orc troops. I don't think Erwight of Entorbis expected his force to be so decimated before it reached the gates. Even if our losses are greater than planned, we were successful," replied Army

Commander Arkondir, looking at the remaining army that had just crossed the second trench.

The fat ugly ogre rode up to the first trench and ordered his men and the gray dwarves, who were lingering by the destroyed war machines, to remove posts and planks from them to make the second trench passable.

As the first ranks of the enemy moved across the second trench, Army Commander Arkondir ordered a retreat. The enemy, now marching towards the third trench, advanced faster than the defenders of Ib'Agier could retreat.

The narrow passage between the trenches and the forest back to the gates offered barely enough space for three horses galloping side by side.

Werlis, who was standing on the defensive wall, realized that the riders would take too long to pass. The rear ranks of the foot troops were already being attacked by Erwight of Entorbis' horsemen. From behind, they struck Astinhod's and Ib'Agier's warriors, killing many of them.

"We have to help them!" shouted Werlis to one of the dwarf officers also on the defensive wall.

"The enemy riders are out of range of our archers," the dwarf replied.

"The ballistae!" Werlis called to him, whereupon the officer nodded, estimated the distance, indicated the direction to throw and ordered the dwarves at the ballistae closest to the riders to fire. Several large, heavy iron balls struck between the enemy horsemen.

Many of the horses shied, some threw off their riders and some were fatally shot. The resulting chaos gave the retreating defenders the time they needed to get to the main gates. They were still pursued by some riders, but when they were close enough to the defensive wall, the riders were finished off by the dwarf archers.

King Agnulix, who was waiting for the returnees in the inner courtyard, praised the men as they came through the main gate on the left. The wounded were immediately tended to by the dwarf priests. Those who were in good health were sent as reinforcements to the strike force.

Wahmubu, who was slightly wounded, was treated by one of the priests and then went with King Agnulix to the plateau in front of the Hall of Kings to get an overview of the approaching enemy.

"How many casualties do we have?" he asked Wahmubu.

"About half!" he replied.

"And the enemy?" the King of the Dwarves wanted to know.

"It's hard to say. I couldn't see the whole battlefield from my position. Not many of the enemy's war machines remain, I saw that with my own eyes! You should ask Gorathdin or Army Commander Arkondir. They surely know more," replied Wahmubu, pressing a hand to the cut on his shoulder.

"Where is Army Commander Arkondir, Borlix and Gorathdin?" King Agnulix continued to ask, but Wahmubu could not give him an answer.

Unbeknownst to Wahmubu, Army Commander Arkondir and Gorathdin were still standing near the third trench, hastily instructing the stragglers to flee into the city.

Both shouted, loudly, to Borlix that he should retreat. He thought for a moment, looked up at the sky to the east then to the north, stood up and ran over to his friends at the outpost in front of the gates. They were just about to walk to the rock face to the west to get back to the gates when Borlix looked over his shoulder to the edge of the forest. A handful of paladins under his command were fighting with ogres, who were beating them with their heavy, spiky clubs. A troop of more than a hundred gray dwarves suddenly appeared behind the ogres and rushed to their aid. Borlix then turned back and ran, screaming, in the direction of his paladins.

"Retreat, retreat!" he shouted as loud as he could, but his men could not hear him over the loud noises of the battle. Gorathdin, who had instinctively turned around, caught sight of Borlix running across the battlefield. He ran after him as fast as he could and when he caught up with him, he threw himself at him, causing Borlix to fall to the ground.

"I have to help them!" Borlix shouted at Gorathdin, pulling away from him with all his might and standing up. Just as he was about to run on, several arrows were fired by some mist elves who noticed him. All but one bounced off his golden armor and stuck in the right side of Borlix's chest, and Gorathdin, still lying on the ground and camouflaged, looked at his friend's pained face.

Despite the arrow in his chest, Borlix tried to get up to reach his paladins, but Gorathdin pulled him to the ground and held him there.

"It's too late!" he said to Borlix, who was trying to free himself from Gorathdin's grip.

"Borlix! It's too late. There's nothing more you can do for them!" Gorathdin shouted at him, needing all his strength to hold his friend. It was the first time Gorathdin had ever seen Borlix cry.

The enemy force came closer to them. Gorathdin grabbed Borlix by the arm and ran back to the outpost, dragging him behind him. When Army Commander Arkondir saw the two approaching and realized that Borlix was injured, he rode towards them as fast as he could.

"Mount up, Borlix!" he called to him. With Gorathdin's help, he pulled him onto the horse behind him and rode with him back to the gates.

"Open the right gate!" shouted a dwarf from the defense tower when he saw Army Commander Arkondir and Borlix riding towards him. The gate opened slowly and the two rode through it past the strike force to the priests who were tending to the injured riders in the courtyard.

Borlix fell off the horse at the feet of a priest who was applying a bandage to a warrior from the Desert of DeShadin.

"Quick, help me!" shouted Army Commander Arkondir, jumping off his horse and bending over Borlix.

Two men from Astinhod hurried over, carefully lifted Borlix and laid him on one of the hides that had been spread out on the ground for the wounded.

Wahmubu, who was still standing by King Agnulix's side on the plateau, saw Army Commander Arkondir, next to whom Borlix was lying injured on the ground, and immediately ran down to them.

"I'll take care of him," Wahmubu said to the priest, who took Borlix's helmet off.

Army Commander Arkondir briefly reported to Wahmubu what had happened and rode back out onto the battlefield to look for Gorathdin, who had still not arrived behind the gates.

Wahmubu looked at the mist elf's arrow in Borlix's chest. He felt his forehead, which was glowing with sweat. Borlix's lips were blue and when he tried to say something to Wahmubu, he lost consciousness.

"The arrows of the mist elves are poisoned," the priest remarked.

"What poison?" Wahmubu asked him.

"Spider venom," the priest replied.

"Do you have an antidote?" Wahmubu wanted to know, holding Borlix's arm.

"I don't think so. Take him to the Holy Hall. Perhaps Groblix can help him," replied the priest.

Wahmubu took off Borlix's heavy golden armor, except for his breastplate, lifted him up and brought him into Lorijan's Hall.

"Borlix! What happened?" cried Master Drobal when he saw Wahmubu holding Borlix in his arms.

"Groblix! Quick, over here, Borlix is hurt!" Wahmubu called out to the chief priest of the dwarves, who immediately answered his call.

"Where is Gorathdin?" Master Drobal asked Wahmubu.

But Wahmubu did not know that Gorathdin was being pursued by mist elves as he ran after Army Commander Arkondir and Borlix. Many arrows were fired at him, but all missed their target. The mist elves, quick and agile like all elves, followed Gorathdin closely. He was within their grasp when several cries rang out. Gorathdin looked over his shoulder and saw some of his pursuers lying on the ground. Just a few paces behind them, Aarl came running towards him. Gorathdin stopped, reached for his longsword and slew two of the five remaining pursuers. One of the mist elves stopped and drew his bow as one of Aarl's throwing knives stuck in his throat. Gorathdin performed an aerial leap with his longsword towards the two remaining pursuers and decapitated them before he landed safely on the ground.

"Thank you!" he called to Aarl, who walked towards him with a smile.

"I thought you were dead. I saw you lying on one of the overturned iron plates next to some archers," Gorathdin said in astonishment.

"You weren't the only one who thought that. Fortunately for me, I have to say. When we were attacked by the spider and lizard riders and then they got reinforcements from the crows, I thought it was better to just play dead," Aarl explained to Gorathdin, waving to a dwarf on the defense tower at the right gate. The gate opened.

Army Commander Arkondir was about to cross the battlefield in search of Gorathdin when, to his great joy, he saw Gorathdin and Aarl, who had been thought dead, at the gate.

Gorathdin briefly told him what had stopped him when Army Commander Arkondir interrupted him.

"Borlix has been hit by a poisoned arrow. He's in poor condition," he told them.

"Where is he?" asked Gorathdin.

"In the Holy Hall," replied Army Commander Arkondir.

"Let's go to him at once!" Gorathdin urged and led them into the Holy Hall, where he found Wahmubu and Master Drobal kneeling next to Borlix.

King Agnulix had also come to Lorijan's Hall when he heard about Borlix's injury.

"We need an antidote, or he will die in a few hours, like many before him," the king said in a depressed voice.

"Wahmubu, can't you help him? Vrenli told me that you know the art of healing," Gorathdin turned to him, but Wahmubu shook his head.

"This spider venom is unknown to me. The only thing I might be able to do for him is to buy him an hour or two, but to do that I have to get to the wound first, which is difficult because of the arrow that has penetrated his body. I can't pull it out, that would be too risky. The poison could spread through him faster," explained Wahmubu.

Gorathdin looked at Master Drobal for help.

"I can try to split the breastplate," he finally said, and since no one had a better suggestion, everyone present agreed.

Master Drobal raised his staff and tapped the center of the breastplate. Small, violet-colored flashes slid slowly from the staff across the golden metal. He waited a few moments and tapped again, this time harder, on the center of the breastplate, which broke in two with a soft crack. Wahmubu carefully removed the left half of the breastplate and could see the wound on Borlix's right breast where the poisoned arrow had penetrated flesh. The small, thin veins around the wound spread across Borlix's chest like a spider's web.

"We should send for Brother Transmudin," Wahmubu suggested.

"He's down in the grotto with Omnigo," Master Drobal informed them.

King Agnulix instructed one of his dwarves to go to the mines to fetch Brother Transmudin. The dwarf then hurried out of Lorijan's Hall and returned a little later with Brother Transmudin.

"What happened?" Brother Transmudin asked those present, who then told him about the incident with the mist elves.

"Spider venom! That's not good! I can stop the poison a bit, maybe for a few days, but I can't cure him," explained Brother Transmudin gloomily.

"What we need is a druid," he added, looking at Gorathdin.

"I will take him to my father, but I need a Scheddifer horse because we don't have much time! The Dark Forest is seven days' journey from Ib'Agier," said Gorathdin.

"You can't leave Ib'Agier. Someone else must take him to your father," Master Drobal objected and looked resolutely at Gorathdin. His diamond-shaped mark began to shimmer light blue and Gorathdin understood.

"Aarl, you must take Borlix to my father in the Dark Forest. You know the way. I can't leave Ib'Agier," said Gorathdin, and Aarl nodded in agreement.

"I'll take him there, but what about the rangers, the wild animals and the other druids?" he asked Gorathdin.

"Call on me, and if you get into trouble, ask for Regindar. He will help you," replied Gorathdin.

"I will accompany you. I'll get my horse and meet you at the west gate near Manamii. You can ride her horse, it's the fastest in the Desert of DeShadin," Wahmubu said with pride in his voice as he was about to leave the Holy Hall.

"How am I supposed to ride a horse with Borlix? He's unconscious," Aarl remarked, looking questioningly at Gorathdin.

"We'll tie him to the horse. Come now, time is limited!" replied Wahmubu, and he and Aarl carried Borlix on a stretcher to the west gate, where they found Manamii, who was still waiting for a message from her foot troops. They quickly told her what had happened outside the gates of Ib'Agier in the east.

Tormenix opened the side gate for Aarl and Wahmubu so they could reach the horses standing in front of the rampart with Borlix on the stretcher. Their arrival seemed to alarm the horses, however, as their fearful neighing suddenly broke the silence, causing the dwarves behind the rampart to sit up and take notice. They ran out of the side gate towards Wahmubu and Aarl, who stood rooted to the spot in front of a huge, upright bear. It roared menacingly and bared its mighty teeth, while a lynx and two wolves prowled around behind it. Three stags with large antlers stood still in front of around two hundred armed elves from the Dark Forest, who stared at Wahmubu and Aarl with their dark green eyes.

A forest-green light enveloped the bear and a moment later, instead of a bear, the druid Mergoldin stood before them.

"Did you really think I would let my son fight the enemy from Fallgar alone? Or why are you looking at me in such astonishment?" Mergoldin asked Wahmubu and Aarl, who then quickly told him about Borlix's poisoning.

While they marched back into the city through the side gate with the druids and their entourage and met up with King Agnulix, Gorathdin stepped forward.

"Father? I thought you had changed your mind!" he exclaimed happily and hugged Mergoldin, then beckoned Regindar to him.

"You didn't really think I would let my only son go to war alone, did you? We were held up by several clans of forest goblins. Hence our delay! But now let me try to help your dwarf friend," said Mergoldin, leaning over Borlix.

"Mist Moor red spiders. A deadly poison. He wouldn't last two days without treatment, even if the wound didn't look like it does. The poison works quickly and there is no conventional antidote. He would have died on the journey, that's for sure," he explained to Brother Transmudin and Wahmubu, realizing that they were both skilled in healing.

Mergoldin gently placed his hand, from which a dark green light shone on the wound, over Borlix. Slowly, the red veins that had already spread from the wound over half of Borlix's body receded. It took some time before Borlix opened his eyes and tried to sit up. Exhausted, he told those present what had happened on the battlefield.

Groblix, having heard that fifteen paladins had fallen at the outpost, began to pray for their souls before the statue of Lorijan. Master Drobal greeted Mergoldin warmly, as if they were old friends, and they whispered something in each other's ears. Gorathdin, Army Commander Arkondir and King Agnulix were discussing the losses on both sides and considering their chances of defending Ib'Agier when several small tremors shook Lorijan's Hall slightly.

"Those are projectiles from Erwight of Entorbis' war machines!" shouted Vrenli and Werlis, who ran into the hall together and warned those present. King Agnulix immediately went back to the plateau, where he looked down on the forces of Erwight of Entorbis, who were firing at Ib'Agier with three ballistae and at least four catapults standing in front of the last trench.

"Their range is further than we thought," said one of the army commanders, signaling an officer below him in the courtyard to return fire. The bombardment of the war machines on both sides continued until the early hours of the morning. Vrenli, Werlis and Gerold managed to destroy a ballista and a catapult, but when the enemy archers, who were seeking cover behind the large defense tower, fired a hail of arrows at the defensive wall and towers for several hours, the three had to leave the wall temporarily. Only when the hail of arrows subsided did they return to their posts.

"The only option we have now is to observe exactly where the bullets that hit here are being fired from and to hurl our iron balls in that direction," said Vrenli to Werlis and Gerold.

Werlis went back up and climbed the battlements. From there, he had a view of the battlefield.

Large, powerful ogres pulled out the metal and wooden stakes that had been sunk into the last trench near the gates. Many of them were killed by archers' arrows on the defense towers.

A muffled signal sounded from a war horn.

It wasn't long before three dozen mist elves on spiders and lizards rode onto the battlefield from the small, wooded area to Werlis' right.

They drove their mounts towards the defensive wall, skillfully dodged the arrows of the defenders' archers and climbed up the wall onto two of the defensive towers.

Once at the top, they finished off the dwarves' tower guards and archers. King Agnulix, who observed this, ordered his axe-wielders in the inner courtyard to recapture the two defensive towers. They rushed up the spiral staircases and fought the mist elves on their giant spiders and lizard beasts.

King Agnulix was startled when a bombardment of catapults and ballistae began on the gates. An incessant hail of arrows from the mist elves, who had moved closer, followed, killing many of the defenders on the ramparts.

Some of the orcs, equipped with battering rams, tried to advance to a side gate, but were knocked out by the gate guards pouring liquid ore on them from above.

"We must attempt an initial attack to decimate the enemy archers," suggested one of the army commanders standing on the plateau with King Agnulix.

"Let only the well-armored warbucks attack. The riders of the Scheddifer and the Knights of Astinhod should wait!" the king said to the army commander, who then gave the signal to attack and shouted to one of his officers that only the warbuck riders should ride out.

The two side gates opened and the dwarves rode their armored ibexes towards the mist elf archers. They decimated their numbers considerably until they were finally driven back by the foot troops of the orcs and gray dwarves. An hours-long alternating hail of arrows and bombardments from the war machines of attackers and defenders followed. The forces of Erwight of Entorbis advanced closer to the gates, step by step, despite heavy losses.

Vrenli and Werlis did their best at the ballista, while Gorathdin and Army Commander Arkondir commanded the men on the ramparts. Wahmubu and Aarl prepared for another attack in the courtyard, while Brother Transmudin and Mergoldin watched over Borlix, who had already survived the worst.

A fierce battle also broke out on the west side of Ib'Agier, as Manamii with Dark Forest elves, Tormenix's men and their decimated foot troops encountered snow and forest goblins attempting to take the side gate.

Betrayed and sold

As the morning began to dawn, Master Drobal sat alone with his eyes closed next to the grayed bowl, near the statue of Lorijan in the Holy Hall on the floor. The silence was suddenly interrupted by a familiar voice.

"Stay seated! You don't have to bother getting up!" said Ornux, who was standing in front of Master Drobal with Erwight of Entorbis. The shadow aura of the mage from Fallgar darkened the Holy Hall.

Erwight of Entorbis looked at the statue of the Goddess Lorijan and signaled to Ornux. The shadow mage slowly placed his hand on the golden statue, causing its golden glow to turn gray.

"Her light is no longer needed," Erwight of Entorbis said to Master Drobal, who was still sitting on the ground. Ornux slowly raised his arms, and out of nowhere, two more shadow mages in black robes and hoods pulled low over their faces materialized at his side, shrouded in the mist gathering on the ground. Master Drobal looked into Ornux's gray, pupil-less eyes.

"I thought you'd turn up here sooner or later," he said to him calmly.

" You didn't think you could do anything against us on your own, did you?" Ornux replied with a sardonic smile.

"Since you have killed all my brothers from Horunguth Island, I suppose I have no choice but to face you alone, or did you think I would present the kings of Wetherid to you on a platter?" replied Master Drobal.

"It would have saved us time. But we'll pay them a courtesy visit anyway," said Ornux, looking at Erwight of Entorbis and laughing out loud.

"Ib'Agier has not fallen yet. You are acting a little hastily," said Master Drobal to Erwight of Entorbis.

"It's a matter of hours. Ib'Agier will fall. But that's not why we came to the Hall of Lorijan, mage!" replied Erwight of Entorbis.

"As you know, a book fell into my hands and I came to get the missing pages," said Erwight of Entorbis.

"Fallen into the hands, you say? Do you call stealing, murdering and plundering 'falling into my hands'?" replied Master Drobal.

"The Entorbis family is not the first to lay claim to a country and thus to all its goods, mage!" Erwight of Entorbis replied.

"As I read in my book, there were several wars in Wetherid, and the enemy didn't always come from outside," he added.

"First of all, the book is not yours, even if you currently possess it, and the internal conflicts of the peoples of a country do not give anyone from outside the right to go murdering and pillaging through the land. You are right when you say that problems have not always been solved peacefully. But nothing that happened in Wetherid is comparable to your greed! You are driven by envy, anger, revenge and a lust for murder," replied Master Drobal calmly.

"Well, as far as I can remember, we made you a peaceful proposal if you gave up Ib'Agier," mocked Erwight of Entorbis with a derisive smile.

"Spare me that kind of conversation," said Master Drobal and stood up from the ground, holding on to his staff. Ornux and the two other shadow mages watched his movements closely, for they knew of the power of the mages of Horunguth Island.

"You are not here to take Ib'Agier, at least that is not your main reason," Master Drobal spoke to everyone present.

"Ib'Agier is an important city in Wetherid and it is in the interests of our allies to take it. But you are right, nonetheless. I have come to take the missing pages of my book. Frankly, I care little whether we succeed in breaching the defenses or not, but as mentioned before, politics demands Ib'Agier," explained Erwight of Entorbis.

"And until we have the pages in our hands, we will abide by this policy. In moderation!" Ornux affirmed, to which the two other shadow mages accompanying him nodded.

"The magic of the elves from the Glorious Valley, which rests in the book, will enable me to conquer not only Wetherid, but also the Northland, the kingdom in the east, Candiras in the west and the island kingdoms in the south! The world will have a ruler who will unite and rule all under the crest of Druhn!" announced Erwight of Entorbis confidently.

"You are very sure that the magic of the elves from the Glorious Valley will make you so powerful. You should never be so sure in life, Erwight!" warned Master Drobal.

"It is undisputed that the shadow mages of Fallgar are the most powerful mages known to us all. The book will increase our power, many times over, and don't think you can stop us, old man!" said Ornux, sending Master Drobal crashing into the wall of the hall with a wave of his hand.

Master Drobal fell to the ground and took a deep breath, but contrary to Ornux's expectations, he did nothing but walk slowly towards them again, leaning lightly on his staff.

"Even if you kill me, the book will do you no good without the missing pages!" he gasped.

"I have to agree with you, mage!" Erwight of Entorbis conceded, raising his hand and making a beckoning motion, whereupon Brother Transmudin stepped through the entrance to the hall.

He glanced briefly at Master Drobal and then lowered his gaze to the ground.

"This cylinder contains the missing pages of your book," he said to Erwight of Entorbis and held up the cylinder.

"Surprised?" Erwight of Entorbis asked Master Drobal with a smile on his lips.

His eyes began to sparkle as Brother Transmudin handed him the top hat.

"Surprised by the falseness of some people? Yes, I am. About Brother Transmudin handing you the cylinder No. I expected that!" said Master Drobal and looked sharply at Brother Transmudin, who was getting nervous.

"You must understand. I am a servant of Omnigo. He has been living underground for centuries. Omnigo must be free and able to fly over Wetherid again. It's not right that he has to live like a prisoner!" Brother Transmudin defended himself.

"You could have informed the mages of Horunguth Island about the existence of Omnigo so that we could look for a solution together," replied Master Drobal.

"A solution? Like that of King Grandhold's father, who even forbade us to use our magic? Is that the kind of solution you mean?" replied Brother Transmudin angrily.

"I can understand your anger, but did you really have to betray everything worth living for? You have trampled friendship, solidarity, helpfulness, truth and hope with your foot!" Master Drobal spoke sternly.

"For us, Omnigo is all that matters!" replied Brother Transmudin, to which Master Drobal realized that no further words were necessary.

"Well, now that you have the missing book pages, I wonder why you didn't take them much earlier. You didn't think I attributed all the incidents on our journey, from which we always escaped without serious damage, to luck, did you? Did you think I had missed the fact that you knew where the pages were long ago?" Master Drobal asked Erwight of Entorbis.

"They say a power stronger than the magic of the elves rests within this book, but I could learn nothing about this mysterious power no matter how many times I read the book. Therefore, since I am also bound by covenants, I decided to let you and the Keepers of the Book go to Ib'Agier to command you here and now to reveal to me this power that I have been told about so often, mage! Here and now, before my allies break through the gates of Ib'Agier!" Erwight of Entorbis commanded him in a trembling voice.

Master Drobal noticed how the Shadow Lord's hands began to tremble with excitement as he opened the cylinder.

"Kondji Jahrandu!" cried Master Drobal, and a bright blue beam of light shot out of his diamond-shaped mark, piercing through the ceiling of the hall and the thick rock of the mountain into the sky and spreading out over the peaks of Ib'Agier.

Ornux and the two other shadow mages recited a verse in the language of Fallgar, whereupon Master Drobal was hurled through the air by an invisible force and finally pressed against the far wall. The force of the impact almost knocked him unconscious. He fell to the floor.

Ornux, with the dark power of Fallgar in his voice, muttered another spell. A shadow shot from his hand straight towards Master Drobal. The mage of Horunguth Island rose quickly and decisively as he created a wall of purple light with a powerful swing of his staff. The shadow crashed into the wall and dissolved into a veil of smoke.

But the other two shadow mages were relentless. They hurled dark shadow orbs, one after the other, at Master Drobal. Despite his wall of light, one of the orbs managed to penetrate the defense and hit him. With a groan, Master Drobal sank back to the ground.

He wanted to stand up again, but he noticed how the shadow around him was draining his life force.

Meanwhile, Vrenli was the first to see the bright blue light above the peaks of Ib'Agier and immediately hurried to Lorijan's Hall.

"I have to see Master Drobal!" he called out to Werlis and Gerold, who questioningly looked after him.

Gorathdin was shooting his arrows from one of the defensive towers near the badly damaged main gate at the ogres and orcs, who were once again battering the gate. As he ducked to avoid an arrow from a mist elf, he glanced briefly over his shoulder and saw the bright blue light in the morning sky. He then jumped from the defense tower into the courtyard and ran to Lorijan's Hall, where he arrived almost at the same time as Vrenli and Manamii.

The three friends froze when they saw what was going on in the hall.

"Now that we are fully assembled, add the pages from the cylinder to the book!" Erwight of Entorbis instructed Ornux, handing him the cylinder.

Gorathdin wanted to run towards Ornux to prevent this. Vrenli and Manamii tried to get to Master Drobal, who was still lying on the ground by the wall, but they were all held back by a wall of shadows emanating from the two mages next to Ornux.

Ornux inserted the pages from the cylinder into the appropriate places in the book and handed the complete book to Erwight of Entorbis.

"At last! What my grandfather began, my father continued and I, Erwight of Entorbis, finally finished. The Book of Wetherid is complete!" he shouted, holding it up in front of him.

At the same moment, the left main gate of Ib'Agier burst with a loud bang. More than a thousand knights of Druhn, gray dwarves, mist elves, ogres and orcs tried to enter Ib'Agier through the main gate despite the arrows fired at them by the surviving archers on the defensive wall, the towers and the courtyard.

The undead, who had previously fled from Lorijan's light, also ran towards the side gates from the adjacent forest.

The few surviving paladins realized that the light of Lorijan had left them and their blessing remained powerless. They could no longer do much against the undead. The undead tried to open the side gates for their allies but were caught up in a battle with the barbarian riders and Astinhods.

The gray dwarves and ogres pushed the battle tower over the last trench, which had been cleared of all obstacles, and advanced towards the defensive wall. The wooden hatches of the tower opened and a host charged towards the defenders on the wall. A fierce battle broke out.

Werlis and Gerold had to flee from the ballista. A mist elf jumped off the wall and followed Werlis. The mist elf laughed out loud when he noticed his missing arm. But before he could strike with his scimitar, Gerold grabbed him from behind and twisted his head with a jerk, causing the attacker to fall to the ground motionless.

Werlis was about to thank Gerold when hundreds of warriors from the Desert of DeShadin armed with scimitars, spears, bows and arrows stormed onto the defensive wall from the courtyard below and engaged the enemies in battle. Werlis and Gerold ran back to the ballista and alone, more out of desperation than strategy, fired some of the iron balls at the enemies still behind the defensive wall.

King Agnulix, who, when the gate broke, ran with two of his army commanders from a narrow staircase down the plateau to his men in the inner courtyard, was heavily attacked by some gray dwarves with axes.

"Protect the king!" shouted one of his army commanders, whereupon several dwarves and knights from Astinhod rushed to the king's aid.

Loud horn signals sounded from the east towards Ib'Agier.

Army Commander Arkondir, who was fighting the enemy on one of the defensive towers, saw a purple light on the horizon that had spread far across the sky and was getting closer.

"The elves from the Glorious Valley are coming!" he shouted several times, as loud as he could. Everyone fighting on Ib'Agier's defensive wall was delighted at the good news. King Agnulix, who had regained hope, gave the order to break out. The men regained their strength and succeeded in pushing the invading enemies back from the destroyed main gate and the defensive walls.

"Those were the horns of the elves from the Glorious Valley," Master Drobal realized, slowly getting up from the ground.

"The elf woman can't help you now either. It's too late, old man, and now tell me, what other power is there to speak of besides the magic of the elves? Speak, or one of your friends will die!" said Erwight of Entorbis threateningly and signaled to Ornux. He hurled Vrenli through the air and pressed him against the wall with a hand of shadow. Vrenli cried out in pain.

Master Drobal clutched his staff, from which purple lightning was rising, but when he saw Vrenli lying on the ground in good health, he decided to do nothing.

"I appreciate that you are wise enough to know when to give up," Ornux said with a grin.

The pained cries of Erwight of Entorbis' army echoed into Lorijan's Hall as the elves of the Glorious Valley charged the enemy from behind, cutting them down with a precision and unity that resembled a sweeping, sharp blade stretching across the battlefield before Ib'Agier.

The call of hundreds of owls, hawks and falcons flying over the mountains from the west and swooping down on the enemy made Gorathdin sit up and take notice. When he heard the howling of wolves and the mighty roar of a bear that sounded across the plain to the Lorijan's Hall, he knew that all was not lost after all.

"You must call the young man. Call the Keeper of the Book. Concentrate!" Vrenli heard a voice within him.

Confused, he got up from the floor and looked at Master Drobal, who slowly nodded slightly. Vrenli closed his eyes and thought hard, with all his might, of the verses he had heard in his dreams. He saw the young man who had been entrusted with the book from the Glorious Valley clearly in his mind's eye.

The young man asked him if he knew where the Book of Wetherid was.

"It is here. Here in front of me." Vrenli whispered and heard Gorathdin, Manamii and Master Drobal whispering the same words.

When Ornux heard this and was seized by a dark premonition, he quickly tried to raise his hand against Master Drobal. But suddenly, a swirl of blue and violet light flashed through the center of the Holy Hall. Out of the shimmering light, an elven youth emerged with a graceful determination, holding in his hands a sword that seemed to be made not of metal but of pure, glassy light. The youth swung his sword, a symbol of purity and strength, high above his head, ready to wield it against the darkness embodied by the shadow mage.

Ornux, recognizing the threat, backed away, but the elven youth, swift and agile as the wind itself, gave him no time to escape. With a smooth movement that seemed to part the air, the youth struck a powerful blow. But Ornux, who was experienced in the dark arts, parried the blow with a shield of shadowy energy that enveloped him at the last moment. A fierce battle broke out, and each clash of their magical weapons created a fascinating interplay of light and darkness that bathed the walls of the hall in a flickering spectacle. Ornux, now revealed in his true form, a shape so dark and distorted that it seemed to devour the light around it, attacked with a series of dark spells. As Ornux unleashed his dark spells, an aura of sheer darkness surrounded him. The elven youth, agile and determined, parried every attack with the elegance of a dancer. Between the flashes of dark magic and the gleam of the light-flooded sword, words found their way, revealing the essence of their conflict.

"You think you can defeat the darkness, youngling? I am the night itself," mocked Ornux,

"The night always gives way to the morning light. Your darkness has no place here, Ornux," the young elf replied calmly, for he was unshakeable in his faith.

As Ornux unleashed a particularly insidious spell that filled the air with a suffocating darkness, he continued to taunt the youth.

"Can you feel the shadows reaching for you? They will devour you!" said Ornux with a sneer.

"I walk in the light, and the shadows you cast cannot touch me," the young man replied, skillfully gliding through the darkness.

"How can you hope to stand against me? I am the end of all things," Ornux hissed as another of his attacks came to nothing.

The elven youth raised his sword and struck, breaking through the darkness around Ornux.

"Every end is also a beginning. Your fall will pave the way for a new light," he said in a voice full of confidence and continued his attacks. With a well-aimed blow, he decided the fate of Ornux, who fell to the ground dead.

The young elf then turned to the two other shadow mages.

"The light shines brightest in the face of darkness. Your time is over," he said.

Before the other shadow mages could turn their horror at their leader's fate into an attack, Master Drobal intervened. With his staff in his hand, he unleashed a volley of purple lightning that flung one shadow mage to the ground, while the other, in a blind rage, turned his dark powers against the youth. But even the darkest spells could not touch the young elf. They slipped through him as if he were a mere shadow of light.

Unperturbed by the attacks, the elven youth took his glass bow, put a silver arrow in the string and aimed at the remaining shadow mage. The arrow, which turned into lightning as it flew, found its target with deadly precision.

Erwight of Entorbis, who had watched from a safe distance as his allies fell one by one, quickly tried to grab the book lying next to Ornux's lifeless body. But his movement was abruptly interrupted.

"Don't you dare!" a powerful female voice echoed from the entrance.

When Erwight of Entorbis looked up, the Queen of the Elves stood before him, along with King Agnulix, Groblix and a group of elven warriors who had strung their bows and were aiming at him.

Erwight of Entorbis, his face contorted with surprise and anger, stared angrily at the queen.

"You think you can stop me? The book is mine and mine alone," he said maliciously.

The queen took a few steps towards Erwight of Entorbis, her eyes sparkling with the calm and strength of ancient forests.

"The book will never fall into the hands of someone like you. You stand for everything we have sworn to fight," she replied firmly.

Erwight of Entorbis laughed derisively as he drew his sword and took a few steps towards the queen.

"And you think you have the power to stop me? I have led armies that would blow your warriors away like leaves in the wind!" he thundered.

King Agnulix stepped forward, his gaze unwavering.

"It is not the size of an army that determines the outcome of a battle, but the strength of the heart of those who fight. We stand united, Erwight!" he spoke in a firm voice.

"Your greed has blinded you, Erwight of Entorbis. Even now, at this moment, you cannot see the power of the unity that stands before you," spoke Groblix, standing next to King Agnulix.

"For every shadow you cast, our light will only shine brighter," said one of the elven warriors, his bow drawn and voice as sharp as the tip of his arrow.

Erwight of Entorbis, now surrounded by the overwhelming presence of his opponents, realized the hopelessness of his endeavour. But instead of conceding defeat, he continued to advance on his opponents.

"This is not the end. The darkness will always find a way!" he hissed threateningly.

"And we'll be there to push it back, every time. Your path ends here, Erwight. The light overcomes the darkness, now and forever!" replied the queen with an authority that filled the room.

In this moment of tension, the elven youth reached for the book lying on the floor, ready to hand it over to the queen. But Erwight of Entorbis, driven by desperation and greed, drew his sword and stabbed, striking the youth. The blade passed through him as if he were made of air, with no visible effect, but at the same time the arrows of the elven warriors found their target. The ruler of Druhn fell backwards and lay motionless. Despite the attack on him, the elven youth seemed unaffected and continued, holding the book securely in his hands, stepping in front of the queen, a picture of victory and hope for those present.

"I've found the book mother! Let's take it to father!" he said to her, whereupon the queen took the book and gently stroked the cheek of the young boy, who was beginning to dissolve.

Brother Transmudin, who could not believe what he saw, knew that he would now have to bear the consequences of his betrayal. He knelt on the ground, put his hands to his face and waited until two of the elven warriors led him away.

Master Drobal, meanwhile, looked at the graying statue of Lorijan, clutched his chest and collapsed to the horror of those present. Vrenli, Manamii and Gorathdin ran towards him and bent over him. Gorathdin slowly unbuttoned his tunic.

"His chest is covered in grey spots and there are black rings around his heart!" Gorathdin realized.

"A shadow spell!" said Groblix, kneeling before the statue of Lorijan and immersing himself in prayer.

But when Lorijan's hoped-for light did not shine, he stood up again and looked sadly at those present.

"Lorijan's light has gone out!" he announced weakly and had to be supported by King Agnulix standing next to him.

The Queen of the Elves opened the Book of Wetherid, leafed through it and when she had found the right place, she read aloud a long verse about Lorijan, who gave her life for her husband, the first King of the Dwarves. A bright light shone from the book onto the statue of Lorijan, enveloping it in a golden glow.

"Look here, Groblix! Servant of Lorijan!" the elf queen spoke to him.

Groblix looked up and when he noticed that Lorijan's light was beginning to shine again, his smile returned.

He knelt down in front of the statue and prayed for the Holy Light. A beam emanating from Lorijan's right hand surrounded Master Drobal. Everyone watched as the gray spots on his chest slowly faded. Master Drobal awoke again, a slight smile on his lips as he looked at his friends and saw the lifeless body of the Shadow Lord lying at the feet of Lorijan's statue.

Wahmubu, Werlis, Aarl and Army Commander Arkondir stormed into Lorijan's Hall.

"The enemy is fleeing back to the east!" they shouted in delighted voices.

When they saw those gathered in front of the dead ruler of Druhn and his shadow mages, they stopped abruptly.

Gorathdin told them what had happened in Lorijan's Hall.

Everyone was relieved.

Wahmubu approached Manamii and kissed her tenderly. Werlis embraced Vrenli with his left hand. Gorathdin strode happily towards his father, who accompanied Borlix into the hall, supporting him. Army Commander Arkondir and King Agnulix shook hands joyfully. The Queen of the Elves held out her hand to Master Drobal and helped him stand up, whereupon Aarl handed him his staff.

"What will happen to the monster under the mines?" asked Groblix, worried about his hall.

"What monster?" asked the Queen of the Elves.

"The dragon Omnigo!" replied King Agnulix.

The queen then began to leaf through the book again and finally tore out a page, which caught fire and burned in her hand.

"There are no more dragons in Wetherid!" she said, addressing King Agnulix, who looked at her in amazement.

The queen then approached Vrenli and handed him the book.

"Take care of it," she said to him gently.

She said goodbye to everyone, especially Master Drobal, whom she kissed on the cheek, turned around and made her way back to the Glorious Valley with her warriors.

Vrenli looked confusedly at the book and then at those present.

"I don't understand. Why did she give me the book of all people?" he asked. Those present looked at each other in silence for a few moments. None of them knew the answer and none dared to make a guess. Only Master Drobal knew that the elf queen was acting with foresight, for this was probably not the last time that Vrenli would go on a journey to do Wetherid a service.

"Send messengers out to Wetherid! Erwight of Entorbis and his allies have been defeated!" shouted King Agnulix.

He then strode into the Hall of Kings and sat down on his stone throne. His army commanders, who had gathered in front of him, began to inform him of the losses they had suffered in the battle.

Master Drobal, followed by his friends, walked from the Lorijan's Hall through the Hall of Kings out onto the plateau. There he raised his staff high above his head and loudly whistled three times. He thanked everyone present for their help, hugged Vrenli and Werlis, and patted Gorathdin, Aarl, Borlix and Wahmubu on the back. Then he bowed to Manamii and climbed onto the haldakie that had landed on the plateau.

"See you in Astinhod!" he said to Gorathdin and was about to fly off when Vrenli asked him to wait.

"Speak up, little friend!" he urged Vrenli.

"Haven't you forgotten something?" Vrenli asked him.

"Not that I know of," replied Master Drobal.

"What power is more powerful than the magic of the elves from the Glorious Valley?" asked Vrenli.

"I said that it is probably more powerful," Master Drobal replied and smiled.

The moment the last rays of Holy Light dispelled the darkness from Master Drobal, he turned to Vrenli, who stood devoutly beside him, his face a reflection of the hope and determination that had carried them all this far. Master Drobal, his eyes now filled with a deep wisdom and an unshakable faith in goodness, shared his realization in words that captured the essence of their struggle.

"The true power I spoke of is not that which can be found in books or achieved through magic wands. It is the power of unity, the unchanging strength of friendship and the ability to withstand the temptations of evil. This power comes from an unwavering conviction to believe in goodness and to do good even when the road is rocky and the darkness seems overwhelming. That, my young friend, is the essence of our power," he explained in a hopeful voice.

Vrenli, who had learned so much and experienced even more on this journey, let these words sink in for a moment.

"I fully understand now, Master Drobal. It was our cohesion that made us strong, our willingness to put personal goals behind the good of Wetherid. By overcoming fear, never giving up hope, even in the darkest hours, we made the impossible possible and defeated an enemy whose power seemed insurmountable. Our unity, our friendship, and our belief in goodness were our true weapons in this battle," Vrenli replied in a voice filled with new understanding and a mature realization.

These words, spoken in the silence of Lorijan's Hall, echoed far beyond its walls. They were a testament to the light that will not be extinguished even in the deepest darkness.

In that moment, as Master Drobal and Vrenli stood in silence, surrounded by their friends and the lifeless witness to their greatest challenge, it was more than just a victory over an external enemy. It was the confirmation of a profound truth that the greatest power is that which comes from the heart, the power of unity, friendship and unflagging faith in the good.

Master Drobal said goodbye to everyone, gave Vrenli another smile and flew off with his haldakie towards Horunguth Island.

"Farewell!" Vrenli's voice echoed across the plateau as he stood beside his companions - Gorathdin, Manamii, Wahmubu, Aarl, Borlix, Werlis, Gerold and Army Commander Arkondir - holding the Book of Wetherid firmly in his left hand.

Together they gazed into the distance. With his right hand, Vrenli waved after Master Drobal, whose figure slowly disappeared on the horizon until the haldakie finally vanished completely from their vision.

"Friends! Come along! King Agnulix has opened a barrel of mead and he doesn't want to drink it without you!" Groblix called from the entrance to the Hall of Kings to his friends, who immediately accepted his invitation.

Epilogue

Twenty years later, Vrenli looked up.

The small oil lamp in the room had almost gone out. He closed the book, put the chair back in its place and blew the flame out.

"Thank you so much for this wonderful story, father," the little boy laying in the bed thanked him in a sleepy voice.

"Tomorrow I'll read to you about the Northmen," Vrenli said to his son and pulled the blanket up a little higher.

"Good night, father," said the little boy and fell asleep.

"Good night, my son," Vrenli replied quietly and left the room.

As it was a balmy summer night, he went out onto the terrace in front of his house and gazed at the stars. More than twenty years had passed since the battle at Ib'Agier and he still thought back to that time with nostalgia. He had only written a few pages in the book since then. He had the feeling that time and the events in Wetherid had fallen into a long hibernation. When the Queen of the Elves handed him the book back then, he had no idea that he was not only destined to protect the book, but was also required to write in it, as many Keepers had done before him.

The sound of hooves clattering could be heard from afar.

Several torch-bearing riders rode hurriedly from the village square towards Vrenli's house. When they were close enough, Vrenli recognized Gorathdin, Borlix and Aarl.

"Vrenli DaFanorlan! We need your and Werlis' help! Hurry up and take only the most important things with you. Time is of the essence!" Gorathdin said to him, whereupon Vrenli hurried back into the house without asking any questions.

He walked to the cellar hatch and, before opening it, glanced at the stove where his wife was standing, filling a kettle with hot water.

"Gorathdin and the others are outside. They need my help!" he informed his wife, who was walking towards him with the hot kettle in her hand.

Vrenli took her in his arms and kissed her.

"Take care of yourself, Vrenli! And the book too!" she warned in a worried voice.

Vrenli nodded.

He opened the hatch to the cellar, descended and retrieved his short sword. This time he also grabbed his glass bow and put on his father's armor.

He quietly returned upstairs and crept into his son's room. With a tender kiss on the sleeping boy's forehead, he carefully pulled up the covers, took the book from the bedside table, stowed it in his leather bag and hurriedly left the room to join his friends.

"I'm going to ride with Gorathdin!" Vrenli announced, mounting behind him and waving one last time to his wife, who was standing on the small wooden terrace.

"Let's ride to Werlis!" said Gorathdin and spurred his horse on.

Afterword

Dear readers,

With the conclusion of "The Chronicles of Wetherid - Legacy of the Elves", I would like to express my deepest gratitude to you. It has been an extraordinary journey through the mysterious world of Wetherid, filled with adventure, magic and unforgettable encounters.

I hope you found in this book not only an exciting story, but also a world you could immerse yourself in to escape from everyday life and discover new horizons.

For more information, exclusive content and news about upcoming projects in the Wetherid series such as "The Keepers of the Seven Artifacts" or "The Secret of the Ice Flames", please visit our website wetherid.com or facebook.com/wetherid/. There you can interact with other fans, discover bonus material and dive deeper into the world of Wetherid.

Thank you again for your support and enthusiasm for this story. May your journey through Wetherid hold many more adventures.

Best wishes,
Christian Dölder

About the author

Since his childhood, Christian Dölder has been fascinated by the worlds of magic and adventure and has set himself the goal of sharing this fascination in his works. The "Chronicles of Wetherid" are the result of a long journey through fantasy, inspired by the epic works of great authors such as J.R.R. Tolkien.

Through years of dedication and tireless striving for perfection, Christian Dölder has created a story that not only entertains, but also makes you think. With the "Chronicles of Wetherid", he aims to take readers on a journey that takes them through the highs and lows of the human spirit as they discover a world of adventure, magic and unforgettable characters.

From its early beginnings to its publication in 2024, "The Chronicles of Wetherid" is not only a story, but also a journey of self-discovery and creative fulfillment. Christian Dölder invites you to immerse yourself in the world of "Wetherid" and become part of an epic saga you won't soon forget.